King of the City

Also by Michael Moorcock

Behold the Man
Breakfast in the Ruins
The Cornelius Quartet
A Cornelius Calendar
The Great Rock 'n' Roll Swindle
The Opium General
Mother London
The Brothel in Rosenstrasse
Gloriana
Letters from Hollywood
The Retreat From Liberty
Byzantium Endures
The Laughter of Carthage
Jerusalem Commands
The Vengeance of Rome (*forthcoming*)

Recorded music

'Sonic Attack', 'Coded Languages', 'Kings of Speed',
'Running Through The Backbrain' etc. on various
Hawkwind albums

'Veteran of the Psychic Wars', 'Black Blade', 'The Great
Sun Jester' on various *Blue Öyster Cult* albums

'The New Worlds Fair', 'The Brothel in Rosenstrasse',
'Dodgem Dude', 'Another Quiet Day in Auschwitz' etc.
with The Deep Fix

Instrumentals and vocals on Robert Calvert albums and
singles including *Lucky Leif and the Longships*, *The
Greenfly and the Rose* and *Hype*

King of the City

Michael Moorcock

WILLIAM MORROW 75 YEARS OF PUBLISHING
An Imprint of HarperCollins*Publishers*

This book was first published in Great Britain in 2000 by Scribner, an imprint of Simon & Schuster UK Limited, a Viacom Company.

HarperCollins books may be purchased for educational, business, or sales promotional use. For information please write: Special Markets Department, HarperCollins Publishers Inc., 10 East 53rd Street, New York, NY 10022.

FIRST U.S. EDITION

Printed on acid-free paper

Library of Congress Cataloging-in-Publication Data has been applied for.

ISBN 0-380-97589-0

01 02 03 04 05   QW   10 9 8 7 6 5 4 3 2 1

For my grandson, Alexander, a fable

CONTENTS

CHAPTER ONE
The Form

Believe me, pards, we're living in an age of myths and miracles.

Call it divine coincidence, good instincts or bad timing, but at the very moment the People's Princess and Prince Harrod-al-Ritz hit the concrete in Paris I was zonked out of my brain, hanging in a frayed Troll harness from the basket of a Hitsu FG-180 hot-air balloon drifting through Little Cayman's perfect skies in the mellow light of the setting sun and snapping the godzilla bonkshot of the century.

Orgasmic flesh rippled like flowing grain. Flanked by luscious palms, sharp and sweet at maximum zoom, that familiar pink arse mooned magnificently into frame. With rhythmic balance and enthusiasm, his perfect pelt glowing and pulsing, feeling no pain, deceased zillionaire Sir John Barbican Begg was skilfully demonstrating the missionary swing to that flower of English womanhood, our good old reliable Duchess of Essex, Antonia Staines.

In a hammock.

A symphony in pink and gold.

Eldo-fucking-rado!

My cousin Barbi wasn't doing at all badly for a dead man. Publicly drowned in London, publicly flamed in Kensal Rise Crematorium and sentimentally remembered at St Alban's, Brookgate, he was easily recognized by his distinctively marked but well-nourished buttocks; she from the idiosyncratic heavings of her bucolic thighs, her Pre-Raphaelite mane, her hearty faraway whoops.

Barbi had been the richest man in the world when he was wacoed. I knew for sure, however, that he definitely hadn't been divorced. His ex-widow, Rose, was my other cousin. My ex-wife, his step-sister, had also married him, which made Barbican my ex-brother-in-law . . .

Some of those relationships went back to the womb but just then old mister wonderself didn't give a Welshman's wank about relationships. *Moi* was bathing in the sensual flame of transcendental onanism. Had hit the $G spot. Was scooping the superpoop. Snapping my place into the tabloid hall of fame.

The balloon rental had cost me my remaining credit card but by tomorrow I would be immortal. And so would Barbi. I was about to make him a legend in both lifetimes. I'd never even liked him up to that moment but now I genuinely loved him. How could I not? He was my meal-ticket to the multiverse.

Definition better than perfect at maximum magnification, back from the dead and bonking like a buffalo, there he was: The Midas Kid. The man who had reaped the profits of a dozen recessions, used the *Fortune* Five Hundred as a shopping list, dumped Maxwell, bought Trump, outfoxed Soros, massacred Murdoch, dismissed Ted Turner as a sentimental amateur and considered Citizen Kane a philanthropist.

My pictures were the prize for weeks of unsleeping obsession, decades of dissatisfaction, a heap of subtle humiliations, some serious inconveniences and miseries. Pix that were every photojournalist's dream. International currency. In a couple of days, when the pix saw print, the island would be thicker with photogs than flies on a Frenchman's fart. Barbican would have scarpered by then, of course. But the game would definitely be afoot; the pack would be legging it to the view halloo while I'd be rediscovering the emperor-size feather bed at the Dorset and phoning down for the full English for myself and glamorous young pard. For a moment I felt profound empathy with the pair below. Frame by zipping frame I shared every delicious nuance of their photo opportunity. The moment was saturated with sex. All it lacked to make it perfect was the sound of a two-stroke as Cathy Tyson arrived to carry me off in her microlite . . .

I only had one crack at the shots. Drunk or sober, mad or sane, I only needed one. As we dropped lower over the convulsing soulmates, I clipped on to the D-ring so that I could lean further out and take some side views, hoping that in their ecstasy they couldn't hear the thump of batty-gangsta rap vibrating from my pilot's pulsing boombox and amplified by our vast silver canopy, or catch a whiff of the roiling cushions of reefer smoke probably keeping us airborne.

Not that you could do much about steering or speed in an FG-180. Plus the volume was busted on the blasta. Plus Captain Desmond Bastable, the pilot, had insisted on bringing two magnums of champagne for the trip as well as a pound of ganja so strong you could get cheerful just being in the same city with it. Also a bottle of Stolichnaya. I never drink on the job, it interferes with what I put up my nose, so Captain B had enjoyed both magnums and now lay spreadeagled on the bottom of the basket-chewing on his dreadlocks and cackling at his own smutty porkboy stories. Every so often he did something amusing with his burner. I didn't care. I had three full rolls of FX-15+ with digital back-up and I was on my fourth. The smoke pacified my mind. I relaxed so much I almost went completely over the side. I started to laugh. Captain Bastable found the vodka bottle. Life was never going to be better.

Five rolls finished and then our Panasonic hiccuped radically from Really Hip Hop into Cat Stevens's *Moonshadow* at full volume. Captain Bastable's musical taste was eclectic but strictly Reformed Muslim.

The air was the clearest it would ever be. I went in for a portrait. Full zoom and still sharp as a stockbroker's trousers. I might have been standing beside her.

Maybe she was telepathic. Suddenly, open-mouthed with glazed confusion, the duchess stared into my excited lens as if into my face. Clickety-click. Then the wind had changed. I was invisible again. I dropped our penultimate sandbag, and we rushed rapidly upward and back the way we'd come. As Rai Twist gave it some stick with their version of the Cheb Khaled classic *Sidi Boumédienne*, I waved farewell to the Isles of Greed and sat down on the floor, zipped up my camera, sealed my film bag, flipped back at the digitals, secured my disc, lit a spliff, popped my last E, sipped the dregs of the Moët, ate my wholefood patty, threw the bottles over the side and saluted the soft emerging stars, wondering vaguely whether Captain Bastable would wake up in time to get us down somewhere near Kingston or if by tonight we'd be trying to bribe ourselves out of Havana with eight dollars, some seeds and stems, an old climbing harness and about six thousand yards of second-hand balloon silk.

An age of myths and miracles, certainly, pards. And wonders. But also an age of disappointments. And, I must say, some confusion. I'm not the first conquering hero who returns home expecting a big welcome only to discover that in the meantime the social climate had gone a bit radical and the mates who sent him off with wild applause are not all that pleased to be seen with him now. Embarrassed silence as Lawrence walks into the mess. I had left the bosom of my nation, or at least Marriages New Wharf, Wapping, one of the lads, popular with my peers, credit at every pub, a well-respected pro people were proud to know. I'd returned to feel like Hermann Goering popping in at his local to down a last stein before going on to his trial in Nuremberg. 'Well, mates, wish me luck.'

In London I had trouble focusing on this new reality for a while. My future had vanished.

My little house in Fogg Yard, Brookgate, was full of threatening messages. That was normal. Everything else had subtly changed. Like in *The Twilight Zone* when you get up in the morning and somehow know this just isn't your own world. For one thing, it's too fucking friendly?

Remember how weird it got for a while? Dianalgesic. It really did happen overnight. The Year of the Woolly. And there I was sporting the pot of gold I'd brought back from the end of the tabloid rainbow! The least I expected was a little professional congratulation. But suddenly all the rules were different. The language was different. The twentieth century's most sensationalized car crash had changed everything.

Friends became strangers. Hardened cynics turned into sentimentalists. Sentimentalists turned into vicious avengers. It was a baby-pink cashmere nightmare. Official reality was at last the fully digitalized, graphically equalized Lord Attenborough™ official movie version. Down we go. Another Prozac nation.

By now, of course, both Diana and Barbican have passed beyond fact. The Princess of Hearts and the King of Diamonds have joined the cigar-chewing Wardog, Old Queen Bessie and the venomous Maggie Moneyeyes as heritage icons. The struggle's over. They've become transfigured, complex works of fiction, compendia of others' dreams and anxieties, public inventions, subject to the public will I suspect they all believed they could control.

A living song, a constant echo.

But at that moment Diana's story drowned Barbican's. No contest. When myth challenges legend, hearts always beat diamonds. Legends are the tales we tell to cheer ourselves up. Myths are the stories we live by. Chance sometimes makes us part of that story.

Barbican had created history in his own way. Of all publicity-loving tycoons he had been the star. The big financial fish Lacey Moloch, the great white shark's little kipper, respected. Richard Branson had been his admiring novitiate. Soros couldn't outsmart him. His successes challenged everything you knew about reality. But Diana went better. She went metaphysical. She actually changed the nature of reality.

You probably don't remember anything different, do you?

It doesn't matter what the truth used to be. Billions of women will forever identify with Diana's misery as she in turn identified with theirs. They thought they knew her. They thought she knew them. She spoke their language. The same as Bill the Cocksman. With every revelation, people knew him better.

Diana hit every woman's heart because her tragedy was the ultimate chick flick scripted by Barbara Cartland, rewrites by Shena Mackay and Joanna Trollope: Suburban Gothic, an Essex Jane Eyre, a Sloane Sylvia Plath. The story works because it's a version of common experience. Mills and Boon folk-history. Harlequin Romance. *News of the World* normality. Innocent young woman's love and idealism invested in dream marriage. Boredom. Isolation. Rude shock of reality. What's this in his sock drawer? Ugh! The bastard! Defeated expectations, disturbing shadows, unlikely explanations. Oo-er! Her noble husband's dark secret! A message misdelivered. Who was the mysterious Lady Tampax? Husband's surly reticence turns to anger. Storms out. Dissolve to Night in Kensington Palace. Strange echoing cries in the corridors. Blonde innocent pauses in brushing locks. Hastily to bed. Sinister silence. Darkness. Premonition. Sits up suddenly. The door creaks open. The virgin bride's huge blue eyes widen in terror. Unable to suppress a scream, she watches as Nemesis in a flannel nightie, whinnying like *El*

Caballo Diabolo, applies her Dunhill to the drapery. That family's affinity for large animals is probably scandalous.

Rebecca never had more dysfunctional relatives and servants. Stereotypes, like most of their class. The remote powerful mother-in-law, self-destructive drunken aunt with shameful secret, dotty grandma addicted to gambling, bumbling, reactionary old father-in-law, glowering sister-in-law, 'modern' slightly iffy younger brother-in-law, husband torn between the lot of them and so on and so on. Strange tensions every morning around the devilled kidneys and bacon. Why did she hesitate when I asked that? Is it my imagination? Were they exchanging significant glances? Hollywood Henry James. The Eternal Twist. The Divine Soap. The final panto. *Jeunesse sans* fucking *frontières*.

The pain of revelation. She throws herself into a life of dissipation. Montage shots of our heroine in shockingly short dresses dancing on the table with shockingly short sheikhs. False laughter, falser friends. But her children console her. She returns to duty. Then comes the next disappointment and the next. Whirlwind romance with Mr Wrong, the son of the sheikh, the cokeboy, and we slide towards *Reefer Madness* – cut to titles – 'Let's get out of here!' – NO, the audience gasps, no, Di, don't – but she takes the inevitable step towards the death car – and the music starts to come up – Oh, no, Miss Scarlett!!! I'm sorry I hurt you, leader of the pack.

Add all the subtleties and complexities you like to it, that's what keeps the punters panting.

That and the tasty realities of the private lives of the overly rich and far too famous, the people we pay to be our puppets, our surrogates, to wear the clothes we'll never wear, to taste the pleasures so frequently forbidden us, to represent us in paradise, to earn our never-ending approval by merely existing. But that existence, of course, can't be in any way private. That's not what they're being paid for.

They're paid because their lives are our soaps and soap characters exist to be stripped of all privacy, exposed to intense examination. We must know exactly what diseases they have, what needs they are repressing or expressing, what they earn, what they eat and how they fuck. We want to see them in hospital, in the ambulance, in their coffins, being born or giving birth. We want to know their deepest shame, their noblest ambitions. We want to know what their skin smells like, what their underwear feels like, what their bodies look like to the tiniest detail. We want to know what it's like to fuck them. To have control of them or to be controlled by them. We want to know about their pets, their childhood fantasies, their secret children, their real stories. They are well paid for these reports. They couldn't exist without them. Ultimately, we have the power of life or death over them. Anyone whom we pay disproportionately to their talent, whether it be an actor or an aristocrat, is fair game. They belong to us. What else have we paid for? They have no unusual skills or even looks, most of the time.

You can't invade their privacy. They've sold their privacy. It belongs to us. Every moment of it. And what a lifestyle they get in return!

The 'Royal Family' (funny notion) sold the last of their privacy when they started earning their living entirely from satisfying public fantasies. They have no other function. It maintains the status quo. Great figureheads, mind you. Profitable tokens. They pull in a fair few million a year for the heritage merchants.

The Royal Family's fortune is based almost wholly on show business. They are *stars*, the way anyone who makes more than a million a year from satisfying public fantasies is a *star*. They are paid to represent the vulgar imagination. I worked with Prince Bigears's official photographer once, some drawling Scotch gillie with a hanky up his sleeve. In the shoot when Bigears and Bigeyes were doing their pre-marriage photos, to go on stamps and mugs and stuff, this bloke told me Charles was so much shorter than Diana they'd stood him on an orange crate for the shots. An Adonis, indeed. Don't send me to Horsemonger Road, guv'nor. Check it out. See how she slumps against that fence? For all I know they dug her an Alan Ladd trench. A foot in the grave from day one.

That's our money they're living on.

We're entitled to know anything we like about royal lives. They're in the public domain. They adjusted the rules, planning to survive. But like Gorbachev with glasnost, they started something that got out of their grip. Populist roulette is like that. New plot twists are generated spontaneously, leading to an inevitable crisis of control. H-bombs for sale to any old warlord. *Came the Reckoning . . .*

A loose cannon rocked the boat. But that piece of wobbly artillery ruled our hearts and circulations while the Royal Family burst into fractal dust around her. How desperately her brother bellowed his distress in the Abbey as he made one last grab at disappearing business connections by claiming superior association with the little princes! As if their own father wasn't a blood relative! And the Queen sitting amongst all of this like Miss Jean Brodie at a Haitian wedding. Meanwhile Muhammad-el-Harrod, his own fortune founded on a successful fantasy, having rewritten the past, starts trying to write the future! Not that easy as Britpop Nulab Toney Blurr knows too well these days. And the poor old Arabs, still living in Macbethworld, think the Queen had Di rubbed out for screwing a lapsed Muslim. They don't realize that the Windsors would shake their manes and enthusiastically paw the ground if they could get a nice Arab into the stock. Who controls the film rights on all this stuff? Send for the resurrection men. This needs a Robert Bolt script.

Richard shouting for a horse couldn't have felt defeat sharper than the Queen as she slowly realized she'd somehow fought and lost a civil war and was now subject to the victor's will. The people had chosen their own queen. Queen of the Fourth Estate. Marlene Dietrich as *The Scarlet Empress*.

Diana had her court, her constituency, her ministers and advisers. Her own consorts. Her own press. It was nothing she'd planned for, of course. She played the hand she was dealt. But she played it like a pro. Few other mythic superstars had that unbeatable form. Check it out. Wonderful supporting cast, solid story, mythic resonance, a perfect tragic ending. Room for some good conspiracy theories. This one will run and run. And of course, if you're also a sex symbol, hang on to the residuals. Especially if there's an element of public sacrifice. Glug the compassionfruit pop, gulp the piety cola. As long as you have big soft eyes and a sympathetic drone, cartoon features, the public's yours forever. You fulfil an important need, create a deep diversion. While you're the epitome of their virtue they can identify with you and feel good about themselves without having to do a fucking thing except put the odd coin on the plate. Cheap at half the price.

Golden syrup. This is how to make the nasty world we live off smell a little sweeter. Go on. It's naughty but nice. You deserve it. That ain't corruption you're sniffing. That's just the icing on the marzipan.

What a need she filled! For a while she put out the best universal crack since Mary, the Mother of God.

Fuck the famous dead, I say. And fuck the famous living, for that matter. My nobody friends are dying by the day and any one of them has left the planet better for having been here, put all that they own on the line, more than any sobbing royal or self-approving Yank superstar whining for an even more banal and compliant press to share his fine opinion of himself. I don't blame the public, though. They're in a difficult position, really. They find it so much easier to identify with the rich.

So what's my chip? My beef? My line?

Call me by the p-word. It'll do fine. That's me, pards. Anywhere, any time. Any word will do that sets me apart from some Austrian fatface meatbrain supermillionaire who hasn't got the balls to take the heat. Such fine heroes for the public. Tom Cruise? He must have eight billion dollars for every one of his brain cells. And who's the dosh doing good for, pards? Nobody but themselves and the sodding Scientologists. Dead money. Damned money. But it don't stop that empty soul from barking. Jesus Christ! Have you ever listened to the abnormally rich whining how life's so public for them? Try living out your entire life on a timeshared paving-stone in Calcutta and you'll know what privacy means. Or watch your house, your well and your generator disappear in a mudslide. Or your family blown to bits by NATO planes. Or wiped out by Albanians, or Turks, or Serbs or Kurds or Hutus or Tutsis. Maybe we should keep that quiet, too, eh? So as not to disturb the world's darlings in their wonderful comfiness?

So fuck you and what you think. I'm Dover the paparazzo. It's an honourable trade. It's the pop performers and the politicians who live *alla tangente*, pards. The culture croppers, the stock-sniffers. Gullible as I've been, nobody's ever paid me off. I did give in to temptation, though. Once, in a big way. Which probably also had something to do with my current bad luck.

Anyway, as my bank manager smartly reminded me, whatever my moral opinion of the world, the simple fact was that pictures that would have made Barbican the hero of a new red-top reading public and assured me a brass-band welcome at my local Barclays were instead doomed to the dustbin of history because an over-tired driver did a few pills too many, had a few extra Scotches and decided to take the tunnel rather than the bridge.

In short, he explained, I had ceased to be an intrepid and courageous uncoverer of cupidity and corruption in high places and was now Social Pariah of the Year. The best he could do for me was freeze my interest. But I'd have to start paying off my overdraft within the month.

He patted my back as I left. A gesture of pity and admiration. He didn't have to say it. I was a vanished breed.

CHAPTER TWO
The Squeeze

Our Di had, according to her myth, been hounded to death by the baying werewolves of the yellow press. Of whom it was now plain I was one. Maybe even the worst of them. Some people claimed they had actually seen me baying. In the tunnel. With the blood of their angel on my hands. Myths, miracles, gossip and the fuck process. Any journalist knows they're all more powerful than mere fact. Especially these days. We're entering an era of unrelenting hypocrisy, half-true spins, wrinkles and twists, mind-numbing relativism, perpetual self-invention, liberal cop-outs, the new bigotry, VR backdrops, feelgoodism, abstraction and distraction, virtual theocracy, the quest for the greatest common denominator. A fruity pasta. Mussolini mild. A century of depths and substances. Richest muck in history. Those depths should be worth a visit or two. Haul up a bucket of that, dilute it to public taste, try some of the substances, and you're in business for a decade. In my business, anyway.

Kaptin Klix, Danny Devo, the Red Snapper? If you were anywhere around in the seventies and eighties, you'd know at least one of those names. Deep Fix? Paul Frame? Bob Calvert? I was always a better photog than I was a guitarist. Half the familiar images in your memory were made by me. Remember? All those great Pistols shots. The Shepherds Bush Sessions. Glen Matlock at the Lyceum. Pat Benatar at *The Worlds End*. Siouxsie on half a dozen classic tours.

Once the *New Musical Express* depended on me for its circulation. *Rolling Stone* begged me for exclusives. Elvis Costello in Graceland. Iggy at the Portobello. Freeze-frame death in the Falklands. Graham Parker at Magic Mountain. Maxwell. Somalia. Cantona. Bowie in Cuba. Bloodbaths in Congo. Michael Jackson afloat. Madonna up the Amazon. Everyone who was where they weren't supposed to be. Trigger-happy UN troops in Bosnia. Princess Margaret under the Virgin table in Las Cascadas.

I did two years as featured photog for the *Mirror*. One more year for the *Sun*. Six months for the *Guardian*. Back to freelance. Umpteen compromised Tory cabinet ministers. Greenham. Cairo. Bombay. The Crustyville Raid. King Juan and the British fishermen. The Demons Bust. Redweird and those Hong Kong Whores. LA. Brooklyn. Dworkin at the barricades. Massive Attack in Morocco. Van Morrison in Monaco. Gulf Two. Bahrain. Cornershop in Kurdistan. That Rwanda story with Fromental. Right place, right moment. I had a low curiosity that had to be satisfied. I did dozens of incidental Dianas, of course, some fairly saucy, though I didn't specialize. Nothing nasty, nothing I had to hunt her down for. Nothing I couldn't show a nun. Just some lucky leg shots. And a couple of tasteful tits. I'd cracked off several small fortunes made from the elusive famous. And now I was suddenly nothing. What the fuck else was I good for? Who needed an unemployed jackal? *Shopping Weekly? The Times of Kuwait? The Washington Post?*

Backwaters? I was spoiled for choice. There were a few people who'd be glad to see the Red Snapper landed at last. I couldn't believe the truth. I was Denny Dover, has-been. Forgotten man. Don't forget the Dover, as my grandad was fond of saying. A play on 'diver'. That was a Tommy Handley catch-phrase from ITMA. Tommy Handley was the most popular comedian of the forties. He always sounded dire to me. Heard of him, have you?

My grandad was a radio man. He lived in a vibrating world. His ears were his only sensual organs. He hated pictures. Telly was an abomination to him. He thought the same about gas. Gas was a ticking bomb, he said. He refused to let the pipe go across his yard. They had to put a special bend in it. We were the only house in the street that couldn't have a gas-stove. My big Auntie Connie was cooking for us on a monstrous black coke-burning Rayburn range until the day she had her stroke.

Now grandad's got a microwave. He's triumphant, a vindicated visionary. It's what he was waiting for all his life. It arrived just in time to save him. He relentlessly points out it was originally called a 'radio oven'. He shows me the *Lilliput* magazine with the original article from 1949. The oven looks roughly the size of a nuclear reactor and was used for fusing plastic.

Because of its evident faith in an electrical future, *Lilliput*, the digest-size companion to *Picture Post*, was the only illustrated publication he would allow in the house. *Lilliput* specialized in tasteful nudes and radically angled deco power stations. Founded by a Hungarian who'd been banged up in Munich's Ettstrasse and Stadelheim by Hitler and escaped to Britain, it had the pick of the surviving European refugee photojournalists in the late thirties. It ran great pictures. Which grandad turned a blind eye to. Or pretended that he did. It folded in 1960, but I could probably tell you every photo in it, and most of the photographers.

I got my sense of freedom from my big Auntie Con. Her side of the family had always been more political. Her best friend had been a Russian anarchist. Mrs Feldmann used to tell us stories from *Neither Master Nor Slave*, which she'd written and published, in Russian, for the children of Nestor Makhno's education train. Exemplary stories for little anarcho-socialists. *How Yuri Learned Self-Determination. Sasha and Natasha: Co-operate and Survive.* She'd known everyone in the East End. She used to say things like 'Take anything you want from the bosses except their rules'. A maxim you could apply pretty generally to school, employers, authorities of every sort. You don't have to swallow the whole pint. You should always blow off the froth.

My grandad's brother, Tom, was a great union organizer. He was in the print, down at Fleet Street. He reckoned himself. It was a dying aristocracy when I was growing up. But I saw those vast iron printing machines running, sniffed the stinking ink and felt the throb of a newspaper battering its way into the world. I saw the end of a tradition. He preferred the late shift so he could always bring an early copy of the paper home. He retired to Tudor Hamlets the year the first presses started moving out to Wapping.

My grandad worked for Mullards, Clerkenwell, all his life. I've still got his wartime pass. He didn't have to fight. He just had to stay in the East End during the Blitz. He retired on a good pension but kept the family home. He owned a crowded two-up and two-down terraced house, jerry-built around 1821, in Bonemeal Street, Brookgate, which was home to me for most of my early life. Dark, smelling of damp, full of little cupboards and loose boards. Bits of radios and lots of books, mostly self-improvement stuff like Winwood Reade's *The Martyrdom of Man*. In his last active years grandad started a business rebuilding old valve sets. He had thousands of valves in his shed, which was the converted outside toilet. Some of those glass tubes were bigger than me. They warmed the airwaves, he said, and made them human in a way transistors never could.

My grandma Nell had run off to Margate with a deaf spiv in 1948. She'd do anything for a small port and a pair of nylons, her sister, said my Auntie Con, who was really my great aunt, Rita's mum. Rita was Rosie's mum. A couple of years after Nelly had gone, Con heard that the spiv took up with another dummy and gave Nell the brush. A few years later Nell started writing my grandad letters. He didn't open them. If anyone asked after her he'd say he hadn't heard a word from her.

I found those letters a few years ago. She'd wound up as live-in staff in a pub on the Kent coast. Broadstairs, I think. A Tudor Steak House renamed in themed-up gibberish. What had been The Oak was now something like The Widow Murphy's Real Old Sailorman's Vaults Under The Sign Of The Magpie and Maypole. Reassurance stops for the lost tourist. The only people in there have maps in one hand. A place all serious drinkers and teetotallers avoid. Grandma's letters were sad, half-hearted attempts to revive a fantasy he'd never shared. The photos she sent revealed nothing but the conventional paint and costume of her class and calling. She could have been anyone's barmaid.

I'm not superstitious, but I do have one good-luck charm I couldn't bear to lose. It's an ordinary bit of London brick. It's blackened, chipped, pitted and it isn't any different to all the other debris from World War Two you're always finding in your flower beds. I picked it up in Mustard Street just before the whole area vanished under the feudal concrete of the Leith Building, Barbican's greatest monument to his own power. He got the Huguenot Leases. I got a bit of brick.

I was born in Mustard Street. In the top back room of The Hare and Hounds. On 21 December 1952. My dad inherited a faith in electricity the way others inherit politics. He was the last real Londoner to be hanged for murder. He must have been London's youngest tram-driver, too. For half a century the best of Brookgate that wasn't freelance or at Mullards worked for or on the trams. Two nights before I was born Dad drew the right to take the final Number 5 from Hampstead into the Holborn terminus. He had the makings of a top-class driver, they said, on the trolleybuses or the Tube. He was skinny, twitchy, wiry. Face pale, all gaunt angles. But everyone liked him. He was a bit serious. Mum said he'd had rheumatic fever as a kid and tended to read a lot. Turned down for National Service, he was just beginning his career. He had a good future ahead of him. He'd already retrained for the Underground. He was contemptous of internal combustion. Its day was done.

My grandad had hooked my dad on this vision of a clean, efficient, all-electric future. Before the judge sentenced him, Dad asked if he could be electrocuted. A lot of people criticized him for that. They said it was un-English.

As usual it was Pierrepoint the Hangman's fresh new hemp that snapped young Dick Dover's neck. He died in Her Majesty's Prison, Brookgate, at eight in the morning, not ten minutes' walk from where he was born. He was twenty-two. Half my age. Old enough to swing. He carried a burden, said my grandad. He always had.

A sweet-natured man, Dad. With an unbearable distrust of everything. Which was probably to do with his mum running off with the wide boy. Since my mum Doreen knew she was pregnant, he had harboured the notion that I wasn't his. He decided that his depot inspector Gordon McAllister was having it off with 'Reeny. I know the story inside out because it used to be the stock in trade of all those monochrome *Man in Black/Edgar Lustgarten Investigates/Calling Scotland Yard* true-crime episodes rerunning on late-night telly. I'd watched them since I could remember. I knew my dad by his full name, Douglas Alexander Marconi Dover, before I knew he was my dad. They used to put a bit of echo on it when the judge settled his black cap and started to deliver the sentence. Sometimes my mum was portrayed as a bit of a tart. Sometimes she was a baffled angel. I got used to thinking of her as played by different actresses. My mum was played by Joan Sims and Eve Dane. A couple of reasonably famous actors got their start playing my dad. Alan Rickman and Tom Baker. Nothing like him, of course. But it gave me a fair bit of credibility at school.

Dad was an introspective, suspicious but good-hearted young man. His side of the family had always been straight. Never violent. Cabbies. Schoolteachers. Craftsmen. He didn't enjoy alcohol much. But this was the last night of the trams. Everyone had to have a drink. He had several. After the celebrations, the speeches and the sentimental songs, Dad took his heavy brass lever from his cab and went into the office where Gordon McAllister was locking up. He'd confronted the bloke and then, unwittingly he said, killed him. Hit him once with the lever on the side of the head. Something about McAllister's laugh.

Nobody thought there was anything between McAllister and my mum. Everyone in Brookgate knew them. Her dad, Micky Shea, had been a famous boxer and was by then licensee of The Hare and Hounds. Mr Shea – 'Grampy' as he called himself to me – frequently aired his satisfaction at my father's execution. He was, he said, no fan of the Becks or the bloody Dovers, Brookgate's oldest families. They carried an evil, ancient slyness. And they gave themselves airs, he said. Too clever by half. They took too bloody much for granted.

The H&H had been that block's only building to survive Hitler almost completely intact. Shea wasn't a month dead before Barbican's big steel balls started swinging. It was just a bit of profit for Cousin Jack but as far as we were concerned they might have been knocking down St Paul's. Which, admittedly, you could see better once the pub was rubble. Barbican did it at night, before the authorities could stick a preservation order on it. Nothing, believe me, could save our street from my cousin's visionary greed. Not once he had the Huguenot Leases. His was a calling, a knightly quest, a mission.

When it came to sublime self-congratulation Barbican was a Yankee matron. He was the very model of a modern major See-Ee-O. A classic money-nerd. The velvet fist, the honeyed turd. He acted like Attila and talked like Amnesty International. Those stingy lips issued pieties and governments fell. In response to need, he dipped gingerly about in his purse, not sure he had any change. That wagging, sententious finger sent small nations into painful oblivion, their assets stripped, their peoples scattered, while he pocketed the profit. Who says there's no money to be made from diasporas?

When I had the chance I told him he was a shit for doing what he did to Mustard Street. He let me know with puppy-sweet compassion that the project employed thousands and put a vast amount of money back into the economy. What was my personal twist worth compared to the chance for people to pull themselves out of the poverty trap and make themselves a dignified wage?

Yes, Barbican was in his own eyes benevolent. If he liked the religion, he bought the church. As a sign of his liberalism, he donated a million pounds to the Green Party. He gave an island to Friends of the Earth. He funded an abortion clinic. He bought a bird sanctuary for the Audubon Society and a mountain for the Sierra Club. He underwrote Virago and a Russian gang. He built a mansion in Hampstead to live in the clouds and congratulate himself with his fellow residents that he'd conquered the moral high ground.

Well, I was doomed never to experience his self-approving authority. If nothing else, I am what I am. All I've learned in my life is to keep schtum and clock the action.

As it was, it soon became clear I was only living on borrowed time. In a matter of days the grief gestapo would start knocking on my door. The electoral register would show how I hadn't written my name in the book of condolences. I'd failed to make proper obeisances at the monuments to the people's princess. I might never work in this world again. Remember all that?

Do we really want lowest-common-denominator populist politics?

Far from being evidence of infamy and sleaze in high places, I soon heard how my Barbican pictures would be invasive 'porn' if they weren't such obvious fakes. Not only couldn't they be true, they shouldn't be true. In spite of my evidence, my certain knowledge of my cousin's topography, in spite of getting his doctor and his surviving ex-wife, Jillian Burnes, the transsexual novelist, to agree with me, I was told there was no proof it was Begg and not some lookalike.

So there I was, spun-up like a NATO communiqué.

Editors who a few days earlier would have sent crowded airbuses out to the Caymans on a whisper of this story assured me they had it from the top horse that the Duchess of Essex was enjoying a well-deserved private holiday somewhere in Florida and they had no intention of intruding on her.

Their breath smelling strongly of the Oban and Perrier, the *Daily Mail* told me they would call the security guards if I didn't leave immediately and take my bloody filth with me. I made them feel sick. The *Independent* was cool, the *Guardian* distant and the *Telegraph* had never heard of me. Equally pissed, on aggressive, acid wine, the *Sun* threatened to blacklist me. The *Star* ran a story on me as some kind of Gallic serial sex-ghoul, but got my name wrong. The *Chronicle* and the *News* considered duffing me up on the spot and possibly tying my broken body to the back of a delivery van, to be distributed in bits through the streets of London. The picture editor of the *Financial Times* told me that they knew for certain that the next time I came to the Wharf I'd be wearing cement overshoes. Economical as ever, the *Express* said that scum like me should find out what it was like to be flung from an aeroplane without a parachute. An opinion they normally reserved for people who stopped fox hunts. I was almost flattered.

They were, as the *News of the World* told me, respectable newspapers. Didn't I realize that my kind of cheap scandalmongering was what had killed the only decent woman in the kingdom? I was the next best thing to a Serbian war criminal. The smoking gun was in my pocket. Saddam Hussein and Colonel Gadaffi combined had a higher popularity rating. Some of them said they felt almost sorry for me. Only the *Observer* showed faint interest until a couple of their own iffy sales-booster stories (*Was Diana Murdered?*) backfired on them and they stopped answering my calls. I got the message. Not even *Scumbag* or *Upstart* were interested. They said that sort of story was dead as a dodi.

And it wasn't any better for me in New York, which I could only afford to phone, fax or e-mail, though not visit in person, because I was still amazingly connected by BT, despite a bill large enough to fund a Balkan genocide.

There're no people more backward than the Americans. A million channels and no news. That's why they're always starting wars they can't finish. Everyone knows more than the Americans, but the Americans think they know everything. Two days in Cuba, one in the Philippines and they knew enough to start the Spanish-American war. A weekend in Cairo and your average Yank comes home an Egyptologist. That kind of provincialism can end the world.

Even English editors get like self-satisfied Yorkshire aldermen once they've been in Manhattan for a month or two. It's strange how they go to New York, isn't it, when there's nobody left to employ them in the real world? Where's Harry? Doing well in the provinces. It's like someone paying you a couple of million quid to go and live in Huddersfield to edit the *Weekly Echo*. A fortune! But you have to live in Huddersfield. Sometimes it doesn't really sink in till you've got the job. And then it's too late. And don't tell me there are worse places than Huddersfield. Agreed. Try Washington. What you thought was civilization was a formica totem. Have you ever talked to any of those people?

Significantly, most Brit journos taking Yankee gold were never Londoners in the first place. They're from the Home Counties and beyond. They only ever really feel comfortable in the provinces. They've found their true niche at last. The State of Essex. They don't have much style but they do understand cosmetics.

Whatever their provincial provenance, Big Apple editors now made it clear that I was no longer welcome on the planet. Those people are the industry's litmus paper. They respond instantly to a change in the corporate climate. They gibber in anticipation of the big boss's whims. They know exactly when to run. They know when to hide. And they know when to stick their heads in the sand and talk out of their arses.

Now, of course, they were willing me into non-existence. I had seen it happen to other embarrassments. I was being firmly shoved into the deepest corner of the closet. If they had ever known me, they didn't remember. I had been erased from their spellchecks.

I've always been a realist. I knew I needed to lie low and pray for a change in the psychic weather. My reputation as an investigative journalist had been flushed down the toilet. I'd be lucky to pick up a job snapping tourists in Trafalgar Square. Which is actually the way I started, when I was ten. That's how long I've earned my living at this. I had a picture in the *Evening News*. Front page. With a credit. And Rosie in it. When I was twelve. I worked as a Wardour Street runner, then joined a Notting Hill commune as a hippy photog's mascot. I'm almost the last of my kind now they can invent any digital photo they want. I made an honourable living, by and large, but you wouldn't know it. Now reality's how you spin it.

I understood at last that I had no allies. The only person who would certainly believe me and be able to help me, my cousin Rosie Begg, was, according to official bulletins, in secret retreat, taking a rest cure. I'd picked up enough earlier to know that she was involved in some huge and maybe seriously dangerous deal involving several of the larger Central American countries her companies controlled and, whisper went, some nukes or chemmies, depending who you heard. The upshot was that none of her many employees admitted to knowing where she was or admitted to being able to get a message to her. I didn't really expect a response. She'd already told me I was on my own. I had to hope she warmed a bit towards me and discovered my predicament before I starved to death. She'd given me my best clues, after all. Without her, I'd never have found Johnny in the Caymans.

Now I was slipping swiftly into social limbo. If I turned up at the Groucho nobody would recognize me. I was becoming less real by the day. As, of course, was my story.

Modern times. Malleable truth. There's no such thing as objectivity. All stories are subjective. Everything is relative. There's only self-interest. Right? The link man on CNN summed it up the other night. Morality, he said, is a matter of personal choice.

CHAPTER THREE
The Pinch

Soon everyone treated my insistence on Barbican's resurrection as a scam, a diversion, or at best a delusion. The nature of the pictures instantly marked them as distasteful, unprintable in any decent medium. They were blaming the messenger, I said. They ignored me. We had a new code now. Drawn up by Piety Blair, the rich man's Cromwell. The Mortlake Mussolini.

Admittedly the woman resembled the Duchess of Essex, but how could you tell who it was mounting the good lady? It could be a husband or some other relative. And those palms could as easily be in Torquay. And the hammock's movement blurred detail. What was required were pictures of Barbi full frontal in a suit and tie, exchanging brown envelopes with someone famous. Preferably the Pope. Preferably in Switzerland. Preferably in front of the statue of William Tell.

At that point I had to give it up. Can you imagine what that feels like? I had spent almost a year and all my credit tracking the nasty little bastard down. He had broken every law there was. He had engineered his own apparent death and last rites. He had conned billions from innocent investors. He was responsible for thousands of public pounds spent looking for his body, scores of suicides, several domestic murders and many broken marriages. His decisions had turned once-productive regions into poisoned wastelands. Every major power in the world had been adversely affected by his manipulations. Now he was living the life of Riley on a tropical island, enjoying the knowing company of aristocratic tax exiles, power groupies and other sweet-smelling beneficiaries of Baroness Ratchet's successful assault on the civic purse. While I, moved by some dim sense of moral disquiet, as well as the need to earn an honest living, was silenced and sent out to the edges. Ruined! You didn't have to be Thomas Hardy to see how that bagel dunked.

But I hung on to my evidence. There wasn't much I could do until people started believing it again, if they ever did. Two things were uppermost in my mind: paying the mortgage and avoiding my creditors. Finances were so bad that cash machines would set off their own alarms if I so much as glanced at them. I needed somewhere to hide for a while, maybe change my tag once again, but all my twists had been about *spending* my fortunes. This was a bit of a stopper. Where was I still welcome?

It was easy enough to test the waters, as it turned out. A couple of days after the Funeral Show I walked down from my flat in Brookgate to Seven Dials, for a late breakfast, and then strolled up Long Acre. It was unnaturally sunny. Smothered in hothouse flowers, London had the fetid stink of the Tropical Fern House at Kew. The gutters ran with mulch. The air had an amniotic taste. Something new and terrible was being spawned from the dark womb of the city. I stood on the corner of New Row, waiting to cross St Martin's Lane, trying to keep clear of a sudden mob. A party of German tourists had come out of a matinée at the Coliseum and were instinctively employing their massive shell-suited bodies in some relentless panzer movement upon Covent Garden. They almost knocked me off the kerb as I reached St Martin's Lane and stood looking across at Cecil Court where I planned to visit my monarchist friend Prissie the Print, who wasn't exactly a Dianista. I wondered idly why this particular street was now always full of taxis.

I spotted a gap in the purring flow and was about to plunge in when, sprightly through the busy traffic, drivers honking at him like outraged geese, darts a white-suited, straw-boatered, cane-wielding goozer from another time, painted cheeks beaming, dapper and sprightly to his little pointed brogues: Old Norbert Stripling, the radio personality, robust as ever, full of the joys of late summer. '*Denny*! Darling! I *knew* I'd see you today! I'm *psychic*, darling. How's Mum? How's your lovely *grandpa*? Still hanging on in that *awful* reservation? I promised him some Harry Roy tapes. Come and have a drink at The Call Boy, dear. Then you can tell everyone what you actually saw in that tunnel!'

It seemed a shame to disappoint him. But I could use a free drink and I needed any wisdom and help I could come by.

The Call Boy was one of the few London drinking clubs that hadn't changed its name since I first knew it. It had been The Call Boy in more innocent days, before the Second World War. Norrie had started coming here regularly after his wife died in 1970. There were a handful of theatrical clubs still surviving in the Soho area, full of smart little old men and women like him, making the most of themselves and never giving up hope of a good part. The ladies were called Doll, Liz or Peg. The gents were Billy, Freddy, Dicky. Most were at least as old as Norbert but few had known his success. He was their smell of stardom. Their luck. They called him Norrie. They had stories to match his. It was expected of them. They had been in show business all their lives, worked with the best, seen the stars of the firmament fall and become newspaper sellers in Leicester Square, shop assistants at Whiteley's, whores in Norwich, minicab drivers in Skerring. Norbert was none of these. He was their own proof that you could hang on and you could succeed.

A popular juvenile lead in London and on Broadway during the thirties, Norbert Stripling OBE had known everyone, appeared with everyone, done almost everything, including a double act with Freddie Earlle. He was remembered in films for his wonderful character parts, notably in early talkies. He had worked with the best. He'd been an influence. Norrie showed *The Trouble With Harry* novel to Hitchcock. The old bastard liked it so much he paid a hundred quid for it, the whole twist. It had been written by our mutual friend Jack Trevor Story who never got another penny. Stripling and Story had written radio scripts for Spike Milligan and Peter Sellers. Even my grandad had respect for them. They'd written a series of Anna Neagle and Frankie Vaughan movies and done some of the best *Carry On* routines.

Norrie had scripted intimate review before the coming of Dudley Moore and the Fringe. His *Old Gold* request show was still high in the BBC ratings but his chief income came from his song royalties. While Radio Two still lived, he earned. He had written *Bloomsbury Blues* for Sonny Hale, *Cockney Carmen* for Jessie Matthews, *Lamps of Lambeth*, *The Pearly Stroll*, *Foggy Weather*, *The Holborn Hop*, *My Old Town*, *London Lullaby* and *Lights in the Smoke*, among many others still requested by those longer-living oldsters. They had all been hits in the thirties or forties. In fact, *Madonna of the Twilight* had been a huge hit for Dickie Valentine as late as 1956 and Norrie's terrible novelty number *Lambeth Twist* got Lonnie Donegan to Number Three in the 1961 Hit Parade. They were all still hits in the hearts of Norrie's fellow members. It was probably why he enjoyed his daily visits so much.

Norrie had a wonderful, crowded flat in the cupola of the Grand Theatre, just round the corner from the club. Everything under its grimy glass dome was extremely neat and shipshape. I remembered when it was a lot less tidy. The rooms had been Wolfit's own offices when he managed the theatre. He had willed them to Norbert who claimed the great Edwardian actor manager had died, still in his Lear, paralysed in his greasepaint, giving himself up to death at last like an old bull. 'I can still hear his melancholy bellow, dear. Calling for his meat pie and Murphy's.'

Norbert had lived in Barnes for years, using the St Martin's Lane place only occasionally, but when Yvonne died suddenly he'd sold their house and moved back to Soho. 'It doesn't do to grow old alone in the suburbs, dear. You're halfway to the grave already. You can't tell when you're dead. Keep plenty of concrete around you and there's no chance of slipping accidentally into the ground before your time. There's a stress to having good neighbours which you never have to experience when you live in the West End. I want to conclude my days, dear, where I can be assured that if I fall down dead in the street, I shall be properly ignored until the council picks me up. It's what I pay rates for.'

He had that stylish natural courage a lot of Londoners manage to find when life gets foul. Not that there was anything much wrong with his health. At eighty-two he seemed immortal, hardly changed from those black-and-white thrillers in which he'd energetically quipped and chirruped after kidnapped cuties and stolen secrets. Norrie's only problem was that he seriously missed his wife. In his heart he had willingly joined the queue moving slowly towards the exit, but meanwhile he thought he might as well relish life as much as possible. 'I tell myself it's for her sake. Isn't that weird, dear?' Every day you could walk to the Tube without disgracing yourself was a day to celebrate, he said.

'She died at the perfect moment of her story, dear.' He guided me with his fingertips back towards New Row. 'We're all of us waltzing on the *Titanic* and it's how we dance and to what music that's the measure of our memory. We invent one another. A simple twist or two of fate and no doubt it would have been Her Highness of Wales doing the Ferragamo wave from the hammock and her spiced-up girl-saga could have continued to feed a million mouths and the imagination of the world (*Diana: A Nation Drools*) while you became a self-righteous tax exile. Is there a connection between our tear ducts and our saliva glands, dear, do you think?'

The club's smart green-and-brass door was at the end of a shabby hallway directly off New Row. Once you'd announced yourself to the entryphone you went through the door, down into a steaming basement smelling of smoke and sweet gin, where Bee Baloo, fat and fluffy as a Texas turkey in her buckskins and beads, with her massive chromed bouffant making her look like Tammy Wynette on steroids, yodelled her recognition as she took our coats and signed us in. Thanks to Norbert, I'd been a member for years. I'd slept down here more than once in times almost as bad as this.

I knew everybody. They were all pleased to see me. Nobody judged me. It was enough that I'd been touched by fame. Being pension day, the drinks came fast and generously and I was soon repaying them not with delicious tales of Di's final moments but with my adventures in the Caribbean and my disappointed expectations. To be fair, they listened sympathetically but obviously felt a little short-changed. Before long, Norbert and I were alone at the table in the alcove, the candle flames casting lively shadows on walls crowded with signed portraits of forgotten troupers. Norrie was doing his best to address my dilemma.

'I'd have thought, dear boy,' he said, 'that the Serious Fraud people would be more interested in what you have at the moment. I mean, there must be half a dozen crimes involved. Isn't it a matter of public concern?'

It hadn't once occurred to me to involve the law. I frowned.

Norbert saw that he was heading in the wrong direction. 'Well, dear, what about his wife, Rosie? Wouldn't she be interested?'

He knew about me and Rosie. I told him she had other things on her mind. She wouldn't be particularly pleased to hear from me. The reason I knew this was that she had told me so herself. Face to face. Before the door shut on mine. And she probably wouldn't even mind about giving back Barbican's life insurance. A few billion probably didn't make much difference to the most powerful person in the world, which was what she was now. As she'd once been fond of saying, she hadn't done at all badly for a little boon bastard from Brookgate. And that had been when she was still running charities.

'Blood, dear, is blood, after all. She's not a poor woman. Though she must get tired of begging relatives, eh?'

Rosie and I still weren't actually on speaking terms. I'd exchanged about eight words with her since the Tower Bridge gig. In fact, she had hated me so much I was surprised she hadn't put some kind of corporate hit out. Or set a couple of her smaller countries on me. She controlled so many, she deserved her own seat in the United Nations. I was grateful for her restraint. There's a certain advantage to being close family. I wasn't rubbed out. I had merely been made invisible. Much as I hoped in my bones she would eventually relent, it wouldn't do at the moment to test her goodwill.

Norbert was a great moviegoer. His solutions to problems usually consisted of adapting some plot he had seen in a film. You could sense him flicking through his mental file index from *Aardvarks Are Amongst Us* to *Zenith, Lord of the Zodiac*. You'd have to hope he stopped on something more appropriate in your case, like an old *Prisoner* episode, the remake of *The Fugitive* or some *Three Stooges* situation.

'Well, dear,' he offered after due deliberation, 'usually in a modern drama of this kind the hero would start doing things with his computer. That would be the key to his salvation. Klickety-klick in darkened rooms. Flashing screens. Funny green light. No luck. Despair. Then, suddenly – YOU HAVE ACCESS!!! Is there something you could do with your computer?'

'I could pawn it. It won't be worth a fuck when they turn the electric off.'

'It wasn't worth a fuck once you bought it, dear. Computers are the perfect consumer item, aren't they? Obsolete even as you carry them home! And so we make abstract economic theory concrete. What a wonder it all is! What power we have! You should get on the Net, Denny! Go online. I have. It's wonderful. I have friends all over the world. You won't have any trouble finding people who'll believe you there.'

I was unimpressed. 'My wiring doesn't come any cooler, Norrie. Or so I was assured by the toddler who installed it last week. I have all this stuff. A thousand upgrades. K upon K. The Net is a cornucopia, a lifeline, but from the few sites I've looked at where I could publish, those people who'll believe me also believe Sculler and Mouldie are secretly married to aliens.'

Norbert waved that one away like a bad smell. 'Scepticism, dear, is wonderful in small doses. But if you live with nothing else, it consumes you. There are perfectly adult parts of the Net where you can contact people of intellect and integrity. People of our own kind, dear. Still, as it were, barking. Tatty, worn-out old sheepdogs who continue to think in terms of the common good. Even you, Den. You can't help yourself. You know you'll never be very rich, any more than I will be. We're both of us dreadfully profligate, dear. Both awful gamblers. And you know as well as I do what a bad streak feels like.'

A few days earlier I would have called that rank defeatism. Now I saw it as grim truth. Some of us weren't meant to win the lottery. Every advantage had to be earned and earned and earned again. The smallest mistake brought ruin. Square One. Do not pass Go. Karma? Dharma? It made you wonder about Buddhism sometimes. Like, Kerouac? I was halfway there. I had always had trouble believing money was real. And the world had never seemed entirely concrete to me. A little abstract. A bit on the absurd side. It's why I was forever looking for a jackpot so big it couldn't possibly all vanish before I died. That would generate itself, the way I'd been told money did.

Barbican, of course, had learned all this before we were both six. Before he was Barbican. He used to read the *Financial Times* in the school break. At parties, adults thought his grave assessments of the world's markets were cute. Later they revered him as an infant prodigy, an oracle. They asked him about their investments. He was still Johnny then, before Rupert Dracks, Lord Barbican, adopted him. He was a child of his time all right. Look at our great captains of industry, our senior statesmen. The geek already inherits the earth. Would you let any of those nerds in your home? But, as my friend Tubby used to say, most people aren't interested in originals. Fame is its own cloak of glamour, he'd say (being that way inclined). Fame makes the ugly beautiful and the beautiful into icons of exaggerated perfection.

Before he was famous, we found my cousin tiresome, smug, dull and very embarrassing. We called them 'goozers' in Brookgate, I don't know why. He went to St Alban's in Gray's Inn so he was in the area a lot. Luckily, after one term, I didn't see too much of him. We moved in different spheres. I was from Brookgate which was Cockney before the Romans. He was from Sporting Club Square and that shabby-genteel middle class, all teeth and teasets, which treasured its status above life or soul.

'You also have to decide whether this pursuit of Barbican is a noble cause or just your spite and envy. You have to think, dear, what it's doing to *you*.' With expressive eyebrows Norrie ordered two more sweet gins from Sylv at the bar. 'The smallest revenge poisons the soul, as they say. It's up to you, dear. If it's moral outrage, forge ahead. If it's self-pity, don't go too far with it. If it's hatred, tell someone else about it and drop it altogether.'

'Why is it you make so much sense and my stomach still goes on churning?' I accepted his drink. 'Why is it certain that my life will be all downhill from now on? I'm going to be forty-eight when the new millennium hits and if I'm lucky someone will hire me to photograph baked beans for a Kampala advertising agency. I might even have to move to America. None of this is very comforting, Norrie. I'd planned to be a little further along in my career by now.'

'It's a rather disturbing world altogether at the moment, dear, isn't it? Everything's upside down. I'm still trying to get used to the idea that we prefer Elton John to William Blake at funerals these days.' He shrugged his neat little shoulders. 'You certainly don't have any doubt your time's over when the only names you recognize are on the obituary page or on BBC Gold.' He got up, pulling out his ancient pigskin wallet to pay for the drinks. 'And no, dear, I can't let you stay with me. Maddy La Font will let you stay with her. You have a dozen ex-wives. Some of them are still alive. What about the twins? Pinky, anyway? No go? Bobby MacMillan? Tubby? I know. OK. Well, I'm a selfish old bastard with my privacy. You might just have to bite the bullet, like a good boy, and give yourself up to the Brighton Belle!' He spoke in tones of subdued irony. He was serious. He looked into my eyes and took pity on me. 'Come on, it's Tuesday. Son of Tarzan's fighting Jack the Ripper Junior down at the Elephant. We'll go to the dogs together.'

I hadn't been to an old-fashioned gnasher since before I went to Rwanda. I'd gone off them. Now I was glad of the distraction. The yellow lights, the powerful smells, dogshit, booze and fried onions, the deep shadows, the floodlit ring, happy unhealthy faces glowing with meaty grease, panatella smoke, the busy betting, urine and sugar, the hyped-up willing mastiffs, what the old goozers called 'the warriors', the muffled yaps and growls, the eager panting, the clatter of the mechanical scoreboard, the shouts of the crowd and the stolid friendly pleasure of the regulars. Win or lose, they were always cheerful.

Indian and black guys run a lot of the dogs these days. Most of them are from Southall or Hornsey. It's still a working-man's sport. There's something honest and wholesome about a dog fight you never get around racing. Even though it's at night. And not that it's any cleaner. You can nobble a dog in a lot of subtle ways. It's better these days, though, compared to when I started going. It's one of the few bits of honest old London left. I breathed in the rich air. I checked out the form. I gave it some pump. I got into it. I borrowed a fiver off Norrie, put it on a jaunty new dog called Shit for Taste and won thirty-six coins. I sent a pound of liver round to Shit, who was grinning like the happy spectre of death he was and paid Norrie back the fiver and half the boss. I thought

I had to be in bad shape if the gods were taking pity on me. I was luckier than I knew. Four days later, Shit got ripped to bits by Big Peter the Third. His only other fight. Still, he'd had his victory, his day.

It was on the way home to Brookgate on the DLR that I recalled Norbert's advice about the Brighton Belle. He was right, of course, but I still didn't think I was up to it. There had to be a better option than retreating to Skerring-on-Sea. But any other option would further complicate things. It's true Pinky would probably be glad to see me. Even Flicky. But I didn't even want Maddy La Font to know I was in town. And I'd never been one to hide under a girlfriend's bed. And some of those women had a lot of reasonable grievances. So naturally I refused to throw myself on their willing mercy. I had a vestige of self-respect.

Still, it wasn't much of a choice.

Every real Londoner worth their salt knows that once you cross the river you're in limbo. Actually go to live there and something starts to eat your higher brain. Go as far as the South Coast and you might as well join the Cocoa Club. You move down to Eastbourne and next thing you know you're telling everyone in the local pub how you used to be a contender, how you told them to stuff their London job. It's the end of the line. After that you might as well walk into the mourning waters of the English Channel. Defeat accepted. Oblivion welcomed. The South Coast is thick with disappointed ambitions, a miasma that rises like morning fog and settles deep in the streets at sundown. Those nursing homes and boarding houses began to look attractive to you and the smell of disinfectant purified your soul. You started looking in the shops that sold spiffy motorized wheelchairs and wondering how you were ever going to lay your hands on three thousand coins. Maybe you could get a second-hand one. One some other bloke had died in. I mean, here we go to the land unknown, pards, choo-choo-choo into the tunnel of the great beyond . . . Drifted to the beach and waiting for the tide to take you out . . .

I was desperate for alternatives. I could keep hold of my Brookgate place all right for at least a year, I was pretty sure. Somebody would cover the mortgage. I had forked the gov enough in social security! So far they hadn't managed to find a way of cutting off your dole if you hadn't paid the appropriate respect to the Holy Gal. However, I had a feeling the DHSS wouldn't be in a mood to square almost twenty thousand quid's worth of credit cards or a three-hundred-sheet overdraft. On their last demand, they should have just told me to give the money to my mortgage company and saved themselves the transfer fees. You're on your own, like a rolling stone . . . Like fuck. Whoever talked me into buying this place?

I'd earned fortunes, of course, but didn't have much to show for it. It had been the Baron's men carrying off my last piglet, or squeezing my last roper in fact, together with a shocking amount of VAT, that had long since put me on my uppers, only about four years after I had been totally krauted by the Revenue. This time bankruptcy looked inevitable. I could see their brands threatening my thatch. Unlike many of my friends I hadn't built that option into my financial system. Even though I don't like responding to threats, I need to pay my crack. In Brookgate we like to think well of ourselves in that respect. It's the way my grandad brought me up. How you got the dosh wasn't as important as what you did with it. You didn't die in debt. You paid your way ahead. You even left a tip for the vicar.

All in all, the nineties had not been good to me. I understood I'd made mostly enemies in the eighties. Any friends I'd made in the seventies were now either dead, vanished, puffed into the stratosphere, become zombie-Scientologists or were just then otherwise unavailable to me. I couldn't help wondering as I packed my laptop and all its bits how I'd arrived at this predicament. I had never until now thought of myself as friendless.

I locked up Fogg Yard and walked to Holborn. I got the bus. For the first time in my life I began to feel lonely. I was almost glad to reach Victoria Station in time to buy my ticket, courtesy Norrie, order an expensive styrofoam cup of full caff at something blazing with fake brass and fake wood and called *Colombian Blast* and see that the 11:22 was running to West Hove as it had always run for as long as I could remember. Even then the privatized railway companies knew to leave routes like that well alone. There are some lines so profoundly well-travelled they shouldn't be altered. They extend into parallel dimensions. To change them would be to unravel the fabric of reality itself. Not that it isn't unravelling pretty rapido at the moment, no?

When the train divided at Haywards Heath I felt my last link with the real world broken. We rolled remorselessly past Parsons Piece and Preston Park. The last barrier.

From the cold-hearted regularity of West Hove, that tall stone necropolis for rich anal retentives, I got the rattling local to poor old Skerring. There was one First Class compartment. I was the only occupant. I never remember to bring anything to read and I'd forgotten my stereo. I sat there like a haughty exhibit, with my laptop on one side of me, my bag on the other. Through the glass partition I looked back at the other seats crowded with bright, busy nylon, with housewives and schoolchildren. Some got off at one station and were replaced by an identical wave of red, green and yellow at the next.

We stopped at a hundred of those bleak little neglected shelters guarded by miserable-looking gulls and offering distant views over scrub of one of the most depressing stretches of shingle shore on the planet. Almost monochrome. As usual, there was a drizzling rain.

Grey pebbles. Grey gulls. Grey skies. Grey roofs. Grey seas. A scattering of cranes and winches. Red aquatic steel. Cogs clogged with seaweed and mysterious filth. Tattered, fluttering rags might have been flags or canvas. Every so often some dismal marina, a concrete oblong full of boats that looked as if they'd been abandoned since D-Day. Who sought these places out? What kind of sanctuary did they represent? Did the boats ever sail? Nothing could take my mind off the reality.

Stop by relentless stop I approached my doom.

Potfield. Shoreham-by-Sea. Fenden. Hampton South. Great Hampton. Wearing Wick. Wearing-on-Sea. East Worthing. Worthing Central. West Worthing. Ooze. Goring. Great Stoning. Ferring. Arundel South. The next stop was inevitably mine. Even the train seemed reluctant to approach its angsty brick.

Skerring Station was an assaulted relic, a deconsecrated temple, tarred, patched, concreted, creosoted and rendered all over its original Victorian tawny rococo. Beyond the station were identical streets of concrete, terracotta and flint flanked by the defeated towers and spires of half-abandoned hotels and guest houses confronting the sea across a tarmac promenade whose railings were bent and scarred, spotted with patches of lead paint.

The most deeply unfashionable resort in Europe with a higher rainfall than Seattle's. It also had the highest suicide rate after Stockholm and Christchurch, NZ.

I considered staying on until Littlehampton, but it would only delay the inevitable. I swung my bags out of the carriage and began to haul them slowly up the platform to where my recidivist stepbrother Bernard grinned an enthusiastic alternative welcome. He raised his hand and affectionately slouched his shoulders. He punched the air. He went through a repertoire of meaningful tics and cryptic gestures. He moved in an over-relaxed shamble, grinning with alarming affection. He smelled strongly of engine parts and hash. He murmured something sincere. He told me to give him five. His skin was veined with motor oil. His lank brown ponytail gleamed with grease. His big, amiable Teletubby eyes shone from a face the colour of much-fingered dough. He demonstrated a lugubrious New Age hug. 'Big hug, man. Bi-ig hu-ug. This'll mean so much to Mum,' he said. 'Did she really ask you to save the baby?'

'Mum? Oh, Christ! What now?'

Bernard guffawed. 'Oh, yeah, sure! Not even the Brighton Belle, these days, brother Den, mate. Not since she had the operation. She's been so much better. Happier, you know.' Still grinning, he reached out his cardiganed arm and picked up my big bag. He pointed through the archway at his parked Montana. 'You know what I mean, Den. In the tunnel. When she told you she was pregnant.'

'*Diana?*'

As he got his car keys out of his overalls Bernie paused and put a serious hand on my arm. A kind of eager piety tempered his mildness.

He nodded, confirming the answer he craved. 'Was she, though, do you think? Is that why the Arabs had her killed?'

I made space for myself amongst the cans and smaller engine parts on the front seat. Sitting down, I felt a sense of profound regret. Yet I also knew a moment of epiphany. Of genuine repentance. Oh, how desperately I yearned to change the past. To go back to a time before my fall from grace, to abort that fatal moment when I had, after a lifetime, finally managed to piss off the only woman I'd ever truly loved.

In short, it was the closest thing to being personally damned by the Almighty anyone not actually in the Old Testament could probably get. Repentance wasn't enough. I was getting the minor-prophet treatment. I had to do my time in the wilderness until I truly understood the nature of my sins.

I gave myself up to Fate, trying to recall if I had any credit left in that area. I knew instinctively that Rosie wouldn't let me back into the world until I was truly ready to redeem myself.

On the other hand, I could just fuck it all off, admit defeat, roll a big reefer and join Bernie on the beach. I mean, does it really mean anything, man?

You know, in the end?

CHAPTER FOUR
The Crack

They say I talk a bit tricky sometimes when I'm with Rosie. What they're usually hearing is the old Brookgate twist.

All parts of London have their special twists, of course, to tell their own particular stories. Combined, they create the greatest common voice in history. The true voice of our group unconscious, protecting and extending our deepest freedoms.

London's that voice's vital heart but not everyone would know it as English. From Brookgate to Bombay to Boston all these rich lagoons of argot and cant, pidgin and patois and parlay spill one into another and make a stream and make a flood that roars back into every gutter and pipe and crack in the London pavement. It's as chaotic, relentless, as practical and as self-regenerating as nature herself. You can't contain it, can't really record it.

Even their dullest TV hackademics say we speak at least two languages. Private and public, dialect and standard. For good fucking reason. Ask any boon. But they're not really two languages. They're one. And they're a zillion. In Brookgate or Moss Side one word has a hundred meanings, minimum.

As Wittgenstein might have put it: The twist defines the crack.

In Standard English you can't afford to have that many meanings or it isn't efficient. We just speak a different language when we need one. Especially these days. And context in Brookgate isn't the context in Brussels, right? In Brookgate we like to call a scribe a scribe. Which in Brookgate is not the poet but the pen.

Nothing's as important as talk. It's our city's lifeblood. It pumps into every side street and alley, pounds down every tube and drain, enriches the heart, stimulates the brain. It carries the silt of centuries in its undertow. It unites us on the most profound levels. It's what keeps the tribe together. You can't print a current vocabulary because it's always in a state of change – responding, reacting, adapting, defending, attacking, inventing new twists, new realities. Like most things, if it's not resilient, it doesn't survive long. It doesn't do its job.

London twist's as impossible to capture as *Alien*. As soon as the media announces a sighting, it slithers away from them, hides in the air systems and the sewers, in the wastes of public toilets, in the scum and the detritus of the pubs and street markets where 'Nobody' goes. Unseen, scarcely heard, it pulses out of sight on the bottom, transforming itself. Then, when it's ready, Nobody comes back, snapping like a shark. Nobody's often raw. Nobody's often truthful. But you can't print what Nobody says in *The Times*. They won't let you. Why should they? Nobody said it.

When people do publish it, they get prosecuted. Or shot. Of course they do. They're threatening the consensual fantasy. The faintest whisper of the winds of limbo from the chaotic chasm has to be deleted. It might hint at the mile-high pile of hypocrisy most of us are crawling about on. The general agreement is that language should be a kind of honey.

I like it to be a kind of speed.

In the 1830s *Oliver Twist* reviewers condemned Dickens for his sensationalism, his fascination with filth. Only the public understood him. My friend Dave went to jail twice for reporting Moss Side twists and faces in their own idiom. A phantasmagoric troglodia of boons, perkies, fleaboys and logjammers. When the God-wielding chief constable up there had something nasty to say about fudgepackers, Dave took his speech, changed the word 'homosexual' to 'Jew' throughout and reprinted the lot in a comic. The goozer and his whole fucking squad were after Dave from that day on. They had the bench on their side. No contest. Dave learned what a lot of people learned before him – trust in the truth and you're as good as banged. At least he didn't have any trouble understanding the blokes in Strangeways when he got there.

Years ago I was in court and watched Lucy Rycroft tell the magistrates what the arresting policemen at the Oz demo had said – and done – to her. They'd talked dirty. They'd felt her up. Found guilty, Lucy also got a heavy reprimand from the bench. 'I hope, young lady,' said the chairwoman, 'that you don't use that sort of language in front of your parents!' City of London, 1971? She was lucky. A few years earlier she'd have been sectioned or burned at the stake for saying less. Instead, at twenty-one she went on to help found *Spare Rib*. And wound up editing national newspapers. Now they can hear her all right.

If they could fix a living language in a printed book it would immediately die and be replaced. Luckily they can't. Partridge's *Slang* is a riot. According to him, phrases used by cockneys for centuries were all invented in Australia in 1950. He wouldn't have known a living language if it gobbed in his yap. Or yapped in his gob.

You can always spot a dead language. The hi-brow weeklies will be full of it. It has rules, perimeters, specificity, agreed interpretations, clear definitions, approved meanings, an original purity. It can be debated. It has to be pronounced precisely. Hackademics love it. Dumb people always think if they control the language they control the world. Maybe they could – if they could control the language.

Virtual language gives the weak-minded a spurious feeling of authority. Like attending a Nuremberg Rally or singing in church. Or macaws in a squawk frenzy. It's a comfort, but is it a survival tool? Watch the fundamentalists falling over their real-world feet, for instance, when they do get a crack at being in charge. Or spin-doctors trying to spin a shooting war. It's more than hypocrisy, pards, it's downright dysfunctional. It's got to be neurotic when you come to depend for your sanity on the consolations of endlessly repeated banalities. It's US pop. They've managed to poison their own tongues with it.

Fake language makes the nutty all the nuttier. It lets them *pretend* to be sane. Hear your local politician go barmy before your eyes. Hear how an unhappy Scientologist supermillionaire can compare himself to an Auschwitz victim. Only in loopyspeak. Fake language is simple and specific. It gives an air of authority to lunatic notions. It simulates sanity. Baroness Hatchet was a great example. Barking barmy, talking like Mrs Bucket and running around America pretending to be the Queen. She'd be sectioned in the blink of a meat pie in Brixton. When the language changes you always see a lot of baffled politicians clumping up and down the corridors of power with staring eyes, untucked shirt-tails, open flies and institutional haircuts, wondering why people start grinning or avoiding them as soon as they open their mouths. They think if they close ranks and use the rhetoric even more aggressively, it will still work. Like banging a dead tower.

The smart ones know that when they blitz your twist your best bet is to create another. Rapido. It doesn't matter who you are. Minorities. Authorities. Bigots. Zealots. Black guys. White guys. Good guys. Bad guys. The isolated. The profoundly paralysed. That French guy who worked on *Vogue*. Give us an eyelid to blink and we'll communicate. We produce words almost faster than we think. If we didn't we'd be extinct.

I used to read those Russians, the ones they said sold out to Stalin? Every sentence was a triple entendre. They're stuffed with meaning. They invented a language on the spot that not even Stalin the philologist could read. Or maybe he didn't care. Maybe it was his secret way of maintaining an intellectual elite. Of course, everyone who bought the books knew what they were really saying. That was the trick in those days. But it's also how the public voice grows and grows, yes? Until one way or another it has to be answered.

Anyway, our native twist kept me and Rosie together more than once.

I grew up with Rosie. Her mum was like my own. Only more normal. We were poured out of the same pot. She was my fetch. I was her ringer. They said we were invisibly joined. Psychic Siamese. Crack pards. We had the same DNA, the instincts and habits of twins. The echoes, the recognitions. More than brother and sister. Our humour, our suss on reality, was identical. Same V, same flix, same print, same sounds, same thoughts. We made up the same words, copped the same spiel, clocked the same points, faced down the same aggro. We got angry about the same things. Injustice. Inequality. Matters of fairness. We were never short of face, me and Rosie. What stallies call smack. What my grandad used to call bottom. Self-respect, really. And a bit of nerve.

We ran a gang of kids. We called ourselves The Brookgate Tygers but Alf Horspool's name for us stuck. The Alley Cats. It was the nastiest insult the newsy could come up with.

Alf hated cats as much as he'd loved dogs. He'd been a Primitive Methodist preacher until his pet lurcher Lightning was struck by lightning in Lincoln's Inn Fields. Alf took this not as irony but as petty antagonism on God's part, a personal betrayal, so in fury he signed up on the spot with the opposition and joined a black-magic coven that had met regularly on Putney Heath with the object of establishing the reign of Lucifer on Earth until the locals complained about the noise.

I think they were sacrificing moggies. You could believe it of Alf Horspool. He had a witchy sort of name. He smelled faintly sulphurous. He had a dyed widow's peak so he looked like the devil with his heavy sloping eyebrows meeting in the middle. No lobes to his ears. Slanting cheekbones. The whole West End production. Boo! Hiss! Shudder!

Horspool saw Rosie as quintessentially feline. He was certainly most vicious to her, but we were all scum, he said, living witness to the decline of western civilization since the War. I think he'd banked on the Nazis winning. People like that always turn to black magic. A natural progression into oblivion, really. Alf's rising nasal shriek gave the word *guttersnipe* a new dimension. And nobody could accurately mimic the way he said *Oiks*. We tried for hours. You'd have to have had his operation, we decided.

Alf said we were the Litter of '52. We should have been drowned in a bucket at birth. None of us was hurt by his antagonism. It was too obvious. We all knew where we stood. We knew we could wreck his business any time we put our minds to it. We adopted an attitude of lordly tolerance. We were, after all, the most powerful gang in Brookgate. Even Mr V.S. Mehta, who was one of the top mobsmen at that time, would give us a grin of recognition when he went into his uncle's appliance shop, which he used for his headquarters.

Mr Mehta was known to have Soho businesses, but in Brookgate he was just a model landlord, always willing to accommodate the genuinely hard-up tenant but wouldn't give a ligger the airspace. He'd trained as a lawyer and knew all the ins and outs of the Huguenot Leases, which controlled so much of Brookgate's land and kept the place looking so old-fashioned. He never overstepped the spirit of the Leases, always respected the ancient customs and beliefs. He had the soft-spoken, straight-backed manner of all successful mobsmen, that cultivated self-control which warned as much as it welcomed, and was a close friend of the Richardsons. His mum had been Muslim, a Bengali princess. His sister Yaz married my nephew's son, Ben. His other sister, Jenni, married Gentleman Jerry Cornell. My step-uncle. A union of titanium. Nothing could break it. An extended family of expert villainy. Thieves, fighters and fixers. Instinctive grafters and grifters. Granite-willed women and men who never stepped outside until every every hair was in place, everything polished, a crease in the trousers, an edge to the cuff, a rake to the hat.

Mr Mehta's dad had started the businesses. He had been a war hero in Flanders, rode with the Bengal Lancers at Ypres, scored the Military Cross, got demobbed in the UK and bought his first properties with his soldier's pension. Mr Mehta was too much of an aristocrat to boss a gang. He just had people who did him favours from time to time.

We took it for granted that Rosie and me bossed our gang. It wasn't like an LA gang or even the stuff you see in Hoxton and Dalston these days. It wasn't macho or flashy. Like most of our generation, we thought uniforms were naff. We were too much in danger of being put into one, probably. Ours was an old-fashioned East London klick, boys and girls, any race or colour. Almost any age. Taking in new members at one end, losing them at the other. We didn't waste our time fighting rival gangs. We only rarely fell back on defensive violence. We could do it all right – short, sharp, secret and nasty, usually – but we thought violence was crap, too. We weren't bored schoolkids killing time. We were learning how to survive. We were scavengers, not predators. Proto-retailers.

Kids who grow up round a street market are like that. The market sets the tone and marks its own card. Aggro gets you nowhere. You learn how to graft, trade, turn over unconsidered trifles, twist for anything tricky. Any bricky. Any bracky. As the Greeks say.

We were a gang because of common interests. Nothing forced us into it. Most of us had only one parent, usually a mother. These days you would call us latchkey kids and we would be a scandal, but then we sensed our liberty. It was the beginning of the Golden Age. I don't know a better time to grow up. It wasn't long after the war. Your mum was still just glad to see her kids running about in the open air, in one piece. They all went to work, mostly at the Old Brookgate factory in Clerkenwell Row. They had to trust you. They had no choice.

In those few hours between school finishing and someone coming home, the world was adult-free, yours to make your own. Which usually meant going to Old Sweden Street twisting for tricky, on the lookout for any small item we could nick, an errand we could run, a chance to turn a tanner.

This was before the Leases got bought, of course. Under all kinds of pressure, victims of unimaginable cunning, Mr Mehta and the others moved into South London, sold out to BBIC and in a matter of a year an entire culture was blown apart. Mr Mehta was the old school. Mr Begg's men were of the new.

The one big lesson American consumerism taught Europe is how to strip your own psychic assets. How to sell your self-respect in return for a handout and the chance of a class-action court case. How to squeeze a handsome buck from a murdered ancestor, maximize the profit on your birthright, burlesque an act of bravery, shit on your own dead to catch a penny from a tourist, replace the family jewels with paste, fake your own heritage, strip the authentic assets of a place and substitute a clapboard fantasy. *Disney's Real Life for Windows*™. *EastEnders* cockneys spouting rhyming slang as authentic as old Richard Attenborough™ movies. It's like New Orleans coon dancers. Real people reviving a grotesque parody of their heritage for a condescending stranger's passing approval. What's it got to mean?

For centuries our Brookgate was controlled by her citizens (or *denizens* as the old journos used to call us) under the power of the Huguenot Leases which, partly because of the plague, made full ownership of the land so unclear it had been disputed in Chancery since 1670. Missed the worst of the Great Fire of 1666, which destroyed a lot of records. Effectively, it meant we all had a say in what happened in our own patch. Any new building, improvement and so on was usually agreed by common consent, usually after some sort of meeting. It was our strongest civic weapon.

These days, of course, all that's gone in the virtual warmth of the glo-flame millennium. Old Sweden Street, with its Heritage-style Tudored shopping parade, fake coaching yards, chain chippies, retainered pearlies, cockneyed-up caffs, nostalgia novelties, tarted drinkers, security pied-à-terres, lamprey-bars, forged pieshops and all its other false-fronted gimcrackery, actually stinks. Thanks to cowboy plumbers, one-slap painters and electricians short of opposable thumbs, you can smell it a mile off. It was once the sticky, permeating nicotine sweetness of the Old Brookgate tobacco factory at Clerkenwell Row. Powerful enough to flavour your chips. Other Londoners could tell at a sniff where you were from. Not any more. Now we're all plodding through the same toxic haze of urine, grease, carbon monoxide and degenerated plastic that has eaten away the city's deregulated gilt and left us coughing up crap.

The concrete-'n'-cosmetic rush spread its tyre tracks all over our city. For a few months Jack Cade's Parade, our hardboard heritage, glowed like Hollywood-on-Holborn. Now it can't tell any more lies. It looks as shitty on the outside as it is on the inside. Talk about gilded flies. The trim's curling and warping. Retail spaces are grimed with cracked promises, crumbling concrete, warped pine. Those still open look like film sets left out in the rain. Leaseholders' dreams of gold transmuted into interminable hours of leaden grind. Some poor bastard stan's learning about the enterprise society the hard way. The cladding's coming off, just like the faux optimism of those awful years. What was sold as Portland stone turns out to be cinders and papier mâché.

And now the street's been blocked, rechannelled, one-wayed, faked up and pedestrianized. It's little more than a dog-leg rat-run between Hatton Garden and Gray's Inn Road with a few miserable *Sweet News* stalls in it. Corporate coster barrows. Teknikolor awnings and synthetic grass. You see them in airports everywhere. In streets they're obscene.

I might sound bitter, and the blank generation isn't supposed to care about these things, but I grew up in Old Sweden Street's final glory, when ordinary spivs still ran a lively black market and only Petticoat Lane and Portobello could boast the variety and complexity of our trade. It was an international market. And a centre for what people now call 'underground' sports: knucklers, doggies, the birds, pig racing, ferrets. People from Paris, Berlin, Milan, Dublin were always there doing business. Funny overcoats, odd hats. But very sharp. You know. Big wads. Heavy links. Plenty of gold.

Originally we paralleled Leather Lane almost down to Holborn. Locals never bothered with the Lane unless they were lazy. It was known to be rubbish. How could anybody *not* look down on Leather Lane market? Even their fishers were crap. They couldn't fry batter. Their chips were always flaccid, their faggots limp. Their saveloys were unspeakably worse than the all-nite Chinese chippy's in St Alban's Passage.

Lanies said we were paupers, posers and wankers.

We knew they were whiners and ponces. Even their branded goods, seemingly identical to our own, were inferior. It was a pathetic market. The traders never took risks. They hardly ever bought anything off you and never gave you a price when they did. They all had coppers in their families. They swore everything they sold was kosher. You knew it was nicked. You usually knew who'd nicked it. They weren't happy with that, either. They hated us because we were clever. We did better because we took chances. We got off on risks. We were part of the twist.

It was how we were in Brookgate. We were that sort of community. In 1900 Brookgate raised a whole regiment of irregulars for the Boer War. They got a taste for it. Played the dutchies at their own game. Hit and run. Never waste ammo when you can use your knife. Never use your knife when you can use your teeth and hands. Always try to get a souvenir. Bunch of savages, it says in the books. We were proud of them. The Brookgate Bastards. They were famous. We put up a great memorial to the lot of them. Alfred Gilbert designed it. The bloke who did Eros? We got it from a bankrupt foundry in Stoke Newington. We lost it somewhere when Barbican knocked down Mustard Street.

Off and on the Bastards had a whale of a time for a few years until everyone but Captain Jerry Silverstein, the famous Kosher Butcher, was snuffed out on the Somme. Lanies said we were naturally rabid, that we didn't have any morals like they had. Guts was what they didn't have. If they raised a regiment, it was the Queen's Own Sweetboys. Leather Lane was notorious for being two-faced conservative cowards. Half of them were chapel. An iffy, unLondon religion that had spread up from Streatham some time in the previous century. How it crossed the fucking river no one will ever know.

In contrast, Old Sweden Street, catholic and cosmopolitan as can be, was flush enough with reinvestment dosh to reward any enterprising young snip. Turnover was everything. So our thefts were largely a one-way flow from Leather Lane's grumbling wimps to Old Sweden Street's stylish mobsmen. They had lay preachers running their stalls. We had eloquent dandies. Retired jacks. They used the good book as an authority for their bigotries and judgements. We were *in* all the books about master thieves, daring cracksmen and ingenious weaponry. Famous fights like the Siege of Bacon Alley. The Dorrington Street Barring-In, when the police were barricaded in their own station for two days. Edgar Lustgarten could have done a whole series, just on us. Our crooks had their names in the Sunday papers and most of them weren't in jail. Our jacks were legends. Names like Lakefort and Mehta, Little Billy Cady, Grandma Fix, Dick Banff, the Gerrards, the Cottingtons, the Lamberts, the Khans. Up there with the Krays or the Cornells. Only less showy.

We were even snotty about what we lifted off the Lanies. Leather Lane had a couple of plastic toy stalls we trained on. Their snap would have disgraced Woolworths. Not worth blacking up for, as the Brookgate Bastards used to say when they returned unblooded from a disappointing trawl in the kraut trenches.

It was a market you could hear, long before you got there. We had new and second-hand toys and clothing at the north end of Old Sweden Street between Hatton Wall and Bonemeal Street; fruit, veg, meat, fish, pets, live fowl, pigeons, rats and domestic products at the south end around Brooke Passage and Little Baldwin's Gardens up to St Alban's, down to Greville Street. Tools, junk, books, gadgets and linen were in the middle, between Brook Lane and Baldwin's Gardens. Clothes were mostly round the corner in Bacon Court as far as Verulam Street which stretched across Leopards Place, through the Buildings, all the way to Fulkes Passage into Brooke Street at the back of the Prudential before the council and the redevelopers started dropping billion-ton blocks of concrete on us.

Our gang never stole from their favourite market trader. Mr Lorenzo Small's Trick Emporium was just an ordinary stall, but with a little awning made of draped blackout curtains, so you had the impression of entering a cave. It smelled of incense, California poppies, patchouli, toilet fresheners. Inside, Mr Lorenzo Small Jnr was incredibly thin and tall with a glass eye he was willing to take out and show you and the kind of bald head that made you wonder if he was wearing one of his own jokes. Like Tired Tim from *Comic Cuts*. His gaunt, long face bore that vague, benign, protective beam of one profoundly terrified of the world's brutalities. His skinny arms and legs stuck out of his clothes like pipe-cleaners. His hands danced like picked bones over his stock. But he liked kids. Nothing wonky. He had a wide but fairly random selection of tricks. He was dependent on what his agents could steal from Ellison's and Gamage's round the corner on Holborn Parade, just before the Viaduct. It's gone now.

Using the short cuts still provided by bomb sites, it took two minutes to run from his stall on the corner of Fulke Street, down Brooke Passage into Holborn and the shops, grand, triple-fronted monsters, with gold decorative lettering, on three or four floors. Five minutes later you could be back with a bob's worth of barter. He paid prompt, the heavy coppers almost too much for his delicate hands, and if he couldn't pay you, he trusted you to take a brown half-quid note out for change. In those days it was almost impossible to prove the stuff was nicked. The stores hung enormous layers of goods outside and it was knowing temptation on their part. They expected to lose a bit. The price of advertising. Local taxes.

CHAPTER FIVE
The Patch

Ellison's didn't just sell jokes and tricks. It had a whole Carnival department, full of Big Heads from nineteenth-century pantomime, vast comic wigs, noses, moustaches, greasepaint, gum arabic, every kind of mask you could think of. Fancy dress for all occasions and tastes.

They were ten times bigger than Pollock's. They had puppets, string and glove. A thousand Punches and Judies. Scarlet and gold. Dark greens and pulsing yellows. Silver, black velvet, vivid silk.

They had toy theatres, and pre-war German cut-out scenery, and cardboard actors and every accessory you needed, down to real limelight lanterns for the stage. They had little cardboard boxes of flat soldiers, straw-packed in tiny wooden crates, from Germany. Cheap paper labels with spreading ink. Furniture polish. Paint. Scented wax.

They had vast walls of tiny brass-labelled wooden drawers which stretched into heaven's darkness and sent down glinting dust whenever an assistant climbed a ladder to find something. *Noses, Red, Large. Noses, Red, Medium. Noses, Red, Small. Noses, Red, X.Small. Opera Glasses. Opera Glasses, Trick. Paint (Glow). Paint (Invisible). Paint (Trick Colour). Roses (Silk). Roses (Water). Roses (Shock). Spikes (Head). Spikes (Hand). Spikes (Adjustable). Staples. Soap (Blackface). Soap (Smelly). Spinach (Trick, Cans). Stink Bombs (Large, Strong). Umbrellas (Filled). Water pistols. X-Ray glasses (juv.). Zipshots (med.)* . . .

Rosie and I visited Ellison's the way other kids might go to a museum. It was an education. We would nick things we didn't recognize and find out what they were when we sold them on. We learned a lot there. Mr Small knew everything. Sometimes he'd circle what he wanted on the back of my *Pecos Bill*. Ellison's used to advertise in all those kids' sixpenny comics, usually on the back page. Remember them? In that weird blue ink? About a thousand little boxes for severed hands, nails through heads, starting pistols, real radios and joke soap. Kids sent postal orders to them from all over the Empire. *Pecos Bill* and *Tarzan Adventures* were edited from round the corner in Brooke Street. We used to blag free copies off the fat little office boy who wanted us to think he was the editor.

There was a lot of printing and stuff in the area, with all the typesetters and block-makers and presses around Fleet Street, St Paul's and the Old Bailey, down Fetter Lane, Farringdon Road, up Ludgate Hill. Flash-fast developers and printers. You took your negs in to the paper and they did the rest. I got used to stringing for them. A lot of us did it. If you got a story followed up you got a guinea and a half – one pound, ten and six — about one fifty-two now. Signed your rights away on the back of the cheque and that was that. Smash and grabs. Lost dogs. Arrests and chases. Grist to the mill. Rosie had a nose for the stories they'd pay more for. And which would do somebody some good. Old ladies alone at Christmas. Cats on a ledge. The human-interest stuff. Genuine causes a lot of the time, right from an early age.

Rosie Beck was my mother's sister's daughter. Her stepdad was George Haley, one of the first Punjabis to work for London Transport and a friend of my dad's. There was no clear record of his real name. Everyone loved Uncle George. He was a naturally kind-hearted man. He'd helped half Brookgate through hard times. He'd always been good for a fiver if you were really desperate. He'd even offer before you asked. He had an inheritance, he said.

Uncle George's inheritance turned out to be his tendency to kleptomania, which had made his dad a jailbird in East Bengal. Eventually he lost his job and did a year in the Scrubs for fiddling his takings after he was promoted to the ticket office. It hadn't been for himself, of course. Most of the dosh went to Shelter, Refuge and the Brick Lane mosque. He was a discreet and pious Muslim all his life. He didn't let his defence use that in his favour. He said that would have been cheating.

When he came out he worked on and off in Old Sweden Street, mostly on the fruit and veg. He was never the same, my Auntie said. In prison he'd turned a cancerous grey. She was disgusted by how few of the people he'd helped ever offered their support. Some were wonderful. Others she could shame or bully into doing something, but some simply refused her. She held a particular dislike for Alf Horspool. The newsagent's shop was directly across the road from them on the corner of Dowling Street. Years earlier George Haley had helped Alf with his gambling bills. Which was why Alf was still alive. His debts of honour had been to Mal 'Lips' Cornell who was very strict about payment. Alf had already had one strong warning. George had also helped him give up the dogs. Alf was now doing well but had never once, my auntie said, offered my uncle so much as a job delivering papers. So none of us was allowed to buy anything in his shop. Which was fair enough. We compromised and only stole from him. Principles were principles. But it didn't make him like me and Rosie any better and barring us didn't do him much good when we had command of Brookgate's finest klick.

Me and Rosie did everything together. We were the core of the klick, unquestioned leaders. Our best lieutenants were unambitious, amiable kids who were as fascinated by us as by the games and adventures we invented. Others stuck with us because we knew how to make money. Most weren't very imaginative but they had a spark of romance. Not all our escapades were victimless fun. Rosie could get impatient, carried away, a bit too bossy. We hounded an old man to his death once. That is, he had a heart attack while we were following him. We thought we were joking. And we almost killed a copper. That shocked us. We tried bullying but our hearts were never in it. Our plan to kidnap and ransom household pets came to a noisy and painful end. We still have the scars. Mostly we stuck to snapping, nicking, twisting, sub-contracting and gophering.

Rosie and me discovered the truth about sex together. It had been on our minds for a while. We went one Saturday to Farringdon Street book market under Holborn Viaduct and paid sixpence for a thick volume called *Guide to Love and Marriage*. I think it's the one Arthur Koestler wrote. A version of it, anyway. We took it back to our floury gang HQ, an abandoned maze of lofts over J.A. Taylor's who had stopped baking on the premises and now got deliveries from their depot at Kings Cross. We inspected the clinical illustrations and compared them to our own dusted anatomy. We discussed the questions raised and found most of the answers made sense.

The *Guide* had told us what we needed to know. We kept the information in reserve. We understood it to be potent truth. It gave us a cheap sense of superiority, to hear our friends speculating so comically. We'd crack up. We'd exchange looks. They'd never know what we were laughing about. We had discovered our parents' secrets. We had their power. We were a junior priest and priestess of Dionysus, privy to all sexual wisdom. Satisfied, we swapped the book for something more interesting. *The Future* by Professor A.M. Low. A world without sin or sickness, a world of shared wealth and noble architecture, clean, smooth-running public transport. A Wellsian vision of things to come. It spoiled us for the reality, I suppose, even though the real version emerged as tower blocks and concrete opera houses.

On the whole I think we got as much out of *Doctor Smith's Lesser Classical Dictionary*, which had been one of the few books my dad had owned. *Doctor Smith's* reproduced some salty Greek and Roman friezes by way of illustration.

It was from the night-school courses his grandfather had done at the old Brookgate Institute. William Morris taught there. Edith Nesbit. Bernard Shaw. H.G. Wells had turned up once a month religiously for years. Grandad had seen him. He was a cocky, charming little pipsqueak, he said. Wells piped his enthusiastic visions and shrilled his indignation at the world's follies and entranced them all.

Chirping away like a mad grasshopper, said grandad, Wells filled them all with dignity and a sense of purpose. Those were the days of self-improvement and working-men's colleges.

And that was our rite of passage. It took about a day. I don't remember any traumas and neither does Rosie. We were interested in our differences and understood their function, we liked the way we felt in charge of ourselves, we liked the buzz of sex, but we just went on about our lives. It must be why I've never been able to relate to that school of fiction where turning thirteen was the most interesting experience of the author's life.

Later the sex and the politics would get complicated but all through the golden sixties it never came between us. Maybe it's because we fell in love with the existentialists at the same time. That is, we watched Jean-Paul Sartre's *Roads to Freedom* in that rich early trinotronic telly colour and were sucked in instantly. Dramatized by David Turner. I could probably tell you who designed the sets. Spencer Chapman.

What a twist! Those faces! Moody Michael Bryant as Mathieu, haughty, tortured Daniel Massey, sexy Georgia Brown, Rosemary Leach, Alison Fiske, Anthony Corlan. There's nothing more stylish than Anglo-Saxon actors pretending to be French. They get high on it. My friend Freddie Earlle was in it, too, as a Jewish soldier in the last episodes, but I didn't know him then. I met him later on the set of *Clochemerle* or maybe *Chéri*. He was doing nothing but frogs for a while. When was *Roads*? BBC, Sunday nights, repeats on Thursday. 1969? We'd have been sixteen. Intellectual ducklings. Ready for imprinting, all right. Kapow!! Sex. Death. Politics. Philosophy. Existentialism. Hip attitudes. Elegant drugs. Spanish Civil War. Lagondas and long-nosed Citroëns. Difficult choices. Ambiguities galore. Cool threads. Moody theme music. The looming advance of Hitler. Plenty of accordion. Powerful cigarettes! Lashings and lashings of ennui, like black cream on bitter chocolate. Paris. The eve of Nazi occupation. The concerns of youth seem to fade. We have maturer considerations now. Real life. Our illusions fall away and we begin to see the brute horror breaking up through the fragile crust of our culture. Obscene cynicism, exemplary idealism.

Oi moi! Nobody mourns their lost youth more thoroughly than a teenager. Nobody understands better the potent anguish, the bleak realization that existence and oblivion are mutually dependent. The series lasted for thirteen luscious, desperate weeks. It was one long sophisticated glorious *complaint*, an elegy to our vanished innocence. A twist more potent than *Casablanca*. As angry as Brecht and gritty as Pabst. Angstier than Graham Greene. God, those Catholics can suffer.

Roads to Freedom should have carried a health warning. It hit us everywhere at the same time. Soul, mind and groin. These days they'd ban it. We spent half Sunday making sure the TV was working properly for that evening and then we relished the repeats on Thursdays. It offered us the complete lifestyle package. We coughed our way through packets of Gauloises and listened to our Juliette Gréco album. We wore sunglasses indoors. We wore navy blue jerseys because Marks and Spencer didn't sell black. We sewed our jeans to our skinny legs. We bought the orange Penguin novel and were disappointed by it. The TV story was a lot easier to follow – time jumps always work better in a visual. Long moral arguments about setting the world to rights. The blind hypocrisy of a middle class unable to see the injustice and cruelty its wealth is based on. Rosie had got her scholarship to St Paul's Girls' School in Hammersmith. She could even talk French. She had an incredible gift for it. By the time she was thirteen she had also taught herself basic Spanish and Italian. She'd soon know German and Arabic and was getting into Russian. She was that kind of girl. She had the brains, I had the sensibilities. She could learn the fundamentals of something and make it work for her. My gifts were for clocking the realities of mood and expression, reading body language, framing a shot, recollecting scenes, anticipating moves, guessing the perfect moment, all that stuff. And I had what they used to call a nose for a story. In that sense, I think, we were probably both telepathic. We had complementary charms.

When I was fifteen I was in my first band, Black Flame. I could play one chord shape down the neck. Chuck Berry riffs. But it would be a while before I had my moments of stardom. Rosie was the lead singer. Singing wasn't her obvious talent. She looked great, though, so we gave her a tambourine to bang until she got bored and went off to do something more useful with her time. I didn't much enjoy it without her. I didn't get interested again until she started going out with Paul Frame.

I was never motivated enough to be a proper rock star. The truth was I didn't have much relish for repeating the same preachy songs every night and no instinct for posing on stage. Don't ask me why, but I was more interested in the famous than I was in fame. I preferred to photograph the posers. And in the end that's what I started to do. It got me into *NME* and *Melody Maker*, but it was *Rolling Stone* that gave me my real success. I didn't have all the chores of rehearsals and there were fewer cold nights on the road. My serious rock-and-roll career pretty much ended with the Tory revolution. The Rainbow, Christmas 1981. I did a few sessions because people asked me to, some Support the Miners and Rock Against Racism gigs, a useless tour of America which I didn't want to do in the first place, then new fashions came in, and that was that. I lost interest. Rock and roll was over for me when Stiff went soft. For a long time there was only pop. And the occasional authentic echo of some sampled chord.

But, like Rosie, I never stopped getting a buzz off a brunette pageboy haircut, an oversize black jumper, a packet of Gitanes and an Edith Piaf song. *La Jetée*? Monotone voice-overs? Verité grain? What?

Existentialism's in my soul. It changed my life. If it confirmed the guess I was born with, that we were all dancing on the edge of the abyss, I didn't take the news badly. I'm a natural optimist. Rather than sit around moping, it seemed to me and Rosie that we might as well enjoy life while it lasted. *I wasn't. I am. I won't be.* Make the most of that. Leave the planet as you'd wish to find it. I think that's how existentialism goes down in a fundamentally secular culture like ours. You've got to have had the pope rammed up your bum from birth to get seriously worried when someone states what is fairly obvious to the ordinary unindoctrinated citizen – viz.: we have one life and we don't know why. What would we be doing if we didn't have it? Like you wake up and find you've got thousands more in your account than you thought. It's probably a mistake but you might as well make the best of it.

Roads to Freedom led naturally to Camus and I was totally hooked. Camus's *Caligula* ran at the ill-starred Phoenix, Charing Cross Road. With Derek Jacobi. For about a week. Including the matinées, we saw every performance, all but the last three from the Upper Circle. There were so few people in the audience by the end of the run that the manager let us sit in the best seats. The actors waved at us. Oh, God! It thrilled us. As the assassin's knives rose and fell, Caligula cried out 'I'm still alive!' and we knew exactly what he meant.

After the closing night we clapped ourselves silly until we got self-conscious, then waited to get Derek Jacobi's autograph but I don't think any of them were very happy. A sort of jaunty sadness comes over actors who know they're performing well in a good play but just can't bring the audience in. We felt we were intruding and walked up to Theobalds Road for egg and chips, round the corner from home. We talked about it for weeks. Real plays. Real people. It made everything more real. Better than movies. And the movies were great, too. We felt a bit impatient with the ennui sometimes. We wanted to tell them to get off their arses, remind them, like Beowulf, that God helps those who help themselves. But that's a paternalistic religion for you.

I found Aldous Huxley about then, too. All of it at the same time. His early scepticism side by side with his essays on faith. *Crome Yellow* and *The Perennial Philosophy*. I was a bit baffled by Simone de Beauvoir. I loved Kierkegaard. Failed with Heidegger. Wittgenstein got too iffy for me. Some of these guys seem to roll the stone off the top of the philosophy volcano and then spend the rest of their lives trying to roll it back on again. But Camus remained tops for buzz. Only a couple of other writers have given me anything like it. William Burroughs was one of them.

Burroughs understood all that stuff about the power of languages. I got to know him in London. I took the Beak Street session photos – him,

Ballard, Paolozzi, Walsh – which everyone says fixed him exactly. He never stopped twisting on in that Midwest monotone of his. Like T. S. Eliot on Prozac. I thought he was joking at first.

Not that he didn't have a sense of humour. Burroughs believed absurdity was fun, too. Ha, ha, ha, he would rasp. Ha, ha. That's funny. And then read a newspaper across the columns rather than down. Life wasn't too bad for an existentialist who had the measure of his own drugs and enjoyed the ridiculous irony of his situation. He was living his life on a thousand levels at the same time, never sleeping, never waking. In the margins. Getting the best out of it.

For a while he was the only writer reporting the authentic speech of all his subcultures. And not just reporting it. He was using it. Reworking it. Inventing it. Giving back as much as he took. Eventually his own voice drowned him. Rosie couldn't stand him. By then she was reading Proust in the original and eating a lot of quiche.

Reading and eating preferences aside, Rosie and I remained almost mystically close. Our arguments scared people who didn't know us but they were works of art, verbal arabesques with a million references. Their ferocity was part of the crack. And we were definitely passionate about our causes. Though neither of us liked joining much. We were mostly happy with it being just the two of us, posting bills, raising money, getting signatures. We had plenty of other friends. Sometimes we'd stay apart for a few weeks, as a matter of healthy instinct. Our friendship was never incestuous. Our developing sexuality seemed complementary, and yet we never really fucked. We tried it a couple of times and it didn't work. Rosie said it felt like a weird form of wanking. All the embarrassment with none of the fun. Like most people, we needed romance; we were attracted by imagined mysteries in a partner, physical exploration. A difference. And Rosie and I knew each other inside and out. Or so we thought.

I took a couple of early girlfriends back to see my mum. It was the thing to do in Brookgate, in those days. I thought the first meeting went fairly well. We left without my mum throwing anything at us. But the girl never saw me again. The second time, my mum started asking the girl questions about her 'intimates' and her washing habits. Neither me nor Kelly could believe it. Yet she found herself answering. I think she'd have gone on seeing me if I'd stopped apologizing. Mum said how nice she thought they both were and often asked after them. I was used to her, of course, and hardly noticed a lot of her eccentricities.

Rosie's dad was from Senegal originally, a US airman. Her mum was my mum's older sister. She was a crack. Always joking. Whereas my mum was merely cracked. That's why my grandad had custody. But I spent more time at Rosie's house than my own. For one thing they had their own telly. My mum could never keep one. Kids always use the tolerant homes as bases.

My mum still lived in Brookgate then. In Felix Court, though eventually she had to take medicine. She loved me and I loved her. She wasn't exactly intolerant. She valued freedom as much as her parents and grandparents, the Radical Mary and Canting Dick of Charles Godfrey's famous comic song. She was Brookgate through and through. She admired a rebel of almost any stripe. But she was unpredictable. Freakburn. She challenged everyone to accept her extremes. My dad being hanged hadn't helped. She was an early acid casualty and needed a lot of comfort. A lot of fantasy. A lot of rainbow roads. A lot of mind-holidays. Everyone liked her, including me. It was just a good rule to keep clear of her. Sweet, dippy, selfish, greedy and well paranoid. Short-lived liaisons, long-term memory loss, kids she probably wouldn't have known as hers. I was a bit vague about my siblings. In certain states she was perfectly capable of eating her own. I still don't like to ask her what happened to the twins. Or their father. Not someone you could generally rely on in a crunch. Whereas Rosie always was.

Rosie busted me from jug once. I mean, they were actually holding me in the old Holborn nick, in an interview room, and she just walked through the lot of them, DCs, PCs, WPCs, uniformed, CID, took me by the arm, told me I was coming home, and walked me out. I think they were too embarrassed to do anything about it. I wasn't even the one who'd found the gun. I thought shooters were stupid. Maybe it was growing up with my great grandad. He knew a lot of people who'd lived in Brookgate around the turn of the century who'd been in gun battles with the police. His brother bought a working pistol in a swap shop for sixpence. A Mauser machine pistol, the class hand-weapon of its day, would set you back a fiver at the Army and Navy Stores, Victoria Street. Guns for anyone, he said. There were a lot more dead coppers in those days. And dead humans. Nobody wants to go back to that.

I'd been identified as the kid who shot the fucker in the knee. Not true, but there it was. For some reason Alf Horspool didn't prosecute. I thought he'd seen who'd shot him and didn't want to say. It wasn't Rosie but she knew, too. She told me years later. Alf had had a relapse into his old trouble and no George to bail him out this time. It was Billy the Brummie – Billy Fairling, working for the Cornells, who he owed a small fortune to. Team-handed. Three other blokes, apparently. Alf was lucky he only got shot in the leg. It was an accident. Billy pulled the shooter, snagged up the safety on his tatty old coat lining, and hit Alf by a fluke. Still, it saved breaking a billiard cue. We didn't have baseball bats in those days.

Alf moved down to Southend for a bit. His spinster sister Doris lived there. He said he was glad to see the back of our bloody slum for ever.

Of course, he was home in a year, limping on a nasty ivory stick that he'd learn to throw like a javelin. It was something of a relief to all of us to have him back. Nobody felt strongly enough to scare the bastard out of the district. He was one of our own, after all. And he'd been shot by one of our own (though really a Brummie), for being a general berk. Admittedly by accident.

So everything was sorted. We were square again. By way of a welcome I bought the first and only Mars Bar I ever paid for over his counter. He was trembling and blinking when he gave me my change. I think he was trying to believe it was real. He died of cancer a few years later, after he'd apologized to Uncle George and accepted Islam. He'd made his peace with Brookgate. Our rejected dead were allowed to go to Clerkenwell Crematorium but we buried Alf in St Alban's Churchyard, between the primary school and Fogg Yard. An imam came from the mosque and helped the vicar with the service. We never saw who threw the old pistol into the grave as the last sods were thumping on his coffin, but I was certain it was the vicar.

Rosie was by then a terrifyingly potent young woman. Seventeen years old and powered to go. A state-of-the-art sex kitten with the self-esteem of a Nigerian field marshal. They looked. They swooned. But they never thought of touching. Even in her school uniform she had authority. In her civvies she was an H-bomb. She was at UCL doing languages and PEP by autumn 1970. She was going out again with Paul Frame, also seventeen, briefly of Ozzie and the Overtones, the hippest funk guitar on the R&B circuit who of course would become one of the driving elements in early Joy Division before he formed Cirque d'Hiver and for about ten minutes found respectable security in Surrey.

Rosie only went out with Paul once a week. She was serious about getting her degree and he was still technically back at St Martin's but was working most nights. So I used to go down to The Limbo in Greek Street every Saturday evening with her. The Ozzies were residents. They really were the heaviest rock-and-roll band around. Tight and tireless. I thought they were great and she got us in free.

Don't think I was jealous. We were far too close for that. If I'd been Rosie I'd have been hanging on Paul's arm, making a fool of myself, which she wasn't quite doing. The bloke had everything. He was handsome. Remember those early photos of him looking like a really cool Jesus? And then punk. His deep eyes. His carved jawline. Skull like a hatchet. Sensitive mouth. And he was a gentleman. His grace was a perfect complement to Rosie's. All exceptional. But on stage he was more than that. He was an authentic guitar hero. A living god. Neither Graham Parker nor Wilco Johnson could match that edgy presence. He had the dash and confidence of early Hendrix. And what a technique. The music just flowed out of his hands. Anywhere his fingers settled on the fretboard something unexpected, energetic and melodic happened.

That's how I started picking up the guitar seriously, in the dressing room when Rosie was busy with Paul. He wasn't touchy about people playing his Gibson/Ford TN29. And it kept me occupied. They wouldn't let me take photographs in those days. They thought it was a wank.

Just being around a guitarist like Paul gave you enough to come away a moderately good musician, which is what I am at best. Little bits of his talent flew across the dressing rooms and overcrowded stages and were breathed in by the rest of us.

My friend Bill Harry knew him in Liverpool. He said Paul was always like that. Too generous with it in the end. Most of the money he made in the eighties went up his second wife's arm. The rest went up his own. Disappeared for a bit. Wandered around Africa. He straightened out, got himself a studio and a family in Brittany and put together a new solo album every year or so. But he was always best with a band around him. You still can't get that early Savoy Joy Division stuff for love or money. It's tied up in legal red tape. Savoy don't have the rights any more. Somebody won't let it be released.

I'd known The Limbo Club most of my life, through a lot of incarnations. It had been The Blues Bunker in 1957 but I didn't go till the early sixties when it was already The Limbo, an attempt to make a tourist-style nightclub with a steel band and tropical drinks. It still had the pastel daubs, the painted palm trees on the walls. And now it didn't matter what it was called. The Limbo was synonymous with tasty urban rock. A perfect name, really, for one of the earliest Blank Generation venues. Of course it later became better known as the club that launched the Adverts, the Damned, Wreckless Eric, Deep Fix, Richard Strange, The Coke Cans, Elvis Costello (with Nick Lowe), The Streets, Siouxsie and the Banshees, The Boyles and Glen Matlock's Autermatix. And of course John Lydon. Dave Stewart and Annie Lennox first performed there, I think, with a lot of tape.

I loved and admired Annie Lennox. She was a pro, like Rosie. She didn't mind working. I'd known her when she was with the Tourists, grafting days behind the counter at Mr Christian's the grocer's in 1977 when I lived in Colville Terrace, off Portobello Road, married to Barbican's alleged half-sister Julie May.

By then the area was getting iffy. The Grove was filling up with liberal professionals – writers, TV producers, models, literary agents, bohemian aristos, film directors, lefty columnists, barristers – the entire fucking fancy. So many wankers that if you went out to the pub your feet stuck to the pavement. The pubs remained, in the main, our own. Speed in the Alex. Dope in the Blenheim. Junk in Finch's. They kept tarting up Finch's and Heneky's and we kept tarting them down again. As my friend DikMik put it late one evening: you could take the needles out of the toilets but you couldn't take the toilets out of the needles.

Really, you couldn't take the needles out of the toilets or the broken amps off the floor, no matter how many fake Victorian globe lamps you installed. Notting Hill's loadies were instinctive, conservative, fixed in their habitual migrations. No amount of orange neon and disinfectant could scare them off their regular settlements.

It took the cracky nineties to terminate them, like they terminated my Julie May. She was murdered in her own bed. Bloodily. There were about forty rockheads living in her flat at the time. Nobody saw a thing. They were all suspects, but I knew who really killed her and so did Rose. As for the loadies, I don't know what it took to ethnically cleanse them, but they're mostly gone now. They were probably poisoned by film production companies. Reincarnated as *Independent on Sunday* readers.

Arthur Lark, who used to run The Albion in Westbourne Grove and was a big radio ventriloquist before the war, was originally from Brookgate. He moved back when the brewery brought in nothing but St David's Lite 'n' Lime, Mordred Mild, Daffodil Daiquiris and Camelot Cola, got a harpist in at Sunday lunchtimes and themed the name of the pub to Merlin Glendower's. He swore that before he asked for his cards they'd had a go at teaching him a Welsh accent.

He and my grandad saw each other every day. They sang elegies for a more wholesome past, when their class held the moral high ground and the political rhetoric more accurately echoed their own prejudices. They still had their tabloids to comfort them. They'd given up on Labour when Nye Bevan died and couldn't stand the Tories, thought the Liberals and that lot were a load of solicitors and estate agents. They wouldn't listen to the BBC any more and they both hated television, so they had very little to distract them from their happy laments and wobbly old tapes of Wee Georgie Wood. Can you 'ear me, mother? Right, monkey!

Rosie grew from a long-legged golden child who could run like Floella into one of the most beautiful women in the world. Our generation's Brookgate Venus. After our famous *Vogue* cover, she only modelled for a year until she had the money she needed for her next project. And she never stripped. She wouldn't.

Still, she said, it was a fairly hairy year for her, without much help, like steering a little boat through very heavy seas. I'd been dropped from the equation early on, as we'd guessed, but we'd built that into our strategy. They said they needed someone more experienced. Like some fucking David Bailey or whatever. Clones sell lots. Originals sell once. What would you rather have your money in? You want your ship to come in once or lots of times?

Boats was the other thing she got into while she was a model. She learned to sail. She was in some famous crew that won a prize. You'd remember, probably. I'm not that familiar with the yacht-owning crowd. I met a few of the goozers briefly through Rosie, years ago. She hadn't thought a lot of them, I remember. She said they were mainly yapping seals. The richer insensates. It didn't stop her making the contacts she'd use later. Or pass on to me.

The ones she enjoyed most were arms dealers. They're not at all the image of Zaharoff the Armaments King, with severe beards, monocles and astrakhan collars, holding their cigarettes at a funny angle. They actually tend to wear Hawaiian shirts and funny shorts. Or off-white crumpled European suits. They usually tell you they sell aeroplanes. They do. But they also do a handy line in accessories, like rockets, tanks and guns. They're charming people, most of them, like all successful salesmen. Plenty of good stories. Generous with their rounds. They were all over the Med when I was doing the St-Tropez trawl for the *Mirror*.

It was when she first split up with Paul, who wanted more of her time than she could afford, that Rosie took a brief, shocked interest in Rupert Dracks, Lord Barbican, the grand architect of the new economic order, chairman of Anglo-American, owner of the South Warwickshire Cricket Club and adoptive father of our own cousin. Johnny Begg was the apple of his eye, the heir apparent, the one who would carry on the Old Consumer's grand design – to eat the whole world. What a trencherman, as they said in the City. What a butcher.

Nobody who knew him doubted Johnny could do it and when he was at last installed in Lord Barbican's place, we anticipated a masterpiece of psychic cloning. That was in 1979, the year the world changed. The Tories were elected and Mrs T used the language of liberal humanism to reinstall feudalism. We were now in a world of permanent conflict. It was the only way to keep the economic bubble pumped up. Somebody had to be blamed. And punished. Everyone had to be kept scared. And promised a kinder, gentler American empire.

Perfect for me in my trade, of course. I joined in like a Brookgate Bastard. Up the miners and take the tin. By 1980 our Rosie had found herself and I was still wondering where to look.

I might think of them as empty years, but I had the lifestyle, if not the investments, of a millionaire and for a while I thought I was suffering for my vocation if I had to take business class because first was full. A flux of dosh, all right. Well-redistributed wealth.

And there's never any point in asking where it all goes.

Norrie told me how he went to court with Jack Trevor Story in 1966. Jack was being bankrupted. Someone presented the evidence that Jack had been paid two thousand quid only a couple of weeks before he declared himself destitute to the Revenue. Big scrap in those days. The judge asked Jack where it had gone. 'You know how it is, judge,' said Jack amiably, 'depending on how much you've got in your pocket you can spend twenty quid or two hundred just going round the supermarket. Two hundred or two thousand, it always lasts a week to a fortnight.'

Jack went bankrupt just to change his luck sometimes. Accountants never get it. They think you've hidden it, invested it, are making it work for you. What else would you do with money?

I really didn't think the dosh would stop coming altogether, though.

I'd always guessed that free money had to come from somewhere and probably had to be paid for by someone. But I think I might have got stuck with the whole bill.

I'm fly but I'm not psychic. Even about Rosie. Although she did, I'll admit, have a mysterious master plan when she married her worst enemy.

If I've learned nothing else it's that sheer brute power is very well rewarded in this world. It's also possible to be pretty thoroughly ruined. Half the taxi drivers in Brighton used to be major names at Lloyd's. It's what keeps the survivors lively, I suppose. Nothing like a visible social abyss to remind you just what edge you're balancing on and at whose good will.

I understood it but I didn't give a shit. I let them know it. I have rights. My ancestors killed a lot of wimpy decadent Italianized Celts to settle this country and make it what it became. I've got freedom in my genes, democracy stamped all through my DNA. Which doesn't necessarily make me a nice person. I wouldn't even be civil to the bastard suits when I met them at parties. They had the souls of Dutch merchants. They were natural yankees. Drawling Boers. Pious appetites. I hated them. I really hated them. And that was what made me so good at my job. When it comes right down to it, I really am not in it for the dosh.

Rosie, too, had nothing but contempt for them and she also didn't give a shit. But she was just a lot better at handling them to her own advantage. She had a steadiness, a maturity if you like, which I've still to cultivate. That's how she got her satisfaction, by waiting for it, by savouring it, by picking her moment. Women are like that. Cats are the same. They actually get a buzz from being patient. A mystery to me. Blokes are generally not at all like that. What I needed to do to feel better was to piss on some plummy plutocrat's marble doorstep. Shit in his shoes. I guess that's how Rosie came by the power to change the world and I retreated to Skerring. You could see how it was going to go when we were kids and had our different ways of sorting Cousin Jack. And of course he really did need sorting.

Looking back at how things developed, you could almost believe that Rosie had planned it this way from the start.

CHAPTER SIX
The Twist

Neither me nor Rosie ever ran a fetcher on Barbican. It was him, desperately trying to thrash himself free of his middle-class public-school repressions, who tagged after us. We'd known him slightly for years and taken to avoiding him.

I got into St Alban's School, Gray's Inn, soon after Rosie scored her place at St Paul's. That's when I met Johnny and found out we were related. He was a day boy like me. We were eleven. I was already earning my living and thought the other kids were wet and he was a prat. I started leaving after a term. I'd see him around sometimes and had no reason to be unfriendly to him, though I never actually liked him. We'd let him come with us when we went to the pictures by the back doors, that sort of thing.

But then he started coming down to The Limbo when we were doing our first gigs with Gordons Riot. 1968, I think. It had to be. By 1969 Paul Frame had split back to Salford. His scholarship to St Martin's only lasted a year. Paul would have been eighteen, naturally hip.

Also still at school, Johnny had already been officially adopted by Lord Barbican in a strange public ceremony, making him official heir apparent. Remember that weird story? For a while in the sixties the papers and telly were full of it. Johnny and his ma were more than happy with their agreement. On the death of Rupert Arndale Begg Ingham Dracks, Lord Barbican, Johnny would change his first name to Barbican. The title wasn't hereditary. It was Lord B's way of perpetuating his honour.

Johnny would sometimes test the name, calling himself Barbican even before he had to. I read that neat drawn signature of his, textbook copperplate, on his Limbo membership card. J. Barbican Begg. Like something out of Dickens. What was he? Seventeen?

He was already an entrepreneur. He had a stock-market portfolio. He had his own broker. But he was still a boy of his time. And however twisted his means of sexual expression, his gonads were firing on all cylinders. He wanted to manage Gordons Riot. He longed to be friends with Paul Frame.

Johnny first swaggered down to the Limbo full of fake bottle backed by a couple of his sniggering studie pals. You could tell it was meant to be a joke. But he stayed on when they left. He was still there when we'd finished. He was eager. He offered us a lift in his car. We had our own van.

We thought we'd seen the last of him. But he paid full crack to get in to every one of our Limbo gigs after that.

We weren't too sure about him. He didn't look like us. His pink, well-tended skin was sleek as soft money. It glowed with private healthcare. With his casual neckerchief, his floppy schoolboy quiff, his shy, staccato sprays of demonstrated idiom (these people are always performing for some authority) he rarely came empty-handed. He geekily offered Rosie huge boxes of chocolates, which she gave away on the spot, along with the odd bunch of flowers. He was usually good for a double in the pub, a few crappy reefers. Posh kids get sold such rotten dope.

The middle class have to own what they love. They don't always see it that way. Someone like Johnny can get genuinely enthusiastic about real nobody culture. But he doesn't necessarily understand what attracts him. And usually he can't help killing it. Johnny wasn't Mephistopheles. Not then, anyway. He generously wanted to give us what he valued most. And what we clearly needed. Predictability. Financial stability. Viability. Middle-class credibility. Ho Yus? So what is it we're hearing? All aboard the Death Star?

We know they mean well, but their gifts carry subtle, sometimes fatal diseases. Not all of us feel at our most comfortable in a top hat and a grass skirt, smoking a Romeo y Julieta.

In rock you can get viable the hard way, by doing so many sodding gigs, getting so much experience, building up so much smack, so much grass-roots respect, that everyone wants you at their balls. The buzz builds. It's like a secret drug. It's the best success. Like the Beatles. They were known as the business long before they got a record deal. But the other band that anyone from up north in the early sixties reckoned to be as good if not better than the Beatles, who gave the Beatles a lot of their inspiration in Germany, was Kingsize Taylor and the Dominoes. Both bands had that something extra. Only the Beatles had Brian Epstein. Kingsize preferred regular work in Hamburg to being a chancer in London. Then he saw the writing on the wall and got out. He couldn't write lyrics, he said. The last I heard he was sued by the Beatles for selling a tape he made when they gratefully jammed with him at The Star Club. You can tell from the tape who's driving the action and it's not the loveable mopheads. Is that why they didn't like it? Kingsize now runs a successful butcher's in Bury. I took some pictures of him there. He says he's happy. Most people are lucky to get a decent house out of a career like his.

I have this story in my head. There was a famous jazz cornet player –

innovative, admired, seminal – called Bunk Johnson. At some time in the late twenties or thirties, when things got generally tougher, he stopped getting gigs. He fades out of the picture. Everyone thinks he's dead. Then some jazz fan discovers him working in the Louisiana rice fields, where he's been picking rice for twenty years. They get him a new horn, they get him some teeth, he does some practising and discovers he can still blow like an angel. Makes a few records. Classics.

So how do you interview a guy like that. Well, Bunk, what was it like, working in the rice fields when some of your old pals were on stage at The Cotton Club? I don't really know what it means. How would Big Mama Thornton feel at an Elvis retrospective? Or Woody Guthrie at a Grammy ceremony? *It was early springtime, and the strike was on. They drove us miners from our homes . . .* That busy old axe. America's lost working-class history of the twentieth century. Billy clubs, boxcars, bullets, brutality and old guitars. Southern trees bear a strange fruit. Syphilis, sadness and disrespect. Josh White got in on the same set of stamps as Woody.

Talent? Innovation? Is that what it's about?

You don't have to become a professor of sociology or work in a rice field to make it. You can get viable the Malcolm McLaren way, by putting money into promotion. It's usually your money, in the end. And promotion requires that you do stunts, live an almost entirely public life. A lie. It can kill you. It never does you much good.

In the end it's the band who keep some sort of smack, street cred if you like, who have the staying power. Self-respect and good judgement. Hawkwind and Siouxsie lasted a lot longer than Adam and the Ants. Even poor barmy, talented Calvert, yearning to be middle-class, always blowing it somehow, would still be down here in the street with us, if he hadn't had that sodding heart attack. He was only pretending to be posh. Real middle-class boys knew their parents' jive too well. They'd heard it all their lives. It was in their bones. And it clobbered them. They were already too interested in power. And the powerful. To us it was all a foreign language. But Rosie learned it as thoroughly as every other she learned, because it was useful to her. But it didn't control her any more than her knowledge of Arabic. It just helped her steer her course. Myself, I just don't have the gift.

You have to be sexy, too, in some ways. Which means you have to spend a lot of time on yourself or have some animal stink that attracts those well-fed girls and boys. Ask anyone who's ever been in a working rock-and-roll band. Ask what it is about our underpants. Those weasely, self-conscious little telly journalists are always mentioning them. Boys and girls, both, as if they've never seen anyone in a pair of knickers. Maybe to them it's like a public school without the teachers, why they always seem to be expecting someone in charge. Whatever they're fighting in themselves, they can't stay clear of our shitty overcrowded dressing rooms. There's a definite chemical reaction in working-class sweat, especially when mixed with testosterone and hash, that is almost irresistible to our betters.

I suspect what turns them on to me is something like the sensations I get from a really tight-haired, tight-assed, glossy PA girl, younger versions of Barbican's step-mummy, airline stewardesses flying too close to the ground, the women who squirt scent at you in stores. My chemistry takes control when I meet one. What is it? Early exposure to Judith Chalmers? Those careful Listen-With-Mother accents? That horrible Estée Lauder, moulded hair-dos, sculpted make-up, Diana-oid clothes, sharp heels, sharper tones. Hair forever yellow. Forever tied up in a black velvet bow. I hate their disgusting social attitudes. I hate everything about them. I would gladly see them sacrificed screaming en masse to Moloch. And yet I know I'll never harm them. We are natural mates. Like it or not, she is the female of my sub-species. I am genetically programmed to protect her. Which could be why I'm no longer married.

What deep drives are running here? Do I give off a smell of health? Enduring genes? Relative vitality? Maybe I'm just an acceptable fucking-animal. A sort of sexual long pig. A throbbing euphemism. So it's not really bestiality for them. I'm halfway between a fido and a dildo. That's bad enough, but imagine my bloody feelings – I have a biological urge to *be* fucked by such people. And, what's much worse, I don't always fight it. Luckily for me I'm usually never more than a passing fuck for them. Usually. Bobby was one of the exceptions, and she was half-disguised.

To Johnny, our urban musical aggression, powered by an urgent desire to climb out of the poverty pit on our own terms, represented vitality and sexual freedom. As Jon Savage would say later. In short, we somehow got his dick up. We were all kinds of cool stuff. He thought our words were super. He knew where we were coming from. That was just how he felt about those old bastards, too. He was going to change everything. Together we'd take over the system. We were definitely the hottest thing that had ever happened to him. Rock on, man.

We were his *Roads to Freedom*, I think. Especially Rosie, of course, who was never officially in the band. But without her being around, banging the odd tambourine, our charm would have relied on Paul alone.

Like Brian Epstein with the Beatles, Johnny fainted at the very nearness of us.

Knickers again. A rich, knee-knocking mix for him – locker-room savouries and a cockney Carmen, this self-confident gypsy, irresistibly combined.

Naturally, he was prepared to pay for his pleasures. He'd been brought up to do it. Anything without a price can't be valuable. He wanted to tell the world how ace we were and he wanted us to be viable, which would involve him making an investment and taking a percentage. It was his risk, he told us. But it was worth it to him. He might never see a return, but if we made money then so would he. 'Believe me, this isn't just because I'm keen on you.' It was enlightened self-interest on his part.

We believed him. Rosie said it was venture capitalism of the best kind, cash backing an enthusiasm. Just the sort of willingness to take a risk that fuelled the Cornish slave trade for a couple of centuries. Sweet poison, she said. On our behalf she told him, amiably enough, to piss off. He was disbelieving. He'd spent weeks and weeks, he said, working out the kind of financing we'd need. Everything was in place. He became disgusted. He'd had such faith in us! We just hadn't risen to the opportunity. And then he actually said it – Maybe it actually was a matter of blood and breeding, after all?

He threw down his spreadsheets and stomped off. This amused us even more. We found everything he did funny.

For a while he washed his hands of us. Then he came back to see if we'd realized what we'd done. Paul rolled his proposal up tight and offered to get the KY. He winced. God, we were childish. So fucking self-destructive! We had no idea of the influence he had. What he could do for us. We could be at Wembley by next year. We were unbelievably feckless. We were crapping on our own talent. No wonder the working classes were in the shit! Short-sighted. Unable to see which side their bread was buttered on. We had no ambition. We'd never pull ourselves out of Brookgate. And to think he'd not only invested his idealism in us. He'd been prepared to invest over five sheets! So we could make a record.

We hoped we'd seen the last of him but he was back soon, saying he'd realized we were wise to give it a year or two. We all knew what drew him to us for every gig. It was Rosie's insouciant sexuality and his own addiction to an authenticity he couldn't even identify.

It didn't last much longer. Our own smack on it was right. Apart from Paul we were a crap band. Eventually he went to Liverpool, then Salford again and, a bit later, Manchester, Deansgate, Savoy and Joy Division.

That's when the predatory classes were still trying to court us. Before they decided they might as well just take us over. Only, of course, they didn't really take us over. They took over the decoys. The prix with the godzilla spex and fake barnets. The singing sponges. From where we were, they just stopped being good for a tenner. Which, of course, was their basic political message. Public contributions to charity went down and down with every Band Aid concert. The whole world got their message. You had to sing their tune if you wanted your supper.

Somehow you never heard Our Lady of the Landmines saying how she empathized with Sid Vicious's unreasoning frustrations and Joy Division's seasonable anger or how nicey-spicy easy it was to identify in your heart with Wreckless Eric and Iggy Pop. Why don't we invite Billy

Bragg round for the evening, your marm? They couldn't stop our lot tugging our foreskins instead of our forelocks. So to be on the safe side the corporate barons started making up their own pop groups. As tacky as their secret fantasies. And fantasies made real are never quite as good as you anticipated. The more you control, the less you possess. That's what they found out when they achieved The Spice Girls and their clones, the people's princesses. Fool's gold. The real hit's always just coming.

But old Sri Reg and the almost-new romantics are there for the groovy wealthies. They even own Dylan's corpse. They wheel it on at parties. Rubbing shoulders with the big gun men. So pleased to be popular. Jolly clothes and rose-tinted hair. Big white spectacles. To sing the brown-nose blues. Along with Little union-busting Stevie Wonder and Mika You-Name-It Jackson and all the other rich giggling geeks who think this is rock and roll, who took the meaning out of the people's music, removed the anger and pain and kept pouring on the sentimentality until it sold at last – unhip syrup, third-hand roses, fifth-hand melodies, disinfected rap. *Wow!* Those house niggers squeezed Blind Lemon dry.

That's what piles up the dosh, all right, but you get nobody's respect. You get subtly dissed even by the plummies you perform for. You're as useful to them as porn.

Those timeless queens of the velvet overground must know what they've lost. They've been well bucked by the system. And paid for their trouble. They were never anything but cartoon rockers. Black and white minstrels. Coon dancers. Every ounce of authenticity wrung out of them before they were twelve. Dissing their own roots. Wet as dux. Politically conscious as a plate of mussolini. But, be fair, handy decoys. Something has to distract the predators while we get our crack at the waterhole. If only they really were on our side.

'God, I could do without their self-approving pity.'

An acquaintance of mine, Mario Amaya, said that. He died of AIDS before he could be further pitied. A few years earlier he'd been shot by accident at Andy Warhol's place. Some woman from Coyote or SCUM. It always seemed unfair, but he felt flattered. And it gave him a sharper taste for life, he said. Mario was a gentle soul. He wrote books about Pre-Raphaelites and Art Nouveau. He once bought forty-two Morris & Co chairs from a club in Cheltenham for five bob each. The woman who sold them felt so guilty about the price she threw in some Burne-Jones watercolours. His little flat was jammed with the gorgeous loot of the whole *fin de siècle*. He had to sell it in the end, I think, to pay for his illness. Blooming sixties summers when only hippies valued that stuff and you could still pick up a good Millais for two hundred quid in Bond Street. Mario had the best of it. Win some, lose some.

Johnny hadn't been coming down The Limbo long before he invited me and Rosie back to Sporting Club Square. We were almost unnerved.

He asked us round for tea. To meet his mother. She's pretty hip, really, he assured us. Far out, we said. We were sure he wanted just Rosie, but knew she wouldn't go without me. We told him we'd think about it.

A Begg hadn't invited a Beck, or a Dover, to Sporting Club Square in recorded history. We weren't too sure his stepmother knew who his new friends were. She was only recently widowed, I think.

Sir Humphrey Begg had been a decent enough duffer who had married a series of crappy old greed bitches, like he was addicted to them. They never left empty-handed and he was lucky when one or two of them drank themselves to death before they actually took him to the cleaners. Which was why they were living in the remaining jewel in the family crown, shabby, vulgar, rambling old SCS, and not South Audley Street, Mayfair (sold 1956) or Low Cogges, Oxon (hammered 1963), and why Sir H., aged about five thousand, went off to work in the City every day until he died on the District Line, suddenly, between Blackfriars and the Bank (heart, 1969, 5 w., 2 s.).

CHAPTER SEVEN
The Sniff

Some people find Sporting Club Square romantic. To me it's always been a hideous bit of ostentatious Victorian greenery-yallery folly. A victim of the speculative boom of the late nineteenth century when huge areas of Surrey farmland had thousands of tons of Buckingham brick dumped all over them. Most of the stuff is the usual terracotta Gothic you get lost in anywhere on the city's fringes. Same designs. Same stained glass. Same mouldings. Early English personalized high-pop mass-production housing. Choose from any one of our five fashionable designs and add your own plaster features.

The Square was an attempt at commercial individuality. They wanted to push Fulham upmarket, turn it into Barons Court and West Kensingon (the real Earls Court and Kensington already being rented to capacity by lower-income aristos of the day), thus extending profitable middle-class real estate beyond the South Kensington Railway. They wanted it to echo Pugin's classy Kensington Gothic but be more modern.

So Hubert Begg, not yet knighted, designed Sporting Club Square in the very latest fashions and fantasies, to attract the demi-monde – the hip young couples who bought *The Yellow Book*, *The Savoy* and *The Studio*. A themed community. The place was a vast square, built on land owned by the Beggs for centuries, including about a score of full-size tennis courts. Tennis was the coolest craze of the 1880s. The courts were enclosed with a mass of baroque ironwork worthy of a decadent shah. There was an unwholesome, heavy, foreign feel about the place. The towers and buttresses, the arts-and-crafts medieval battlements and Gaudí-esque escarpments were a nightmare by Harry Clarke, that weird Edwardian artist who made Beardsley look as bland as Disney.

Just as SCS was finished and Begg moved his entire home and studio there, the Great Depression of the 1890s put a sickening dip in the upward mobility graph. The thrusting young stockbrokers were happy to be in any work and only the shabbiest of genteels moved in. They started reading *The Time Machine* and getting angry about the future.

After the First World War the flats were full of spinsters and widows.

Sub-lets slid it even further downmarket but it kept a kind of dignity. An uneasy pocket of misses, of failing middle-class memory and aspiration. In a determinedly miserable Fulham slum. They hung on to their standards, their status, until the sixties, when their alarming grand-children and great-nephews and nieces started to find the turrets and steeples quaint, some confirmation of their awful Tolkienoid dreams.

By 1970 every liberal longhair with a shabby-genteel relative was settling in Sporting Club Square. Within months the place was thick with journos, publishers, loud liberal lawyers, literary agents, actors, admen and aggressive after-dinner novelists. Felix Martin had a place there for a while until he was burgled. By 1975 the Square had become the most upwardly mobile address in London, outstripping Notting Hill for Range Rover occupation. The shit crack being that those bitching oldsters who would have voted for Goebbels if he'd had the sense to stand as their local candidate, who had hung on with elliptical complaints and pursed lips and many secret phone calls to the police through the hippy invasion, were suddenly, thanks to the pioneering self-same hippies whose straighter relatives were now moving in, stinking rich. They were able to sell their horrible unsanitary, poky, unmodernized, original featured, nasty ecclesiastically-stained-glass-little-comfy-camelets and buy the posh mock-heritage home in Hampshire they had always known was theirs. Thank you, Bilbo fucking Baggins Properties PLC. You flogged your bloody hobbit-hole at last. I always said Tolkien had the soul of a Midlands alderman. And that's why there's no fucking justice, pards. Not much, anyway.

Johnny Begg's particular stepmummy had proceeded in the con-ventional way, becoming his daddy's PA and then shafting her pre-decessor who in turn had shafted her predecessor Moira, Johnny's dam, and so on, to become the fifth Lady Begg. Baboons are subtler. They were all identical. Social climbers with nowhere to go. Strong ambition, bad judgement.

By the time Lady B5 was ensconced, all that ensconced her was the large flat at the top of Begg Mansions which, in 1980, became a protected Class II historical building. Johnny's old dad hadn't done well on it. By seventy his lolly had been licked to the bone. And Johnny had inherited his mother's soul. He certainly hadn't inherited it from Sir Humphrey. Which didn't surprise anyone who knew his power-blonded mother.

Johnny looked a lot more like Max Wheen. The handsome lefty had often been around to pat Lady Moira's well-manicured hand while her callous husband slogged away meeting his debts of honour. And Max had made himself useful. He published a hi-brow quarterly that came out about once a year and was called *The Left*. It ran all the usual Robins and Kingsleys and was entirely dependent for its existence on how many rich women Max could prong. Norrie thought *Dexter* would have been a better title for the magazine. He estimated that Max had got about fifteen thousand quid a result in stud fees. Seven babies at least. Norrie had also worked out that, given the rarity of its appearance, *The Left* had cost about four hundred pounds for each of its seven issues. A clear profit of fourteen thousand, six hundred coins. Over fourteen and a half sheets. Which in the 1950s wasn't at all bad. Probably a lot more than the PM was getting. Not a cheap stud. In fact, the most expensive in the country. A pedigree to be proud of.

Sir Humph hadn't been an actual father since 1935 when Johnny's half-brother, now the well-known expatriate liberal lord, Dick, was born. Who knows? The old boy might have been happy to pretend to plonker power that hadn't lasted him past wife one in real life. Besides, he was used to doing what he was told. He'd been trotting to someone else's tune since he was born. Like most of us, he preferred familiar miseries to mysterious ecstasies. Sometimes you thought he was still alive. Meekly haunting. If you saw anything, you saw his twin brother, who lived on in the uncharted basements of Begg Mansions, a confirmed recluse, trusting only his gargoyle housekeeper who serviced him, we heard, in uncomfortable ways.

So, after talking it over, Rose and I took the Circle Line to West Kensington and walked down North Star Road, following the twists and the turns of mean little North Fulham streets until we got to Sporting Club Square. Which Rose loved and I'd hated on sight. See? Not always the same tastes.

I thought we'd never make it up in the lift, which was all rattling brass and sparking steel. To a dark, unwelcoming landing where Lady Begg opened her black lacquered door to us.

Not only the door was lacquered. She, too, was almost entirely lacquered. From head to toe. Nails, hair, legs, neck. Parts of her creaked and powdered as she moved. She had a tiny, watchful face. The flat had no trace of her character. A neat set. She smelled strongly of some aggressive scent. I found her confusing. She referred to us as 'Johnny's band' and sat eyeing us as we ate her shop-bought fancies. She asked Rose what school she went to and was half-satisfied. One status point. Made Rose a little whiter.

Lady Begg asked me my favourite music. I told her I liked Schoenberg, Messiaen, Julie Driscoll, Woody Guthrie, Zoot Money, Alkan, Liszt, The Beatles, Mahler, Long John Baldry, Grainger, Elgar, R. Strauss, J. Strauss, the Who, Leadbelly, Dave Berry, James Brown, Beethoven, Steampacket, Offenbach, Ives, Lehar, Hendrix, Brahms, Memphis Slim, Mozart and Kurt Weill.

'Ah,' she said, 'The Beatles.' She told Johnny to pour us some more tea. Then she began to wonder about making a phone call.

Later he took us up to his loft. 'My den. It's a no-go zone here.' Under its eaves he had all his expensive recording equipment, his guitars and the other toys he'd offered to lend us. He called the place his studio. It had a warm, slightly bitter smell. Rosie said it was the smell of long-vanished wealth. On the Tube home she showed me what little she'd stolen.

The joke was that Johnny got me back in touch with the underground press. That would have been around 1971. The best alternative paper then wasn't *International Times* but *Frendz,* an even more chaotic breakaway from *Rolling Stone.* That's where I met Lucy Rycroft. She was about twelve. They had offices in Portobello Road, two doors down from the *New Worlds* offices, and they shared typesetters, printers, distributors, sometimes staff. Johnny took me in there one busy Friday when the market activities seemed to spill through the doorways and carry on in the passages and stairwells. The editor was a mate of Johnny's from St Alban's, a year or two older, an Oxbridge poser called Jeremy Something, and he seemed out of his tree most of the time, but he loved my photos. They were so used to trying to decipher red print on red paper that my b&w reality was a whole new trip to them. They didn't really pay very often, but they were generous with their dope, used a lot of my material and usually remembered a credit. Some of it you could even see. It was the first time I felt like a pro again. It's how I met Calvert, too, come to think of it, and started gigging with Hawkwind. Then we formed Deep Fix with Paul Frame.

It wasn't really my first affair with the underground, though I'm not sure *New Worlds* counted. The NW crowd didn't have any rocks to get off on the page. They had strange geniuses like Ballard. The *Oz* people were mostly middle-class Australian wankers and worse. *Colons* who represented themselves as the colonized. NW people had more experience than qualifications. They'd fought guerrillas in Malaya or been in the Horse Guards or made record mountain climbs. Ballard was the oldest and about the best educated. He'd dropped out of Cambridge after a year or so. Most of his education as a kid had been in Jap concentration camps. I only met him once. He reminded me of a mad but amiable suburban bank manager. He told me what my images were really about and how they should be more like his. He almost persuaded me. I didn't see much of any of the others except PixEd Nigel whose style was all over the thing. He used more photographs than *Life* and always paid for them. Not a lot, but in cash if you wanted it. Which suited a nineteen-year-old with a taste for reefers and flash stock.

The pix editor started off as Nigel but changed his name to Simon because he thought Nigel sounded wet. There you go. He was younger than I was. One of the other editors had torn Nige out of his public school before they could harm him. Some sort of scholarship kid, he still had most of his own North London voice. We got on well. He was eccentric, rather than weird. Carried his own smack. He sewed all his own clothes out of scraps of denim he cadged off the Portobello traders.

He lived on a ledge made out of a door placed above the office stairs. It was his bed, his workplace, his library, his territory. But he got interested in bikes and started bringing more and more of them indoors. Whenever *New Worlds* hit one of its periodic patches of white water he earned his dosh from the bikes. Wherever there weren't bales of back numbers there were bits of bike. The last time I saw him was in 1983. Somebody had left him a bit of dosh. He was living with his wife and kids in Queens Park. She was Indian. Really beautiful. The entire house was full of oily bike bits except for the kichen and one downstairs room, and the garden, which was her territory. By then he was building custom bikes. Mine was made to fly like a bird and look like a dog. It's never been pinched. But Simon moved to the country for a healthier life, biked his kids to school one day and coming home was killed by a truck. Went the way of Barney Bubbles. If the drugs don't get you, the rural life will. God hates good picture editors. They all die young. The old farts hang on forever.

Barney was another good friend of mine. He created the Stiff Records image. His style dominated the seventies. Before that he was art editor of *Queen*. Then he rejoined the underground and started doing layouts for *Frendz* when Jon Trux was editor, sleeves for Hawkwind, Mighty Baby, Third Ear Band, Quiver, Brinsley Schwartz and some of the other underground bands of the early seventies. Sometimes he'd build the sleeves as models and have me photograph them. He did that for the ticket booth on *New Worlds Fair*. It's in one of those poster books Mick Farren edited. You still see it. But the Stiff stuff was his best.

Other designers worshipped him as an innovator. He kept me going during those years. Costello. Dury. Calvert. The Adverts. The Damned. Graham Parker. The Feelgoods. Check the credits. Almost every photo he used was by me. They didn't come any kinder and gentler than Barney. You hardly ever saw him out of a pair of blue overalls with coloured patches. A classic old hippy. Sharp, gentle, troubled. I heard he topped himself when Mrs Thatcher got in for the second time. God knows what he'd do now.

Around 1971 Jack Begg, as he had become, decided he was going to finance a drug deal. Someone had got hold of a hundred thousand tabs of Swiss Silver. You couldn't score any better. It was legendary acid. All totally kosher. Thirty thousand quid. Even if you only sold at a pound a tab you'd make seventy thousand just like that. True, I said, if you had seventy thousand customers. Or say just seventy customers, he said, with a thousand pounds. You can help me, Denny. I'll cut you in. I need your contacts. You'll get fifteen per cent on every customer you bring in.

That'll be maybe fifteen customers, I said, with a fiver each. It was out of my league. It made me sweaty just being near it. Again, he couldn't believe that I was turning down such an opportunity. He went ahead with the deal and did all right, selling on at a smaller hike to bona fide dealers. A clean transaction, as he saw it. Nobody was caught. I just couldn't calculate his profit.

'You would have made four or five sheets out of that, easily,' he told me when I next went round to his big white shaggy Chelsea pad. He showed me the figures.

I'd gone to blag a few free samples off him. I had a reason. He was always willing to treat me as some sort of exception. Normally, he couldn't bring himself to give anything away. But in my case . . . that's what he'd say: 'In your case, Denny . . .' it was almost affectionate, the way he treated me. He was the same with Rosie.

Me and Rosie shared one of the tabs the next day. She'd come back for the final time from Brussels and her Grand Passion. It was intense for a while but she never told me who Mr Magic was, except that he was married. A Euro politician, I guessed.

She told me Johnny had been at her again to marry him. Or work for him in his new City firm, which he'd founded on his drugs profits. All he needed, he'd told her, was a suitable mate – an equal. Together they could take over the world. It was all too much, she said. She needed to wipe her tapes, get back to where she belonged. I was disturbed by a new sadness in her. I hoped it was temporary.

She said she couldn't have asked for a better holiday, reminiscing over our past, all our good times. Then she told me about the baby. A little girl, she said. Very cute. I'd love it.

I said I hated babies. She knew that. Then I had a thought. 'How old is it?'

She winked. 'Old enough.'

'It is yours?'

'Oh, she's definitely mine.'

'But not mine.'

She laughed. 'First cousins don't make the best combination, Den.'

The baby had been left with a good friend in Begat, where she'd been based for her volunteer training. She was missing her a lot. There were some medical problems. She didn't offer to tell me about the father.

She stopped wanting to talk about it, after that. She said she'd see how we went. But she hardly mentioned Kim for years.

A telepathic shutdown. A silence. I could only respect it.

We took a boat trip on the Thames. To Kew. We always did that when we wanted to wind down. Find each other again. Do some good acid or roll a powerful joint. Lie in the grass, take in the buds and the blooms, the bees and the birds, check out the sensory overkill, the sexy amniotic mud of the primeval fern houses, and communicate, in the language of colour and form, with the gorgeous cuttlefish in the marine gardens below. No sweeter trip. We were one again under blue skies.

Even the tight-arses who live around the Botanical Gardens were nice to us that day. We didn't look like crusties.

We were twenty-one and had long since reached our maturity. The sun was getting low as we took the boat back to the Tower. We got one of those astonishing London sunsets. The clouds turned to ochre. Waves of scarlet suddenly rolled over the little slate roofs, the bricks and grey gardens, as if heralding some happy apocalypse. The water became glimmering jet. Deep, long, old-fashioned shadows. Painters' shadows. Then it was twilight. Growing dark. Quiet. We sat together in the stern. The sounds of the engine grew distant. The air turned sweet, chill, a little misty. There were only five other passengers, some Japanese tourists all grouped together at the prow. The wizened helmsman in his khaki balaclava had his back to us. His little engine house was alive with more comfortable, domestic shadows. Its fumes smelled of hot oil, fried eggs, toast and strong tea. We didn't say much on the way home. It was dark by the time we went under the silvery beauty of Chelsea Bridge. We looked back at a fantasy by Whistler.

'I'll miss all this,' she said.

It was almost a relief to leave fairyland behind and see Tower Bridge bulking up out of the early fog, her yellow lights marking the borders of our native turf.

As we disembarked, Rosie told me she'd applied for a job with The Lady Montague's Trust and was going for an interview in the morning. It would take her to Africa or South America. She had the qualifications. Working in the field, first. Then an administrative job.

I didn't know what to say. Before we went home to my place and bed, I brought up my camera and took a couple of snaps. Something to remember her by, I said, when she became respectable. I've still got the best one. Her hair's a massive dark corona surrounding a golden head as perfect, as poised as Nefertiti. She's grinning, mucking about. Tower Bridge is behind her and the rising fog makes the lights flare like dying stars.

That night was probably the happiest I'd known until then. Just delighting in her. Loving her warmth, her body lying in my arms as we talked ourselves into a deep, delicious erotic sleep. I dreamed that we were married and had kids.

She got the job.

I said goodbye at the airport. Hanging around in the cafeteria, I told her I admired her but I was beginning to wonder if it wasn't too late to try improving the world.

'Oh, there's a bit of time left, Denny.' Unconsciously, she was looking through her handbag, checking for her tickets in that obsessive way she had. She hated flying. 'Maybe the twenty-first century will see a world of self-respecting equals. Mature, sane governance, humane practices, minimum rules.'

'I know what you're talking about,' I said. 'I read about the war to end wars. I saw the movie. *Things To Come*. 1936. Wonderful vision. Peace and harmony. The rule of sanity. Admittedly a paternalistic peace and harmony. A kind of ideal Nazi state without any bothersome non-Teutons. Five years later – World War Two. I don't know, Rose. Can we change anything for the better? Don't we always wind up making things worse? I mean, what started the trouble you're trying to clear up? And how can you stop it?'

'The slave trade,' she said. 'Money.'

I didn't have her clarity. That's why I knew she couldn't love me.

A month later she was almost in hearing distance of Albert Schweitzer's mighty Wurlitzer, a few hundred miles up the Congo, seeing what she could do for lepers. I was proud of her. I felt guilty for not being there. I missed her like hell.

This feeling had faded by the end of the year. I had fallen in love with Julie May.

CHAPTER EIGHT
The Score

Barbican's half-sister came to Sporting Club Square to be finished. The former Lady Wendy, now the former Mrs Belstaff, her mother, unable to afford a flat for her while she went to The Mayfair School in Kensington to learn how to walk and talk, asked her ex-husband's widow, Lady Moira, if, for a small contribution, Julie could stay in one of the several unused rooms at Begg Mansions. Lady Moira must have been feeling the pinch. Her Wheen-pulling days were well over. She graciously agreed and took a cheque in advance.

Julie's long blonde hair made her look a bit like Marianne Faithfull did that time the real People's Princess was brought down to the Limbo by Chas Chandler and Eric Burdon to hear us play. Miss Faithfull was very polite. She stayed ten minutes.

Julie had a still, quiet quality that some people found mysterious and I thought was self-protective. She had a slightly mannered grace, as if she'd already been trained to walk with a telephone book on her head. She had an accent, I was told, that made foreigners wet themselves. She was assured of a good position. A PA, a foot on the ladder her mother had climbed. But this time, her mother insisted, no more Missy Nice Girl. By which I suppose she meant murder 'em, don't bother to milk 'em. But it was impossible for Julie not to be nice. She was sweet-natured, a bit silly and not stupid. Traumatized, maybe? Dazed? Every bit of her mother's hypocritical sentimentality had been taken literally by her and she tried to live by that yardstick. The superficial had gone deep into her soul. She was almost saintly in her passion, her honestly meant platitudes, her inarticulate love for the whole world and everyone in it. She couldn't pass a collection box without searching in her purse. Panhandlers spotted her at once. Try getting through Covent Garden on a Friday night with Julie. You had to take a pocketful of change if you ever wanted to see the picture on time.

Apart from Julie, nobody knew who Julie's father was. It clearly wasn't Rodney Belstaff, the tiny, dark dancer whose name was on the certificate. She believed, perfectly blissfully, that daddy had been Sir

Humphrey. She loved him intensely in retrospect and for a while turned against Lady Wendy who, she said, should have remained by his side, fought for him, rather than going off with Rex Martin, the famous farting novelist, who happened to be on a binge in a nearby flat. Fartin' Martin and Lady Wendy stayed together long enough to marry, produce two testy novels and one legitimate issue, the dwarfish Felix, whom Julie loathed. Mai Zetterling told me that when they were filming Rex's novel *A Winning Pair* with Peter Sellers, Rex had propositioned her one evening with his now famous pick-up line – 'Want to see my Aertexes?' And farted as he leered. Sellers, flattered to be his pal, had been hugely appreciative and had attempted to emulate him. He'd wound up failing and doing some funny voices instead. A literary gent of the old school, that Rex. As, of course, is Felix.

Julie was in solid denial *re* her nearest and dearest. The only antecedent she could identify with was conveniently cremated. She knew in her heart that she was a Begg and loved her mother's dead ex-husband accordingly. Some people just need that extra bit of security. She was certain, therefore, that I was her second cousin. And therefore we had a special rapport. A frisson of illegitimate intimacy. I was in a state of mind to verify this. I knew what real twin souls were all about but I accepted her estimate. I did a chart of our family relationship. Yes, I said, we were cousins. The same blood. We bonded. It's so easy to fall in love.

Sir Hubert's mother had been Effie Beck, last great star of Sir John 'Mad Jack' Parker's Famous Follies, the actual, original Brookgate Venus who became the first Lady Begg when Queen Victoria honoured her husband. Family legend says she gave her last request performance for the old queen in 1900, a year before she died. Her brother, Garnett, married my own mother's great-aunt. Which was how lowly Brookgate spread into nearby Bloomsbury and helped weaken the defences of a savagely exclusive middle-class enclave. Or strengthen the bloodstock, if you like. When sentimental or attempting to call on a spurious street cred, Barbican would sometimes refer to his Brookgate roots . . .

Pick a heritage.

As it happened, I didn't meet Julie through Jack. She didn't know I was a relative. She just thought I was cool. I was performing under the motorway, doing a free Saturday lunchtime gig with Nick Lowe, Brinsley Schwarz and a scratch band made up of anyone we could find who could stand up before noon. Basing Street was only round the corner. Half the people we knew did session work there. Some hadn't gone to bed yet. Martin Stone hadn't been to bed for three years. His black beret was twitching on his scalp. He was beyond gaunt. His black little eyes were somewhere in the region of his cortex. He was so skinny you could use him to chop his own lines. He mumbled in a guarded, abstracted monotone. His guitar was getting edgier and edgier. He said warningly that it was all right, he was still warming up.

It was a benefit for Erin Pizzey's Women's Shelter. She was there with her journo husband. She'd only recently started it. Nice dope. Good vibes. Happy audience: youf, rastas, oldsters, hippies, proto-punks, all together. Naturally there were prune-faced ex-colonial protesters with lifted telephones at a couple of distant back windows. The first chord we played, they called the police and complained about the noise. The jollies were only too happy to respond. Call them out on a rape and see how long they took.

We opened with a nice fast selection of Nick's best rock-and-roll songs and some ragged Chuck Berry stuff. Then we had to stop and sort ourselves out. As we tuned up, I looked into the audience. I'd never seen so many good-looking women. No-contest stunners. Swedish flower children. American yippies. French ippies. And Julie May, a Saxon virgin, with daisies in her yellow hair, serene and tall in her tie-dyes and a perfect image of the perfect day.

I should also mention the lust. I longed to have my camera with me. To record the moment. It was frustrating. Then Nick's disciplined, insistent rocking guitar put my mind back where it should be. But I played every note for her. Normally I never looked at the audience when I was on stage. My eyes were usually on the middle distance, listening to the others. It was the way I worked. And that day I was, needless to say, also whacked out on the nastiest speed money could find. Wired for sound.

I was all over the stage in those days. It's a wonder I didn't spin myself up in the cables and vanish. There's a lot to be said for that really raw yellow Iranian whiz. While it lasted, it was our muse. Our inspiration. Don't say the Ayatollah's all bad. You could say he tried to silence one man, but actually he got an entire generation talking their heads off. The crowd had packed itself into the tiny theatre, made from a motorway bay, and spilled out over the whole of Portobello Green saturated in sunshine. Any time I looked forward I stared directly into her huge blue eyes. And got a godzilla power jolt. She was a Russian Earth Goddess.

Epic Hero v. the Beast! I turned into a spastic maniac. I was helpless. In the grip of a rock-and-roll orgasm, a holistic fit, I was flung back and forth like a Jack Russell's rat. And the way she kept moving closer in to the stage told me she was definitely there for the best reasons. Crouched over my instrument, I must have looked like I was being buggered by the Invisible Man.

If I'd been a pigeon I'd have had my chest puffed and my tail feathers flared. As it was, my hair seemed to be standing upright from my head. Which was blazing with copper fire. My eyebrows itched like scabs. There were suddenly thin red scars all over my fingers. I can remember the riffs, each one a rippling wall of colour, the way the set built and built. Every bone in my body was jumping to a different beat. I was hurting. Solid unrelenting pain. I found chords I never knew existed. My teeth screamed. But I couldn't and wouldn't stop. I never once lost control. My guitar was beginning to make Martin's seem mellow. I was electrocuted by love. Jazzed with the joo-joo juice. People still remember that gig.

The day continued to bloom into something exotic and fabulous. There was no coming down. I had its measure now. Mach One. Mach Two. Mach Three. Approaching the speed of light. I believed I was probably going to die but I certainly didn't mind. No body, no human heart, no brain could stand this ecstasy, this bonding harmony with my music and the girl of my dream. (One dream but very powerful, when I was eleven. Julie was in it. An echo. A recognition. I think she saw the same in me.)

I began to believe I was doing something alchemical, musically creating my own Rosie substitute. A glamorous fetch. A perfect mythago. Then I dumped the idea as pointless and tricky. Julie met my eye and smiled. Suddenly I was at the heart of the sun. Yow! Master of the universe. My Rickenbacker was bucking out of my control, screaming with complicated lusts, radiating funny black light. Its strings were silver rays piercing infinity. Roadways through the multiverse. Va-zooom. I had the feeling the Rickenbacker was tripping. I wondered what it was on. Iranian daze. It's never been the same since. A spent machine.

Certainly the Rosie void was filling pretty rapido for me that Saturday. I was a Ukrainian reactor. **KABOOM!!** That was it. One chance meeting on a Saturday afternoon and it was love and madness for four long years. Sex and drugs and rock and fucking roll. Pictures and paranoia. Black-and-white nightmares. The Silver Age. Follow your nose. Snorting our way towards social suicide, boarding the oblivion express, getting tired of politics just as Maggie and the Hatchetmen started hauling in their equipment. Bad timing. Is that the story of your life, too?

The set lasted for over an hour. Then the jolly peelers muscled up with a dog in tow, armed with some garbled by-law to prove we shouldn't be irritating them by having fun for nothing. We dealt with the dogs in the usual way and they were soon running about whining to themselves, but finally the jollies turned off our power and we finished with the traditional chanting and drumming until we all got tired of it and the poor dogs sat down, their eyes and tongues lolling. They never could work out how we sorted their dogs. Always nice to leave a baffled bobby behind you.

Julie came over while we were packing up our gear. I felt her warmth against my cold sweaty back as I turned, pulling off my T-shirt. I winked at her. Friendly. Already intimate. She smiled uncertainly but had that familiar determined stance. This was her day for getting laid. She wasn't going home until it happened. I don't seek out female company just for the sake of it. I like being on my own. So I wasn't seeing anyone else.

I was still technically married to Germaine and living in Colville Terrace, but it was well over. I didn't yet have a drum of my own and Germaine's living room didn't seem the right place for the occasion. So I took Julie with us when we went up to the Princess Louise in Portobello Road. I thought she was foreign at first. The usual score. I thought she was a tourist. Her wide, pink face looked more Slavic than Surrey. Her father must have been that Polish Count she'd sometimes mentioned, who was a friend of her family's in Shepperton. I said she looked like some epic Northern heroine. She laughed and showed me the little bit of coke she'd bought at school. We did it all in the ladies' toilet before going on. It was getting cool and neither of us had much in the way of clothes.

After a while we went down to the Princess of Wales off Portland Road. I had a desperate idea. I was lucky. I scored a couple of half-an'-halfs off Little Ronny and an ounce off Geronimo and caught sight of Germaine who'd just come in with one of her friends. No need to tell her anything. She gave me the keys to the Pink Panther, her van. I didn't like to ask if the mattress was still in it.

The van was parked in a lock-up behind St James's School. A few minutes' hasty walk from the pub. And the mattress was still there, if a bit damp. Julie seemed perfectly happy with it all and took everything for granted. She told me later she'd no idea what was normal.

I apologized. I thought maybe she expected more from a rock-and-roll hero. But she was in heaven. She thought it was romantic. About as far from Shepperton as she could get without a spaceship. It made her gently randy.

It wasn't too much longer before I was engulfed in her slowly relished appetites. She enjoyed it from the first moment. And so did I. I was never a breast man, but those tits and buttocks were primeval. They took me back to the dawn of time, to the long slow pleasures of genesis, spending like mercury. At one point we did a bit of speed and then obsessively rolled enough joints to stone an army. We set the controls on cruise and didn't get up till Tuesday. You're dead right. We *were* having a better time than you.

Check it out. 10 October 1972. I was almost twenty. Maybe you weren't even here then. A golden age.

Barney Bubbles, banging on the side of the van, brought the age to an end. He only lived up the road, in a big Gothic studio built by Burne-Jones in 1905. He'd had a message from Germaine. The police had been round to Colville Terrace looking for me.

Jack had decided I was a bad influence. So he'd told the police she was missing. That I might have been the last person to see her. It was his way of warning me off.

He knew exactly who Julie was with, because Germie had reassured him on the phone Sunday morning. Julie was over eighteen, her own woman. She phoned him to say she was OK. But Jack knew better. She was his responsibility, he said. His sacred charge. How could he face her mother – or his mother – if anything happened to her? Julie put the phone down and came out of the booth. She was grinning. She'd guessed all along that he fancied her. 'Just a jealous guy,' she said. And hummed the tune.

But Jack, of course, wasn't going to leave it there. He gave up on involving the jollies, because they were getting more interested in his motives than his story. They'd already apologized to Julie. They knew a thwarted suitor when they saw one.

He tried to appeal to my decent side. Was it fair to take Julie away from a good career? She was missing weeks of school already.

'She can walk and talk,' I said. 'She's passed. She can send in for her diploma.'

Jack said I was cynical and selfish. He said he shouldn't have expected anything else from a Brookgate wide boy. He'd been brought up to take his responsibilities seriously. What kind of protection could I give Julie? What would her mother think?

I told him that Julie didn't seem to need protecting and that, in the absence of a handy goat, her mother could fuck herself and his mother, too.

That, he said, was exactly what he was trying to keep Julie from. What drugs was I pushing down her already?

You ought to know, I told him. I'd bought quite a lot of them from him. Is there something wrong with the quality? Do you have something better for her?

He called me a shit. He said I was the lowest scum on the face of creation. I said his higher education wasn't improving his English.

That showed how much I knew, he said. He was at the London School of Economics. Mick Jagger's old school.

I got tired of it. I said I was going to have to punch him. He was terrified of physical violence. And fascinated, of course, the way they are.

He thought this over, then went rapidly into denial. He switched to that reasonable tone they all have.

At least let me pay for a decent flat for you both, he said. I mean, Julie's used to a very nice house. For her sake.

I started laughing. What a predictable cunt you are, I said. If you'd had everything stuffed up your arse that should have been stuffed up your arse you'd be a fucking medical miracle by now.

He said he had no idea what I was talking about. The shit was doing something to me.

I mean, look at you. Another month with you and Julie'll be a junkie.

It took a few years, actually, and I did everything I could to stop it.

I've never been able to do junk on its own. It's just not my drug. Even ordinary speedballing gets to me in a way nothing else does. You can always tell when you're losing it, when your paranoia becomes really banal. You start hearing yourself saying the sort of things you hear from any loony in the street. I hate drugs that make me stupid. That's what's so nice about modern designer drugs and the Philip K. Dick Pharmaceutical Companion. Somehow, in spite of the ludicrous rhetoric, we're setting up our own standards and controls.

It wasn't a bad few years, all in all, though Jack was never reconciled. He said at one point that he thought I ought to have some consideration for Rosie. As if she was my wife, not my cousin. For someone who generally understood people as appetites and needs he seems to have registered me and Rosie as almost as real to him as he was. Almost as important. We were about the only human beings he didn't regard automatically as commodities or obstacles. Early sibling imprinting, I suppose, before his marvellous unconscious confirmed that sympathy and loyalty are never survival traits either in work or sex.

A complex but unsubtle mind, as Dorian (Tubby Ollis) Theakston said. Tubby had Jack's measure better than the rest of us.

Julie and I went to stay at the Mill. In those days Jack didn't know about Tubby.

Julie and I saw a lot of Tubby even after we got our own place. He became one of our best friends. An innuendoist to his roots, he'd describe himself as an ex-skin-thumper who hadn't touched his kit in years. He'd been a jazzman originally. They're all like that. It's their generation. Humphrey Lyttelton. Ronnie Scott. Johnny Dankworth. Bad puns and cool jazz, as Tubby used to say. That was who Dorian really was: Tubby Ollis.

The drummer on a lot of our gigs, Tubby had been in the family scrap trade originally and his first business had been architectural reclamation. He'd never really needed to work. He was one of the three best percussionists in England but he's only on a few records, like Pavli, who was too bored to play rock-and-roll bass and took up the classical cello after hearing a piece by Kodály.

Tubby inherited an incredible house on the crown of Tufnell Hill. It's that old converted windmill you see from the top of the 138 as it stops beside the gates. It had part of its original sails. He'd deliberately let it look a bit neglected, but it was neat as a pin inside. Rhododendrons all around it now. And larches. Evergreens. Huge brambles. Like Sleeping Beauty's palace.

When Tubby first got it, the whole band did it up. Then for a while it used to be full of miscellaneous musicians, mostly members of High Tide. That's where I met Pete Pavli and Simon House. We were all hard to tell apart then. We all looked like fucking Jesus. In the end Tubby kicked out the last few Jesuses and now it's just him and his oriental cats. Which isn't to say he doesn't have a pretty active social life for an overweight recluse who sometimes claimed he gave up drumming because it made his wrists too tired for wanking.

Don't believe it. Women flew in and out of that hive like happy bees. Whatever he was offering, they couldn't get enough of it. Powerful women, too. He'd made several fortunes on the phone, thanks to their tips. Old friends are allowed round on Tuesdays or Thursdays. Any time. Those are his days off. His talking days. He says he has to take care of his heart.

'Most women are like cats. Men are like dogs. Women enjoy routines. They actually like being patient. It gives them a sense of security. They relax like cats. And like cats they're naturally conservative.

'Men are ready to go walkies any old time, especially if there's a hint of somebody on heat somewhere in the universe. Women are attracted to me because they always know where to find me and can plan their days around me. It makes them randy just knowing that I never ever go out. What else would they find so attractive about a fat hairy old fart who sits in a chair watching videos all day?'

It had to be more than that. Rosie said he was simply lovable, all soft fire and honey. And still, under those blossoming cheeks, so fucking, heart-stoppingly Elvis Presley handsome. Even I could agree there was something sweet about him.

'Incorruptibly sweet,' is how Rosie put it. 'When he dies he'll crystallize. He's like some of those great Sumos you meet in Japan. It's not like ordinary sex. It feels safer and happier somehow. You're willing to try out any fantasy in the Mill, because you know in your bones you can never come to harm with Tubby. But the fantasies you have there are never predatory or humiliating.'

Only me and Rosie were allowed to call him Tubby. He was Dorian Theakston to anyone else. When asked by *NME* why, on his fortieth birthday, he'd decided to change his name to something so eccentric he said that it was a signal to his friends that he was now officially an Old Peculier. That dark Theakston's was a cross between a milk stout and Murphy's as far as I was concerned. Too much going on in it. I avoided both. I'm not one of your jolly tankardmen. Ackroyd's Mild keeps you trucking and if they don't have that on tap I'll have a Campari. Rex Martin told me mild was an accountant's drink and the other was an office girl's drink. You could tell a good beer by the strength of the farts it made. I was happy to believe him.

Tubby would still drum for us occasionally, but we had to go to the Mill to record him. He had his own studio there. State of the art. High Tide lived and worked there rent-free for ages. They produced one album in three years. Three long tracks. Don't play *Talking Rats* unless you've a very slow evening ahead of you and everything's tickety-boo.

On the other hand, if you're already contemplating suicide, bugger *Gloomy Sunday*, this is the album for you. Tunes from an alien time-zone. It makes The Cowboy Junkies seem like Jerry Lee Lewis. Then there was a raid and some other trouble. Pavli moved in with his girlfriend in Barnet. House joined David Bowie. Jik Green killed himself. Graham was arrested for dealing. After that Tubby made a rule. Only tried and true friends to stay. And for a limited time. He knew how to get rid of anyone who overstayed their welcome. And as his friends died or went mad, there were fewer and fewer of us. It was a good place for me and Julie to be when we were first together. Julie loved Tubby and he showed her the sort of vulgar respect he reserved for his favourites. She was fascinated by his books and his toy soldiers. He'd read all the books and enjoyed the soldiers, but he had no proprietorial feelings towards them. He'd bought both collections from Alex Harvey. They had identical tastes, he said, and Alex had got bored with it all, needed some money and sold it for its market price.

He was a classic mixture, Alex. Aggressive, complicated, sharp as a diamond, Glaswegian. Dead now. What can you say? We were trying out some work together just before he died. His Jacques Brel stuff, which he growled in a kind of Mississippi Clydeside, never sounded more sardonic, and he could shout out a blues with the best. Another Star Club vet.

Not always an easy man to work with, Alex had read more books than the British Librarian. I wondered what it was like for him travelling with Tubby, who'd also read a lot.

It was miserable, Alex said. All Tubby would do when they were touring was make infantile puns, tell dirty jokes, get drunk on some offensive local ale and sing Shirley Bassey hits. He'd pick up a pretty girl after the gig and always fell asleep before he could do anything about it. Every hotel the band was in you'd see Tubby snoring his head off somewhere in his room while his latest prize sat on the edge of the bed looking sheepish and wondering what she was going to do about getting home.

The life suited Tubby even less than it suited me. At least when I was taking photographs I could get to bed early if I wanted to. He just gave it all up. The Mill was his. He had some small investments and he still got good money from his jingles and two albums he'd made in Germany in 1970, *Over the Edge* and *Shoot the Drummer*. It had been the last time he'd left the country and almost the last time he'd left the house. While he was gone he rented it to Jillian Burnes, the transsexual novelist, and when he got back there was some problem about her leaving. They settled the dispute by getting married. It lasted three weeks. Her significant other is now her fellow modernist, Felix Martin. They live in separate flats. Rosie says she can understand that. She had a one-night stand with Felix. It was the kind, she said, that made you wish you'd stayed indoors and washed your underwear. Jillian and Felix pretended not to be a couple. They co-parented a bottled child, a sort of changeling. Very artistic. They've got a house near Tubby in Tufnell Hill, a manse on the Scottish border and a place in Little Bavaria, Spain. They're bound to meet occasionally.

Whatever the story, Tubby took against them both and, typically, planned and executed a thousand minor revenges, by every medium available, leaving his chair only to lick a stamp or get his mail. Hunched like the Phantom of the Opera over his electronic keyboards, he was hoping to kill them, he said, by slow degrees.

Graham usually goes in to see if there's anything he's short of, but mostly Tubby has everything brought in. Mostly by international beauties. His cupboards are stuffed with exotic foods from the finest shops around the world. Airport luxuries purchased on the run, usually for the look of the jar. Most of it's pretty good. He lets you eat what you like. There's plenty more where that came from. And his place is always spotless. When they're not buying and selling airlines, some of his lady friends love to clean for him.

'What sensible animal would bother to go out?' he asks.

He was never, he says, agoraphobic. Neither did he have anything personal against most people. He just preferred the life he led. It wasn't as if, he pointed out, he was short of exercise. He was, his doctor assured him, impossibly healthy.

'And here I am,' said Tubby. 'Living the life I love, with my beautiful friends, my beautiful lads and ladies.' He was speaking of the elegant oriental cats that covered his lap and shoulders. They loved him. They purred and smiled whenever they set eyes on him. Their tails twitched with the ecstatic knowledge that he existed. Sometimes they'd rouse, arch, stretch, preen and go back to sleep, content in the reminder of his wonderful presence.

You could tell how his girlfriends felt about him. It didn't take much imagining to see those lovely women slipping out of their street clothes with much the same urgent, elegant movements as their feline fellows.

The eighties would see Jack's first attack on the Mill. It was one of the last really prime properties left in London. Tubby would not give up his home, no matter how many millions and millions it was worth. But for years he was in a state of siege, doggedly refusing to acknowledge the threat, until Barbican's persistence got to him. He lived in fewer rooms which he kept dark, burning candles and scratching old Leonard Cohen vinyl, always a sign of serious depression. Especially in a drummer.

In the end he became something of a symbol. Of the old enduring London that Barbican for so long failed to conquer. Or so it seemed.

Jack got Julie in the end, of course, but I don't think he could have been very happy with his prize. She didn't come back in the condition she'd left in. No fault of mine. I tried a hundred times to pull her out of whatever personal vortex she fell into. When she married Barbican the sunshine vanished from her soul. A bad, bad bargain I never really understood. You can't hide those lyin' eyes. Sex and drugs and deep black holes.

Life goes on. Obla-di, Obla-do.

Well, it does for some of us, right?

CHAPTER NINE
The Scrap

Me and Rosie used to go mudlarking, usually when it was a low tide and the river was a shallow stain. We weren't the only kids to do it. It depended on what your parents thought. Posh kids only rarely got down there. They didn't last long. You saw them bundled, squealing, into furious cars.

Brookgate kids went mudlarking the way country kids went scrumping. There wasn't much paid casual work in Brookgate except thieving, so mudlarking could be a profitable way of making some easy non-dodgy money. There was an old bloke in Hatton Garden who had a jewellery business. I don't think Mr Marks was a professional fence, but he was always a realist. We used to take any bits and pieces of trinkets to him and he always gave us something, just to keep us coming back. Sterling silver got a bit extra. If it was gold he paid accordingly. I dreamed of some miserable diamond merchant, rejected in love, gnawing on his gold rings, fleeing with his wares to Blackfriars Bridge and flinging himself into the welcoming water, to be washed up, complete with bag of high grade tom, just as the pair of us set foot on the mud below Marriage's Reach. Some hope.

Mudlarking was delicious. Anyone who's ever done it themselves knows what I mean, which is why we were never stopped from going.

It was best to get there at dawn with a cold sun rising out of West India Docks and the mud flats etched with detritus and half-sunk boats, a profound promise of plenty. Long, shifting veins of light running like bridal ribbons in the thin metallic water. Shadowed by flustering silver gulls, who seemed to wake up quarrelling, we'd head straight down to Blackfriars and then walk until we got past the Tower and into Wapping, where people didn't bother you. You get filthy. You get lucky. These days you can get a few new diseases, too. You go home looking like a walking dog turd. Thames mud is a stew of everything the city wants to lose and sometimes, if you're unwary, you can sink into a patch of quicksand and when you get out stink like a sewer for days. A stink so foul that only the initiated can believe it comes from living human flesh. Maybe that's why I didn't ever think it was much of a social let-down to be a paparazzo.

I've never had a problem about the ways I scrap a coin. What you see with me is pretty much what you get. These days I hear all that 'How can you live with yourself?' crap which has to be a sign of a really hypocritical culture, no? I mean, who the fuck buys those papers? Show me a woman who'll pass up the latest *Hello* or *People* and I'll show you a faulty clone. You can't tell me all those intellectual housewives aren't frigging away with the best of them over the latest Antonio Banderas cozzy pix. Live from the Costa Fortun. Zip-zip-zip. ZORRO ZORRO ZORRO!!!

So what else do you want? More saggy Ivana Trump shots to make the older reader feel good? Iffy twat snaps for the gents? Unlikely willies? Sleazy embraces? Grimacing faces for all seasons. Heroes and villains. Villains and legends. Faces and characters. Suits and skirts. Vicars and schoolgirls. Tarts and duchesses. Salt of the earth. Bread on the table.

Some people always want to know how an underground guitar hero and investigative photog turned into trash. I'm not a different person. I'm what's left of the fourth estate. As I see it, in a popular democracy it's the journalist's job to represent the underdog and the outsider, to be their eyes and ears and sometimes their voice. To represent the best the mob aspires to. The good it achieves. To mock the worst. That's all my songs were ever about – peace, love and understanding, freedom and justice. In a popular arena. Nothing sentimental. Not Donovan or Donny or Dopehead I-wish – but good old-fashioned anger. Don't push my buttons, please. I'm a mutt. I bite. But I'm always happy to play by your rules till you break them.

The rich don't need more laws to protect them, they need fewer. Privacy? They can't pay for good bodyguards, moving environments, modern electronics? What do they want for their free money? Freedom? It's not that kind of money. And what are the predatory super-rich actually protecting themselves from? The public that created them? Well, there's a dilemma.

The people who really need the protection of the law are the people who can't afford it. Do you think I ever went after some nobody for a cheap shot? Check it out. I'm a specialized predator. I prey on the rich and powerful. You won't find any beleaguered gays, rape victims or any other half-fictionalized minor actors in the ongoing world soap with my credits on their private parts. My pictures try to tell true stories about the abnormally rich and powerful.

No, I never compromised my ideals, Mrs Kleen. I just compromised everything else. And I never felt I had to reconcile my own self with some other goozer's idea of what that self should be. I'm the cockney existentialist, aren't I? I'm happy with the contradictions in my character. And the vulgar, messy human race. Take us or leave us, Mrs Kleen.

I got my first real break on the flats below Greenwich. Authentic enough. Rosie and me found a corpse. A victim. It was the Union Jack Murder. Much more famous now than my dad's. He'd been strangled with a flag. A youth. Brian Canning. A nance. And I'd lifted a tasty instamatic only two hours earlier from a tourist on Tower Pier.

Of course Canning was covered in mud, but we hadn't been sure he was drowned, so we'd lugged him out and wiped his boy's face, thinking to give him the kiss of life. Rosie quickly realized he'd been dead a while. She drew back, her smooth, smeared cheeks suddenly white in the risen sun. And I got a perfect picture.

The *Evening News* gave me five pounds for the rights. And ran a little story about me. That's how we first met Jimmy Lakefort, one of Brookgate's legendary mobsmen. He had a permanent smile powdered on his creasing pink face. He looked like a holiday-camp host. A ballroom-dancing promoter. Merry blue eyes. A double-breasted pinstripe. An old school tie. Plenty of shirt. Big links. He drove round to see us in his famous eggshell-blue Roller. My auntie made him a cup of tea. He said you couldn't beat a Brookgate brew-up. He gave her some vouchers for his restaurant. 'Bring the family,' he said. We never went. Too posh. And my mum was in the home at the time. Jimmy congratulated us on being responsible little citizens. We deserved a reward. He asked the familiar questions about how we'd found the victim, where, what he looked like, and so on. He wondered if, in recent days, we'd picked anything up near the body. A friend of his had lost his watch around that stretch of the river and it was of great sentimental value. We told him we'd keep a lookout for it next time. 'I think it was a watch,' he said. 'Just get in touch with me first if you find anything like that at all. Here's my business card.' I guessed he had some motive, but it didn't bother me. After he'd asked me a couple more vague questions, vaguely answered, he slid me a monkey and patted my shoulder with an unforgiving hand. That visit, the dosh and the picture put me well up in the local kidarchy. But that was about the last mudlarking we did. Soon after, Rosie started at St Paul's. They never caught the murderer. The boy was gay, a known Berwick Street cruiser, and they more or less wrote it off, the way they do.

The *Evening News* picture was a professional credential. It began my distinguished career into oblivion.

Some time after that I started working for Barney Bubbles when he was art editor on *Queen* and did a lot of his sleeve stuff when he went freelance. I snapped demos and love-ins and free festivals for United Artistes, who gradually turned into a regular agency and slowly stopped paying me my cheques on time, but I'd had their facilities and learned their expertise and it was easy to go out on my own. I became the Red Snapper at a bad moment for the fortunes of the free press – low wages – but it got me back into gigging. And it made me more ambitious. Not that I ever really deserted one career for the other. There weren't too many people who could do both reasonably well. For a while I was fired up and some jobs led to others, photo sessions one day, guitar the next, but then slowly I started getting too clinical and I didn't much care for the result. Words, pictures and music. Yackety-yack, clickety-clack, twangety-twang. That was my state of mind, more than anything else. And Julie's junk. And probably mine, though I always had the sense to stop as soon as I thought I needed it. I hate routine.

They should classify the drug-users rather than the drugs. Some of us never get addicted. Some of us are addicts from the moment they put their first Tizer to their youthful lips. Julie was a junkie. She would have been addicted to Abingdon if she'd stayed there. If there was nothing else to get addicted to. And she loved the rituals, the little do's and don'ts of junkiedom, the idiot rationalizations, the perpetual repetitions. A nice person, like a lot of junkies. The world was too hard for her. She should never have crossed the border from the Shires. But I suppose she's all right now. She went through an identity crisis after her divorce from Barbican when she got out of hospital. All that confusion and litigation over blood relatives. She was only thirty. For a while she joined a commune of Marxist mystics, but even their complicated rituals weren't enough for her. She got into every loony cult going and one night a Ladbroke Grove nobody cut her to bite-sized bits.

But Julie wasn't the reason I started to get itchy. I was depressed by my modest success and bored by her recycled heart. The first year was great, if crazy. The second year was crazy, but great. The third year was just crazy and I didn't know how to handle her passion for drugs. The fourth year was hideous, grey, down the toilet. Maybe it was my fault, but I thought I was helping her to find firm ground. The most memorable thing I remember her saying was 'Is that a line of something for me?' She really shouldn't have taken that train up from Bagginsville. And I shouldn't have fallen in love with her. She went on looking like some sturdy, sweet-faced Alice almost her whole life. She was innocent. She had a beautiful nature. But she was also a junkie. A lethal mix for one and all. It isn't the junk that's the problem, as they say, it's the lack of it. You'd have to be a rich enough pop star to be invited to Princess Di's funeral to make Julie's Christmas white. And Julie wanted every day to be Christmas. If she'd had any taste, she'd have followed Rosie's example and not touched me with a barge pole. That's right, pards: every other compromise and evasion in the book, but I never compromised my calling. Just my heart and soul.

Julie was a junkie,
A dedicated junkie,
Got a little funky,
But she was still a junkie.

Rock-and-roll careers like mine always sound better in retrospect, with the high points condensed. Soaring stardom. The heady fruits of success. The crash to oblivion. Actually it was more like the early history of flight: a lot of bumping along the ground and a few sudden wild moments in the air, over almost before you realized it. I used to pretend I'd chosen photography above cheap stardom, but the truth was stardom had never come cheap to me. I got some lucky breaks but I didn't really want them. I wasn't suited for it and I never got offered it much. Here's the full story: I start as a reasonably proficient counter-culture guitar hero in Notting Dale, coming up from the bottom, and I bottom out in America, drowning in syrup. Famous for a hamster's lifetime.

In Black Flame I'd got reasonably good on my Rickenbacker 12, which isn't everybody's instrument and is a bugger to keep in tune on stage, but at its best, if you resist the string-grab and if you use the patent 'Rickosound' output with a bit of wah-wah, it sounds like you're controlling a choir of bells and I've got a choppy, melodic right-hand style that some people like. I switched between that and my ES-335, one of the earliest that Gibson made in 1958, with two '57 Classic humbackers, the works. Deep cherry finish. I got it cheap at the time because it was a left-hand conversion. There isn't an instrument like it. It plays itself. Wild and easy. And you get the credit.

Of course, no guitar ever beat the Epiphone Black Bird, but we haven't got to that, yet.

We didn't do badly for a while. Most of our releases were in the top hundred and we had an album that got to number three in some charts. But Paul Frame grew as bored as me and first our stage stuff and then our albums got more and more experimental for their own sake and we were playing all kinds of weird rhythms and keys, most of which only he really understood. As a result we fell away one by one, usually joining other up-and-coming bands who were based in blues and R&B like us. Let's face it, the kind of girls attracted to that sort of music weren't there because they had exciting lives. Some nights we looked out into a void in which huge tinted pairs of round glasses glinted, clustered in tiny groups here and there in the vastness of the unfilled auditorium, like watching harpies, stern owls. And only Paul was enjoying himself.

'I hate to think of you with all those groupies,' says Julie out of the blue one night.

'Don't worry,' I told her, 'they're too deaf and blind to catch me.'

I went back to smaller gigs, larger audiences. Lots of fast 4/4 bass and drums. ROCK AND ROLL!!!! Work up that luring sweat. Four sets a night. Hamburg hours. More lines. More sweat. Get the air stewardesses in town for a one-night stand. That was what it was all about. And it was good for a couple of years unless you were a psychopath or Neanderthal. Then you had to take a lot more drugs just to install the necessary brain damage. The secret was in shortening your attention span to that of an amoeba so that it all seemed new for night after night after night. And when the do-it-yourself lobotomy kit failed, you topped yourself or went back into teaching or the family grocery business. C'est la vie. Let les bon temps rollez. And enjoy them while it lasts, eh?

So I got gigs. Martin Stone had me in Chilli Willi long enough to do three tracks for *Teatime on the Prairie*. I took over on bass when Pavli temporarily left High Tide. I'm on most of Calvert's albums. Banjo, mandolin and Yamaha on *Lucky Leif*. Rickenbacker and Gibson on *Hype*. He often got the best out of me. *Stormbringer*. Sessions with Sonny Browne and Nick Lowe on early Elvis Costello at Stiff. A few gigs with Arthur Brown. Paul Rudolph, Trevor Burton, Twink and me in The Pink Fairies. Danteleon's Chariot. The job in The Police was between me and Andy Summers. Paul Kossoff suggested we form a band just before he had his heart attack. And then that long run with Calvert, Deep Fix and Hawkwind. *Sonic Attack. Choose Your Masks. Maddy Font Live, Lucky Leif. New Worlds Fair, Taking the Shots, Vein Fancies, Faster than the Mainstream, Kings of Speed, Aiming for Zero*. My finest moment? A single. *The Greenfly and the Rose*. Recorded for Flicknife at some terrible little studio in Covent Garden. One of the simplest records I was ever on. Calvert paid me himself, the same night. A day's session fee and proud to have the credit. An elegy for all our pasts. A presentiment of the rise of the Grand Consumer. Check it out. It's still in some of the shops. There's a thinner version, pretty much a demo, on Calvert's solo *Hype* album, the last new thing that came out before he died in Skerring or some other godforsaken resort. Deep Fix in its last classic line-up of Calvert, Pavli, King, House, Frame, Turner, Gilmore and Colvin – and occasionally me. The last session work I ever got paid for. 1981? It's silly to be proud of a job on which all you did was backing vocals and a few well-placed basic licks. Then, a bit later, there was the ridiculous few months being promoted in the US and everything going really crazy in West Hollywood. Everyone else had gone home. Maddy La Font was with me long enough for us to make those two LA albums. Maddy persuaded me to take one of the old cabins behind the Tropicana. And then she disappeared.

A phone call from Rosie pulled me out of that. She was in Kinshasa, changing planes. She had some leave. She was going to be in LA for a couple of days. Something to do with the UN.

When she found me at the Tropicana Motel I thought she'd be tickled by my crazy lifestyle. I told her how Maddy La Font, still at that time the Scarlet Lady, had dumped life with me for a night with Dylan. I felt almost proud. I showed her my new pictures, played her my new tapes, explained how they were meant to sound banal. It was ironic. We did up my last line or two. She stayed overnight and in the morning I woke to find everything packed. She'd even had a ticket FedExed round. Four

hours later we were flying back to London. It was the first time I'd
travelled economy class.

As I shivered into some kind of consciousness on the plane she asked
me if I knew that Lloyd Stokes was fighting his last professional match
in New Jewry that coming Saturday.

Rosie always had witchy powers. It was as if she'd touched me with
her magic wand and brushed the dirty sugar off my psyche, brought my
wiry little body back to life and reminded me who I was. I'd followed
Stoker's career all my life. He was the last of the old time bare-knuckle
pugs. The original Lord of the Ring! I was surprised to know he was still
slogging it out with the raw 'uns, as the Prince Regent's rules punters
used to call it.

I couldn't believe my own enthusiasm. 'At the old *Corinthians*? Who's
he fighting?'

She watched my face. 'Sonny Portillo.'

'Tasty.' Sonny had been one of our minders. He used to block the
dressing room doorway and still have some of himself left over for the
surounding walls and ceiling. He loved the authority of being a roadie.
A natural NCO. I knew him better than I knew the Stoker but I didn't
like him as much. And I also guessed the Stoker still had an old-style
toughness that could take Sonny in a fair fight any day.

'I got us a couple of seats.' She was grinning. 'The wonders of modern
communications. I called Jimmy Lakeforth from LA.'

'He'll be glad to see you.' I kept touching her hand. I wasn't sure this
was actual. 'I know I am.'

'God, you're clammy.' She made me go to the toilet during the first
movie and give myself a body wash. That started me shivering again. She
held me in her arms for half the flight. We watched *Down And Out In
Beverly Hills*. I soaked one of her shoulder pads.

She came back with me to Fogg Yard, got me settled, made a few
phone calls and said she'd decided to stay with me for a bit. She was only
in London to pick up some medicine for the kid. Stuff that would take
weeks to get there. But she had to wait a few days while the amounts
were prepared and approved. So, she said, she might as well get me
sorted out while she was waiting.

'What's the matter with the kid?' I asked.

'Oh, just problems,' she said. 'Just problems.' It was the one thing she
wouldn't trust me with and I didn't know why.

CHAPTER TEN
The Snap

Rosie said she fancied some old-fashioned Sharps Alley bloodworms and taters that Saturday night, so we went to Turpin's in Smithfield. It was crowded with City types in weekend uniforms, but the food was as good as you could get in the area now. We thought we'd walk afterwards to the Corinthians, just over the river. The black sausage was a lot tastier than I'd expected. I ate too much. So did Rosie. We washed it all down with halves of A&S mild.

In the end we felt so fat we took a taxi to Fish Wharf and, hand in hand, walked over London Bridge planning to reach the Corinthians by midnight. In the middle of the bridge we stopped and looked towards Blackfriars. There was something solid and inviolable about the city seen from here. Maybe because there were fewer lights. The almost invisible domes of St Paul's and the Old Bailey. Cross, sword and scales. A city of love and justice, a true new Jerusalem, complex and profound. I gave it all my attention. I was still getting my head round what Rosie had said to me about her daughter. I did my best to sidebar that as much as I could. I had a feeling she'd told me all she was going to tell me. Tonight was a conspiracy of escape, for the warmth of being amongst our own.

New Jewry, the district behind the station, was where the old House of Conversion had stood. It had itself been converted around 1800, when you didn't have to be a Christian to become a citizen. Bought by 'Dandy Bob' Begg, our remote and rather more attractive ancestor, it became the finest sporting hostelry in London: THE JOLLY CORINTHIAN BOYS. Almost all the famous boxing prizefights were held here in the great bare-knuckle days. But her fortunes sank through Victoria's middle reign and she got a bad rep as a charnel house, no-holds-barred slogging matches and worse. But gradually she became a music hall and by 1900 her only rival south of the river was the Canterbury.

The Boys had once dominated Baal-Zephan Street (which locals called Bells-Evans) until the coming of the railway and its viaducts. Even after the flyovers were built the district had somehow retained its integrity and had survived Hitler's war. All the street names around there were originally Jewish before the redevelopment. Melchior Street. Ship and Mermaid Row. Jove Street. Sign Street. Manuel Street. Jesus and Mary Yard and Vinegar Street sound a fair way from the original Hebrew. Rebecca Street. Isaac Street. Zachariah Mews. Now all the Jews have long since been absorbed into the South London mix, which is as much Gypsy, African or Irish as it is Anglo-Saxon. A sturdy gene pool. And here was Sonny Portillo, Borough born and bred, boxing in the tradition of the immortal Brookgater Dan Mendoza who, I had always been told, was my real great-great-grandfather, Dickens's hero. Anyone with uncertain Jewish ancestry claimed Mendoza or Disraeli as an ancestor. But I indulged the fantasy. Mendoza and Dutch Sam had dominated boxing at the cusp of the eighteenth and nineteenth centuries. Mendoza was four times heavyweight champion of Great Britain. The face who put the science and speed into the manly art. Made boxing a skill. The Ali of his day. Ran a pub and school of boxing in Whitechapel. Turned out a lot of tough Jews. From what the old Victorian social-studies goozers used to call street Jews. Old-clothes merchants.

New Jewry had been a crash course in assimilation when the House of Conversion was running at full blast and the practice of Judaism was regarded as a disgusting affront to Christ. To their credit, Londoners generally confined their attacks on Jews to newspaper tirades and demands for their expulsion. But assimilation happened so naturally, without a dramatic change of habits on anyone's part, that everyone had a Jewish relative in no time. Listen to them talking. Look at the body language, the strength of those genes, and tell me where saxon, celt, gypsy and blackamoor end and jew begins? It's still happening. Every thoroughbred was originally a successful mongrel.

The Jolly Corinthian Boys was the castle on the cockney borderland. Once a shade outside the City's stricter by-laws, but in easy reach of most citizens, a sporting tavern of fame, she had been a watchword for riotous and bawdy behaviour, her bloody combats too much even for the bleeding hearts of the 1840s, who tried to get her closed.

They failed. There were royal connections involved.

Set back from the road, in that gap between Leathermarket Street and Morocco Place, she was a cocky monster. Her busy, beating heart forced life through her deadly surroundings, brightening the stained cladding of the apartment stacks, classic symbols of social spin, chipboarding over the chaos within. But they couldn't put their Lego cosmetics on The Jolly Corinthian Boys. She was a South London matron and she knew she was supposed to look like a blonde success in scarlet plush and pearls, silver and gold, winking like a diamond. She was a stronghold. Her car park was vibrant with smart motors. Her paint and brick were bright, her stonework scrubbed, her kitchens raised to an Ajax glare. Survivor's principles. Fresh make-up, clean knickers and a big smile.

She was the last bastion of the old South London knuckle fights, Prince Regent's Rules, which were nothing like the brutal knackerings the travellers favoured these days. You could smell her insides from half a mile away. Beer, floral colognes, cockles, cigars, sparkling wine, whelks, grease, whisky, baked potatoes, jellied eels and hot wine. There wouldn't be a suit or a frock at her several bars who didn't have form, fame or both. Inside, form was everywhere in contrast to the collapsing structures outside. Smart clothes meant self-control and self-respect. Quiet voices meant casual power.

Everything was always up to snuff at the long bar of the Corinthians. Her mirror was a portrait of the generations, from gypsies to rastas, but all sharp, all skirted and shirted and showing their best, with that cool sense of caritas and gravitas the best Elizabethans cultivated, for this was really still a seventeenth-century culture, following customs that had kept it safe and strong for ever. It treated its own wounds. It issued its own warrants. An all but indestructible cultural root system that survived the upheavals of religion, politics and total war and kept South London together from Lewisham to Lambeth and formed an invisible link with the East End. Not as good as a mature democracy, not well adapted to deal with race-killers, but better than the available alternatives. And useful in a crisis, as Churchill discovered when he expected us all to panic in the Blitz.

At the Corinthians glass shelves rattled and glinted with the best of everything, with Bayley's Irish Cream and Extra Fino ports, old cognacs, Gaelic malts, reinforced wines, posh bubbly, fashionable vodkas, exotic gins, rums, richly coloured aperitifs and digestifs, her smoke wreathing leather rooms decorated with sporting prints and signed caricatures of forgotten personalities.

Since the 1800s, when the old medieval building had been torn down, her Gothic-Greek exterior had welcomed the London mob. It had made her its own. She embraced it, warmed it, comforted it. Marie Lloyd's favourite South London hall.

What had been an open courtyard big enough to take a dozen coaches at a time was now covered by an ornamental cast-iron skeleton holding a glass roof made by the same firm who did the Crystal Palace. You could easily imagine stepping through its huge double doors into the great covered yard, now an amphitheatre with bench seats stretching to the eaves, and seeing the coloured gaslight playing on the saucy features of Our Marie as she asked the audience if they thought her dress was a little bit – just a little bit – and winked in that way she had while the orchestra rattled and thumped and brayed and banished all memory. Harry Champion, Hetty King, Vesta Victoria . . .

He says you can't sleep there,
I says Oh?

He says I'm Rothschild, sonny,
I say that's damned funny,
I'm Burlington Bertie, from Bow . . .
I just 'ad a banana, with Lady Di-ana,
I'm Burlington Bertie, from Bow . . .

Lupino Lane, Jessie Matthews, Max Miller, Nellie Taylor, Tommy Trinder, Arthur English, Max Wall, Max Bygraves, Alma Cogan, Dennis Lotis, Lonnie Donegan, Ruby Murray, Freddie Starr, Diana Dors, Joe Brown, Roy Hudd, Barbara Windsor, Mike Reid, Ian Dury, Jack Dee, Eddie Izzard and Lemmy James all played the Corinthians and half the great London songs were first sung on her stage. The *Lambeth Walk* started there, though the Locarno, Streatham commercialized it. In her heyday she and the Canterbury had been out and out rivals, each proprietor suspected of arson more than once, the greatest and bawdiest of the notorious South London palaces.

Her polyglot audiences were volatile, rowdy, her comedians shocking, her chanteuses lewd. The police made raids and the great and the good were discovered amongst the trawl. So the police rarely raided the South London halls that became a great voice of popular sentiment strong enough to topple kings. But tonight the Corinthians was offering a scene straight from her earliest days, when the Prince Regent and Beau Brummell and all the bloods of the Hell-fire Club came to display their own protégés and lay the price of a labourer's life on the turn of a card or the outcome of a fight that in Brookgate we still called a knuckler. Originally, there was no time limit. Now the fights go to thirty rounds. Usually there are a variety of warm-ups to the main event – wrestling matches, women's fights, football tricks, up-and-comers, even variety acts. But all this is a preliminary to the big fight. A Sensational Display, as the Masters of Ceremonies used to shout, of the Noble Art. Bare knuckles, toe to toe, five-minute rounds, Prince Regent's Rules. It was like watching a ballet, when two good, evenly matched boxers went at it. It's more like fencing than modern boxing and nothing at all to do with those brute smash-and-maul all-ins you get in Poplar and Canning Town.

Rosie loved the Ring. If she was hooked on anything it was the manly art. We had come since we were kids, because her uncle worked here. In those days they were running a film club, to get round the GLC regulations, showing offbeat movies with sexy overtones and he was the projectionist as well as the best referee in the business. That's how we got to see Stoker's great matches and all that *nouvelle vague* stuff during our existentialist period. The punters thought they'd be throbbing to a flash of French titty in the heat of Latin throes, not trying to work out what the fuck was what in *Huis Clos*. They were sexy to us, of course, but in a rather abstract way.

Posh movies aside, the Corinthians was never one of your middle-class enclaves, like the Roxy Cinema in Brixton, where eager liberals went to slum. I did the photos at Angela Carter's memorial service there. It never got taken over, like The Cricketers' Arms in Mitcham, the one by the pond, that used to be the last authentic bit of suburban London before it turned into Surrey green belt. The old tram terminus. Now it's called Bats, looks like an upmarket toilet inside and is owned by Virgin Entertainment. Cricket was Mitcham's traditional sport but, because so many gypsies had settled there, it was rivalled by less public pug shows: all-in knackering, no-holds-barred, teeth-and-testicles contests, usually on a patch of bare ground in a ring formed by the punters, that could leave one fighter crippled for life and the other earning three hundred coins. They depended entirely on word-of-mouth arrangements.

Jimmy Lakefort and V.S. Mehta, the Boys, well-known Brookgate partners and the most famous of our high mobsmen, had long since stopped promoting illegal fights. Now the Corinthians was totally kosher, a private sporting club giving displays of Prince Regent's Rules pugilism and other revived athletic competitions. The Boys drew the line at modern aberrations, like those messy bird fights that got so popular around Edinburgh for a while or the spiky-monkey fights they're still putting on in Willesden. But most contests that got blood over everyone in the first ten rows had taken place there, either by advertisement or private word, though they couldn't any longer get the boars, the bulls or the bears for the really traditional bouts. Only the cocks. I'm not sure that either of the Boys liked to-the-death violence. But they still had that queenly taste for rough and tumble that brought in the black-leather crowd on Wednesday evenings, attracted to the faint smell of bloody Saturday-night sawdust hidden under the stink of booze, fags and cheap meat. On those two-pint shants and straight glasses brimming with good old English ale, there was a lingering taste of broken bones and pulpy flesh, of blood and phlegm and the pain of centuries.

In minutes we'd reached the Corinthians' vivid red brick and glinting stone. Towers, battlements, columns, gargoyles, caryatids and fabulous beasts were spotlighted, festooned, illuminated, murmuring and winking with crystalline electrics that made deep shadows of the surrounding railway and motorway arches, challenging the outer darkness, the silhouetted towers. And she really was our citadel. She always had been. Once she'd been owned by the Cornells, but they'd lost her to Mehta and Lakefort. Our Boys had always wanted control of the Corinthians and immediately made it their HQ. The Cornells hadn't minded much. They had given up South London and were moving into Notting Dale property development.

Believe me, pards, I see no virtue in villainy or any particular merit in working-class customs. Most of the guys I know who talk biggest about looking after your mates and never grassing on a pal and rather cutting off their cock than hurt a woman turn out to be the worst bullshitters in the end. Ask anyone who's been inside.

The code of the East End (or the North or the South) didn't do any better than the code of the West against Barbican's sustained attack on our last strongholds. In a lot of ways that code's a fantasy, like organized religion, which tends to let you down when reality rolls over you. The rhetoric and bullshit is one thing; the actions are another. For me, going down to the Corinthians was a bit like a fast-track health farm, the best kind of holiday. Because I knew the body language as well as the idiom. I knew how to get and to give a big welcome. I knew how to behave. And don't think me cynical. By and large that community knew a lot more about equity and common justice than Toney Blurr and his Sultans of Spin. Mostly, though, it was the sense of unconditional acceptance that you went for. Just like being on stage at your own gig.

This of course was BC (Before Canonization) rather than AD (Après Di). When the Boys didn't approve of you, that was always another matter. And that's why I drew the line at joining the whole dodgy tradition. I know the value of my culture and experience. It doesn't have a lot to do with the Krays or the Boys or the Cornells. It does have a lot to do with tradition and endurance, self-protection. We celebrate our own robber barons, our own heroes, but their legends aren't always authentic. They don't have to be. Our heroes aren't always very heroic either.

The Cornells at least admit they owe their power to the old Irish families of Notting Dale. They know they'd be nothing without the culture. Half of them are my good friends and relatives, but they're still robbers. And they're not pacifists, either. But I'm not like them. Our family never was and we were respected for it. I don't respect them for what they do, only for who they are. Bent or straight, I'm still a Brookie, still sustained by what's left of that eternal tribe. They call it anarchy, these days, that kind of strict local law. They don't know how many rules there are. You could be in the army. And that's the big attraction for those of us who were brought up by it. We can forget the complex world outside and pretend everyone's as good as their word and every virtue we claim for ourselves is real. Doing the Lambeth Walk. Nothing like a cockney knees-up. Or a Baptist prayer meeting. Or a formal fist fight. Oi!

When the pair of us waltzed into the long bar, most people were already heading for their seats. The warm-up stuff was over and the mob was getting focused on the Ring. I saw Jimmy Lakefort up under the Dandy Bob figurehead he'd bought at an old fairground auction. He and Dandy Bob were beaming distantly down on the little clique we called the flea circus, that bunch of short macho novelists who'd cultivated the place in recent years. Jimmy was the only one who seemed relaxed. You had the feeling they would rather have watched this on telly and then pretended they were there. You could tell the fleas by their self-conscious swaggers. They all looked like well-dressed extras out of *Me And My Girl*, leaning on the bars, their peripheral vision flickering like the clappers, their lips approaching their lifted pots as if they were flutes. All they needed was string round their trousers, Equity cards in their back pockets. But the Boys were flattered by the pieces the fleas wrote in the Sunday heavies, so everyone got some fantasy catered to. Except, of course, the culture. Ask any boon.

Felix Martin, himself a tiny goozer, was there in body if not spirit. But he always looked as if he'd rather be somewhere else. Felix's grumpy dad, Rex, was alive in those days and had rolled his bloated old body down for a reluctant change of booze and a fuzzy taste of the real life he'd never known. Farting didn't go down too well with the Corinthians' regulars, and Felix had so far diverted his snarling sire from his familiar performance, but Jimmy and his friends found his opinions agreeable as long as he stayed off the subjects of poofters, dagoes, Philip Larkin, little girls and underpants. They'd given him a big pewter shant pot full of gin and water and, grumbling, he'd settled on a bar stool like a messy mashed-potato sculpture and seemed to be developing a crust. The Corinthians was about the only place you could still get those quart shants that used to be all over London. Jimmy insisted on his guests having them.

Felix's pot was as big as his head and he was embarrassed by it. It almost took him two hands to lift. His petulant eyes shifted awkwardly, unsure of any of his relationships, or even his own tenuous identity. He shared a place at the bar with ice-cream-suited J.G. Ballard, whom I hadn't seen since my *New Worlds* days. He rarely left his house for anything but the Ideal Home Exhibition. The only original talent in the lot. Looking like someone had dragged Lord Jim home to face his fans. Every so often his face would split into a huge, terrified grin. In fact none of the litry boys seemed very relaxed. I reminded Ballard of the last time we'd met, the confusion, the fun of it. 'Great days,' he said. 'Great days.' I waved to Jimmy Lakeforth and we passed on. Rosie didn't know them at all and it seemed a waste of her time to introduce them. She was busy mouthing hello to old acquaintances.

There were so many people crowding around Stoker's dressing room that we went over to Sonny's instead. He was sitting there, puffing on his panatella, grinning like a locker. He was surrounded by minders and tarts. He thought we'd come to support him and we didn't tell him any different. He let us know our money was safe. All that black bastard would remember was stepping into the ring. By morning he'd be scrap. They psych themselves up like that, the new breed.

I guessed Stoker was at his stretcher as usual. He wasn't the only knuckle boxer or ex-sailor to enjoy embroidery. The chances were he wouldn't be able to make a stitch for weeks afterwards, win or lose. He never made anything more elaborate than a nice William Morris bookmark or the occasional antimacassar. That's how much time he usually had between healing up and getting his next fight. Well-wishers had brought him dozens of bigger designs from Needlewoman, but he was keeping them for when he retired. He'd promised his wife new cushion covers and a bedspread.

The noise drops a bit once we're in Sonny's dressing room.

I told you I'd be famous one day, says Sonny, making a halo of smoke around his face.

But not this famous, I thought. First he'd failed to be Conan, then Conan's stand-in, then Conan's stuntman, then the stuntman's standby, but maybe would have muscled his way to stardom if he'd had a better temper. That temper was rarely turned on us when he roaded for us, but it was a fearsome and chilling thing when mustered against someone giving us grief. It had got him kicked out of *Gladiators*. I felt my money, on Stoker, was safe.

Sonny seems to think I'm eating crow. He's as flashy as ever, black hair, white skin, pale green eyes. A pointed chin and the ultimate in acne screamed roids as plain as if he'd just had an Olympic blood test. Roids had always been his weakness. And they wrecked his judgement.

As we left Sonny punched the air with a fist like a folded bacon flitch. 'If you see Stoker – tell him tonight's the night we sink the *Titanic*!'

Nick Shakespeare, just back from Peru and bound for Morocco, was about the only healthy face in the place. He stopped me outside. He was bigger than Sonny, but with better taste. His huge, sweet heartstopper's face, under his mop of silvery hair, was genial. His effect on strong women was famous. Rosie's body language changed. Her smile improved. She ran to hug him. He greeted us equally enthusiastically. We'd worked together on a couple of jobs for the *Telegraph* before he'd become the literary editor, got sick of that and went freelance again. He'd done some novels, too. Got a fund going for crippled kids in Peru. Couldn't help himself. He was one of the best writers on London. His mother had been a famous Mais sister, one of the two most beautiful women in Oxford. He was doing a series on underground sports for the new *Chronicle*. He'd interviewed Stoker and was going to Sonny's dressing room now. Was I here for a paper? The tannoy started playing Sam Cooke. The house lights dimmed. There wasn't much time. He gave me his card. I said I'd bell him.

The big klaxon cried and the display systems started flashing down the minutes. The distorted soul music and the crowd's voices ebbing and flowing blended into a rhythmic roar.

Felix and the circus were heading slowly towards Stoker's dressing room, supporting the snorting Rex on their tiny arms, so we went the other way, slipping up the narrow concrete stairs to the office where V.S. Mehta and some of his Hong Kong suits stood about, watching an electronic board and talking money. But it was stock-exchange stuff, not sport. The office was like the observation deck of a liner. You could look into the arena in every direction. You didn't need a CCTV up here. V.S. was pleased to see us, especially Rosie, and switched off immediately, asking his associates to excuse him while he hugged and kissed us and offered us his world. Once the suits had gone he was an excited, delighted flouncer. You saw his shirt turn pink before your eyes. He trusted us. He also felt he owed me something. It probably had to do with the Union Jack murder. The favour I did him was a mystery to me, but not one that kept me awake. Somehow, we'd put ourselves in double-well with Brookgate's most admired mobsmen. And what was even better, they were the only villains to operate Michelin-rated restaurants on both sides of the river. While they and the Met had an arrangement, we'd never be short of a gourmet brunch.

The businesses were pretty straight. The methods of running them were traditional. Their managers were loyal to the death. As well as the Corinthians, V.S. and Jimmy Lakefort owned The Friends of Mrs King, in Hampstead, The Two Queens, in Brookgate, The Knave of Hearts, on Tufnell Hill, The Three Tars, in Brompton Road, and The Pair of Jacks, at the top of Portobello Road. They also ran their own lottery, a kind of goodwill/protection tax, that drew in millions and that they distributed to handicapped children, homeless people and the arts.

Jimmy was always adamant that he was foremost a creative artist, a comedian, and was always flattered to be recognized as Lemmy James. Jimmy dealt with the charity and arts side mostly, with V.S.'s approval, because V.S.'s real passion was for soldiers and old cars. He collected classic cars. He restored them. He had Duesenbergs and Lamborghinis, but he'd work on your kid's pedal-sportster if there was nothing else to get under and test. The problem was, he was a superb mechanic but the world's worst driver and whenever he'd got one of these massive expensive motors fixed up he'd drive it up Clerkenwell Road and have an accident. He was thinking about too many parts working at the same time. He spent more money squaring the jollies than he did on the cars themselves. Holborn nick depended on his contributions for their annual skiing holidays. He'd never passed a test. He could't get insured.

'My boy,' says V.S., putting a chubby brown hand on my shoulder. 'I knew you were coming and it's lovely to see you. Believe me, you picked an ace night. You know Stoker. Portillo's a good match.'

'Think he'll win?'

Suddenly he looked like one of those happy Hindu gods. He rolled his eyes. He gave a little swagger. 'Come, come, Denny. Nobody wants that.'

'Except Sonny.'

'Sonny'll get points out of this and Stoker'll go home unbeaten. Don't worry.'

The noise of chanting was pushing up through the floorboards, coming through the walls and windows like a persistent storm. It would be another fifteen minutes yet before the Champion of Britain and his adversary showed themselves.

I couldn't believe V.S.'d fix this fight, even for Stoker. He reassured me.

'You think we'd pick someone who could beat him? But it's still going to be tight. Still hard to judge. And it all depends on Stoker's will. So it's an open book, really.'

A large tinted window in his office looked down on the ring. The crowd was settling in, getting ready for the business. The roar was steady. V.S. poured us drinks and asked what we thought of the new benches he'd installed down there. They were padded, he said. 'Luxury class.' He handed us our rattling Waterford tumblers. 'We had to put the prices up last year.'

Rosie stared down through the smoky glass. 'So how come the poor's luxuries get dearer and the rich's get cheaper?'

V.S. winked at her. 'It's the politics of consensus, beauty. Everything meets in the middle.'

'Well,' she said, 'it certainly populates the margins.' She had moved to the illuminated glass cabinet behind his desk. It was full of old toy soldiers. 'Spanking smart,' he used to say. He'd built up the collection himself. It was his other passion. He pretended sexual ambiguity but it was a boyhood hobby. He'd never knowingly fucked a soldier in his life.

He knew all about these, though. The special makers. Even the people who did the modelling and painting. They were troops of the old British Empire. 'Because they have the best uniforms.' Miniature Gurkhas marched beside the Black Watch; Zulu impis shared space with running Zouaves. Lancers charged. Hussars reared. Royal Sussex and Royal Gloucesters aimed at invisible enemies. Guards marched in step with Ugandan infantry and behind them came Egyptian camel squadrons, Indian cavalry, Australian rangers. The colours were glorious. The flashy legacy of imperialism. In miniature. With added brightness and none of the brutal reality of their function. In the middle, he even had old Queen Bessie taking the salute for the trooping of the colour. Even down to that strained expression she wore that gave you the impression she had a drumstick up her bottom. Not that I said anything so blasphemous to V.S. He loved the royal family. He avoided all current debate. He revered them as icons of decency and nobility. He refused to hear stories of family squabbles. As far as he was concerned Prince Bigears was the soul of England and Princess Bigeyes was his saintly sidekick. He stood beside Rosie, staring at his armies. It seemed strange that a man so powerful in the real world should get pleasure from commanding tiny toys. 'It's relaxing,' he told Rosie, opening a door and taking out an elephant, complete with mahout and all the elaborate furniture of a state occasion. 'Blimey,' she said. 'It's heavy.'

'As lead.' Carefully, he took it back. 'I've only recently got into elephants. My camel collection's probably the best in private hands. Lauren Bacall's my only real rival. We do swaps whenever she comes over.' His tiny brown fingers again browsed amongst the lead figures and lit on a prize. 'Look at this—' a Gatling mounted on a Bactrian. 'Deaf camel, eh?' He pointed out the detail on one identical guardsman compared to another. Triumphs of the hollow-caster's art, he said. The benchmark for all other soldiers. Scarlet and gold. Royal blue and imperial crimson. Silver bayonets and buckles. Flags. Flags. Flags.

'Those were the days.' V.S. replaced the camel, a chink of metal, and closed the door.

'For some of us, anyway.' Firmly Rosie shook her head as she sipped her drink. I think she found V.S.'s admiration inappropriate. But he had been raised in a different world. 'I never accepted the Kipling crap. All the mysticism, the obfuscations and hypocrisies. The gaudy nonsense that was so naturally Hollywood. But I respect those poor old devils of the Indian Civil Service, those Indian Army imperial patriarchs who really thought they were helping. They believed it to their souls and died believing it. It sounds great. It idealized and ennobled what was cruel and unjust in our national character, but in the end the idealism outlasts the injustice. As does the glamour.' He spoke in those soft, juicy tones, full of mockery and guarded intelligence. Apart from us, his hidden paramour, Blakey, was the only other person he shared such confidences with.

His plump delicate hand indicated his soldiers, his crowds, his operation, the punters, the people. 'At its worst it's an acceptable sentimentality. Harmless nostalgia keeps the community coherent and strong. The actuality now is meaningless. Why should they care about it? What they're enjoying are those mysterious suits of armour left behind by feudal lords. Now they're romantic absurdities. Stock comedy props. Yet, when it was functional, sight of that steel would make ordinary people shit with fear. We have a habit of reducing the symbols of forgotten power to fairy stories.' V.S. was interested in power. He had as much of it as suited his fundamentally solitary nature. Nothing that was too much of a burden. Saturday night was his social night. He knew the importance of keeping his feet on the ground.

He made an even more expansive gesture. 'The fruits of empire are now back in the mulch, Rose. The price of empire is almost paid. It's made everyone so much more relaxed!'

She kept her mouth shut. V.S. had never known Rosie's options and therefore never sensed her frustrations. She had none of his respect for inherited authority. In some ways he was more of a true Brookgater than people like us, who questioned too much and tended to make an atmosphere edgy. V.S. was a natural mobsman – conservative, respectful of authority, moralistic, cautious, arrogant, formal and generous to his own, and he'd never had trouble being brown in Brookgate, especially with his father's reputation. They used to call him the Prince. And everyone liked him at school. He went to St Alban's, too, and then on to Oxford, I think.

In England, it's the people with options who have the trouble. It's the white upper classes who don't have any black relatives. And it's those temporal drop-outs still living where most other people don't want to live. Like Skerring-on-Sea. That's the 'nationalist' vote. Those are the fortresses of our heritage. Thatch and cobbles. Cobbles and thatch. Those poor bastards feel threatened by everyone. And, like paranoid Arabs and Midwesterners, suspicious of predatory raids on all they hold dear, nobody even knows they're there. In pockets of wolds and fells where *All Creatures Great And Small* is on perpetual re-run, British towns and villages still live in what to most Londoners is the remote past. Periodically they get alarmed about mobs. They've only just stopped worrying about Old Boney coming. They're still not too sure about the Tunnel. They avoid large cities. They refuse to use motorways. They think *Lord of the Rings* is literature. They're still wondering how to stop it all before it goes too far. Those who aren't still pretending we don't exist. Well, live and let live. They'll be back to spinning by hand without us. Maybe that's what they want? Their past restored. An eighteen-hour minimum working day.

CHAPTER ELEVEN
The Lick

'You'd better get in there.' V.S. looked at the big brass clock. 'Give me five minutes and I'll join you.'

He stepped to the side door and unlocked it for us. We went two floors down the wrought-iron Victorian spiral steps leading straight to the coolness of the tunnel and from there to our ringside box. The seats were deep, blue plush. There was a discreet minibar. Solid brass fixtures. An extraordinary view. A little world of its own opening directly out over the crowd, almost on a level with the ring. You could see every crack in the canvas, every twist of the ropes, every stain. You could smell the rubbing alcohol, the warm soapy water, the hemp and rags, the disinfectant. And you could smell human bodies. The stink hung in the air like ectoplasm. You could almost see it, almost reach out and tear a piece off. A quintessence strong enough to travel between the stars, a gaseous DNA. Our tribal immortality. Our blood.

Before we knew it, we were absorbed. Wherever the crowd's attention went ours went. The noise became a constant musical note. We were suddenly standing: from the far tunnel Sonny's seconds ran, blaring music, megaphone aggression, banners, slogans, chants. Glaring spots all over the place. Strobes. His fans were going berserk. There were a lot of them, especially the women, who thought Sonny could wipe out the oldster.

'Su-nee! Su-nee! Su-nee!'

He was lighter, harder, faster and, above all, younger. Now the spotlight found him and it seemed he was drawn upwards by the noisy will of the crowd, drawn from the darkness into the light, a copper demigod with blazing muscles and strong, white teeth, his Union Jack trunks bulging with unopposable manhood. Oh, those yearning cheers, that manly crowing – 'That cock is mine and I am that cock.' That vast shout became an all-drowning white noise that reduced every human anxiety to the veracities of the ring, voicing ecstasy without conscience, lifelessness without death, Fuck Oblivion. With a Kingfisher beer and a vindaloo to look forward to when it was over.

Better than soccer. Authenticity. The business. Nobody faked injuries in the Ring.

'Saaaaaaaaaaaaaa-neeeeeeeeeeeee!'

Sonny was supported all the way to his corner, punching and waving and grinning and happier than he'd ever been. His glinting sinews were crimson runes raised in his flexing flesh. He was the lads' boy, their face, their muscle, their challenge to the old order. He stood there and bounced on the ropes, shadow-boxed, roared and bared his teeth and got the crowd on its feet again. Then it was just his dedicated supporters shouting. Heads were already turning.

The Stoker had appeared without fanfare, walking almost unnoticed to the ringside and swinging himself in. He wore a white bathrobe, white shorts, white boots. The spot found him as he sat down in his corner, handed his embroidery bag to George Melt, his old trainer, and flexed his heavy hands on the ropes as his robe was drawn away. Stoker was monumental. He was King Kong. He had a chest you could land a 747 on. It looked as if Henry Moore had carved him out of a block of obsidian and then got Zeus round for a home visit to breathe in some life. His tight grey curls and grey stubble broadcast his years, but his face was ageless, immobile, almost insentient. He was what they had tried to make on Easter Island. The hooded eyes gave Sonny the once-over. The stakes were high. They were fighting for more than the ten grand prize money. They were fighting for the Prince Regent's Sword and the Meadley Cup. Both of which Stoker had kept for fifteen years' steady knuckling. If he won this fight, he kept them for ever.

Without apparent emotion, Stoker went through the warm-up rituals while Sonny screamed and insulted and strutted and challenged and addressed the crowd. Most of us were yelling for the fight to start. There was that acrid smell now that came with the promise of a climax.

Rosie's Uncle Alf was down there in the crowd, but it was a younger relative, Benny Patel, who was doing the honours tonight. He was popular and had the best eye in the business. He got a big cheer after Lemmy James, told a couple of old jokes and introduced him. Lemmy always made it clear that the ref was under his wing. It saved trouble later. Benny was true blue, but there were always loonies who felt cheated when a referee stopped a fight – usually because of badly broken bones, internal injuries or damaged hands.

The Prince Regent's Rules were called. There was to be no kicking, gouging or blows to the groin; no biting, holding or excessive elbowing and each contestant would comport himself in a gentlemanly and sporting manner. Light shoes to be worn at all times. Any blow struck after the end bell would automatically be scored in the recipient's favour.

I caught an unexpected glimpse of Tubby Ollis in the front row to my right. He was beaming like a Buddha. He seemed to have six or seven ladies with him. People must think him a successful pimp. He glanced up and saw me. He waved a fat hand. He had all his old rings on. Was that Barbican beside him?

Ding-dong. The first round.

The pair are in the ring now. Stoker lets Sonny do all the work, taking his measure, each of his slow-feinting hands as large as my head. Stoker wastes no energy, but his eyes are hard, concentrated. Sonny frowns, grimaces, snorts, tries a cut to the face. Then another. His balled fists are literally pickled. No standard glove would fit them. The punches don't land. Stoker's left comes up and blocks both of them and we hear his right's knuckles swiftly snap something.

Sonny backs away, panting. No blood drawn.

I can hear Tubby yelling over the crowd. His voice is like a drum, thudding into the air. '*Kill him, Stoker!*'

Sonny comes in again, fast, and dibs two futile blows in to the Stoker's stomach. As he positions his third punch, Stoker takes him on the heart and then in the kidneys. Stoker's extraordinary body moves slowly, almost gently. He wears an expression of amiable concern. It reminds me of Ali handling Cooper. Almost slo-mo, almost gentle. The bell goes and they step to their corners. Sonny's green, but he hasn't got his second wind yet. One good foul could finish him. But – and this is what helps make it sweet – Stoker isn't going to use a foul. He never has. We'll have to wait and see what Sonny's position on that is.

Sonny's still full of piss and fizz, shouting back to the audience, laughing at his opponent whom he keeps constantly in the corner of his eye, as if he thinks Stoker will attack him before the start bell.

Bong! Bing! Bong! And Sonny's dancing around like a mad gazelle. A tidy round, each man taking time to feel the other out. A few light punches exchanged. The crowd's screaming for blood. Back to the corners.

At the third round, V.S. joins us, just as the seconds duck out. He doesn't say anything. His whole attention is on the fight. He's chewing something. Another good one, but nothing dramatic. We all appreciate the finesse. A fourth and we're beginning to want to see a little more action. We don't get it until the sixth, after Sonny's seconds have said something urgent to him.

As soon as the bell rings Sonny comes in low, ducking down and trying some fast jabs to the Stoker's navel. Stoker blocks them all. Then he skips backward, light as a lurcher, and brings Sonny in after him until they're dead centre under the spots. It's as if Stoker's set up the shot. His left elbow smacks in hard on Sonny's ribs, while the right fist grinds through his guard to the heart and winds him. A quick chop upwards to the jaw and Sonny's doing the backwards foxtrot towards his own corner. And sits down as if he thinks the bell's gone. Which it does. Just in time for him. He looks around and he's still smiling, still growling, still waving at the crowd, as if he hasn't started fighting yet. Their roar is incredible. One massive, terrifying, yelling primeval monster. And we're all part of it. We're the mob.

In my mild acid daze I let my ears form words out of the crowd's noisy surf.

WE *ARE* THE MOB.

WE *ARE* THE MOB.

The Stoker's tired. Next round's the seventh. He's sitting back on his ropes, letting George soothe him, getting the oil into those stiffening joints, situating the pads and towels, fanning, fanning. He touches a hand to his side. We notice dark patches on his chest and ribcage. He's bruised, but still looks invulnerable. Like blotchy flint.

V.S. chuckles and nudges. 'Hee, hee, hee,' he says.

Rosie's nose is twitching. She's a cat. A panther. 'You're smelling blood,' I say.

'This round,' she says. 'Or the next. He's running out of time.'

I don't really know what she means. Then I do.

Sonny dances in, confident of his kill.

Stoker stops and hesitates as if he's wondering if he turned off the gas before he left home, and Sonny's got two good ones in. This reminds Stoker of his business and almost absently he brings up his left and lands a strong lung punch. Sonny oofs. In comes the right. And Sonny oofs again. Stoker seems to be about to give him the elbow when Sonny uses his own weight to land a cracking right-hander to Stoker's ribs. Within seconds we see dark patches spreading under Stoker's skin, as if he's haemorrhaging . . .

'Su-nee!'

Ding-dong. The ref comes in for a quick word. Stoker reassures him. Benny warns him and then dodges off again. The crowd's all on Stoker. Is he really going to lose this one? Even Sonny's supporters don't seem to want that now.

The bell, and they're suddenly locked together. Stoker staggers back, vinegar fists, hard as oak, streaked with blood like sap, protecting his body, and Sonny grins as he puts two more into the face. Stoker's left eye splits. His lips split. His nose bleeds. Small crunches sound like breaking teeth. You can hear the bone smacking bone. Smacking bone. Smacking bone. There's no sound like it. Stoker's head rolls back. You'd think his neck was broken.

Someone's going to stop the fight. But nobody wants that. Stoker doesn't want it. Even as he returns to his corner and another anxious conference with the ref, he's saying he's OK. I can read his lips. It's strategy, mate, he's saying. His head looks as if something's been gnawing on it all day. Honest, it's strategy.

So the bell goes for the ninth.

And Sonny's rushing in low one minute, staggering back with his face bleeding the next. Stoker stands there with a little smile on his face, his fists bloody bones at the end of his pulsing arms.

Sonny does something uncertain. Stoker slices up fast, his knuckles like razors, and knocks Portillo's face the other way. Sonny loses it at last. He screams. He starts swinging at Stoker who leads him around, tiring him like a bull, his jabs sudden and daring, like Errol Flynn in a sword fight.

Then Stoker pauses again. He takes his own time. Sonny's trying to recover himself but it's far too late. Now it's all style. Like Ali and Cooper. It seems minutes as, blow by elegant blow, Stoker brings Portillo down exactly where he wants him. Blood's pumping from both men, but Stoker's a machine and Sonny's fists are open hands now, just trying not to get hurt, and then he drops to his knees at Stoker's feet, his broken teeth still grinning through his ruined lips, his pulpy eyes disbelieving, wounded. Both heads are unrecognizable and the bodies are slippery with blood and phlegm. Blood gouts from ears and mouths, eyes and noses like gargoyle fountains. Even as Sonny falls forward and sprawls on Stoker's untriumphant boot the ref comes in with the count.

Stoker seems to smile as his arm's lifted for the victory. The crowd's approval is total. A thousand of London's best on their feet and cheering.

'STOKER!!!!'

And echoing and fruzzing over the sound of the crowd is Benny Patel's rounded pronouncement.

'The winner, nine rounds and a knockout, ladies and gentlemen I give you your friend and mine Mr Lloyd Stokes, undefeated Champion of Britain. He keeps the Cup. He holds the Sword!'

A perfect ending.

For a second Stoker lifts one dripping mess of pulped flesh and bloody bone into the air in an affectionate wave of acknowledgement, his modest thanks to those who worship him. Somehow, Sonny's vanished. Benny does the last honours and the crowd goes manic again. Yet even as they begin to converge on him, the Stoker slips out of the ring, picks up his embroidery and dressing gown from George Melt and retires into the tunnel as discreetly as he'd arrived. He'd come back later to show off his cup and sword to his supporters. They would have chanted themselves hoarse by then. Lloyd owned a bar in St Malo, his old home port, where he intended to display the trophies. *Le Coup de Grâce.* His wife, Yvonne, would do light meals.

We didn't follow him to his dressing room.

Rosie spotted Barbican as we moved towards the bar. I wanted to pretend I hadn't seen the bastard, but she was already dragging me through the crowd towards him. He wore his usual City duds, a slightly feminized version of the mobsmen's threads and probably from the same Jermyn Street tailor. Dark blue suitings, pink-striped shirtings, the universal S&S. Those guys always remind me of really nasty villains in WW2 movies. You keep expecting them to sprout horsewhips that they slap significantly into their palms, or smoke menacing cigarettes. Their dialogue isn't very different. They're always asking you to be reasonable. They always start smiling when you raise the subject of human misery or other consequences of their actions. They've heard that one before. Now they know where you're coming from. You'd better talk to our publicity department.

It didn't pay me to have that kind of lambeth with Barbican. I learned a bit more if he thought I was on his side. So we shook hands, the way friends do these days, and he took us over to a private table where a selection of drinks was waiting, minded by a creature twice the size of the defeated contender. As soon as we arrived King Kong went out to climb a tall building. His only job had been to make sure nobody spat in Barbican's beer. I picked up a glass of O'Dowd's. It looked a bit cloudy to me. But it tasted all right. Rosie was next to Barbican, showing him pictures of Africa. He seemed uncomfortable and kept saying 'Very nice, Rosie. Wonderful. Wonderful.' I asked after his umpteenth bride. 'Very well,' he said. 'Wonderful.' He didn't offer a name. (Jillian Burnes, three days and annulled). He had the air of an excited tourist, uncertain of his surroundings, but I suspect he was a bit uneasy in an environment he couldn't readily control. His strange, geeky, handsome, soft schoolboy face gave me a contradictory eye. Something warmed in that ice when he looked at either Rosie or me. He was trying for friendship. Or at least marriage. If his way of looking at Rosie was a little different, that only emphasized the quality I thought I detected – some peculiar sense of kinship with us that made him want to be of use to us, though always on his own terms, as when he had tried to manage the band.

'How's business, Johnny?' I asked him. We had settled on 'Johnny' since he'd dropped 'Jack' in favour of 'Barbican'. 'Do you own the world yet?'

He took this as a compliment and his responding grin was relieved, almost cheeky. 'Not quite,' he clipped.

He'd grown plump and sleek since I'd last seen him. His good looks were already fading, to be replaced by something far sexier, the gloss of wealth, the deep lines of power, crow's feet and self-indulgent belly that turned on even ardent radical feminists and sent them shaking to their support groups. Even I fancied him sometimes. Though I'd have charged him at least two million to fuck me.

As it was, of course, he fucked us all for free.

Tubby came out of the toilets and waved at me. He was dressed in a vast black velvet suit and his face was powdered clown-white. I thought he had a disease until, sitting down, he explained how he felt he looked far too robust for someone who had spent most of his later years in an easy chair being fellated by supermodels, so he felt he ought to look a little paler. His eyes had a glazed, rheumy look as they peered from his snowy skin. I asked if the fight had been worth whiting up for.

'Well worth,' he said. 'Oh, yes. End of an era, Denny, eh?'

He was right. But it wasn't the end of the Corinthian Boys. A few years later Johnny decided to buy it. But that's a different thread.

Johnny had arranged to see Tubby here. He had another business proposal. After a bit of chat we left them at the bar. Tubby was beginning to get that edgy stance he took when he didn't approve of what he was hearing. We went to have a drink in V.S.'s office with Stoker while he waited for his limo. In his silvery Savile Row double-breaster, Lloyd looked even more of a monument. He could have been the Invisible Man, so much of him was bandaged. When we asked about his injury, the blood under his skin, he said he had some bizarre auto-immune disease controlled by steroids, which he refused to take before a match. 'Come Monday, Den,' he assured me, 'I'll be back on the tablets. But it looks good, doesn't it? They always think they got me bleeding insides bleeding when that happens. Makes 'em relax just enough. Strategy, mate.' He opened his mouth and uttered the huge laugh that everyone now knows from his breakfast sports show on Sky. He couldn't stand it in retirement.

I told him I'd like a few pictures of him and his trophies sometime. He reached towards me. 'Number seventeen,' he said, 'don't let the graffiti put you off. I'm going in a week.' A heavily bandaged hand gave me his card. Aneurin Bevan House, Fulham.

It wasn't cool to take pictures at the Corinthians. But, of course, you could draw anything you liked, and that's why people never really believed the flea reports when they first came out. Who can't do a bad drawing? Or prove its provenance? It was the all-ins that got the real publicity, with those hidden cameras at Mitcham and on Wormwood Scrubs. And that was almost the end of everything. It wrecked proper knuckle fighting, too. There was a time that every family had its amateur boxer, ready to try his luck with or without the gloves. Now it's only football. And look what's happened to that. It's best to let them go on thinking that things you value don't exist. They really don't want the truth. They punish people who alarm them. So why have this impulse to force the whole story on them? Look at me now. Don't believe a word I say.

After the fight, Rosie and I went home to Fogg Yard. We didn't talk much about anything, but we were very close. We lay together, half-awake, all night, hardly speaking.

In the morning she came with me to the grave, directly behind the high wall at the end of the cobbled mews. In those days, before there were so many thieves, there was a little wicket gate that led into the churchyard. As well as being part of the Huguenot Leases, St Alban's had its famous Royal Grant that made it, among other things, one of the few London churches able to bury its own dead in its own soil. Dad had received some kind of dispensation from the prison to be here. It was almost next door. By then hardly anyone knew the old churchyard. Battered, badly patched Norman church, odd-looking tombs, gnarled yews and fragrant herbal hedges, rose briars everywhere, lush with endless life, it was all hidden behind sightless red-brick warehouses and decaying courts of flats. Everything was taller than St Alban's steeple.

To be buried here, you had to be born and bred in the parish. But you only got a limited plot. Our family grave was so crowded I had the impression of them forever shifting and fidgeting, trying to get settled, like a charabanc party. When I was a kid I thought I could hear them all grumbling ritualistically about their arrangements, the way they always had. My dad's stone was a nice piece of polished granite, very nineteen-fifties, set amongst our rose bushes, which family legend said were almost three hundred years old. The rosemary had grown heavy, the scent intoxicating, but the roses had mostly blown. Their browned sodden pink petals completely covered our grave. I hadn't known my dad, of course, and tended to feel resentment towards him more than anything, but it wasn't only him I was visiting. The patch was crowded with weathered limestone and granite, marking the remains of the wealthier Dovers and Beggs. Many of the poorer ones hadn't even made it here. They'd been quicklimed in one or other of London's many epidemic diseases. Or blitzed.

It was an uncertain morning, with the sun shivering in the sky and a light mist falling. I could hear the click of water on gleaming rhododendron leaves, the distant slushing of the Holborn and Clerkenwell traffic, rapid footsteps, the gargling Fleet somewhere underground to our east, the dull thumping from the Central Line, the buzz and swish of a solitary milk float: a symphony of discomfort. There was a damp, oily stink coming off Gray's Inn Road. Rosie shivered in her big navy coat. She glanced up at the stained walls, at the dirty nets flapping in the blank windows of abandoned flats and wondered if anyone was looking down on us. It wasn't likely at that time of the morning. She said she was beginning to yearn for the relentless African sun. It made a change from the relentless English rain. Then she held my hand.

We stood there crying, the way we always had, since we were kids. I'm not sure why.

Maybe we knew how lucky we were.

CHAPTER TWELVE
The Drift

Dorian Theakston had inherited Tufnell Mill from his uncle, Lord Garstang, the Quaker chocolatier. In the 1850s when it featured in a highwayman novel called *Old Highgate Heath* it was known as the Red Mill. A popular melodrama based on the book, *Hannah Cornwell; or, The Miller and his Men*, was still running in the odd provincial rep when I was a kid. And, of course, most people know it from the stylized trademark on old tins of Pearson's sweets.

When the bakery-merger price wars of the 1860s threatened to sink him, John Tuftnole, a great-great-grandson of the original miller, began specializing in elaborate chocolates. Bon-bons were his natural trade. His 'London fancies' became famous. Londoners couldn't get through Christmas without a box of Red Mill.

With the arrival of public transport, the miller continued to coin it. Tuftnole's Tea Rooms were the East End's favourite Sunday-afternoon fun spot. Thanks to his political connections, Alderman Tuftnole shook hands with the transport company (which needed to cross his land) so Red Mill was where the horse-tram's round trip to Shadwell began and ended, a heavy haul for a double team, even on the freshly metalled road. With everyone gasping for a drink by the time they got to the top. John T. put in a fancy stone horse trough. He built modern stables. He added a large Tudor-style extension and gave it an upper gallery. Then a stage. An outside menagerie. A summer orchestra. Peacocks and fancy roosters all over the place. Shetland ponies. For a penny you could pass through a wicket gate into the bluebell wood. And, naturally, propose to your sweetheart. Half the mashers of Brookgate had received their answers in Lovers Lane.

By 1890 Tuftnole's was a household word, the size of a village, the Six Flags of its day, with a beer and cider licence. Then railways and motorbuses slowly took away the trade. It was too expensive to come up the hill. People went further afield. The tram company failed and sold its assets to Universal Transport, who only wanted the concession rights, not the line itself, and didn't think it economical to run electricity up the

hill. Tuftnole sold off everything but the bluebell spinney and the Mill.
In 1902 the A1 extension road cut through the southerly corner of the
old tea gardens and suddenly, between the Mill and what remained of
Tufnell Park, there was a busy chasm, full of rattling scarlet and sparking
brass. Plans were blagged to pull the whole place down and put up some
kind of crystal fantasy, to bring people back, but it was a bad time to find
dosh. Tufnell Hill became steadily more isolated. John Tuftnole was
elected Liberal MP for Holborn North, moved to Lincoln's Inn and died,
on the steps of the Reform Club, after dining with G.K. Chesterton the
day before his maiden speech. A by-election got us Montague 'Monty'
Collins, one of the first Labour MPs to be elected from inner London.
Brookgate put him there. The Mill's abandoned tearooms and limping
sweet trade remained a Tuftnole family company until Pearson's took it
over in 1912, first for offices, then for storage. It was thought dangerous
to use the upper floors. Pearson's was gobbled by the Callard and
Bowser confectionery empire, but the Mill remained Lord Garstang's. It
was a rat-ridden wreck when Tubby came into it.

A chipper old goozer, straight as a die, all beaming pink health and
exploding white tufts, Arthur Pearson, Lord G. visited Tubby when we
were living in Notting Dale and invited him for tea at the Reform. He
said we could all come. We had the sense to avoid the general
embarrassment. We had no interest at all in the 'establishment' – only
middle-class kids knew all about that. We didn't want to break down
that kind of barrier. It would be like startling a lot of institutionalized
old lions and telling them they were free to return to the jungle. They
know their place, those old buffers. Eventually they'll extinct themselves.

Lord G. turned up at a couple of festivals where High Tide was
playing. He loved all the peace and love. He couldn't see the hippy
hucksters, the liggers, the rapists, the pervs and pushers and long-haired
free-loaders. He said the power of youth could set a golden example to
the world. High Tide was spreading the message of universal love.

Tubby told me Uncle Arf had arrived at this conclusion around the
same time he'd smoked his first reefer. Which cured his rheumatism and
helped him break the ice with a woman of his own age, Annie Rollup,
who became the last Lady Garstang and died of happiness within a year
of the wedding. Garstang in the Lords continued as an earnest advocate
for dope's medicinal use long before most of the Commons had any idea
what he was talking about. The weed hadn't stopped him being a devout
and high-minded Quaker, however, and this idealism remained invested
in Tubby. Good judgement. But that's the way it is with weed.
Encourages too much altruism. The antithesis of free-market capitalism.
The enemy of consumerism. You can grow it cheaply yourself. You can
see why they hate it.

Lord Garstang had willed most of his remaining estate to General

Graf von Baudissin's Institute for the Study of Peace in Paris. A conscientious objector himself, he'd lost all three sons in the Battle of Britain and his daughter had been killed when they hit the Mitcham margarine factory. His wife's house had received the only direct V2 hit on Hampstead Garden Suburb. I met him a couple of times but talked to him only once, backstage at the Roundhouse. 'We make the best of it,' he said. His lively old eyes reminded me of Harpo Marx. He was stoned out of his brain. He told me that Tubby was a cherub. I didn't laugh. I knew what he meant.

Arf Pearson's first wife's branch of the family had been Fortnums. Which was how I'd first met Flo Fortnum. She'd been fifteen. In an Oxfam shirt and denims two sizes too big. Accompanying her grandad to our gig. Her twin, Patience (Pinky), had refused to come with them at the last minute. More a compulsion than a habit, it turned out. I met Pinky later and we became instant friends. But beyond her own large apartments she was pathologically shy.

Flo, of course, was neither shy nor homeloving. It was as if her twin's energy was on loan to her, so that she had twice the vitality, aggression, will-power, determination, eloquence of any other human being on earth. I loved Flo. She irritated everyone. She was too much. But somehow I was always touched by her incompetent generosity. Flo could talk her own case to death, manipulate what was best left alone and produce firm resistance in people who had previously needed no persuasion. It was why she had failed so thoroughly as a charity lobbyist, a publicist and a wife, but she remained captain of her own ship. Or ships, I should say, since she periodically wrecked them, to swim, disbelieving, back to the shore, dry herself off, and start building another. People offered her jobs in order to get her contacts. They didn't know that Flo's connections avoided her like they would a Zippo on the *Hindenburg*. They didn't trust anything about her except her blood. She had a bottomless fortune, controlled by old Victor Fortnum's knowing will, and spent it on a dozen causes at a time – lost souls, underdogs, political prisoners, church restorations, foreign relief – into which she threw herself – or selves – with devastating commitment. Few were safe from her charity.

For a while I became one of her causes. It was like being cared for by a tornado.

When Lord G.'s dust settled in the Brompton Road family sarcophagus, he'd left Tubby the nearest home to heaven he had. Rising from gnarled North London shrubs and ancient evergreens, framed by cedars and poplars, still allowed her patch of bluebell oak wood, the Mill was agreed to be the highest building in London proper, after Peake's Point observatory, downriver. Her garden had gone to bramble sharper than razor wire. It would take a singing prince with a magic sword to get through it when Tubby locked his gate but the top floors had views everywhere. She'd remained a landmark, a courting spot. Although she still had the remains of her anchored vanes and a working shaft, she'd been disused for at least a century. The Mill had disappeared completely from public consciousness when the road and rail builders pushed out towards fresh markets and created that miserable ditch up from Kings Cross that contained all the putrid human detritus they'd discarded in their glorious enterprise.

Through most of the century Tufnell Hill was surrounded by a mephitic moat of collapsing tenements and gloomy grog-shops, full of the dispossessed and the never-owned, where few babies saw the light of day, let alone a month's life, in the uncertain hands of their child-mothers. No incendiary could scour it. For a hundred years, its dour, threatening air had challenged the casual visitor, until the modern gentrifiers moved in with a breath of fresh paint.

Neglected, the Red Mill and what was left of the nearby village had survived various modernizing crazes and remained pretty much the same as in those early photos of her heyday showing the thatched tearoom extension and jolly cockneys at long bench tables, playing ukeleles, changing hats, comically cross-dressing, sporting teacups and stone shants, taking their evening pleasure before getting the horse-tram home. In a quiet twilight, you could almost hear the strains of 'My old man, says foller the van . . .' disappearing into the Edwardian mist.

The Tudor extension had gone in the Blitz, of course. Blazing for two days and visible for miles. But the incendiary had only blackened and shaken the Mill's original brick. They'd put a great steel S-tie through the whole building and she'd been sturdy ever since. The bluebell lane was still miraculously there, though now it had a fenced public footpath, an avenue of planes, chestnuts and birches. The Mill wasn't nationally owned, but she was Grade I Listed and in those days still a bit of obscure old London, considered as inviolable as the Siege Perilous.

Tubby had accepted the bequest as a trust. He got daft about it. He felt, he said, as if he was defending the Grail Tower. A proper little Parsifal, I said, if a touch on the plump side for an ascetic knight. We'd gone through a Wagner craze together.

The band called her Rat Castle when we first moved in. Cockroach Hall. Creepy Grange. But with a little speed and some real dedication we had enough skills between us to do her up inside and enough money from the record company to get the roof fixed and the brick repointed. Which in those days, even including the cost of scaffolding, wasn't that much. Graham freaked, decided the Mill was haunted by evil presences and left for a while. He came back with the right mantra and got rid of the demons. And then we had this great pad. My room was the coldest, right at the top. I could get up in the morning and look out across the whole city.

Apart from his bit of clunky self-ennoblement, Tubby generally speaking had his feet on the ground. He agreed that changing his name by deed poll had been a momentary barminess, like deciding to pierce his privates. Nonetheless he was used to both by now and, on suitable occasions, enjoyed them with great pleasure. He had a thing about pseudonyms, he said. Disguises. Virtual worlds.

He still thought the name rang with a more dignified tone, in tune with his inherited responsibilities. I said he sounded like a second-rate rep actor or a Victorian brewing baron out of a Trollope lollop. Everybody said he was barmy to do it. Letters generally came to the mill as T.O. Peculier or O'Dowd Stout, from absent-minded friends. But by and large, if they weren't official, in buff oblongs, they were usually very private, in scented pastel squares, with cultivated handwriting, in posh coloured ink.

Tubby hardly ever opened the pastel envelopes and never in my presence, but he always studied official letters carefully. He took such things seriously and his books, apparently, were kept impeccably. They should have been. One of the richest financiers in the world had developed the system for him.

She was Trixie Fong from Toronto, who'd occasionally been privileged to stay more than twenty-four hours. I'd seen her address on the back of a lilac envelope. She always used the Mill as her base, until she went down into total ruin and degradation after running up against BBIC on ethical grounds once too often. Got the treatment Barbican reserved for a major irritant. These days it isn't enough to ruin someone financially, you have to degrade them sexually, too. Full trumped-up scandal coverage in the Moloch press. **Lesbian High-Flyer Stole My Wife, Says Actor.** Wiped out by a series of financial strategies designed to trap her.

They say Trixie killed herself. Tubby took it personally and concluded that Barbican was the Antichrist. High Captain of the Brute Dominion.

I couldn't argue with him. It was the rational thing to think by then. Tubby was already heavily into computers. He'd found the right weapon, he said, for this particular incarnation. A way of fighting back, he said.

Tubby wasn't scared of the evil he perceived, but battling it drained him sometimes. He'd fine-monitored two prime ministers and Rupert Moloch for years. He had a file on Rupie that, released to the rival tabloids, would result in his red-tops losing circulation so fast their shares couldn't be given away in supermarkets. He had unbelievable visuals. Quarts of what we in the trade used to call gravy. High-quality stock. The unforgiving goods. The long video testimony of Moloch's ex-wife, in which she gave details of his joyless tastes, with graphics, wasn't for the under-forties. Secretly recorded audios. Grunts and yelps. Tears and wails. Niffy. Minicam moments. Even a confessional! The stuff of modern political show business! Nothing I'd ever knowingly been close to. All thanks to the World Wide Web that, until he could control the sun *and* planets, Moloch would never own. And that Tubby could broadcast over any time he felt like it.

At other times, Tubby told me, he grew exhilarated when he was able to help change the world for the better. He was especially interested in getting generators to Third World villages and that's how he stayed so regularly in touch with Rosie who had begun to specialize and was working for Womankind Worldwide, installing light machinery in impoverished countries, training the women with the most self-interest in maintaining them, developing solar-powered portable computers and wind-up short-wave radios, simple, efficient water-purifiers. From his Lay-Z-Boy recliner, especially made for him in America, Tubby was a weaving spider, expertly operating his extraordinary cyber-station, a computer designed for him by Sizemore, the guy Bill Gates failed to buy.

'Nobody's much in control of much, really, Denny.' The world on his screens was a reflection of the general chaos. 'There are just a few badly dysfunctional shitbugs like Moloch who've gathered more shit in their corners and are greedily eyeing the other piles of shit in the other corners. And then there are the worthy politicians, pretending to steer the ship of state. Pompous Gilbert-and-Sullivan admirals, mostly. Professors of pop. Spin sisters. They keep coming up with new charts. Just a matter of getting the right grid on the terrain . . .'

Tubby thought most politicians started with good intentions but got addicted to the adrenalin. Then mistook this addiction for a vocation.

'The first thing you have to realize about any ship of state is that it's actually a raft going down a river fed by erratic rains. States are rafts of different sizes. Big ones have heavier momentum and appear to be more in control. Little ones often get smashed on the rocks. But, big or small, the people holding on to those crude tillers are not exactly steering forward. They're just hoping to control the rate of drift. The rest of us are clinging on to anything we can find and hoping to survive. Some devote their entire energies to dropping more anchors. Most of the time our rafts are rushing between rapids. In quiet water, they can pretend to steer a bit, but as soon as the river speeds up again, they're useless. I love to hear heads of state going on about leadership and decision-making. They're babbling crazy, most of them. The best politicians are like old Lyndon B.' (Tubby's hero). 'He understood about the raft and how to get what he wanted during those patches of calm water.'

One quiet afternoon I'd asked Tubby what he was doing on the net all day. Surely not just tracking iffy politicians and low-browed captains of industry. And I couldn't see him watching porn.

He was delighted to tell me, chuckling like a dirty-minded five-year-old.

'Assassinating Christians,' he said. 'Well, any nasty trouble-making bigot, actually. For instance, I have a file of seriously deranged anti-abortionists. The kind who publish lists of people who've had abortions and go around inciting their fellow loonies to murder doctors and bomb clinics?

'Anyway, in common with a few fellow souls I track their activities on my computer. Sometimes we'll also sue them. That worked well with the Southern Poverty Law Center against the Klan. Our physical base is in Brussels. Every so often the opportunity arises to take one of them out. It costs a bit. A suicide volunteer, a mob hitman, a moonlighter, whatever's most appropriate. But it's worth it. We call it post-foetal extinction. PFE. Euthanasia's an unpopular word these days.'

He spread his plump, sensitive hands. He smiled his wide, seraphic smile. 'I just adjust the balance. The only way to deal with people that crazy is to lock them away forever or kill them. The cheapest and most effective option, Denny, old mate, is the second. Yankee economics. Bang! And we all get a bit of peace and quiet.

'We have to shoot back. Only the declared followers of great prophets feel righteous about murdering everyone they disapprove of. Constantly baying for blood, that lot. Especially in America. That fish on the back of their cars ought to have a dorsal fin. These people are truly disturbed. Predatory Neanderthals. America has whole states full of them. They're the kind who decide to put square lines on land masses and insist that all city streets should be gridded and numbered. Poor bewildered buggers. They straighten out rivers where they can. Organize forests. They need help. Only the gibbering crazy invent rules like that for themselves. The rest of us rub along all right, following the lie of the land, the grain of the wood. And somehow in the process we discover a profound aesthetic. Not something you could say for the unrivalled magnificence that is Chicago. Wonderful folk art, but it's minimalist aestheticism, that. Borrowed motifs. Anyone with a bit of graph paper and a ruler can do it. The trick was never in the art but the engineering. It's aestheticism for people who don't trust their own taste.'

I wasn't sure killing homicidal anti-abortionists was the most effective method of improving the world, but later I discovered he didn't really kill them. He was having custard pies thrown in their faces. *Entartement*. That's why he had links with Belgium. Those guys had been doing it for years. Wherever they went, the pompous and the spectacularly greedy, the cruel and the careless, the uncaring powerful, never knew where the next pie might come from. Moloch himself had felt the kiss of the custard more than once. Sleeping, waking. In restaurants, in restrooms, at conferences and churches and their own living rooms, frequently on camera, occasionally on the job, they would be relentlessly pied, he said, not once, but until they drowned in their just desserts.

And that, by and large, was how Tubby waged war on barbarous bigotry, second-rate writers, monstrous criminals and bad politicians.

You've seen the footage. Raspberry tarts oozing down respectable noses. Rex Martin *à la crème*. Toney Blurr with chocolate icing. Janet Reno's *bombe surprise*. Trent Lott's *French Cherry*. Rex Reed's blackberry whip. Billy Graham's treacle tart. Ken Starr got a spotted dick.

Strawberry flans crumbled on to impeccable shoulders. Syrup puddings clung to skulls as tight as napalm. The occasional trifle crowned the dignity of some nation's mighty chief. It improved political rhetoric, if nothing else. Though their eyes shifted about more. Tubby's friends and their agents were everywhere. Tubby's ploys on Gingrich alone are legendary. But he said getting Gingrich was hardly sporting. It was Tubby set him up to write that embarrassing schoolboy book. And had his computers suggest most of his disastrous speeches and campaign strategies. Talk about leading with the balls. 'He believed anything,' Tubby said. 'Largely because he was no longer entirely sure what the truth was. But you had to admire that bloke. Show him the merest shadow of his foot and he'd shoot at it. Like any successful politician, he got lucky and thought he'd planned it.'

Pat Buchanan got the Klan Flan. Louis Farrakhan got the Rainbow Roulade. Anyone who described citizens in terms of stereotypes got a Mississippi mud-pie.

'Terror by Tarte Surprise,' says Tubby, smacking his lips. 'Vivent les sans-gâteaux! Allons, mes marshmallows! Take the syrup to the Savile Row. The toffee to the tweed. The nougat to the nylon. Saturate the silk with sugar, flour and milk. There's no greater power than the power to Pie! *Why kill or die when you can pa-pa-pa-pi-pi-pi-pi-pi pi-pi-pi-pi-pa-pa-pa-pie-pie-pa-pie-pie-pie, pa-pi-I-I-I-I-I* . . . in the words of the popular song.' It wasn't a popular song at all. We'd left it off our last album. The Pious Pie Song, we called it. But Tubby remained attached to it and resented our decision. Which is why he always brought it up. He never bore a grudge he didn't tell you about. Anyway, this was Tubby on a talking day, glowing and pink and jovial, tipsy with his own eloquence. Not your usual drummer. He allowed himself the luxury twice a week. By the time I'd known him five years or so he was ready to pass on to me his fundamental understanding of life. 'It can be offered in seven words.' He was only faintly sardonic. 'I wasn't. I am. I won't be.'

I liked the sound of it. I felt a pang of nostalgia. I could smell the Gitanes again.

'The rest's speculation. We do our best with the stories we have. But can your dreams ever come true, I wonder?'

He offered me a box of beautifully crafted reefers. As a child one of his lovers, now a rich society hostess, had rolled cigarettes for a living in Haiti.

'But by God, Denny, you might as well make the most of that middle bit – the *I am* bit – while you're here. And enjoy it. And, as you said, try to leave the planet as you'd wish to find it. What else but civilized courtesy do we have between us and the infinite void?

'This is the best I can do,' Tubby had indicated his screens. It had been state of the art then. Primitive hacker's gear by today's standards. But, like now, way ahead of its time.

Today it's open access, direct link, serverless, independent, D-tagged to infinity, organo-teknik, dark plush and brass, rich screens, green baize surrounds, elegant boards. Muted, complex Morris and Voysey. He relaxes in his chair's embrace. Programmed to love him and him alone, it cuddles around him as he leans back from his smiling machines. The chair doesn't really have to be programmed. Everything animate, organic or electronic, loves Tubby. Just being near him cheers it up. There's a merry energy to his screen savers. His keyboards are kittenish, his mice lively. And naturally each one of his cats has a distinct personality. It's like being in an original Disney movie and not an ersatz Disneyland version. *Fantasia* rather than *The Hunchback of Notre Dame*. At a certain age, one's an authentic experience, stretching the medium, the other's a familiar comfort, a dummy, a *pasatiempo*.

Tubby's big round living room was festooned with cats. They lounged on every surface, across consoles and keyboards. His electronics filled a quarter of it and he'd put cushions all over them. Everything accommodated his cats. The mask of Sekhmet glared from the central shaft, in permanent watch over her kind. At the same time his fabrics and pictures, his murmuring displays, had a textured, technicolor warmth. Once you got inside the Mill, all the contrast seemed up and the colours were richer, brighter. There was vibrant personality in the furniture, the wallpaper, the curtains. The metal glowed, the wood shone. Rugs glinted like the pelts of living creatures. It was a perfect acid trip. You started seeing colours and patterns you didn't know existed. Layers of order. God's enormous plan. Even when Tubby played records you'd listened to all your life, you'd hear things you hadn't heard there before. Whole melodies. It wasn't just the dope, but maybe the dope left its mark.

Maybe after a while so many intense fantasies can form some kind of reality. A triumph of the trip. On one hand Thatcher's Little England, Diana's Cuddly Charity. On the other, Tubby's Mill. Maybe those happy cats, those ecstatic free souls who came to visit him, had something to do with it. Maybe it was just Tubby. And the fewer of us there were left, the better it seemed to get, as if all our dead, happy, generous pals had left the best of themselves here before their dissipating spirits took Flight Zero Zero to Limbo International.

It wasn't. It is. It won't be. Yet I'm absorbing the stuff of the living and the dead with every breath I take in this city and the odds are you'll find a DNA match with mine any time you dig up a graveyard or a plague pit or a Roman mausoleum. For a moment or two, one of us scraps gets to be conscious, then it's over. We go back to being bits of drifting dust, shards of bone, an image or two in a rotting magazine. A couple of words. A message in a bottle. Sometimes, pards, I'll tell you, I really look forward to drifting away again.

Listening to classical music in Tubby's room was better than the best concert hall. That's where he first played me the Boulez version of Messiaen's *Turangalila*. One of the most sublime pieces of music in the world. Or we thought so. Julie, who tried to like it, found it mad. But then it wasn't us who were barmy to begin with.

Or so we said.

I mean, what was sane about my actions? Marrying poor, sweet Julie. Carrying her off to live at the Mill with a bunch of musical dead ends and dedicated horsemen, whose love for their needles communicated itself as a benign, seductive glow to all around them? To be fair, when it was over Julie was the only user Tubby would let through the door, and then under strict supervision. It's the one thing you learn in life – the one other thing, he said. I wasn't. I am. I won't be. And never trust a junkie.

And would she still be alive, if it wasn't for meeting me?

The answer's simple.

Probably.

In Staines or Sutton or Skerring or somewhere.

So who should we trust, I wonder?

Julie used to say that a year of life with me was worth ten anywhere else. Well, that's about what she got. Soon after we started living together Deep Fix took off with the other Flicknife bands. In those days we were the fastest speed-band anywhere and Flicknife was the coolest indie label to be on. It was run by Frenchy Glogauer and his formidable partner Queen Congoroo (formerly Marie Whitbread) whose first child was born with a black leather skin, blond dreadlocks and silver studs in its forehead. They had a loyal Angels following. The only problem with the Hell's Angels I ever found was that they're motoring bores, always going on about the best routes to wherever. The sort of nerd you'd tell to fuck off if he wasn't sporting a useful length of bike chain, had biceps the size of the Goodyear blimp and tattoos on his eyes. Instead you listened politely while he offered the various arguments for taking the B909 road from Tufnell Hill out to the Al and then going off at the Fairview Road roundabout just before the Blue House, which was now a Crook and Shepherd pub, 'though it used to be great when the old landlord ran it, but now leathers are banned, they'll find out what that means one day. I mean, do we ever look for trouble, Dennis?

'Well, you take that little turn-off that says Wycombe and the West (make bloody sure it ain't Middle Wycombe or Little Wycombe or you're in total trouble and will have to go all the way up to the Highbury Corner roundabout, but that's another story), do another right and a left down a couple of private roads, which brings you out at the park, right?

You follow the park until that road just funnels you back into the A1 and you've missed that bottleneck at Finchley West.'

Saving all of half a second. Life amongst the Angels. *Travelwatch* with Peter Fonda and Dennis Hopper. On the road with E.L. Wisty. Would you want an Angel for a father-in-law?

Which wasn't a problem I had with Julie. She hardly knew who her father was. She'd picked the fantasy that suited her best. Old, wise, decent Sir Hubert, she thought. All she ever wanted was a world she could love.

For a while Flicknife was a friendly rival to Stiff – getting what was left of the buzz after Stiff had started to lose it. Like all record companies, they had no judgement, just luck, and for some reason we seemed to fill the gap – so we got famous for a while, some of us.

Deep Fix only played the really big venues when we were supporting another band. The best we could feature was at the Marquee, Dingwalls or the Nashville. But even when we'd gone our separate ways some of us would always guest with Hawkwind on sentimental occasions, usually at the Hammersmith Odeon.

It was at one of these big parties, actually at the Rainbow, Christmas 1981, that Calvert and me had our famous fight – performing on stage like pros and then dusting it out in the wings, with Jammy, Shitty Schmidt's girlfriend (whom Calvert was screwing), Chrissie Hynde and Gay Advert shouting for us to stop and Lemmy trying to calm everybody down and Captain Sensible making things worse and beer spilling everywhere and God knows how many roadies, ex-wives and girlfriends milling about and half the road crew suddenly holding Calvert so that I could hit him (he wasn't popular that year) and me refusing and getting hit by Jammy, who then turned on Shitty and began to whack him with a bit of mike stand, which is the least he deserved, until she made him cry and stopped. Shitty was our notorious manager.

By then Chrissie and Sonny Portillo were holding me. I turned to tell Captain Sensible to shut up. And that was when Calvert socked me, on the side of the face. I remember noticing his strange, hesitant heavy hand, the scratched knuckles, the bitten nails. A thoroughly intellectual blow, I said. Distinctly premeditated. He hated fighting. I had a bit more experience at it. I toecapped his shins and punched him twice in the stomach and the bastard kept throwing up through the rest of his set. Limping on the walking stick he'd brought to beat me with. Probably just as well that the roadies had fucked with his sound-system so nobody could hear him. It wasn't much of a sentimental parting. But the band played on and the fans were delirious with the good spirit we radiated from the stage. Throughout the whole thing Dave Brock had kept the music surging on. Nothing was a lie. That was how it was. We always gave our best to our public.

I'd been at Mike Dempsey's funeral all that morning. He was the Granada editor, a cut above the nervous little rabbits who generally process books these days, who'd also managed the Adverts. Father of one of Emma Tennant's kids. Nice kid. Also a Rose. A mensch. A mate. He put out all three of my photo books. Two of them are still in paperback. The Catholic church is that one you almost miss in Fulham Road. It had been full of punks, publishers and priests. Our Lady of Sorrows, Fulham Road. The vicar apologized that he couldn't offer the sacrament to non-orthodox Catholics and directed the rest of his liberal message at the hard-faced Jesuits from Manchester who were sitting with Dempsey's miserable-looking parents in the front row, giving aggressive responses. Dempsey would have laughed. When the massive bruiser of a Jesuit, who looked like a sergeant in the Foreign Legion, started his oration, I thought Dempsey would bust out of his coffin, roaring. Bellowing his contempt and his mockery. The bastards had him at last. They only have to wait till you're dead.

Anyway, that was still with me. Haunting me, you might say.

I got through my numbers, put my Gibson in its case, and left before the encore. Flicky had a taxi waiting. Her pretty little oval face was alive with all kinds of indignation. She was telling me how she'd told me so and how that bitch Jammy had a lot to answer for. I said I thought Jammy was trying to stop the trouble. Flicky said if I thought that, there was no point in talking to me now. I got the picture. I knew that conversational roundabout. I turned off my mental engine and idled in neutral for a while. I was beginning to get a hint that this was not going to be my merriest Christmas.

That's right. You guessed it. Flicky had just started screwing Calvert. Which of course I didn't know. Season's Greetings to all our readers.

The beginning of the end, I think. It was my birthday. I was thirty.

Flicky Jellinek was twenty-four. She eventually went into politics. After marrying Barbican for two years.

Calvert, of course, never got to forty-five. He had a heart attack not long after Julie had married Barbican and I'd just married Pinky or Flo Fortnum. Tubby said forty-five was the dangerous age.

'You have to maintain your body more carefully, like a well-kept car, and then it can still use the same fuel, go the same distances. Take the same risks. But it's a question of judgement. Of paying a little more attention to the road.'

And poor old Calvert had no judgement.

'It,' I sing on one of the last backing vocals I did for *Hype*, '*was not a tragedy.*'

But it came close.

Tubby hadn't bothered to make it down to Calvert's funeral. By then, he hadn't gone beyond his front garden for almost eighteen months, but he said he skipped the funeral because he didn't want to hear the eulogies from those same extravagant worshippers who'd helped get Calvert to the bin and eventually to the grave. You never did want to hear that crap if you knew and cared for the real person. It's true that the oratory always rings false in the face of irrefutable fact. Nonetheless, I did go. It was my fourth funeral that year, all drugs, but I wanted to see the old bastard off. I still had respect for him. And of course what actually happened was that I spent most of the time cornered by some distant Calvert cousin telling me about rooting shrubs out of season, or else autographing Order of Service cards for the less sensitive mourners. Most of Calvert's wives and kids signed in, but I didn't get to talk to anyone. We were all sick of the sight of one another, I think.

Maddy La Font came with me up to the Mill afterwards. She wasn't saying much that day. She was unusually reflective. I was miserable. Tubby was philosophical.

I got a meal together from his freezer. Everything not from Harrods was from some other internationally famous deli or food hall. Beldonni's in Houston Circle, New York. Buffet Fraiche in Paris. The kind of stuff admirers brought, forgetting that elaborate eating wasn't usually what they wanted at Tubby's. I cooked French roast beef with a kind of American Yorkshire pudding, green beans from Nairobi, spuds from Egypt. That was about the simplest meal you could make out of that gourmet freezer. Desserts were frequently a glorious mystery.

Maddy's strange mood stayed with her after we'd eaten. She decided she'd load the dishwasher. I had a bit of Marakshi jet with me and we smoked it in one of those big brass opium pipes he favoured. I told Tubby that I thought we'd both been pole-axed by the fact of death that year, Maddy and me. It got you worried for yourself.

He said I was pathetic.

'If you can make it past forty-five, Dennis, you'll probably survive until you hit the cancer zone. If you miss the cancer zone you become one of those exemplary old bastards that everyone points to and says "drugs can't harm you". Which is a bit like saying the Black Death can't harm you. It can't, if you're immune to the Black Death. Here's to Lady Luck, pard. Pack us another pipe.'

That was how much time Tubby allowed you, or himself, for self-pity.

Sometimes life seems a series of clumsy hopeless swoops between a line of inevitable disasters. That's why I like Americans. They're optimistic. They can see a future. They're living on the fringes of civilization, in the still water, and they think they can do something about death. They think they're in control. Maybe they can. Maybe they are. They should never come here, to the centre, where you get an unspoiled view of the walls of the maelstrom swirling around you as you make your brief, conscious bow to the multiverse and prepare for the next stage in your substance's relentless journey to the ends of time.

Which is where reading too many Frenchmen gets you, yes?

Thanks for the angsts.

Obla-di, obla-deux, pards.

CHAPTER THIRTEEN
The Jack

I first met Madeleine La Font in Paris, at the old Quai d'Hivers, where, as her family would say, nobody of any reputation is ever seen. She wasn't hard to spot, dressed from head to foot in 1950s movie scarlet, a tiny Lotte Lenya trying to look like Lucille Ball, with scarlet lipstick and nails, her pageboy hair hennaed, a scarlet pillbox hat sporting a scarlet cockade, all to emphasize the paleness of her skin, her vibrant ugliness, the intense focus of her ruby contacts, the quickness of her skinny hands. This was long before she started performing on stage, though she already saw me as someone who could help her. Of course I didn't know that at the time. She didn't tell me she was a journalist, either. I just thought she was a loony. Which, of course, she was. The kind of loony I'm fated to foster.

It was seven o'clock on a cold autumn morning, with the usual oily mist rolling off the canal basin. I'd been up since midnight and was breakfasting on a bowl of mussels and a glass of Ricard. I'd done a good night's work.

I was winding down. I had my eyes off the job. Then Maddy advertised herself from across a crowded formica table glazed with the smoke of a million cheap cigarettes. She picked up my light meter. I took it away from her. She seemed to approve of that. I didn't give a fuck. I didn't want any mind-games at that time of day.

'I think I know you.' Her French was tinged with a faint North African accent. Definitely sexy. From the bar, shoulder to shoulder, the red-faced boatmen and their pale lounging customers argued and joked and kept an interested shufti on us both.

I'd been doing a commission for *Adios* of Barcelona. An old-fashioned photo-essay. They tired you out.

Though I knew the area well, I'd never seen her before, but apparently she was always here. Every morning. She had friends: beaky, pock-marked, blonded Madame Stepp, Monsieur Vermuth, the sweet-faced lizardoid *belle époque* bookseller, and a fat, black US deserter we knew as Uncle Sam, who claimed to be the father of George Whitman's daughter, Sylvia Beach. He'd left the army, he said, in order to get some action. So far he'd failed to find a job as an African mercenary and had been turned down on medical grounds by the Foreign Legion. They thought he was a US Intelligence plant. So did we.

They came for the food. It was cheaper, healthier and better than anything else they could afford. The smell was rich enough to keep you going all day. The accumulated juices of the centuries. There was a Colombo Brothers accordion tune on the jukebox. *Germaine.* The TV news blaring somewhere. *Maroc et Algérie. La Paix. Les Fundos. La Guerre. La Nation.* A whiff of coffee. The stish of the stoves, the whine of the ventilators. Arguments in the kitchen. Pans and threats hissing in harmony. Nothing changed at the Café Terminal.

The bargees were a conservative bunch. They left you alone mainly because they didn't want to have to deal with you. As long as you weren't authority, they were friendly enough. But they were watchful. They could see us reflected in a long, spotted mirror set behind dusty bottles of Norris and Duchem, incongruous ads for Michaud roulades and Jansen beer, and the best selection of anis outside Marseilles. The substantial fog off the canals dragged itself down the windows like dirty sperm, leaving brown smears in its wake; and its long fingers seeped through cracks and windows to snatch at the warmth of the living, at the piquant sweat, steam, billowing grease and cigarette smoke. An addictive atmosphere for someone suckled almost from birth on *L'Atalante.* I couldn't get enough of it. In the evenings there was a gnomish accordion player, in a red bolero jacket, silk trousers and a gypsy sash, like an animated, mummified monkey. He smelled of chicory and rosemary. He had a huge yellow grin. He called himself Little Pete and half his repertoire, sung in a high, sweet voice, was Cajun. *Joli Blanc. Grande Mamou. Ai-eee, ma Houston.* His stories were even better than his songs.

Apart from the odd *vérité*-junkie like me, few strangers ever seem to hang around at the Quai d'Hivers. The public preferred its *vérité* virtual. Literally the name means 'Quay of Winters', and the place was said to be the site of secret executions under the Bourbons, but it's actually named for Les Hivers, the area of Paris set behind the Cirque d'Hiver on the Boulevard du Temple, not far from the Place de la République. It's the old canal terminus, where the city's six great underground waterways convene, bringing boats from as far as Nizhni-Novgorod, Vienna and Istanbul. But most of the trade is in the familiar Lowlands cargoes whose carriers have used these routes since the late sixteenth century. What the Flemish boats brought and how the cargoes were exchanged was the stuff of countless *policiers*, given real atmosphere by Simenon. The little bistros sold nothing but eels, freshwater shellfish, lampreys and catfish. It wasn't the delicate, delicious catfish of Mississippi, but the dark, oily monster of the estuaries and outlets of metropolitan France, sliced and fried with vinegar. A speciality. Not to my taste. Admittedly, if you cooked it right, you couldn't tell it from rat. I was at the Café Terminal, though, because they had outstanding *moules*. And *frites*. The best substitute for fish and chips on the continent.

'Well, Monsieur "Dennis"?' She pronounced my name sardonically, as if it were French. It was the first time I heard that thrumming, vibrant, persuasive tone, like a sardonic cello. 'I had no idea you "slummed"' (she said that word in English) 'in the capital. I thought you preferred the South's private beaches. Surely there aren't enough ex-princesses with sagging tits and bulging stomachs to suit you here?'

I was just out of Belfast, but I wasn't upset. I started laughing at her. I was flattered, of course, that she recognized me. I'd never been that famous. Of course, she secretly knew much more about me than she suggested and saw me as useful to her. It was how she habitually conducted her affairs. She generally began a relationship with a well-prepared, well-learned dossier. She was good at it. Her meetings with potential lovers almost always seemed spontaneous. In later years the net became an invaluable research tool. *International Who's Who* was her bedside reading. She was a natural competitor. She played only to win. Which could be fun sometimes, though generally tiring. But that first time she pretended she only knew of me as an intrepid photog. Which of course had me preening a bit.

The reality was that she'd met Rose in Casablanca two years before. She'd seen my photo. Rose had talked about me enthusiastically. Rose loved me. I'd find this out from Rose herself later. Even after all the shit Maddy put me through, it wouldn't bother me. I had some sense of how the relationship was going pretty much from the start. But initially, at the Terminal, Madeleine had the advantage of me. Which, of course, turned her on. Naturally, I just imagined she fancied my rough cockney charm.

'Oh, yeah,' I said.

I'd first come to the area with Frenchy, who was born there. One of his second cousins pretty much ran the district below the Boulevard du Temple. He was the notorious half-Tunisian, half-gitane dwarf, Avram LeVec, much respected *patron* of Les Hivers. Stern but fair. My association with him had brought me a lot of good manners. Like having my own cruise missile. So it was a comfort for me to hang out down there. A psychic trip back in time. The way the East End used to be. Dangerous for them but safe for me. You knew where you stood. I almost always used expensive Rochester black-and-white stock for those shoots. I was really only after the faces.

Much as I hung out there, I wasn't prepared to see the likes of Maddy at the Terminal. I was usually only there at night. Not really clocking her as I read my *Libération*, I thought at first she was a high-class whore going off duty.

'I enjoy your features.' She reached down into a red leather handbag and pulled out a copy of *L'Actuelle* that had run some of my most recent Kashmir pix. The magazine looked as if someone had wrapped meat in it. She tried to smooth it and then waved it away. I gave it a varda. Not much of an issue and a pretty lousy spread. Shit printing. Hardly worth blacking up for. But she had me by the ego, the key to every man's penis. I was already hooked. I stayed hooked, off and on, for another couple of years, until Rosie rescued me from the Tropicana.

It was October 1981. Flicky Jellinek, whom I'd married in a blackout, said she needed some space to get her head together, so I'd borrowed Professor Dave Harry's place for a couple of months. I could use it as a base and it had a decent darkroom. I meant to sharpen some of my old Parisian contacts. But in the end I hardly left the flat.

My old friend Bill's brother, Dave, was a famous rugger player, an academic, big on postmodernism and all that, who'd bought this apartment up a tiny alley on the Ile de France for a song in the sixties. The only problem with it was that it had no lift and the building was vertically about twice the length of the street. Eight and a half floors to Dave's flat. It had been servants' quarters, of course, and I suspect once the servants were taken into the house in the old days, they never saw the ground again. Or else developed inhuman thigh muscles. You should have clocked Dave on the rugger field. Those Paris holidays paid off. Faster than a speeding cabinet minister.

I was accepted in the street the moment I arrived. Everyone called me Docteur 'Arry or M'sieu le Professeur. They'd read this on his mail. I was about his height and weight and we had similar colouring. We were both English. They thought I was him without his beard. It was easier to let them go with that. My credit was good and stayed good. I paid my bills in cash. I had an arrangement with the local newsagent and baker. Every morning I lowered a basket all the way down to the street. They filled it with *Libération*, milk and croissants, sometimes a thermos of fresh coffee, and I hauled it carefully back up, trying not to knock against my neighbours' windows. It kept me in touch with the rest of the planet. That and the World Service on my little short-wave. Great reception.

Once up there, you didn't fancy leaving. Unless it was to run across the grey, twisted roofs in the moonlight. A Quasimodo-eye view of Paris. You could drink your coffee and think yourself back a hundred years, in the city's golden age. With the right drugs, you could easily imagine yourself swinging between the oddly angled chimneys and spires, all the way to Notre Dame to rescue Esmeralda.

And in the street, whenever I got down there, everyone was pleased to see me. 'Bonjour, m'sieu!'

'Bonjour. Bonjour.' I was an identity they recognized. Already an institution.

Familiarity. It was all we wanted. What a comfort. How happily we slip into these aliases, as if we were born to them.

Not that modern Paris didn't have a lot to offer. Maybe not solid gold, but close. As far as I was concerned those first few weeks with Maddy seemed at least solid silver. After she'd buttered me up so much I was pulsing like an eel pudding, we had lunch at the Restaurant Voltaire, where the food always makes you feel wonderful, and walked along the quays pretending to look for some old sheet music she said she was interested in. She darted about me like a brilliant red bird. Sometimes she seemed to disappear altogether then reappear suddenly, a flashing cardinal.

I wasn't really interested in the stock, but I was surprised at how many blatant forgeries, of popular Steinlein posters and Willette pierrots, of entire books, were now being sold. The last time I'd looked, the stuff had all been real.

The Seine hadn't changed, and was a muddy, busy glow in the late-afternoon light. The smell of braziers, of roasting nuts. Red, white and blue awnings. Ranks of slender trees. Green baize. Elegant silver stones. A distant hurdy-gurdy. The quietening dusk. An Impressionist glaze.

'Time for a hot toddy?'

'Why not?' No hesitation.

It was only a step across the bridge to my tower. She made it up the cobbled alley in her heels, but she wasn't really ready for the ascent. The one thing she hadn't researched. She almost didn't finish the climb. The stairs got steeper, the spirals tighter. She removed her hat. I thought she'd die. I don't think she'd been sleeping much. But, by God, she was radiating appetite. I think it was for sex.

She was righteously pissed by the third floor, but she held herself together. I could sense some conflict, but had no idea what it was. Her face writhed occasionally. It was like one of those SF movies, where the alien's trying to take over the human's brain. A dybbuk. She was mumbling to herself, cursing herself, her voice echoing everywhere in the big empty stairwell. She wouldn't take off her ruby shoes. She staggered up, in and out of darkness, landing by landing, resting on the rickety banister, groaning at the distance ahead, gasping at the distance below, cursing the builder and his building, bringing half the neighbours out to look at her. I think she was also reminding herself of her aspirations when she lifted her eyes up towards the filthy skylight far above and gave herself a murmured admonition. Her tone wasn't pretty. A stifled snarl. A lurid complaint, an impossible offence. My neighbours became agitated. Her colour threatened their familiar glooms. Her salty Algerian French offended their silences, pricked their worst fears. And any hope in their minds that this might be the professor's little student, or even his niece, had vanished. In extremis, Maddy looked like something you'd pick up on the Place Pigalle, if you were into ugly little transvestite schoolboys.

By the time she got to my flat she was quietly outraged, clearly blaming herself for something, and sat panting, staring through the window at wet grey slate, holding the coffee I'd made for her and not at all sure the climb had been worthwhile. It took half the coke she'd brought just to revive her. But after that, we didn't leave the flat much. I was ready for her tricky fucking. It suited me. I was good at it when I wanted to be. Rolls of roles. I'd had enough of hearts and flowers. In the back of my mind I knew why Flicky had sent me away. They always say it's to think things out.

When we were spending more time on the floor or in the toilet than in bed, when the coke never quite lasted long enough and we were gladly cutting it with raw whizz, I was ready to try to work things out with Flicky again. So I went home to Ladbroke Grove and she was even more distant than ever. I told her about Maddy. She said that was great. She'd often thought I needed two girlfriends at least.

I didn't have to be telepathic. Ho yus?

But I didn't have time to think that over. We were rehearsing a short tour that would run through most of November and finish up at the Rainbow just before Christmas when we'd share the bill with Hawkwind, who we'd also join on stage for the kind of big 'party' that had become a tradition with us in London.

Deep Fix rehearsals were a bugger. Calvert kept making jokes and goading me in a funny way. Then he'd bridle at the slightest criticism. I couldn't work out what was going on. But I didn't like it. Mysterious references. Too many guilty secrets, it turned out. So the tour was shit, badly prepared, constantly spoiled by quarrels and ego trips. I left twice and went home. But, of course, I wasn't welcome there, either. When I came back, Calvert left.

I wound up taking Maddy La Font to Tubby's regular Thanksgiving party at the end of November. Flicky, sunk in her huge sweater, her great brown eyes about as shifty as I've ever seen them, said she wasn't feeling sociable. The party sorted me out, left me more cheerful, so I went back and finished the tour. I only missed the Reading and Oxford gigs. I was hoping the big Christmas gig would make up for it. We usually did them at Hammersmith, but the Rainbow was an even better venue. It was supposed to be a celebration. Great atmosphere. As well as both bands, everyone we knew who was still alive was back stage. Lemmy, Tom Baker, Glenn Matlock, Dave Vanion, Pavli, Siouxsie, Graham Parker, Wilco, Norman Watt-Roy, Billy Bragg, Simon House, Mo Collier, Snowy White and, of course, Calvert. He was going to open with some solo stuff he'd got sorted out with tapes. Then we'd do a set. Then Hawkwind. Then all of us.

Flicky came with me to Dempsey's funeral, but she left before we went to the pub with the parents and the disapproving Jesuits. It wasn't like her to be rude. I thought I'd done something wrong. Or that Flicky was overwhelmed. As, indeed, she probably was. Or at least overstretched. It was a mess we were too tired to sort out properly.

That's how Flicky and I were on the night of that Rainbow gig, with the band effectively broken up and some of us ready to fight to the death. I never did discover why she didn't want to tell me about Calvert. Probably because she was afraid he was going to dump her. Though the whole thing between us was well and truly crapped by then, she didn't know her bum from her barnet, with her jealousy no doubt focused on Calvert rather than me, and I was beginning to miss Maddy's calculating tongue.

I'd seen Dempsey last at Tubby's Thanksgiving, joining in the Burning Dance, arms linked with Jack Trevor Story and Angela Carter. He'd been talking up the new Irish publishing company he wanted me to work for. A book on the emerging Irish bands. His round, enthusiastic face, topped by his frizzing dark hair, his big glasses, his scarred lips (from where his mouth had been sewn shut by the Cornells), always gave him the air of a startled schoolboy. But keen. You kept expecting him to show you how he'd invented an entirely new kind of mountain bike. He was full of hope and booze and spitting contempt for anyone not prepared to risk their entire career, and possibly their life, on backing him.

Dempsey himself had backed so many outsiders he was known as 'Longshot Larry' in the fancy. He'd started his career as the racing correspondent of the *Tatler* while still at Cambridge. He said there was no such thing as an honest flat race. I used to go to some of the southern tracks with him, usually during the flat season. He never won a thing. Any money he ever made was off steeplechasing. His bets were enormous. His winnings were sometimes uncountable. After a successful win, he would invite me on a coke pick-up with him to his usual dealer in Crouch End, half a k or more, and then we'd go round to his place in Fulham and, using kitchen knives, lay out foot-long gram lines across his old marble washstand, snorting them into our systems until our veins and brains were quicksilver crystal. He could do the same with smack and not seem to suffer any consequences. Not me. And he had a penchant for sexual experiment that left me cold. Maddy knew him. They'd met at a Sex Pistols gig in the mid-seventies.

Strangely, it wasn't excess of anything that killed Dempsey. Just a bit of bad luck. An accident. He was hiding from his creditors at Jilly Cooper's old flat. I was talking to him on the phone just before he died. He told me he was going out for some fags. A few minutes later, according to the reconstruction, he fell over a banister and went down four floors. Nobody found him until the morning. He died some time that night of a ruptured lung. He'd been going to publish Bill Butler's poems. The thing was typeset and pasted, ready to go. I wrote a song for them. A couple of bands have recorded it. And that was that.

A lot of people took the big step that year, but Dempsey was one of my best friends. There's still enough of him left, hanging around out there, for me to get pissed off with him from time to time and tell him what a stupid prick he was. He tells me to fuck off. He's not the only dead friend I blame for my situation. You should hear what I say to Jack Trevor Story.

Jack was also at the funeral. Afterwards I saw him listening with familiar dreaming politeness to a woman with a black velvet bow in her hair telling him how everyone was getting into units at the moment. She had the sharpened-up look of the day. The Lacey Moloch special. Everything plucked and primped. The very best she could do with that ordinary, greedy little face. Jack's look of polite attention signalled his complete failure to understand her argument and the sudden realisation that he was all right for tonight.

'What,' he said, 'you mean kitchens? My mate Bill's selling kitchen units. He says you'd be amazed at the mark-up.'

'Oh, it's all marks, these days.' She was young enough for Jack. He was now showing an interest I'm sure she encouraged. I know they left together.

Don't worry, I'm not really crazy. Those friends only exist in my mind now. They weren't. They were. They're not. He wasn't. He was. He isn't. Easy. But what's wrong in weaving a security blanket occasionally? I mean, what is it we invent in our friends, anyway? Over to you, Jack.

Tubby's Thanksgiving parties were famous all through the seventies. He only gave one party a year and it was for everyone he felt like inviting, but originally he'd started having them because he felt sorry for American friends living in England. Bob Dylan had been at the first one. It's an important ritual to Americans. I remember the writer Toni Morrison asking Tubby why he went to such trouble to celebrate a specifically American holiday. Tubby said that the Pilgrim Fathers were thanking God they'd arrived and we were thanking God they'd left.

Maddy had only ever heard of his legendary parties and was thrilled by the prospect. A lot of these same guests would be at Dempsey's funeral the following month but today Dempsey was still alive and on good form.

In spite of her strong sense of outrage – to use the Tube was like exposing yourself in public – I took Maddy by underground to Tufnell Park, then got the bus up Junction Road to St John's Grove and went into the park through the Pemberton Gardens entrance, which still had that run-down rural look: a ragged picket fence, dusty hedges, old fag packets, a pitted tarmac path over some muddy turf to the smoke-mottled trees. You could see the top of the Mill as we climbed up the steep hill through that chilly, rainy morning, but you couldn't tell what it was. Maddy wasn't curious. Maddy hadn't stopped complaining since she realized we were taking the train. As it was, she kept getting the shivers. It was the time, she said. She was never normally up this early.

Then we had passed under the low branches of corporation chestnuts and into little crooked Bluebell Lane, NW, with its old wrought-iron fence. The noise of the city fell away around us until suddenly all we were aware of was birdsong, the squirrels rooting in the leaves, the occasional deep creaking shudder, as if the old machinery of the world were turning a painful inch or two.

Almost silence.

It all startled Maddy and she began to get edgy, aggressive, but I told her not to worry. I led her through the spinney towards the big brick building that now thrust up out of ivy and evergreens to dominate the hill. Another gate in a high privet hedge, with a corporation-green 'Private: No Entry' sign, and we were in the shadow of the Mill's pitted terracotta, with her dark ivy, her brown, reflective tin shutters, complicated woodwork and scarecrow vanes, with nothing but the surging grey sky behind her. Like something out of *Jamaica Inn*.

Again Maddy reacted with exaggerated alarm. 'My God! It's far too *massive!*'

'An important bit of industrial engineering, in her day,' I said. 'Big news in the 1770s.'

She glared at me. She loathed and feared history. Most dates, any reference to time, made her feel sick. She growled contempt in her hideous private French. But when I reached into my Liberty bag and took out the hat, collar and cuffs of my old pilgrim fancy dress, pulling them on over my ordinary jacket, she made a gesture of defeat.

'Denny! What is this? A lodge meeting? Am I to be inducted? I'm too small.'

I led her on up the path to the big, solid oak door Tubby had reclaimed from a church and that looked like something off the set of *Frankenstein*. Overhead were ranks of tiny windows, surrounding the big central grain doors which Tubby would open in the summer, still with their eighteenth-century stonework, their ornamental shutters. Above the grain doors was a gallery with a kind of rail carrying a hoist capable of travelling the whole circumference of the tower and worked by a winch. Rusted hawsers anchored the ruined vanes. The hawsers kept the whole upper chamber from turning, but the wind still moved those tattered wings and the great cogs still grumbled against the restraint. That was what you could hear as you approached. Like a giant's senile soliloquy. It scared the shit out of local kids.

I turned Maddy by her padded little shoulder to look back.

She was impressed. In spite of herself.

Through the gap in the old trees, to the south, over the roofs of Tufnell Park, the whole of London could be seen as far as the river. At that time of day the mist was lifting and the contrast sharp, so that every familiar landmark, from St Paul's to Big Ben, looked as if it had been etched into the grey air.

'Best view in London,' I said. 'A living map.'

She snorted. It was very nice. To get to the roof of the Samaritaine was less effort.

There was already a warmth escaping from Tubby's door, the scent of spiced wine, coffee and hot cakes, an enveloping mixture of stimulus and comfort, promising everything that Tubby's parties usually delivered.

I lifted the great copper Voysey knocker, but before I could let it drop a voice behind me cracked through the air like a horsewhip.

'Wait for us, Denny. Let's all go in together!'

I really hadn't expected Johnny Begg to turn up that year. I expected him to be doing powerful things on islands or in mountain retreats. He swung round the side of the Mill at the head of a whole bunch of familiar faces. He'd walked up from Whittington Park arm-in-arm with his hardy new mistress Bobby MacMillan. He was glowing a bit, wheezing faintly, his soft charm already coarsening to fat. She looked like a mourning Greek goddess in all her well-pressed cool black. Anaemic, sad, but taking no shit. And not even slightly out of breath. The business editor of the *Daily Mail*, she'd been one of the first to have her hair blonded and tied back in a black velvet AIDS bow. I didn't think it was any coincidence that the bow had appeared at about the same time as the middle class became aware of AIDS. Within weeks every ambitious woman in London was wearing one. My guess was that they flourished it as a talisman, to keep their backs covered against the disease, which otherwise might drift up their bottoms. (You have to remember this was the early voodoo age, when Thatcher's and Reagan's mumbo-jumbo was just beginning to take over and people who had been educated to learn nothing were now ready to believe anything.)

At the gate, they had joined forces with with Sir Bryan Mupett, his companion Michael Dickens and their spaniel George. Mupett's 'Hollow Earth' Symphony was going down a treat at the RFH. It was the hit of the year. Chucky Osborne in the *Daily Telegraph* had been adamant – Mupett was the late-twentieth century's only substantial composer and Dickens the only voice fit to sing him. The two of them seemed to be floating on a golden cloud of public approval. They were aglow with it. Even the dog looked like he was getting good reviews.

The old gents were a riot of toning tweeds and casually flung cashmere scarves. Butch by L.L. Bean. But a nice enough pair of painted queens at heart. Mupett wasn't so much mutton dressed as lamb as a well-presented roast. One of the vividly living dead. Like his music, he was all balance and tradition. Maddy, a natural fag hag, gravitated instantly to his arm, leaving Dickens rolling courteous eyes up at an expansive, golden Johnny, billowing in a loden green raglan, who now introduced me with unexpected enthusiasm. 'You know Micky Dickens, of course.

And Bryan Mupett? I gather they're doing great things at Glyndebourne these days. You know Bobby MacMillan, I expect?'

She offered me a hearty handshake, a bit of a grin.

I'd met her when she was still married to Harry MacMillan, when he was briefly editing the *Sunday Telegraph Magazine* and keeping me well in work. I'd always fancied her. She leant towards my cheek, a scented peck. I hated her. She was my perfect type. Ugh.

Maddy was a natural groupie. She greeted each star as if she had never heard of them before. 'And what is it you play?' she asked Sir Bryan as with deep dismay he noticed what her lipstick had done to his lapel.

Johnny found her a bit alarming. He kept grabbing my shoulder. 'Great to see you, Dennis,' he said. 'Great to see you, old pard. How's tricks? Still coining it, eh?'

'Can't stop,' I said. 'And your good self?'

'I'm not complaining.'

Yet his eyes were full of frustrated longing.

Looking back, I realize now he was anticipating deregulation. The era of the terminally, perversely wealthy was about to begin. The Second Second Empire. That year they'd been testing the waters. Thatcher must have been poised to knock the plugs out of the public barrel and Johnny was looking forward to the moment when he'd get his trough under the spigot. The trick then would be to get all the other troughs. And make one big trough, which he controlled. The best of his kind. The Grand Consumer himself. What fair competition and free enterprise were all about. Johnny was at last turning into Barbican. The Man Who Ate The World, the man we all learned to hate. At that moment, though, he was only one of the richest men in Britain.

A hardy little hand lifted itself from behind Johnny's shoulder pads. 'Hi, Denny!' Flo Fortnum's smile was all over the place. She was handbagging a squat little dude in a camel hair overcoat who I mistook at first for the Sultan of Mauretania. She introduced him. Tootsie Fade? I'd never heard of him. He could have been a local Greek gangster. He shook my hand viciously, grinning, power-seeking eyes searching the rest of the group. 'Fugging brilliant,' he said. 'You going to take some pictures with the queen? Let me know, you won't be sorry.' I checked to make sure he hadn't slipped a tenner into my hand.

There were several I didn't recognize in the party now gathering at the Mill's elaborate entrance. Some were admiring the Georgian stone-mason's rather showy workmanship, including a marble lintel, added on as an advertisement to the miller's increasing prosperity and engraved with his name and future, *John Tuftnole & Sons*.

A little prematurely, Maddy darted forward, put the tips of one gloved hand on my forearm, raised herself in her ruby slippers and slapped the great copper knocker against the booming resonator Tubby and Ginger Baker had discovered on one of their famous field trips to Africa.

The growl of the drum faded into the Mill's heart.

Tubby, of course, had seen us coming. Beaming, he threw back the massive door, a golden pilgrim, a benevolent peach, a benign Dionysus. He raised his arms. From the shoulders up, Tubby looked a bit like the guy on the Quaker Oats packet with his black hat on his curly hair, a wide, starched collar laid over his pink tweed suit. He was framed by an aura of warm orange light, his short, pink fingers flaring from his yellowing cuffs, his welcoming arms offering to scoop us all into his embrace at the same time. You never felt more welcome than when Tubby was pleased to see you. You never felt happier.

'Dear old pards!'

He drew us all in.

As we handed our street clothes to Mandy Moonglum, actually Tubby's transvestite zoologist cousin Maurice in full hat-check girl kit (his annual treat), I heard Flo's escort snort in astonishment. 'Where's the fuggin' daleks? It's like a fuggin' Tardis in here, innit?'

I'd often thought the same. Outside, Tubby's tower was substantial, full of history, a London landmark, but, inside, it was a whole world. With its high ceilings, its oak panelling decorated in Voysey copper and Knox silver, its muted Morris fabrics, it looked like a cross between a set by Grot for *The Sea Hawk* and some Tennysonian Camelot. All tall, black beams and glittering shadows, lit by curvaceous Benson oil lamps and warm yellow gas. Yet layered into this were Tubby's sophisticated electronics, his consoles and monitors. Every screen was alive with discreet sequences of images and information, yet the air of ecclesiastical tranquillity remained. Nothing intruded. Everything in that huge central room radiated from the hub, which was the massive millstone itself and its great brick shaft house, stretching up into the darkness and connected at the top to gears originally turned by the whirling sails. This shaft also now carried all Tubby's pipes and cables. Its brick sides were decorated from top to bottom with Tubby's memorabilia, his gold and platinum discs, pictures of his family, his lovers, his favourite cats; some drawings his father had done, a few paintings and sketches with personal associations, some framed comics and press cuttings. Nowhere else did Tubby display so much of himself. Yet nothing of his anger was there. Some of us saw the shaft as a glamour, designed to draw attention away from the real, self-created Tubby whose secret wisdom he sometimes shared with the world. He called it his Pillar of Shame. He said the pictures were subtle mocking pasquinades, *memento mori*. It was a useful ice-breaker with new guests, who could study it as they got acclimatized. There were also a few cats they could pet, but by and large Tubby's orientals preferred to observe their company from the shadowy tops of beams or from ledges let into the naked brick. Every so often a flame would find reflection in a yellow eye.

There was still not much mingling. There was instead an air of expectancy. A few old regulars had their collars and cuffs on, but sans the outfits, the party always got going pretty formally, with a speech from our host at twelve sharp. Although it seemed awkward and old-fashioned, this routine actually helped warm things up. Tubby would have made a great conductor.

I'd noticed on several recent occasions that all the puritans who came refused to wear fancy dress. The people who chose to wear the costumes were usually the least puritanical. An enthusiastic masquerader, once Maddy understood the deal she told everyone she'd come as *The Scarlet Letter*.

Then I rounded the pillar and felt almost sick with pleasure.

I hadn't known Rosie was going to be there. I thought she was still in Begat, heading the UN teams. I'd seen her once on the nine o'clock news, holding a wounded child, looking straight at the camera and speaking softly of the unspeakable. She was still superbly photogenic. And she radiated moral authority. But she didn't like her face made public and had taken, because she worked predominantly out of North Africa, to wearing a casual veil. The UN were getting into the habit of using her for their most ambitious appeals. Her image, almost always with the light veil and covered head, like Benazir Bhutto, was becoming as well known in charitable circles as Mother Teresa's, but she somehow resisted all attempts to glamorize her. The subject had to be her cause, not her response to it. Which didn't make her quite so easy to identify with as Princess Di, but it gave her a lot more credibility in the right places. She made full use of Di's well-meaning sentimentality whenever she needed to.

Elegant in her Berber fabrics, her abundant hair, Rosie was talking to a striking young woman in a blonde crew-cut and fashionable motorbike gear. I approached them and they both turned. As Rosie rushed to hug me, my eyes met those of her companion. I was almost flustered. That green savvy gaze might have been Rosie's own. Her relationship to Rosie was obvious. She had the same self-contained tawny vibrancy, the amiably distant air of a very superior cat. A queen. A goddess. You could almost hear the purrs from the surrounding shadows. Cats beamed on Rosie. They recognized their own.

Rosie took my hand and put it into the girl's. 'This is Kim. Denny. You've heard of old Den, Kimmy, eh? Uncle Den?'

'Hello, Uncle Dennis.' The leathered gidget was smart and lively. In the subtle curve of her cheekbones, the angle of her eyes, I saw something about her that wasn't Rosie. Maybe a touch of South East Asia? Korean? Vietnamese? Kim could be from half a dozen countries. I liked her a lot. Her slender hand was warm in mine. Judging by her smile, she'd heard mostly good about me.

It was what she said next that confirmed my dawning guess.

'Mum's played me all your records. You and Michael Jackson are my favourites.'

I had a feeling Michael Jackson got more airtime than I did, but her familiarity with my dodgy musical career wasn't the real surprise, of course. Given that this child looked seventeen (actually she was ten) and that Rosie was the same age as me . . . That's where I went wrong with the math. But this had to be the 'baby', the 'little girl' with a medical problem. A picture was coming together so rapidly I was almost lost for words.

'Don't judge me by that crap,' I said. But I left off the next line. It didn't seem appropriate. Rosie was grinning at my discomfort.

'So this is that baby.' I reached towards her. All I could do was enjoy Rosie's delight at my confusion. I kissed Kim awkwardly on the cheek. 'So this is the family.'

'Well, some of it.' Rosie seemed to be warning me. Too late. His eyes looking every way but north, Jocky Papadakis, all spaniel nose and careful mouth, sidled in to remind her that they'd met at the Savoy Oxfam bash and to tell her that he was her greatest fan and what an incredible job everyone at MBM thought she was doing for the undeveloped world.

We were used to handling this. 'Take the west fork,' I told her. 'I'll meet you at the pass.' Jocky was still MacEnery Business Management then, still wearing that awful beard, a freelance corporate hit man, an accountant-assassin, a humourless, geeky bubble, an international Uriah Heep, a Glaswegian super-jobsworth, who, apologizing for a hiccup, had downsized the dreams of millions.

I'd given up trying to work out why Tubby invited certain unsavoury people to these events. Maybe to make sure he'd covered the spectrum?

I had nothing but loathing and contempt for Papadakis, but found myself almost sympathetically listening to his problems with his new BMW as Rosie and Kim slipped away to talk to Goerda Flockinger, the sparky little jeweller, already attracting Maddy, who took a sensual North African delight in gold.

That was how it was at Tubby's. Whatever he did to achieve it, or whether it was actually some kind of supernatural phenomenon, the Mill radiated an all-embracing geniality on these occasions. Elsewhere famous literary antagonists were already enjoying a reminiscent joke or two rival actresses were bonding on shared-husband stories, savage news commentators were exchanging recipes with infamous politicians and blood enemies from the City were finding how much they loved the same holiday spots. Clive James had his arm round Germaine Greer's shoulders. Richard Dreyfuss was telling Al Pacino stories to a producer he'd sworn never to work with again. Michael Cimino was talking gratefully to someone who'd never heard of him. Alan Bennett was mystifying Tom Wolfe with some provincial irony. Or Wolfe was mystifying Bennett in the same way. I had the feeling John Lennon would walk through the door and embrace Paul McCartney. Lennon had only been shot a year ago and the fact hadn't really sunk in. You met everyone at Tubby's parties, even the recently deceased. I have lived too long in anticipation, wrote Fioro Lorenetti, so have come in advance to mourn the loss of all I love. I have nothing left to mourn. Nothing left to love. The old pop-futurist was there again this year, quoting himself as usual.

Well, here we are, back in the past. Back in that last secure moment before the Grand Consumer took his first big snap at a bewildered world. And we started running about in terror. What was it like, children, you ask? Before Thatcher and her brisk apprentice Tone decided that the world could only be American and that politics was just the PR side of accountancy? Who seriously believed that appetite was a moral quality. That grids and scoreboards actually worked and the business of America was business. The crime business. The prison business. The crime-prevention business. The crime-protection business. The lawyer business. The show business. The accountancy business. Private enterprise is crime. Crime is private enterprise. The Russians aren't idiots. Merely a little naïve. They innocently understood that America is a country whose internal economy *depends* on crime. Without it, half their domestic trade would collapse.

John Peel's American mate was there. The guy who got killed in that microlight crash over Wimberley. Gene Poudakasian. We all knew him as Professor Poo and he ran that insane Beefheart show for two glorious Capital Metrosonic seasons. He looked like a massive version of Peely in his Hawaiian shirt and decorated overalls, smoking a reefer the size of a Christmas cracker. His voice was as American, as sublimely sane as Jimmy Stewart on Acapulco Gold. *Mr Deeds Does The Weed.*

'That's why we're always coming up with new crimes. And hairstyles, of course. You know what the Baptists say: the higher the hair, the closer to God. And new diseases. We need plenty of those. You can't blame business for doing what's natural. The higher the profit, the closer to God. All seamless. It has to proliferate. The health business is always expanding. New cures. New diseases. New drugs. New food additives. Carcinogens. Hormones. It's a consumer culture, man. Everything works together. Junk food makes you sick. Junk drugs cure you. Other junk drugs deal with the side effects and those side effects are treated with more junk drugs. New causes. New diseases. New drugs. Now that's one that will run and run. Whatever you can afford. And they always know what you can afford.'

We'd attracted the questing ears of doddering old Frank Foot, the local MP. 'Unless pre-Revolutionary England is our model for modern governance, we have no business looking to America for leadership.' His horrible sports jacket and flannels made you think he'd been buried alive for a year. He seemed surprised when we listened to him, almost flattered. I don't think he'd realized he *was* alive. Something in him warmed and sputtered. 'Those puritans only moved to America when reality steadfastly refused to knuckle under and obey their lunatic simplifications. Which created a paradise for lawyers, book-keepers and preachers. Gridthink. That's what happens when you raise a system – communism included – over common sense. Keir Hardie, of course, knew this . . .'

'Yeah?' I said.

Tubby took the expansive view. 'The Great Fundament is logically the other obvious end of the Grand Consumer. A single organism. Gobble gobble gobble. Shit shit shit. It's all that's required of us. Fundamentalism.' He waved farewell as he rolled up-board to his big black carving chair. 'Back to basics.'

The talk took a topical, if predictable, turn as we looked for our own places at the vast table.

The Mill's central room was long enough for the huge wooden trestle that Tubby had commissioned and that he stored in sections for the rest of the year. It had a William Morris sturdiness to its red oak and was very comfortable. Dovetails an inch thick. Some of the chairs went with it, but over the years Tubby had assembled enough Windsors and wickers and country ladderbacks to suit every shape of guest.

The meal would begin with pink champagne, pâté de foie gras and Beluga caviar at twelve noon and move towards the great central moment of the mid-afternoon, when the eight twenty-four-pound turkeys and a dozen other roasted birds were brought out of the old bakery's updated ovens.

The smell of those fowl, of the mince and pumpkin pies, hush puppies, the dressing, vegetable casseroles, mashed potatoes, gravy and the yams must have drifted across the whole of north-west London. A reminder of Christmas yet to come. With Tubby in his hat and cuffs, his sharp linen and burgundy waistcoat, like some clean-shaven, off-duty Santa at the top of the table, tilting claret jugs and sharpening his silvery knives and spreading limitless goodwill, a benign spirit. No animosity could survive Tubby's extraordinary aura, no quarrel could be sustained at his table. He'd often invite ancient enemies and seat them side by side so that, for one day at least, they could behave as friends. It was a quality he had always had. He was forever patching up some unnecessary falling-out. In those last rotten days of The Deep Fix, Tubby had kept the band together against all odds.

When I found my name-card I was delighted. Tubby had been kind to me. I was surrounded by interesting, beautiful women. Maeve Gilmore, widow of Mervyn Peake, was on my right, Goerda Flockinger on my left, and opposite were Julie Christie and Siouxsie Sue. They were flanked by Norbert Stripling and a Tunisian writer called Jahloun. The poor buggers were sat across from Tootsie Fade and Anthony Cheetham, the publisher, but it didn't matter. The two were soon oblivious of all others as Cheetham purred to Tootsie's admiring fiddle.

'It's like a Rembrandt tapestry.' Sylvia Gupta was staring up and down the table. Her long features seemed permanently amused because of her short-sightedness. She was still only eighteen and had just won the Wigmore Prize. I knew what she meant. More like a Frans Hals peasant feast, I thought. All those vivid faces. All those rich crimsons, greens and golds. The glare of puritan linen. The dancing amber and winking ruby of the silver-lidded wine jugs, the blood of angels. The ivory cloth and mother-of-pearl napkin rings, great dark bone-handled Victorian chop-house knives and forks you could dig a grave with. Heavy pewter *belle époque* table furniture by Gilbert and Levallier. Mysterious condiments. *Beaux arts* salts and grinders. Georgian tureens. Red Mill table crackers, pine branches and mistletoe, under those black Gothic beams.

We weren't allowed to sit next to partners at Tubby's, so Maddy, an animated postbox, was miles away at the other end of the table.

That year Tubby wore his pink tweed Cardin suit, a white shirt, his waistcoat. He was flanked by Johnny Lydon on his left and Glen Matlock on his right. He had brought them back together. Johnny was talking a lot. Glen seemed a bit sad. He kept looking up and grinning, as if he hoped for the best. He was getting puffy, overweight, while Johnny was as lean and nervous as a vixen at a chicken coop. I knew Glen pretty well but I'd always had Johnny down as a bit of a bullshitter, generally inclined to pump up the drama, whereas Glen just couldn't help being good-natured and sensible. It suited Johnny to characterize Glen as a wuss and a wet, but Glen had given the Sex Pistols the substance of their success. You need the anger, but you also need good songs. Without them, they really would have been about as memorable as Bibi C. Who was also there, fresh in from Majorca, where he was running, he said, a rock-and-roll theme restaurant.

Goerda Flockinger was a tiny, humorous woman, full of ideas and enthusiasms. She was like a wise, sardonic cockatoo. A bright eye. Fascinated with precious metals and jewels. Making organic, exotic rings and necklaces, blending gold, silver, diamonds, emeralds, sapphires into work that lay on your flesh as if it had grown up out of your bones, fed by your soul. We usually bumped into one another every other year or so. She was amazed that Tubby's cats were so well-mannered. Like him, she lived alone with her Siamese cats but hers had taken over her house, she said. She spoke with wondering emphasis. She'd made each one a golden throne, studded with tiny diamonds. As soon as the thrones were finished, they had exiled her to her workroom, the kitchen and, occasionally, her first-floor sitting room.

'The ingrates! Really!'

The rest of the house was entirely theirs. Her furniture was destroyed, her rugs in tatters and whenever she had a visitor the cats sprayed their coats. I said it sounded wretched but she waved her fingers and laughed. 'I usually warn them in time, these days.' She seemed to delight in her own helplessness. 'What can I do?' she implored, flatteringly.

I've a feeling I'd be like that with cats, once I decided to settle down.

I told her about my dream of retirement. A warm house in the London hills, looking towards the Thames. A few oriental shorthair cats, black, silver and marmalade point, a reliable border collie, maybe a golden retriever and a good view. Then I'd read everything I'd ever wanted to read and listen to all the music I wanted to hear and watch the city in all her aspects and slip contentedly into non-existence. One at last with that amniotic dust. She said she hadn't thought that far ahead. She just hoped she'd keep her eyesight. 'I suppose that makes me a bit of a shallow person.'

Goerda was one of the world's best jewellers. I'd bought a ring of hers in 1972, for Julie. We'd stayed in touch. She made me a couple of things when I was flush. Goerda eventually got an OBE. Had to get kitted up to see the Queen. She bought some new boots for her presentation. She'd meant to buy something practical but she wound up buying highwayman thigh-highs. She said she felt like Prince Charming or Puss-in-Boots in a panto. Long strides all the way to the Queen. It was all she could do to stop herself slapping her thigh and shouting 'Mornin', Dick.' A trick to curtsy, as it turned out. 'And really difficult to back up in, you know. You start to totter. The momentum starts to take you backwards at quite a lick. Luckily there was some chap there to catch me.'

The hors d'oeuvres were already on the table – blocks of pâté de foie gras, mountains of Beluga caviar, great dishes of toast and biscuits and bread, bricks of butter, plates of sliced Italian sausage, Lyonnais *saucisson* and all kinds of tapas, whole fast-fried artichokes, tureens of soup and salvers of asparagus.

Tubby was miked up. His voice came from several speakers. It was like the voice of Oz the Terrible. We all looked in his direction. The doors were closed. Few latecomers ever got in. Those who were here would see the Jack and join in the dance of the Burning Man.

'Dear Pards, welcome!' was all it took to bring silence fairly swiftly to the table, though Johnny's aggressive modern yap (a tone that would proliferate in the coming years) – 'Ludgate Circus? Americans think Harrods is London's true centre . . .' carried on for a few seconds with Tootsie Fade's 'Fuggin' too right' as the last touch of counterpoint. The Egyptian was even more fascinated with Johnny than he was with Cheetham. He craned to hear him down the table. Maybe Johnny represented a vision, an aspiration.

Then Tubby raised his carving knife in one hand, his carving fork in the other, and rested his fists on the table.

'Dear old pards! Again we gather to thank providence that we've survived another year and the signs are that we'll be able to preserve a few civil and humane habits in the face of an ever more powerful Chaos and Old Night. Here, at the Mill, the resistance goes on. Some of you here today look on me as an impractical idealist, I know, but experience has shown me that realistic altruism – enlightened self-interest, if you will – actually advances all our interests, whereas formalized greed advances only the narrowest interests for a short while and results in social disaster.'

If this was a sermon directed at Johnny and Co, it wasn't getting through. Tootsie Fade was frowning, desperately trying to understand the meaning and shaking his head in his failure. You could see he thought he'd missed something important. He cupped his ear to hear better. 'Fuggin' too right,' he murmured.

Johnny, of course, hadn't heard a word. I had the impression that mentally he was on the phone.

The babble started up again. Time whizzed by until suddenly there came the sound of a great booming gong and to my surprise I realized it was time for the main course.

Far away in the darkness the twin doors separating us from the kitchens below crashed open and I was hit by the intensity of the smell, the fizzing fat, the bubbling veg, the roasted fowl, the bacon, the chipolatas, the stuffing and the gravy, the Brussels sprouts and French beans and broccoli and spinach, the vegetarian casseroles, the sweet potatoes, the roast potatoes, the mashed potatoes, the sauces and the spices, the fresh cranberries, the pumpkin pies, the mince pies, the custards and the creams.

It brought a further hush to the table as we all breathed deeply.

'Dear pards!' Tubby was seraphic. 'Please raise your glasses to toast our passing year and herald in the new.' He lifted his glass of Smith-LeVec. Crystal and wine caught the flickering light so that he seemed to hold up a glorious beacon. The Grail itself.

'I want no small appetites here, for this is the feast of the harvest. Here's our celebration of the world's bounty in which we share equally for one day, at least. Tuck in, pards. Make the most of it. That's all I ask.' And downing his wine, he raised his flashing carvers over his head. 'Bring on the birds!'

From kitchens where meals had once been cooked for hundreds, borne by twenty of Mandy Moonglum's most glamorous friends, all in black and white, with massive high heels, sashaying like cakewalkers, with platters held elegantly overhead, came the goose, the turkeys, the pigeon, the ducks, chickens, pheasants and grouse, all under vast pewter domes out of which seeped their savoury juices, their irresistible essences, all the refined piquancies for the predatory palate.

Every roast but the goose had been subtly carved, so that the lines of the knife were almost invisible. As they were set on the table they fell elegantly into slices. But the goose came to rest before Tubby who lifted his knife and made the first incision to the breast. Great applause and a faint pop of crackling. An almost overpowering essence.

As all the vast dishes were set on the trivets and served, Tubby began the swift, delicate slicing of the bird, layering the surrounding platters until his goose was suddenly a picked carcass, a vulture's perch, which was switched away discreetly, to be replaced by Tubby's own modest plate that allowed him to taste a little of everything. We had been brought to a moment of sublime greed.

Mr Fox was that year's band. A nice hairy folk-rock band, playing seasonal stomps in the background. The old place had never been more like some Merrie Englishe feast hall without, thank God, that awful mead or the burned peacock. Or too much farting and burping.

As usual it was a lively table. At every new course, people would reposition themselves, continuing conversations, starting new ones. Angus Wilson, the novelist, who bore a striking resemblance to Margaret Rutherford, the actress who originally played Miss Marple, was talking to a small theatrical group, including Patricia Hodge and Rosie's favourite, the ebulliently rotund Simon Russell Beale, then just starting with the RSC. Sheridan Morley, Giles Gordon and a few other critics, chatted manfully to Johnny Begg and Tootsie Fade. I heard Clare Short, not long an MP, talking to Andrea Dworkin, not then demonized but wearing a leather jacket anyway. 'If we're forced to sentimentalize our lives for public consumption, we're already telling a lie to the people, aren't we? Then we're supposed to live up to these sentimental lies and, if we fail, we get clobbered. Wouldn't it be better to get rid of the sentiment and just tell the public the truth? In the long run they've always been happiest with the truth.'

Dworkin shook her head. With dark hair and eyes, she was small, plump, delicately boned, listening courteously to Short. She smiled. She was apologetic. 'I'm really sorry. It's my jet lag. I didn't get any of that.'

Iris Murdoch, settled and self-contained as a cat at a wake, sat smiling into the middle-distance while Felix Martin explained the H-bomb to her. 'So interesting,' she said vaguely. 'Really? That's extraordinary.' You could tell Felix was convinced he'd made a convert. He was almost on the verge of inventing CND. John Bayley, Murdoch's genial, queeny husband, was talking to E.S. Turner, the ancient essayist, a puck in tweed. I'd read his *Boys Will Be Boys* when I was a boy. It taught me everything I knew about the activities of the big comics publishers who surrounded Brookgate in those days. At one point I'd wanted to be an artist for the *Eagle*. I recognized Alan Brien, the *Guardian* columnist. I'd illustrated a couple of his books, including the one on the Pakistan/Bengal conflict. I heard him say he was thinking of going in for novel-writing. He was talking to the stately Maeve Gilmore, who somehow, with her fey sadness, her pale gold hair, reminded me of Guinevere after the deaths of Arthur and Lancelot.

Maeve was a famous stunner. Mervyn Peake had drawn her constantly. Dylan Thomas and half the poets in London had been in love with her. Her beauty had blazed out, pure and guileless, against the Blitz. A little distant, dignified, feminine, old-fashioned, she was quietly her own woman. I knew she was a painter. I began to wonder about her work. A few weeks later I would arrange to photograph her and those extraordinary murals she'd painted all over her Drayton Gardens house. Fairy-tale scenes for her grandchildren. Vast playing cards. Darker, more symbolic paintings revealing her own startling agony at Peake's pain. Allegories of loss and desolation, of quiet, catholic hopes. But that night I apologized for not knowing her work, though I recognized her from Peake's poems and drawings. I'd been a bit of a fan of Peake's poetry but wasn't familiar with his fiction, which seemed a bit too monumental for my shallow tastes. I fell in love with her like the others. Someone else asked her about Dylan Thomas. 'He wasn't very trustworthy,' she said.

I've met few women with her elegance. I'm glad I took the photographs. Some years later, when she died, Rex Harrison's wife bought the house and had the murals whitewashed over. And that was that.

Martin Stone was there that year. I think this was his annual meal. Chilli Willi had broken up. He'd stopped gigging, he said, and was dealing. Books. He'd discovered a nose for them. He could spot a rarity with almost supernatural regularity. Martin was never plump, but I've seen meatier skeletons. I was beginning to be afraid he'd disappear altogether one day. But he seemed very happy. He was thinking of getting married, he said. I don't know what came of that. He slipped away early, I think.

About half the guests left after lunch, perhaps in anticipation of how shit-faced the other half were going to get.

As the afternoon continued, those who stayed all got slowly, cheerfully stoned until everything became a flowing, wonderful, dense memory of scents, sights and personalities, sharply defined faces emerging from a magic carpet of furniture, fabric, clothing, people and voices.

At one point I, Rosie and Johnny were all talking intensely. I can't remember anything about it. I know I wanted to ask her more about Kim. The child was too old to be hers. But I couldn't get the chance. They were hardly ever apart. The kid would join in any conversation that interested her. I was beginning to enjoy the bafflement on the faces of guys who thought they'd scored with a tasty young thing. But she was never in any danger. We were all stoned blind by that time, which was rare for Rosie and almost unheard of for Johnny now that he was a responsible captain of finance. Johnny was telling Rosie how he loved her and would do anything for her. How he loved me and would look after me in spite of myself. I think he genuinely meant it. We didn't just represent his softer side – we were all there was of it. He'd begun to talk of his dreams of utopia, of a world run by a council of wise people who represented the interests of everyone. 'But not heavily ruled. I mean, small government and low taxes every time.'

We'd sobered up sufficiently when Tubby turned down the gaslights until all we could see were the winking screens, the yellow and green eyes, the spots of living light, like stars.

'Pards! It's time to set the Old Man dancing.'

We cheered and we felt a bit queer in our bones.

Some of the guests only came for that legendary dance. Some people were more into that kind of thing than others. Tubby had revived the custom from the first year we took over the Mill. An old, bloody myth. The Jack hadn't always been made of straw. Tubby had discovered the story in one of those obscure Mummery's London histories. Every year, when the place had been Wiccam Hill, in the full moon in the last quarter before Midwinter's Day, the people would light a great fire and burn a man. Usually in effigy. It was a corn king, an Old Man they burned, to ensure a flourishing spring. Later the festival was overtaken by November the Fifth and the burning of poor old Guy Fawkes (or occasionally, still, the Pope). I was one of the few members of the band that never went in for all that mystical crap, but it was running rife in those days and I got to quite enjoy a bit of pagan fun once in a while, if sufficiently primed on a few juicy Thai sticks.

By four o'clock only the hardiest control freak could resist the Mill's vibe, part of which was solid dope fumes. By six o'clock (and after a prearranged phone call to the council) we were getting ready to go outside. At the door we were handed tarry garden torches. It was a misty twilight, with the distant roar of the Thursday-night rush hour, glimpses through watery gaps in winter trees of the diffused yellow lamps and storefronts of Tufnell Park Road.

Eventually we were all standing around the dark bulk of the Mill like shivering extras in some bloody James Whale horror film. Then from above, in the gloom, we heard the groan of chains, the crunching of old machinery. Something up there creaked. A door opened and spilled light on to the shadowy gallery below, which began to squeak and judder. I thought I heard a high, despairing whimper and then, from almost directly over my head, a huge black shape fell. I thought it would crush us all when it stopped suddenly in mid-air and began to thrash and shriek as if in severe pain.

It was the Jack. I was shaken by his threatening features. He hated us. Others saw that face now. There was a murmuring, but no loud voices. People were genuinely caught up in the scene.

Vibrations. Rattling. Tubby had opened up the Mill's big overhead loading doors. Now, with running lines, he unhooked a massive link and, from the Mill's crown, swung out the elaborate wrought-iron hoist. The dark shape was dangling from the hoist, outlined like a gallows against the rising moon. It was the bulky figure of a hanged man, turning slowly and smelling strongly of spirits. It looked nasty and real.

Johnny made a nervous joke about how Tubby had excelled himself this year and found an answer to the homeless problem. Not that we had much of a homeless problem, of course, in 1981. Not in comparison. The thatchers had only just started to get busy.

In the light of the residual glow on the horizon and the slowly rising moon, we saw now that this was a well-made creature of straw and wicker, a solidly woven figure with elongated limbs and twig-like fingers and toes; a wicked, threatening glare from beneath mossy brows. He was a convincing woodmantle in an old felt hat, his poor, rooty face more like a pissed-off Wurzel Gummidge than the sinister Golem.

The Old Man was the business as far as the witching trade was concerned. He was made for Tubby every year by Randy Sandy, the Witch of Holloway, who used to have a shop in Kentish Town Road until BBIC ran their new scheme through. Her old name for her creature was 'The Jack'. It's what they called him near Wokingham, where she was born. They were supposed to be able to bring them to life down there. Until this century it was a local cottage industry. Jacks. Dollies. Wax manikins. Darkmen.

Sandy hadn't been able to get to Tubby's party herself. There was a significant witch conference in the West Country that whole week.

Tubby had long since lost any interest in Wiccam Hill and the London mysteries, but he kept the annual ceremony running anyway. If he hadn't organized it, someone else would have. He said he didn't think he could stand the idea of a bunch of barmy crusties stomping about in his front garden.

Now the Old Man's swung out overhead and begins to turn slowly. As if under his own volition. To cast his dying curses at every one of us. Then Mandy and Co were making us widen our circle and telling us to be careful with our flambeaux because here comes Tubby, a rotund druid, still in his hat, with some kind of wide-nozzled gun in his hand.

We fall back.

One shot of red fire and the Jack's dancing in his harness. He's alive with copper, emerald and golden flames. As he burns he grows in substance, rather than diminishing. He's huge!

Born to burn, that boy. Jack's been lovingly made throughout the seasons of the year, bit by bit, stitch by stitch, stick by stick, weave by weave, plant by plant, through the whole year, spell by spell, conscientiously obeying strict rules of magic, just for this one night.

This wasn't your ordinary druidic folly. Not your crusty Camelotic do-what, straight out of a bad British horror picture. Call it crap, as I usually did, but this was a careful piece of considered witchery, faithfully obeying ritualistic actions taken at exact hours, in exact days and months, mostly by moonlight, to prepare the ingredients, to weave the willow and the corn, to produce this simulacrum, this greenjack. This Power. This Old Man.

Now, under Tubby's guidance, we lifted our torches and touched them to the Jack. And the Jack touched them back. In our hands the brands became alive and agitated. Hot, unpredictable.

The Old Man's our year. Our gains and our losses. Everything we've consumed until this moment. All our sins, our pleasures and our unfulfilled yearnings. Our brute dreams, too. Our evil thoughts. He's also our promise of another chance. Jack died loudly and reluctantly that year, cackling and crying to us, whining out his pain, seething his torments, begging for an end even as he skipped and pirouetted in the air like a mad harlequin. He had enjoyed an extraordinary year, but he wasn't the bravest Jack we'd had. While he danced, we danced with him, round and round the Mill, our torches rising and falling like a manic sea.

Then Tubby's discarded his gun and has his black cowhide drum under his arm, his fingers coaxing deep growling notes, threatening, ecstatic notes, throbbing, visceral notes. Notes to make you empty your bowels. Notes to make you want to fuck yourself. And climb up your own spine all the way to heaven. Oh, Tubby's drum was irresistible. It moved your guts and soul at the same time. It made you sick. It changed the nature of reality. Ancient music. Organic music. You could feel the whole hill shake itself and come to life. Magic music, to make all this the true world and all that, so distant now, an unsteady dream.

Dum dum dum dum dum. Subtly at first, but then with increasing effect, thanks to Randy Sandy's expert craft, the herbs began to cook inside the Old Man. Gradually we were engulfed by an atmosphere almost as powerful as the one we'd left inside. Yet this was like getting a faceful of the roasting, fecund womb of Mother Earth herself. It was everything that lived. Every beast and flower. A distillation of the planet, turned into an atmospheric soup, the essence of the world. You breathed it in as you danced, whether you wanted to or not.

Above us the flames flickered, then faded. It seemed the corn man wore only a few fluttering washed-out rags. Then his finery flared again. Into fresh, new colour. His feet and hands began to move in time to the unremitting drum. And I swear he whistled a tune. He seemed to be cheering up. His cares had been burned away. Old Jack wasn't your average Guy. And this wasn't your average firework night. We were dancing on the edge of time.

There was a subtle change in the drum's voice. The Old Man's arms jerked and flapped, his legs jigged, his head moved from side to side and

I'll swear that for one horrible second I saw his cold, doomed eyes, oozing with something like blood, staring into mine.

A heavy body struck me so hard I fell off-balance. My assailant cried 'Fuggin' clumsy bugger' and danced by, a portly, sweating dervish in a camel-hair coat, his torch all over the place. Tootsie wasn't holding himself back. I took advantage of the interruption. I should have carried a camera. I stood in the shadow, with my back to the Mill's brick, the Jack burning and singing above me. I watched the others dancing by. Tubby led them, his drum encouraging no rest. Some, like Maeve Gilmore, had the happy air of parents joining in a children's game. Johnny Lydon was either constipated or bored. Jocky Papadakis seemed utterly traumatized, totally terrified. Yet nobody tried to break from the circle. Nobody put down their torch and everyone went on dancing. Rosie and Kim were thoroughly into the whole thing, as were most of the women, though Flo Fortnum turned her heel so was hopping erratically and getting in the way of the others. They had a proper, covenly look to them. Even the severe ones, with blonde hair, black suits and AIDS bows, looked right. But some of the men, in their formal weeds and clerical overcoats, had the hopeless, desperate air of cabinet ministers caught on Clapham Common with their trousers round their ankles, watching their car and briefcase disappear with their partner of the evening.

Johnny Begg, of course, was used to the whole ceremony, though he hadn't been to a Thanksgiving party in years. He danced carefully, perfectly, in an almost exemplary way, as if he had set out to learn all the moves before he turned up. Maybe he had.

Bobby MacMillan was dancing with him, as if she, too, had rehearsed this before she came. She was rather elegant. Like a Belgravian hostess doing a folk dance. Her legs in that tight black dress were clones of Cyd Charisse's in *Silk Stockings*, which I'd watched eighteen times on French-language TV for a week in Marrakech when I was eleven, getting a free holiday (but precious little pocket money) while my uncle Charlie Cops Cornell used me as an innocent cover for a dope run (all my toys were carved out of blocks of black). I'd fallen in love with Cyd. That movie had a disproportionate effect on my sex life.

I could smell Bobby every time she went by. The fecund odours of the Old Man actually complemented her own sophisticated stink. I could smell her through him. I had a notion she and the Jack might be about to copulate.

Bobby caught the vibe. Whirling by, she was the only one who saw me resting there. I think she winked. She certainly smiled. I had a feeling she was going to slip me her phone number, if she got the chance. My natural mate. A super-air-hostess. Oh, calamity! Half of me prayed that I never saw her again. The other half was already reaching for her body under the sheets. How is it a man can survive junk, crack and all the other minor narcotics, including nicotine and booze, and yet always fucking succumb to those dangerous glands?

I didn't care what happened to me because the moment was too good to waste and it was lasting forever. I was drunk on sex and fire and ancient blood, on custom and familiar grotesquery, on friendship and a sense of frozen time. It seemed that the Mill was a node, right at the centre of a whole variance of time streams. Past and future converged here even as the machinery high above began to shriek and mutter, rumble and moan, and suddenly the whole top of the Mill was vibrating, powered by the motor Tubby had long ago installed, turning slowly, as her sails had once turned her, moving the hoist. Jack swung wildly, mindlessly. His legs and arms were miraculously uncharred, his blackened face still sporting a manic grin as his innards flared with a spectrum of darting flame while snakes of amber, turquoise and silver wove a chaotic robe around his agonized roots.

The next time Johnny came round, his face was seraphic. He was genuinely enjoying himself. For some reason this cheered me even more. To see something human in him. Rosie went by and I stepped casually in beside her and took her hand. She was as delighted as I was. Then Kim took my other hand and we danced on. Rosie was casting the spell she hoped would ensure us at least the illusion of fulfilment in the year to come. We secretly hoped it wasn't a dance of death.

Slowly the fire fades, our steps grow heavy.

Gradually the dance ends, the Jack becomes black dust and it's over.

We're all momentarily surprised, hoping for meaning.

'Do well, pards. Do good!'

Tubby waves as his guests begin to head down the hill. Some of them are excited. Some are embarrassed. Jocky Papadakis is running as if the Fenris wolf is on his tail. Most are heading for the bus stop or their parked cars.

The last I saw of Maddy, she was going through the outer gate with Tootsie. I must admit I was a little relieved. Those two were soulmates. I had a feeling they married at some point later, for a little while. Or that could have been his brother. I lost touch. Flo had gone home in a taxi.

I arranged to see Rosie and Kim for lunch the next day, embraced everyone who was still there, and got a lift home with Johnny and Bobby in her nippy little Porsche. She dropped me off at the top of Fogg Yard, even though I told her it would be all right to let me out at Holborn. 'What a sweet house,' she said, when Johnny pointed mine out. 'You're like a snug little hobbit in there, I bet. Cosy! Peter Pan and Wendy.'

'No Wendy,' I said. 'At the moment.'

It's amazing how the love of power goes hand in hand with the power of love. Or, at least, banal sentimentality.

Bobby found out what a pit my Never-Never Land Wendy House actually was about an hour later when she came back. She didn't care.

She'd exhausted her sentimental vein, she said. Did I mind if she didn't smile much for a bit?

'I'd had enough of Barbsie for one day. Anyway, he needs an early night.'

'What?' I said.

Which was about all I did say for a while.

The music goes round and round. The world turns. The plot twists.

The end of a perfect party. An unlikely but welcome liaison. A sense of belonging to something. Of having friends.

It was all downhill after that.

CHAPTER FOURTEEN
The Queen

Speedballing was always my weakness. And I always got into it when at my most depressed. Which was usually at Christmas. And Christmas 1981 by anyone's standards was a righteous bummer. One to escape and delete. If we'd had PCs in those days at least I might have found someone equally miserable at Scrooge dot net, so instead I phoned my mum, who was in the 'quiet ward' in Bethlehem Mental. There was a lot of cackling and hooting in the background. I think that was mostly the nurses who were off their sedatives so they could drink. She said they were having ever such a good time. She let out some kind of yelp. Oo-er, she said. She had a present for me. She'd give it to me when I came later. I said I'd be down to see her as soon as I got off the job I was on.

'Are you coming to take me home?' That was a button I'd hoped she wouldn't press.

'See you soon, Mum,' I said. 'See you soon.'

This in turn made me feel guilty about Flicky. Was it my fault she was spending the hols down at Viv Stanshall's horrible houseboat with Calvert? The writing had been on the wall for months. You can tell a relationship is coming to an end when your partner actually contradicts or questions everything you ever say. Like, 'Did you post that letter to the DHSS?' and you say 'Yes,' and they say 'Are you sure?' and you say 'Yes, I put it in the box as soon as I left this morning,' and they say 'Only because if you haven't . . .' You say 'Looks like the sun's coming out' and they say 'No, it isn't,' even as the rays hit them full in the face. Well, that's how it was with Flicky. She blocked every chance of a conversation. So in the end I'd given up and let it all run downhill, even though I knew I could probably save it if I tried; but what would that be worth? Another month and back to 'No, it isn't' and 'Are you sure?' This has more to do with their anxieties than my being a congenital liar.

I'm too lazy to be a liar. If a lie's working in my favour I might sometimes not bother to counter it, but otherwise it involves too much time and energy with the follow-ups. So, for purely practical reasons, I rarely tell a deliberate porky. Even to slip through some self-important wanker's special Forbidden Zone.

So it starts to get up my nose when, as far as the person you're sharing your life with is concerned, you are in constant need of cross-examination by a team of top QCs just to find out if it was you who forgot to change the toilet-paper roll that morning. It's a sure sign that someone wants to write you out of their script. And I couldn't blame her for that. I'd been shit to live with for months. I'd become used to working on my own and the strain of rehearsing and interacting had all been taken out on Felicity. Once again I discovered, to my psychic cost, that I really am a loner. I'm a good team worker, but it drags everything out of me. I feel threatened. I don't get enough time on my own. When I get home I don't want a relationship. I don't even want a fuck. Even to prove I'm not fucking anyone else. I suppose she had every reason to throw up all her mental defences, however unconsciously. Going off with Calvert, who made the average egomaniac seem like *Snow White*'s Bashful, was probably not her best option.

I stayed in bed, smoking some nice grass, but then I had to get up because the smack and the coke were in the fridge. I did a couple of lines and turned on the V. Jingle bells and holly. Like a 24-hour *Playschool* run by paedophiles. A couple more – smack to the right nostril, coke to the left – and I was ready for Her Majesty.

The Queen's speech was very vowelly and regal in those days, my hearing enhanced by some medium-strength acid, and when she said 'People in all walks of life – whether soldiers, policemen or nurses' (soldeahs, pleesmen or narsus), I was moved to tears and found myself bonding with the entire British Commonwealth. It was like the last scene from *Nineteen Eighty-Four*. I was weeping with love for Big Brother. After that, depression set in and I lived *Crime and Punishment* for what seemed the whole time the book usually took to read. Watching some God-awful remake of some God-awful TV original took up another thousand years, but it was a drop in the bucket of infinity. My recollection is that I was trapped in a candy-pink gas cloud with *Benny Hill*, *Are You Being Served?* and *The Monkees* on perpetual rerun. I watched Cilla Black and Tom Jones for at least a couple of millennia. And no normal brain can take that without snapping.

I went under for the third go when *Disneytime* hit the Winnie-the-Pooh spot. Groo. If anyone ever wants to put kids off drugs, make them watch Dumbo and the crows in *Seen An Elephant Fly* on a combination of junk, coke, Thai sticks and a tab of matured Marin County 4X acid washed down with some cans of Newcastle Brown and a pint or two of Wild Turkey and Jack Daniels. If they survive, they'll never take so much as a junior aspirin without shuddering. *Kubla Khan? Opium Eater?* Things have come on a bit since the Lake District Loadies' Club. We've expanded the limits of human tolerance in almost every direction. My guess is that our metabolism adapts readily to most drugs we care to chuck down us, so it doesn't really matter what drugs we do. We are helping the process of evolution. Our children will thank us. Our bodies will absorb the new information and make use of it. With some drugs, I'll admit, the adjustment takes longer than the average lifetime. But eventually it'll all be speeded up electronically.

Anyway, that was my logic as I pushed back the frontiers of human endurance, all but incapable of movement and having lost the will to punch the OFF button on the V control when Dick Van Dyke began his traditional cockneyoid grotesque. I was drowning in self-pity whose transparent banality filled me with further self-disgust. Which naturally increased the self-pity. Self-conscious, moi? What is this stuff, anyway? Oo-er, guv'nor, ain't that the baby cryin'?

That's Baby all right. Baby's all the shit you really should have dumped by now but somehow haven't. Baby gets jealous. Baby gets vindictive. Baby gets tantrums. And just then, not far from the surface, Baby Dennis was howling his soul out. Baby wanted to be heard by everyone in London.

Poor Baby. All alone at Christmas and not one fucking phone call. Poor Baby. Make Baby feel better. Suck, Baby. Yum, yum. This called for some maudlin opium inhalation, rolling the ball, priming the pipe and puzzling out the complexities of a Hayley Mills movie. Then came the nightmares and then there were the bad nightmares. Baby stops crying. Flash. All those starving eyes. All those jumbled joints, those piles of mangled dead, the abandoned faces of all the stiffs in all the fucking wars and all the cruel disasters of the last decade. Flash. Huddled women. Flash. Running women. Flash. Wailing women. Flash. Raped women. Flash. Stunned women. Flash. Shaking women. Flash. Falling women. Flash. Dead women. Flash. Rotting women. Flash. Tiny girls whose lives you could save if you had one useful fucking thing in your fucking bag that wasn't a fucking lens. Another thousand years. Flash. Pop stars pretended to fuck themselves on stage. Flash. Film stars describe the psychic scars suffered by being photographed fucking on holiday. Flash. Michael Jackson takes another fucking cut to the face. Flash. Scars, bones, red fucking flesh, miscellaneous body parts. Dismembered Africa. Fucking Africa.

I settled my arse comfortably on the edge of the abyss and looked down into the darkness, into the gravity that sooner or later had to overcome me. Demographically it could only get worse. If 25 per cent of people in the world are actively vicious and 25 per cent are actively altruistic, that leaves the other more or less passive 50 per cent who tend, on the whole, to get roped in by the bastard side. So it isn't your imagination. There are actually more evil bastards in the world. And they're doing their best to kill the rest of us off. I still don't know how to identify them, let alone suggest how to stop them. 12 October 1999.

The six billionth human being was born. So that's a billion and a half absolute bastards right there.

It's bound to get worse and worse. Because the evil bastards are also the ones doing all the active damage, who have the simple needs. *We*'re the ones who said they'd never shell Dubrovnik. I think what infuriates and drives them is the knowledge that they're not quite Cro-Magnon. Not like us. Remember they found that half-breed in Portugal, proving Cro-Magnon had married Neanderthal and could breed. We didn't kill them off. We absorbed them. They're the 25 per cent of full-strength evolutionary *huis clos*. Dead-end genes. The N-gene. N for Neanderthal. They know their brains don't work properly. Why shouldn't they want to destroy us and all we've built? I still thought it would be funny to turn them into pet food. Something made me laugh, anyway. Then it was bleak for a bit. I watched the stars of various soap operas do vaguely lewd acts in panto cross-dress. Cat Whittington and his Dick. Little Boy Blue sat on Little Bo Peep's Pussy. Slap those thighs. Wink those eyes. Bold Robin Pud. 'And what's your name, my strapping fellow?' 'John Thomas Little.' 'Then I shall call you Little John Th—'. Oo-er. What a carry-on. Morecambe and Wise. Perry Como. And other institutions.

Still nobody phoned. How could I blame them? I was a turd.

But I was a proud turd. I wouldn't phone them, either.

The truth was that people always thought I had an incredible time – a glamorous rock-and-roller like me – wine, women and wacky baccy! Every fucking day, mate! Glug, glug. Pant, pant. Puff, puff. They knew that if I wasn't fucking I was fixing. What I wasn't licking I was loading. If I wasn't enjoying unguessable ecstasy with a model I was bonking a basketful of beautiful groupies. I had that kind of image. I never encouraged it but I gave up discouraging it after a while. If they thought about it for five seconds they'd realize most models are untouchably fragile and bonking one is a bit like humping your Great-Aunt Matilda's most delicate whatnot. It's sometimes a relief but it's never relaxing. And most groupies look like Lips Lewinsky. With differing thicknesses of mascara. You have to be heavily into funny underwear to get the most out of girls like that.

Actually, I have a feeling that just then I was everyone's fantasy life. People were always disappointed when they came to Fogg Yard for the first time and discovered this poky little slum house with a back window looking over gravestones covered in brambles, crisp bags and pages of the *Sun* that had been read, used to wrap chips in, thrown away and pissed on by more than one drunk. On the other side, the nondescript brick wall with its wired-up window could have been a warehouse as easily as a church. Apart from the dates on the papers and the logos on the Mars wrappers, you could have been a hundred years in the past, only the house now had its own plumbing. Photo crap everywhere. Bedroom made into a darkroom. Books shoulder high, six deep. Filthy old fifties armchairs, velvet curtains, nice fireplace, pictures on every possible surface. Piles of ancient correspondence. The kitchen was usually tidy and everything clean because that was what I did when I should have been working. That was their second surprise, the kitchen. Not that I was a gourmet chef. Just heavily into cleaning agents. I'm always trying out some new kind of toilet duck.

That Christmas Day I ate five one-pound jars of Sainsbury's sweet mince and a two-pound jar of Tesco's Big Value marmalade. I ate a variety pack of Marks and Spencers Chicken Drummers and I would have eaten a five-pound Harrods plum pudding but I forgot about it and it fused with the bowl I'd been boiling it in. I'd assumed the cloth was linen, the bowl was china and the pudding real fruit. So I ate a tin of cranberry sauce to make up for the disappointment. And did a few more lines.

I was maudlin about Rosie as usual. And I was beginning to tell myself what a wanker I was for not persuading Kim to stay for Christmas. We could have still had it at the Café Royal. But it was all regrets that particular year.

I'd taken Rosie and Kim to Heathrow the night before. Put them on the plane for Paris. We'd been going to do the whole Café Royal experience. In the Grill Room. Plush. Gilt. Mirrors. Carolling waiters. She'd asked me to cancel it. I said why didn't I come and spend Christmas with them in Begat, but Rosie said I knew it was an emergency. She would be taking a Royal Air Maroc flight to Marrakesh, then a UN turboprop over the Atlas and down into the territory of the Berber S'r'wi who were trying to hang on to their tribal homelands against the usual Maghrebi interests.

There'd been a nasty little three-sided war a few years earlier, which I'd covered briefly for the few people interested because nobody else wanted the work and I was trying to get taken seriously. I hadn't spent any time in Begat, the region's only city. Now it had some UN monitors and a bunch of agencies, coordinated by Rosie, who were trying to help the region set itself up for independence. The country was coveted for its strategic position rather than for any wealth and had a pretty good idea of its place in the world. It was now effectively united in its willingness to back a guy called Ibram-al-Rikh' (ironically, the 'Sand-storm'), a charismatic strategist who had brought the tribes together without resorting to religiosity. I'd seen him once, taken some pix, but like the blue-veiled Tuareg he never showed his face. Always wore gloves. They said he was badly disfigured from leprosy, but that didn't explain his weird eyes.

The Berber S'r'wi trusted him and he was the only guy who could really bring stability to the region and establish its nationhood. For some mysterious domestic reason of their own the Americans had thrown one of their spanners in the works at the UN and everything had slowed down. The S'r'wi began getting itchy trigger fingers. Sheikh al-Rikh' could probably keep them together, but wasn't sure he wanted to. He needed reassurance. He needed to have plans of his own to offer his tribal leaders. Rosie could give him the background and let him know how she thought things were going to go. She'd tell him the truth. At that stage she really believed that faith, transparency, respect and honest debate could move mountains. She could convince him to try legal strategies, to be patient. She could give him her ideas of the odds. It wasn't a job you could delegate. She said Kim could stay with me while she was gone. She seemed to want me to persuade Kim, who was, I gathered, a high-maintenance health responsibility and better off over here, but Kim definitely didn't like the idea. Neither did I. I mean, she might have been my kid. I hadn't been able to find out much. And she freaked me. I couldn't help myself. I was the kind of person who debated the moral problems of owning a goldfish. Though I'd come to think a lot of her.

Rosie and I had managed to have lunch a couple of times, but Kim had been there too, so we hadn't talked about much personal stuff. It was almost impossible to believe the child wasn't a bright teenager. You couldn't help responding to her as if she was a young adult. You had to stop yourself asking her if she wanted a drink. All your senses told you she was older. She had the bearing and body. I would have suspected some kind of complicated wind-up by Rosie, but it wasn't her style. It was only at the end of that second lunch that I could really accept that Kim was ten. It was her enthusiasms – ponies, ballet, dollies – that made her convincing. While Rosie was paying the bill I got a very serious lecture on why the Appaloosa was prettier than the Palomino and why people who said the Palomino was prettier were really really stupid. It made her a lot easier to like. If you didn't know better, those uncertain silences of hers were snottiness. Of course, it wasn't her maturity that confused her. It was the world that was confused. Rosie had raised the child in her mould. Kim was self-confident, curious, adventurous. But she was often baffled by the world's responses to her. It treated her partly as an equal, partly as a monster, partly as some kind of Erdegeist. When all she was was a nice little girl who felt a bit isolated at her Swiss boarding school.

I'd never talked to kids or animals in any tone other than my usual one, and they seem to like that. So we got on well. But it wouldn't have been right to pump her. She did know Begat, though, and had probably been born there. She spoke Arabic casually, as well as French. A chip off the old block, I thought. However long I'd known Rosie, I could never get over that aquiline beauty.

Eventually I saw Rosie on her own for a drink in The Shakespeare, Westbourne Grove, which was near where she stayed when she was in London. She told me about Kim. The kid had some kind of inherited disease that rapidly accelerated her lifespan, brought her swiftly to maturity and would kill her before she was thirty. Except Kim wasn't likely to make anything like that distance. She was also HIV positive. In fact, that HIV virus could have activated her condition, which was rare and didn't always develop. Drugs kept her more or less healthy, but you could never say when her entire system would turn on itself and kill her. It could happen in a day.

'Jesus Christ!' Rosie was telling me all this at a tiny table in a crowded corner. Two Jamaicans were arm-wrestling immediately behind me. I could barely get my pint to my lips. 'And the dad?'

Rosie sneered at me. 'Does it matter who her fucking parents are?'

'I don't know,' I said. 'It seems to, yeah.'

'Well,' she said, 'there's something in me doesn't want to make that clear, even to you.'

'And what the fuck does that mean?'

'It means I'm disappointed in you, Den. Sometimes all you are is blokeish ego.'

'And you're defensive,' I said. 'I don't get it, Rosie.'

She took what I said as a fair rebuke. She shrugged. 'Okay, Den. It's how I want it, OK?'

'She's clearly your kid,' I said. 'I mean, really . . .'

This got her huffy again. 'Great. Then what more do you need to be told?'

I was sorry I'd put her on the spot but I wasn't used to her blocking me like that. She was straight as a die normally. We'd never had to have important secrets. Just around Kim. It seemed crazy of her not to trust me of all people.

'Well, it's not like you,' I said. 'Not between us.'

'No, I know.' She started that stuff with her bag. I asked her about the weather in Begat.

So I never found out how the kid got HIV.

Boxing Day morning I made it round to Noreen and Alan Chang's all-nite chippy in Bonemeal Passage and not only was it closed, it had been shut down for months. Noreen and Alan had fulfilled their dream and retired to New Zealand. They probably had the best chippy in Christchurch by now. Up to Liquerpond Street and even Morrie Singh's Bombay Beef Kebab stall was closed in celebration of the Saviour's birthday. So I had a reluctant pint and bought a carton of fat-free milk off Beefy Walsh, landlord of the Queen and Country, inevitably, gloomily, defiantly open for me, the only customer. He'd driven most of his regulars away by trying to recruit them to the anti-European cause. The place was full of Union Jacks. Red, white and blue tinsel. I wished him a Merry Christmas.

He was only about thirty, with a massive aura of auburn hair, pasty skin, scowling in permanent dismay out of a narrow, inbred head. He wore a clashing England football shirt and he pulled my pint with angry solemnity as if he was crowning an unpopular monarch. 'Yeah,' he said. 'All right.'

A week earlier his wife had run off with their solicitor. A day later the brewery had told him to stop using the pub as a political campaign headquarters or he'd never get another house from them. And the Friday before Christmas he'd been told he had to go into Clerkenwell General for exploratory surgery. He always was a sour bastard and this news hadn't done a lot for his attitude. He eventually noticed what Christmas Day had done to my face. 'Something wrong, Den?' he asked hopefully. 'Wife thrown you out?'

'Run off with a wanker,' I said. 'Good riddance.'

Beefy began to whistle.

But it was Rosie I was missing. I didn't even finish the pint. I seemed to have hit one of those abstinence days. Drugs of any kind weren't welcome. The body knows when it's beat.

And the body was also telling me what it needed to restore itself. I had to get down to Ray's for the full English with double everything and do my best to wipe the last drop of egg off the plate before I drank my last mug of tea.

What can I say? I have an unsophisticated body.

It was the right sort of weather for suicide. Grey skies, grey streets, grey buildings, slushing rain, a bitter wind blowing from the east. Christmas Day is never as grey as a bad Boxing Day. Christmas, you think everyone's inside enjoying themselves. There's a tradition of at least interior warmth. The churches look bright and warm. But Boxing Day's public. You can see the truth. There are just enough miserable people on the streets to make it feel solidly desolate. A bored boy limping beside a new bike. An old bag lady pushing her trolley down the deserted length of High Holborn. In those days people didn't graze giant consumer fields in their free time. They had arguments, fucked, darned socks and made model aeroplanes. Or walked about the streets in sodden anoraks, looking in the windows of closed shops, wondering about the sales. Or visited relatives. Or went to watch rugby.

Half an hour of being out in that and I was already beginning to feel better.

Damp weather's meat and drink to a Londoner like me. Grey moisture's our natural habitat. It offers that gloomy solace which actually revives something in you and keeps you going. It's crucial nourishment. Without it you start to shrivel.

As soon as I reached Staples Inn on the other side of Holborn my spirits improved. A solitary taxi went by and soaked my right leg. As good as cheap sex. The edgy drone of the approaching diesel engine, the swash of water as it hit the puddle, the swipe as the water hit me, the swift hiss as the cab disappeared round the corner into Chancery Lane:

it all did something to my soul. A kind of positive bleakness increased with every step I took in the direction of Seven Dials. I crossed Kingsway, walked down towards Drury Lane and the Opera House, but turned into Little Wild Street and was relieved to see a light shining from Snatcher's Island. A stone's throw from Covent Garden, Snatcher's was at that time still a bizarre holdover from the reign of Charles the First, and a total eyesore or a picturesque ruin, depending on how you valued the land it stood on. Potentially one of the most valuable bits of ground in London and, like Brookgate with her Leases, nobody could buy it or build on it, which was why half the houses were permanently shored up with a mixture of wooden and metal scaffolding added over centuries and some of it was fenced off from public view. A tumble of bad brick, hard black beams and shingle that smelled of the solid filth of centuries, a deep, antique stink. People of my age remember it mainly as a squatters' warren where you wouldn't want to stay overnight, not because it was particularly dangerous but because it had no city services, no running water, no gas or electricity and was a breeding ground for crabs, fleas and bedbugs. Mostly inhabited by anarchist squatters, the rickety houses formed an inner court full of electrical and mechanical junk. Early in the morning, when they still had the big public WCs on the road island in front of the Shaftesbury, where *Hair* was playing forever, you saw the Snatcher's queuing to use the toilets and washbasins. There was no point in trying to get a pee there until at least ten a.m. And you might as well go down to Leicester Square any time you wanted a crap.

Snatcher's was technically foreign soil. It was probably the last patch of London not an embassy that had that privilege. It had been a sanctuary for petty thieves since the days of the Great Fire and a slum since Drury Lane grew famous as the haunt of whores and actors. It was supposedly built on ground owned by the Queen of Paphos, bought by her, according to Steele in the *Tatler* (26 July 1707), 'before the days of Christianity'. But it was owned by the Duchy of Crete. The notorious Duchess of Crete, a Romanian, had her embassy here towards the end of Elizabeth's rein. The Duchy passed via various European bluebloods to the princes of Wäldenstein, which became part of Czechoslovakia after 1918 and part of Germany until 1945; the legal tangle around the ownership made Jardine and Jardine's most protracted cases seem swift. A case had been running in Mirenburg for years. The Czechs were attempting to get a clear deed so that they could then tear the place down and build a skyscraper on it. The rents on that alone would probably double the country's income. But the whole thing was as impenetrably tangled as the Island itself. It had been named after the pickpockets – wipe-snatchers – who ran here to escape the law. Jonathan Wild and his famous Bow Street Runners besieged the place for a year once, without much outcome. With the cloud low and the drizzle filtering everything, the dilapidated walls could have been a scene out of one of those 1940s English movies, with James Mason dying somewhere inside.

Ray's was a gourmet greasy spoon. He had at least a dozen distinctive kinds of grease, every one of them delicious. And the All-Day Full English had most of them on it – perfect free-range fried eggs, crisp fried bread, best back bacon, tomatoes straight off the vine, fresh portobello mushrooms, Savoy black pudding sent specially from Manchester, tasty baked beans, Fourmantel's Carlisle pork bangers, Trevithick's Cornish butter. If you can think of it, Ray had it. These days he'd be in every restaurant guide in the world, but that was before a mania for populism blew the whistle on our secrets. The only people who went to Ray's were people you didn't mind rubbing shoulders with. Mostly people doing work in the area. A bunch of regulars – a few actors, writers and stuff – but Ray's was best known as a hang-out for jazz musicians. That's where Tubby got fat. It's where he got most of his best jokes. Ronnie Scott had one of the darkest senses of humour of his generation (which could be why the poor bastard killed himself). Mildred Bailey. Humphrey Lyttelton. Cleo Laine. Ivy Benson. Johnny Dankworth. Kitty Kallen. King Oliver. All the American guys over on tour. As a kid, I was in there when the entire Duke Ellington band came to try one of Ray's famous specials, Sweetbreads and Roast. Jack Trevor Story introduced me to Billy Strayhorn. Jack told Billy he wouldn't find better chitterlings anywhere. And he should know. He'd started life as a butcher's boy. Jack was playing with the Swingliners at night and writing scripts for Frankie Vaughan during the day. *These Dangerous Years, The Trouble With Harry, Live Now, Pay Later*. Music, films or books, Jack put phrases into the language as fast as other people pinched them. *Snatch the Snatch* wasn't one of them, but it was the Swingliners' popular finale number. They play it at every revival. All the big band buffs remember it. But Jack's favourite was *Ray's Tripe*. There wasn't a sliver of offal Ray couldn't turn into a religious moment. If he liked you.

I never recommended the place to anyone. You had to be introduced if you wanted a chance at Ray's grade one treatment. People wandering in casually got a perfectly adequate grade two meal and left wondering what all the fuss was about. Which was how Ray seemed to want it. A few appreciative bons vivants, rather than mere customers. And Ray's All-Day Full English was what earned him his steady reputation. As Somerset Maugham said, it's nonsense to say you can't eat a decent meal in Britain. You can eat one three times a day, seven days a week, so long as it's breakfast. And, of course, if you have a constitution that can take it. Which I had. Check out my medical.

Snatcher's Island through the drizzle looked a bit like a wreck that had just erupted from the seabed and dumped itself on shore. Its dark, unwholesome timbers were festooned with mysterious weeds and lichens, rotten ropes and tarpaulins. There were even a few gulls today, driven inland by the foul weather. Miscellaneous bits of roof, timber, chimneys, walls and scaffolding made mysterious shadows, sudden shafts of grey light in which an occasional figure moved. Ray's yellow lamps might have come from the cabin where the drowned captain had your articles waiting for you. Once you'd signed them, the whole monstrous hulk would take you back to the bottom. Doomed to navigate the depths for eternity.

I pushed open the door. As usual a V was up behind the counter, running some soundless rugger game, and Ray had his back to you, controlling his huge stove with conscious style. Every flip of his skillet was a little bit of perfect choreography. Each red formica table had its squeezee bottles of brown sauce and tomato ketchup, piccalilli, Worcester sauce, and vinegar, and shakers of pepper, salt, sugar, almost all empty. Today he had no real business, which was unusual for Ray's. No builders, of course. Just actors. His usual trade was done between six a.m. and six p.m. He didn't cook dinners. Breakfast, lunch, tea and what he called high tea. And then he went home to Fulham where he had a nice little house overlooking the Bishop's Park. Nobody had ever met his wife, who we suspected was really another bloke, though Ray always referred to him as 'my other half' or 'the ball and chain'. He'd been a cook in the navy and we guessed the person we always referred to politely as 'Mrs Ray' was a shipmate.

'Wotcher, Den.' He didn't turn. He could see me in the steamy mirror over his deep-fry. 'Thought you'd be somewhere warm this time of year.'

'That's why I'm here, Ray. Nowhere else to go. Couldn't stay away from your breakfasts.' I spoke to his reflected, glowing bald head. He wore a tight black T-shirt, tight jeans, a blue-and-white-striped apron. His muscular arms were all tattoos, most of them terrible. When he turned, his little bright blue eyes were grave in kind, prissy features.

'You say that,' he said, 'but you'd be surprised.' He never had known how to take a compliment.

'Indigestion city here.' A familiar voice.

I hadn't seen him there at first, but I knew that droll face well, glittering up at me with a mixture of wariness and good will. Freddie Earlle, the low comedian. Jimmy Durante with irony. Who had been in *Roads to Freedom*. And therefore could do no wrong. 'This food's killing me.' His Glaswegian accent always thickened when he was joking. As a result people didn't realize he was being friendly and he'd been punched more than once for trying to flatter someone.

'How are you, buddy?' He got up and opened his arms to hug me. He was a dapper little devil in a sharp tweed overcoat and a snug red scarf almost up to his mighty nose. I was fond of the bastard. I'd met him when he was doing a job in Germany, a Holocaust presentation, and he'd been brilliant. He was always at his best when he was performing in line with his own politics. But he could be touchy and, while he should have been doing Brecht at the Tricycle, I had a guess that he was working the season in the West End. He hated leaving home unless he had to and he wouldn't have been here today if he wasn't going to do a matinée somewhere nearby. 'Theatre Royal,' he said before I asked. 'Fucking Cinderella.'

'What? On stage? Harlequin O, *Calcutta!* It'll run and run. Do we get to see you in the buff?'

'Shut up. I'm the comic. I'm a funny copper. Tommy Trinder's the other one.'

'Bloody hell,' I said, 'what is it, the all-wheelchair production?'

'Tommy's as fit as a flea, the bastard.'

'I wasn't thinking of Tommy.'

Something in Ray's brought this kind of banter out of the most laconic customer. It was probably the musicians setting the tone. If you're touring a lot in cramped transport and dressing rooms it can be the only safe way of letting off steam. It's gallows humour with those old jazz men. Someone told me how Ronnie Scott had done his back in once but wanted to go to the funeral of one of his best mates. The other old jazzers were all there at the cemetery. Ronnie had only been able to make it by lying down on a board in his station wagon. His mate Humphrey Lyttelton looked into the car after the service. 'Blimey, Ronnie,' he said, 'are you sure it's worth you going home?'

Freddie was finishing up his kidneys and bubble. He was doing an early show. He'd hurt his back taking a pratfall two nights ago. His wife had insisted he keep working. 'God, I hate Christmas,' he said. He had a big family and they were always glad for him to be doing something over the holidays. 'What's up with you, pal?'

I thought I'd tell him about Flicky. He was often a sympathetic ear, even if he never really heard a word you said. He should have been a confessor. Then he looked at his watch, yelled at Ray to chalk it up, he'd be in tomorrow, and told me to phone him soon. He got to the front door and stopped suddenly, his eyes opening wide as he saw someone he recognized. Then, with theatrical gravity and a vicious bow, he opened the door for his old enemy and ex-partner, Norrie Stripling. Tiny, dapper, frosty antagonists.

'Thanks so much, dear. I'm sorry I haven't any change for you.' Norrie swept his eyes pointedly towards me. 'Morning, Denny, dear. How's Mum?'

I didn't hear Freddie's retort. He was off into the flushing grey, a warm shadow heading up to Drury Lane and his first call. I was relieved I didn't have to talk to them both. It was always a bit awkward. They had been a double act briefly in a series of successful little thrillers one of the Boultings had done in the early sixties. Black and white. The usual Ealing rep cast. If the faces weren't familiar, you felt uneasy.

By the time the formula had arrived at *Carry On Lowest Common Denominator* it was as strict as kabuki. You never see those earlier black-and-white movies these days, even on telly, but they're full of actors who seem to have been around since the start of the century. Before they became stereotypes. Cardew Robinson. Terry-Thomas. Peter Sellers. Spike Milligan. Kathleen Harrison. Jack Watling. Bonar Colleano. Quite a few of them were written by Jack Story, mostly Frankie Vaughan vehicles, I think, for the Wilcox production company. Another one had Anthony Newley in it. And Adam Faith. Marty Feldman.

I watched everything that ever came on late-night or afternoon telly. It wasn't just a fascination with an alien culture, when we had our own film industry. I studied those movies the way a Mexican might study Mayans. They promised clues to my obscured and revised past. Most of the films were B-movies. What they called quota pictures, because British cinemas in those days had to show at least a portion of home-grown stuff. Made around the time I was born, when there was still an Empire market.

It's another world. It looks safer, though I know it wasn't. They were just less likely to show the truth. You really don't see so many scarred faces in Brixton these days. Almost all white blokes. I was in Soho at the end of that era. If you didn't have a scar nobody took you seriously. Yet even the Teddy Boys seem charming, compared to modern yobs, though I know some people couldn't walk down Balham High Street in the 1950s without getting their clothes slashed and I've heard what it was like in Fulham or Notting Hill then. Nothing but confrontation. Flick knives. Cut-throat razors. Coal hammers. Bike chains. Stilettos. Broken bottles. They didn't have our sophisticated attitudes but they were just as good at violence.

Maybe it was worse then than now, but not as bad as it had been. I don't know. My fascination with the period was obviously to do with the fact that I had a dead dad and a mental mum. One I couldn't ask about his world and the other I couldn't trust her answers. Mum had a set of personal myths, elaborate fictions, so anything she told me had to be adapted to fit her invented plots and anecdotes. Which caused her to get a bit funny sometimes, even downright belligerent if she was having trouble fitting an unlikely anecdote into an appropriate time slot.

I know she'd told someone that my dad was killed in the Battle of Britain, but she'd dropped that when even she couldn't explain the dates. She'd turned him into a heroic older brother. She had more characters and story lines running than *EastEnders* and *All My Children* put together. Though the result was more like a Mel Brooks comedy. She could have been another Carla Lane, if she'd been a shade less barmy. And to some extent the barminess was my dad's fault. I guessed she was really ashamed of what she felt she'd caused, though she was certain of one thing. She'd always thought Gordon McAllister was slimy and the idea of sleeping with him made her sick.

But there was something else there occasionally: a hint of guilt? She was too fly for me. She dodged off that as soon as she got within a mile of it. I might yet find out the truth before she talked herself into the grave.

Maybe she still wondered if somehow she'd led him on, at least enough for my dad to get jealous. Maybe she over-responded to the bloke because she didn't like him. Smiled too much, maybe. It was hard to separate it all out now. She had moments of coherence but the more coherent her memories were, the quicker she ran away from them. It was easier to patch a picture together for myself, talking to relatives, neighbours, checking family documents, watching old movies. And it was easier for her to make up a romantic fantasy, though her adherence to her own particular vision of the world was what got her into the bin from time to time. She was inclined to insist on her version, sometimes emphatically, and regard anyone who contradicted her as a mortal enemy.

Mum was in the bin now because she'd taken issue with her next-door neighbour over the matter of whether Dame Edith Evans was dead or not. My mother insisted she had dined with her at the Café Royal only the previous week. That's when Dame Edith had given her the tip about Steve Davis and the snooker. She found her neighbour's insistence threatening and had decided there was a murder involved. She'd called the police. Which was probably the best thing she could have done. They knew her well enough to get the doctor in. Instinctively, she knew when she needed to recoup. She signed herself into Bethlehem.

Norrie was sorry to hear all this. He told me to keep my chin up.

Norrie was also working in the West End. Strictly speaking it was the South Bank. He was playing his classic Baroness Bonnybuns in the National's *Puss in Boots*, a wonderful full-scale Victorian revival, with lush, rich costumes, lots of red plush and blue velvet and gold tassels, designed by Agnes Trigvisdotter, the Icelandic wizard, following one of the original scenarios and keeping all the original parts. Simon Russell Beale. Elaine Stritch. Judi Dench. Mel Smith. Glenda Jackson. Antony Sher. Transformation scenes. Big heads. Freddie's panto wasn't much more than a string of tired variety acts, minor TV stars, with Freddie and Tommy Trinder keeping some kind of professional life in it, leading the sing-songs and the look-behind-you routines, but Norrie was doing the class show, which in those days had massive public funding and paid off a treat. Freddie could have been doing his Dan Leno act if he hadn't been so touchy and refused to work with Norrie.

I told Norrie my tale of woe. He said that what I needed was a good Boxing Day dogfight. He got some tickets out of his wallet and offered me them. 'It's your lucky dog, Dennis. Son of Gnasher the Bold. Nine o'clock tonight. Put a fiver on him.'

I told Norrie that watching a variety of belligerent, crazed, hungry mastiffs tearing one another to hamburger meat was probably not going to lift me out of my angst. He raised an eyebrow. Hoity-toity. I felt like a prick even as the words came out of my mouth. 'Well, take them anyway, dear. Real death can work wonders for one's anxiety. I can't use them. This job's wearing me out. I shan't be doing it much longer. The address is in the envelope. It's a pub on the Isle of Dogs. The Lady Jane Grey. Big ring at the back.'

In those days I'd lost interest in blood sports. It was before I'd done all those photos in Bosnia and Rwanda and became addicted to death. Might as well get the most out of it. I said I appreciated the thought. Norrie heard a familiar jingle from the telly. 'Oh, it's the news,' he said. 'Good.' He turned away from his liver and brains to look. 'Isn't that a picture of your Rosie?'

'No,' I said. 'She hates going on telly.'

It was a still picture. A bunch of library shots. Begat. S'r'wi tribesmen.

As it dawned on me what was happening my first thought was how glad I was I'd had my breakfast. I shuddered. Ray didn't need me to ask. He turned the sound up.

The UN plane from Marrakesh had gone down somewhere in the Far Atlas, as it was beginning its descent towards Begat, the region's only city and the only civil airstrip, on the edge of the Sahara. There'd been some radio contact. A forced landing rather than a crash, but no real information, except to say that the area was threatened with 'instability' and that the hills were full of 'S'r'wi fighters'. Rescue operations were already under way. The S'r'wis wouldn't accept help from French, Algerian or Moroccan teams.

I got Ray to lend me his phone. I talked to every picture editor I could contact. I needed to convince someone that I was the best guy to express out there. I told them Rosie was my sister. The editors kept calling the S'r'wis 'the Arabs'. I told them I knew 'the Arabs', that I'd already interviewed their leader. Two hours later I was on my way to Marrakesh with a planeload of Thomson tourists singing 'Roll out the barrel' and 'Maybe it's because I'm a Londoner' and advising me to cheer up, it might never happen. Only it had happened.

In Marrakesh I had a pre-arranged liaison with the French press blokes. *Libération. L'Actuelle. Paris-Match. Le Figaro.* We were ferried out to a plane that looked like an unsuccessful prototype of something Hitler had hoped to fling against the Allies as a last resort. It had five propellers, only two of which seemed to be working, and a very nice line in electric blue and white fifties streamlining, but we were reassured when we were met by a UN Press Attaché, who spoke American with a Dutch accent and amiably persuaded us all efforts were being concentrated on our behalf. Although hostage-taking hadn't become epidemic in 1981, we all had the Iranian hostages well in our minds. They'd been released less than a year earlier. Ibram-al-Rikh' was no Ayatollah, but he was a super-strategist. He knew how to take advantage of a situation.

There was still no information about the passengers. Then *Libération* turned up lucky for me. Their guy was called Jean-Luc Fromental, a journo who lived in Les Hivers, who I knew from the Café Terminal when I was covering the student riots of the early seventies. He arrived late. I had the feeling he'd grabbed the tailplane and stopped the aircraft. He was the biggest human being I'd ever met. His head, frowning amiably, blocked out the light. He had massive dark eyebrows, a huge square skull. He looked like the sort of guy Mussolini would send round to your country to show he meant business. You had the feeling he was nicknamed *Il Brutto* in Genoa or had held the Vatican Palace on his back while they did necessary repair work. When he spoke, smoke poured from his mouth. He stank of the little Indian bidis he constantly chained.

'God, man, it's fucking good to see you.' His hand engulfed mine, warm, with that habitual gentleness you associate with animals careful not to make casual use of their strength. He had to be six foot six and he was wearing the biggest leather trenchcoat the world had ever seen. It was from the First World War. It looked tank-proof. He was about the only human being with a frame capable of carrying it. It should have been in the Guinness Book of Records. When he died, it would go on display at the Louvre, like those famous suits of armour made for giants.

There was something massively comforting about him in that coat, perhaps because of his instinctive recognition of our physical difference. He was like a mammoth. He'd always been bigger than anyone else. You knew you were safe with him, that he might hit someone on your behalf, and he might get a bit out of control sometimes, but he was never going to hit you. And for people of average height or less like me this offered a rare sense of security. It was a natural alliance. I patted gratefully at all that leather. I made room for him. I offered him my reefer. 'How's it going?' He sat down beside me with a great sigh. He accepted the reefer and blew mournfully on it. 'God, man!' We had a lot in common. A lot to talk about. Also he helped me get my awful French into some kind of shape. We spoke back and forth in both languages. Both of us were rusty. Catching up. Our jobs. Our mothers. Our wives. Our frustrations. Then he brought me up to date on Begat.

It passed the time and kept me from going totally out of my box with anxiety. Rosie was in danger. It could have been the first time I thought of Rosie as being unable to handle something, as being vulnerable. I'd always assumed Rosie could take on the world and win. But out there her chances were bad. By now she could be injured, captured or a lot worse.

I told Fromental I'd found the S'r'wi Berbers courteous and not characteristically predatory. He shrugged. They were seasonal nomads, living in permanent settlements for parts of the year. Grazing the semi-desert for the rest of the time. Herders. Occasionally, in their history, they'd rustled a few camels or wiped out a rival clan but, in their distant past, they'd ruled a great interior empire, from Timbuktu to the Near Atlas. Their horsemen were still famous. They had sent their chivalry against the invading crusaders and defended Mecca and Jerusalem. This past was as fresh to them as their exploits against the al-Glowie clan, who had ruled most of Morocco in alliance with the French until the 1950s. The French had never defeated the S'r'wi Rif. In fact the S'r'wi Rif had never been defeated. Their legends told how they had driven the Romans back across the Mediterranean.

Those were the people I'd photographed. Today, of course, they could be just another gang of disinherited peasants, furious at how cheaply they had sold their souls to the West and a lot more anxious to get their hands on a pair of RayBans or an AK-47 than the vote. It never took long to convert most people in the world to some form of consumerism.

Fromental was obsessed with the place. He'd done a couple of books on it. He wrote thrillers with a shrink called Landon and most of them were to do with the region's politics.

The French had the same romance with North Africa that Britain had with India. The conqueror's affection for the conquered. And they're always upset by their former colonies' failures to meet their romantic orientalist ideas.

Fromental was more of a realist. The kind of frog who clings to the truth like a Jack Russell to a rat. You can't beat those bastards at their best. Something to do with their brand of Catholicism, I suppose. His father had served as military governor of the region for the few years that it was a French protectorate. Jean-Luc had been born in Begat and thought of the place as home, he said. 'Which is ridiculous, but that's what it's like for children of empire like us, isn't it?' Certainly the S'r'wis weren't going to welcome him back to his birthplace like a long-lost brother. Very confusing. He complimented me on my grass. 'It's American, isn't it? You can't get anything like that over here.'

The ride grew bumpy the moment we left Marrakesh, her red walls and green palmeries merging with the sharp white peaks of the surrounding mountains. I loathe flying but I thought there could be worse places to die. It's a city with few surviving monuments. Built around the same time as the Tower of London, razed to the ground with every dynastic change, with a nice old bookseller's mosque and her famous Square of the Dead, best known for a vastly overpriced and vulgar hotel, Le Mammounian, her beauty is of a piece, it comes out of the work and the ordinary houses and the antiquity, the commerce, good humour and casual cruelty that characterizes every tasty city. I'd spent a surprising amount of time there, usually with Rosie, and would normally have looked up the odd friend. But the only S'r'wi Berber I knew was running the Sony concession in Rue de Voltaire in the modern district, which they still called the French City, and could give you a very nice price on a VCR but wasn't often in touch with the old homelands.

Fromental admired al-Rikh', who'd been educated in Paris, Mirenburg and Berkeley. 'He knows how to play the big guys off. Morocco and Algeria. France. Spain. But it's a very difficult game, yes? And these days there are a lot of people who see the Ayatollah kicking ass in Iran. So they think they'll get themselves a few useful Nazrani hostages, too. Take on the big guys. Earn some points. Get some prestige. Show the fucking UN who they're dealing with. That fucking plane could just have fallen into someone's lap, man.'

'The S'r'wis always struck me as being pretty reasonable, smart people,' I said.

He looked at me with contempt. 'Noble savages? People are people, man. Circumstances change them. Some circumstances are better than others. Some times more people are reasonable than at others. Come on, man. Context. Context. When were you last there?'

I took his point. The frustrations and aspirations were universal. So were the attempts to make something positive of those frustrations. And so was the anger when, against all the efforts, some distant political decision turned to foolish nonsense all you'd ever worked for. 'Most people aren't normally violent, Den. God, but you know, neither will most people confront violence or examine the nature of violence. They ignore it or romanticize it or try to legislate it out of fucking existence. But sooner or later, man, most people get involved in violence and hurt by violence, whether it's in the London Blitz, Vietnam or Rwanda. You know. It's the fucking truth, man.'

After that the conversation got less coherent. During their stopover, the *Actuelle* guys and a Czech photog who'd blagged a lift had loaded up with executive-class Sultan's Reserve, the blackest, richest hash you've ever inhaled, and while the little prop plane was thrown all over the sky in one of the most terrifying thunderstorms I've ever been in, we were telling Belgian jokes, sucking on bongs and making happy references to lost horizons. At one point the cabin was so thick with smoke and bits of smouldering dope, I thought we had to be on fire. There were a couple of tight-arsed UN Swedes up in the front seats who gave us those frosty smiles which is their arctic version of stabbing you ten times in the body and cutting out your eyes before throwing bits of you to their dogs. They refused our pipes, cigarettes and bottles with fastidious bonhomie, like Ken Starr being offered a cure for his constipation.

We were stretching their training to destruction, I think. The cooler and stiffer they got, the happier it made us. We started telling Swede jokes. There's nothing like a Swede for a straight man.

I was glad to be travelling with the frogs. By and large French journos are a jollier bunch than the bifs and a lot more adaptable. And they know their territory. It turned out I was the only bif in the entire operation. Nobody from TV. They were having a hard time finding crews to work on Boxing Day. I'd made an arrangement with the World Service guy in Rabat to do some audio for the BBC if anything developed before they could get there.

Naturally, being from *Libération*, Fromental was all politics. At some point I stopped being able to follow him. The upshot didn't sound very promising. 'They've nothing to bargain with,' he said. 'And now America's in the game, they have even less. Poor bastards. What are they likely to get for a few hostages? It might be more economical – more satisfying, anyway – to finish them off.'

I thought I heard something snap. The plane began to fall suddenly, like a broken elevator. I hit my head on the luggage compartment, grabbed at my harness, fell in Jean-Luc's lap and threw up into my seat. The lights went out. Another lurch put me squarely back in my own vomit. The lights wavered back on.

Jean-Luc was a vast nanny, dabbing at me with tiny bits of Kleenex. 'You OK, man?' His concern was almost comical. It was his charm. Nanny Bluto. I tried to kiss him, but he held me at arm's length, like in a cartoon. He stood up and his face disappeared somewhere overhead. As the plane continued to buck like a mad steer, he made his way up the aisle towards the toilet, bracing his shoulders against the roof of the plane whenever it hit another air pocket. He was the only human being I knew who could have done it. People started applauding him. His progress towards the toilet became a famous epic, told wherever there are journalists and bars.

He admitted later he was terrified, but anything was better than sitting next to me in that condition. He came back a bit later with some water, disinfectant and a roll of paper towels. I must have stunk, but hash always blocks my sinuses, so I couldn't smell a thing.

When we were through the worst of the storm and could actually see the white crags of the Far Atlas below us, he got me to the toilet and I cleaned myself up properly. There weren't any attendants on the plane, only officials and two old Free French pilots. No hot water. No soap. We did our best with the mess and changed seats.

I spent the rest of the trip with my belt on, pretending to be asleep, while Fromental's colleagues made the usual jokes about the dignity of the biftecks. Fucking frogs will always take advantage of a decent Englishman. It's not our fault we have more sensitive stomachs than they do. My grandad told me why it is. 'It's all that grease they eat,' he told me. 'And snails and reptiles.' Their problem was they didn't get enough fish and chips. Any time he had a bad stomach he'd settle it with some corned beef or a nice bit of fish. He reckoned it was the iodine. I thought it was probably the vinegar. I don't think it could have been the chips. But there's no doubt about it, whatever country you find yourself in, they all have a magic food cure that would kill anyone with the same condition in another part of the world. You tell me how that works. Acid stomach? A can of Heinz tomato soup, two slices of Hovis. Fixes you right up. They're not antidotes as such. They don't have a lot of nourishment, probably. But they're perfect anti-stress agents. Americans are forever pouring Coca-Cola down them, the way the Irish do Guinness. Doctors recommend it for everything. My friend Bonfiglioli reckoned whisky and milk did the trick for him. Flicky always went for tuna salad. Mostly it's some form of nursery food. Cheaper than nurses. Feel good. Get better. Two medium-boiled eggs and ten brown-toast soldiers can cure most cancers and we all know what chicken soup can do for the common cold. A can of Crosse and Blackwell baked beans once pulled an entire family through an outbreak of cholera in East Bengal.

I started to fancy baked beans on toast. It was the dope.

Which was pathetic.

I knew I wasn't likely to find a can of beans when I got to Begat. In fact, there wouldn't be much in the way of shops. And I could forget about bacon. And probably eggs. Not a chip for a thousand miles. Not a potato. A lot of mutton. A lot of goat. From now on it was going to be all tajines and roasts and mysterious couscous, if I was lucky. I began to remember what it was like. I could easily get used to it. Great grub at its best. I was salivating. Then I had a thought. Maybe I was salivating for nothing. Then I felt like a bastard. I just couldn't remember if the Begati people were starving or not. It was easy to get confused between needs and causes, between small, beleaguered countries and refugees. A tide here, a tide there. Displacement on displacement. Everyone running to the guns or from the guns. Taking revenge. Digging their own graves.

I was too ashamed of myself to ask anyone how Begat was. I decided to wait until we arrived and find out for myself.

I'd been right to fear the worst. They didn't have any fresh eggs in Begat when we got there. The Germans had eaten all the chickens.

The place was even poorer than I remembered. As the plane came down into glaring sunlight a herd of skeletal, long-necked camels scattered awkwardly in front of us. Then we started making dust and you could hardly see a thing. A few straggly palms. Some dead ornamental shrubs at the end of the runway. The crew wouldn't let us off until the dust had settled. We stepped down the bouncing ramp into ninety degrees, trying to dab the grains out of our already swollen eyes. I prayed there wouldn't be a sandstorm. It was getting very close to sandstorm season.

The Swedes and the other UN people separated themselves as soon as they could, taking a blue and white jeep across the strip to a single-storey building flying the green and black flag of Begat with a big, beautiful sign in modern calligraphy telling us that this was Begat International Airport. Let God smile upon us and peace remain with us.

I had half a suspicion that the Swedes had asked the authorities to keep us suffering in the sun for a little while. Waving goodbye, the pilots walked slowly towards the admin building. I took my collapsible panama out of my pocket. It was filthy. I couldn't remember what I'd last used it for. Something to do with a car. I put it on anyway.

A team of munchkins in overalls came running from round the corner and began to push the plane back the way they had come. I recognized it from this angle. It was one of those O'Bean machines. The guy had turned out weird aeroplanes the way Boeing turned out dull ones. The thing looked like it had taken the beating I'd feared it had taken. It was pitted and dented all over.

We stood on the sticky tarmac, with our equipment scattered about our feet, trying to stay upright unsupported, until a *Le Monde*-chartered Mercedes bus that looked as if it had been taken off the Munich–Nuremberg route in 1926 arrived to drive us a bone-shaking mile to the hotel. Le Grand. Which wasn't that different in size and general amenities to those places off Praed Street the whores used. Places where you got a discount if you stayed the full night. Paradoxically it was bulging with German tourists, in bright white shorts and with Pentaxes round their necks, complaining that nobody was helping them. The sad little lobby was piled with equipment boxes. Sound technicians were testing their stuff on the Germans. 'Tell me, Frau Plumenfumpf, how long is it since you asked for a plumber to look at your potty?'

Hand-wringing managerial flunkies, most of them smooth, round-faced young men from Agadir in lightweight suits, bowing and scraping. A little bobbing of scarlet tarbooshes from God knows where. Maybe the waiters' uniforms. Police? Everybody was sorry. Everyone had different explanations. It was this. It was that. It was being attended to. Nobody had any news. Phones weren't working properly and someone was waiting for a part for his transmitter. This was in pre-digital days. Satellite links were special features. No cell phones. No laptops. Primitive times, pards. TV crews were still using film. Flying it physically to Paris and processing en route. They could do it in record time. Employed a lot of people.

Fromental knew somebody. He got us a private duplex in a little guest house at the back. No lines to the outside world but the internal phones worked and they were still doing room service. Particularly if you were evidently a favoured customer. And a good tipper. There was some pleasure in enjoying cooling drinks and eating a reasonable *croque monsieur*, looking through the shades at those smooth, pink thighs, those precisely tied Reeboks, those glittering buttons, those beer-nurtured faces growing redder and redder as they marched about in the sun waiting for whoever it was someone had told them was in charge. I think they were on a package and had come from Ouarzazate. They'd been caught up in events. The S'r'wi had closed the roads. This was supposed to have been a picturesque overnight stop, not the entire two weeks! Where was the swimming pool? The sunbeds weren't out. I had a suspicion they couldn't have paid much for this holiday.

Fromental had lost it at last. He was mumbling something about his proud forefathers. Who I understood to be opera singers. I left him sleeping and went to see if the missionaries were still here. Begat had a population of about three thousand but it was an old, walled city with no real streets, just narrow alleys between houses, and it would be easy to get lost. I saw a bunch of boys watching me as I came out of the hotel into the small square they had called the Place des Internationales in the hope of attracting a foreign dollar or two. Hotel and square were the entire tourist industry in Begat. I had a feeling their resources were already overstretched.

The boys didn't swarm, the way they did in Marrakesh. Their parents could keep a better eye on them in Begat and S'r'wi Berbers are a bit touchy about their kids shaming them by appearing to beg. But a leggy little brown-eyed urchin in a ragged grey jersey and a pair of Manchester United sweat pants came running over when I signalled. He spoke good French, a bit of English and a suspicious amount of Swedish. I think he doubled as a catamite at weekends. We negotiated a deal. He got me to the mission on time and was more than happy when I paid him with a five-dollar bill.

I was beginning to understand what Fromental had been saying. When I was last in Begat the streets were full of flashy horsemen with customized Lee Enfields and Martinis, glittering burnouses and raw, red gold bracelets glaring in the sun and the only money they'd accept was sovereigns or Turkish silver. Now there were UN vehicles all over the place, trying to negotiate passages crowded with camels, donkeys, old men carrying vast burdens, handcarts, mule-carts, mopeds, herds of sheep, goats, brilliantly dressed locals. Few Berbers veiled, so the full chador you saw further south, in Arab Morocco, wasn't fashionable here at all. These people dressed very colourfully, more like Bengalis. But their clothes were in bad shape. Still very easy on the eye, a lot of them. They had handsome, aquiline features, pale dark-ivory skins, chestnut hair, green eyes and looked a lot like Rosie. They might have come originally from Egypt. But that beauty was marred by quite a few pockmarks, general signs of untreated diseases, rheumy eyes, cracked lips. Scabs. They were going downhill. Bad nutrition. Bad healthcare.

The mission's front door was like every other door in the little street. No crosses. No Latin. Just a name in Arabic. His door was painted sky blue. Presumably it was where the missionary lived, where he held services and so on. I wasn't sure how you handled a Christian mission in these parts.

Father Riche reassured me. He was a slender man in his mid-forties, with dark grey hair, heavy glasses, square, leather-tanned face, a downturn to his lips that gave him a weary, disapproving appearance. He wore an old linen jacket, a T-shirt advertising *The Whole Earth Catalogue*, sagging jeans. I was reminded of one of those sad, white-faced clowns. He was unhappy with events here, but in the outlying regions the tribal people were still amongst the healthiest in the world. Still full of integrity, he said. 'It's just here. With the situation. The Europeans . . .'

Begat, since it became a UN protectorate, had actually got wealthier. Permanent officials had brought local jobs. Trade had improved. People bought second-hand cars. Fuel came down the old military road from Ouarzazate, via the UN and also, so he'd heard, on camelback from Libya. Cans of refined petrol crossing the old Saharan trade routes. He didn't really believe it. 'The evaporation,' he said. 'But it comes from somewhere. Cheaper than water, they tell me.'

This was in the days when in Begat a Catholic priest still had some kind of respect amongst ordinary Muslims, especially if he was seen to be working on behalf of the people. But he was getting an increasing number of threats. 'I don't intend to stand against them. If they do not wish to have Christ in their country we must wait until they come eventually to Christ and we'll pray for their souls until then.' He winked. 'As they pray for ours.'

Rosie had told me about Father Riche. He was one of those old-fashioned lefty Catholics who do all that heroic stuff in South America. I said I thought he had a fair chance of being murdered here, if he carried on. Wasn't he worried? He smiled a little bit. He'd made a pact with God, he said, that he would not become a martyr. 'God knows I don't hold with martyrdom.' The first sign of real trouble, he told me, and I'd see him on the newsreel, waving Begat goodbye from the door of an ascending Sikorski. 'But I'm fairly effective. I think I have a few friends, even. So I haven't packed my crucifix yet.'

He hadn't received any hint of what had happened to Rosie's plane. He took me out into the little courtyard where a couple of scrawny black cats nosed about in the dry dust of a disused fountain. Hollow windows looked down on us from all sides.

'But Rosie knows these people as well as anyone could. They won't hurt her.' A surprisingly fat, unconvincing chuckle from such a slim man. 'She knows how to appeal to Berber chivalry, if nothing else.'

'They could be tenderly bringing her in on a stretcher slung between two camels,' I said, 'and covering her with prayers and poultices. But that doesn't mean she hasn't got internal injuries or whatever. I'm not saying the plane's fallen into the hands of the Evil One. I'd just like to know how the passengers are.'

Father Riche started to nod. He couldn't offer me much. But if I was going to be stuck here for some time, he could give me a decent game of chess, he said.

I opened his door for myself.

I asked him to let me know if he got any news on the grapevine.

In the guest house Fromental was snoring so vigorously I half-expected to see the roof rising and falling, like in a Tex Avery cartoon. While I'd been away he'd showered and changed and now lay across his bed wearing a colossal Bugs Bunny nightshirt. He'd been listening to a tinny shortwave radio whose aerial he'd stretched around the little living room in what he'd determined was best for ultimate reception. He woke up suddenly and nodded at me, rubbing his eyes, looking around the room, and went back to his radio. He could understand the Arabic but made me shut up while he listened. 'It's real information, man.' He'd tuned in to some official channel.

'They've found the plane.'

I think he was listening to helicopters or something because he couldn't make out much more for a while, then he lost the signal altogether. 'I don't know, man. They didn't seem to find any passengers. No bodies. So is that good?'

I asked what he thought about going into the hills on our own account. Getting to the crash scene first.

'There's only one road. The old French road. It was bad in my dad's day and I don't think anyone's worked on it since. It's falling apart. We'd be better off on horses.'

Man Mountain Fromental on a horse wasn't easy to imagine. The locals were tiny and wiry. Their ponies were pretty much in proportion. Finding him something he could ride without his feet dragging along the ground would be a bit like trying to find a bike for Gulliver in Lilliput. He needed an elephant. 'We'll hire a good jeep or something that flies,' I said. 'We'll get Hoffmann to fly it for us. He's got a licence.'

He didn't think Hoffmann, who was then working for *Le Temps*, was willing to go that far for what wasn't likely to be much of a scoop. And who was going to pay for it? Assuming we could find one. I was going mad. He began to wind up his aerial. For all we knew, someone was bringing Rosie, Kim and Co back to Begat and we'd see them, safe and sound, in the morning.

What he said made sense but it still took about half an ounce of Sultan's Reserve to get me to sleep. And it took nothing to wake me at dawn the next morning.

The pretty little boy I'd hired the day before was in the room, shaking my arm. 'M'sieu. M'sieu.'

He'd come from Father Riche. Father Riche had some urgent news for me.

I hoped it wasn't to do with chess.

Fromental woke up as I was leaving. He looked like Bacchus after a bad night in Nymphtown. I told him where I was headed and to go back to sleep. I'd let him know what was happening. The muezzin's calling from the square, blocky sandstone mosque. The dawn streets of Begat are all deep shadows and domestic business as people take advantage of the coolness to get their morning work done. Sheep and goats bleating. Cocks crowing. Pots clanging. Women getting their families up. The boy padding in front of me, never looking back.

His attitude had completely changed. Instead of being cocky and streetwise, he was grave and responsible, as if Father Riche had charged him with a matter of life and death. I prayed it wasn't some bad news about Rosie. We loped through the souk, a weave of light and shade. We went under arches, down conduits, followed the wall for a while and eventually came to the little alley and the mission. The boy banged on the bright blue door but it wasn't immediately opened. He stepped away from it, signing me forward. 'Min fud'luk.' Then a grille was pulled back. A woman's eyes. She opened the door to us. She was tiny, dressed in an ordinary long-sleeved, full-length dress of a local design, but I knew immediately that she was a nun or an ex-nun and that she was screwing Father Riche. Which was a bit of a comfort, for some reason. Small-featured, pale, dark eyes, brunette, a typical bright provincial French finch, who smiled at me apologetically and murmured that she was here because of the circumstances. Father Riche had thought it appropriate. Poor, poor child, she said. She closed and locked the door. Then she led me up the stairs of the house to the roof where, under an awning, a thin foam mattress had been laid. Father Riche stood staring thoughtfully down at the mattress. It was only gradually that I realized someone lay on it. A slender form, hardly denting the surface.

Kim still didn't look her age.

Her little old woman's face was relieved when she saw it was me. 'Hello, Uncle Denny.' The eyes were still those of a child. The skin was yellow, the flesh dry. She had lumps. Two or three pustulating sores. She looked as if she'd been left out in the sun for a year. When I'd put her on the Air France plane she'd been lively, healthy, undoomed.

'A tribesman brought her in an hour or two ago. He knew nothing of the plane but had been given the girl by a cousin. He had been told to take her while it was still dark to the mission. He understood the orders to come from al-Rikh'. But the child tells me the others are all well. Probably prisoners.'

The woman spoke quietly from behind us. 'There was the note. Evidently the shock of all this accelerated the child's condition. I gather it's not unusual. But, you see, we have no facilities here.'

'I don't want them to send me away,' said Kim. 'I want to stay here until they let Mum go.'

Father Riche sighed. 'The plane's already left. It will eventually bring back supplies. And more planes might come. But . . .'

'There's no chance of my leaving, right?' Kim's spirits improved. 'Don't worry if I look a bit sallow. It's some kind of jaundice. I've been through it before.'

I felt a hint of hope.

'Here's the note,' said the nun.

'Mum said there was a chance you'd get here.' Kim's voice was frail but assured. 'The note's just about my condition and that. I have this disease and I need special medication. You can only get it on prescription.'

'We'd better find someone with a radio,' I said. 'Do you know if any of the medicines on this list are available here?'

'We can ask at the hospital,' said Father Riche. 'I wonder, Barbara . . .'

She took the list from my hand. She folded it carefully and fitted it into a bracelet.

She began to descend. 'Ten minutes.'

'Impossible without her.' Father Riche looked up at me from his lowered head. He seemed to think he owed me an explanation. 'But what do you think? Are these the consolations of the wilderness? Or do we seek the wilderness for her consolations?'

I'd brought my camera with me. I knew what Kim's little face would mean in terms of the sympathy and money it might be possible to generate for the S'r'wis. I felt like a traitor when I asked her if she'd mind me taking a couple of shots.

'I'd rather you didn't, Uncle Denny. My eyes hurt. That sort of thing always makes me uncomfortable.'

'Me, too,' I said.

When Sister Barbara came back she brought a couple of battered Tintin and Asterix books. She also brought several Libyan pharmaceutical boxes. The labels were in Arabic and French. I had a feeling these weren't the crucial drugs. But it was something.

'I told the hospital she was a journalist.' Sister Barbara looked to Father Riche for approval. 'They're radioing for the supplies, but we will have to pay. They insist on francs or dollars. Is that all right? And a doctor might have to see her.'

'I think a doctor had better see her right away.' I started to come to my senses. The kid was in terrible shape. There were UN doctors here. Surely Rosie hadn't persuaded their captors to release Kim just so the little girl could die on a roof in Begat? I knew that no strategy of Rosie's would involve sacrificing a child, especially her own. My guess was the message had been garbled by the people who had brought her here.

'Exactly.' She was deeply relieved. 'I'll go back now. I'll bring someone.'

Father Riche began that rapid nodding of his.

I gave Kim the doses they recommended on the packets. She told me what she needed. No doctor came. I read her *Tintin and the Magic Cup* until she fell asleep. Eventually, at about three in the afternoon, an off-duty nurse came by. When she understood the situation she acted quickly. Within an hour, Kim was in an isolation room in the local hospital, a long, single-storey building with red crescents painted all over it. I was with her the whole time and for most of it she was conscious, asking after Rosie, wanting me to read to her a little more. Sister Barbara stayed until it began to grow dark and then she had to leave.

The nurse brought back a Turkish doctor who apologized for knowing so little about Kim's condition. He examined her with a respectful tenderness and gave her a couple of injections. He assured me he had wired for the supplies. They had to come from Switzerland. It was all right if I stayed with her. He got me a bottle of Vichy water.

She never really woke up. At one point her breathing sounded like speech and I strained to hear what she was saying, but it was impossible. She was dead before dawn.

I sat beside her mattress tearing the Tintin book into little pieces.

I wasn't looking forward any more to seeing Rosie.

I took some pictures. I used my whole roll. I wasn't hurting or betraying her. These were for me. Maybe for Rosie. They weren't for anyone else to look at. I just wanted to remember her. I've never known such grief. It threatened my sanity. I couldn't stand it. I didn't know how to handle it.

By the time al-Rikh' had gone public and was telling us his terms for the return of the hostages, I was back in the awkward arms of Jean-Luc Fromental, crying like a schoolgirl while his huge hands thumped at my back and he grumbled angry helpless words of comfort.

I wish to fuck I'd never taken those pictures.

CHAPTER FIFTEEN
The King

I don't know who it was had brought the tape recorder, but what began as Elvis Presley soon started sounding like an Algerian funeral lament as the batteries ran down. Fromental went across the courtyard for a few minutes and when he came back the noise had stopped. A little while later it was *King Creole* again. At normal speed. Fromental shrugged. 'I gave him some, you know, *piles*.' He hadn't said much since the kid's death. He hardly knew what to do with himself. At one point we went up on to the roof of the hotel and I took some shots of released hostages coming in. Rosie wasn't with them. She was one of four left behind, all senior UN people.

There were a few injured, but they'd been well cared for and they were all pretty cheerful. They seemed to be under the impression that the S'r'wi Rif had rescued them. Fromental went and did a couple of interviews. He was only gone for an hour or two. 'Lousy copy,' he said. 'These people are full of praise for al-Rikh' and his guys. They think they'd be dead if he hadn't come along. That's a five-minute happy story. I'm here for the politics. I need a new angle.'

'My sister's still out there,' I said.

'Tell me about her.'

I'd been crying anyway. It didn't make a lot of difference now. I spoke of Rosie's incredible dedication, her controlled, positive anger, her sense of urgency, her intelligence and her sublime common sense. I told him about all the projects to help people become self-sufficient, especially women, of the work she'd done round the world. Africa. Asia. South America.

'A saint!' He was chain-smoking bidis again. 'Is she good-looking?'

You can guess why I did it. I showed him a picture.

Four hours later we were cresting a hill, wondering if we were still on the road or whether we were looking at its remains. A ribbon of irregular brick, shale and rock winding through high valleys already touched by those vivid wild flowers that brought so many Victorian botanists to the region. It's the flowers that stop the Far Atlas from being a fairly boring range, reminiscent of the less picturesque parts of the Scottish Highlands.

The region's Berber clans had a lot in common with the Scots. Their equivalent of a single malt was a superb, clean hashish that filled your soul with hope and your body with ease. They didn't break the stuff out for anybody.

'I think they tried to blow it up,' Fromental had an old oil-stained linen map in his left hand, under his thumb on the wheel. A bidi between his fingers. He was wearing a pair of Road Runner shorts and a Wile E. Coyote cotton jacket with the sleeves rolled to the elbow. He kept trying to tune the jeep's radio which we hadn't been able to turn off since we started out. Every so often it uttered a burst of static like distant gunfire echoing around the surrounding crags. The Swedes, still neatly stiff in their harnesses and uniforms, bounced in the back and occasionally exchanged a quiet, significant word. They were pretty sure they were in serious trouble. But since we had claimed to know both the way and the local dialect, they'd reluctantly agreed to let us drive them, the preliminary negotiating team.

Actually, I knew nothing of the S'r'wi Berber dialect, which varied considerably even from the Rif dialects of the High Atlas. But Fromental had grown up here and I counted on the fact that everyone spoke at least a bit of Arabic. We'd had to exaggerate our expertise, just to con the UN guys.

We weren't exactly trying to get Rosie free. Al-Rikh' wanted certain matters put in the fast lane and he was willing to deal with the UN only if Rosie were present and only if Rosie vetted any deal they came up with. We weren't entirely sure if she was there against her will or not. The other passengers seemed to think she and the others had elected to stay, but she might have done a private deal with the Rif.

The radio came on suddenly. Sounded like Oum Kal Thoum. Yearning music for love and the love of God. *Inta al hob*. It is the love. You are the love. You, God, are the love. All the subtle meanings of the most beautiful Arabic in the Middle East. A thousand profound aspects of a single word. And just as the hills were alive with the sound of music Fromental took his attention off the track to look up and drove us straight into a drift so the wheels started wailing over air filled with the sand devils they were spewing up. The noise was hideous. The crags were screaming in reply.

Fromental was almost mindless with self-disgust. 'Oh, fuck, man. Fuck, fuck, fuck. Shit, man, I'm a fucking cunt, right?' He set the engine to idling and thought about it. We got out of the jeep to look at the problem. We could push some rocks down under the wheels and be on our way in minutes. The radio was back to broadcasting static. Then we heard the distant sound of an Arab newsreader. Then silence. Above us, on the rise, a veiled horseman appeared.

Another four hours and our jeep was being towed by four camels as we walked beside it. The UN guys were a little way behind us, moving with well-trained economy. We'd all had a turn on the horse. There were about a dozen veiled Rif with us. The jeep was being towed to save the benzine. We were in the steep, bleak Valley of the Phoor'n which I had never really believed existed, whose secret waters and hidden greenery were legend. Not so green. Brackish water. But it made the Hole-in-the-Wall seem as public as Wembley Stadium and it had never been taken. In the 1930s, Fromental said, a Foreign Legion division had gone to find the valley and never returned. Radio contact was almost impossible even now. As we got further and further in, we trod on bones, stumbled over bits of rusted ironmongery, as if an army had lived and died laying siege to something.

Ahead were tents of black, brown and dark green felt, grazing herds of goats and sheep, horses, camels. It had the air of an ordinary prosperous Saharan market town, all in the shadow of a weird basalt cliff. There was a core of single-storey square buildings but it was from the big black felt tent under the cliff at the edge of the camp that I heard the soft, steady rhythm of Ellington's *Take The A-Train*. Vocal by Mel Torme. '*If you ever want to get to Harlem . . .*'

Ibram-al-Rikh' was definitely here. The Rif chief had the finest collection of swing tapes this side of the South Sahara. When I'd first visited him, one of his first questions was whether I'd met Lambert, Hendricks or Ross. He wasn't by any means a simple man, but he was an enthusiast. He had fond memories of Ronnie Scott's club and that little street down near St-Julien Pauvre – Huchette? – where all the American musicians had played in one tiny bar after another. Jack Teagarden. Thelonius Monk. Davis. Coltrane. When he was a student in Paris he could stand outside and hear all the greats for free. You had to buy a drink if you went inside.

This was all in the interview I did for the *Telegraph* magazine.

I wonder what it is about ambitious politicians. They all need to be soothed by some mouth or other. Hitler had enjoyed nothing but operetta throughout his entire career (while pretending to like Wagner) while Saddam Hussein's extraordinary attempts to get the latest Whitney Houston CD are well-known. Remember Colonel Gadaffi offering that deal to Michael Jackson? And didn't the boss of the *Sendero Luminoso* play Julio Iglesias and Los Tigres del Norte over and over again, or was that in a Nick Shakespeare novel?

I suppose I should have been grateful. I'd read about the poor bastards made to stand around listening to Hitler playing *Der Zarewitsch* and *Das Land des Lächelns* selections day in and day out. I didn't have much against Count Basie or even Bob Wills. And with luck the bloke wouldn't have time to put on his anorak and bore me with the entire discography.

The buildings turned out to be a miscellaneous collection of barracks, stores, offices, a rough-and-ready field hospital. The kid would probably have been better off waiting for us. Then I realized al-Rikh' would never let the helicopters know where he was. So had Kim died to preserve his stronghold's secrecy?

Rosie came out of the black tent pitched in the shadow of the basalt. She looked wrecked. She was wearing a white, dirty djellaba, with the hood covering her head. She had a piece of paper in her hand. She was picking grit out of her tired, beautiful face.

'Hi, Denny. How's Kim?'

'Doing fine,' I said.

I couldn't have lied to her at any other time and got away with it. But I'd rehearsed this.

'Great,' she said. 'I'll tell you, I was more than a bit worried there. The shock, the heat . . . Did she tell you anything?'

'She didn't seem to know much. I read her some Tintin books. She slept a lot. And then the plane came. She'll be in Switzerland by now.' It was the nearest I'd ever come to offering someone the consolations of religion.

'She's a great kid, Den, eh?'

'None better,' I said.

It was a relief to her to be able to put that concern aside for the moment. It was all I could do for her. I doubted that she'd thank me for it.

She didn't suspect me because she wasn't used to me trying to control her. What's the ethical consensus on that one? All I did was delay a moment. The sort of thing you can only get away with once and even then it wasn't certain she'd be deceived by me. We were usually telepathic.

I think she believed I'd kept Kim alive. When she hugged me I felt as if I'd swallowed razorblades. Just fucking great. Then she was telling me what I could and couldn't photograph and suggested if Fromental wanted an interview he might as well do it after the preliminary negotiations were sorted. He was hovering over the two of us like some anxious superhero, wanting to help but only able to leap tall buildings or stop express trains. Rosie asked me in an aside if he was sick.

'Just knackered,' I said. He'd done most of the driving. She accepted that and started walking towards the main building where the UN people were waiting for her.

'They won't let any journalists in on this.'

We hadn't thought they would. 'But you'll be able to give me a brief word or two for our French readers?' Fromental spoke in the slow, deferential rumble he reserved for these delicate situations.

She liked him. She said she'd do her best.

After she'd gone inside I felt his hand settle carefully on my shoulder. 'Jesus, man.'

I got some shots of the Boss, with his veil, eyes like a laboratory rat's, his strange, distant whispering voice, as if he spoke from beyond the edges of the universe. His English was excellent, but with Rosie and the Swedes he preferred to speak German.

He was no Yasser Arafat. He was a much better diplomat. His demands were practical and possible. He knew he could get what he wanted without setting a bad precedent while keeping everyone's goodwill. Of course Rosie was helping him through it. Interpreting the offers for him, second-guessing the Swedes, suggesting where he could cover himself. It was virtually an acceptance of the region's independence under UN protection and wasn't at all what the French, Algerians or Moroccans wanted. Hassan of Morocco was himself a dab hand at high profile gestures. Al-Rikh' was learning the wisdom of hiring a good PR company.

But he knew as well as we did that without Rosie he wouldn't even have been a starter. That's probably why he was so nice to the media. And we were nice to him. And it's why the Brits still think of him as a hero when anyone else would have been a 'terrorist'. Even the French started dealing with him properly after Fromental's three interviews appeared in *Libération*.

By the time our papers got my pictures they had their 'Red Shadow saves Britons' angle. It made a change from combat fatigues, RayBans, monster noses and stringy beards (some of which they all had under their mysterious robes). But a nice bit of romance. Got popular opinion behind the S'r'wi Rif and the Algerians off their turf. Sometimes, as Rosie always used to say to me, a touch of orientalism works a treat. We were all in the right place at the right time.

Apart from the kid, that is.

Fromental took my pictures back with him and got them to the papers. It was one of those dream jobs everyone had to use. They all loved me, the red-tops. The *Scratch*, the *Sniff*, the *Spit* and the *Stain*. It's the story that really made my name. As it made Rosie's.

I stayed on with her in Begat for a while. The day came when we were due to leave the camp. All the negotiations had been worked out and it was about as firm a deal as anyone could get. A successful goal for the rule of law.

Before we started our journey back to town I had to tell her about Kim. After that she didn't talk to me much. She didn't blame me for it, she said. She would probably have done the same.

The efforts she went to after that to avoid the kind of publicity she was getting tended to build up resentment in editors. Women who resisted their benign narratives were especially dangerous. Revealed not as angels but as man-hating feminists likely to snick off your knackers at the drop of a bra. So she tended to get the Princess Anne rather than the Princess Di treatment. She just wouldn't flutter those lashes and dip those shoulders. Though I'd seen her come close, once or twice, when it was the only thing that might work to get a regional water-purification plant or convince some silksuit at the IMF to cough up the odd billion for some country he'd never heard of.

But she was never the People's Charity Worker, the way Benazir Bhutto was never really the People's Prime Minister. Some women just have too much dignity for their own good.

Those pictures are still turning up, though. They have a kind of before-and-after look if you know what order they were taken in. Rosie smiling, full of herself, shaking hands with al-Rikh', chatting with the UN negotiators. She had everyone's respect, including her own. The other shots were of Rosie doing her best to look as pleased with herself as she had been before she knew the kid was dead.

'She couldn't have stayed at that camp,' I said. 'Either way, I think she couldn't have made it. The plane crashing was what caused it, Rosie, not you.'

'But I could have been with her.' She didn't respond much after that and I didn't push her. I had a fair sense of how she was feeling.

There was, of course, no comforting her.

Kim's death was hardly mentioned in the press. We hadn't given them the angle.

A good time for getting busy. And after Begat I was really busy.

About a month later I was in New York doing the Houston Circle photos – Iggy Pop – Bob Dylan – Beefheart – Snowy White – Paul Frame and a few others on those legendary lost tapes. Not that they were *lost*. I could tell you the story of how the tapes got wiped and so could Mick Farren, John May and Jon Trux. But there are some mysteries to which you never provide the solution.

The weird thing was that I met Johnny Begg down there. That's like finding a can of Beluga at an Arkansas fish-fry. The area behind Canal on the edge of what these days they call TriBeca. It was mostly warehouses and whores and dangerous shadows in those days, before the new Mayor sold his city to the Gap. You could get in there from Lispenard and a couple of other streets, but it didn't work as a short cut, so there was hardly any through traffic. Just the odd lost soul.

A lot of the places were rented by hippies, who had turned part of the central park into a garden and play area. It was a few years away from the final middle-class colonization, but the early settlers had broken the ground. A little alternative paradise.

There was an old Irish pub on the west side of the circle, with a run-down hotel next to it. Both built of the same sooty brick. Flaking gilt. Cheap repairs. We'd stayed there once or twice when Shitty was trying to break us into New York on a shoestring. You couldn't get to sleep at night for occupants of other rooms either yelling to be let out or hammering to get let in. Not so much a loony bin or domestic violence as very badly painted-over doors. We'd guessed there were people had died behind some of those doors, still whispering for help. But Doyle's was OK. I started going there every day for a couple of pints and a chat with the shifty old landlord. He claimed Houston Circle was where the first Irishman had raised the first tavern. This was a more recent hostelry, put up on the same site. He was thinking of having a sign painted – 'Oldest pub in America'. You had to make use of any angle these days, didn't you? Maximize your assets.

I went in one lunchtime, before the session was due to start, hoping to get a pork pie, though it was a bit late. There weren't many places in New York you could get a decent Irish pork pie and a pint of stout that wasn't icy Guinness. I usually had two of the small pies but they were all gone. 'This gentleman ordered them,' said Corny Doyle, indicating a well-tailored back and a haircut they couldn't often afford in that part of the city. Occasionally you'd see those expensive threads wandering about, trying to find the World Trade Center, but never sitting down. And never ordering food. There's nothing much more xenophobic than an international businessman. This one was definitely Savile Row English and was cheerfully at home, elbows working, jaw moving.

I moved round to confirm my suspicion. Johnny Begg. Looking as if he'd just been thrown out of a glossy magazine ad. I could even smell the Ralph Lauren cologne over the subtler flavours on the table. He had half a dozen pies, a jar of Branston pickle, some Daddy's Sauce, a hunk of bread and butter, some Cheddar cheese and the only shant of O'Dowd's this side of the Atlantic ocean. He nodded and smiled at me and gave me a thumbs-up. His mouth was too full for him to speak. He was sitting there on his own, in his Park Avenue overcoat and his trumpoid trouserings, tucking in like a Tipperary trooper after a hard day's work massacring some Sioux.

'*Was gibt?*' I asked.

'Have you tasted the food at the local Hilton?' He forced himself to take a breather. 'And the prices they charge for that muck. The hamburger du jour? Fucking Vienna steak and chips you'd throw at the waiter in Brookgate.'

If you didn't mind him throwing it back at you, I thought. So Johnny was in his man-of-the-people, rootsy mood, desperate for an authenticity that was never his in the first place. That went with his lust for pies. I remember him at fifteen telling me how revolting, fatty and full of horrid goo they were. Almost as bad as jellied eels. But now the East End had an image. It stood for honesty. Old values. Real life. Coherence. Ripe for colonization, in other words. It was as if he was calling spuriously on the yeomen of England (or at least Wicklow) to support him in whatever he was up to here. It was weird. At this rate I'd find him ordering up a plate of fresh lampreys and throwing coins to his foot soldiers.

'I couldn't stand it any longer. It's all so fake.' He'd eaten half the jar of Branston. 'I could do with some chips,' He signalled to Corny's daughter who came reluctantly to help at lunchtime. She didn't seem to have much time for her father.

'Try the bloodworms. They're better than anything you'll find in Smithfield, these days. Most American food is a kind of replica, a bad memory of the original recipe, the gaps filled in with hot spices and sugar. A sort of nursery forgery. But New York food is a golden memory wrought real. Better than the original. So the fantasy's made substantial. The American dream at its finest. Who told you about this place?'

'Nobody. I just found it. You know me, Dennis. I've a nose for the quaint and out-of-the-way.'

'What are you doing in town?'

'Oh, this and that. Business.'

It wasn't like Johnny to look awkward.

'You're not involved in this big Marks and Spencer/Brooks Brothers/ Fruit of the Loom/Hanes takeover, are you?'

'Old news, Den. There's rather bigger and more urgent matters afoot in little old New York right now.' He'd begun to slip into that strangely pugnacious nasal accent that lads of his background seem to think is cool, tough and American. Felix Martin was inclined to sound like that when he was losing an argument.

I think Johnny was high on the pies. He grew glossier by the second. He couldn't finish the last two and pushed them towards me. I didn't care. I got a bag for them and put them in my pocket. Snowy would eat them if I couldn't. He was from the Isle of Wight. Pork pies are a gourmet delicacy there. If you don't believe me, go over.

I had some of his chips, too. Nothing like a hot chip and a bottle of Daddy's on a cold New York lunchtime. By the time I was on my third pint of Murphy's and he'd sipped his way down to the bottom of his shant I was feeling very good indeed and Johnny didn't seem such a bad bloke after all.

Generally we talked about the past. He didn't remember how we'd been so contemptuous of him. He looked back on those days with extraordinary warmth. Remember when you, me and Rosie did this, Rosie said that, you said that funny thing I'll never forget. And Rosie standing on that embankment, pretending to dive off . . .

It was a very odd feeling, because I'd known what a rat Johnny had been since he was a nasty little kid. I was certain he'd be hugely irritated if I mentioned the cost in human dignity, anguish and life his greed created in the world. But *only* irritated. A cracked record, he'd say. If only it was that simple, he'd say.

So I let him go on while I ate his chips and watched through the window, across that weird little park with its old dovecote still there in the middle. The studios filled three basements of the houses immediately opposite. I could see who was arriving. So far, nobody had turned up.

'Great days,' I told him, by way of paying for my lunch. 'Too bad they end, eh, Johnny?'

'Absolutely! It's a hard, hard, hard old world, Dennis. I read all about Rosie and those Arabs. You got some good pictures. In all the papers. Must have cleaned up, eh? But why was everybody veiled?'

'Different reasons. Privacy? Modesty? Some kind of statement. I don't know. Rosie finds it easier to deal with these people by respecting their customs. Doesn't seem a bad idea. Not unless you're heavily into control. You know, trying to change people's customs. Telling them what to do. To make them good consumers.'

I laid it on. I'd read some piece of bullying nonsense proclaimed by Rockheart Reagan, the amazingly popular president who had already bankrupted California and was now rapidly in the process of shoving the National Debt up to where his Star Wars technology was meant to be and notions of public service where the sun didn't shine. Easiest way to get popular. Borrow a lot of other people's money and spread it around for a while. And bingo, you have an economic miracle. Obviously Johnny was already impressed. But there was a strange, ideological strand to some of what sounded to me like borrowed Yankee notions and he mentioned the KNTO significantly and when I didn't know what he meant added: 'It's not anti-Semitic. There's plenty of Jewish people with us. So don't go nosing about.'

The initials sounded like an American radio station to me. I still thought of myself as a second-rate rock-and-roller earning a bit of dosh with his photography, rather than as a tabloid newshound sniffing out the depraved and the dodgy. I wasn't interested in his nasty wheelings and dealings.

Maybe I should have been. Maybe I should have poisoned his fucking pies there and then. But he was invulnerable in those days. You sensed it. You reflected it in your attitude to him. Maybe he'd sold his soul, suckering some second-rate devil into giving him eternal life. He could have pulled the deal off, probably. But more likely he just went and made an aggressive takeover bid for Hell PLC. Stripped the assets. Sold all the eternal-life options to corporate sponsors, kept the best bits for himself and rented the rest out to a theme-park developer.

Maybe that's why he was catching a plane for San Antonio the next morning. To get a feel for the possibilities.

He tipped an imaginary stetson. 'Howdy, y'all,' he said. I gave in to my embarrassment and got up.

I told him to check out Kinky Friedman, to say hello to the Alamo and to give my regards to LBJ. Then I went and listened to that weird wailing session with Iggy, Beefheart and Paul Frame. Like a lament for the end of the world.

Mick Farren was there. He could tell you what happened to the tapes, but I never saw them – except when they were going round and round on the deck. I don't even know who started the rumour that Trux and I had ever had them in our possession. Trux and I went back on the same plane. He'd even forgotten the presents he'd bought for his girlfriend and I had that light bag I always carried. And my camera stuff. And that was that. No other luggage. And if you think you can get those old three-inch reels into a camera bag I'll show you the bag and a reel and let you work it out. It wasn't Charlie Murray's fault, but that *NME* story has dogged me for years. Dylan won't talk to me but the last time I saw Iggy in the lift of the Portobello Hotel he looked up at me from where he'd sunk to the floor and told me that when the tapes turned up as bootlegs or got sold at Sothebys he'd believe they hadn't been wiped. That's Iggy.

But pretty much everybody else thinks I must still have them. The questions come round every few years.

Flickfnife did put out *The Greenfly and the Rose*. It was the last thing Calvert and I did together. We didn't do any gigs. We didn't do any publicity. I'm not even sure I was ever sent a copy of the single. I hardly noticed. I was too busy being an intrepid photog by then.

I didn't see much of Rosie for a while, even when she came to London. She was frank about it. She said she didn't want to be in anybody's story for a while.

The last time we spoke at any length for some five years, I wasn't long back from Angola and the Houston Circle pictures were appearing in *Rolling Stone*. I was now the flavour of the month, jetting here, jetting there. She had some business in the Hague and phoned me to say that she didn't want to talk very much but that she loved me and one day would have a lot of questions to ask me. She wasn't resentful. She was just grieving.

The sun set over Fogg Yard, a sepia moment, and I lay deep in my old armchair staring through the drizzling air at the lost graveyard, the bones of all those Dovers. I was angsty again. Back pretty much where I'd been on Boxing Day. Except I was listening to Elvis Costello a lot more. *A Good Year For the Roses*. Quality depression.

Which at least gets you sick of yourself faster. I developed the pictures I'd taken of Kim. When they were ready I put them in my folder with some others I'd done of Rosie and the Rif camp and I walked down to Chancery Lane tube. I changed at Tottenham Court Road and waited for the Tufnell Park train. The Central Line was crammed with loving couples, brilliant with blooming scarlet and rustling cellophane, soft, simpering teddies and boxes of Thornton's the size of Manets. I tried not to imagine the tons of peculiar and uncomfortable underwear that was in the wrapped boxes. Even the buskers were wearing flowers in their hair and singing love songs. What a complicated way of reproducing ourselves. Come on cloning, I say.

At times like that, when the scales were dipping a little too far on the side of the group fantasy, Tubby was my only hope. Some kind of reality.

It was one of his open days, so I didn't bother to phone him.

At Camden Town some early drunks got on and sang 'Valentine, Valentine, please suck mine for Valentine.'

Which at least provided a rough shelter against syrup fallout. 'Oi! Oi!'

I was lucky and got a cab coming down from Dartmouth Park Road. As usual I had to direct him all the way. Taxi drivers tell you that there are certain bits of the Knowledge, the book of lore all cabbies have to memorize before they can get a licence, that they are doomed never to recall. Like parts of the driving test.

Once they've got their licence, they have these blind spots for destinations their entire career. Ask any cabby. They'll agree. And try getting a cab driver to take you to Sporting Club Square, which every driver does in the Knowledge. In the Knowledge, see, but not in the real world. Expunged from the race memory. 'Oh!' they exclaim. 'I know that. We did it in the Knowledge. I'd forgotten all about it.'

When I used to stay there you'd see the cabbies going round and round on their little mopeds with their clipboards on their handlebars checking it off. It's not exactly unobtrusive. Maybe it's too much like a Victorian fantasy to remain in our twenty-first century reality.

There are certain areas of London that I suspect retain their integrity and beauty only by becoming invisible. Threatened or abandoned, they fade slowly into an astral plane, an alternate universe where all the forgotten buildings and ruined architecture of the world still exist, still function, are still inhabited. Sometimes I think I only have to turn round suddenly at the right time to see an ectoplasmic Brookgate shimmering through all that glassy concrete Barbican stuck in its place.

Anyway, we got up to the Whittington Park entrance and I paid him off while he shook his head in wonderment. 'I haven't been here, in what, thirty years,' he said.

It was dark as I climbed the long, patched asphalt path. Fairly warm for February, with watery stars overhead and the fluttering lights of traffic in the streets below. A couple of old dears in woolly hats walking decrepit four-legged creatures of uncertain species said 'Good evening' in perfectly friendly tones, as if they hadn't yet learned to be suspicious of single young men coming towards them.

'Not too bad, this evening,' I said.

'That's right, dear,' they said. Approving my loyalty to convention, I suppose.

Then I'd pushed open the creaky municipal gate, mounted the brick and concrete steps and was back in the little cul-de-sac that ended at a fence and a notice that said PRIVATE. The area behind the fence appeared to be completely overgrown. Its big iron gate looked daunting. But I knew how to open it. The post was so poorly seated, I could jog the eight-foot gate off its lock and put it back again after I'd gone through. Almost everyone who visited Tubby from the Whittington Park entrance knew how to do that.

I was looking forward to the warmth as I walked the last few yards to the Mill's baroque marble porch. For everyday use, Tubby had one of those electronic locks you had to punch a number into. It was about the only number I ever remembered. 49406. He's changed it since.

I'd expected to find a lot of people there but after I'd hung up my coat in the little lobby and pushed open the door to the main room I hesitated. The place seemed deserted. Then I heard low, murmuring voices from overhead and I looked up into the shadows where I made out the silhouette of Tubby and a couple of other people in intense conversation. Shorter than Tubby. A man and a woman, so I presumed I wasn't interrupting anything.

'Wotcher, Tub!' I peered up at the iron gantry that still fanned out from the shaft-house above. This Mill had been one of the most advanced machines of its day. It had paid for itself in the first two years of its operation. Iron stairs ran down from each arm of the gantry where steevers had once raced with buckets to cool the whirling metal and the rasping stones pouring out high-quality flour in moments. I'd often wondered what it would cost to get the sails fixed properly and the whole thing working again. But it would have disrupted Tubby's routines, so we'd never know.

'Tub?'

There was a pause when they heard me, then silence.

'Tubby?'

I recognized the voice that answered. It wasn't Tubby. It was Jocky Papadakis. 'Hi, Dennis. Many congratulations, my friend. Wonderful pictures in the paper the other day.'

This wasn't my idea of a good time. 'If you're busy,' I said.

'Not a bit.' That was Tubby, grim and angry. What the fuck had I stepped into? 'I just told this bastard to leave.'

Then they were talking together again and I couldn't hear anything that made sense. The third figure moved away from the others and began to climb down the ladder to where I was standing. It was a woman in thick tights and a grey pussy pelmet. She was wearing a huge orange sweater. It was Flo Fortnum, negotiating the rungs in high heels. She looked like she'd been given an *It's A Knockout* handicap. What with Maddy's recent problems on my stairs I was beginning to wonder if these women fixed their shoes on with superglue. What was it about something so flimsy, so easily shed, that came to represent such profound security? Apparently, the moment the stocking touched the tarmac the world would end.

I once asked Julie why she wore high heels when they hurt so much. 'I have to learn to do it,' was her answer. Baffling to me at the time.

Anyway, Flo got down and came trotting perkily over to me as if she'd just stepped out of a limo. 'Darling, darling, darling Dennis!'

'Easy, Flo.' I took half a step back while extending my hand. 'How's tricks? What happened with that nymphet you were PR-ing for Malcolm McLaren?'

'I'm working for Save the Children now. And the Heritage Council, of course. Which is why I brought Jocky along.'

'Do what?' I didn't really care because I thought Tubby would tell me what was really going on if he wanted me to know.

'Well, it's a question of money,' she said. She giggled aggressively. 'Isn't it always?'

'Seems that way,' I said. There was a thump from overhead. Relentlessly Tubby was rolling along the gantry in pursuit of Jocky who was holding his shoulder and squeaking with outrage. 'Don't you people understand anything about self-interest? Don't you want to be helped?'

I'd heard that one before. And from the horse's mouth. I grew alert, the way you do. That same horse had eaten five small pork pies in Doyle's only a few days earlier.

Tubby smacked Jocky on the other shoulder. I knew what Tubby could do when he got angry. He was the only member of the band Sonny Shapiro had been scared of.

'Tubby!' That was me. I didn't want him to get into trouble.

Jocky scrambled down the ladder radiating a mixture of mindless cowardice and self-righteous aggression. He reached the bottom and stood pulsing there, his horrible beard twitching on his pale little chin like a dying rat.

He placed a moist hand on my arm and gave me an emetic smirk. He thought I was on his side. 'Thanks, Dennis. See if you can talk sense into him, old pal. Love to Maddy. Tubby's not himself. I understand what it's like if you never get out of the house and see the real world. Family all well, I hope. I don't hold any grudges.'

The little fucker was grudge from bald patch to corns.

'I was like a brother to him,' he told me mysteriously as he hauled an apologetic Flo out of the Mill. To give Tubby some time, I went and watched them huffing and fluttering down the path towards the gate. Flo's attempts to soothe Jocky were having their usual effect. As they reached the gate, he turned and hit her in the eye.

So suddenly, hating them both, I'm running down through the drizzling darkness shouting at Jocky, who didn't know how to get the gate open.

I jumped it out of its lock with one angry fist and shoved him through.

Flo looked at me and then looked at him. She drew back. She held my hand, almost like a child. So I told Jocky to fuck off, which he was doing anyway, and I reluctantly took her back to the open door. 'I'll get you a taxi,' I said.

'Marvellous,' she said. 'Honestly, Dennis, I blame Tubby for this. He *knows* Jocky's half-Greek.'

Tubby didn't come down until she'd gone. He'd had a shower and was wearing that big white robe he loved. He was carefully towelling his hair and styling it as he went. He was very vain about his barbering. He wore a kind of discreet Elvis. I think that was the first time I noticed that he was dyeing it.

'Thanks, mate,' he said. 'Sorry about that. You didn't mind—?'

'What? Calling a taxi? You're a fucking troublemaker, you are, Tubby. What the fuck did you invite Jocky for?'

'He came with Flo. She was bringing me some flowers. Poor bitch. Any bastard can con her. That man ought to be buried on a special site, he's so fucking full of toxic waste. We owe it to the public? *We owe it to the public.* Heard that one yet, Den?'

'Owe what? To do what?'

'To sell him my fucking house. The whole fucking Mill, Dennis! This! My trust. He's got Flo involved because of this charity she works for. He says it's a public monument. He says he wants to buy it as a gift to the nation.'

'And you didn't laugh?'

'I couldn't. I have a fair idea what he's really up to.' He got that Cassandra look on his face. A grim prescience.

I didn't pump him on it. Tubby tended to keep his speculations to himself. He only liked accurate gossip. He'd tell me when he was sure. In his own time.

Absently he made some calculations on his nearest keyboard. I told him that if he had a lady friend coming round for this special day I'd leave.

That made him laugh. 'This is a definitely neutral day,' he said. 'No special visitors. Blanket rule. Saves embarrassment all round.'

We spent the next hour or two listening to Schoenberg and Mozart, smoking a little Natchez Nouveau and breathing easy. After a while I told Tubby where I'd been, what had been happening. Was he sure he had the strength for it?

'Show me the pictures,' he said.

Around us his monochrome screens murmured and twinkled and his cats moved a little uneasily, vaguely disturbed by what had happened with Jocky and Flo. Tubby kept talking to them, reassuring them, and slowly they settled down.

Tubby remembered Kim from the party. He didn't say anything when I laid the photos out in front of him.

A bit later Paul Frame came over. He was on his way home and had his bag and his old Yamaha acoustic. He told me how they'd lost the tapes. 'We can't find them. The spools are marked, but everything's blanked. Either someone came in and wiped them, or somebody's substituted blank tape for the originals.' He had a couple of partial cassettes. That's all you ever hear on the bootlegs, too.

I never felt more like playing the blues.

So that's what we did. 14 February 1982. Another month, another moon. The Year of the Rat. That's what we did.

Played the fucking blues.

The government got more and more full of itself. Foot proved an ace at shooting his own feet and Labour lost any chance of being taken seriously. Even their supporters knew that particular hierarchy didn't have an ounce of authority any more. Foot wasn't a leader, he was a compendium of every learned bit of socialist orthodoxy there was. Put a shilling in the jukebox. Not so much an analysis of our problems as a litany of what should be. His reality centred on the comradeship of the Aldermaston march, the wagging fingers of the concerned middle classes. He would teach us the secret of nirvana but first we had to learn to speak his language and adopt his beliefs.

Not the public's favourite figure.

The public loved their Maggie and willingly sought her approval. Theirs was a language that was naughty but nice: be good to yourself, go on you deserve it, go on put your hand in your knickers, go on feel yourself up, go on make yourself comfortable, go on your majesty, give her a cuddle, go on make yourself feel generous with a quid in the red-nose tin, go on have another, go on you need it. Go on. Nobody will notice. Go on. Nobody will judge you. Go on. Treat yourself. Go on have a good cry. Wasn't it a lovely funeral? Go on.

With increasing recklessness and ignorance Maggie Hatchet started destroying the fabric of centuries as if it was so much heritage junk. Ancient liberties. Common law. It was all dry rot to that classic kulak mind. And the more her government got away with, the more they despised the public. People who know what's good for us are always like that. People who know what's good for us always want to be in charge. They always want to be the government.

I know one thing about governments: In 1939 the government prepared for the bombing of London, expecting the population to panic and that vast numbers of shell-shocked people would rush into the surrounding countryside.

And I know one thing about the public: Within hours of the first great bombing raid on London, which sent street after street roaring with fire and turned the world to shrieking chaos, Londoners began to take control of their city – in *spite* of the government.

It's a fact. My grandad and my mum know it's a fact. Grandad was in the ARP but he helped rush the Tube station and force the authorities to open it up as a shelter. He organized the rescue teams and manned the anti-aircraft positions and hardly missed a day's work at Mullard's from

1939 until 1945, when the workshops got a V2 and had to be relocated. Most of the crucial stuff was being done out of London by then. He was in the office.

Brookgate seemed charmed. Clerkenwell, Holborn, the City were all getting hit hard, but it was as if they hadn't taken our measure. We had an ack-ack gun in the Fields. Barrage balloons drifting over Lincoln's Inn. I wish I'd seen it, in a way. Surreal. All I remember, of course, is the ruins. And they were disappearing as I grew up.

But that's when the mob was king. And looking after things. We should always be proud of that. The Germans don't like it and even the French aren't too sure about it, while the Americans think it's OK from a distance – but for us it was an authentic moment of epiphany for the national soul, the way Stalingrad was for the Russians.

The Germans are always ready to put that behind them. If their army had turned on Hitler and refused to follow his orders, they too would be able to remember a great moment of national heroism. But up to now they haven't had much of a record. I want never to put that behind us. Any more than we should put Amritsar and Malaya and Cape Town and Wounded Knee and Kent State behind us.

Only rarely do people come together at their very best against tyranny and brute evil. Londoners seem to do it more often than most. At least on their own behalf. It helps you remember that there was and can be a world maybe a bit better than this one.

We talked about a world like that. Where mob rule means the rule of common law and mutual respect. Wasn't it what most people wanted? And were so ready to give up at the promise of another dollar, the threat of another depression. Tubby and I kept on that theme later when Paul had gone to catch his early train up to Manchester and we were all wide awake on the Iranian Orange Paul had scored on his way to the Mill in order to make sure he stayed up until his train went. He left the best part of a gram with us because he didn't want to get paranoid on the train and he was carrying about a pound of tightly packed California Gold in the accessories compartment of his guitar case.

I've always been partial to cheap speed. The subtleties of cocaine are the same as a wine, but the charm of something like IO was that one snort and the back of your head blew out out out, bone and flesh and hair, and suddenly everything was working very well and very fast. And you were a king.

Some people do badly on speed, but when you play in the kind of rock-and-roll bands I played in, you learn to get on top of any drug and not to take a drug you can't stay on top of. So me and Tubby got behind the speed and let our hair down. Played a bit more. Spun some discs. Watched the uncut version of *Heaven's Gate* Tubby had scored from someone at the studio. I loved it. I still love it. But I didn't take it all in. We couldn't stop talking. We talked through the night and well into the next day.

My life was looking pretty useless to me, especially in comparison to
Rosie's. I didn't know what to do – whether to ride the zeitgeist as I'd
started to do – follow the curves and twists of the real world in all their
complications – or whether to settle back from it and join in the telling
of the group story, our race's mighty self-reassuring cluck. There is no
death. There is no oblivion. There is no nothing.

Went to the Union Station, mouth full of much oblige.
Went to the Union Station, mouth full of much oblige.
I asked the Man to tell me which train shall I ride?

Where did all that American history disappear to? The history of the
American mob? That Woody Guthrie sang about. The American
working-class heroes who stood together against corrupt government
and often lawless National Guards in the pay of some state boss. The
Americans in worn overalls who got shot down because they dared
demand a fair price for their labour. Who got arrested and stigmatized
and ruined. Who suffered famine. Who got wasted by their own
generals. Just like the Scottish lords wasted their own clansmen and sent
them desperate to America. To kill Indians. To begin again.

The Americans that Steinbeck celebrated and Josh White celebrated
and all those poets and painters of the New Deal celebrated, black and
white, English or Spanish. *This land is my land. This land is your land.*
Where are those brave Americans? Where are the Vietnam protesters?
Who's protesting now?

Workers of the World, Unite!

Guthrie was indicted by the House Un-American Activities
Committee. As proof of his communism they produced a picture that
showed him when he was serving in minesweepers during the war with
the slogan *This Machine Kills Fascists* painted on his guitar. They
hounded him as he died of a terrible disease and now they've put the
bastard on a stamp. *I've been doin' some hard travelin', I thought you
knowed . . .*

I mentioned how strange it had been, meeting Johnny in New York.
Tubby got alert and asked a few leading questions. I told him the little I
knew. But I didn't remember about those initials. I said I thought it was
something going on at the World Trade Center.

'All part of the same pattern', said Tubby mysteriously. 'What are we
going to do about it?'

'About what?'

'About the Grand Consumer.'

I thought that one over for a bit. Then I cut another line.

I'm still not sure what it was exactly that defeated us.

CHAPTER SIXTEEN
The Pull

The few times I've been in prison I've usually been lucky. I've never had an experience that wasn't useful. Of course, I was reasonably welcome in English prisons, having done so many gigs. There's always an advantage to knowing the odd Angel. Because a prison with Angels in it offers a very useful support group. Particularly since I hate football.

I used to be fairly tolerant of it all until the football business boomed through the nineties and every bloke who used to use his socialism or his war experience to give his banalities moral weight now used his loyalty to Man U or his ability to put the side of his foot to a plastic globe and move it across a flat space.

I used to get pissed off during recording sessions when the whole fucking band would take off for thousands of pounds' worth of studio time just to watch a bunch of people running about, kicking balls, waving their arms and periodically simulating injuries with all the subtlety of Coco the Clown. It's one of those cultural things I can't seem to connect with. The sentimentality, the mysticism, the sheer lugubrious stupidity of the managers and teams, not to mention the fans, makes them no better than a bunch of boozed-up hobbits, in my view. Aggressive anoraks.

Disliking football tends to isolate you in prison even more than it does in rock-and-roll bands. People get suspicious of you. They don't know who you are. You've got to be a shirtlifter.

I met Christopher Lee once. That is, I stood with my head somewhere near his hip and stared upwards, vaguely wondering why his teeth looked wrong. Amiable but very English, he was doing a sojourn in Hollywood. He had the philosophical air of an exiled king forced to work in a theme restaurant.

I was out at Gene Wilder's place doing those *People* pix that women always remember. A pool party. While I was taking his picture John Vernon, a Canadian actor I've always admired, came up to Lee and greeted him warmly. 'How's the cricket going, Christopher?'

'Well, old boy, Kent's declared at 230. Yorkshire's doing well, though

Hopkiss was bowled out early . . .' and so on and so on. I'd never had
Lee down for a cricket bore and said something about being surprised.
He chuckled – which in him is a bit like Etna reactivating – and shook
his head. 'I'm not a great cricket fan,' he said, 'but everyone out here
assumes that I must be. I meet all the cricket buffs. I don't like to
disappoint them, so before I came out today I tuned in to the World
Service and checked the cricket news because I knew someone was
bound to ask me the question.'

I wasn't prepared to go to those lengths just for a couple of months in
the nick. There's always been a weird bit in me that thinks if that many
people have gone collectively stupid to the extent that intellectuals are
rationalizing, explaining and justifying their stupidity, I don't really
want to join. You start looking around for a fresh planet. To me
excessive interest in sport goes with a decreasing quality of public
debate. Look at America. All that holds the middle classes together is an
interest in baseball or football. It's all they have to talk about most of the
time because nobody ever tells them the issues. And sport's a great
leveller, isn't it? Brings out the best in people, eh?

Divide and rule. Bread and circuses. Empower the Walloons.
Representation to the provinces. Most of what that meant was that
instead of the government getting stick for dividing up a small piece of
cake, everyone gets to fight over who gets the whole slice.

Maybe that was what kept me and Rosie so close, too. Any game that
involved running around in pursuit of a ball, puck or pill might do
something for your animal self but when it came to satisfying animal
selves we had rather more direct pursuits. If I get involved in a
competition I want to be sure one of the contestants is going to die or get
brain damage if they lose. It's why I only used to play for high stakes in
that poker school I belonged to in the Elgin, Ladbroke Grove, for years.
We all did. Until we ruined one another. And then those travellers got
murdered and the survivors were banned from the Kensington Palace
Hotel, so they came over and you could never get at the pool table and
the school broke up.

Luckily, I had this other identity. I never did more than three months
anywhere and you don't exactly get the bad-boy treatment if you're
doing time for contempt of court.

When I got out of Oxford nick in 1983 (it's a long story) a bloke I
mistook for a warder came up to me and saluted before I'd taken two
steps down the cobbled path. It was Barbican's chauffeur in full kit.
Including driving gloves. He handed me a square envelope and offered
to give me a lift. I had gone to prison with some publicity and was a little
surprised to find none of my fellow pressmen waiting for me.

I told the chauffeur I wasn't sure where I was going, but if he didn't
mind waiting a bit while I nipped over the road for a quick quan-tong,
which I had been promising myself for weeks, I'd give his offer some

thought. He became vaguely agitated. Expressed some uncertainty about parking. I said where I'd be and when I was likely to be done. Then I went straight into the Manchu Munchee and ordered the Mongolian Medley. When I waddled out, the Roller wasn't near the prison any more. But as I set off towards the station, it appeared at the intersection, so I got in. I felt like someone out of a classic noir movie. Alan Ladd. Except there was no Veronica Lake with her exquisite legs crossed waiting for me in the car. No sultry once-over. Not even a silver-haired stooge or a rat-faced punk or a cop with a message to lay off the case. Just a deco bar, a television and a whiff of Gentleman's Relish. I sank into the horsehair. Why not?

The invite was to attend a weekend house-warming at Johnny's new Oxfordshire seat and 'another place' which would be named when I got there. I was curious. Low Cogges, between Oxford and Witney off the A41, was a house associated with Johnny's aristocratic ancestors – Dutch tradesmen ennobled under Queen Anne. No wonder he got on so well with Yankees. They came from the same time zone.

It was in the days I received occasional invitations from people like him to go to places like that. They still thought of me as a musician who took photographs rather than as a tabloid muckraker. And I had a bit of glamour to me. They wanted to know what it was like in prison. I was just the chap they needed. Even though I'd only been to prison for refusing to name my sources. We were all doing it at that time. Miners' strikes. Government leaks. Shoulder to shoulder. Side by side. Always the groom and never the bride. A different world. But one you must be fairly familiar with. The reason I don't go on about it is because my grandad used to complain that the anarchists (he never missed a meeting at the Malatesta Club, Red Lion Square) had been sold out to the communists who had lost the Spanish Civil War at such and such a battle and my Uncle Pete would go on about World War Two and the comradeship and the rationing and how they'd been sold out by the Americans over the Battle of the Bulge and his friend Jack Curren, at that point running Westminster Council, said we'd be living in Utopia now if Attlee hadn't sold us out to the Americans in 1947 and you know in your bones that your important names and symbols are just about as important to someone else as theirs are to you. But it's a passion hard to convey to the next generation and everyone who shared it knows what you're talking about anyway. Like being in prison. Or like the people who came out of concentration camps. What was there to talk about? What do the disempowered usually talk about? Free will?

Or how God's looking after them?

I was slipping into the edgy eighties. All my pictures started having rain in them. Concrete. Rubber. Heavy shadow. A resistant harmony to that nasty, mean-spirited little grocer's miss from some crap dormitory town that wouldn't exist if it wasn't for London. That sounds like it was faked up for a Trollope mini-series. I knew that she couldn't be eliminated. She had a thousand clones. Each clone came up for tea at Derry and Toms with her handbag on her arm and her husband puffing behind. Putting on airs. Airing a few put-ons, too. Throwing her weight around with the waitresses, that grim grin that said comply or die. The banal stuff of natural spiritual poisons oozing through her desperate clothing. When she dies, no region accepts her corpse. They have no choice but to regenerate her again and again. Otherwise that degree of poison would have to be buried at the core of Vesuvius. See? I'm doing it again.

Only people who've never been inside think prison's a doddle. Even your average police nick is a pretty disgusting place. Prison isn't a holiday camp. Unless the holiday camps you know stink of urine, testosterone and a repressed, raging madness. Of brute terror. Of life-threatening banality. Of filthy toilets and stinking slops. No fundamental privacy. You are their property. You get driven deeper and deeper into yourself, more and more unlike yourself on the surface. Inescapable reality. Not for everyone, of course. The levels of macho fantasizing beats anything you'll hear in the pub and people spend as much time bullshitting as pumping iron and it drives you mad. Sometimes the only coherent word is the name of a football team. A reality you are forced to face twenty-four hours a day for as long as you are in there. Maybe that's what it's supposed to do for you. Show you just what shit life really is. So when you come out you've lost any aspirations that might have driven you to crime. Take the McDonald's minimum shilling, buy a third-class ticket on the consumer gravy train.

For some reason I'd been moved to Oxford two days earlier. At Luton, it turned out, I'd had more than a Roller waiting for me. There had been a TV crew and reporters. I was a passing celebrity because I wouldn't reveal my sources in the closures leaks. It had been Flo Fortnum, who had embraced the Hatchet enthusiastically and worked as a PR for some high-up in the DTI until I'd persuaded her that what she was doing was immoral. And she got me the pit list they published in the *Mirror*. And I snapped the secret meeting between the DTI guys and Ray the Rat Arkwright that would have sold out the West Midlands. Not something I usually do.

My other English stretches were all short. Refusing to hand over negatives. Greenham stuff. I was there when Joan Baez came to see the women and advise them to go home and sing about their anger. There's a moment in those photos when she seems almost troubled by what she's saying. *Don't sing love songs, you'll wake my mother.* What levels of ego are we dealing with when Dylan shakes the Man by the hand as if he were an old friend? What could he need to make him do that? What must he have betrayed? Changing times, pards.

The Roller swung me up the newly costumed drive on gravel that looked as if it had been chipped from a bank vault and threatened to savage the tyres. Severe topiary on either side. Crunch. Purr. Whisper. Silence. A vast Tudor manor house. Moated, with the drawbridge down. Kelmscott but even more so. A fantasy? I couldn't tell. Astor's Hever Castle looked like something out of Douglas Fairbanks's *Robin Hood* (*c.* 1920), far too good to be true. But this was low, solid, enduring. Mature willows, oaks, chestnuts. It was a lot better than anything I'd expected Johnny to buy. An extended manor farm rather than one of those huge Frenchified cathedrals to their own success that the Spencers and Churchills and Villiers, put up all over the place. More like eighteenth-century cinema foyers than houses. With romanticized histories and well-laundered views. Blenheim. Built by the greatest Essex man of his day, that pile. Unusual in its persistent vulgarity. But then, look at the family.

Johnny's dark red weathered brick and black beams was two storeys with dormers, close to the ground as if to avoid danger rather than confront it. United with the earth by old vines and deep roots and iron ties and buttresses, under a heavy Cotswold slate roof. Wistaria from the beginning of time. Hollyhocks. Roses. A working building that had grown and warped over the centuries. Beautiful because it had responded only to its function and environment. As opposed to the titanic baroque of Queen Anne's courtiers, posing with all kinds of continental pomp.

The real thing.

And then the door's being opened for me by the chauffeur and I step out into a fantasy of Merry England, of topiary and beams and herb gardens and all the rest of that picturesque oldishness, heritage nonsense provided by some posturing ersatz Inigo Jones (who has a lot to damn him, too) who every American matron with more than twenty-five million pounds will court and promote and praise until the moment he goes out of fashion. A day or two of execration and then he, too, will be vanished. His successor will begin all over again. Because repetition is a sign that you are still alive. A kind of architectural fugue.

The house could absorb most of these indignities, but beyond the unfakeable yew hedges, the whole of the surrounding farmland had been turned into a golf course, which encircled the grounds. The distant clubhouse was a thatcher's fantasy. Gables, chimneys and soft straw. The heritage shrubs and flower beds were all recent. It looked like someone had taken a nice bit of wood-grain formica and perked up an Elizabethan sideboard.

I'll be seeing you in all the old familiar places, down the pub and at the races, we'll have a do the whole night through . . .

I felt like a fool, whistling as I crossed the drawbridge, passed under a portcullis and came face to face with Barbican.

'Dennis, you old lag!'

'Hello, Johnny. You want some tekno?'

'Ha, ha, ha. Is that one they tell in the *joint*?'

His hand fell on my arm. His fingers gripped my elbow. 'There's all sorts of people want to meet you.'

'Blimey,' I said. 'Is this my coming-out party?'

'Why not? Why not?' He chuckled loftily as he steered me towards an inner courtyard. I heard the sound of horses clopping, harness, soft-voiced ostlers.

'Like it?' Johnny was pleased with my response. 'It's the soundtrack of the new movie we're doing. *The Highwayman*. Based on the song by Phil Ochs. And the original novel by Harrison Ainsworth. All the old romance. Merry England. Dick Turpin and the Bow Street Runners. All-English. Makes a change from the fucking wild west, eh?'

Things couldn't have changed that much in three months. I felt vaguely as if I'd wandered into the world of *The Old Men At the Zoo*, which so accurately predicted the rise and the tone of Thatcherism. And which the hatcheteers buried. Wilson would have had an embarrassing nose for New Labour's posturings, but he went ga-ga in some East Anglian nursing home. Familiar territory. Peake. Murdoch. Graves. All the Celts. Ga-ga. Don't ask me why. Maybe it goes with the genius gene. The Normans and the Saxons just get dull and self-important. I'd known Wilson slightly since the mid-seventies. The only one of his kind I got on with. And he took great pictures, with his shock of white hair, his prissy little pink Scottish face broken by that wicked smile, those knowing eyes.

I could have done with an ally like Wilson at that moment, but I was suddenly surrounded and no longer breathing air. Instead the atmosphere was a rich mixture of expensive scents and pricey smokes. A bit of a shock, really, after urine and sweat. You could smell Jermyn Street on the laundry marks. Being barely three hours out of the nick, I was very glad I'd eaten the Mongolian Medley and so prepared myself in stomach if not in spirit for the rush, that physical assault on my senses that soothed all judgement away. They couldn't help doing it any more than the Creature From The Black Lagoon could help pulling damsels down to his dark domain or Dracula could help sinking his incisors into some nymphet's neck. It was how they fed. It was an instinct, as unconscious as a shark's sense of smell, that allowed them to exude this lulling psychic web, wrap you in it, keep you in suspended animation until you were ready to eat. Or discard. And just as a lioness purrs over her captured prey, even as she kills, so they purred over me.

I'd been battling would-be buggerers and creepy warders and was on a somewhat different defence system and here's one of Maggie's generals, Douglas 'the Nerd's Nerd' Hurd, who is about eighteen feet tall with a shoe size to rival Little Titch's and wearing the upper crust's favourite anorak, a Barbour oilskin. Showing me his teeth and telling me he admires my guts. He's Low Cogges's local MP, he says. Just dropped in for a quick one. Got the Range Rover outside. And half a dozen identically Barboured Special Branch. Going home to unwind. Like most of his kind, that bastard was so tight the only thing he could unwind was the clock he and his seedy gang were trying to put back. You could tell by the way he held his glass that he thought of himself as a man of conscience, a pretty good guy. He beamed on me in that vague way frightened people do. Douglas Home had the same fixed grin. Unfashionable glasses. Short-sighted people look like that sometimes, to be fair. They hope if they keep smiling no one will hurt them. Or notice what they're up to.

Why did I feel that I was the quick one the old bastard had in mind and that his reasons for admiring my guts were more culinary than moral? There was something about that wide mouth, that Desperate Dan chin, those gigantic, clumping brogues, that upset my blood and shivered my timbers. Colonel Gadaffi once told me that he had it on the best authority that in order to gain membership of Maggie Bonehead's inner council you had to eat human flesh and swear on the New Testament to bring about the destruction of Islam. The Colonel's grasp of religion wasn't the product of years of contemplation, but I was inclined to believe him in the broad.

I was beginning to discover what Billy Bragg meant by 'class enemy'. Hurd was as amiable as the rest of them, though he was inclined to have trouble doing two things at the same time, but I felt like the pig invited to a pork roast. I had a feeling if there was a blackboard with the day's specials, then I was the recommended entrée. No wonder they liked the look of me. No wonder they were salivating. What the fuck had Johnny pulled me into? I was thinking twice about going on to the unknown address. Three months is a long time in politics. For all I knew they'd reintroduced human sacrifice and were planning to read my entrails.

'We're well aware of the potential hardship,' Hurd was saying to me, 'and we intend to do everything we can about it. But this is for the good of the country.'

Hear that, lads? Toot toot, parp parp. Here comes Mr Toad.

It was already pretty clear to me that in hatchet-speak 'country' meant 'the ruling elite'. The people who really, badly felt they should be in control. But that was Mr Toad for you. Toot toot. Parp parp. Out of my way. Here comes Toady's motor. A crude, hugely wasteful motor able to move you at great speed at enormous cost to everyone around you. That's Lady Hatchet's marvellous economic engine, borrowed from nineteenth-century expansionist America. It presumes you consume infinitely and people had better get out of your way. And they wonder why kids are more aggressive, swear more forcefully, vandalize more thoroughly, murder more efficiently. They're part of the cost, the way bad air's the cost of cruising your supercharged roadster through the Shire's rolling roads. Some fucking hobbit has to suffer.

They introduced me to the Chief Constable, too.

He described me jovially as 'quite an old lag'. He acted as if we were now in the same team. None of them seemed to understand what prison was. Or what my sentence meant. Does anyone understand the meaning of their sentence?

The Chief Constable was tickled about thwarting the press. Shifting me like that. He radiated happiness. It was like his team had won. Cops 1, Press 0. I think he wanted me to congratulate him. I was saved from an embarrassing scene by a little bloke who looked like an off-duty Nazi who bustled up and stuck out his hand, announcing himself as 'Pee Wee Wilson, the JP' and clearly expecting the CC to know who he was. He started going on about 'these filthy travellers'. The copper's smug grin disappeared and a more troubled look crossed his face. I slipped away from that one and went to look through a leaded window at a scene good enough for Disney's Winnie the Pooh. Lawns, hedges and rolling hills. Landscaped at huge expense to look just like Bagginsville. Telly Tubby paradise. These days I'd suspect it was computer-generated. But this was authentic. Real sod.

It made a change from bars and concrete. I'd started to feel dangerously relaxed when Bobby MacMillan came up behind me and briefly touched me on the left buttock.

'Hello, sweety.'

Fresh from the nick? I must smell so good her knickers would take a week to dry. I was quality rough and no mistake. She'd have had me on the hand-looped William Morris if she hadn't been certain the Chief Constable would instantly turn up with a bucket of cold water.

'How's things?' They'd put some sort of cocktail in my hand now. I could feel it heating. 'How's life with the Captain of the *Titanic*?'

She was in full formal kit – blonde hair tied back in a black velvet bow, little black dress, seamed dark stockings emerging from a pair of stilettos you could deliver a *coup de grâce* with. She held a glass between her thumb and middle finger and smoked a small Cuban cheroot.

'We're splitting up,' she said. She had her head lowered slightly, as if she was about to charge.

'Oh?' How complicated could my emotions get? I was a mouse who wanted nothing more than to be swallowed by the python. 'Johnny didn't mention that.'

'He doesn't know yet.'

Now this was weird. When I'd gone to prison, it had been from the court to the cells, to Wandsworth, to Coventry. Nine weeks of a three-month sentence and it would have been shorter than that if I could have stopped myself answering back.

What I was wondering was how in a couple of months I'd stepped from the reality of strikes, class confrontation and prison into this vaguely Hollywood scene. The closest it felt like was when Robert Donat (or whoever you've seen in it) gets to that big house in Scotland (*39 Steps*) and discovers all the people aren't what they seem to be. They're all in the plot. At what point had life gone from being messy reality to this sort of glossy fiction? I didn't remember any of Johnny's other celebrations feeling quite like this. Donald Sutherland in *Invasion of the Body Snatchers* gradually realizing that he's the only actual human in the group?

I could have been in the sequel. The contrast was too high. Everything was too glossy, especially the people. But, of course, that was part of Bobby's fatal attraction. I stood there helplessly, waiting for her to do or say something.

'You look like you could use a decent bath and a nice bed,' she said.

I had a feeling I'd get the bath after the bed.

When Barbican asked where we were going she told him I was knackered, needed some sleep and she had some work waiting for her in town. She'd drop me off, she said, on the way in.

'But I had something important to talk to him about. It's a proposition, Den. Stick around for a couple of hours and you can sleep here. Believe me, you'll be interested. It's right up your street. You'll love Pilbeam's island. Lots of toys for the boys, eh?'

He didn't seem too pleased with Bobby. And she clearly didn't give a fuck what he thought.

I enjoyed the ride back. I'd never been in a Bristol with the roof down. Just what I needed. By the time we got to Fogg Yard the sun was setting over the graves. The windows were filthy but my bed was neatly made and clean. Somebody must have been looking after the place. When Bobby saw the pristine sheets she seemed almost disappointed, but since she was already slipping out of her knickers I had the feeling she planned to stay.

CHAPTER SEVENTEEN
The Touch

As we lay exhausted and sweaty in my no longer pristine pit, Bobby told me where the elite of the party was heading when it left Barbi's Oxon retreat. A private plane was flying them from Luton, via his own airfield, to Sir Hornsey Pilbeam's mighty manse on the Isle of Morn.

I'd heard about the house he called 'MacLear'. He'd bought it with the original dosh made from his patent windscreen-cleaner. He'd started in the fifties as a door-to-door tallyman, selling car accessories. The economy got better, more people bought more cars, and Pilbeam's fortunes improved. His AutoWear chain was still doing well. Bobby said he'd built up a massive fortune with major holdings in several big American and French companies.

As far as I was concerned, if you chose to live on the Isle of Morn when you could live anywhere you liked in the world you must have something seriously sick in your psyche. It was deeply wet. He thought of it as home because he'd been born in Glas while his mother was on a day trip from Ireland. She'd given birth to him in the toilet. She knew it was the Ladies' but she couldn't remember much more about it.

'Or hadn't wanted to tell him,' Bobby squinted at a jar. 'Did you know this coffee's stale?' She was standing naked in my kitchen going through my stores. She sniffed disapprovingly at canisters and cups. 'I think you've got mice.'

We were drinking the coffee when Billy Fairling knocked at my door. The disgusting old fucker had spotted the posh motor in the mews. I knew it was Billy Fairling because only he had that pseudo-confident rap. Billy was that Brummy who'd been settled in Brookgate since I was a brat.

Billy was the slag's slag, the abuser's abuser, the creep's creep. He was in his seventies and would have been rehoused years before in some New Town if he hadn't been running so many social-security scams he couldn't afford to leave. It would take him too long to build up the complications of his story with some new authority so that it was again impenetrable. He had one of the old alms-houses across the graveyard.

He was supposed to do it up when he moved in. When he died they'd bury it with him, it was so full of rot.

It would be easier to get rid of Billy than have him hang around all morning. So I closed the bedroom door and went to ask him what the fuck he wanted.

Damp, in a charcoal-grey, grease-seamed suit, an open-necked golfing shirt, nasty sneakers and a hat that looked as if it had been knitted out of his own hair, his red eyes shifting, his pallid skin glowing like a dead fish, he stood there with a soaking wet paperback in his hand. It was the size of a small sideboard. I never had Billy down as a Catherine Cookson fan.

He did something with his mouth. I think he was trying for a conspiratorial smile.

'Welcome home, Den. Nice car, the Bristol. How much that set you back, then?' His red nose was pinched in a jealous point. 'Or was it a gift? I heard you was in the pokey. Somebody made it worth your while to keep shtoom, eh?' His wink included me in a catalogue of slippery options. 'Ready for some good news?'

'No dosh, Billy. No nothing. Fuck off. What's that book?'

'I was going to show you this. About me. We're all getting famous round here, these days.'

I didn't think the smell coming off him was alcohol, but something had got him going. I'd warned him before that he was too old for glue.

The book was a London guide by a hack I knew slightly called Chrissy Herbert, a card-index anorak who turned the things out in truckloads. Computer-generated heritage guides. Second-rate versions of the Mummery Guides.

'That crap'll only confuse you, Billy.'

'Crap, is it?' he says. 'I fought in World War fucking Two for you lot.'

'What fight was that?' I asked. 'Inside Wormwood Scrubs or outside The Green Man?'

He'd cracked the book's spine and it fell open in the rain. Water was about the only thing that was holding it together.

'There you are.' He pointed to an entry in black type. Fairling, Wm. Some bloke who'd been a famous nineteenth-century Brookgate boxer and had a school that rivalled Mendoza's. 'That's my grandad.'

'You're a Brummie.' I'd had enough of this.

'Originally, yes,' he admitted.

'From Birmingham. It was where you were fucking born, Billy.'

'I returned to my roots. To my home turf. And now I'm about to fulfill my fucking destiny.'

I was already closing the door. 'Fuck off, Billy.'

'I'm going to open a gym,' he said. 'And train the next world champion. You can have an early share. Sonny Shapiro's in.'

'Sonny's going to wear powder puffs?'

'Don't be daft. We'll do knucklers. I'm going to train him up. But the first thing is to get the gym going. We already have our main finance worked out.'

I could see the *Sporting Life* stuck in his jacket pocket. 'Where's it running? Aintree?'

'This is straight. Guaranteed.'

'Then good luck,' I said. 'And now fuck off.' I hated slamming the door in his face only because everyone slammed the door in Billy's face. Except the woman he once lived with, who pushed him under a bus and got his ribs broken. The whole neighbourhood felt disappointed for her. She'd hoped to kill him.

Eve was never charged. It would have been a waste of time. A hundred of us would have sworn we saw Billy fling himself under that bus while she stretched out her hands to save him. Brookgate clubbed up to send her to Majorca, where she had a job in her uncle's bar. She married a local and runs a leather business. Brookies always get a discount. My old leather jacket's from her.

'Come on, Dennis. The times they are a-changing, mate. Let bygones be bygones. Live and let live, eh?'

There was a fiver in the jar behind the door that had been there since before I went inside. I'd meant to pay the milkman. I offered it to Billy.

'OK. Here's a deposit in good faith.'

'I was thinking more in thousands. I've got the handle on the Huguenot Leases. I can get us the perfect premises. Honest, Den. I wouldn't be here if it wasn't top-notch. One payment's all I need – and we get control of Bonemeal Court.'

'Do you want the fiver or not?'

He accepted it with dignity. 'I'll give you till tomorrow morning. And even then you'll be out of the game if I've got me capital prior-sorted. This is big news, Den. The real thing. You'll thank me for the rest of your life, squire.'

I didn't know what the hell he was talking about. I went back to Bobby's greedy arms.

'Who was that?' she asked.

'Billy fucking Fairling,' I said.

'And who's he?'

'Billy fucking Fairling. Ligger. Shot somebody once. Waste of time.'

'Come here, quick.'

Her attention was back on the business in hand. She was ready for more. I hadn't realized it was Saturday.

She had until noon, she said. I wasn't sure whether that was meant to be extended opening or early closing.

It was the old Huguenot Leases, of course. And only Billy could have got hold of them. And that's why I'm not a zillionaire.

Sometimes the advantage of being perpetually face down in life's wheelie bin is that very occasionally they'll throw something in on top of you that they don't realize is valuable and it'll hit you so hard on the arse that even you realize it's too heavy to be plastic. Come to think of it, that smell hadn't been glue, after all. Just the accumulated essence of all the gutters and garbage Billy had lain in for a lifetime waiting for his luck to change.

Not as dramatic a change as he'd hoped for, but we'll come to that later.

When Bobby had gone, leaving behind some stains and her small stash, I lay in bed, looking out of the streaked windows, enjoying the first real tranquillity I'd known for months. Some of the people inside don't seem to mind as much as I do. They're more sociable. I don't reject company, but I need at least twelve hours a day alone. And this, rather than Bobby's attentions, was what I'd been promising myself.

I turned the ring off the phone after the first call. I let the machine take the messages. It was flashing away like a mad lighthouse, so I obviously already had a lot waiting. I put on a Bing Crosby CD and lay back while *Begin the Beguine* gently washed my brain free of all the crap. *You have to acc-en-tu-ate the positive . . .*

As a journalist, I hadn't exactly been sent to Stalag 19 and the warders, well aware of the possibilities of turning up in the *Sump*, had watched their behaviour as much as they could, but the boredom had been the worst of it.

Even that one time I was systematically worked over by those guys who really enjoy their job, who train at it and take courses in it, it grew routinely, hideously boring. You should check out that erection next time someone's beating you with a truncheon all over your body. It might be boring for you, but it's great for them. I remember the Greenham women talking about the soldiers getting huge hard-ons when they had women trapped inside barbed wire.

I'm not making anything of my few days in the Oakhurst Federal Institution, before they found out I was English. And not some dumb 'illegal'. And realized they hadn't got my camera. But I must admit that's what finally altered my attitude towards the greatest democracy in the world. I suppose I should have been grateful it was happening at home. The Americans might have trained Pinochet's torturers and set the Taliban upon the people of Afghanistan, but at home they have problems explaining themselves to their mothers.

I heard some smart Yankee on Radio Two suggesting that it was time for Americans to take a hard look at welfare and think the unthinkable.

Fat chance, I said.

They haven't even started thinking the thinkable, yet.

I'd seen enough television inside, so I didn't even try to find out if my V was working. I put Graham Parker's *Steady Nerves* on the player and sat back to enjoy Bobby's high-quality grass.

My state of relaxation lasted an hour or two before I began to realize that I was getting very depressed and didn't particularly want my own company, after all.

So when the next knock came at the door I was eager to answer it. And very glad to find it was Norrie Stripling, pink and beaming, in a straw hat and a blazer, dapper as a Dutchman's dipstick. He'd come round with a basket of special grub, a present from Tubby, whom I planned to see the following Tuesday. I told him I was wondering if there were any original members of the Poisonville Social Club still around, but he said most of them had gone back to America and died. The couple of old members he'd met recently had returned as tourists and now didn't seem any different to all those other Americans. 'They argue between relativism and bigotry, dear, and think they're having a debate.'

He began complaining about American film stars embarrassing themselves and everyone else on the West End stage. I think it was Jon Voight playing Othello. In blackface. That was the autumn of '86, wasn't it?

'Scientology appears to be at the root of it, dear. Or maybe they're all Baptists and Hasidim. One of those weak-minded religions that appeals so thoroughly to the undereducated and the insecure. And, of course, advances only the interests of their own addicted egos.' He winked. 'And it takes one to know one, dear. Do you have a corkscrew, still?'

I was glad I'd let Norrie in. I felt depressed, as if I'd been doing stupid things in my sleep and was only just realizing it. I would never normally have let Barbican's Roller pick me up, or have done most of the other things I'd done.

Prison makes you switch too much off. How thoroughly had I been manipulated already by Barbi and his gang? Or had Bobby really buggered up some plan of her fiancé's; was she really dumping him or were they in this together? Or was he dumping her, so she was planning some pre-emptive revenge? Involving me.

And what, come to think of it, had Billy Fairling been going on about?

I couldn't see much of a conspiracy. All in all, things had seemed to happen at random. I was sure some plan might have been afoot, but I hadn't behaved predictably, so the rest of the plan had collapsed.

I discovered a long time ago that conservatives, by nature, only have one idea. And if that idea fails to get them what they expect, they apply it over and over and over again, with increasing vigour and resolve. Neanderthal genes?

The Germans used to set up a machine-gun and wait for the Russian lancers to come charging down the road towards them. Relentlessly, in a column. Again and again and again, until there were none left. I put this to Norrie.

He was cleaning my glasses. 'I think it's what happens to the powerful, dear. The aggressors can only afford to have one idea. But the defenders have to have lots.

'You only need one idea, dear. If you have all the firepower.' Norrie was fastidiously cleaning my knives. He'd lived half his professional life in the US and loved it. He knew all the American musical people. But he had become embittered after the fiasco of Vietnam and the Chicago Democratic Convention. Reagan's nonsense had been the last straw. Evidence that power in America had been wrenched from the hands of the sane and delivered into the control of the barking barmy.

'We have been defeated by the cynical and the greedy, dear. Bigots and bullies have set the tone. I really think we should disband NATO as quickly as possible. And, since they don't seem to be prepared to do it for themselves any more, isolate the USA from the civilized world. We in turn must remind ourselves of our intellectual traditions, our fierce sense of freedom. America has no intellectual traditions, only a few traditional intellectuals, indeed a tradition of anti-intellectualism, and a fierce sense of authoritarianism. Too much faith and not nearly enough analysis. That's partly what makes them so self-important, like the Boers in South Africa, and so oddly vulnerable.

'It's up to us to help them, dear.' He had started on my forks. At this rate, I'd have nothing compulsive to do. 'We must be kind but firm and tell them to stop interfering in other countries' politics, because they really aren't very good at it and create so much extra trouble for everyone, swaggering around and shouting and doing all those silly things they do in their training. As if their training had anything at all to do with real life. Or real death, for that matter. Certainly it tends to let them down in real wars.'

'They mean well.' I was becoming defensive. 'Too nice to make good soldiers. They're good-hearted.'

'True. As good-hearted as the average cockney enjoying the benefits of Empire. Soldiers Three. Amiable contempt for the occupied people. Unquestioning paternalism. Imperialism in its purest form. We just can't afford to think of them as benign any more, Denny, because they clearly aren't. No matter how well they think of themselves, the rest of the world is getting a very low opinion of them indeed. We've got to start telling them off and give them a chance to improve. Our first action should be to slap massive tariffs on American goods and high charges on American planes using our airports. We're getting a bad reputation by association, dear.'

It sounded unfair to me. I didn't have anything against Americans. Except they never paid their bills. My contempt was for the New York media and Washington power politicians. Corrupted institutions and bad governance.

But it was all sky pies. This was when the Hatchet ruled parliament

and could break international law with impunity in order to do her
Ronno a favour. Clinton and Lewinsky? Nothing. Think of La Hatchet
and Da-Do-Ron-Ron alone in the Oval Office. And you thought you
knew the last word in obscenity. If they ever get his inanely grinning
head up on Mount Rushmore it will be the end of that grandiosity. Some
reasonable citizen is bound to blow the whole fucking vulgar shit-heap
sky high. I mean, what else could you do if you feared for the sanity of
your nation? It would be more to the point than blowing away
schoolkids or even Baptists.

   It was 1986 and the civil war was won. It was all over for us. The Big
Bang was blowing us across the world. Dynasties were being founded.
Lacey Moloch was emerging whole from her father's powerful arse.
They were in charge. Their garrisons controlled our towns. We were like
Alan Breck heading for France. 'Fare ye well, Sir Advocate. May your
poor compromised head lie easy on its pillow.' The distant cry of a gull.
A fair wind for the Continent, a sudden cultivating of our own gardens,
the discovery that our language of generosity, kindness and concern was
old-fashioned. Wet. And it had sounded so authoritative when we first
started using it. Another retreat from liberty. Another nail in our public
coffin. Once only Americans were famous for using words like 'God' and
'Democracy' to give their crap ambitions authority. And now we're all
doing it.

   'Why didn't we just enjoy the best of what they produced instead of
getting into the bathtub with them? Muddy. Woody. Buddy.'

   None of these were heroes to Norrie. His favourite American was
Cole Porter. He was an old *New Yorker* reader.

   'I suspect it can go a lot further, dear,' says Norrie, laying my table and
ostentatiously setting aside an ashtray with a half-smoked joint in it.
'Our Maggie has that certainty, that single-minded idea, that leaves
enemy strategists gasping, much as they gasped at Hitler, who did the
unexpected only because his grasp on the complexities was so poor. We
always think these people are acting in full knowledge of the
consequences. What was their strategy? How did they plan this, make
that mistake? They must have a tremendous sense of strategy. Not a bit
of it. They're like bad chess players making wild moves and confounding
the conventional player. Those moves only work for part of the game.

   'They got lucky. Nobody could believe they would do what they do.
Because it was so stupid. These people are running on bad rhetoric and
brute instinct. That's why, when things go wrong, they're forever taking
to their beds in dismay. Gradually their followers sneak out of the
shadows and gasp at the discovery that their leader is not merely mortal,
they're positively barking. Puts you in a difficult position. Especially
when the Russians start knocking on the door of the bunker.

   'Still, if nothing stops you, it looks great for a while. Reactionary non-
strategy. Then people start noticing the gap between what you're saying

and what's actually happening. They don't see the complexities and therefore they don't see the damage, therefore it doesn't exist. And if it insists on existing, it shouldn't.

'It stands to reason they wouldn't be doing any of it if they weren't yelping barmy. And if you look back, you'll see the pattern through history. It's one continuing story of some poor bastard trying to talk reason to the world and getting his or her head chopped off as a consequence. The people who are addicted to control are self-evidently nuts. Who, in the end, controls what? Except God the Father, dear.' And Norrie crossed himself, an ostentatious Catholic all his life.

'Their actions define them, dear. *Sartor Resartus*, as they say. It's never been a good idea to have vision, sweetheart. Look at Carlyle. Look at Blake, dear. It's much better to keep a clever set of books. Look at Venice.' Which became a very lively anecdote about a production of *The Gondoliers* he'd once put on in the Sinai, during the War.

I was surprised that my laughter was so unspontaneous. We both got alarmed at the same time.

Norrie gathered himself in. He adjusted his cuff. He glanced at his watch. He asked how hungry I was. Not much, now I'd found my vacuum-packed speed at the back of the knife drawer.

He told me to get my hat and jacket. We were going for a good, long walk with a top-class pub at the end of it. You didn't get many late-October evenings this pleasant. I said to give me a minute.

At Norrie's insistence, we strolled through a dreaming evening down a half-empty Kingsway to Aldwych to stand on Waterloo Bridge and watch the sunset sprawling over the river and the South Bank, warm and easy, the very last of a long summer. You could already smell November on the air, a hint of gunpowder. And in the gathering twilight, parliament, Big Ben, the defiant GLC flying mocking red banners from across the river, the last of Ken Livingstone's furious rabble. Another year or so and they'd be gone, too. And we still didn't understand the profound nature of our defeat. You sell the public's utilities, you sell the public's power. You lose your absolute rights as a citizen and get a charter, a contract, with options.

It turned out that Norrie had met Sir Hornsey Pilbeam. 'Portly chap with a rash. I organized a couple of concert parties for him, when he was still living in Holland Park. And then, later, I went out to Morn.'

I was breathing in the last of London. What days. What times. Such rascals abroad. 'So what's he like?'

'On one level he's a typical successful businessman. He had some luck, some reasonable judgement, a couple of good guesses, right place, right time, and now, of course, believes himself to be a very fine fellow. An oracle, dear. Believes he can run the world better than the corrupt and shilly-shallying politicians. They all go the same way, but some have the sense to confine their banal dreams to the family sphere. He belongs to that expired Brookgate Masonic lodge they revived and all belong to now. You must know about it.'

'The old Masonic hall? It's closed down. Failed as a bingo venue.'

'That's right. But they have a new building on Pilbeam's land. On Morn.'

'A long way to go.'

'That's probably why they have the private planes and things, dear. Anyway, he's one of those successful Perot-style tradesmen who thinks he can run the planet as efficiently and luckily as he runs his businesses. Which are actually, of course, hugely inefficient, downsize their experienced staff periodically and have to solve the same problems over and over again. And can only exist as part of a whole.'

I wondered if it was worth writing that book I'd talked about: *Dover's Delusions of the Rich and Famous.* Would that get the pack sniffing my anal glands? I asked. Would I become rich and famous and deluded as a result of my book's success? Were our motives always low? Was there no such thing as altruism? Or is all that embarrassing? What's so serious about peace, love and understanding?

Norrie said I should calm down. He took me across the bridge and into that warren of tiny streets around the Old Vic. Waterloo's a funny area. It consists of one or two whopping arterial roads, the station, and then a maze of little cuts, alleys and cul-de-sacs. He'd played the Vic, off and on, for years and was well known in the district. He'd done his *Malone* at the Young Vic and packed it for the full month it ran. I'd been to this pub with him before. It was one of those multi-decker Victorian red-brick gin palaces called The Nest of Vipers and it was a hang-out for the junior Cornells. Lacey Moloch was said to go down there disguised with some of her mates to trawl for rough.

But it was chiefly the favourite pub of the dog-fighting fancy. It was full of stuffed dog-heads, dogs in glass cases, dog cartoons, dog novelties, dog paintings, dog adverts, stuffed dogs having a tea party, stuffed dog musicians, stuffed dog hunters. The ceiling was thick with plaster fauna, with a great broad-bladed fan sweeping the nicotine fumes around the ornate arches, which were supported by pillars wound with realistic snakes.

The pub had originally been built by 'Lord' George Sangral, who had lined the walls with glass tanks, heated by gas, in which he had kept his vast collection of pythons, cobras and rattlers. And, of course, a nest of vipers. These days the only live snakes were wriggling in excited jeans, though it was rumoured they'd tried out mongoose-and-cobra fights, but the mongooses were so efficient there wasn't much sport in it. It was like pitting a Jack Russell against a rat. No contest. *Riki-Tiki-Tavi* tended to talk up the danger and difficulties for dramatic effect.

Only when they substituted Siamese cats was there any kind of real contest, but it was never a popular variation and the cats were inclined to direct their energies at the human cause of their misery rather than the snakes. Like mongooses, they're not much affected by snake venom. But it doesn't stop them being pissed off. A clear-sighted, firm-minded animal, your average Siamese.

As Tubby often said, you'd never get an ordinary Oriental shorthair to take the shit we were all getting used to. It was like Reconstruction in the South, or the German conquest of France. You had to eat it. If you were one of the defeated, it eroded your psyche, destroyed your perspective. Your words tasted funny to you.

I touched my lips to a pint of Finnegan's Mild. It's not a beer to swig at the best of times, but certainly not when you're straight out of the nick. Lighter than stout, but tasty. It's got a lot of flavours going. It reminded me that variety was the spice of life. I began to cheer up.

'So,' I said, looking about the crowded house without moving my head, 'you'd say Pilbeam's a loony.'

I was really more interested in the publican's fat little blonde daughter. She wore a black and tan dress, black and tan sneakers. She had a mastiff puppy in her arms. She was grinning much like the dog, except her tongue was a bit shorter. They were clearly related. They were both looking forward to getting bigger so they could tear some rival's throat out.

I must admit my focus in those days was still what you might call a little retrospective. I still didn't know I was beaten. I was more in the position of feeling nostalgic about pastoral scenes of the gallant South. Still talking of regrouping, of fighting guerrilla battles, all the consolations of the thoroughly trounced. Saving our Old Labour currency. Our embarrassing leader Gimpy Le Leftfoot assures us of glory, of our righteousness, of our popularity. Falling back around Clause Four. Here come the fucking Normans. Now we'll see how the flower of feudal chivalry lasts against our withering Marxist dialectic.

I felt like Hereward the Wake wondering whether to stay in the marshes or split for Denmark. That prison sentence they gave me should never have happened. They were showing their power. I had a lot to think about.

Instead of being merely in sympathy with the miners and the rest, I was now thoroughly pissed off. So I wasn't hugely curious about Hornsey Pilbeam's eccentricities and what I'd missed by not sticking around at Johnny's party. It just sounded like a standard *Harpers and Queen* story. I hadn't begun to see how simple it really was. I hadn't started to look in the right direction. I still thought we were engaged in some sort of democratic debate. Big business was already establishing its keeps. Normans 10, Saxons 0. All we'd been doing for the last couple of years was skirmishing. We hadn't noticed them building the Tower of London.

No wonder Barbican felt sorry for me and brotherly towards me. But not a bit afraid.

I assumed the position, with my back to the bar, with my well-polished heel on the brass rail, my niftily suited elbows on the mahogany, my half-shant in my fist and a reefer between my fingers. I wore my coat collar half up and my jacket sleeves pushed back to reveal sharp lengths of well-Persiled cuff, some silver links. I had a decent crease in my trousers and my boots were buffed. I was glad I'd made the effort. I can't help myself in pubs like that. I revert to type. If I don't look smart, I'm not comfortable.

Norrie, on the other hand, held himself in, with a look of generous amusement, sipping a sweet gin and daring anyone to remark on his pink handkerchief and natty spats. No regular ever did. He knew they wouldn't. He was their star. They'd seen him on those panel games. He was their guy. A sporting gent. No side. Norrie had a talent for being the people's choice. He'd always used his fame to get the life he wanted.

'Any danger?' I asked. 'Pilbeam?'

'Not really. Only if he got much richer, dear. He's a great argument for heavier taxation, especially on the rich. At the moment he's a mere millionaire. He can only dream and do a bit of covert publicity. But I think he had some idea of buying Morn and setting up his own government. It's already sovereign territory, of course, so he couldn't buy it anyway. Nowadays, I gather, he has enough local influence to be the effective feudal laird. The Pilbeam of Pilbeam. Private airstrip. Entertainments. Friends of mine have performed there until fairly recently. A bit weird. Sense of him watching you all the time.

'He's a genial old tyrant. Self-made. Rough diamond. Bought his K. Bit resentful of those who know it. So he dreams of owning the world and showing his critics what-for. Fell out early with La Hatchet. Not sure why. Personalities too similar, maybe. Increasingly reclusive.

'Ronnie Scott did an All-Stars gig there when Pilbeam first took the house over. I arranged it, but I only went over that once. Ronnie said it was creepy, like doing a private function for Heinrich Himmler. CCTVs everywhere. Pilbeam doesn't look a bit like Himmler when you meet him. I think he has some sort of psoriasis. Embarrassed about it. Makes him like disguises, maybe. Suits him to have a little bit of theatre in his politics? He was going for influence at the time, but he seems to have lost any direct interest now.'

'So why the fuck would he invite me to one of his dos? A scumbag supporter of his class enemies?'

'Because your cousin vouched for you? Maybe they're scouting you, dear. It wasn't that long ago that you discovered the CIA was funding half your left-wing publications and about a quarter of your organizations. *Encounter*? Maybe he'd rather keep an eye on the opposition by buying it. Nothing particularly sinister. It's part of their ordinary policy. Maybe Sir Hornsey needs a friend in the popular arena? Your cousin Johnny wants to be friends with you. This might be all he can offer. An invite to the secret source. Were you the only journalist invited?'

'I don't think so.'

'He could be forming some sort of quisling contact group, of course. Enough money and power to be attractive, but not enough to move significant bits of the world. He could be working on that. Oh, dear, where's Lloyd George when we need him? Did you ever read an awful novel by Conrad and Ford, *The Inheritors*? In 1900 *everyone* was convinced that big business was taking over the world, creating wars, manipulating markets, making and breaking small countries, but then look what happened.'

'What?'

'Well, dear. Bolshevism and so on.'

Since Norrie was meeting me halfway, I didn't debate that one.

Then a couple of Norrie's South London friends turned up, Jill and Vic Warburton, big, jolly people with peroxided hair, bright sheepskin jackets and pastel shell suits, with their good-natured daughter and their graceful, handsome Nigerian son-in-law. It was drinks all round, handshakes, shoulder-slaps, iffy jokes, panatellas and dogs, dog, dogs.

It was a wonderful change.

Bloody football.

CHAPTER EIGHTEEN
The Smack

'I value the approval of the forgotten dead over the respect of the living. I suppose you could say that's my main problem. It makes me appear increasingly unsociable.'

Tubby sits in his E-Z-Boy eating health mints. He has to be depressed. That's when he always starts talking like this. A Chris Rea record speaks to his anxieties. *This is the road to hell . . .*

I was about to tell him that me, Pavli and Paul Frame had reformed Deep Fix and were set up to tour America. I knew he wouldn't want to go, but it was only right to ask.

I hadn't had a chance to say anything because Jillian Burnes and her little husband, Felix Martin, the pocket Peacock, had dropped in. They lived nearby.

The stately Jillian, in full organdic splendour, her petticoats stiff as a clipper's sails, moved significantly, like something out of *2001*. You expected to hear Strauss pounding from the speakers whenever she turned. Slow-motion bones. My eye naturally followed her frame from the tip of her enormous feet to the top of her extraordinary wig, slowly, the way the camera moves over the Death Star. She was all detail. Chaos Theory demonstrated. Every feature was a perfect representation of her whole. I could have photographed her for ever, just like they endlessly paint and repaint those long bridges. She'd made herself into a genuine objet de tarte. When you were around her, the self-created Jillian, you were in the presence of a work of authentic genius. To meet the artist was often a disappointment.

Helmut Newton did a lot of her at some stage. Fetishized, distanced, safe. But I didn't snap a thing. Not that time. And never at the Mill. After prison, I lost my interest in photography for a while. There was a kind of anger in me that could only come out in rock and roll.

In the end the band that flew to Toronto a year or so later was only me, Pete Pavli, Snowy White, Simon King and Paul Frame. Paul went home in disgust after Cincinnati because the gig was being sponsored by the United Fruit Company, which he was boycotting. Snowy quietly resigned in Denver and Simon King lasted until Austin, where he fell in love. We picked up Alan Clarke in Austin who drummed for us until we got to LA where Pavli went home and Lemmy joined us for two gigs and we split up.

The last honest work I did was with Blue Öyster Cult for the *Heavy Metal* movie, *Veteran of the Psychic Wars*. The money went through my veins faster than a rat up a rope. Then I did those two ludicrous Motown albums with Maddy. And that's when Rosie found me at the Tropicana Motel. I think I was in serious denial. Not freshly disillusioned but thoroughly lost. Snort music. Heavily into soul. Caught in a trap. Can't go back. Because I love you too much, baby.

Felix was snarling about some slight he'd received in the big people's world and Jillian was beaming, as if at the charm of a favourite child. In those days, they were in perfect union. He spoke relentlessly about himself and his self-concern and she sailed sublimely around him, using his gravity as her anchor. It was a bit like Venus orbiting Pluto.

Felix's ancient publisher had just been taken over by an American entertainment conglomerate, which in turn had been taken over by a big German entertainment conglomerate, which had been taken over by a French entertainment conglomerate, which had been taken over by Disney. All in about a week.

He was complaining that at this rate he'd be paid in vouchers for the Jolly Olde Englande Ride. I said he had a secure future just so long as he kept wearing the mouse suit. He was, after all, the right size for the job. Jillian looked on approvingly as his nose twitched but he didn't say anything for a while. I had a feeling he was afraid she'd put him back in the teapot. Then he couldn't resist adding urgently:

'It's serious, this. We could all wind up with just one dominant worldwide publisher.'

'Does it make any difference if they're all publishing the same crap?' asked Tubby. His eye was on the electronic future. He saw a world of cheap free speech, a fourth estate worth the word. 'They keep saying they're getting leaner and tougher. But they're still lean, tough dinosaurs. Too big to sustain a hard winter, pards. Ice-age casualties. Consumerism's a lousy basis for publishing. So's conglomeratism. It doesn't function appropriately.'

'What the fuck are you talking about?' Felix picked up an apple, wondering about it.

'Always too slow to respond to public taste. Always taking a dive on the last saturation. You know. Boom and bust. Boom and bust. No honest currency, as they say these days.'

'Well, they'd better remember who they rely on for their money.'

'Who?' Tubby asked.

'Me – you – and a lot of people like me.'

Tubby started to laugh. 'And I thought it was just the fucking public.'

Felix sank back with his apple. He'd had it with this tiresome hair-splitter. 'Feel like scorching some rubber, sweetie?'

Jillian became winsome. A memorable moment. 'Not half, darling.' She drew on one of Tubby's Churchillian reefers. 'Just let me finish this joint.' Her mother was looking after their strange little changeling. While they had the chance, they were visiting all their friends.

Felix had never reckoned me much. He hadn't liked the photos I'd done for *Vogue*. I'm not sure what he'd hoped I'd make him look like.

Felix was also convinced I'd turned Rosie against him because she'd resisted his aggressive courtship during his recent brief visit to Marrakesh to confirm his suspicion that he'd hate it. As far as he was concerned, he'd said, the only people who wanted to spend any time in Morocco were either poofters or dopers or both and he wasn't interested in either. It was too hot, too crowded and altogether too fucking foreign. And little boys kept bothering him with offers of their arses or lumps of hash. Jesus. It was worse than Notting Hill Gate on a Saturday night.

Of course, he hadn't told Jillian what had really happened with Rosie. He glared mournfully into the fireplace.

'God, I hate dope.'

Control freaks always hate dope. So do most drunks. Who are often failed control freaks. Or control freaks using their drunkenness. Felix was suspicious of everything that might seem untoward in a 1950s Surrey suburb. Inside he was always yearning for his ancestral Norbury.

His books were a wail, a lament, as if he was searching for something he'd lost but that most of us probably wouldn't have missed yet. His literary tastes were like that, too. Larkin & Co. Thin gruel. Anything that confirmed a mean life-view. A grey, cold little place, his England. Needs massive comforts to sustain its pallid blood, to hold off the dark and the cold and the brutal evil that forever threatens to engulf it. What a wormy turnip. Sometimes, when Felix was dirging on about some fashionable after-dinner anxiety, I thought I'd almost prefer to hear the sound of his father's grim, despondent flatulence.

Marrakesh was the first place Felix had really spent time with Johnny, who was also staying in the glorious sub-deco vulgarity of the Hotel Mammounian and who was out there, too, to confirm a suspicion – that someone was botching the local figures and the Spanish-owned Casablanca United Palmeries, in cahoots with the French-owned Société Générale de la Tête Noire, PUC and SGTN were holding out against his passing attempt to control world date distribution and were a lot more vulnerable than they believed. SGTN had an important handle on the African fruit trade.

Barbican didn't really want or need world date distribution but it might be a useful card in another game he was playing, involving a bunch of American banana Republicans (politicians owned by the US fruit conglomerates). He'd gobble them up the following week. And trade them off a year after that in order to get them, by two more ruthless moves, and the corporation that bought them, back into the fold but now with an operating infrastructure compatible with his own that could be seamlessly downsized.

My cousin bought small corporations the way fishermen buy flies. To see what he could catch. It was his whole strategy. And when he was ready he was like a giant ray. First he nosed out his prey. Then he followed it to the source. Then he engulfed that source. By a variety of different methods, of course. First rule: never attack from the same direction.

Imperialism? Certainly not. Private enterprise. Rugged individualism. Ask Cecil Rhodes. I consume, therefore I prosper.

Felix was getting up. 'I must say, I thought he was a lot taller than that. But Jillian thinks he's mad, don't you, sweetie?'

She passed me the remains of the reefer. 'I call it the Alexander syndrome. The more you conquer, the more resources you must use defending your conquests. Then, when you've conquered everything, you have to start worrying about defending yourself from contenders within. I mean, can we really be in the power of such banal people? With such arid ambitions? Is this the democracy we imagined? But what was he doing out there personally? I mean, he must have hit men for that kind of job? Dates? He'd just bought Exxon. Or was it Shell? I mean, he was trading in whole countries at that point.'

'It was his way of relaxing,' said Tubby. 'And of getting in touch with the real people. Renewing himself. Absorbing that authentic vibe. Sometimes you have to go back into the arena yourself, get a sense of what's really happening.'

We looked at him in surprise and he shrugged.

'That's his story. Believe me.'

He jerked his thumb back at his screens.

'I've got it on tape, if you're interested.'

I preferred my own guess. But later I realized we were all probably right. Not that it did us a scrap of good. You don't reach for *The Interpretation of Dreams* when the real shark is coming in for the final feast.

I remember when Barbican bought his first media complex. He challenged Moloch and the BBC in the name of free speech. This amused Paul Frame. 'To predators like Johnny, free speech is only something that gets in the way of their hunting. That's why they like to have it potentially under control. That's why they all love America. One vast game reserve for them. The media is big business and big business is the media. Identical interests. Say what you like so long as it doesn't harm consumer confidence. Baroque Orwell. The subtle reality. The best-tamed nation in the world. Well, after Luxembourg.'

Of course, he didn't say any of that until we did that horrible tour.

Barbican had spent more of his time with Rosie in Marrakesh. She was taking one of her regular breaks and had flown in from Nairobi. Marrakesh was always where she went for her occasional R&R. She had good friends there, in the medina, who'd taken her into their family. As a kind of social pastime, a celebration of her visit, a chance to gossip, the Berber women gathered to decorate one another's hands and feet, often with elaborate, multicoloured patterns, designs as old as Africa. She'd shown me her hands and arms, her feet and legs, with swirling patterns of white, ochre, red and yellow, pricked into the skin with henna-tipped sticks. Like bridal bracelets. The bonds of Africa. Extending the family, giving you their strength, expecting nothing less in return.

The patterning was a great social event. Women would come from all over the city to visit, to meet Rosie and hear her stories, especially of their S'r'wi Rif relatives. She in turn was glad of a chance to watch CNN on their satellite TV, to drink lemonade and sherbet and eat the delicious little tiger fish the grandmother always prepared. She loved to hear the news, all the news of all the children and grandchildren and great-grandchildren, who brought further strength and honour to the family. Of the women who brought wisdom and those who brought patronage through marriage and made good marriages between their children. Who moved to the coast or to Rabat and so continued to extend the family, an uninterrupted chain, and built a root system that only democratic consumerism could threaten.

As Rosie's kin, I'd been made welcome more than once. A brother. A son. There's nothing like that kind of acceptance. You begin to understand the appeal of Islam. Especially the Berber version.

The grandmother was a religious woman who taught me my prayers in Arabic and who thought so highly of me she would always try to offer me the joys of her faith. Her faith was good enough for my faith. It cheered me up a treat. She had more deep-rooted integrity than Sam Spade. Berber Islam can be a bit like the best Protestantism – rigorous, generous, broad-minded, humane and not much given to empty ritual. City Berbers, they usually only wore the veil in accordance with Arab notions but had a tradition of educating women. Successful desert peoples learn how to value every resource.

They're also admittedly a bit narrow-minded in certain areas. On the subject of Jews, for instance, Berbers generally rival Martin Luther. It's only a few years ago they were made to stop slaughtering Jews every time a *harka* against some other tribe overshot or otherwise failed to engage. But whatever it was they did when they turned their scimitars into combine harvesters, their fruit and veg is a lot tastier than Israel's. They used to be delicious when Marks and Spencer stocked them. But the EU squeezed them out in favour of Spanish and Portuguese crap.

Forget about the Rif's Revenge in North Africa as long as you stick to the pulse and veg. It'll do you good. You'll love it. Not that the mutton's at all bad. Or a really good home-made couscous *royal*.

Anyway, Rosie was hanging out with that family when she met Barbican by accident in the metal-workers' souk. He was buying a long, ornamental dagger, decorated in silver and ebony. He'd been bargaining since dawn. She arranged to see him at the Mammounian but she hated the place. It was always jammed with tourists walking through, like Harrods Food Hall. She took him down to the booksellers' mosque and then for an evening stroll around the Djema al F'naa, the great Square of the Dead, full of jugglers and storytellers, snake-charmers, fortune-tellers, kebab-sellers and instrumentalists. He told her with some awkwardness that it certainly showed you what progress meant. She hadn't known how to take that. She wasn't working for the UN at that point but for Womankind, an organization that sets up women in their own businesses, helps them get their rights, control the means of their own production and all that, mostly in the Third World. I'd done a couple of features on them, some of the only sets of pictures Rosie ever let be used. Not that she always had a choice. But it's amazing how people who really don't want to be photographed can make sure they aren't. A picture is only as valuable as the subject's notoriety.

Rosie moved around a lot now. She was running crucial aid programmes all over the world. She was needed everywhere. She spared Barbican the time because she was hoping to get a billion dollars out of him for some planting project in the West Indies. It might come in the form of seed from one of his agrochem conglomerates, or machinery from his Caterpillar subsidiary, or water-purifying equipment from his Platt and Whiting plant. Rosie would get what she wanted from him and all the other volunteer outfits would marvel. Barbican was notorious for asking what was in it for him.

I think he was also a bit scared of Rosie. Or, anyway, he needed her good opinion.

Sekhmet looks out at the universe. She's got one eye closed. When she opens both eyes her glare will dissolve the world. Sekhmet, Mother of Cats. Our Lady of Destruction, Our Lady of Love and Justice. We are the drinkers of blood. We are the eaters of brains. We are the punishers of your unjust souls. The agents of your destruction. We are the warriors on the edge of time and we're tired of making love. Coded languages.

You can take the boy out of Hawkwind but you can't take the wind out of the boy.

All Tubby's cats seemed to be sitting upright and keeping an eye on us in those days. I felt they were expecting something better of us. They gave no hint of what it was. Nothing but that cool gaze from the shadows, the occasional remark.

I was enjoying some mild pastelly acid and getting so fucking mellow I was almost ready to switch off the burglar alarm in my head and open myself to the vibe when round the corner from the entrance hall, still in his Rhinelander's overcoat, peeling off his gloves, James Mason as Rupert of Hentzau in *The Prisoner of Zenda*, steps Barbican Begg, glowing like the ruins of Atlanta, to offer us all an expansive hand as if our favourite boy had returned to the fold. He's a shark, that Mackie Messer, dear . . .

Johnny was so used to approval he didn't actually notice, except in some vague, abstracted way, that he was being sort of snubbed. He removed his Tyrolean titfer and swept back his floppy locks. But it still didn't make him very welcome. Jocky Papadakis, with no apparent memory of any previous encounter, had been round three times with various strategies to try to get Tubby to sell the Mill to Barbican or some stooge company or fake heritage charity owned or influenced by Barbican. Tubby had told him, as usual, that it was his sacred trust, willed to him in good faith by a man who understood the meaning of the place and to fuck off.

Now here was Barbican, whose strange 'R&R den', all recovered Victorian decorative cast iron, looked like a very fancy gigantic budgie cage designed by a mad Prince Albert on top of his 'other' tower (the first being over the river, with a reconstructed famous fish restaurant on its roof and the main BBIC offices below) has just been in *Hello*. He also has a full-size Wurlitzer cinema organ and what looked like a version of those toys he used to show us in his attic, like fancy guitars, amps and stuff. I wondered if this was to take attention away from a basement where business rivals are racked and roasted for their industrial secrets. And who plays that shit? I have a sudden vision of Barbi, Rupert Murdoch and Donald Trump having a night's jam together. My cousin, of course, exudes benevolent might from every well-nurtured pore, from every well-oiled joint, for it was true, he knew, that his interest and the general interest were the same. If he felt good, it followed the world must feel good. His self-enrichment meant that all were rich. Anyone unable to share this view of himself was either mad or evil. He was confident enough to worship.

And, of course, as usual he was innocently delighted to see me. 'Den, boy!' He used that traditional BBC cockney of his. I'd heard Guards officers, trying to sound like their men, do a better job. Why was it that sight of me always put him into man-of-the-people mode? What did I really represent? I sometimes wondered where all this egalitarianism was showing a dividend. There had to be a motive. Why else would he bother to be friendly?

But of course I always forgot. He was a specialized predator, mindlessly willing to destroy the world in his determination to gobble everything up, but, like most specialized predators, he had certain irrational affections. And, as far as Johnny Begg was concerned, Rosie and me were his blood kin, who had his grudging but unbudging loyalty. He automatically believed us to be on his side, no matter what we said.

We were his notion of a family, of what he could have been. We were almost him. It's an odd feeling. Like a mouse being admired by a friendly cat who thinks you're his brother. You just hope he doesn't forget that he likes you. Or why. Or plays too rough.

'Here he is,' I said, 'the man who bought the world. Sorry about the bomb.'

One of Barbican's big insurance companies had been destroyed by the current spate of IRA bombings, carrying an attack into the heart of British enterprise. Better than blasting Harrods and killing all those Americans who might have helped fund you. Better than blasting schools and streets and bandstands. This, like the bomb that was meant to destroy Hatchet and her Cabinet, was beginning to threaten the Lords and Ladies of Distance. If you want anything done, these days, you do it yourself or threaten the lives of the rich and powerful. A lot of City barons, Barbican amongst them, now knew they were not that invulnerable.

Lady Sekhmet, Lady Sekhmet. Must you destroy us?

Wouldn't you?

Cryptographic anxieties.

On the road again.

Investigate the meaning of your sentence.

We are the lost. We are the last. We are the unkind. We are the soldiers of the end of time.

Tramp. Tramp. Tramp. Tramp. Marching up and down, boys. Marching up and down. Just hoping to make a little time. A little time.

Mother of Justice,
Mother of Death

Pavli's inspired, clever bass was beginning to beat in my head again. The swell of the synthesizers edged at my memory like surf. I could feel myself with a stage pounding under my feet, with my guitar singing its own song, like Ahab aboard the *Pequod*. Riding the wild, wide sea in search of the great white whale. Confronting the brute. I could have done with Tubby's drum, but there's nothing like a touch of angry urban space-rock to get that angst into your veins and powering your system. Not for every audience, of course.

'Are you still doing that old crap?' Barbican lets out a comradely guffaw. 'Freedom, maaaan. Justice for all, dooooooood.' He pretends to be Neil in *The Young Ones*. He raises his fingers, a mocking scout. Sitting there as if he already owns the place.

He took a fast, contemptuous pull on Tubby's massive spliff, handing it casually over.

'You bugger,' I said.

'No hard feelings, Den. But you really do sound like yesterday's news.'

They'd got themselves a nice fake language and were disempowering ours as instinctively as their ancestors reduced the Gaelic. It might sound like scientology to me, but to the world their words were the words of authority. Our old common speech had become a rough, uneducated tongue. We now spoke a dialect without authority. Picturesque at best. The language of the conquered. And like the fucking Scots, we had only ourselves to blame. Too bloody sure of winning. Because we were so righteous.

'Do you *really* want universal justice, Den? Do you know what it would cost you, personally? What it would do to the UK economy alone, the standard of living you take for granted? You'd soon groan when you saw it on your tax bill.

'We don't always get the justice we feel we deserve, Den. Do you want every Pakistani to receive a fair minimum wage? Do you want every tin of cat food you buy to be made with humanely slaughtered cuts of only the best quality? Try putting your moral money where your moralizing mouth is. You'd have to do a Tolstoy on us. And you haven't. You've enjoyed the benefits of all this wicked capitalism as much as the rest of us. And you congratulate yourselves you've kept the moral high ground by calling Maggie a witch. But you're enjoying the benefits of her cynicism and wickedness, aren't you? Even as you sing about how horrible and mean she is. Why shouldn't you be a people's martyr? It's not in your self-interest to be anything else. Only a hypocrite wouldn't admit it. Because if you really hated consumer capitalism, you'd go and live in a hovel somewhere in the jungle. Or join Angela Davis or someone and blow Mr Imperialist Whitey to smithereens. You'd refuse to be caught in the rat race. You'd take some action. You'd take your stand.'

He was right. I'd made a mistake. I'd thought we were all in this plot to make the world more civilized. I believed what I was told. I thought the moral argument had already been won. I hadn't understood my ideas to be naïve.

'Some rock-and-roll rebel,' he added. 'Reinvented as the Bishop of Berkshire.'

'I've never had to reinvent myself,' I said. 'I've always been who I wanted to be.'

'Nobody wants to be a loser, Den. And you don't have to be, either. You just need to get your attitude right.'

Remember *Rogue Male*, that movie where the guy has Hitler in his sights and doesn't kill him? Then spends the rest of the movie being hunted down by Hitler's agents. Wishing he hadn't baulked at murder?

So maybe I didn't have the sense to turn down the lotuses as they were handed out. But I was only just beginning to realize what I'd been swallowing. Prison had done me a lot of good.

In the pause, Felix and Jillian made their excuses, rushing for the exit when they heard new visitors arrive. A flurry of scarlet and green, as if Robin and a couple of Merry Men had swung in. But it was only Maddy

La Font, full of fireworks, and our ex-wife Julie Junk in emerald velvet, looking good enough to feature in a famine commercial. Apologizing as always. 'Hi, everyone. Sorry to barge in.'

Barbican was airy. He didn't get up. 'Hi, girls!'

'My God, Barbi darling, you're looking luscious.' Maddy went straight into flattery mode. It was a matter of principle with her. An instinctive response to power. A flash of scarlet and Julie suddenly didn't have a friend any more. I went and led her over to where I was sitting next to Tubby.

'You seem well,' I said. These things were relative with Julie. By that I meant that she looked like Janis Joplin after a night out with Jimi Hendrix, Jim Morrison and Keith Moon. Her beauty was still visible, almost painfully, like the remains of an exquisite Roman villa sacked by Vandals. Its ruin broke your heart. But you also knew she was dangerous, because if you got addicted to Julie, you got addicted to what Julie was on. There was no other consequence. So we were all wary around her, in our different ways, even Maddy.

'Magnificent!' She applauded something of Barbican's.

He was still on a roll. 'It's unrealistic to think anything else. We're all bloody predators. We make laws to ensure we don't turn on our own, we make laws to ensure we don't get too inbred . . .'

This seemed to be directed at Julie who said she had to go to the bathroom.

Barbican swept his hand towards a row of cats on a beam overhead. 'And we look after species with whom we have some kind of symbiosis. What separates us from those cats? Why do we have to justify what they do naturally?'

The cats were looking at Barbican in that way they had, as if they certainly recognized a predatory equal, but considered his hunting habits crude and unsporting.

'Don't you get bored, gobbling things up?' Tubby took another monster reefer from his box.

'Oh, come off it, Tubs. It's a game. You get into it. A game. You'd be doing the same. You get hooked on it. Always a new goal. It's natural for man the hunter. As natural as anything your cats do.'

Tubby had had enough of his own mood and of the conversation. Whenever someone included his cats in an argument he started taking diversionary action. He touched something and got *Ziggy Stardust*. I didn't complain. That album is a defining landmark in my musical life. Mick Ronson, buggering everything in sight and giving it all some heft. Forcing all that was good in Bowie to come out, sharp and bright as a line of Iraqi Silver. The year David Jones of south-east London turned professional. What a performer! What a talent! You could feel it through your own bones. Every inch of his flesh raw with astonishment at what he found he could do. Giving authority to all the elaborate and sophisticated twists his career took. Still the defining album for people like me. What we needed after the Beatles collapsed under the weight of our demands. After Hendrix died. After the Who self-destructed. Before the Pistols. How the hell did we start to confuse musical actions with political ones?

Ziggy played guitar . . . And to think me and Lindsay Kemp rolled skinny Davey in a carpet and almost sold him to a Saudi we met at the Metropolitan Hotel the night we were trying to coax Calvert in from the balcony. And Viv Stanshall ruined the whole strategy by jumping ahead of Calvert because he couldn't bear anyone else getting so much attention. Down into the car park.

Straight on to some poor bugger's Morgan soft-top. He broke his leg. Dragging Calvert and carrying Davey in the carpet, we slipped out of the hotel with as much dignity as possible, given the pharmaceutical content of our collective bloodstreams.

Julie had helped us get the carpet and its contents into a taxi. Lindsay knew where we were going. On our way to Covington Square he patted Julie on her knees. 'Sit on him, dear. That'll make him sober up.' And Lindsay had done his motor-car joke. And when we arrived our hostess, one of those excited Chelsea honourables, had sent out for the finest drugs.

Golden days. Every word that fell from your lips was interesting to the powerful. They disdained money. They wanted the velvet and silk. The power of the flower. The better sex they imagined we had. The clean consciences, the uninhibited appetites. I was only sixteen. Those women couldn't keep their hands off me. They disdained money. They were embarrassed about it. They apologized for it. They gave it away to left-wing wankers. But they were really buying flesh and bone. Because ours was the boss culture. We were the magic. Those young merchant bankers and their glorious sisters were still trying to do it our way. Before money got so alarmingly sexy. When girls fucked me just because I was young and my eyes were whizzing round and round in my head and they just had to. A unique moment in our history, pards. Sex, drugs, ideals and ambition. Rock-and-roll suicide.

Then suddenly we all became fucking Prussians. A stock in every pot. Realpolitik in every home. What a promise. What a future.

He was all right. The song went on for ever. It still goes on. It's still there. The band was all together.

Watch me, now.

Touching base.

I can make the transformation.

We *can* go back. We have a starting point. We *can* go back and begin again. We can go back. We can.

At first I enjoyed playing in the band. That was never the problem. If it had just been rehearsing and performing we probably all would have done fine. But couple that with so much travelling and discomfort, so much disappointment, such bad drugs and mismanagement, and it probably wasn't a surprise to anyone when we fragmented. I was never a natural front man. I liked playing against someone else's lead, staying in the back of the stage, out of the lights. But in Deep Fix I was the main vocal, so I had to take the centre mike and stand there every night getting whatever easy attention there was to get. Doing mostly familiar stuff. *Rolling in the Ruins. Brothel in Rosenstrasse. Dealer Man. Kings of Speed. The Greenfly and the Rose. The Entropy Tango.* We pulled pretty big audiences. Good-sized venues. The problem was that we were underfinanced, underadvertised and underenthusiastic.

We were doing this, most of us, because we wondered if we still could. And we found that we couldn't. It was all wah-wah and fuzz and skilled effects, but no real energy. Not as the tour went on. Not worth it. Not for the kind of money we were taking. We should have stayed in the studio for a year and made a definitive album, let it get some word-of-mouth attention, and then gone out with it. New tensions. New problems. Fresh energy. I tried, but my heart wasn't really there after LA. I'd sung my blues. The music had served its turn for me, at least for a while. I'd got something out of my system.

Rolling. We're rolling in the ruins.

Did we believe that by chanting the old rituals, singing the old songs, dancing the old dances we could somehow turn back the tide? Ghost warriors. Painted, prancing and howling against the night.

Choo. Choo.

Look out, Geronimo.

Here comes the iron horse.

CHAPTER NINETEEN
The Shaft

Sex with twins is probably the most astonishing kind I've had. In more ways, you might say, than one. Déjà vu multiple orgasms, sweet confusion.

Flo and Pinky Fortnum set me up for it. In those days my life didn't have much room for extra fantasy and I'd never even dreamed of being in the same bed with those sisters. It appeared to be something they'd not only dreamed of, but planned for. Or rather, Pinky had. She didn't go out enough.

Admittedly, I didn't go out much for a week or two myself.

I married Flo Fortnum (almost certainly) at the old Kensington Registry Office in St Mary's Lane. On a beautiful May morning shortly after the first big Can't Pay Won't Pay march. Did my heart good, that march. People 1. Thatcher 0. It was the start of the end. The public challenged Hatchet and won. It took the Labour Party years to follow their lead, and when it did, it blew it. Sometimes it's hardly worth putting up the fucking barricades. Villa and Zapata must have got righteously pissed off after a while. Doing all that hard fighting and then having the left-wing politicians suddenly become conservatives. They didn't blindfold her and put her up against a wall, but the Hatchet never had quite the same support again. I lost my old Minolta and my favourite Pentax in the riots, which meant I had no shots of the police arresting the juggler, the event that started it all. One minute the poor bugger was juggling, the next the jollies had him by the elbows. But I got some good stuff later on my back-up Olympus. The Minolta was smashed by the police. My Pentax was nicked by a Red Guard, whoever that was. But this wasn't a communist plot. This wasn't Bill Bragg's singing. This wasn't a bit of spin. Or a publicity success. Or a cult. Or a bunch of loonies. Or a bunch of axe-grinding radicals. This was the public showing its disapproval, deciding it had had enough. And every copper knew in his bones that he was on the wrong side. And the pictures were heroic.

Family pictures. I've got them in my special book. My old, sweet, darling mob. My good old London mob. Not lads. Not yobs. Not bastards. Not bitches. Not a problem. Not the marginalized. Not the insane. Not the desperate or the hungry, not the envious or the weak, not whingeing professional victims: just outraged men and women with a strong sense of how things should be. And even Tony-boy knew he couldn't keep that mob spinning for ever. A government can only betray the public interest for so long. And a tabloid can only betray its readers' interests until it realizes it had better follow their lead. The press is slow to read the public mood. It always thinks it's in control. It's always hurrying to catch up.

Over the years, as they'd come on the market, Pinky had bought all the flats in D'Yss Mansions and rented out about half of them. The rest she had made her own. The building looked much the same as the other blocks, but behind its bland walls were new stairways, shafts, passages and doors linking her various apartments together. Because of her sitting tenants, she had been forced to circumnavigate some flats by peculiar means and sometimes you'd find yourself opening a door to what seemed to be a cupboard and discovering a dumb waiter or even a staircase.

The mansion block had taken on a very weird atmosphere. The tenants themselves were all pretty reclusive, like Pinky. As you climbed the stairs and approached the landings you saw the doors softly closing on either side. Which suggested they interacted but hid from visitors. Not that there were many visitors. The postman was only allowed to deliver as far as the front door of the block, usually handing over the packet of mail to a nameless old woman who had made that her duty. Normally he'd deliver to each individual apartment in Sporting Club Square. The milkman wouldn't have gone inside even if you'd told him Demi Moore was in there naked and whispering his name. Every morning on their steps were thirty or forty pints, half a dozen packets of butter, a dozen loaves and other miscellaneous dairy products. A doctor occasionally visited and sometimes an ambulance had to be called. No newspapers were delivered to D'Yss. Any animals kept there seemed to be exotic, giving unfamiliar cries and whistles and you never saw them, either. Just the odd scrabbling basket coming and going.

You'd expect a warren like that to be spooky, but in fact Pinky's fundamentally cheerful nature gave the place her own atmosphere. The reason she never went out, she said, was that she hated to be disappointed. This way she could think the best of everyone.

That could be why she'd had the incestuous relationship with her sister for so long. I suppose I should have been flattered they allowed me to marry them. They were such fundamentally generous women I found it odd they should have turned out as they did, but they rarely offered a clue to their earlier lives.

Their father had been Sir Richard Fortnum and their mother the former Honourable Emma Tenniel, Lord Graglynch's radical daughter, who'd taken to drink about a year after her marriage and now wrote sequels to popular Barbara Cartland romances. One of those desperate private lives so many women of her class seemed to enjoy, knowing too much of the world but not being prepared to engage with any of it. The twins spoke distantly and a little contemptuously of their father. But their judgement of him seemed more to do with his theme-restaurant empire than anything personal. I got the impression he hadn't spent a lot of time at home, either with Lady Emma or the twins.

They were pretty, boyish women with small breasts and wonderfully rounded limbs, muscular, but soft, like a cat's. Their skin was extraordinarily vibrant to the touch. To lie in a stoned stupor on the bed while these tigerish sisters sat in front of me, odd mirror images of each other, staring into one another's eyes and masturbating, was eerie, but it was the sexiest thing I'd ever known. Their mutual washing rituals had a distinctly Children-of-the-Damned touch, I will admit. They wanted me to take photos and I did. But I gave them the negatives to develop themselves. Sometimes you know you really have snapped a piece of someone's soul.

I was staggering out of D'Yss Mansions one perfect summer morning, with the air still and the traffic distant, nothing but blackbirds and sparrows, butterflies whizzing around in the gardens, roses and hollyhocks all over the place, when I wasn't surprised to bump into Norrie Stripling.

The old trouper had seen me as I locked the door behind me. He stood on the gravel of the little crescent driveway, whistling as he waited.

I agreed with him that it was a perfect English morning. I knew from the tunes he was chirping that he'd been visiting his old friend Jessie Matthews, who'd lived in Sporting Club Square since she stopped doing *Mrs Dale's Diary*, sometime in the early seventies. Norrie would go over once a week and play the piano for her. You could always tell when he'd been with her because he was inclined to whistle hits from her most famous shows – *Over My Shoulder, Mirror, Mirror, Lambeth Talk, Evergreen* and *Once A Girl*. I knew them all, of course, because of my grandad. He and Norrie could recite a litany of lost stars.

I could tell you who was featured on the bill at the old Kilburn Empire at any time in the forties. Put me on *Mastermind* and I'll remember the names topping every London Palladium bill of the sixties and a lot of the supporting acts. You've probably never heard of any of them.

Alma Cogan. Max Bygraves. Jess Conrad. Dennis Lotis. Matt Monro. Their records and movies were stomach-turning, but I can't help knowing who they are. Like Catholics can't help being Catholics. Or knowing the names of saints. There was one glorious period when people like Buddy Holly and Muddy Waters topped bills because they were still playing the old package circuits round the music halls. Gene

Vincent. Eddie Cochrane. Otis Redding. Five living legends a night for a couple of quid. Soon, the variety theatres started folding in twos and threes. For one brief moment Morecambe and Wise featured in bigger type than The Beatles. Then it was finished. Bands did either pubs or stadiums. The theatre circuits gradually collapsed. The theatres became bingo halls, multiplex cinemas, warehouses, high-priced sites.

Freddie Earlle couldn't believe what I could tell him about his Variety career before he went into TV. I just knew his name from the bills. Norrie's collection of posters was famous. People were always borrowing something or other and you never saw a book about the English theatre or cinema without Norrie getting a credit. The Empire, Edinburgh, The London Palladium, The Manchester Hippodrome. Freddie was on the bill with Frankie Vaughan, in between Roy Castle and Pinky and Perky, in Startime, 1958. I saw him there. March, 1958. I went with my Auntie Rita and Rose. We were five or six. She'd won the tickets in a competition. We were bored stiff through most of the show. Standard stuff. But, of course Auntie Rita thought she'd died and gone to Las Vegas. She had all Anthony Newley's records.

What a burden. I was helpless.

I joined in the harmonies of *When We Smile Again*. He'd done the original role of Emil to Jessie's Pandora. By that time Jessie had made too many enemies amongst her peers, stolen too many husbands, and American-style musicals, slicker, less quirky, less outspoken, were coming in.

'A short run, dear, but a wonderful run. Jessie was never fresher. I had the feeling I wasn't giving her everything she needed. Maybe nobody could, dear. From the start she was wonderful to work with. Disciplined, cheerful, helpful to the other performers, but then one night something snapped and it was as if all her energy had been used up in that performance, the performance of being Jessie Matthews, good companion, the public's little trouper. She became abrasive, to say the least.

'You weren't altogether sure, dear, who the private Jessie ever was. She just seemed to offer a series of characters with which she tried to get your approval. If she failed to get that approval, she felt thwarted. And if she felt thwarted she was inclined to turn on you. Even in the bedroom, dear.' But he wouldn't pursue that. It would be pointless to try to make him.

'Some people don't have inner lives, Norrie. Some people don't feel the need for them. They exist in a world of physical effect, a world of struggle and conquest. Their futures are hideous. Apes in the mud, Norrie.'

'Please, dear. We don't mention oblivion and we don't mention the baboon colony. We agreed that conversation isn't about realities, dear, but reassurances. Like grooming, dear. Like stroking and petting and

purring, dear.' And he feinted at me with his stick, tipping his hat over
his left eye and winking with his right, all the trademarks of his old stage
persona. You can see him from his earliest years on film, with a tennis
racket, or a ukelele or a golf club, his little face polished like an apple.

As we strolled towards the east exit with its fancy Russianate
ironwork and over-the-top *fin-de-siècle* mademoiselles, now picked out
in smart paint, Norrie asked me if I liked the change.

'It probably reflects the times. A triumph of style over function.'

They'd landscaped the big garden square and done up all the old
mansion blocks. Emphasized architectural features in different pastel
colours, like the San Francisco painted ladies. It looked like something
from *The Prisoner*. A set. There was a small fairground now, with a little
kiddy merry-go-round whose central shaft was decorated with pink and
white stripes, like a surgeon's pole. A snack stand paid rent to the
Residents' Association in order to keep down service charges. It gave off
a strong smell of vanilla and onions.

All this had been introduced because the new leaseholders felt the
younger residents were not sufficiently catered to. The younger residents
paid much higher rents and leases. And now they bought hamburgers
and sideshow tickets where a year or two earlier they'd sat reading while
their kids played with a ball and a dog. You couldn't keep that
unprofitable tranquillity, so someone suggested it would be wise to
worry about the safety of your kid, helped you start buying more and
more expensive lures to keep them at home, not to go out into those
dangerous streets and consequently die. Crime remains a growth area,
integral to any modern nation's economy. Why should the people
making the profits want crime to stop? Everything works to the besuited
white man's advantage. No matter what side of the law the combatants
are on, he gets a cut. While the hamburger stand helped stimulate
moribund areas of the economy. Which was to everyone's benefit in the
end. Or so the new leaseholder, my cousin Barbican, had been telling me
last time we met at Tubby's. That hamburger stand was the symbol of a
healthy, dynamic entrepreneurial society, a growing economy.

I've watched it since. It's all on tape, of course. Tubby couldn't help
himself. His little cameras were everywhere. In a way those of us who left
the bullshit on the doorstep when we visited the Mill came over a lot
better than those of us who remained concerned about status, power and
lust. Something in an obituary has always stayed in my memory. I can't
remember who they said it about, but it was a good description of Tubby
– *Strike him where you will, he rings true.*

Barbican, on the other hand, was a synthetic orchestra, a muzak
symphony. Greed does that to you. It turns you into a specialized
appetite that automatically lies, that will say anything to make an
immediate gain and will then compound that gain and compound it
again. Using any resource to achieve the end, unconcerned by any value,

any importance, save cash and control. Gobble, gobble, gobble.

'You don't hate the changes, Dennis? The coarseness they bring to our lives?'

I'd never thought much of the place. 'Come off it, Norrie. It was a vulgar Edwardian fantasy and now it's a vulgar Thatcherite fantasy. So?'

'It looks as if Disney had taken the whole thing over.'

'Well,' I said, 'there's worse things to worry about in the world than a spot of middle-class angst over a disappointing paint job.'

Serves me right, then, I suppose.

Funny how sentiment colours your read of the world, isn't it? But I really didn't see why they should enjoy a privileged tranquillity which the people in the council flats a few streets away would never know.

Why is there always something more important dividing us?

I wasn't really listening to Norrie talking about the end of the Conservatives. In 1992 it didn't seem entirely likely. I think the Labour leader was either Neil Two-Right-Feet Kinnock or the reassuring John Smith who had an unreassuring heart attack and let Tony Blair become leader. Talk about an exemplary story for modern times. And you think I should show more respect?

'These pompous crypto-socialists will discover how little they can deliver on their promises, how little public power is left, how much their predecessors will have sold to private enterprise, dear. Believe me, things have been out of kilter since we lost Harold Macmillan. Hate him though you might, he had some understanding of how to maintain civic justice. When you give up public control of utilities, dear, you also give up the power to level the playing field.'

We had crossed North End Road and were strolling up Old Brompton Road, past the Tube station and towards the cemetery, wondering whether to walk through to Fulham Road or take Earls Court Road to High Street, Kensington. Either way we'd avoid Harrods and the horrors of Knightsbridge. I suggested the northerly route and Holland Park to Notting Hill, which suited him perfectly he said. 'So long as we don't have to go any further into Notting Dale, dear. It's even more yuppified now than Sporting Club Square. I remember the good old days when it was all prostitutes and steel bands and you could relax in an ordinary pub. Where the only serious assaults on your ears were the Irish jigs. When my brother was writing his books.'

Derek Stripling had been known as Colin Chance and had done a series of low-life novels based on his own experience living in Ladbroke Grove from the mid-fifties. A couple of them were filmed, when it was still cheaper to use black-and-white stock. Freddie Earlle and Norrie did character parts in both. Their timing was perfect. It galloped along. But the scripts had given some trouble. Derek's drinking hadn't helped. The films had never been anything but B-features.

Stripling was no Gerald Kersh, but he'd captured the atmosphere of grim poverty and dumb anger that had permeated the area before it became a hippy haven. He'd been a mate of Peter Rachman's and for a while shared Mandy Rice-Davies with him. They were all seedy, he'd say, but they weren't all crap. His fund of Christine Keeler stories showed her as a rather bewildered, exploited woman. She trusted him to ghost her life story and in his last years he became her confidant and supporter. The only time she left her flat at World's End was to go to his funeral. I saw her a few years ago, when she asked me to take some photos. She'd stopped dyeing her hair and was hoping to get some work in TV. I did my best. She said she didn't trust anyone. Not just men, she said, but everyone. She sent her best to Flo, but felt Flo had betrayed her. Something Flo had tried to do with the social services. One of her usual acts of misjudged generosity.

Christine was a potent myth, but she hadn't sought that potency and couldn't deliver whatever it was people expected. She had, she said, given them everything she had. She had nothing left for herself. She hadn't started out with a lot. She'd been flattered by the attention. She'd ridden high on it all for a while. But, like Monica Lewinsky, all she had to offer the world in the end was her notoriety. You can only lift your skirt and show your knickers for so long before people start casting around for a new diversion.

There was a gusty breeze. It made Norrie hang on to his hat. We went up the seedy red-brick bazaar of Earls Court Road with its horrible scattering of formica, its burger bars and pubs shrieking with billboards and banners, tuppence a pint off O'Dowds, two cocktails for the price of one, full English toast and tea, lunchtime specials, deals on high teas and suppers, theatre tickets, plane tickets, train tickets, car rentals, flat rentals, freakless freakshows, *Der Spiegel*, *Herald-Tribune*, *Al Misra*, the pavements busy with backpacking antipodeans looking for an address their parents used in 1965, with German students, French boys, Arab boys, Italian boys, Greek boys, crocodiles of giggling Swedish schoolgirls, with tourists on walking tours, with touts and shouting shopkeepers, and Middle Americans in London Fog raincoats with maps in their hands who had just discovered to their horror that most of the world isn't on the grid. And that far too much of it walks. Whores, pimps, coppers, grifters and grafters.

The Earls Court Road might once have known some kind of character, if not elegance, but now, with its busy bus routes and cut-throughs, it rivalled Queensway for a level of tackiness normally only found at the centre of things, in Leicester Square and Piccadilly Circus. We paused outside a Bar-B-Q, recently a Pizza Hut, which had previously been a Taco Bell, which had previously been a Wendy's, who'd taken over the Wimpy site, and Norrie asked me if I remembered George Pal's *The Time Machine*, where the passage of decades is reflected in the fashions changing in the store window across the street.

'These days, dear, they could do it with fast-food logos and we'd realize what was happening.'

I laughed. 'Remember when it was all ABC Tearooms and Lyons Corner Houses round here, Norrie? In the golden age of cafeterias. It used to be nothing but automats for as far as the eye could see. Strong tea was still one of the dominant smells. Chippies, offal shops, saveloys, faggots, butties and patties, pasties and pies, hamburgers, kebabs and enchiladas. Call it what you like, it's still flour and sugar and grease, spuds and batter and spitting fat. They all kill you pretty much the same. What's the fucking difference between the fashion in one fast food and another, Norrie?'

'There was always a chance of being pleasantly surprised, dear.'

I sniffed. And wished I hadn't. We began to move on.

'People who like to control everything, to standardize everything, Denny, are very alarming people. They are reducers, dear. They're anti-life. They're death personified, dear. They are the friendly face of evil. The ones who boast of the jobs they create, the lives they improve, the nutrition they provide.'

'Greedy hypocrites is all,' I said.

'Powerful hypocrites, Denny, dear. They've created a *culture* of exploitation. They have whole departments founded whose business is to deceive, to confuse and, in the final necessity, to silence any questioning voice. We used to recognize their kind in the community. We could choose not to do business with them. Or they would need the goodwill of the people enough to behave themselves a little better. Now we have no choice. Show them a reassuring international logo, a familiar sign, and people's judgement seems to disappear. You're probably too young to remember the curiosity, the excitement of visiting the first McDonald's just up here, in Ken High Street. But I brought my kiddies. It was wonderful. Strange how we always welcome these people and how they always shaft us, one way or another. Nobody ever trusted those shifty lowland Scots and now, through the politicians and institutions they've taken over, they're running the world.'

I was feeling too good to get worried. 'The traitor Campbells,' I said. 'Shunned by Scotland, embraced by America. Come back with a vengeance, the scallywags. If they get nasty, God knows what they'll slip in our soup while we're asleep.'

We headed on to the top of the road and crossed over to the gates of Holland Park and the Commonwealth Institute. The flags of all the old Empire countries were flying and Norrie stood to inspect them. He liked to keep up on any new designs. As he stood there, the wind gusted again and blew a piece of the *Daily Mirror* round his leg. He brushed at it with his stick.

'At least with a political empire, dear, there's some kind of dialogue, some understood option, some sense of what should be. You can use the sentimental manipulations of Empire for only so long. Then that sentimentality has a habit of backfiring. People take it seriously. They want it to be true. And if it isn't true, dear, they go about making it true. A vision is nothing without a moral imperative. Some sort of mirror that shows us how we're perceived. But international business recognizes no moral imperative. There are no real options. No information. Stale, unquestioned notions. There's no dialogue, little sense of right and wrong. Profit and loss are their only methods of moral measurement. It represents nothing but its own self-interest. Idealists are consigned to helpless politics. The Indian National Congress, according to Richard Attenborough, hung around while Gandhi kept to his hunger strike and achieved freedom without bloodshed. We can debate morality as a people, but as individuals we become relativists. Don't it all look barking barmy to you, dear?'

It always had, I said. How many fundamental lies can you found your civilization on?

We sauntered into the park with its great spread of lawn. A couple of teams in full whites were playing cricket over on the far side. Their commands and cries were echoed in the nearby rooftops. Puff puff, whack. Puff puff, swish, thwack. Howzat! Lots of running about and waving arms above heads. Dogs sniffing. Kids racing. Nannies and priests and dapper ancients. Not such a cosmopolitan park as Hyde Park, but more domestic, less of a dominant eighteenth-century notion of natural order. Still in the old dream.

Holland House had been firebombed towards the end of the war and was only a shell, a Walpolean ruin, picturesque amongst the exotic vegetation Lord Holland the botanist had planted. Then the place was a jungle of papyrus, yuccas, buffalo grass, banyans, oriental cedars and other wild imports mixed in with the native oaks, chestnuts and birches. The old wooden snack kiosks had blended with the wistaria that covered them. Fancy pheasants, peacocks and chickens roamed at will, their horrible cries occasionally biting through the dozing summer air.

Holland Park had that slightly frowzy, neglected air of some amiable elderly intellectual. If it could speak, you'd expect it to give you long quotations in Greek and Norman French and compare some current event to a forgotten Mesopotamian wrangle.

Sporting Club Square had until recently had that same slightly run-down, comfortable air and I realized what Norrie was missing. Who were these rehashed sets meant to appeal to?

I'm glad we had that walk. It was the last time I spent in the park before new managers came in to maximize the space's assets and tidy them up a bit, to encourage visitors. But no matter what they did to make the park tourist friendly there was always the hovering shadow of Holland Park Comprehensive, less a palace of education than a hive of killer bees, that twice a day disgorged a bunch of little berserkers to loot and pillage the surrounding territory. People in the know listened for the school bell. As soon as they heard it, they gathered their charges and dear ones and hurried to the nearest exit.

It was early evening by the time we were walking through the woods down to the Holland Road entrance and everything had the luscious warmth of late summer. We'd gone a bit slower than I'd planned and I realized it was getting late. I decided to take the Central Line home. Norrie said he'd join me and get off at Tottenham Court Road. The Holland Park elevators were out, so we had to walk down the long, curving staircase, around the central air-shaft, which tended to emphasize just how far underground the line actually was. I tried not to think too much about it or my claustrophobia would get the better of me. Down and down, round and round, our footsteps echoing a counterpoint to Norrie's cheerful complaints. 'Look at this stuff. Your old engineers sought to serve and astonish. Now all energies are devoted to reassurance. Government is a fat whore, dear, with her legs permanently open.'

You disgusting old horror. Keep your language to yourself. Filthy old bugger. They get off on it, don't they, that type?

Norrie was visibly repentant. He seemed to pale. He looked up at me with genuine dismay.

'My dear lady. I had no idea. My deepest apologies.'

The bodiless voice was not to be mollified.

And now he's a comedian.

'At last,' Norrie helplessly removed his hat. 'Recognition!'

We didn't hear our invisible auditor, even on the platform. The train had arrived before we got there and was just about to pull out. Norrie hurried me aboard.

As the doors slid shut on our almost empty carriage he asked how Rosie was. He'd seen her in Ray's that morning, before he went off to the Square. 'She could have just got in, of course. Were you expecting her?'

I felt stupidly alarmed. Rose hadn't been due back for a month.

It had to be some sort of emergency.

Suddenly I was depressed and I didn't really know why.

CHAPTER TWENTY
The Skin

Rosie had settled in by the time I arrived. She'd always had a key. She often used the flat when I wasn't in London. I knew she was there as soon as I opened the door. She'd got *Love Is A Stranger* on the deck.

The living room was oddly neat. Books upright. A vase of flowers. The bedroom had a woman's touch. There were old, battered brocaded African bags stacked in a corner. They didn't have much of a woman's touch. They looked like they'd been dragged out of the heart of darkness.

'Are you living somewhere else?' she asked. 'This kitchen's not up to your standard.'

'I've been too happy.'

'Well, that makes a change.'

I always forget what a stunner she is. Every time I see her after a period of separation it hits me. She's wearing a big, bright Sudanese dress with short sleeves rolled back; a dish-mop in one hand, an oven pan in the other. Her hair's still all over the place, which means she hasn't been out. It takes a lot of attention, big combs and small machinery to get that mass the way she likes it.

'What's up?' I reach towards the vase to stroke one of the fresh, bright petals. 'You been fired already?'

She'd left the UN a year or so earlier, worried about a growing American understanding that the UN had to be an arm of their own foreign policy or they wouldn't pay their share. *They corrupted their own institutions and now they're corrupting ours . . . The UN's in danger of getting a bad name. I didn't like the way people started feeling awkward around me.* Because of what was going on, aid workers were now often seen as US stooges, the imperial power's missionary priests and nuns. Internationally, America was only just beginning the process of civic corruption she'd completed at home.

As governments hurried to give up their moral responsibilities to the voluntary sector, the power shifted as well. States became increasingly unable to respond altruistically, humanely or even in enlightened self-interest. Sentiment was no substitute for justice.

For some while Rosie had believed that the real power was now with the voluntary agencies and its supporters. *If you're given the power, you might as well start using it . . .* And she needed power, she told me. She needed as much as she could get. Organized and coordinated, the main voluntary agencies were powerful enough and had sufficient moral authority actually to have real influence on the actions of at least nominally democratic governments.

I didn't really think she was going to tell me she'd been fired by her new employers. She'd been asked to set up CAAW. The organization had only recently been formed but was already doing a lot to coordinate different aid agencies around the world. There was talk of the power of the charitable corporations, the threat that they might become the thing they were supposed to resist.

When she didn't reply I asked: 'Work going all right?'

She moved to stand against the window. Behind her the sun set in a pastel blue sky, pink tongues of light tasting the warm brick of the church, green juicy brambles, lichened grey stones, deep shadows. She stood very still, turning to look back at the graveyard. I thought she was about to tell me something. I felt like an actor who'd given her the wrong cue. She seemed to be gathering herself in, as pantherish as ever. Then she relaxed again.

Maybe because I'd just come from the twins, I found myself really noticing Rosie's sexuality. Her figure was fuller and more rounded than I'd become used to, and she gave off a rich, womanly warmth as if she'd just come thrusting out of the womb of Africa. It was like having the whole fecund continent in the same room with you. You could almost faint if you inhaled it. Was she pregnant again?

There was nothing to do but swim in her atmosphere. A subtle bonus after my tasty night with the twins. The trouble was Rosie herself had something on her mind. A bit of a fly in my unusually soothing ointment.

'Are you going to tell me what's up?' I said. 'Or am I going to have to bribe it out of you with bloodworms?'

'Let's go for the bloodworms,' she said. 'Got anything to keep me awake?'

We did the rest of the coke I'd scored when I married Flo and which I hadn't needed at D'Yss Mansions. Rosie was making an effort to get herself up and I was there to help her. She'd have done the same for me. She wasn't much into avoidance. I doubted if she'd seen a line of coke in a year. It meant she needed it.

She and I had an agreement – one week's self-pity every three months. In normal circumstances anything else was excessive. About a month in a year. So I guessed how serious it was.

Keith Varney had just moved his premises out of Sharps Alley and over the road to Toffee Corner, which still had its eighteenth-century bows, its Georgian courts. The wormshop now occupied the premises of the old kosher butcher (no disrespect involved) and some of his tackle was hanging around the place, though the knives had gone in a stockbroker fight on opening night. Since then the Pictish sorcerer Varney had barred suits. It was probably the only place left within the old City walls that refused uniformity as a matter of principle. Varney himself was at his back counter that night, dwarfishly short and enormously fat, his huge eyebrows dripping with moisture, a thin roll-up in his thick grinning lips. His shirt and apron were spattered. He was a steaming crimson. He seemed swollen with blood, as if he'd been feasting on buckets of it, gorging himself under the pulsing pig as it jerked its life into his mouth. What a monster. What a chef.

Varney saw us come in. His eyes held their usual sly triumph. Some of us were drawn to him in spite of ourselves. The cellars were crowded with men in oddly-fitting velvet and peculiar shirts and pullovers – all prepared to risk a night in mufti for a taste of Varney's worms. And, of course, to boast of it as they smoothed back into Threadneedle Street the next morning.

Varney didn't mind. My guess was he was thinking of some new hoop he could make the greedy bastards jump through. They didn't even know they were getting a different menu. He called them 'lordies', same as in Brookgate. They were underwriting the weekly feasts Varney gave every Sunday morning for the local poor.

I can't say something in me wasn't intrigued by these incognito bankers. But even watching them closely, I couldn't work out exactly how some were able to guffaw and swallow at the same time.

Of course, I also had a fair idea why Varney was smiling.

As well as a fair idea of what the gents were eating.

'Good evening, your honours.' He greeted us with his gypsy wink. 'And how's the real world?'

'Terrible as always, captain,' says Rosie, brightening up just from the familiarity of it. I knew she was salivating. Her eyes had gone funny, as if she was about to spring on something. Beautiful, dangerous slits.

Varney had been running a wormshop forever. His dad kept the old Pudding Pit on the other side of Clerkenwell Road while his mum was Mother Fat's grand-daughter. We moved past Varney towards the stairs but, with a faint movement of his head, he directed us to the back, through the heavy oilskin curtain with PRIVATE painted on it in scarlet gloss, where Polly, his pissed-off Rottweiler, growled at us absently. Her tail fell in disappointment when she realized it was just friends. She cast about hopelessly for some real enemy to sink her teeth into.

On his tacky old record-player beside him he was playing Kingsize Taylor and the Dominoes. Kingsize was his role model, the rock-and-roll hero he'd never be.

The back room wasn't always open. Neither did it have any of the beamery and sawdustery of the front rooms. Plain lino that looked as if it had been there since *Upstairs, Downstairs*. Some hideous ruched pink curtains covering a window that seemed to stare into the void. Rocky old draw-leaf tables. Miscellaneous chairs. A glimpse of the kitchen through the inner doorway.

Varney mostly used it when the public rooms got too full and he had to trust you. You might catch a glimpse of something. To get their flavour, the worms had to be made with fresh pig's blood, which meant the pig was being hung and bled somewhere nearby, completely at odds with every city law since the beginning of the world. And they didn't die quietly. Over there was near the old loony bin. You knew it was haunted. You'd never find anyone who'd heard anything. There was a lot of illegal stuff went on at the back of Toffee Corner, in that old rat's nest of streets running up to the station. The police kept clear of it if they could. Going in there was like turning over a tip.

But once you caught a whiff of those tasty worms, you didn't care how illegal they were.

Taters, black carrots and parsnips. Fried broccoli with macaroni cream. Curried scullions and Killarney faggots. French beans in mint or rosemary scurd. Garlic jelly. All specialities of his house. All horrid to the uninitiated. And when cooked by Varney himself they were unspeakably tasty.

It didn't matter that you could hear his sweat spitting into his grumbling cauldrons and snapping skillets, his strange, almost sexual groans as he tossed the worms in the slithering grease, the nasty snarls of the dog who refused to move from her place by the stove and was covered in tiny burn marks. Obviously she considered any discomfort worth the chance to chase a random sliver of sausage through the air before it could reach the straw-strewn floor. The dog was as much addicted to the stuff as anyone else.

It wouldn't have mattered if we'd been told that Mrs Lovett was doing the cooking and Sweeney himself was doing the preparation. There is a moment in any predatory carnivore's life when it must choose between an ultimate moment, where almost every sense is brought to its fullest expression, and a lifetime of regret. But, of course, once you'd tasted Varney's specialities, you never forgot the pleasure.

And sooner or later you started going back for more. The family were all addicts, too. *The Feast of Blood*? Remember the old melodrama? That was about an ancestor of his.

Rosie had eaten far more exotic and oddly-prepared dishes in a culinary world where snake was often a staple and neither of us felt that twinge of naughtiness, that secret, primitive sensation you often saw in those stock-spinners' eyes. In certain cities of the world, which considered themselves civilized, you had to pass by the evening's bleating dinner before you could get into the dining room.

Why do westerners like to pretend they're vegetarians, the way they like to pretend they're children? Itchy-koo, itchy-koo, with the blood dribbling down your chin. It seemed to me that a nod to the screaming steer, a moment or two to thank the twitching pig or the beheaded lamb wasn't too much to offer in return for a tasty Sunday lunch in some lovely old beer garden. But nobody likes to think what's on the other side of that neat, cosmetic hedge.

Old McDonald had a farm. Ee-aye, ee-aye, O!

We didn't talk much while we dug in. That moment when you first slice through the thin, crisp skin and watch the dark, meaty oatmeal erupt from the gleaming black tube is a moment of worship. You could divine the future in those entrails.

We were on the Stilton and kvass before the noise from the public rooms fell away and we felt alone for the first time.

I settled into my chair with my glass. 'So how's the job?'

'Great. It's a great job. I designed it, after all. I'm doing what I always planned to do. And just in time. We need as much coordination as we can manage – getting the aid to the people it's meant for, helping people establish the infrastructure that puts the power in their own hands, all that stuff, especially since the gun trade is booming and donations are down for the poor and the sick . . .'

'You've stopped pressuring the governments?'

'That's not where the real power is, these days, Den. We have to deal with big business. And big business doesn't feel it owes anyone anything. It requires a different approach.'

'What? Cap in hand? Are you saying you're ready to suck Barbican's dick?'

'I've refused four times.' She smiled suddenly, her eyes brightening with a happy memory.

'Do what?' I couldn't imagine Johnny getting up the nerve.

'Well,' she said, 'he calls it a proposal of marriage. He proposes to me every time before he gets married. That's how I remember it's four. Julie. Flicky. Jillian and Roberta. No, five. He proposed again recently. So that means a looming divorce and another marriage. Do you know who he's got in mind?'

'Hang on a minute,' I said. 'Did he actually marry Bobby?'

'Oh, yes. At St Hilary's, Skerring.'

'Skerring?'

'They wanted a very private marriage. Even the Press won't go to Skerring. And Bobby's father's from near there. I can tell you a lot more of this stuff. I had an earful from Johnny on the phone. It's that call, of course, brought me back so quickly.'

'You accepted?'

She put down her cheese and cleaned her lip. 'Fuck off,' she said.

'Anyway,' she added shiftily, 'I might be seeing Paul again.'

'Paul Frame? But Paul *is* married. Once. To his wife. Ulrica.'

'Always.' Rosie sat back from her plate. 'You knew anyway.'

'If I did, I didn't want to.'

'There it is.'

Now I was depressed.

'Sorry, Den.' She patted about in her bag until I handed her a joint.

Then she started crying.

'Oh, shit,' she said, 'I shouldn't have eaten that last worm. You can't be this miserable and have an appetite that hearty.' She started snuffling through her tears. 'I feel awful. I need a beer.'

I ordered a couple of shants of O'Dowd's.

She said she'd never really stopped seeing Paul Frame. She was addicted to him, she said. 'But *he*'s only addicted to junkies.' She grinned in a ridiculous, undignified way.

She was awkward, all over the place. She hardly knew how to break down.

In those years since Kim's death she'd stopped confiding in me. Now she was trying again.

In public. Because she felt safer here.

She cleared her throat.

'So you came over to see Paul?'

'What?' She lit the reefer. 'No. He's still in Burundi, isn't he?'

'We drifted out of touch.'

'He could be in Nairobi by now. Lost cause, all that, I think. But you never know.'

'What's he doing?'

'Singing for peace.'

I took a sip of my shant.

'Well,' she said, 'it's a travelling show. A bunch of idealists. Ulrica's dedicated to it. She was an actress before she got married. Paul's quite famous, you know. They buy his records over there. World Music. He's always on John Peel. And he's the only white boy in the show. Not quite as good as Bob Marley turning up, but almost as good as Eric Clapton. He loves it. They love him.'

'I saw that documentary. I didn't realize he was still doing that. What happened to Nantes?'

'Nothing. Still there. It's his home.'

I just looked at her until she began to laugh.

'Oh, fuck, Dennis.'

I decided not to go to Sporting Club Square that night. I phoned the twins and told them that Rosie was in town. We needed to discuss some family business. They didn't seem to mind much.

We went back through that moist, whispering darkness. Down Farringdon Road as far as the Viaduct. Then up the suppliants' stairs, where beggars murmured to you from shadows stinking of urine and methylated spirits. To High Holborn. And stood looking down towards Ludgate Circus and the river. You could almost hear the old Fleet running under you. We often stood there like that, feeling fierce and positive, the way we had as teenagers. Get the wind in your face and you could be on the city's twenty-second century control deck, taking her up into the spaces between the stars.

'So why did you come back early?' I leaned against the heavy ironwork and rolled us a small one. 'CAAW biz?'

'Us biz,' she said. 'Barbican was really pressing with his offer this time. He had a present for me, he said. A wedding present, of course. Nothing for nothing. Or not much, anyway. This time he thought he had an offer I couldn't refuse. He was full of himself, how he'd achieved his coup after years of planning. The various parties he'd had to deceive and threaten to get what he wanted, the various officials who'd required "a little envelope" and all the usual stuff you hear these days.'

'How else could you measure the numinous and relative? How else could you control the spirit? Look at Lord Jim.'

She took a bit of damp cotton and began to dab at the moisture on the thick, ochre balustrade. 'Well, anyway. I was telling you about his offer.'

'Palaces and jewels, no doubt. Exotic islands. Didn't he just buy Mustique? Wasn't it him who got the previous owner his first hundredweight of heroin? The first hundredweight's always free.'

'I've no idea.' She wasn't ready to smile at a weak joke. 'The point is he says he's got control of the Huguenot Leases. That's most of Brookgate, Den. That's our home turf.'

'The leases are worthless, Rose. Almost, anyway. You get about a florin a year's rent on any one of them. Which in today's coinage is ten pence. It's like buying Lord of the Manorships. No manor. No land. Nothing but titles.'

'Johnny says not.'

'He's just bullshitting you, to get you to say yes.'

'I think even Johnny knows that's a short-term gain not worth making.'

We'd started walking again, up towards the *Mirror* building and Hatton Garden. The Holborn traffic was heavy for that time of night. Most of it ploughing away from the West End. Shards of soft glass. Yellow stars bleeding into the haze.

'What can he do with them?' I asked.

'He can rebuild on the land,' she said.

'He can't just move in and knock people's houses down. I mean, there are laws to protect citizens from attacks by predators. There have been since the Danes settled down. You can't just raid a whole neighbourhood and put it under your heel. Not any more, Rosie. Can they? Maybe they're still doing that sort of thing in bits of Africa, I don't know, but even in Thatcherite London a chap can't ride out of the hills with an army of mounted ruffians and claim a town and its castle for himself.'

'He says it's one of the sweetest real-estate deals in the history of the universe. He says it cost him a pittance.'

Naturally that blurred conversation with Billy Fairling was coming back to me. The time he came round trying to borrow against his ridiculous expectations. Said he had the rights to the Huguenot Leases. That he was onto a good thing. Couldn't lose. And Bobby MacMillan, then Barbican's affianced, had heard the whole thing from where she lay, naked and greedy, in the bedroom.

'Was Bobby MacMillan involved in this coup?'

'I think she was mentioned. Oh, yes, it's one of the main reasons for the divorce. She insists that half of the Leases are hers. He says that she's crazy. She did none of the hard work acquiring them. All she gave him was a tip, and she received a marriage in return. That's what he says.'

'She'll get them in the settlement.'

'Don't be silly, Den. Barbican's lawyers have already proven that the Skerring vicar who married them wasn't properly ordained. They have a rumour running about the vicar's sexual assaults on children, a suggestion that he goes to gay nightclubs every evening, and that he's a bigamist who visits prostitutes in Chichester. That's the first thing they establish, these days. They haven't even started inventing Bobby's private life yet.'

'Why would they want to look into Bobby's private life?'

'Come on, Den! What business are you in? Moloch's already done a story on the vicar. Serves that poor bugger right for getting involved with the Great White Spider. He who spins fastest, spins last, Den.'

Always the bridesmaid, never the bride. At that moment the enormity of what I'd missed began to inch up on me. The human consciousness doesn't have the capacity to take that kind of information all at once. Not when you have only yourself to blame. 'Seems unfair,' I said lamely.

'Why?' said Rosie. 'What about Roberta?' They'd both been to St Paul's, but in different years. 'He seems to be treating her with his usual courtesy. A cavalier, that Johnny. But Roberta herself doesn't mind, does she? I mean, there's got to be a settlement. She'd have made that calculation before she ever went up the aisle with him. I doubt if she's changed much.'

I doubted it, too. I'd never told Rose about me and Bobby and this wasn't the ideal time to start. 'Probably not. She's a tough girl. Knows what she's doing. Knows the kind of game she's in.'

'You make it sound like gangsters. Like that Anjelica Houston character in *The Grifters*.'

'I would guess Bobby could take the odd slam in the stomach with a bag of oranges. If there was a large enough stake for her at the end of it. Broker's balls, Rosie.'

'You're too fucking cynical, Denny. You always characterize the rich, even when you don't know anything about them. There's a lot of decent people, concerned people, who work with us. Billionaires. Yet they live simply and give it all away. You couldn't meet better people. It's not money that makes people selfish, Den. Money's just the easiest thing for selfish people to acquire.'

I stopped at the pedestrian crossing, looking across towards the pink glory of the Prudential, one of the few old buildings left standing on that side of Holborn. It has a big part in E. Nesbit's *The Phoenix and the Carpet*. My grandad saw the Pru as an intruder, even though its Gothick brick had been there since before he was born.

A piece of expensive folly bought at the price of our insurance premiums, he reckoned. He'd paid a shilling a week to the Prudential since he was a boy. And now he had his pension. Seventy pence a week. If I hadn't got him the lady who came in twice a day, he'd have gone into a home. It was my Saturday for going to see him next and Norrie was coming with me. We'd found him a whole bunch of new radio cassettes. Hours and hours of the Archers. Months of *The Goon Show*, *Take it From Here*, *Ray's A Laugh*, *Life With The Lyons*, *Bedtime With Braden*. *I'm Sorry I Haven't A Clue*, *My Music*, *My Word* and *Round the Horn*, of *Dick Barton* and *ITMA* and Billy bloody Cotton. They'd keep him alive and cheerful for another year.

By that time, the BBC marketing department was sending these rejuvenation kits out by the millions. All the old buggers were clutching at them as if they were Shangri-La shandies. It was a perpetual trade. It put them in a kind of comforting coma that stopped time and helped them live forever, buying more tapes. Nothing like a good laugh, my grandad said, to keep you young. At least he had his cronies and I didn't have to listen to them any more. As far as I'm concerned Hancock and Williams killed themselves because they were overwhelmed by the thought of the shit they'd foisted on an easily pleased public. In fact, they said pretty much the same. Men of taste. Men of judgement. Farewell, well-fooled world.

A news van washed by. The *Chronicle* still left from the Farringdon Road depot in those days. It was belting through the night to make sure every newsagent and stand had their copies before six. That's something computers are killing.

'Well, I can't believe his lawyers can sort out a case that's been running for at least three hundred years and is more tangled than a nest of cobras. There's people in France, Holland, Sheppey and the Isle of Wight who have claims. There are royal warrants, German bills of title, Australian claimants. Scottish courts. Belgian writs. Everything. Nobody in a court of law wants to touch it. Which is why it's gone on for so long. There are about five hundred people deeply embroiled in that can of eels at any one time.'

'He says it's cheaper to pay them off so they get something than carry on for another hundred years. You can't think in all those zeros, can you, Den? People will take fifty thousand now rather than billions in a future where the Morlocks are pulling Eloi down for supper. What would five hundred fifty thousands add up to, Den? Twenty-five million? You can't even buy a decent GM soya plant for that, these days. Twenty-five measly million for the chance at a real-estate area that is worth that a square foot? You've always reckoned without the power of money, haven't you? You've never wanted that power. But, Den, once you have it, you can get pretty much anything you want. That's one of the things that makes them all such addicts.'

'It can't be done.' I was adamant. I'd been into that story a hundred times. Everyone knew it was unsolvable. Best left alone. Believe me. After all, wasn't I the seer of Brookgate? I told you, don't listen to me. And if I give you a tip, never put more than a fiver on it.

'Well, I know him better than you in some ways. I'm worried. We must try to stop him, Den, if we can.' Her hand folded into mine. I could feel her taking me over. We were becoming the same person.

'In which case,' I said. 'We'll go and talk to Tubby tomorrow.'

I couldn't see how I was going to get around to telling her about Bobby. It was probably a secret best kept, all in all.

But when we went over to Tubby's he was dealing with his own problems. He did his best to engage with ours, but it was hard for him. He was white-eyed with tiredness, focused on yet another looming case. His screens were blipping and flicking as if someone had slipped cyanide into their circuits. Racing figures. References. Statistics. Church records. Photographs of weather-worn gravestones. Photostats of old documents. Some vast ongoing legal battle between him and Barbican's lawyers in which he was having to prove every ancestor since King Canute and verify every document published since the late seventeenth century. His only bit of luck was that several of his lady friends were international lawyers and were working free. He was babbling. He talked of all the stuff he could reveal about Barbican. How, if he wanted to play dirty, he could dish the bastard for eternity. Rosie and I knew it wasn't in Tubby to play like that. Or, said Rosie quietly, he could take the four million quid Barbi had offered him. Which, of course, we knew he wouldn't. On account of his holy trust, partly. Mainly, however, because he was a hard-headed bastard who regarded Barbican as what he called the Grand Consumer, the Original Appetite.

'Sure,' he says, 'and I'll put the KY up my own arse. What would I do with four million quid? Buy myself a new inheritance? Besides, the cats hate change. We're all too settled to move. He's going to have to kill us to get the Mill. And he'll be able to, soon, with impunity. As big business consolidates and centralizes, governments and nations disintegrate. Shouldn't we be worrying about this?' Tubby apologized for his obsession. He could tell we didn't have a chance. He told us he could recommend several good lawyers, but they were all a bit overworked at the moment.

Too late, anyway, to do anything. They're always ten jumps ahead of you. Because that's how they spend their time when you're at the pictures. It means everything to them. Scheming. Outsmarting. Winning. And Barbican was used to getting applause every time he pulled off another mighty stroke. He expected the conquered to cheer his triumph. To share his sense of well-being. To give him the thumbs-up when he got away with murder, suffering no more than a slap over the olivers. He thought we'd congratulate him. After all, he was going to get Brookgate back into the modern world, make those spaces produce. He had all kinds of plans for livening the old place up.

In other words, it was a *fait accompli*.

He'd planned and built it without any obvious inspiration from the gods, then he'd found someone to open the gates for his Trojan Horse. Probably in negotiation with Jocky Papadakis. Its belly had already burst and the bastards were fanning out through the streets, burning, looting, raping. Trampling our memories, stealing our treasures, destroying our history. Stripping our assets.

Thanks to me, Barbican would soon be enjoying all the usual rewards for hard work and determination in a go-getter consuming society.

CHAPTER TWENTY-ONE
The Spit

The rest is history. To you and everyone else, maybe. But to me it's an enduring nightmare. A stain on an already pretty grubby personal twist. Over and done with now. Like accidentally betraying your friend or watching your country killing a lot of innocent people in your name? It's a crack you have to get used to living with because you can't make it not have happened. And, of course, I also had a guilty secret to make it all the more pathetic.

Once Billy's incredibly doubtful descendancy from the Huguenot De Verlanes had been proven by Barbican's professionals, once the Leases were in hand, the only remaining important thing to do was to buy up the leaseholders' sub-leases (which was what they all essentially were) and you were in sole possession of one of the most profitable pieces of real estate in the world.

To grasp the whole of the sordid scam you need to be one of the people who reads the Business Section before the news. Which means you probably know a lot better than I do how it was done so quickly. Even down to squeezing out the old gangsters and bringing in the new kind. The Jocky Papadakis kind.

One minute our ancient patrons were there, the next they were gone. That's the problem with feudalism. You never know who's going to sell you on. Look what happened with the Highland Clearances.

Getting those Leases finally made our cousin Jack the richest man in the history of time and space. Whatever he wished to control, he did control. If the City and Wall Street acknowledged a Holy Trinity then it was God, Washington and Barbican Begg. The other gigantic corporations he treated like his own deer in his own deer park. Every so often he was forced to cull a couple and make good sport of it at the same time.

Barbican's will was almost unchecked. The only power greater, and that was disputable, given the circumstances, was the USA. It was disputable because so many US politicians were in BBIC's pay. All those mysterious military actions that seemed to serve no national interest?

Barbican's interests were, as he put it, above nations. But the congressmen had the authority and the firepower to loosen up reluctant markets. Poisonville politics. Red harvests.

Remember that old Russian joke about Noah? He gets all those hundreds of pairs of animals aboard, the feed and the family, and the rain comes down and the tide comes up and off they go in the Ark, sailing about looking for land. Time goes by. No luck. Eventually Ham and Japhet come up on deck with pegs on their noses. 'The shit down there's getting pretty deep, Dad. More cubits of compost than fleas on a Philistine. What are we going to do about it?' It's a problem. Noah realizes there's nothing else for it. He tells them to dump it over the side. They sail on, lighter and happier, and nobody ever saw that shit again until Christopher Columbus discovered it in 1492. You started hearing those jokes again after NATO's big Balkan birthday celebration.

Slavs had that same cynical, useless fatalism that coloured their attitude towards communism. They were fucking crap at politics. But you couldn't help seeing their point of view.

With Brookgate under siege and Tubby fighting his own desperate battles, the only consolation I had at all, as I carried my load about like some drifting pilgrim, was that within days of getting his pay-off Billy Fairling died of exposure coming home from the pub. He didn't live long enough to pick up his new signboard. His money went into probate, Ellie made no claims on it, so consequently he paid the public back at least some of what he'd been screwing out of us for years. William De Verlane's Traditional Sporting Academy would never bring Sonny Shapiro before the public. Which didn't make me miserable, either.

There wasn't anyone else to inherit Billy's ashes, so I picked them up. I told the funeral parlour that I'd come to take Billy home. When I got into Old Sweden Street, I dumped him into the nearest dustbin. The plastic urn's still on my mantelpiece. Full of that old, nasty yellow smack I found at Julie's when Barbican asked me to go over there and sort out her things. The smack was all I could find of Julie that didn't have at least a splash of blood or a bit of skin on it. Tubby's cousin picked everything else up in his truck and took it down to Bermondsey Beaches to have it burned in the traditional way. Courtesy of the Cornells, who by that time controlled the private waste businesses and were always willing to do a mate a favour when it came to disposables.

So Billy, me and Bobby MacMillan had all, in our different ways, been shafted by Barbican. Bobby had disappeared, apparently scared of Barbi's vengeance. Or maybe some stirring of conscience. Or a secret lover? Rosie thought she'd joined a nunnery. I had to put that one out of my mind. Sometimes the sleaziness of my own sexual fantasies appalls me. I asked, casually, if it was one of the stricter orders.

'Probably you're allowed to live at home and only come in on Sundays, if she's the same old Roberta. The Order of St LuLu the

Sybarite.' Rosie had an amiable knowingness about Bobby that chilled my blood. Put that together with our telepathy and it would take her seconds to put two and two together. I prayed to all the gods that they should never meet. Or at least never talk.

Barbican said he didn't know where Bobby was. I suppose she understood him well enough to know where she could hide. Not, he said, that she could be hiding from him. After all, he owed her so much. He had made her a very generous settlement. He didn't say a lot more about her and I didn't push him. I really didn't want to go there. But I also knew Bobby and I knew how hard it is to give up power.

'So why buy the Leases if you don't want to change anything?' I said firmly. Rosie seemed impressed by my unusual directness.

Barbi thought he was reassuring me. He was genial. 'I said I wasn't going to make any *bad* changes. Improvements, yes. Restorations, yes. And a certain amount of refinancing, repositioning. You mustn't worry about Brookgate, Den. I love the place as much as you do. I've got as many attachments. I almost grew up there, after all. And we're not going to touch Fogg Yard or the Church or the graveyard. We're making them a feature. I'll show you the plans. They'll gladden your heart. The best of the old with the best of the new. And think what your little place will be worth with property values shooting up. You'll have a bit of dosh for once. And if you'd give in and let me make a few investments for you with your own money . . .'

I don't know why, really, but I didn't want a share in the new prosperity. Not that kind of share, at any rate. I preferred to make my money exploiting the rich and famous rather than screwing the poor and obscure.

We were having lunch with him at the time, a private one catered by Blues downstairs. He'd just got his knighthood in the New Year's Honours List. We were trying to get him to keep his hands off Brookgate, let it stay as it was and develop naturally. He said that the acceleration was just to bring us up to date.

We ate off the finest glass. We had a wide view of the Thames just below the Tower, looking down towards Wapping and up towards the Festival of Britain tourist bridge that was at odds with but added to the city's visual complexity. In this bomb-proof cocoon, Barbican sat back in his elegant executive armchair, boyishly coiffed, subtly oiled and perfumed, wearing one of those suits that seems to be made of living silk, looking with benign contentment on his fiefdom. It was clear he regarded everything he could see as his personal constituency. He spoke in familiar, affectionate tones of the Bengali populations of the East End, the black communities of the south, the old Irish and Jewish families of the north and west and you got the impression each and every one of them was a personal retainer of his. Sometimes I could have been listening to Prince Bigears talking about how his tenants were the salt of the earth. I kept expecting him to tell anecdotes revealing his people's respect and affection for him. The tenderness of the farmer for a profitable field of sheep. The kinder, gentler face of modern feudalism.

The thing about Jack was that he was invulnerable and knew it. Almost nothing scared him. Where Moloch or Judd might feel threatened, enraged, he wasn't even mildly irritated. There was something at least monumental about an ego like that.

I suggested that in his insensate wish to consume the world he was gobbling up and shitting out everything of value. This was a bit of a rib-tickler. He chuckled so hard he had to put his wine down. He gave me the impression that I was no more than a toddler on the road of life. He explained how his activities created work and increased the per capita income of every consumer in the kingdom. Which increased the nation's power. Which increased the value of its goods. Which increased its wealth. Which was, when all was said and done, the only realistic measure of one's worth. How else did I propose paying for all these social services I wanted?

That was the twist I lost him at. Was he actually talking about the market value of human souls?

I was wondering if Tubby was right. Could Barbican really be the Antichrist and not just some grubby, unimaginative, lucky little goozer with the right rapacity, ambitions, and character for his job?

'You can't start these great charitable programmes of yours without lots of dosh from the dosh-creators, pards. It's trade that creates social stability.'

'Depending on the trade, I'd have thought.' I'd just learned BBIC was the primary stockholder in Vickers, Lewis, Walther, Bofors and Martini. Which now gave him the major European weapon-makers to add to his interest in the American LTV consortium. He now commanded more minutemen than George Washington.

Rosie tried firmness, letting him know that he could never win her approval if he carried on this way. 'Your life's a one-way street to oblivion. How can it be anything else?'

He shook his head, as happily entertained by her as he had been by me.

'You'll admit I'm right, Rosie, when you see the elegant new blocks of flats and offices, the green spaces, the clinics and shopping arcades. And the better health and education that accompany all this. You know it in your bones. I'm a visionary, too. But a twenty-first century visionary. You're hanging on to the old ideas. As bad as the unions. And look what's happened to them. My people know how to get it right and keep it right. A stimulated economy is a smart economy.'

'Do what?' I said. I wondered about his sanity. Sometimes a look of sheer barminess would cross his face as he offered another extraordinary opinion. They were speaking a kind of Esperanto, a language founded on abstractions and pseudo-authoritative managerialisms rather than concrete experience. These were the beginnings of a radical and novel spin that would flower as New Labourism, but of course we didn't recognize it. All we knew was that it was an advanced form of consumer capitalist Nuspik. We still hardly realized they'd commandeered our lingo. It's how the Nazis confused the commies. We were floundering around in a goldfish bowl of contradictory call signs. Words no longer meant what we thought they meant. I felt physically sick for a moment. I thought he'd drugged the plonk.

'Lovely view,' said Rosie, getting up and walking over glass towards the glass wall and the river beyond. Subtle refractions. Laser light. It was almost like having gravity in space. You could be an Olympian, floating above the world, looking down on the workings of mankind. Below us, through the one-way mirrors, we saw the happy, efficient, regulated hive that was BBIC HQ, stretching tier upon tier far beneath. A million screens. I felt like a piece in one of those multidimensional chessboards you can conjure up from the net these days.

'Reflections on transparency,' he murmured to himself. We didn't know it, but we were listening to the future.

'Openness,' he added. 'You know. Glasnost. Tearing down the walls.'

'That reminds me,' I said. 'I'm due in Berlin in an hour.'

'A scoop?'

'Not for me, thanks.'

I'd given up. He shook his head and smiled at my whacky, bohemian ways. 'Sniff on, Mister Newshound. See you later, Den, boy.'

It was cold when I got outside his office.

Rosie stayed behind as we'd planned she might. We hoped she could tempt him by other means. She might even pretend to be warming to his idea of marriage. She'd have a go at vamping him. She wasn't the most convincing vamp I'd ever known and Barbican had been vamped by professionals, so that didn't get very far, apparently.

She tried to convince him that Brookgate would be worth far more if left intact. She said you couldn't tear down a city's psychic infrastructure without disastrous consequences. But he knew best. Her arguments were all familiar to him. He'd seen them in the papers. People writing letters. Tony Benn droning on in Parliament. Over-excited provincial MPs in badly made clothes and worse haircuts. John Pilger in the *New Statesman*. *Tribune*. He supposed they meant well, but they weren't exactly realistic. You couldn't do anything for anyone without money. He wasn't sure what motivated these people. Jealousy? A bitter hatred of others' good fortune? Wouldn't they behave like him in his circumstances? Who was doing the most good? Who was it, he asked, who was providing so many people in the world with jobs? With dignity and self-respect? With the money that would buy them the best healthcare, the best education, the best quality of life? Giving them a future?

Rosie met me back in Fogg Yard. She told me how she'd failed. It was like arguing with a junkie, she said. Exactly the same. Arguing with an addict. No logic. Just appetite. A craving that, if you didn't have it, you couldn't understand. They only turned nasty when you came between them and the addiction.

Rosie stayed in London for another week or two, seeing people, getting stuff done. Then she was ready to start work again, she said. She couldn't stand thinking about Brookgate any more.

In spite of the problems, she'd resigned from her posh admin job and taken a new CAAW project in Africa. A big one. I got her letters. They started to cheer up. She was becoming enthusiastic again. The area lent itself readily to self-sufficiency and sustainable growth, a perfect profile for sane, steady progress and prosperity. The people were bright, friendly, pretty sophisticated and ready for new ideas. Any divisions had been created by the Belgians. Good to see the back of them. She had a lot of French money interested and she was sure she could make this one work. She invited me to come and visit her out there in beautiful Rwanda. It was only a little country, about the size of Wales, and you really felt you could get something going there.

I locked up my flat in Fogg Yard and ran away. I couldn't bear watching Barbican's long-necked tripods standing astride the ruins of our old integrity.

You can go to Brookgate yourself now, of course, and witness what's happened. Go in from the Leather Lane side and see what you can find under the concrete and glossy, curving marble, the bulging stone sails, the frozen command ships and false fronts of a pompous and relentless orthodoxy.

I couldn't stand it. I didn't want to watch. I didn't want to be near it. My roots were being chopped off. I might as well become a European.

I started doing more jobs with Fromental who found me a flat behind his in Les Hivers. It was a comfortable place to hide. The area was getting a bit more bohemian. It had started to remind me of the nice, shabby bits of Amsterdam. Little shops with their battered shutters and perky, peeling paint, all with their front doors opening straight on to the towpath. A reasonably pleasant mixture of ordinary daily commerce on the wharfs, with bookstalls, cafés, art galleries, Vietnamese stores selling cane furniture and cheap, jolly china, a Moroccan potter, a health-food restaurant. Nothing much was changed, except the atmosphere was a bit less miserable. One or two of the bargemen were selling their vividly painted carvings in the craft shops. Grotesque pre-Christian jumping jacks, pecking hens and dancing dragons with working jaws. The old bistros were washing their windows more, but not too much.

Maddy La Font visited fairly frequently. So did Flicky Jellinek. And Flo Fortnum. But always on their way somewhere else. Maddy was into TV presenting these days, she said. And theme restaurants. Flicky was involved in Europolitics. Flo was bent on breaking the charitable will of Brussels as thoroughly as she'd broken London's. I had a couple of casual local girlfriends, but really I'd lost interest in relationships. Both Fromental and I, for our own reasons, became obsessed with news. With being where it was happening. I think we were driven by some vague notion that we could change things for the better by doing that. We got plenty of work. Fromental was fearless and I was careless. South Africa. North Korea. East Timor. West Texas. Kurdistan. Somalia. I hardly did any original pix for the UK. We worked for the French, Spanish and Italian papers, mostly, and the US or UK bought second rights. By basing myself in France I guess I was making it a lot easier to avoid the truth I wasn't prepared to believe. Watching consumerism going from being an economic option to an unexamined culture, an orthodoxy. The French, like the English before them, were convinced it couldn't happen to them. Maybe they'd be right. I didn't argue about it. I wanted them to be right.

In London, I stayed at Tubby's rather than sleep at Fogg Yard. Brookgate was in ruins. There was no way I could deal with it. It hurt too much. I didn't take a single picture. Of course, Tubby himself was totally out of his tree. Couldn't be talked to. Kind as ever to me. But his grasp on the rational multiverse was a little loose. Whatever I tried to say he somehow routed back to Barbican and his designs on the Mill.

You couldn't blame him. Barbican's efforts to acquire the Mill hadn't stopped in any significant way since 1982. I doubt if he believed his own senses, but everyone he had co-opted to help him get hold of Tubby's place had failed. Money had failed. Blackmail and false arrest had failed. Sexual temptation had failed miserably.

Threats and legal loopholing had failed. The Council had failed in seeking to find the Mill unsafe. They had failed to find it lacking some vague planning permission, in accordance with some pre-Norman by-law. Barbican's wholly owned subsidiary stooge foundation, The National Heritage Council, had failed to claim it as a site. He had a whole raft of similar outfits working for him these days, covering every aspect of his ambition. The Web was full of his 'Information Councils' and 'Public Interest Groups'. He had more fronts than a Monsanto tomato. More altruistic bullshit than Dupont. Both of which companies he would eventually own.

By a very weird little coincidence, we got a job that took me back to the UK. *Alliance* had a tip about some private rocket site off the north-west coast. Some sinister millionaire's dream of world domination. It sounded as tired as an old James Bond plot and I thought the editor was nuts. He wanted a scandal too much. They were best not manufactured. I wouldn't touch anything with a spaceship in it. Sensational crap, I said. Flying saucer story. Something for the *National Enquirer* or the *Daily Star*. I didn't want my name on a twist like that. Not simply because it was daft, but because I'd get shit from anyone I knew in Wapping. And also because there was no real money in it. Those papers never paid for real stories, let alone something like this. I told Fromental to get someone from *Arthur C. Clarke's Mysterious World* if he wanted to go off on a wild-goose chase in the Irish Sea.

'Channel,' he said. 'I think. Anyway, it's the Isle of Morn. Do you know it?'

'Of it,' I said.

'And this Pilbeam? Sir Harold?'

'Hornsey.'

'Oh, the rabbit.' Sometimes Fromental saw everything in terms of rabbits.

'What's he up to?'

It was all I had to say. He had me hooked. If I'd accepted Barbican's invitation to chopper over to Pilbeam's mist-shrouded manse, rather than letting Bobby drag me off for a bonk, I would be a less troubled man. And Brookgate would still be Brookgate. All my problems, it seemed, had started with that one bad decision. So maybe I had something in the back of my mind suggesting that I could somehow start again on Morn. Whatever. I let Fromental get out a big French naval chart. 'That's what they want us to look at.' He pointed to an isthmus of land, a kind of tail to the main mass of the island that vaguely resembled a dog sleeping on its side. 'That's where the rockets were reported taking off.'

'For where?'

'Space,' he said. 'Naturally.'

It still felt a bit like *Boy's Own* and I wasn't a natural industrial photographer, but the story could be good. Pilbeam's connections with the Teutonic Templars, or whatever that Lodge called itself, were occasionally puffed up into a story by the more desperately rabid red-tops, but never developed and never denied. Most of Pilbeam's business seemed to be in communications. The recluse had acquired the French-owned Communications Informations Telephonics and Digital Electronic Locators (Oxford) PLC, jointly known these days as CITADEL, which of course was one of the first and most successful consolidated media research engines. They also owned Barnes and Brown Electronic Locators (US) Inc.

Before we left Paris, I checked a few more facts and told Fromental there wasn't much point in going. It turned out there was no secret to Pilbeam's private Mission Control. The launches had all been officially cleared and were specifically to put communications satellites into space. They were financed by an international private consortium. Just another phone-and-cable company throwing expensive junk into space.

Fromental said he had an instinct for the story. He still thought there was something worth following up. And since *Alliance* was paying handsomely for everything, I decided I might as well satisfy my curiosity.

To find myself in a malfunctioning, freezing little motor boat bobbing about where the North Sea meets the Irish Channel, totally fogbound for all but a couple of hours before twilight, when we were able to get in close to the long isthmus and take clear shots of the rocket pad and a sci-fi set that might have come straight out of *Doctor Who*. I mean, it was that crappy looking. Even in my best pictures, it's clear we made it ourselves in *Playschool*. Everything could have been made out of old toilet rolls and cornflake packets. Towers and coils and wires and dishes and domes and cones. The usual asymmetrical paraphernalia of the modern commercial communication complex. Apart from the rocket pad, the site was like many others of its kind. I'd seen SKY's, CNN's and the vast BBC location down at Tudor Hamlets.

If there was anything on that bar of land that was iffy, we couldn't tell from our little boat bouncing about in the middle of the leaden ocean, while the steady north wind chilled our bones. It was the logical place to do that sort of thing. I wanted to go home. Fromental wanted to go to Glas, the main harbour on the other side.

We were about to head for Glas when two high-powered launches suddenly came droning round the point. They were playing standard recordings, asking us to keep clear of sensitive equipment and reminding us we were in private waters. I tried to shout back, asking if we could perhaps meet Sir Hornsey. That silenced them for a bit, but when their engines came on again they somehow seemed more menacing. We had to leave, we were told. We had no choice. We pointed the boat towards England, with the idea of sneaking back to Glas when the boats disappeared. But the boats saw us well on our way.

Arguing, we returned to Whitehaven. We got in at some awful time in the morning. We'd lost our deposit and felt like death. On to Cockermouth, where we were staying at the Wordsworth Arms. A bit of black pudding and fried tomatoes put me slightly back on form. Fromental stoked down the grease with the best of them. He had that perverse French relish some of them get for our food. As he tucked away his fried bread he was still for 'infiltrating' the island. Demanding an interview with the mysterious millionaire.

I was too cold for any more of it. I had a better idea. I persuaded him to take the early train to Lancaster and catch the Intercity to Euston. I wanted him to meet Tubby. Tubby would know anything there was to know. On the way to London we made up a leggy showgirl sex-and-murder story to go with the terrible pictures. From a phone box near the taxi rank Fromental almost sold a 'Did the spaceship carry a beautiful corpse into space?' story to *Noir*. He had hopes for that one, but you know what the French privacy laws are like. A lot tougher than ours. And, while they're not always effective, they do offer pretty good protection to the already powerful. No contest. Pilbeam didn't have to put much pressure on *Alliance*. They'd expected a nice exposé, a tasty bit of investigative. So the scam died. And so, in passing, did *Alliance*.

Sometimes it looks like all these laws and constitutions were put together by a few white blokes for their own convenience.

I phoned Tubby and he sounded tired. He said it was fine if we wanted to stay over. He couldn't guarantee he'd be very entertaining.

As usual Fromental wanted to pick up a Big Mac but I needed some real food. We got a taxi up to Tufnell Hill and Tubby was only too pleased to find a fresh audience in Fromental while I dug a joint of French superbeef out of the freezer and sorted some vegetables. My two friends were naturally on the same wavelength and the Frenchman managed to cheer Tubby up quite a bit. 'Shit, man,' he'd say, 'it sounds like this guy's the Big S! The Ultimate Horror! I had no idea he controlled so much.'

They were talking, of course, about Barbican.

I did the washing up.

When I came back Tubby was in his E-Z-Boy, his mouse in his right hand, his left doing fast things on his keyboard. Now he was giving the illustrated lecture. Barbican's spider web of influence. The major brand companies he controlled directly. Those he controlled indirectly. The countries that were in his debt. The high-level politicians, civil servants and newspaper owners who were in his power.

I tried to change the subject.

'What's an electronic locator?' I asked.

'Big earners in industrial espionage,' he said, clicking an image of Barbican on holiday with Judith Major. 'Started as ordinary search engines. Now it's a nice word for a sophisticated spy. A hacking engine, if you like. Satellite snoops usually involved. The works. Bugging. Tapping.'

'Legal?'

'Most of it. Why?'

Fromental explained about what we'd seen on the promontory. Tubby shrugged and brought up an aerial picture a lot more detailed than mine. 'Originally, he got into all of that because of that barmy Lodge he was running. Certainly he and Barbican had differences and I think Pilbeam's fielded the odd unfriendly bid, too. But Pilbeam owns most of his own stock and Barbican's having a hard time getting at him in the conventional way. Pilbeam's cybers are still the most sophisticated around, so Barbican probably needs access to them.'

'What for?'

'Well,' said Tubby with an odd droop of his eyelids, 'you know, information.'

'The most valuable stuff in the world.' Fromental, under Tubby's spell, had become an expert.

'Any kind?'

'Anything useful.' Tubby turned back towards me. 'Same as mine, really. Except nobody quite knows what I have here.'

'What *do* you have here?' Fromental glanced up into the darkness and blinked with surprise as he met the cheerful stare of a young black oriental.

'Nobody quite knows,' said Tubby.

CHAPTER TWENTY-TWO
The Rap

Next morning I made breakfast and the three of us sat watching the world break up on telly. You know what the early nineties were like. A boom boom here, a boom boom there. Something new and nasty every day while the Dow Jones and Co rose and rose and rose and rose: the crescendo of the thundering herd. How the East was won. A tiger race to the edge. A gold-rush to oblivion. An oil-slick to cover the planet. Release the beast and glory at the power of greed. The Moscow crime rate was going through the ceiling. Market experts were predicting the worst.

Fromental was wearing one of Tubby's duvets round his waist. He smelled of almonds from his shower. 'The Russians have been studying America for years. They know what good business crime can be. You sell the tools to the burglars and the security devices to the burgled. You privatize your prisons and bingo, you have a perfect business. Aren't any of us going to do something to help those poor bastards sort themselves out?'

Tubby was taking a breather over his unexpected meal. 'Do those drooling City jackals only see the fall of the Wall as a chance to snap some foul bonanza, strip what's left of their public assets, scoop up the windfalls of civil collapse? If *we* behave like bandits, rapists and looters, won't *they* give it the same twist? We're talking a language they can understand. Jesus, this stuff's tasty. Almost makes me want to head for the bayous again. Laissez les bons temps rouler!'

Breakfast at Tubby's. Louisiana boudin and couscous.

'On the contrary,' said Fromental, then paused politely while he chewed. 'Most of them were always bandits. Banditry was their only trade before communism. It's their only trade after communism. Balkan brigands always specialized in assassination, kidnapping and abduction. All those wonderful nineteenth-century prints of guys with massive hooters, big moustaches, embroidered vests, baggy trousers and bandoliers of bullets. Bashi-bazouks?'

'Weren't those Turks?'

He shrugged. 'I was including the Turks.' He'd inherited his prejudices from his colonial father and Italian mother but he didn't take them very seriously.

Suddenly Tubby laughed with a dark relish I'd nearly forgotten, 'Somebody has to feed the crows. We're predators, aren't we? That's why history is such an unpopular subject these days. We've all done our fair share of ethnic cleansing.'

'We're supposed to have had higher standards since 1945.' I was eating shredded wheat. I couldn't keep up with Fromental's extraordinary appetite. I'd cooked about a dozen boudins, mostly white, and they were all gone.

I turned round to get some marmalade when a massive thump shook the kitchen area. I tried to look where it had come from. Another, smaller impact. And another. Then nothing. I thought for one wild moment that Fromental had exploded, but the bleary Frenchman was as baffled as me. Only Tubby went on eating calmly. He waved his fork in the general direction of the counter. 'What's the time? About nine? Hand me that remote, would you?'

I gave him the control while he finished chewing, swallowed, wiped his lips and pressed a button. The screens overhead tilted so that we could see them easily. 'You'll recognize all that, I expect,' he said. 'Tufnell Hill.'

They were like very high-quality CCTVs, covering every bit of surrounding land from the rooftops of Upper Holloway to the remains of Tufnell Park. 'I've got a more elaborate control board in the living room. But you can do quite a bit with the remote.'

One of the cameras focused in on a group of young men hanging around near the gates. Nothing special. A bunch of youfs, lads in their late teens. Doing something wholesome. Playing football.

Then I found out what the thumps were. Every so often one of the lads would give a quick look about him, reach down into a sports bag, take something out, whirl it around his head like a sling and fling it towards us. I almost ducked. Thump.

'What the fuck is that?'

'Paint.' Tubby uttered a terrible chuckle. 'Aimed at the outside cameras.'

'They're not very good shots.'

'They're not bad. It's just that they keep hitting the dummies. I wouldn't make my real cameras obvious. They think they're dealing with the Met and their clunky old equipment.'

'It must be drenched outside.'

'It would be if it wasn't for some very expensively treated plexiglass that I suspect they're dimly becoming aware of. Didn't you notice it yesterday? This is the sort of stuff I could anticipate and deal with.

'The battle's been going on for years, Den. And a lot subtler than this.

It makes you paranoid. I started thinking of worst-case scenarios. To keep myself busy, I planned for them. This isn't the worst that can happen by a long shot. Jocky's a nasty litle bastard, getting nastier as Barbican's power increases and his attention gets spread wider. Not that I really thought it would come down even to this.'

'A fucking siege?'

'This really is nothing, compared to the mind-games and all the other shit I've had from Jocky and/or Barbican. This is just them trying to get on my nerves. Goad me into doing something illegal. It's Barbican's cannon fodder, his mass infantry divisions. They're permanently employed to hang around the Mill and irritate me. I don't bother to retaliate. I could, but, you know, there are risks. It's always better to let them underestimate you. Of course, they've no direct connection, even with Jocky. The police's hands are tied, apparently. They have to catch them up to something.'

'Why the fuck would Barbican be that petty?'

'He doesn't see it that way. He thinks he's playing a game. And he plays every game to win. Every angle. He doesn't want to know the details of this one, of course. He expresses a general desire, translated by Jocky, who passes it down the line and so on. But it's covering some more elaborate bets. And these days, when the One Great Maker comes to handing out the dosh, he asks not how you played the game, but if you won or lost.'

'I've never understood why he wanted this place so badly,' I said. 'It hasn't even got decent public transport.'

Tubby put down his knife and fork. He folded his napkin. 'Oh, it's pretty simple, really. Even he can't build on public land, which is what the rest of this is. This is the only private bit. He likes the view. Or, I should say, he *wants* the view. I've seen all the designs. He was trying to persuade me to let him build *over* me at one point . . . a bizarre modernistic Eiffel Tower. But he really wants the Mill, too. I honestly don't know what it represents to him. Maybe it has something to do with the industrial revolution.'

'A shit beetle who literally wants to be top of the heap?' Fromental reached for the toast. Whereas I was inclined to indulge myself with a Full English occasionally, Fromental could eat a Full International. 'Is that the only logic to this?'

'Tyrants don't have to be logical,' I said. 'In fact it's a disqualification for the job. That's why they're so hard to second-guess. Sometimes they don't even behave in their own self-interest. It's a vocation.'

I couldn't stop looking at the screens. The lads playing football. Reaching into their sports bags. Throwing a paint bomb. Back to playing football. A policeman strolled by at one time, not even looking towards the Mill, which must have been streaked.

'The one advantage I've always had,' said Tubby, 'was my infantile fascination with electronics and my partnership with Sizemore the Programmer. It tends to put me a bit ahead of the game. There's nobody Barbican or his new partner Bill Gates could hire who's better than us. Not yet, anyway. I hope. Also,' he was gracious, 'I have the support of many other valuable friends.'

'How long's this been happening?' Fromental was scratching at himself with profound feeling.

'A few years,' said Tubby. 'It's intensifying. Now they're around pretty much twenty-four hours. I'm surprised you didn't see anything yesterday. And before you ask about the police and all the rest of it, believe me, Jean-Luc, there isn't anything I haven't tried, not a law going back to before the first Celtic settlements. And I have some very good lawyers. None better. If it wasn't for my various contacts, and a few native skills, Barbican would have made this place his fortress years ago. As it is, he has to make do with owning Hampstead.'

I'd heard what had happened to Hampstead.

That reminded me. I needed some of that old Fochkolor 140 film that wasn't made any more. I had to go over to Fogg Yard and get it from my fridge. I asked Fromental what his plans were.

He was still interested in Pilbeam, he said, but no longer so hot on returning to Morn. So while he was here he might as well call a couple of papers to see if they needed a feature on the lure of London and do a bit of sniffing around to see what contacts Pilbeam had with the City. And maybe unwind a bit. In other words, he was cutting his losses. He'd also check our answerphones, see if anything was happening in Paris.

I took the bus down to Tufnell Park, then waited on the platform for twenty minutes for a Tube to Tottenham Court Road where I got the Central Line to Chancery Lane. It was bright, patchy, breezy. Some of the buildings on the Brooke Street side were hidden behind boarding or billowing, flapping plastic, but I hardly paid any attention. I turned into New Fogg Lane, planning to go straight up it to Fogg Yard. Except the old narrow street wasn't really there any more. Just a sort of line through the rubble.

I'm not sure I've ever felt such a weird mixture of sensations when I saw what wide devastation lay behind the unaltered façades of Gray's Inn Road all the way down to the Prudential building in Holborn. Like having your life-computer crash, losing all memory to a fluttering, fading screen. Gone. Irrecoverable. An absent fact.

Some of what I was feeling was different, though. It made me even more confused. Nostalgia for the ruins of my childhood. Memories of happy hours running through the rubble over near St Paul's. But that was other people's rubble. I felt physically sick.

Apart from a few clusters of Victorian buildings the whole area was one vast demolition site. Trucks. Bulldozers. Cranes. The usual drone, rattle and wail. Mysterious shouts. Where had everybody gone? Where

were all the families? My relatives? I'd expected destruction, intrusion.
But I hadn't expected anything on this scale. Barbican had wiped out
almost my entire past. Torn up my references. And presumably turned
my neighbours into refugees heading for the borders, for the bland
miseries of Hampshire, Essex or worse.

I hurried up what was left of New Fogg Lane, between hoardings and
cement mixers and reinforced concrete and Portakabins, and got into
Fogg Yard as soon as I could. The old mews walls were still there and if
you didn't know better you wouldn't have been aware of any change. I
was still in a daze when I walked through my front door, vaguely
surprised at finding no mail. A sense of sanctuary. Even when I looked
out of the back window the graveyard wasn't much different, or the
church beyond it. A layer of fresh, pale dust. I tried not to raise my eyes
and look over the wall at the huge, muddy pits full of cranking,
groaning, whining machinery.

As I turned to go to my little darkroom I realized that I was smelling
coffee. I checked out the counter. Mr Coffee was whispering away to
himself. Just made. I blinked. Then Paul Frame came into the kitchen.
'Hello, Den. I hope this is all right.'

At least he was wearing his own dressing gown.

'Rosie said you wouldn't mind.' Paul got two of my best Sunny Jim
cups down from the shelf. I never used those cups casually. 'Want some?'
He poured the coffee. 'She lent me her spare key. She said you were living
in France, these days.'

'She's got a fucking cheek.' I was only just realizing that I didn't like
him any more. What were they doing? Using my flat as a bonking gaff?

'I really am sorry. She was certain you were in France. She didn't
know your address. I was surprised you hadn't been in touch. But you
get sent all over the planet. This place was full of old mail and shit, so I
knew you hadn't been here recently.'

I couldn't argue with that. I wouldn't have argued with anything, if I
didn't now know that Rosie had been humping this married bastard for
years. And him poncing around the world like the Flying Nun. Mr
Idealist.

'How are you, mate?' he said. He was still good-looking, but a bit
scrawny. Greying. Eyes slightly shifty.

'So what are you doing over here?' I took the coffee mug and put it
down on my counter. Outside the engines roared and rumbled. You
could hear the moaning, fallen bricks, the scream of tearing metal, the
whispered protest of demolished walls. Those memories weren't dying
without a fight. 'Playing?'

'Bit of session work. This new Canadian company got in touch with
me. Made me a decent offer. So I'm doing an album for them.' He
showed me one of his old grins. 'Just trying to drum up a bit of dosh, you
know. To keep the cornflakes in the bowls.'

Obviously, Rosie hadn't told him I knew about them. And, to be honest, it was easier for me to pretend nothing much had changed. Except it was obvious to him that I wasn't particularly glad to see him.

'On a job?'

'Yes,' I said. 'I came back for some film I need. Is it still in the fridge?'

'Come on, Den, don't be like that. I just tidied up a bit. I haven't touched anything. I'll have my own place soon, if everything works out.' He sounded pathetic. I wasn't used to that.

I found the film and put it in my pocket.

'I thought you were living in France,' I said.

He shrugged. 'Well, I need somewhere in London for a bit.'

'You're welcome,' I said.

'As I said, I shouldn't be here long.' He was trying to get our old relationship back. He didn't know where it had gone.

'Fuck you.' I headed for the door. 'You can have the fucking place. Rosie, too. Enjoy it!'

'Fuck you!' He was still standing there, his face all weird, his coffee in his hand. 'My wife just died.'

'Fuck you,' I said again. 'Why should you care?'

I slammed the door. I wasn't used to feeling so emotionally mixed up. I heard someone yelling after me, but I was hardly aware of leaving the Yard and getting back on the Tube. I was at Mornington Crescent before I started to calm down. I was shaking. I was in a state. What the fuck was the matter with my body? It was like some horrible junk hangover. I hadn't done anything for weeks. And as for my mind – angst. Paranoia. Blind rage. Where was it all coming from? I suppose I preferred Rosie's lovers secret. But I'd never felt a twinge of jealousy. I'd never minded about Mr Mystery or shown any particular interest in her sex life, except what she wanted to talk about. Why was I feeling so jealous of Paul Frame? Why did it seem to me that I'd been evicted from Rosie's life as thoroughly as I'd been driven out of Brookgate?

'Fuck him,' I mumbled as the blackness trembled and sparked by behind the only other passenger in the compartment, who sat directly opposite me, firmly reading an *Evening Standard*. 'He's a clapped-out old has-been. Probably down to working on a Beastie Boys album.' But I didn't say it with any conviction. It wasn't him I was really hating. Just as well, really, since he was soon to become beatified in his own lifetime.

That was almost the last I saw of Paul in the flesh, before he became all sanctity. His career took a definitely upwards turn. But he did nothing after that to make me like him any better.

I didn't really want to go back to Tubby's, so I called Sporting Club Square and got Pinky. I was still officially married to her or to Flo. She'd be very glad to see me, she said. I changed to the Circle Line at Kings Cross, got off at Brompton Road and walked down Lillie Road, going in through the Margravine Gardens side.

Sporting Club Square had a definite Disneyland quality to it, these days. People preferred fakes, so the real thing was now being touched up to look like a copy. There were a few added towers and turrets and two of the buildings had been reclad in fantasy fibreglass, with gargoyles straight out of *The Hunchback of Notre Dame* and ancient plastic tessellations that looked as if they'd been built in the Philippines and shipped over. Having no special affection for the place I still thought it looked tacky, like some sub-Hollywood development. Barbican certainly had a knack for tearing the soul out of things. In fact only D'Yss Mansions, originally one of the weirdest of the buildings, was largely untouched. Pinky still owned it outright but apparently had aroused Barbi's completist instincts. It was a bit ironic that D'Yss was named after the famous Victorian theatre designer, who'd begun life as an architect. Begg Mansions nowadays looked like something out of that artless *Dracula* which wasted Gary Oldman. The Morris manor-house style of the original had been covered all over with *beaux artistries*. Little spiky railings and plaster cherubs. Well rubbished. Dick Van Dyke himself would have felt at home. Poppinsesque. I wondered if old Squire Begg was still living down there in the basements with his wizened housekeeper or whether he'd been pensioned off to the country. Or was pushing up the daisies. All Barbican had to do in the end, to get existing rentals back, was make conditions so shocking for the old residents that they'd died in their beds in droves.

Pinky seemed as much in need of consolation as I did, so we had a good time for a while, though we were both inclined to drift into a sort of gothic depression, given half a chance. She had some decent coke, which helped.

I called Tubby to tell him where I was, left a message for Fromental, and stayed a lot longer than I had planned. About a week. I might have been there now if I hadn't got a phone call from the French giant asking me to meet him somewhere. Pinky said it was all right if he came over, so I told him how to get there.

When Jean-Luc turned up he stood at the front door resting his hand on the upper lintel, completely filling the opening. He looked like shit. His vast, dark brow and troubled mouth made you think he was about to tell you he'd accidentally killed another rabbit.

'What's up?'

'I've got a lot of stuff on Pilbeam,' he said. 'The guy's a freak.'

'You wound up looking like that just to find out what we knew?'

He became concerned. 'Why? What do I look like?'

'Wrecked.'

'Oh,' he said, 'that's nothing. That's just last night. Oh, man! I had to get up early.' He shambled in and with shy politeness shook hands with Pinky. A murmured bit of French. She loved him.

'You still at Tubby's?'

'Kind of, man. I met this lady, you know. So I've been over in Stoke Newington for a couple of nights. Stoke Newington?'

'You've only yourself to blame.' We sat down in Pinky's huge fluffy easy chairs while she got a cup of tea together. 'What's up?'

'I went back to Tubby's this morning. Hoping to find you. I'd heard from *Libération*. We're in favour again. They had a good job for us. Anyway, when I got there the gate was open and nothing much looked disturbed, but there was nobody in. Or nobody answering. I tried phoning Tubby, but there was no reply. Just an answer message, you know. Man, I got worried about that guy. I mean, he never goes out. I went back and tried to get in again. Then I noticed a couple of spots of what looked like blood on his step. So what do we do?'

'I'll take a shower.' I got up and helped Pinky set the tray down. 'Then we're going over there.'

'You think somebody's killed him?'

'I'm willing to believe anything. Let's hope not.'

Pinky got us a taxi and waved us goodbye. 'Your friend's nice,' she said. She allowed him a kindly, disconcerting wink.

'Who was that?'

'My wife,' I said. 'I think.'

The taxi driver was useless and went up Brompton Road straight into the Knightsbridge traffic, so we paid him off and got the Tube, changed at Leicester Square and got another taxi from Kings Cross. Heading north at that time was still a problem, but at least we kept moving, going in and out of Gospel Oak in a failed attempt to dodge the main flow, so that it was early evening by the time we got to the park gates to find St John's Gardens full of police cars, Black Marias, ambulances and all the usual paraphernalia of a modern emergency. A chain of walkie-talkies, torches and uniforms all the way to the top. We could see lights flashing up near the Mill. Chattering electronics, distorted radio voices. *Roger X-ray Zebra Zero*. Flashing, twisting yellow, red and blue lights. White lights. Bulky figures shifting, talking in low voices, raising eyebrows, the usual jolly gestures. This looked serious.

Suddenly there was a lot of shouting. A megaphone bellowed something. Then four men holding a bomb box came running down the hill. It was our best chance to slip off the path, into the shadows. It was habit with us to avoid officials as much as possible, at least until we got close to the goal. The bomb squad got down to St John's Gardens and their van. There was a moment's silence. Then the row started everywhere again. We'd actually made it to the Mill's tall iron fence, but there was no way of getting in. And I wouldn't have wanted to try. The tangle of brambles behind the fence seemed to be occupied by an army of apes. The noise coming out of it was bizarre.

The nearer we got, the stranger the noise became. A mixture of very loud grunting and guttural, aggressive whines. Was it human?

Then we started to see that there were a couple of ladders leaning against the walls of the Mill. Bunches of skinheads blundering about in the bushes. Some of them had their clothes shredded, with thin streaks of blood all over them, as if they'd been attacked by cats. They were dead drunk or drugged or otherwise out of their skulls. Not aggressive, really, just blotted. Their mouths were open and their eyes were popping or screwed tight shut. A lot of them were yelling in that strange way people have when they think they're singing along to a record while wearing headphones. They were stumbling, holding themselves, raving. Some of them fell over. Police led others down towards the parked vans. They could hardly put one booted foot in front of another but continued that incoherent, almost anguished yelling. It was like something out of Monty Python. *Awfugnbarstdunmeearsin* . . .

A frowning jolly was holding his notebook and pencil towards one of the quietest. 'Maybe you could write it down for me, son?'

Forget reading or writing. Some of those bastards hadn't even learned to talk yet. It was like somebody had put silly *Playschool* clothes – big braces and baggy trousers – on a bunch of Neanderthals.

Fugncuncarnearnar . . .

'Pardon?' I heard one policeman say.

Another policeman said: 'They were put up to this. They couldn't have planned it by themselves. They're retards. I bet they're all from Friern Barnet. The leaders are long gone. What bastards. Dirty tactics. Like using kids.'

All released into the community at the same time, armed and sent off to attack the Red Mill? This was definitely *X-Files* stuff. I wondered when they'd bring in the Home Office boffins. I half-expected to see Tom Baker come billowing on to the scene, the quintessential Doctor with his special screwdriver on the pulse of history, to baffle us with confidence and reassuring technobabble, a dismissive quip or two.

Meanwhile, two other constables were moving about in the surrounding bushes gathering things up. They'd collected a fair selection of baseball bats, stilettos, lengths of pipe, a sword, a chainsaw, two sledgehammers, an axe. They kept emptying armloads on to a blanket and then going back in for more. Handy. A nasty little urban army. In defeat. Some of them were holding their tattooed heads and mouthing pain. One or two had nosebleeds. And what did we see through the big window today? Andy-fucking-Pandy, children, with blasted eardrums and swollen tongue, with popping eyes and jerking joints, like they cut most of his strings.

Tubby and the Mill at least seemed intact. The jollies hadn't been in action. They were treating him like a normal householder. Yet something had defeated these dummies.

We made it as far as the area just by Tubby's big gate, the one you used to be able to bounce out of its lock. It was open now. They'd taped it back, but there were only a few onlookers. We could see Tubby up near his front door talking to a couple of plain-clothes goozers and a uniformed inspector. We waved, but he didn't see us. At least he was alive. And they probably hadn't arrested him.

Another officer started moving towards us and I shouted:

'Tubby?'

Tubby saw us, said something, and we were beckoned up to the front door.

He was quick to prime us. 'I told them you lived here, too. I was expecting you about now.'

'Any ideas about all this, gents?' The inspector had huge ears, half the length of his head. They threw everything else out of proportion. It looked as if his face had shrunk. 'What those subnormals were after?'

'Not really,' I said.

Jean-Luc began offering a long explanation, part of which he had to give in French, until the officer realized slowly that he was foreign and therefore had nothing relevant to say. He was the kind of witness you used as a last resort.

'So you weren't here, sir?'

'Long enough to understand the forces at work here,' said Fromental. 'Long enough to recognize the foot soldiers of the Grand Consumer.' He looked to Tubby for confirmation. Tubby tried not to seem embarrassed.

'I've had a bit of trouble, Inspector, as you're probably aware. An old place like this becomes a kind of focus for bored lads with nothing better to do. This was a bit more than that, of course. But you know how it is today.'

'What are they, Mr Theakston? I don't know the proper word. You know, mentally undevelopeds?'

'They seemed normal enough to me, from my perspective,' Tubby told him. 'If a little loutish. But then I wasn't really able to tell much about a large group of young men blundering around in my garden on a Thursday afternoon. Carrying weapons, by the look of it, too. They were like those race thugs, but I can't see what they'd want with me. I was born in Paddington.'

'Well, if they haven't done much damage, we can't charge them with as much as we'd like. There's the bomb, I hope. A lot of possession offences, of course, what with what we found on them and the rest.' The inspector was encouraging. 'Did they break anything?'

'They tried to break the gate, getting out. They must have locked themselves in somehow, failed to get my front door open, failed to get the shutters on the windows open, and were probably giving up when they discovered they were trapped. I had, of course, called you in the meantime. I've always had an excellent relationship with the local police. But you were a little late arriving.'

'I'm not sure what that was.' The inspector removed his cap to smooth his head. His ears looked even bigger. He enjoyed a moment of private concern. When he frowned his ears moved like flags, like an African elephant's. You half-expected him to lift his large nose and trumpet a baffled note or two. 'The message seems to have gone astray.'

'Well, you got here eventually and happily the lads weren't able to get back over my fence. They'd come in through the gate, of course, but when they closed it they must have jammed the lock.'

Fromental at last saw the sense of keeping his mouth shut rather than helping the police with his theories. And eventually everyone dispersed. After arranging to interview everyone again, the cops went off with their cargo of skins that sounded like a whole school of barking seals and Tubby, very weary, ushered us back into the Mill.

'What the fuck happened?' I asked.

Fromental told Tubby how he'd tried to get in earlier and all he'd found was that spot of blood on the step. He'd become very anxious.

'I saw you out there. I hadn't realized about the blood.' Tubby was sorry. 'But they were already on their way and I didn't want you involved. They'd have been here a few days sooner, I think, but they were making sure you two had gone and that I was on my own.'

'I could have helped.'

'No,' said Tubby, 'you might have got hurt. I couldn't be sure. It would have been irresponsible to involve you. It was a bit of an experiment on my part. I had to take a risk.'

'Risk? Experiment? What the fuck have you turned into? Professor Frankenstein? Is that what frightened those skins? Or are they all your own creations, gone horribly wrong?'

'Calm down, Denny. That's Doctor Moreau.'

I was getting tired of waiting. 'Are we going to have to read about this in tomorrow's papers?'

'I hope not. They didn't know anything. They weren't supposed to know anything, most of them. Just as the jollies weren't supposed to know anything. That inspector says he's going to make enquiries. I hope he means it. He could embarrass more than one of his colleagues at the local nick. But you'll be all right. You can see the whole thing on TV.'

'Oh,' I said, 'no newspapers. Just the fucking BBC.'

'Well, almost,' he said. You could tell he felt like showing off. He was almost his old self.

He'd recorded every moment, of course. The skins had been using mobiles to gather their forces, so he'd tapped into all their signals and had fair warning long before they even appeared on the horizon, only a little while after Fromental had legged it back up to Archway (having got lost looking for Tufnell Park) on his way to find me.

Tubby had let them all come in. He'd deliberately left the gate ajar. They were convinced the CCTVs were out of action. He'd seen them take the pipe bomb out of its bag, but it hadn't worried him. Only amateurs made bombs that crude. This was supposed to be a frightener. Maybe not even a real bomb. Otherwise the police would have to get involved. Besides, Barbican didn't want the Mill hurt.

Tubby's shutters looked like shit, but they were titanium-strong. When the baseball bats and the shotgun and all the rest of the vicious paraphernalia had been handed out, one of the mean-lipped leaders swaggered up to ring the bell.

Seated comfortably in his E-Z-Boy, Tubby had spoken through a vocoder. It was a fair impression of Oz the Merciless booming the shivers up the Cowardly Lion.

'Bugger off.'

The skin adopted a stance that showed not only wasn't he fazed, he was bored and pissed off and about to do something violent. 'OK,' he said. 'Does anyone want to buy any double glazing?'

Screens split, now, to Tubby's flying fingers, his instant editing. We saw the overgrown brambles all around the Mill, the cursing skins trying to get through the bushes, trying to raise ladders up to the higher windows.

'We're gonna winkle you out of there, you old fucker.' The skin put his hand on the bell again. And screamed.

'Good old-fashioned trick,' I said. It was worthy of Mr Small's in Old Sweden Street. Tubby held on a shot of the skin's raw, red palm.

'That's why I didn't really want you to keep ringing the bell,' Tubby told Jean-Luc. 'I had to switch it over. Very little of this stuff's been tested under any proper conditions.'

The skin was now belabouring Tubby's ecclesiastical door with his baseball bat. Although not using a wide vocabulary, it was obvious he wasn't deaf and dumb, either. Maybe this was one of the leaders the jollies had referred to? More cuts to surrounding skins, setting the bomb, having a go at shutters, raising the ladders.

'This is why they had to pick a day when they were sure I was on my own,' he said. 'They can't stay off their mobiles. Face to face they'd still rather pose on the phone. So I knew every boring detail. Except the day. Until today. Jocky probably sent the word down. I'd hoped it would be today. I had other reasons for not wanting you there. If anything had gone wrong, if anyone had been killed, I just wanted me to be blamed.'

'Killed? Jesus, man. This isn't the Wild West.' Jean-Luc was carefully watching the screens.

'Certainly not,' said Tubby. 'We're N19.' He had that snobbery common to most North Londoners, who know in their bones they're superior to other Londoners, especially South Londoners. This is borne out by South Londoners who, the moment they get the chance, cross the river and move to North London. East Londoners also move to North London when they go up in the world. West Londoners don't tend to move much, unless it's into Middlesex. Central Londoners have to have their roots poisoned before they'll move.

One with his instrument, a Buddha of the mixing desk, Tubby brought a bunch of screens together to make a big one.

The skins had carried the pipe bomb up to the door but were arguing over how to prime it. Meanwhile all around and above came the thumps and crashes of baseball bats hitting the walls and windows. Bang. Bang. Bang. Rattle. Rattle. Rattle. Worse than a night out with John Cage. Like that sound in the movies when the cons are banging their cups on the bars of their cages as Cagney walks Death Row. At this point we cut to a shot of Tubby, his stately hands moving over his mixing board. We see others, forming a kind of guard in the background, ready for any attack or threat of police. A decently planned operation. Nothing at all random about it.

Tubby's hands slide up the board, degree by degree. And suddenly the skins on the screen start shaking their heads, wincing, dropping their weapons, shoving their fingers in their ears, running about, falling off the ladders, falling in the brambles, kicking and pushing one another, staggering to the gate only to find it locked.

'I got 'em where I wanted 'em,' said Tubby. 'And I slowly increased the intensity.'

'Jesus, man!' Fromental was impressed but disturbed. 'Jesus. What did you do to those guys?'

Tubby turned to me. 'Remember the dogs they used to have waiting for us at gigs. How we dealt with them through the PA?'

'Bloody hell,' I said. 'It never did that to the dogs. Ultrasound?'

'Straight into their fucking skulls. Bust most of their eardrums, I'd guess. Not likely to hear again. Of course I wouldn't do that to a *dog*. Even a nose dog.'

'Blimey!' I wasn't sure that what I felt for Tubby was new respect. 'A bit ruthless, yeah?'

'Oh, no,' says Tubby. 'I was easy on them. I could have shaken the teeth out of their skulls. I could have given them epileptic seizures. I could have blinded them. Light and sound, mate.' He wasn't happy. '*Son et lumière*,' he translated for Jean-Luc's benefit.

'Oh, man,' says Fromental, thinking back to his boyhood, the writer who had made him want to learn English. 'Towers open fire, eh, man?'

'Spot on. The original deep fix. Of course, I'd be fucking useless against a real bomb. Anything serious and Tubby goes bang. But that's what it'll take and it's the one thing Barbican doesn't want to do. Except as a last resort. Blow me and the Mill up and build a replica . . .'

I was still digesting what he'd done. 'He'd be the first suspect . . . But permanently bursting someone's eardrums. That's illegal,' I said.

'Oh, fuck off,' said Tubby. 'We used to do it every night on stage. And make them vomit. Anyway, they deserved it.'

'For failing to attack you?'

'No.' Tubby got out of his E-Z-Boy and made his stately way through to the kitchen area. 'For killing a friend of mine. Any creature prepared to take life so cruelly and casually, not in self-defence, is not fully human. You have to deal with them by different rules.'

'Fucking hell,' I said. 'That's a bit iffy, Tubby. Vigilantism. What is this, *Mortal Enemy Seven*? It's not bloody *High Noon*.'

'When public law fails to deliver justice,' says Tubby, 'we fall back increasingly on other forms of law. The law of the blood-feud, for instance.'

You couldn't blame him, but the poor bastard had lost it. Every marble loose and whizzing around inside his skull like a bunch of rogue comets. Very complex comets. Unpredictable trajectories.

We followed him into the kitchen. I noticed the smell first. Not unpleasant. But familiar.

In Tubby's basket chair, on one of his best towels, lay a dead cat. It wasn't one of Tubby's elegant orientals, but an ordinary big, soft English tabby. I'd seen her around outside more than once. She'd always given me a friendly look, a twitch of her tail.

She was bleeding from the side and from the mouth.

'That's where the blood came from. What you saw. They put her on my step this morning. They shot her with some sort of airgun,' said Tubby. 'I expect they thought she was mine. But she wasn't. She just liked mooching about in my shrubbery.'

With the back of his big, fat hand, he gently stroked her head. 'I gave her a few scraps occasionally, if she asked for them. Didn't know her name.' He put his hands in his pockets. 'Anyway, if they do anything like that again, I start getting serious. They were lucky I kept control of my temper and only deafened them today. They can't prove a thing, either. I'll kill the bastards, if I have to.'

'You used to say brutality never makes anything but more brutality.'

'There are always exceptions,' said Tubby. 'They killed a cat. They killed an ordinary, innocent, trusting old cat. Not because they hated it in particular, but because they thought it would be a good joke. A good way of putting the shits up Tubby Theakston. Yeah? Well, that's exactly one fucking dead cat too many. One fucking murder too many. What's her life worth, Den? What's anyone's life worth, these days? I thought things were supposed to be getting better.'

What could I say?

An hour or two later, because Tubby wanted to be on his own with his cats, Fromental and I went out to get a drink, down at the The Jolly Miller. That's when he remembered the job *Libération* wanted us to do. I told him I didn't give a shit.

'We really are back in their good books,' he said. 'They saw that feature we did on Somalia. We can leave tomorrow.'

'Take your own instamatic.' I was still brooding about Rosie and Paul Frame. 'I'm not sure what I want to do, but I don't fancy Africa.'

'Come on, man.' He rose, picking up both shants in one hand. 'Same again? It's a nice one – and you get to see your beautiful cousin.'

'What?'

'Rwanda, man! The Belgian UN troops are pulling out. The French are backing the incumbents. Could be civil war. They want us out there. You know – Hutus and Tutsis? Isn't that where your beautiful cousin's working?'

So I took the job.

I thought it would be the quickest way of confronting Rosie. The first chance I got I'd ask her exactly what the fuck was going on between her and Paul.

CHAPTER TWENTY-THREE
The Reds

And that was history, too, right? What a fucking century. You start with the first concentration camps, an Imperial war, carving up Africa (or actual Africans in Leopold's case), add a chorus of all the agonized millions calling from the dirt of no man's land, into the Russian Civil War, the Chinese Civil War, the Spanish Civil War, Stalin, the rise of Fascism, the Holocaust, World War Two, Hiroshima, Korea, Vietnam, Cambodia, Afghanistan, Iraq and Bosnia, Rwanda and East Timor. And Kosovo, of course. What a century, pards. What a bloody century.

Remember zero population growth? Crap. That's not what you do with numbers. You people just don't understand about consumerism. It's nuts to hack your market's arms off or shoot it in mass graves. That's peasant thinking. That's old-fashioned and primitive. Instead, you feed your market Prozac. That way, don't laugh, everybody's happy.

World money despairs of these peasants. They just won't come in to the real world. They keep cutting down the middleman.

It's been happening since Europeans bought into the slave trade. Since it became even more profitable to make war on your neighbours and sell your captives in the nearest market. Rum and sugar for human souls. Destroying the civilizations of one continent to feed the industry of another. Genocide and diaspora became their mutual shame.

Soldiers spreading across the map of Africa like blood. Red miasma rising from the cities and the rivers. The buzzing of black flies. The cold flapping of crows. The taste of sweet remains. Nothing but red arms rising and falling, red bodies sprawling on grey concrete, in dusty killing fields, in suburban streets, in prisons, in churches and mosques and synagogues. Killing teachers. Killing nurses. Killing nuns. Hacking the brain and the humanity and the active decency from the culture. Red walls. Red gutters. Red stains. Bloody metal. The stink of cordite and human pain. Nameless graves. Nothing.

A lot of it's in my display books. You know, what you take to editors to show them what you've done. A file of work. You can turn the clean, plastic pages. Nice, glossy eight-by-tens. Picture after picture after

picture. Book after book. Print after print. Transparency after transparency. Catches your eye, red. You'd say I had a fascination with it if
you didn't know this was just my job record. Take your pick. Any
country you like. Atrocity pictures? Ten a penny, mate. Corpses to the
left, rape victims to the right. Roll up. Newspaper files full of them. Can't
give them away. You feel like death. You build up a tolerance.

And tolerance is what it's all about, right? I mean, live and let live.
Everything's relative, right? Morality's in the mind of the beholder, OK?
Cowards? You'd do the same, wouldn't you? Disappear a neighbour.
Watch them next door dragged off to become nothing. Hack a couple of
kids to death in front of their mother's eyes. Make them nothing. Rape
the mother. Hack her arms off. Make her nothing. If you can't loot it,
burn it. You would, wouldn't you? If you had the choice of hacking or
being hacked? Or even risking the disapproval of your peers? Make it all
nothing?

But our public can't stand too much anguish and slaughter. They get
uncomfortable and they feel awkward. You can hear their remotes
clicking desperately. Go away. Be nothing. The editors tell you the same.
They're the representatives of the fourth estate. What we really want is
a nice leg-shot of Di, or even better a nice tasteful tit shot while she's
doing something with landmines. Or lepers. Or some other sort of loser.
Naughty but nice. Compassion, certainly, but with a bit of glamour.
Keep your fucking distance. Who wants to think about the flesh they eat
coming back to life in their mouths?

We're too refined for that. Diana always said she preferred the dying
to the living. You have to admit the company's better.

Pictures unsuitable for public sensibilities. We can't show you these
horrific scenes. The picture was too horrifying for publication. Public
events, right? To be kept from the public? Can we hear ourselves? Can
we really?

Rwanda? I didn't want to know. Did you? Makes the Huguenots or
the Highlanders seem like small beer, eh? The only difference between us
in the seventeenth and eighteenth centuries and them in the twentieth is
that we weren't being sold such efficient weapons.

Never again, eh?

Pass a law. That'll stop it. We're idealists, aren't we?

Can we hear ourselves? Pass a law, that'll stop it. We're idealists,
aren't we?

Our idealism is going to create a stable market, sound money,
predictable income from investments. A stable market is worth any
amount of human life. Best that you're willing to kill for it. It saves you
getting confused later.

Rwanda was the pivot, I suppose, for me. The way it was for Rosie.
Not for Fromental, though. We thought it was because he was too big to
kill.

'It's a fuck-up, believe me, man. We're fuelling it, too.' Fromental's relatives were all professional soldiers. His size. Tough bastards. Free French. Maquis. His father had been a WWI air ace. Soldiers hated politicians. They sent them to inevitable defeat, like the last stand of the Legion at Dien Bien Phu. So these relatives still talked to him. You always know when things are bad, he said. The professional soldiers start getting tight-lipped and refusing to comment on government decisions.

'What's the motive? Why would the French be interested?'

'Alliances. Spheres of influence. Inherited romantic imperialism. It's totally notional, man. Totally abstract. It's always a bunch of idiots in some distant capital playing really dumb strategy games. They have to be dumb because you see the result. They can't be high-level because of how they fuck up in real life. They almost always have the wrong map. The Battle of the Bulge said it, man. Soldiers on the ground going crazy. German tanks and artillery all around them. No, says intelligence, the tanks can't be surrounding the Allied troops. Intelligence hasn't reported any . . .'

Fromental started to laugh that terrifying silent laugh of his. You thought you were experiencing a ten-point earthquake until you realized where it was coming from. But even then it felt like there was a strong chance *Alien* was going to come bursting out of his chest.

'Domino theories. Corridor theories. Field theories. The national "interest" idea was invented by intelligence agencies who have, of course, become utterly corrupt, self-perpetuating bureaucracies and have long since forgotten any function they were originally employed for. They draw the maps and describe the plans, the "corridors", the "zones", the potential alliances and misalliances. They have no experience of reality, only of power, so they always get it wrong. Their intelligence is of the usual limited kind that people who join intelligence agencies possess, and they have about as much respect for individual human life as a couple of Columbine High School butchers dressed up to look like The Man With No Name. They are, Dennis, well off the surface of the planet. And by now they have good reasons they could give you as to why they should stay off the surface. Man, have you ever met any of these intelligence guys?'

'Anoraks,' I said.

He lit one of his limitless little bidis. 'Precisely.' He glanced out of the window. His huge head looked like something carved out of a single piece of rock. You couldn't credit the signs of ordinary humanity in his softened, troubled face. 'Is that land?'

I was heading towards Rwanda fairly blind. A small poor country. Bit of tourism. Gorillas. Not my territory or area of interest. You pick up a general sense of things in this business. You know not to listen to the official bulletins or, if possible, use official maps. All I had was what I'd heard from Rosie, a high-level volunteer working as a coordinator between Médicins Sans Frontières, Womankind Worldwide, WHO, the Red Cross and other outfits, using her experience to its best advantage. The usual nominal democracy that changed its governments by assassination and violence. That's the American model for you.

Are you sure you're on our side, God? I'd have thought you'd have preferred the company of the Mountain Gorilla, if you had any discrimination at all. You're no better at organizing this lot than the bloody CIA. Why don't you get off the fucking fence and either end it all or make it better? I mean, enough's enough. That was a century in which we multiplied the most and murdered the most. And imprisoned the most. And destroyed the most. And consumed the most. The Consumer Century. We consumed it all. We thought somehow there'd be something left in the next century for us. Probably there is. Desert Justice. Just Desserts.

As I heard it, the Egyptian lion-headed goddess Sekhmet was both the goddess of justice and of death. Her job was to bring about the end of the world. Always seemed a bit of a paradox to me. Now I understand. Because if there's any sodding justice we all deserve to die. We do. We do.

If only because of what we let happen in Rwanda.

Getting into Kigali, the Rwandan capital where Rosie was usually based, was easier said than done. There was a lot of bad electricity buzzing around and the UN were playing things as tight as they could. Press not really welcome. Hard to get a fix on it. In Paris, Fromental had got his visa reasonably fast, via the paper. They wouldn't let me have mine at first. Then they agreed. We'd tried getting a flight but we weren't allowed on military planes. Air France was fully booked and wouldn't make any concessions, and the other possible airlines had no flights or had suspended everything.

Eventually we had to go back to London, fly to Nairobi on the Kenyan airline, get a decent flight from Nairobi to Kampala, a Uganda Airlines puddle-jumper to some stretch of flattened field in the middle of nowhere with a hut at one end, and then take a private Westland chopper with horrendous engine problems to Kabale, still in Uganda, where we were told there was a decent main road leading to Kigali, capital of Rwanda.

A place most of us now know about only because of what our governments let happen there.

As we travelled, Jean-Luc filled me in as best he could from the bit he knew and the stuff he was reading, mostly detailed reports from MSF – the Doctors Without Frontiers outfit, which was French-based.

He didn't know much. The Quai d'Orsay was now involved with the country but Rwanda had first been part of the German territories, mandated to Belgium after WWI and run by them on a simple policy of divide and rule, first defining the tribes (who were ethnically and culturally identical) and then raising the minority Tutsis over the majority Hutus. Another fucking tribute to the lasting power of colonialism. And the latest weapons technologies, of course.

By the time they're all murdering one another, under Belgium's cheerful nose, the game's started in earnest. The paternal power watches approvingly while the Hutu organize bloody revolt. Tens of thousands butchered. Tutsis get thrown out, creating the first great wave of evacuation into nearby countries. Get some backing and return as a Revolutionary Army. Hutu hardliners turn against moderates and plan systematic genocide of Tutsis still in country (as 'collaborators'). Do what Goebbels did to the Jews. Start calling the Tutsis cockroaches. *Inyenzi*. A word on the radio. A word that won't die.

The UN sends in troops. But the French materially back the Hutus, and bingo, anything people on the ground are saying, anything the UN is hearing, anything the majority of ordinary Hutus are warning of, becomes nothing. They can't be heard. Intelligence agencies all over the world say it isn't happening.

Our United Nations said that Rwanda wasn't happening.

Intelligence agency? Definitely a contradiction in terms, especially when you start confidently bombing the shit out of major embassies.

Fromental and I had long since learned to ignore official sources and go for the real reports – from CAAW, UNICEF, Red Cross, Red Crescent, MSF and some of the others with people on the ground. People who knew the subtleties and also the horrific simplicities. People who were used to taking risks but who were getting frightened, understanding what they were witnessing. Why does nobody listen to those people? Has experience no substance? Does that mean that reality has no meaning? Are they nothing, too? Like the professional soldiers in the Ministry of Defence or the Pentagon who went unheard when the politicians decided to give their recalcitrant local wide boy Milosevic a day or two's light bombing. What is this obscene lack of respect our politicians show for the real world? Why would they cultivate that obscenity? Why do we let them?

Or are we all the same?

We had a few hours' very uncomfortable travelling time and a lot of hanging about in empty little airports. Plenty of leisure for Fromental to give me the basics. Some Belgian UN guys had been killed. As a result of public demand, Belgium was pulling her troops out. At the time they were most needed. But votes never gave way to principle. It looked like they were pouring oil on troubled embers. The local expatriates all reported increasing murders of Tutsis, an ongoing problem since independence. Bitter rivalries developing between northern and southern Hutus, different Hutu factions. Extremists getting armed by France. Tutsi rebels moving in from Uganda and Zaire. A holocaust waiting to happen.

'What the fuck has Rwanda got that anybody wants?'

'Not a lot. Like Burundi. Position at best. Francophone sphere? The Germans took it because nobody else wanted it. *African Queen* area. Tiny countries surrounded by great big ones. Heavily populated, rural economy. Too many people, not enough land. Kulaks in power, creaming off the top. Peasant problems, my friend. Usually solved with old-fashioned peasant remedies. Stalin knew what to do in the Ukraine. What Serbia's all about. Growing and grazing. It's always *Lebensraum* time.'

People in Kabale were friendly enough, but we couldn't find a car or driver to rent and wound up buying a battered old Renault jeep that still had all its own gears and whose paint didn't entirely hide its military origins. It could do speeds of up to fifty miles an hour. Which, it turned out, was far more than we wanted to do a lot of the time along a road that was partly cracked tarmac, partly flattened red earth and partly stones running through the green spring fields and copses. By now we were used to bad roads. They went with our territory. In the end we fell in behind the Byumba bus, made friends with a couple of minor officials when we all stopped for a rest break. No particular delays at the border. No particular delays.

We stayed in some kind of Christian hostel when we finally got to town. Clean, simple and not that uncomfortable. But an edge. You could taste it.

There was a lot of uncertainty. A history of recent bloodshed. Fear of repetition. Speculation. Reassurance. With the UN still around, with all the other complicated political ramifications, the extremist Hutus would be too wary to act. They needed as broad an alliance as possible against the invading revolutionaries. A political invasion, but they preferred to describe it as a blood threat. The invasion of the cockroaches. The Jew-rats. The Yellow Peril. The Darkie Menace. As we got closer to Kigali the radio was full of fear, broadcasting it like adrenalin across the country. Nasty fear. That's when I first heard the word. *Inyenzi*. Not very PC, the authorities. Definite views. What we used to call bigotry and they now call conservatism. Back to basics. Call a spade a cockroach.

Naturally, I was hardly taking in a third of what Fromental told me. I was rehearsing in my mind what I'd say to Rosie. What she'd say to me. How it would work out.

No serious problems at the border. No particular delays. Careful checking of papers, but then we were in Rwanda. Ochre clay, limestone hills, silvery forests, distant ridges.

The Renault broke down just as a bunch of boys with rifles turned up out of the hills and started shouting at us. Not one of them had a safety on his AK-47, but since I couldn't see any actual bullets I had a feeling we weren't going to be shot. One or two had berets on their heads and a bit of khaki to suggest some kind of authority and spoke some French, so that Fromental was able to crack a joke with them, ease things up. They were fascinated by his size. They didn't know whether to sell him as the eighth wonder of the world or kill him as a trophy. Which bought us a bit of time. A grown-up arrived. He struck me as being a bit like a seedy Scoutmaster, some local Hitler, but he had most of a uniform and an air the boys respected. He checked our papers and suddenly we're being dragged along the road by the local Akela's own dib-dib-dib, dub-dub-dubs, transformed into jolly good-deeders at his command. Baden-Powell would have been proud. Kipling would have known they had the right stuff in them. We had to pay almost as much as we'd paid for the car to get it fixed in a dusty village by a local blacksmith whose name I never heard. Then, after the hovering official had been sweetened, insisting on carefully writing out 'official passes' for us, we were off again to the capital.

The road improved a bit as we got closer and there were more vehicles, mostly UN. We talked to a couple of blue berets. Canadians. They had a grim, disgusted air, replying to us in lowered tones as if someone was eavesdropping on them. They were witnessing murder and not being allowed to talk about it. Because if they talked about it, it would be real and the UN would have to do something. Keep it nothing. Whatever it costs.

We asked them if they knew where we could find the offices of CVS, Rosie's outfit, but they weren't sure. There were so many agencies in Kigali, so many sets of initials, it was hard to tell them apart. They suggested we go to the MSF HQ near Place de la Libération. If we waited, they'd finish their tour and be back for us.

We waited for an hour and then did what we'd usually do and picked up a local boy to ride with us. Usual African capital. Poorer than many. Less showy than a lot of them. Sets for things to come. False fronts representing the luxuries in store. Low-rises. Some local capo's collapsing monument to himself, some crumbling business investment that allows him to be landlord of the lost, king of his local shit-heap. Sun-faded signs over bike repair shops and little drink kiosks and dusty cafés, the cosmetics all failing like the shade-trees browning in the glare, the public buildings left by the Belgians, the big gates and the gardens, the schools. Dark blue skies. Funny looking trees. The police stations. Signs for local beer, for Stella Artois, for photocopies, Fujifilm, Kodak, movies, *Flammes des Tuareq*, *Asterix*, *Tintin*, *You Only Live Twice*. Butchers' slabs. Fishmongers' slabs. Calves' heads. Slick, dark scales. Black flies. Pierrot Gourmand, Ricard and Pernod. Hard heat. Awnings. Shadows. Eyes. South.

We found Rose in a tiny office in a back street off the Rue de l'Ancienne Provenance. An outside flight of wooden stairs, a slatted door, and there we were, filling the place up. Electronics all over the place. Paperwork. Big books. Faxes. Phones going. A TV displaying a permanent sign I couldn't read. Files. Locals coming and going. Expats, mostly white, busy coordinating. But tense, you know. You felt you were intruding. Wasting their space and time.

My cousin was in the middle of it. An exquisite, calm heron in a frenzied aviary, reassuring, recommending, praising, helping. The moment she gave you her attention the world felt somehow a bit more manageable. I hadn't seen her doing her job much. I could see immediately why they all wanted her to work for them.

She looked up, saw me, grinned and shook her head. 'What the fuck are you doing here?' she said.

I reminded her who Fromental was. She was friendly, but still abstracted. 'Lot on,' she said.

So we went to find a room and told her we'd be back when we knew where we were staying. She didn't offer to put us up. She said we should be all right at the hotel. Most of the journalists had left after they'd got what they needed about the killings of the Belgian UN guys. I asked who had killed them. She shrugged. 'Take your pick.'

It was easier to haul what we had down the street to the hotel. Everybody seemed to have a weapon. Every youth, at any rate. I'd never seen so many civilians with guns hanging around. Who the fuck were they planning to shoot?

I met that BBC guy, Nick Allard, in the lobby while Jean-Luc was signing us in. He was always in these hell-spots but never seemed to get the sun. His big, sad friendly face was sardonic. He said everyone was pulling out just as we were pulling in.

'Everyone?'

'Well, not me,' he said. He gave me a kind of sly, weary glance. 'I never do, do I?' He was stuck with a reputation for bravery, he told me later, that had gone away a long time ago. Now all he had to sustain him was fatalism and the occasional snort of something. It might have been the remains of courage, I thought, but it was a damned sight more than most of us had. He missed his kids a lot. He was afraid that if he didn't do these jobs he wouldn't be able to support them. He was hoping he'd be offered something substantial at home. But the public wanted him, didn't they? He was their lad. He was their best. Five years later it would be Serbia.

We had a drink in the bar. The guy running it was an old colonial hand. There were a few French soldiers in there, with red berets tucked into their battledress, talking quietly at one end of the bar. The bartender joked in picturesque French, shaking his cocktails, mixing his shorts. He didn't like us much. He seemed more comfortable with uniforms.

Allard told me that the authorities were arming civilians left and right, under the helpless observation of the UN people. They were creating more militias, so-called home guards, *interahamwe*, to defend against the threat of Tutsi rebels, battle-hardened in Uganda, already massing at the borders and in places making inroads, but Allard thought the guns weren't for Tutsis that far away. 'They're preparing a genocide, old boy.' He started smirking horribly. For a moment he lost control of his face. That was the first time I'd heard the word attached to Rwanda. 'I've talked to half the commanders here. Not those bastards over there. They're what's backing up the arms distribution. God knows what the French think they're playing at.'

Fromental believed these things got their own momentum. Their own plots. Their own villains and counter-villains. Because most of the people who joined intelligence agencies were romantic and invented characters and situations to fit the fictions that inspired them. They always preferred dramatic simplicity to complicated fact.

'Could be, old boy.' Allard tasted his brandy. 'Anyway, it's light-blue-touchpaper-and-stand-well-clear time, if you ask me. The president's due back from that conference tomorrow. Unlikely he's done much in the way of progressive thinking. Probably just building up his power base. He's threatened from all sides. I'm talking about the Hutu-only extremist parties. There's always in-fighting. It's in the nature of that kind of thinking. But if they find something to pull them together, we could be in for some serious mayhem.'

'Like what?' I asked.

'Tune in to RTV-Colline sometime, if you know the language. Like getting rid of all potential Tutsi opposition. By getting rid of all Tutsis.'

I thought he'd gone mad and felt sorry for him.

Fromental and I went back to Rosie's office. It was getting to be dusk. I thought the shadows were populated with gunboys. The office was relatively tranquil but Rosie was gone. Some sort of emergency. She'd left a note to say she'd try to have breakfast with us at the hotel.

This wasn't exactly what I'd anticipated. I wanted to ask Rosie about Paul Frame, not the fucking United Nations. She didn't turn up for breakfast.

She called me at six in the morning from the lobby. She wanted to see me. Preferably in the room. Fromental was engulfing the bed next to mine and was in his usual terrifying coma, so I thought it would be all right.

'I would like to see you alone,' I said, when she came in. 'Sometime.'

'Here I am.' She gave me a big, warm, weary hug. 'Oh, bloody hell, Dennis. Are you here to take some atrocity pix?'

'As soon as an atrocity comes up,' I said.

'Well. It might not. Not really. If we can get a bigger UN force. These people are getting gun-happy, Dennis. It's worse than an NRA meeting at full frenzy.'

'So are you all right?'

'Better than most. They'll protect me while they think they need me. It's not the whites we have to worry about at this point.'

'Look,' I said, 'before we start on all this . . .'

'I'm fine,' she said. 'Really. But thanks.'

So that blew that gambit.

'I saw Paul Frame in London,' I told her.

'Poor bastard,' she said. 'Was he all right? His wife's murder was shocking. Down there in Burundi, too. Terrible mistake. They were working so hard. They had so many friends. I was only talking to her on the phone a couple of days before. I suppose you read all about it over there. Did they say what was done to her? God!'

Some days aren't the best for pitching your own case.

Rosie gave me a briefcase. She said that she might need my help, if we were sticking around. So of course I assured her we were sticking around.

Fromental started to stir. Rosie blew me a kiss. The door closed. I put the case in the cupboard.

I went back to bed. I couldn't think of anything else to do.

Fromental and I breakfasted in a nearby café. The croissants looked right and the coffee smelled right. But the rest was a mystery. He began to complain. As if we were sitting in the Terminal, waiting for the fresh bread. I didn't mind the greasy pastry, the thick condensed milk. But I didn't have his expectations.

I don't remember exactly when we heard the crash and saw the smoke, but that was when somebody shot a rocket at the incoming presidential plane and took out not only the Hutu top dog Habyarimana, but his colleague President Ntaryama of Burundi, plus a few incidental fat cats and crew. But it was a signal all right. The broadcast hatred intensified and hours later the killing began.

I only understood one word of Rwandan, apart from *Hutu* and *Tutsi*. *Inyenzi*. Cockroach. It was the word you started hearing most on the radio. Out of the loudspeakers. Out of the houses. Out of the shops. Kill the cockroaches before the cockroaches kill you. Kill your wife. Kill your husband. Kill the secret aliens. Kill the traitors and the spies. Especially if they are your relatives. Your fellow villagers. Your neighbours. They are the ones who must die. And anyone who defends them or refuses to help in the killing, they die, too. It's that kind of world, these days. Like Wall Street, pards. Kill or be killed. Joe McCarthy would have been proud of them. Welcome to the twenty-first century! Life has never been cheaper. The market has never been more aggressive.

It was orchestrated killing, too. All over Rwanda. In every village and town. Kill the cockroaches before they kill you. They take your food. They take your work. They take your women. Those who do not kill are themselves our enemies. See, that's the difference between them and the Germans. Most Hutus did their own killing.

One of my best-ever pictures came out of that, though. It's always in the books and collections. We'd got caught up in a door-to-door just as we were leaving, after days of running about on rooftops with zooms and hoping nobody took a potshot at us. They were killing according to lists. Street to street. House to house. *Very* reminiscent of good old Europe. These bastards had a few guns, but mostly they had pangas. You know. What the Mau Mau used on the British in Kenya. I had one for years at home. Some Brookie had brought it back with him. I used to split firewood with it. They weren't paying too much attention to us as they harvested the corpses. I have those shots of gutters actually full of blood, right? And all those corpses of men, women and children piled in the alleys. And the four youths hacking the little boy to bits. Great shots, right? From the roof of this house. We'd jumped about eight places to get to where we could see what was going on below. Blocks of flats. We had to go down eventually, and the steps led straight into someone's living room. This family huddled there, waiting to be killed. They listened to the radio. They knew they were cockroaches.

Anyway, we had five adults and six children, mixed Tutsis and Hutus, all terrified. Herded downstairs to wait while Fromental went for the jeep. While the nasty little murder-maddened mob got closer and closer. Brrrrrrm. Round the corner comes the Renault. He jumps out, starts pushing kids up on to his back, showing them where to hang on the straps of his vast bush-jacket, gathering them up in his arms. And only then did I realize he'd been cut or hit in his left shoulder and his right forearm. 'Nothing,' he said. 'I'm not even losing any significant amount of blood.'

So there's my picture. I'm proud of it. It has that rare resonance you long to capture every time. It has a soul in it. Fromental, like Porthos at the well, festooned with frightened children, his AK-47 in his teeth, running for our Renault, which now has its old French markings crudely restored, to make us look more official. He's wounded on both arms. Bleeding into his khaki shirt. Behind him is Hutu graffiti. Kill all cockroaches. Behind that, the cautious adults, knowing not to trust us.

Six hundred years they lived and worked and socialized together. Western civilization soon stopped that. Harmony's the enemy of free-market consumer capitalism.

Rosie needed to get to Ngara in Tanzania. 'I have some children up there,' she said. They'd let her expatriate workers go, but they wouldn't let her out. I think they had her targeted for some reason.

'Jesus Christ, Rosie,' I said, 'how many kids have you had?'

'Oh, fuck you,' she said.

Ngara was just across the Kagera River from Rwanda. She'd got workers with the refugees. Going spare. No transport. It had to be us. If she could get over the border, she could take it from there. She had the impression we knew the terrain better than we did. And that we had a better car. And that the AK-47 Jean-Luc had bought off a boy for ten US dollars came with ammunition. We'd learned the lesson early. A gun without bullets is better than no gun at all. It clears your way a bit faster.

And you never know
When you're going to find some ammo!
Or when a mine will blow
You to zippedy-do-dah! Zippedi-day!
Just never fucking know.
Oh, Lord, when you'll be blow-n,
You will be blown away . . .

as Jean-Luc sang operatically and incessantly while he drove us through the night towards the border. We went through villages that were just one, horrible scream. You started to smell the blood.

'Tutsi soldat! Tutsi soldat!' Fromental would shout, gesturing behind us as *interahamwe* boys wondered about blocking our path and nervous Hutu military waved us through. 'The only fucking advantage we have,' he said, 'is that they think we're French and therefore on their side.'

But he got us all up to the Kagera bridge in time to see the bloody waters clogged with corpses and the carrion-eaters spoiled for choice. I was told by one of the refugee children that the bigger animals preferred babies. She'd had nothing to do but watch the river.

So we got into Tanzania and that new nightmare. But at least we'd brought a few kids out. Oh, I went back and took more pictures. But how many communal graves can you put a different angle on? How many spins of the same old record?

That was how we wound up spending so much time in Africa as the Tutsis turned the tables and all the Hutus started filling up the camps. That was in the autumn. The camps were ghastly. Auschwitz at least had a way of getting rid of the corpses. Local warlords running them. Threatening aid workers. Killing whoever they pleased. Controlling the food that the sentimental world started sending. A market economy in a flash. You don't want these people to become welfare victims, do you? And every fucking aid worker building up more saint points than Mother Teresa. Every doctor and nurse and crabby old nun, risking their rich, sophisticated, intellectual, spiritual, valuable lives to save the lives of the damned. Working in conditions that the TV describes as indescribable. They're not indescribable. They just don't want to do it. Too many people would switch off, wouldn't they?

Isn't it terrible, what those people do to one another?

You don't have to look. You don't have to stop playing games to check out the volunteer websites that do describe the indescribable. In report after report, detail after detail, horror on horror.

One job followed another. They wouldn't let us leave. We'd do a job on the murders in the Zaïre camps and then someone else would want us to do a 'day-in-the-lifer' in Johannesburg, an interview with some poor, distinguished bastard in a nicely trimmed beard and a tribal garment, trying to bring some kind of harmony and civilization back to his bleeding continent and beginning to understand that he was actually an endangered species. All the extraordinary diversity of a continent ploughed under by imported tanks. The extent of the misery, the inventiveness of the cruelties, the voiceless despair of millions, gets you down pretty quickly. You begin to dislike the victims. You don't want to hear the atrocity hit parade. You spend all the time you can damping down your brain.

You can't take any more evidence.

The Rwandan holocaust was a short-lived business, by holocaust standards. Now it's more or less over. It pops up here and there, of course, like a kicking corpse. A raid on a town. Some gorilla-tourists chopped up in areas of designated natural beauty. But it isn't really over, this masque of the red death, because of the displaced millions who are rotting to death in camps, so many of them 'suspects' in the previous holocaust, packed in so tight they have to sleep upright while their feet rot off and the gangrene finishes them. Girls. Little boys. Men and women. Still in the red madness. Learning nothing. They all say the same thing. They're all innocent. Nothing but innocent.

It seemed like you were watching a continent strangle in its own entrails. The thinnest people in the world slipping down the cracks of drought and despair while the fattest in the world despise them as beasts and feast on their bounty even as, occasionally, they toss them a coin or two. If America cared for the continent she had helped ruin, she would not be 'apologizing' to the people who were the most successful local slavers. She would be screaming in shame.

Months after our race for the border, I got a message from Rosie. She was going to be in Bulawayo for a few days. That suited me and Fromental.

Fromental and I met Rosie at the airport. We'd heard the World Service news. She'd just been thrown out of Nigeria. She was part of a deposition trying to get the death sentence lifted from Ken Saro Wiwa, the writer, and his fellow 'dissidents'. She was hopeful.

We went to some fancy steak house. It could have been a Hilton, I don't remember. You hate to admit it, but after months in Central Africa you seek out places like that. The dimmer, more air-conditioned, more anonymous, the better. French wine. Soft bread. Which way to the Café Analgesic? It's where you go when the shells are landing in the streets, when the cries of murdered women rise higher than the shrieking loudspeakers, when the little girls are being violated, when the babies are being tossed on bayonets, when the young men are being shot or forced to join the brutes, when the refugees are crying out for your help, when there's fuck-all you can do about anything. You want to hear some flunkey murmuring about the dish of the day. You want to have a cooling drink. You want clear water and soothing muzak. You want to take advantage of everything you can and you don't give much of a shit what your conscience has to say about it.

So that's where we went.

Rosie looked ill. She'd never looked ill before. I said she should stop whatever it was she was doing. She needed some R&R. She nodded slowly, not denying it as she normally would. She kept nodding, even when I'd stopped.

'You're still nodding,' I said.

Fromental came clumping back from the gents, like the Incredible Hulk trying to look inconspicuous. He filled his chair and picked up the menu. Then he looked at Rosie.

'These lights,' he said. 'Do I look as ghastly as you?'

She laughed without energy. 'Well, I was planning to go home after this, anyway. I had another proposal from Barbican. That means he's going to get married again. I'm curious to find out to who.'

'What happened to Bobby?' I asked.

'I don't know. She seems to have faded from the scene.'

Well, at least the murder was on Barbican's conscience, I thought. You get used to thinking like that. Second nature.

She drank too much. She flirted with Jean-Luc. She even flirted with me. I knew what she wanted. I couldn't give it to her. All I could do was go to bed with her later and hold her while she sighed the night away. It made me feel useful for once.

Next day, still in the hotel, we heard that Ken Saro Wiwa and the others had been executed. Nigeria at her worst, saying 'fuck you' to the world and killing some writers to show us we couldn't push the big guys around. The next news was that Begat, after heavy rocket attack which had levelled the city, had been annexed by Algeria while the world turned a blind eye. The S'r'wi Berberim's leader, Ibram-al-Rikh', had been killed resisting arrest.

'What are you going to do about it?' I asked her.

We were sitting at the television in a room that was half indoor swimming pool. A bunch of young Japanese athletes were enjoying a boisterous few minutes behind us.

I listened to the sound of an ambulance. I was so far gone the noise was reassuring to me.

Rosie had suddenly become thinner, frailer. The only thing that seemed alive on her was the fabric of her dress. Her smile made me feel sick. Everything was gone from her. All the light.

'Oh, nothing,' she said briskly. 'Nothing now. There is nothing I can do now.'

'Then do something for yourself,' I said.

Her answering look shook me. 'I intend to,' she said. 'I'd actually had something entirely different to propose to you. Too late now. We go to Plan Z. That was my last try, Denny. I don't do this any more.'

'You're getting a London job?'

'No,' she said. 'I'm retiring. I'm going to put my feet up and be a proper lady.'

'You can't afford it,' I said. 'You couldn't stand it.'

'Oh, it's a lot easier than that, Denny. I've a position waiting for me. I'm about to phone him now. I'd already thought all this through. All planned. It's my worst-case scenario, but at least I have it in place.'

'Phone who?'

'I'm phoning Barbican. I'm taking him up on that offer. There'll have to be a few negotiations first. I'm not a fool. Just a realist.'

'What offer?' I was a fool, not a realist.

'You know,' she said. 'I'm going to marry him.'

CHAPTER TWENTY-FOUR
The Whites

Yes, of course I tried to badger her out of it. I played every twist and crack I knew. What about South Africa? I said. That was improving. Wasn't it? Kashmir seemed to be settling down a bit. The Chinese politicos were beginning to turn their heads and peek out of their own authoritarian arses. And there was some progress in Israel. And people were starting to listen about East Timor. And the Kurds. And Burma. Tibet. And Ireland could be resolving. And sooner or later we were going to get the Tories out . . . And Washington might discover a principle other than the survival principle . . .

It didn't really convince me, either.

You don't yomp free of the century's second-best, cheapest and perhaps most efficient genocide feeling optimistic about the positive power of human persuasion, about the natural dignity of mankind. Rosie shook her head slowly, grinning at me like a death mask. She was still beautiful. Worse than usual. Lacey Moloch, who spent millions on trying not to look plain, would have given her inheritance and her father's overburdened soul to shine like Rosie shone on a bad day.

I wondered if my cousin's beauty hadn't at last become too much of a distraction, no longer compensated for by the power, the effect she could get from it. I wished we were talking about that now. The way we used to talk. How do you deal with knowing you wouldn't have been able to get half of the problems of the Punjab addressed if you didn't have the most magnificent profile in history?

We'd been discussing it since she was twenty. It's what I would rather discuss. We'd never really come up with the answer. But that definitely wasn't the problem for her at the moment. Every time the conversation drifted in a different direction, she brought me relentlessly home. I wasn't getting it. This was Plan Z, she said. Not to be unsealed lightly. It was her last resort. 'I've had enough of this, Dennis. I've decided to take it easy. Take it easy?'

'The world needs you.' I felt like a goozer. But if she was giving up, who else would do what she could do? Because it needed her genius.

'The world has fucked itself,' she said. 'Eight corporations are asset-stripping the planet. Haven't you noticed?'

'All the more reason . . .'

Fromental rumbled some excuse about a video game he'd seen called *Rabbit Attack* and went to find it.

'I'm sick of this vicious circle, Dennis. We're just making it easier for the predator to pick and choose what he wants from the wreckage. The public pays but has no influence. Public money and sympathy are systematically utilized to facilitate private greed. Capital takes the profits. The public pays the price. The people pay all the costs. About ten white men in suits are making all the money. At our expense. Our whole stock market is a bubble dependent on the fortunes of a handful of international companies, mostly American, mostly keeping their momentum through size and luck. Certainly not intelligence. Those smaller shareholders are as vulnerable as anyone. Everyone pays except the piper. And nobody seems to care enough. Nobody. The system's on self-destruct, Dennis. At least, as we're applying it. Nothing's working for the common good. Unless we fork out huge sums, rich people like me aren't paying the fair cost of our survival. A huge publicity machine works to ease our consciences, to tell us what good-hearted folk we are. Naughty but nice. But private people like us are paying for the multinationals' education in predatory power politics. How to control us without question. To make us cull ourselves. Saddam knows how to play this. He puts his dissidents in his front line and has us burn them to death for him. Read my lips.'

'So joining the establishment will do that, will it? Make the world better?' This was lame. I twiddled a breadstick. If it was a breadstick.

'I didn't say that.'

'You really are giving up?'

'Plan Z – get married and settle down. Pick the most powerful individual on earth and marry him.'

'Johnny's a prick.'

'Most blokes are. If they weren't they'd leave the planet as they'd wish to find it. You know that Washington doesn't make a decision without including him. He's a prick they all want to keep taking the Viagra. The entire pharmaceutical industry depends on the state of his digestion. That's got to mean something. He's smart in his own way. He controls everything he wants to now, Den. Too many other people need him in place to want to topple him. They control themselves. He controls everyone. He might not own the world, but he has the controlling interest. He owns us.'

'Not Tubby,' I said, 'and not you.'

Rosie was all feeling. All sense and sensibility. Johnny was only persuasion. An artificial engine, an unfertilized egg, a cold muscle. It was obscene to think about.

'And you, Den.' She tried some sort of comforting gesture.

'No, Rosie. Not me.'

Oh, Rosie!

It was a turning point for both of us. For all of us, probably. For the whole fucking world, come to think of it.

Oh, Rosie . . .

And personally, I'd had it with Africa. Fromental had become obsessed with Rwanda. You could understand why. It sometimes seemed he carried the whole business on his great big back. He wasn't just reporting now, of course, but doing a lot of what Rosie had once done – trying to coordinate services and get people what they needed before they rotted to death. For him it had gone beyond cause and effect, reasons and warring interests. All he could see was dying children everywhere. Everywhere. But he didn't need me. I was useless at dealing with the kind of wankers you so often had to placate. I just got angry and walked away from them. You needed a different sort of personality.

Oh, Lord, girl . . .

I didn't klik dying kids any more at all. There were no pictures left to take. The stuff I was doing then still turns up on Page 10 of the *Independent* or the *Guardian* pretty regularly whenever they do their 'conditions in the camps' stories or background reports for some new atrocity. But I wouldn't go out on a new story like that. I gave up those when Rosie got married. There seemed no great point.

With your long hair, your long hair, with your long hair hanging down . . .

Rosie didn't talk me into it. Nobody talked me into it. I just twigged: if she could see the writing in the sky then we were well and truly buggered. What good was I going to do, a fly on the dying face of the world? Might as well hang out in the gilt, round the sugar with the better-looking flies, where the nanny state gave way to the nana state.

I went back to Paris. The third empire. I'd been away over a year but I didn't expect what I found. Quai D'Hivers had moved into the twenty-first century.

My flat was fine, one street back from the quayside. Nothing had been done to the insides of many of the buildings, but now the whole pool, where the canals met, had been partially roofed with glass, been dolled up with a lot of busy neon and looked more like an unholy union between Las Vegas and Miami, with more of the usual giant Australian ferns. The canal waters were tinted and floodlit and had jazzy pleasure boats on them. The Café Terminal was now called Maddy's Place, in glaring scarlet neon. Everything buzzed with Disney colours, with vanilla and indigo, emerald and lemon. There were ice-cream booths and VR booths and game and music booths and all the displays were moving and shaking and 4/4 and disco-dandy and we were UP UP UP. Who were these cool, sanitary, international stereotypes sipping long drinks at one another? Anti-bacterial airs wafted from a sophisticated system. Nice, clean surfaces, easily washed down when the wankerazzi went home.

I got exhausted just moving from the bridge, along the quay and up the cobbled side street to my flat. Bad acid. The world had turned to bad throbbing acid. What had happened to the boats? The bargees? *L'Atalante* . . . ? It was pathetic, really.

Particularly since I'd been so unkind about Norrie's favourite havens. Now it had happened to one of mine and all I could think was that I was glad it hadn't happened sooner. However completely reconciled to this inevitable drift of everything I touched turning to dross, I was cursed to wander the world and leave a trail of tacky plastic behind me. It was my due. Payback for what I'd let happen to Brookgate.

Rosie was right. The whole planet was being asset-stripped. Unfortunately, part of it was definitely my fault.

After a couple of hours spent trying to get my flat sorted from the debris left by my sub-let and recovering the few bits of important mail he hadn't managed to let his dog piss on, I went out. I took my Pentax. It was curiosity, mostly. I wanted to see exactly what they'd done to the Terminal. The same kind of morbid impulse that used to make people go and look at the corpses of the violently dead. The quayside had been cleaned up, a smooth padded walkway, and the canal made safe with chains.

The Terminal was still there in a way, behind a perspex shield, a kind of atmospheric wall decoration, almost as its old proprietor had left it. And sitting in front of it, at a high winking scarlet scratch deck on a tall scarlet stool, was the Red Queen, Maddy La Font, Hostess du Spinne, who would be personally welcoming you all that first week. It had only been open four days. It looked to me as if it had been there forever.

'Dennis! My God, you are so tanned and lean and mean, darling.' She yummed all up me, like a sly retriever. 'Oh, you are so good-looking! A pocket Robert Mitchum, sweetheart. Ym,ym,ym,ym,ym!'

I didn't have to pinch myself. This was too terrible to be a nightmare. I was an animal watching its environment rapidly transformed into a theme park. I was a fucking tame dinosaur. Or any current animal, really, I suppose. I was coming out in a rash. I could feel it under my shirt. I was beginning to wonder if I hadn't picked something up. Her perfume drew me down into her ugly flesh. 'You're mine for the evening, darling. You'll be amazed how many famous friends I have now.'

She was right. Every poncey plonker in the universe had decided oh ya Maddy's was bad, bad, bad and just the job for them. That's the night I got my best Di shot ever. Never got a better. Remember? Jitterbugging with Linford Christie? Phew! That's how I found out in a big way the difference between snapping ugly death and lensing the good life. Hundreds of thousands of pounds.

Of course, I had to pay for this break with my own body.

It was the easiest way to clock what else was going on. Not that I really needed to trade my body for that information. It was pretty public. You guessed it. BBIC Entertainment, who also had the next-biggest share in EuroDisney, had bought the Quai D'Hivers for Maddy La Font. Or swapped it for something she had been able to do for them. Probably shafting Tootsie. Everyone shafting someone, eh? You wouldn't think we had the energy.

Well, it was no worse than going to New York and finding a Starbuck's and a Baby Gap where the old pub and hotel had been – or still were, in cartoon versions of themselves. The Café Irische? Mulligan's Tavern, Oldest in America. Barbican had found Houston Circle so quaint he just had to buy it, too. He had a real eye, that lad, for the unusual. Bluefish. Postcard gallery. Charles Rennie Mackintosh shop. A neon store. He could sniff out integrity like a smackhound sniffing for Grade One Burmese, and gobble it up, just like that, leaving a repro, a whiff of paint to mark his passing.

So I went back to Brookgate, to find myself entirely surrounded by vast stone-clad piles. Glassy citadels. Mushroom monuments to Barbican's unfailing vision. The apocalypse was over and we had the feel-good factor back. We had our new security. The graveyard had been tidied up and there were now benches for certain privileged office workers. The buildings around it were so high it resembled the bottom of an air shaft. Our grave was all right, except there was an enormous wrought-iron fence around it (Barbican no doubt being sensitive to his ancestors). The church had been touched up in funny ways and had a fibreglass air. Elastolin stone.

But my place was all right and to be honest I didn't mind an airbrushed view. As long as I didn't go out, I could enjoy the security, the pleasures of my old, familiar flat. Nothing much moved or changed. Paul couldn't have stayed long. Just one of Tubby's friends looking in to do a bit of dusting and make sure the boiler was all right. I might not have been away. I felt like that bloke in that weird witch's cottage they had in *Metropolis*, in the middle of all this monumental machinery for working in.

I had no heart for grafting.

To keep myself from getting any further down, I developed the Maddy's rolls and sent a few round to my agent in the hope they'd cover the various bills I still had. When my agent went ecstatic I thought he was on something. When he told me the kind of dosh he'd got for all those pix of sweaty debs and their oily escorts, let alone the astronomical sums for the jitterbug shots of Di and Linford, things settled down in me. I got cool. I became realistic.

And, as you know, I became a celebrity. More famous as a jackal than a hound. I still sent the old atrocity stuff out whenever the *Independent* or the *Guardian* wanted to do a midsection background on the camps now, or refer to some current atrocity, but mostly I went to parties. And read the odd gossip piece. Barbican to marry the famous 'Angel of Begat' Rose Beck, the little coloured cockney girl who made good. As *English Life* put it. Most treated her with much more dignity, even awe. To some this was like Mother Teresa deciding to shack up with Satan, Son of the Morning. The Queen of the Public Sector, marrying the King of the Private Sector, as the feel-good doctors of the time liked to put it. Most, you'll remember, celebrated this state as a true harmony. The Third Way on the Yellow Brick Road. No Elton in those days. Not quite yet.

The exemplary middle-class couple became royalty. It was a lot easier than trying it the other way round. A relief after the Bigears and Bigeyes scandals. Here was something even the heavy leader writers could celebrate, just to show how right the world could be. Speculation by guests and media about Barbi's increasing charitable interests. Were we going to see his human face? What checks would he pick up? You know. Like Ted Turner and Jane Fonda. Only even snazzier. The alchemical marriage that would bring a balance between the worlds temporal and spiritual. All they needed was the Sangreal as a font. And some sort of sword, probably. Feudal chivalry in all its mighty splendour. Order restored. The world redeem'd. The world fixed up.

They got married in St Paul's with the Hanover Band, in grey silk, giving it full baroque belt, echoing fit to bring the dome down on us, and Barbican's old friend D.B. Beesley, Archbishop of Southwark, doing the honours in his fattest, most sonorous flute, blessing them with the dignity of ancient days. Him so fine in morning grey and her so sleek in white. Tubby was asked to be best man, but refused. He couldn't leave the Mill, he said. So I gave her away and Paul Frame was best man. I didn't like any of it much. Everyone else was well satisfied. We were a step away from a *Vivat!* We had a mythic couple again.

All the great knights of the city were there, all the barons and the lords and ladies of the land, including the Duke of York and his lovely companion. The Harrodses and the Mothercares. The Gaps and the Body Shops. Celebrity darlings. Then for the chosen few hundred there's a reception at one of BBIC Entertainment's newest, hottest spots, with Annie Lennox, lured from her offspring to give a private concert, Tom and Jerry's behind London Bridge station.

That's right, pards. Barbi's done up The Corinthian Boys and now it's got a restaurant called The Arboretum and even more gigantic copper buckets of those big Australian ferns. A stage for entertainments and a sporting motif throughout, in green and brass, with some nice prints of former prizefighters and a few long-lived mastiffs, with toilets marked DOGS and BITCHES and spittoons to dump your fag-ends in. You wouldn't recognize the old place, though Jimmy still arrives like clockwork twice a week to do his 'Great Days At The Corinthians' act.

It's even been on Radio Four. He tells me about it when we withdraw to the nice fumed ebony and gold bar. He puts a powder-blue elbow down and picks up his pint. I can see the shants. They're grouted in rows behind us, part of the interior decoration.

'You like the new style do you, Jimmy?'

'Great, mate,' he says. 'You have to attract the young people, don't you? They do a disco now and everything. And I only have to turn up a couple of times a week on comedy nights. Of course, I miss some of the old clientele, mate.' Noblesse oblige.

A bloke I know is a neighbour of Mad Frankie Fraser's, another of the most feared villains in the East End. Every morning Frankie walks his poodles up to the park, enjoying a tranquil and leisurely retirement. A well-contented man. A well-earned retirement. A little safe garden set aside from the world's troubles. What else could any of us hope for? It's certainly a plus when considering a career. Good choice, Frank.

I asked how V.J. was doing.

'Marvellous,' says Jimmy. 'He bought that motor-racing track up north. North of Leeds. Old speedway track, really. Aldthorpe? Anyway, he does up his cars and toodles 'em round the track and only every so often hits a great big bale of hay. Happy as a fucking clam, mate. Him and Ray.'

'Ray who?'

'You know. They've been together for years. Just led separate business lives. Ray, who used to have the caff in Snatcher's.'

Used to?

That's right. Nothing. All gone. I stood there next morning like some Rip van Winkle, looking up at a great big grey block of concrete stretching into the clouds, wondering how your past, your whole fucking past and the past of your ancestors, their past and its past, can suddenly go blip, like a crashed program, and never have been. Nothing.

Tearing out everything organic and replacing it with perpetually decaying, perpetually profitable processed iron and lime. Kneecapping our culture. Making us walk on their crutches.

I found that V.J. and his family had owned a title to the Duchy of Crete, and therefore the property, for years. But the Czechs still had their counter-claim. So he simply cut a deal with the Czechs to let him get the best price for them all. V.J. didn't sell it when it was cheap down at Seven Dials, because the place's old sanctuary laws were useful to him, and when the land got more valuable V.J. wouldn't sell so that Ray, with whom he shared a Victorian manor overlooking the Bishop's Park and the river, could stay doing what he liked to do. But when V.J. lost control of his Brookgate interests and sold up his Soho stuff, he decided he might as well let BBIC have the lot. It helped the Czechs and the Slovaks get fairly amicably divorced.

V.J. had wanted out, out, out as his old power seemed to dissipate with his self-respect. He and his generation had taken too much for granted. They were like Jews trying to board the last train leaving Vienna. V.J. and Ray got a very nice price for everything, bought a spectacular house overlooking Watendwater in the Lake District, within an hour's spin of the Aldthorpe race track, and entertained the Alan Bennetts a lot. Within hours of Ray supervising the loading on to special trucks of his beloved stoves, Snatcher's was rubble. No more sanctuary.

Hamstrung? I always thought of these little unique bits of the city like the knots in a hawser. Too tight to be untied, they have to be cut. Every cut weakens the overall structure exponentially. It stops being able to function unconsciously. Needs more care. More help. More goodwill. More money. More business.

I did all right with the wedding photos, too. Especially the evening dresses giving it the old knees-up at the fresher, more famous Corinthian Boys. Sons and daughters of the crowd, eh? But every one notorious for being well known and that's what mattered in the great soap opera that had become our only properly recorded history. It certainly brought in the dosh like disaster or rock and roll never had. In fact, what with Rosie and Tubby tipping me off to this and that, it wasn't long before I was Mr Saucy, the red-tops' favourite photog. Look at the credits. Politicians and pop stars slipping in and out of public toilets, trousers down behind the sheds, propositioning whores, dobbing in the dosh, fucking the favourites. They started taking a particular dislike to me.

But I wasn't one of your 'Over here, darling' goozers, hanging about in the rain for two-penn'orth of flash from some overprized pop star. I was there first. Frequently it was only me. My nose became a legend. Not a journo on the Wharf wasn't pleased to know me, so he could talk about me. It was like that, then. They envied me. They knew I had inside info, who my cousins were. Well, some of it was true. But as far as joining any inner fucking circle was concerned, I was resisting easily. And I hadn't actually been asked. And as far as any inner fucking circle was concerned, Barbi himself rang me up once a week to suggest getting together. He had one of the set, after all. He wanted the pair. He wanted us all to be the gang he wanted to be in when he was seventeen. He really had fond memories of those times we were pissing on him. Best years of his life. Was this their secret? Was this where Miss Whiplash entered the equation?

I just couldn't bring myself to join. And I didn't need to, really, either, because I was still seeing Rosie. So I got my crumb of consolation without having to eat it off some burgher's flash cloth in the company of a score of barking captains of industry.

We met about once a week. For lunch. In places where they were calling it luncheon, again. Well bunkered-up nostalgia parlours. And naturally not cheap. Good safe time travel is pricey. Rosie couldn't afford to mix.

It was about the only time she could get away these days, she said. The problems of being a society hostess! Feeding the overfed was harder work than feeding the hungry, that was for sure. She said things like that, I thought, to challenge something. But I wasn't taking the bait. There was nothing in me that responded. The meals were always a bit odd. She paid, usually, at John Adam's, The Creeper or The Cup, or one of those other posh places you only get taken to. But I always felt we were meeting in an elaborate prison visiting room. Like the time she'd come from Kigali or somewhere to see me in the nick. But it wasn't me that was in the nick now. She was highly defensive, as if she guessed what I was thinking.

I wasn't thinking much, actually, but I suppose I was mourning.

It was ludicrous how much I missed her. More than Brookgate or Snatcher's or the Boys.

I was seeing less of Tubby, too. Increasingly my time with him was a matter of business. He was giving me some of my best leads, but everything was getting too different, too nuts. He had this huge information bank at the Mill. Also, he'd fully restored the sails, now working to supply him with electricity and water pressure. Vast bloody things, like an early aeroplane wing, and equally aerodynamic. I'd never seen the technology close up. He'd been forced to do the restoration. The electric company, under some by-law discovered by Jocky Papadakis's lads, had stopped supplying him. Tubby hardly noticed. Those powerful vanes could pour more juice into his computer banks than a nuclear reactor. No shortage of wind on top of London. He still had mains water and sewage, but was taking steps to provide himself with alternatives. The Mill was said to be built above an underground spring, the source of the Fleet, and the original reason for siting it there. He was searching now. It was horrible. He was living under permanent siege, constantly alert to some new move of Barbican's. Paranoia had become second nature to him. Good old positive Tubby.

Tubby tried, because of who he was, but he just couldn't keep his mind off his problems. As he'd once put it to me about something else – a frightened animal can't fuck. Neither could he talk about the old days without somehow coming back round to the Mill, its deeds, his duty, the threats and what he was doing about them. Half the time he was a catalogue of technobabble, an anorak on grade-one whizz. It got tiring.

What was worse, Paul Frame seemed to be seeing a lot of Tubby and I still couldn't get on with Paul. Especially now.

Under Rosie's patronage, through his constant seen-withs (Barbi, Bigears, Bigeyes, Dicky Attemthorough, Maddy, Madonna), he had suddenly become superfamous. Barbican finally had his pop-star pal. He'd always, always, always wanted Paul Frame for his friend. They turned up at functions together. They saluted their favourite charities together. They appealed for sanity and decency together. Art and business. Also in harmony. For Paul, I had to admit, it was a career opportunity not to be missed. He'd become that hero for our times, the pop saint. Saint Cliff, Saint Bob and now, best of all, Saint Paul. The posh end of the relief business. He was the quiet, principled guy from the seventies who'd never sold out. The pop musician who had turned his back on a glamorous career in order to help the poor and the weak. The adoringly handsome, sensitive guy who'd lost his beloved wife in the service of Africa. The moral authority of a world-class conscience easer. Almost as good as having Nelson Mandela hug you with his blessing. He was the best colonial hero since Gordon of Khartoum. He seemed to like it.

I remember seeing a publicity still from when David Cronenberg was making Burroughs's *The Naked Lunch*. Three men face the camera, nicely lit. Cronenberg stands with a bland, proprietorial fist on Burroughs's shoulder, Burroughs looks sheepish, the actor playing him stands accommodatingly on the other side. Well sanitized. Out of the truckstop toilets and into the commoditorium. Burroughs is shiny with glossy light. He looks like a political prisoner hauled up for videotaping to prove he hasn't been beaten. There he is on the plate. Just tell me where to sign. What have they done to him? The man whose craziness drove him scuttling like a cockroach, as eloquent, elegant as Blake, bubbling with junk, babbling across continents, to shit in the confections of the world. Stuck like a butterfly, stung like a bee. And what did happen to Ali? Another ersatz parade. Was he the last American who had the knack of walking the walk?

Paul became Mr *Charity* to Di's Princess *Hope* and Lord and Lady Begg's Mr and Mrs *Faith*. The Grand Consumer's own holy family, appropriately only a little larger than the original, taking relief to the victims of famine and war and natural disaster. Red noses and blue largesse. Only the natural disasters, it seemed to me, weren't a consequence of the ambitions of the GC himself. And these days you couldn't be too sure about them.

I didn't bring this up much at our lunches. When I did, Rosie tended to get a bit impatient. 'You've turned into a prig, Den, like most tabloid journos. You have to think you're better than your victims, don't you, otherwise you couldn't justify what you do. You simplify a complex problem and blame someone else for not solving it simply.'

'That's true of all us old colonials.' I'd shrugged. 'Self-justifying to a fault, eh?'

'And not even right,' she said. 'Not even close.'

'Sorry. I forgot you were now married to the source of all truth.'

'Don't go on with this, Den.'

And that's the way too many of those expensive plates of rubbata and placento got tucked down for no good reason except it was easier to eat than just sit there in silence.

My contact with the rich and powerful didn't stop the VAT and Inland Revenue coming after me with iron bars, threats of fraud and other equally bullying suggestions, when they knew perfectly well that people in my trade never save money, never have investments and never quite get the time to open secret bank accounts and wouldn't know how.

My chronology is measured in disasters, prints, gigs, crises. I don't have a money calendar. I don't measure myself in terms of money. I still haven't got the knack. This doesn't stop them asking you rhetorical questions like 'Well, what did you spend it on, then, Mr Dover?' And they're talking about 1982! Or 1992, it wouldn't make any difference. The money comes, the money goes – usually to some impatient creditor. Or a friend. Or one of Rosie's causes. The more you make, the more you blow. So here I am, the perfect consumer, the ideal upon which our modern society is based. I have recycled my dosh like a drunken sailor and instead of praise I get hassled, finger-wagged, up before the inspectors. They go after freelances and taxi drivers because they know they're bound to have a bit of money. Meanwhile the millionaires are doing fine in the Caymans. Is this fair?

They didn't think it was fair. They thought I was a prat, though. For not having sheltered. The only people they seemed to loathe were people who hadn't tried to cheat them. Or maybe they were just hoping to placate me and stop me calling them names they can probably still remember vividly in nightmares. Threats so grotesque they'd turn the stomach of a Clive Barker fan. But they're used to all of it. They don't close your file just because you've suggested what they like to mix with their drinking urine. They just go on rolling over you like a fucking tank and that's that.

We are, basically, temperamentally at odds, tax accountants and people like me. We don't actually speak the same language. Even the inflections mean something different. And, of course, you don't realize that you are prey. They are actually out to get you. It's a matter of honour, ego, self-esteem. They have to characterize you before they can catch you, kill you and eat you. Naturally, they don't believe a word you say and begin by thinking you must be pretty shifty in the first place to be in this situation.

You, pard, are probably a good law-abiding citizen and have no idea how bizarre these meetings with tax officials can be. I was having a series of them. A serial series at that. Round and round and round. How could they keep such a simple thing spinning so long?

Here we are. Two guys and a woman, looking like Judge Dredd crossed with Judge Jeffreys. Ready to hang me. Or maybe one of them, the woman, has a human glint. No, just a trick of the light. They're framed against huge windows. Their shadows are long, unsavoury and where they touch me I become faintly alarmed.

Kafka? Nothing so fucking funny.

'What about Mexico, Mr Dover?'

'What about Mexico?'

'How long exactly were you there?'

'Where exactly?'

'In Mexico.'

'What, Jalisco? Oh, I don't know. In and out.'

'But how long were you in "Mexico", Mr Dover?'

'Not out of it yet,' I told them. 'Eh?'

'How much time did you spend in Mexico on that trip, Mr Dover?'

'Well, Mexico was just the base. I went to a lot of other countries. You know, stories?'

'Let's stick with the Mexican story for the moment, shall we?' Pursed-arsehole lips. A face that should never have been exposed to sunlight. And two more of them flanking the bastard, like clones, their tonsures twitching from keeping an eye on the pecking order. Monkish, half-formed creatures, these pious undead. They liked to ask questions, jot down notes, buzz amongst themselves and then ask more questions.

'OK.'

'How long were you most recently in Mexico, Mr Dover?'

'I don't know. A few months.'

'Six?'

'Sure.'

'Nine?'

'Absolutely.'

You don't know it, but you're competing in a game of his devising, in which only he could score. What I was actually doing was confirming his deepest suspicions. Proving everything he'd guessed. I was shifty, feckless, trying to slip away from giving factual answers. From my point of view, of course, I was answering as honestly as I could. No way could I easily remember that old drift. He was contemptuous of me, because he thought my methods of deception were primitive.

'Six or nine, Mr Dover?'

'Seven-and-a-half? A market compromise?'

'In 1981.'

'There you have me.'

Every honest answer drove a nail into my coffin, confirming any guilt, my refusal to supply the truth. They had never been facts, at least not to me. They had never existed. They had been other peoples' facts, maybe. Fair enough. My life was in the public record, nothing hidden, nothing much to hide, a record of newspaper spreads, headlines, exclusive snaps. Where had I been? Check the pix. But it was, said my snotting little Witchfinder General, more complicated than that. We had responsibilities. To whom?

To the accounts.

Barbican knew about it, of course, because I had to moan to someone.

But no way would I let him pay. I tried to explain to him that the only thing anchoring me to the real world was my debts.

There were still a few institutions Barbican could only manipulate but he didn't have to do any more than that because they were conservative institutions, happy to self-regulate to his guidelines. But he still couldn't tell the government what to do or square the police or influence the law. He could pay my taxes but he couldn't disappear any taxes. To be fair, I'm not sure it would have occurred to him to attack, in any direct way, those bits of the infrastructure, perhaps because he sensed they were his only real strengths and that the rest of his dangerous fantasies were based on a financial system that could go wild and dissipate at any moment. At last, I thought, he was playing a game against himself.

My sex life was crap. Casual sex didn't do a lot for me. I need more substance. More danger, maybe. I ran out of things to do with Flo and Pinky. They started getting a bit edgy and Flo went mad, taking charge of a heritage centre in Whitechapel that she razed in the name of preserving it. This led her into all kinds of conflicts with the locals, with civil liberties groups and preservation councils and God knows what and the thing spread from street to street, scandal to scandal, with her shrieking on top of the thing, saying she was in control, that the whole of the East End depended on her for its history. Without her, she told me, the East End wouldn't have any history. I think she thought she was the East End. Pinky gave up on her and left London eventually. She travelled at night, in a vast caravan, by road and sea, rerooting herself on Morn in Hornsey Pilbeam's old house, which he had offered her, apparently. Some long-ago crush.

I was having to work even harder, to pay off the tax, and I was going to have to work harder to pay off the tax on the money I was earning to pay the tax and it was at that point I began to wonder about going back to the Continent. Or joining Pinky on Morn. Or not really settling anywhere for long. You didn't have to, these days.

After all, a happy paparazzo would be just as able to work from Rome as from London. Except, of course, that London was London. And who knew what had happened to Rome since I last saw it? I'd be better off asking Jimmy L. to sort me out a new identity. Which is always a problem when a lot of what's earning you your money is your existing name. Also my sources were still too good. No matter how uncomfortable Tubby made me or how awkward it was with Rose, they always slipped me the real goods. Even Barbi called me once or twice with cryptic tips, though I couldn't really understand them. It was another way he tried to bond, I think. I didn't know where he found the time to think about me. That was the kind of bloke he was. So it was bound to disturb me a little.

I was very wary of him, and found myself increasingly less direct in my dealings. Directness didn't work. Once, in order to avoid a visit to his 'den', his private playpen, also overlooking the river, with its wrought-iron Victorian reclamations, I let a naïve new editor on *Le Monde* send me to Serbia.

Luckily it was more like a *Hello* job. Snapping the young and wonderful at some new disco hell where Milosevic flapped about a bit to show he was one of us, but I got to take some nice street shots. Felt like old times. Back via Bosnia. A quick what's-it-like-now piece. Listening to the café talk, I noticed how far more open the political argument had become. Yet, for all the sophisticated method, the Marxist and post-Marxist constructions, you were still reminded that the Balkans was a world so frequently repressed and tyrannized that it had necessarily held unrequited grudges for five hundred or a thousand years. Not an infrastructure you'd want to tamper with lightly. The clan feud was almost a modern method of law in this part of the world. And everyone was feeding in arms, from what Fromental told me a few days later when we met in Old Compton Street, by accident. He was still after the elusive Pilbeam, he said. I was looking for a bit of tart to shoot, I said.

'I know what you mean, man,' he said miserably. 'Like rabbits, right.'

He always got cryptic around rabbits. Those years of working for Warner Brothers had permanently affected certain higher brain functions. We went and had a jar in the French. They were doing the mild again. Cookie was still alive in those days, sitting in one of his usual spots, drinking sweet gin with O'Dowd's chasers and telling your stories back to you faster than you could recount them. He was a walking fucking *Morte D'Arthur*, that man. An epic cycle of heroic Soho, Paris and beyond. You told him something that had happened to you and, by the end of an hour, he was remembering it. It had happened to him. And you were inclined to be convinced.

Cookie looked like an ad for a French chicken stock, with his scrawny neck, beaky, fleshless head and black beret poll, his beady eyes behind his Mr Chips glasses, his affability offering his approval and you willing to accept it, feed him anything he wanted. He lived off our charms and provenances. Stout and gin, too, of course. He kept himself alive by the rituals of talking, by providing you with anecdote after anecdote of adventures, a folk bible whose heroes and villains were the Krays, the Cornells, the Ranjits and the Blooms, whose urban mysteries were conducted in the alleys off Gerrard Street, negotiations on the borderlands. God knew where his stories had come from. Some from us and others you recognized, but there were millions more. He talked and talked, even, ghostly, amused. He had the class Quentin Crisp always longed for. I'd enjoyed his novels as a kid. Stories of posh boys gone wrong and wrong boys gone posh, hectic affairs. That ensnaring, romantic narcissism, with its echoes of *nouvelle vague* and Chandler, the roots of noir and cyberpunk, of real experience mixed with myth.

Powerful stuff at its best. But Cookie was always better than Robin Cook, MP, or Derek Raymond. Were all those others ever such charming drunks?

It was great to see him on the bestseller list but it was a lot more fun listening to him in the pub. So that improved my spirits a bit, but then when Cookie was off for a lavatory break, and then stopped to talk to Iain Sinclair and a couple of goozers he knew from the *Telegraph*, Fromental sank back into a litany of mumbled anger and contempt.

'This is a profound cop-out, man!' He was moody, like a frustrated volcano. Africa was still boiling in his veins. All the betrayals. All our European and American complicity in the destruction of a complex variety of cultures who, when we first encountered them, were at much the same stage of civilization as ourselves. Africa wasn't a problem until we discovered it. What was left of Africa were the scraps we hadn't bothered to cart off in our stripping of a continent. They had sold their own remains. We had returned them to the savage state. Our racism was the convenient explanation for our part in destroying the infrastructure of a continent in a couple of hundred years. Because if there was a market for slaves, there were slavers – strong peoples willing to raid weaker peoples and carry off the survivors to sell, ultimately, at the Slave Coast, bound for Jamaica and Haiti and Charlotte. Breaking the heart of Africa. All the usual misery.

Out of friendship I let him rant. And agreed with him. But I wasn't going to be drawn in. I was a glamour photog now.

We parted in Charing Cross Road. He was looking for some report. I went home. There was a message from Rosie. I called her mobile and she actually called me back in less than a week. I was fed up with the way our meetings were going. I wanted to find out how she was and she wouldn't tell me. I couldn't really understand why she wouldn't want to confide stuff. I was pretty trustworthy, generally. But maybe my role as supersnapper of the world's superficial meant I had been put, thanks to her patronage, on the other side of the pale. So how many kinds of isolation was that?

As I said. I suggested we go somewhere other than a posh stockbroker trough. I wasn't trying to control anything. I didn't mind her stroking it, but I wanted ordinary grub. I suppose I had some idea of getting us back to some sort of reality. I didn't like how all of us were growing apart. Even Fromental and I didn't have much left in common except the past. Everything was getting behind me. I only have about ten friends and time's shifting along, dissipating fast.

She took me up on it. She told me to meet her at New Marshalsea Market, over in Bermondsey, at five-thirty that next morning.

I thought she was joking. Or at least challenging me. But she was laughing when she put the phone down. She sounded like my sister again.

There were two markets left that I still reckoned and in a way I dreaded anyone else I knew going to them. Rosie was too near to Barbi to trust. But since she'd suggested it, and I hadn't eaten there in years, I thought it would be OK. The other market, that I used to know as a kid down by the river, was New Billingsgate, now over on the Isle of Dogs. That, too, still had a bit of their old spirit, but it was gradually getting standardized, what with the eurobores and the heritagers and the site asset managers and the increasingly hyperbolic rise in City land values.

New Marshalsea didn't deal in fish. It was mostly live poultry. Plump, dioxin-free, grain-fed chickens, pullets, guinea fowl, turkeys, ducks, geese. They also sold live farming pheasants, grouse, ptarmigan and other game birds whose sporting chances had been reduced to nil.

Strutting dusty chocolate, glaring ebony, pulsing scarlet, crimson, yellows and verdanta. Fancy white tiles streaked with vividly coloured shit. Old iron beams hung with busy wicker and wire, swift, dark eyes, defiant beaks. Gorgeous ruffs around huge, clawed feet. Caged flutter everywhere. Squawks, shrieks, defiant bellows and joyous whistles. Posturing. Those strange, mysteriously prolonged echoes you get in all masses of birds. A second of truth. Sudden moments of thought. Blizzards of panic. That deep musty smell. Gobbling, clucking, quacking. Brown feathers, red feathers, blue and bright green feathers, all the tasty birds. Vivid colours in shafts of sudden light. New Marshalsea was like a gathering of Victorian regiments: imperial scarlet and gold and royal blue, periwinkle and evergreen. And every one an officer or a lady. Proud to be fowl.

As a kid, when the market was still on its old grounds, but quite a bit smaller, there used to be a hunting-bird section, too. Peregrines, mostly. That had gone with various regulations and moves.

The market was circular, gridded, converted from the old tram terminus house, so that it was a riot of dusty glass and Egyptianate cast iron. Her elaborately decorated beams were from a time when Universal Transport was raising palaces to its own glory. Set across from the fancy bird dealers, the restaurant was the old tramworkers' cafeteria, with its *fin-de-siècle* tiling and its murals to the golden age of public transport. But it hadn't been given the California cuisine yet, thank God. It was, of course, mostly a poultry and game bird restaurant, but it also did, at that time in the morning, the best Full English I'd had in a million years. Eggs straight from the chicken. Bacon sliced from the pig. Black pudding that wasn't dead yet. All singing in its own delicious grease. Even the fried bread had a slightly feral quality, as if it could slip away from you at any second. Portobello mushrooms that seemed to have been torn from the secret vaults below us. Tomatoes that seconds before could have been bouncing on the vine. The toast was Polish rye with Jamaican *Walkers Wood* cane sugar marmalade. First Press Assam in the pot.

The only moment that wasn't perfect was when Sonny Portillo came looming out from the back, even bigger in his vast white coat and hat, to shake me by the hand and declare that breakfast to be the pride of the place. His face had never really recovered from its last fight with the Stoker, but it had gone puffy, filling out with fat. Not too bad. He was the catering manager now, he said. He thanked me for my support while he was doing the boxing, but he was glad to be out of that world. 'It's all up to me here, Den.' Conan had at last found his destiny. And an honourable one at that.

What is it about some markets that they demand such high-quality grub? Half a mile apart sometimes. Others seem to sell nothing but weak tea and soggy Wonderbread sandwiches. Microwaved back bacon.

'I love markets,' I said. 'Real markets.' I was watching the chicken porters balancing the baskets and cages on their heads, carrying the more passive birds in their arms.

'Not too many left, are there, Den?' She was dressed in shirt and jeans so ordinary they only encouraged you to look at her beauty. Tangled hair, perfect symmetry, still a tigress. Those eyes wouldn't go out. They just focused harder and, I thought, with increasing difficulty.

'Where are they all going, Rosie? I just can't buy this stuff about economics. Or heritage preserves. Where can ordinary people buy and sell their own goods?' I really could hardly understand it. I reached for the Daddy's. I'd arrived at the third stage of the taste experience. There's a ritual to eating a proper Full English as complex as a Japanese tea ceremony, but unlike the tea ceremony those who practise it never offer a public glimpse. You wouldn't know what I was doing, unless you knew what I was doing. I got myself some fresh Assam from the big samovars they had on the counter.

'Centralizing, I suppose. In a way.' She became a bit all over the place for a moment. 'It's not like when we were growing up in the market, Den. Mr Small's trick stall? We've gone from real-world economics to virtual economics and it's playing havoc with these poor bastards still in the real world. They hardly know what's hit them. It's given us all the rules to suit ourselves. Well, in the short term, anyway. And there's no long term left.'

'How would you make it real again, Rosie? Without destroying a lot more lives? You going to bring back communism?'

'I've nothing against a multiplicity of real options, Den. Or the free market. I know how much harmony civilization can bring to the natural world, how it can contribute to nature and our own natural preferences.'

'Now who sounds like a sentimental old hippy? Where's that from? The Prince Bigears School of Economics?' I poured the Daddy's precisely on to the right part of the plate. 'But you didn't really answer. How would you make it real again, Rosie?'

'Swords into ploughshares.'

'Oh, sure. What motive?'

She moved her food about on her plate. I helped myself to her mushrooms. She spoke with her eyes down, looking at the table, tracing a pattern with her fingers. 'France never bought the consumerist logic. The economics pan out about the same but you have to work hard at zero population growth. Remember that unfashionable concept? Before consumerism realized it needed an infinite number of consumers if it was going to survive?'

'Still sounds like bullshit.' I sliced a large piece of dark toast and heavy marmalade. I looked at a big Cochin rooster, glaring white with brilliant red wattles and crest, trying to get its leg cuff off. It looked up at me. Black eyes full of bafflement.

I didn't know what to say. I turned towards Rosie. 'London's a market. All cities start like that – a fording place, somewhere to trade, somewhere a bit neutral. London's been the most successful market in the world, pretty much the core of world trade, of the economic system that still rules the world.'

Rosie looked up into the misty moving light, the glittering glass roof.

'We were brought up in markets, Den. We know markets. And we're for free markets. We know how they work. Organically. Naturally. Cities are free markets, I agree. But consumerism is the aggressive imperialist face of the free market – a contradiction of what the market is supposed to do. It controls rather than responds. Instead of discovering the realities of supply and demand, it seeks to *create* those realities. Instead of regulating itself it justifies its own excesses. And what you actually do is cut out other possibilities. You start creating a vacuum, because you never were creating anything in the first place. Only consuming. And that's where the damage starts when you decide to control the whole market culture for the benefit of the few. And it's that aggression, the mindless consumerism itself, together with the idea of planned obsolescence, that you have to counter. A culture that suggests you get the health, education and social services you can pay for. That makes education a cheap competition, a sporting event. Something to do with scoreboards. Cynical manoeuvres by both boss and bossed. That's what leads to the violence, Den. We have to resist that. With a bit of conscience, I suppose. Keep the capitalism, resist the consumerism. The built-in obsolescence. The lies. There *are* better models, Den. Plenty in Europe.'

Nicely delivered. Very liberal. But no solutions, right? I didn't have to put it into the air. She was getting well into a very caring spin. Nothing wrong with the system, eh? Just with the people running it. This was the old Monsanto serious-and-responsible line. Feeding the world all the food it could afford. I was hearing it a lot at parties.

'Oh, you should have a bit of conscience,' I said. 'A bit of relief.'

She shrugged.

Suddenly, I wondered. Was she up to something funny?

Then she went firmly back to the subject.

'Trade's a question of choice. Consumerism's a question of conflict. And I told you, I've settled down. I've had it with conflict. I'm cultivating my own garden now.'

How big a garden?

I kissed her for luck. And just in case.

But she drew away fast, so I only got her cheek.

Drew away fast. Faster by the day, after that.

Rosie!

I was getting uncomfortable. I think I was lonely. I was an astronaut adrift from the mother ship.

When does a loner start getting lonely? I was used to avoiding company. Finding my own space. I enjoyed being alone. It was a very odd sensation for someone like me, who had avoided casual friendships. But there it was. Lonely.

We watched for signs of Rosie's benign influence on Barbican. He funded a couple of orchestras and an orphanage or two, but nothing spectacular. There were mechanisms in place nowadays, what with the lottery and everything, which took care of such things automatically, cutting out reliance on private conscience. He told me that himself, in one of those weird conversations in his cast-iron den. He saw it as harmony.

I was off to the Continent by July, snapping the Season, and only saw the odd English paper holding someone's sunbed space. The Barbican stories began to describe him as a great English character. He was considered the best kind of eccentric privateer, in the role of Drake and Raleigh. Some thought he was simply a bit nerdy and dull, like most tycoons. Others, more daring, spun stories asking if he weren't catching the Howard Hughes bug. Up, up and away. He bought Man U. Then he bought the Dynamos. Then he turned up in full flannels and protection at the Oval with the English cricket team and played a ball off Imran Khan. He didn't do much worse than the rest of the team, as I recall. There was a feature about this lonely, noble figure in his tower, a prisoner of his own fortune. I had a feeling there were stories running which the papers were sitting on. You can usually pick up a vibe like that.

Yet Rosie, when I dined with her at the Old Cavendish on a rare evening, was adamant. 'He's just loosening up a bit. Marriage to the right person works wonders for a man.' She winked at me and I went off to the gents to spit bile into a marble urinal.

But it was the next meal we had that I knew she must have found out about the Leases. An underlying frostiness. It had to be the Leases. I greeted a ticking bomb. Before she sat down she gave me a small, cream-coloured envelope. For me, she said, from Johnny. She didn't know what it was about. She was as frosty as I've ever known her. Giving me no leeway. Nothing. Blocking everything I said. I asked her why the fuck she was here, if she was going to be so fucking unpleasant. In fact, I said, if I didn't know better I'd take her manner to be pretty close to hatred.

You know. I expected her to deny it.

So we sat there, across the dimly lit table, while the flunkeys did all they had to do and got our little responses from us.

'Is this about Bobby?' I asked.

She was pretending to eat now. She seemed sadder, as if the anger had dropped out of her. I began to feel defensive.

But I didn't have any defence.

More silence.

Then she spoke into it. Quickly. And I thought the whole restaurant was listening.

'I saw the photos you took. In Begat. Of Kim.'

'What?' This was out of the blue. 'Kim?'

'You remember. The little girl. Older than her years? Just another job, was it? You remember, don't you, Dennis? Eh?'

'Come on, Rosie. Of course I remember. I took the pictures so I'd remember. She was a lovely kid. Rosie! Why did Tubby tell you about the pictures?' I couldn't see how Tubby of all people could be so irresponsible. This was betrayal. He had known how I felt. I'd told him how Rosie felt. I'd talked mostly about Rosie. Why, Tubby?'

'You showed them to Tubby, too?'

'Not "too", Rosie. He's the only living human being ever to have seen them, apart from me. I was mourning her, Rosie. That was it. That was all. I haven't dug the pictures out. One set developed, still in the file. Jesus Christ, Rose! You know me better than that. I might not have played it right, but I did my level best.'

'Are they published anywhere I might not have seen them yet? Was she dead or dying when you took them? In some she looks as if she's still alive.'

'You're not listening, Rosie. You really aren't. Listen to me. I never showed those pictures to anyone but Tubby.'

'Then why did I find a full set in plastic envelopes, name, time and place, properly marked, only yesterday evening?'

'Where?'

'A BBIC executive's office.'

'Nobody ever had access to my negatives, Rosie. Tubby only saw the one set of prints. That set of prints is in my filing cabinet. With the negatives.'

But she wasn't bothering. She'd only come to say goodbye.

'You rotten little liar, Dennis. You lied to me about her dying. About everything. Your own daughter, you said. You dirty, dirty— oh, you treacherous little wanker, Den.'

'Where did you find them, Rosie?'

'I found them in his special files. Why would you let him, of all people, have them?'

'Johnny?'

'Stop it, Dennis!'

'Jocky? Never! Rosie, those prints never left my files. Hang on!' It was getting telepathic. She was bound to believe the vibe. 'I'm not lying. Rosie!' I reached to take her hands. She'd always known what that meant.

She got up.

She'd had enough, she said. She left me to pay the bill.

I had to sit there for a while, everybody giving me the corner of their eye, until I stopped trembling.

I went straight back to Fogg Yard. The shots were still there, a bit battered. The negs were gone. I remembered the place being too neat that time when I got home. I didn't suspect Paul. Not then. I felt almost flattered. Jocky Papadakis or one of his goozers trawling for anything that might come in handy later. They would have taken an interest in me just because of Tubby. I had a feeling, though, that my pal Johnny hadn't, in fact, set me up. This felt sleazy enough to be all Jocky. And, of course, it was water under the bridge, too. Nothing I could do now except weather it out and hope Rosie calmed down soon. I knew she wouldn't go on with it once she'd thought it through.

But she did. On and on and on.

I was locked out well and truly.

And I think she said I'd witnessed the death of my own daughter.

So I'd been right about the night we came back from Kew.

Or I'd misheard her. Or she'd said something different. Or she'd asked a question. And there were no replies to any of my calls or messages. She'd meant it. My picture was facing the wall. I was being mourned as if dead. That ain't disco. That's your shiva you're hearing. Like a ghost. Smoke. Locked out in Limbo and you don't know how you'll ever get back to the rotten old planet again.

And the irony was that Johnny started calling me more and more, cheerfully unaware of any rift between me and Rosie. From that private tower immediately across the river from his corporate stronghold. He had all kinds of plans for the space, but most of it was still unoccupied. On the very top, he'd had a kind of museum built. It was a riot of cast iron, of pillars and beams and spider-webs of metal, of all the fanciful industrial work of the industrial revolution, pushing itself to wild invention for the sake of it. The bones of the Crystal Palace. The size of a small museum, and with huge ceilings, his 'den' reminded me of a very complicated Gothic Meccano construct, secret behind his smoked windows with their view of the working river. Something to play with. Something to die with.

It was fascinating, though. So once or twice, I took him up on his invite, walking through those strange empty downstairs spaces, each guarded and locked, to get to the fantasy on his roof, that Victorian baroque riot of cast iron reclaimed from every folly and railway station in the land, looking straight back and down to Tower Bridge and the busy river.

I'd sit in an elaborate old dentist's chair, feeling like a patient at the shrink's, while Johnny talked about the good old days and what fun we'd all had. What I wanted to do was ask him how Rosie was. But I had a feeling he didn't know. She was wonderful, he said. She had made a new man of him. He was reinvigorated, ready for anything, full of plans now that he would soon be fifty, and he wanted the world to remember him not only as a successful merchant but as a patron of real progress in all areas of human life. At one point it occurred to me that he was doing too much E. The depression, the knowledge that I was actually denied Rosie, was beginning to get me down. I felt I needed some sort of father or mother figure. I felt like a child.

I had to wait for my Fairy Godfather until a Saturday morning in September, listening to the radio as I developed some of the previous night's hot shots.

Norrie Stripling had been away on tour almost every time I'd been in London. He did his *West End 1936* show up and down the country, filling all the good provincial theatres between runs of *The Mousetrap* and *The Caretaker*. He'd never been the friend that Tubby, Rosie or even Paul had been. He was more the father figure I was after. And he enjoyed the role. So there we were.

I heard him being interviewed that Saturday morning on *Loose Ends*, chirping away to Ned Sherrin's savoury prompts. Back in London, Norrie? pipes Ned. Always am for the autumn season, dear. Wouldn't miss it. New radio series starting next week. *The Great Feud of Shaftesbury Avenue*. TV memoir of Una Cornell and Jessie Matthews. Running battle over Jack Buchanan and Al Bowly while they were still married to Binnie Spinetti and Sonny Hale. Some talk of a National Theatre gig. New book coming out. An active retirement, dear. It's best to keep your hand in.

So, on the off chance, I walked down through the glinting concrete to Youd Street and The Grand. Saturday tourist crowd in Long Acre. Everyone shopping. Was there life before markets?

The little round Gothick playhouse was, like many London theatres, still pretty much itself. Perhaps because it was already theatrical. A lick of paint hardly ever did a theatre much harm, especially when they were converted, like the Grand, from a music hall.

The place was always busy because it was small enough to put on short runs to maximum halls. They were getting ready for a revival of Peake's *The Wit To Woo*, and ironically Freddie Earlle was the lead, nothing to do with Norrie, who only had the lease and flat. The management was still independent, a Jewish family who lived in Hampstead Garden Suburb.

Norrie had only just got to the theatre himself. He still had his hat on as the dusty lift rattled up to his penthouse and almost threw me out at his feet.

'Dennis, dear! You can't stay.' He embraced me.

We had a cup of tea and then he took me to Theobalds Road for a fish-and-chip lunch. He had plenty of time for me today, he said. How were mum and grandad? He'd talked to grandad on the phone about some old Street Singer 78s. He was a walking encyclopaedia, dear. And mum?

'Just on the phone,' I said. 'You know I never go down there, Norrie.'

'She's a flower, your mum. Like Jessie Matthews. Easily bruised, Dennis.'

'But bruises back better, Norrie. Come off it.'

It wasn't a season for reconciliations, really.

I told him how Barbican was courting me. What was it about people like that? They already effectively owned our bodies. Why did they keep on demanding until they got our souls?

'Because all the flavour's in the soul, dear.'

And he ordered us a couple of nice, fresh Dovers. Matzoh batter and the best chips west of the Fleet.

I wasn't sure he was right, though. As I took my knife down the long centre bone of the fish and folded back the white flesh to fillet it, I said I thought it might have to do with control.

Like the Normans. The towers only work so long. You spend your time keeping your rebels down or watching your left flank or whatever. But if you convert them to a particular culture, a particular way of looking at things, your serfs start working in your interest. They stop seeing any difference. The reassurances that Barbican and his kind needed – directors of industry or directors of movies – were those that told you your well would be safe when you next needed a drink. I had a feeling he wanted me around because I was the only factor he wasn't wholly sure of. Not that he was necessarily planning anything special. It was instinct with him. He needed to be the hundred-per-cent share-holder.

Norrie thought all this obsession with power was distinctly naff. He gave me advice when we parted on the corner of Kingsway. 'You need some time in the wilderness, Dennis. That's what Kevin Costner would discover and he would go out there and come back redeemed.'

'I'm a city boy, Norrie, not the fucking king of the jungle.'

'Well, it kept Tarzan together, dear.'

Besides, I thought, when I got home and sat down in my chair to light a spliff and stare out at the graveyard, there weren't any wildernesses any more, were there? Nothing that wasn't covered in blood. I remembered the note Rosie had given to me and fished it out.

Dear Den,
*   Just to let you know you have a mate here who's always glad to see you.*
All best,
Johnny.

I sighed and looked at my watch. Still a long way to go until sundown. It was bleak. I put my hand towards the phone. This wasn't making me feel any better.

I dialled Johnny's special number.

'Wotcher,' I said. 'Gotcher note.'

'Wotcher, Den,' he said.

He sounded as bad as me.

So I was soon back in the dentist's chair, but I was asking questions. He didn't really like what I was asking. This wasn't the deal, I supposed. I was there to remind him of that old feeling. Maybe any old feeling. He couldn't help me much. He made irritable movements with his fingers and kept going to the view, as if to restore himself. He had people, he said, looking after all that sort of thing. He would never give an order to burgle me and if it turned out Jocky had done so, then Jocky would be out of a job within the hour. He'd never work in this world again. Who did I think he was? Richard Nixon? Crime was the one thing you had to avoid in business as much as possible. Surely I didn't really believe Jocky had actually broken into my flat? There were legal ways of doing everything.

But Jocky liked to burgle. Jocky was a natural cribsnapper. Other people's secrets, no matter how innocuous, increased his sense of control. He felt safer after he'd done it. Yeah?

'Jocky's a bit iffy sometimes, Dennis. But he wouldn't – I wouldn't let him – I mean, really, Den.' He was almost crying. Suddenly, it wasn't Christmas any more.

I was honestly astonished by this response. And utterly convinced.

'I believe you,' I said. I patted at his luxurious threads.

I hadn't told him where my information came from. And he hadn't once asked me how much of it I had got via Rosie. It was as if he was avoiding her. I was beginning to suspect that Rosie's real relationship wasn't with him at all. She was really seeing Paul Frame. Was that why Barbi was so restlessly desperate for old certainties? Was that what he thought he'd get from marrying her. Yet how could a man with double everything feel worried about his judgement? How many times do you have to conquer the world?

I couldn't get him to talk about Rosie herself, only about what she'd done for him, how she made him feel. He remained enthusiastic, too. It wasn't like the other wives, who had usually lasted about a week in real terms. And he wasn't worried about her. He had her in place. Maybe that's all he wanted of any of us.

I continued trying to contact her. I didn't make a campaign of it, but I always dropped her a note and left a phone message. Back again to Barbican. Another evening of R&R for Mr Big. Another evening where I tasted at every reference to her and wondered how he could enjoy being out of her company.

For me, she'd vanished. Deliberately. As if she'd pirouetted three times in the air and popped out of the picture. Gone. Nothing.

I couldn't believe it.

I saw the sad prospect, though. Since he was now my only close contact with my cousin, I supposed I'd be seeing even more of Johnny.

At least until Rosie came to her senses.

CHAPTER TWENTY-FIVE
The Blues

Barbican was enjoying a late mid-life crisis or it might have been an early second childhood. Either way, he was getting much more out of life than the rest of us. Meanwhile a shameless Tory government played increasingly to its loony right and John Major made speeches against gypsies, as if he thought he was back in Bohemia, doing his best to Balkanize Britain. He hadn't so much dropped the ball as forgotten what a ball looked like.

That creaking Whitehall farce wound its way in concert with a similar farce in which the American public elected Billy the Plonker, the Republikan stooge, who started telling the world what-for in the name of his business backers, whom he called Democracy or The American People. The kinder, gentler face of rapacity. For a while everyone else had forgotten who they were and these Yankee dogs just came sniffing by one day and cocked their legs on us and claimed us for their own. Lucky Yankees. Lucky us.

Consuming to live. Living to consume. Is this our long-term plan? To eat the world? And then what? One another? The American Eagle with its beak up its own arse, chewing on its its own liver.

Oh, I know. Rosie was right. I was claiming high ground that I hadn't actually climbed to. I could sit there spitting rage, but what had I done to improve things? Taken a few snaps and sold them to the highest bidder. What good was I? How was I helping myself? I was part of the problem. I'm part of the bait as well as the prey.

It's a fine day, says Brecht's worm to the angler, *let's go fishing*. I'm joining in, aren't I? I'm shimmying on the hook and Barbi's got me well and truly sorted by now. I'm fucking stuck in this, just about. That sudden separation from Rosie's done my head in. And Barbi's my only sure link to her. The only slim likelihood I have of running into her. Anything for the chance to talk to her, make her stop hurting. Stop her hating me. Because my guess was she'd been set up to find those pictures. Probably by Jocky, who was still on holiday in Malaysia. They said. We were all denizens of Barbi's domain now. Almost all of us, anyway. I wasn't in as deep as the rest of them, at that point. But at that point only Tubby was well clear of the Man-Who-Owned-The-World and that didn't look like lasting too long, either.

I'm still not entirely sure how it gradually happened. I had a mixture of motives for going to see him, usually on his own, on top of his tower, in the cast-iron cathedral he was putting together from some of the finest Victorian fancy iron, stripped from some of the best buildings in the kingdom. I'd had no better luck working out what Rosie had meant. But then, I didn't have any habits of second-guessing her, or interpreting her. Since we'd been born I'd never had a reason to examine my relationship with Rosie. Only what she wanted to examine, casually, over the years. There hadn't been much to examine because there had never been a crisis before. We'd never fallen out in any real sense. We didn't discuss the fundamentals of existentialism much, either. Or why we did what we did. Or who we were. Or what we were doing. We took each other for granted. Why shouldn't we? We were a team. We'd always been some sort of team.

Not any more. Always it wasn't. Like the Berlin Wall went up and that was that. Suddenly there was twenty feet of solid concrete between me and the only woman I really cared about in the world. I just couldn't believe she wouldn't give me a chance. Answer at least a couple of questions. Hear me out.

Now you could say this was all transference on her part. She was blaming me instead of herself for Kim's death. But we all knew what happened. Kim had insisted on going. I'd tried to go, too. I'd got Kim as much help as I could. I'd done my best. We'd all done our fucking best. And our fucking best had got us a dead kid. Lots of dead kids, actually. What are we doing, rushing around the world like this, interfering in everyone's business? Making their business our own? Oh.

So why did Kim die?

Because she was a proper little madam, a chirping victim of history, a child as old as her times. Because she was unlucky.

One of these days, we're just going to have to teach the public what this great big game of chance is really all about. A bit of judgement, a bit of skill and a lot of luck. All we can get. Failures of imagination. Failures of idealism. Failures of kindness. Failures of nerve.

Meanwhile, we go on being disappointed when life fails to match the grid we put on it.

I had a dream after one of those regular evenings with Barbi. Something special, I suppose. A buffet supper with Barbi, Tony Blair and Bill Clinton, among other mighty people. I'd spent most of that evening talking to Flo Fortnum. In the dream, something like the world's ectoplasm seemed to be disappearing off the planet faster than the atmosphere. As it shredded it left pieces behind. Immediately a specialized insect developed. The insect ran about gathering up the pieces and rolling them into a ball. When it had a really big ball, it would roll towards another big ball and make it stick, rolling the two into one, then rolling over some more medium-size balls, crushing their insects, until there was just one insect with one ball.

Barbican Begg, in this case. And meanwhile, of course, he was having a much nicer dream. You wouldn't believe the ball *he* was thinking of rolling, either. His dream was developing naturally from his comradeship with Paul Frame. There wasn't a major charity event left unopened by Barbi and his new best friends. If they weren't compassion-bonding with our Lady of the Landmines, it was usually just the three of them: St Rosie, St Barbi and St Paul. The Three Saints.

The Three Saints had even presented the Oscars. A bit ham-fistedly, you'll recall. They almost forgot to thank the wonderful sponsors. All in a good cause. Later, gracefully, they manifested themselves at the Albert Hall, with the Three Tenors, the Two Ronnies and the Four Seasons.

But Paul's success was taking him away from London. He had become a world-class Benign. If he wasn't sitting down in a semi-lotus for a cup of tea with the Dalai Lama, he was thumbs-upping on jeeps with jolly South Americans or playing a game of cricket with happy geeks. Never off the front cover, always in the news. Doing his bit for everyone. What a lovely smile. Our ambassador of peace and charity. Our best man.

Which meant, unfortunately, that Barbi had one less friend available and even more time for me. And he needed his playmate, this goozer. He wanted me on call.

Originally, his power over me entirely depended on his being married to Rosie. He was my only way through to her. Now, if his power was getting stronger, it was probably something to do with my awful airline-stewardess problem.

Could I be conspiring in my own entrapment? I was certainly becoming unusually fascinated by Barbican's power in the way Isaac Babel was fascinated by Stalin's. Not entirely sure what it was, but profoundly curious, barmy, drawn in closer, the way Babel was drawn in by his nearness to the seat of power until, snap, they took him, backbrain bang, nothing. Gone. The last charge of the Red Cavalry was probably about a kopek for the bullet. He knew what was coming to him. He couldn't help himself. Compelled towards the vacuum. The void that's the wellspring of evil . . . I couldn't easily stay away from Barbican now. Not because of him, or anything he was doing, or trying to do. But because of what he was and who I was and who Rosie was. Because I hoped for hope, just a whisper, that Rosie had read a letter or listened to one of my phone messages. I was pathetic. She was unmoved. This was total blockade on contact and communications.

Barbican wasn't much use as an intermediary or as a weathervane. I'd ask after Rosie, casually. He never gave me an answer that was worth anything. He wasn't deliberately twisting me, but you could tell where his real interest lay in that relationship. When I asked after her, he was always enthusiastic.

'She's brilliant, isn't she? I can't tell you what she's done for me, Den. Just given me a new sort of energy. You know. And she looks after my health. Vitamins and antioxidants and all that. And helps me let my hair down the way I never did before. Just enough, you know, to start relaxing, realizing who I am, who I really wanted to be. I was worrying that I was going to get tired, lose my grip, especially over this last big T&C deal with BT, BA and Virgin, but then it all starts happening in my head, you know. Not just the spreadsheet details, but who to square, who to flannel, where to get the authentications, who needs reassurance, what PR angle to put on it. Bingo. Everything.'

He looked questioningly at me, as if I didn't believe him.

'Just like that,' he said.

He frequently stayed up late, sitting in the dark, looking out over the river, down towards the Isle of Dogs, watching the lights, the long constructions, the encroaching millennium. I often found him and left him where he sat. He'd taken to spinning old Stiff sides. Graham Parker. Nick Lowe. Madness. Martin Stone. And increasingly he was playing the stuff Calvert, Pavli and I had done with Deep Fix but only partially released. Spacey versions of *Rolling in the Ruins*, tight, laconic semi-tek like *Lord of the Hornets*. Strange to come in on him in that huge baroque iron security cage, semi-circle crossing semi-circle to form a kind of comb, an impenetrable security zone of deep shadow and sudden shards of light. All looking out over the black, night river.

There was a track playing faintly now, *The Greenfly and the Rose*. I never thought to ask him how he'd come by those tapes. It was one we'd done for Flicknife. At the Rock Garden, I think. Paranoia flashes. I took control of myself. As Charnock had sung, before Texas and all those nasty best-sellers, *Playing in a band, you don't understand where the time goes*. Or the money. Or the life. Or the work.

'What's this got to do with Rosie?' I asked.

He was rolling a giant, messy reefer. I took it away from him and remade it. Powerful ganja. Amsterdam skunk. Oh, oh, oh. No wonder he wasn't entirely in this world. He told me he knew where she was, who he was, where she was coming from and all he really needed to know now was where he was going. 'Direction. You know. New goals.' He cast his eyes towards the world.

'This has to do with Rosie?'

'It's her. What she's given me. A hundred per cent, Den. What she's put in me. A new kind of feeling. I mean, she's taught me what it's like to be young again. Young for the first time, really alive, you know, because you learn, don't you? That so much of what you think you want isn't really what you wanted. She's great, eh, Den? I only wish she had more time so that we could all get together, just like we used to down the old Limbo, but with all her openings and galas she doesn't feel like going out in the evening any more. I'm working on it. Even I have to make an appointment with her, these days, ha, ha. You don't think this suit makes me look fat, do you?' The cool material rippled as he moved.

'It's all relative,' I said, 'but you seem to have extra-long sleeves.'

'That's to allow for growth.' He winked. His huge smoothed features folded gracefully in the contentment of finely filtered memory. He was wholly enviable. He'd created a universe fit for him. Now, to make it actually universal, we all had to *be* him. It was our only crack at continuity. Mutual self-interest as he saw it. Our inevitably logical choice.

He threw back his head and laughed. I think he was developing a personality.

He would have done anything for me, my cousin.

He'd have paid my income tax for me, if I'd asked.

As it was, he came up with the scheme to get me out of the vicious circle. Well, he came up with about fourteen different schemes. Every one of them legal. All involved me getting paid by someone in some other country. And doing something spectacular for charity. It was too tiring for me to concentrate on.

I knew it was twisting funny when Barbi bought himself the Epiphone TG40, one of the rarest guitars in the world. A Black Falcon. Called 'The Bird' by every musician who knows it. Eight made before the wood ran out. Elvis had one. Clapton has one. Ry Cooder has two and Merle Haggard lost one. Two are in private collections. His agent had bought it at auction at Sotheby's. It had a provenance as long as your life. It had belonged to Eddie Cochrane and was fully authenticated. You can see pictures of Eddie playing it on stage in Liverpool and Glasgow during that incredible January 1960 tour with Gene Vincent. Eddie had been strumming it only hours before his fatal car crash. You could almost smell the blood on it. They didn't say who bought the guitar in the papers. They just said someone had paid four hundred thousand quid for it. Which was about three hundred and ninety-five thousand more than it would normally be worth.

He asked me to look at it for him. I don't know why. Just to reassure him that it was the instrument it was, I suppose. You can't be sure, can you, if you don't play it? He said he was having a bit of trouble tuning it.

It tuned to a touch. Someone had been looking after it properly. Beautiful, fine nuts. Good strings. What was the trouble?

He was embarrassed. He had a bit of a tin ear for tuning, he said. I told him about electronic tuners. That cheered him up.

The guitar was big and chunky, but it was definitely a masterpiece. It gave you everything it promised. Warmth, voice, response, maturity.

Nice. I handed it back to him.

He held it carefully, his fingers feeling for a chord shape. He put them down hard in E. Strummed. G. Strummed. C. Strummed. D. Strummed. E. Strummed . . .

The guitar sounded baffled, vaguely uncomfortable. Like a thoroughbred horse with an amateur rider.

But Barbi was in heaven.

'With your lead and my rhythm,' he said, 'we'd be back in business in no time.'

Definitely in a world of his own. I let him stay there. He wasn't bothering me much. Not then. *So you want to be a rock and roll star.* So fine.

I bumped into Norrie outside Sotheby's the day after the auction.

Norrie said it happened to chaps in early middle age. Hadn't I noticed? Everyone of my generation, he said, wanted to be a rock legend. Until he mentioned it, I hadn't realized just how many of these fabulous instruments were racking up large prices mostly from rich guys who thought if they had Eric Clapton's Strat it would somehow give them soul. Like putting Excalibur on the block. Usually sold for charity, they were better than Monet. And, of course, they had far more resonances and meaning to the likes of Barbican. Barbican didn't have a lot of time for Old Masters. You couldn't pose in front of the mirror with your paintings or your companies. Norrie says the famous-instrument business turned over faster than St Hilda's laundry basket. Holy relics, full of power, full of meaning. Full of life. They had real authority, those expensive Gibsons and Fenders and Rickenbackers. Usually winding up on the wall. Hang 'em high. Air music.

'Like Planet Hollywood, dear.'

'Who the fuck would want to live in a theme restaurant?'

'Everyone, Denny! You're not looking. Most large modern homes are decorated like theme restaurants. Where else could they get that taste? Themes are simple, dear. This is the age of the simple person.'

'I can't tell the difference any more.'

'Well, that's a sort of harmony, isn't it, dear?'

Norrie was about my only anchor in a world where I had more and more recognition and less and less effect. It was making me uncomfortable. I was drifting too far, unable to get a fix on anything. Without Rosie I felt like nothing. How could that be?

I saw a lot of her. All in the papers. There she was, grinning at the opening of some new charity ball. Here she was, bringing out the gentleman in Bill Clinton as she stepped aboard his boat. And over there she was speaking of the benefits of modern business to the economies of the Third World. Almost everyone surrounding her in those pictures looked like a first-rate scumbag. Out of horseshit came forth *Molly McGredy*.

Her mum died. My auntie. I went to the funeral. I tried to go up to her, say how much I'd loved her mum. But I couldn't get past the security people.

I think she made her benefits-of-business speech the same day as Bill Clinton apologized to the Africans for enslaving them. Since he apologized to the very tribes who had grown powerful on the benefits of the slave trade (the less powerful tribes had been enslaved), they had some difficulty getting the gist of his meaning. And since they had been successfully reinvented as consumers, they were still trying to get the hang of his expectations. They really wanted the money, those local politicos, but they were confused about which hoops were the right ones to jump through. Just like New Orleans.

Barbi introduced me to Bill at that party that gave me the nightmares – Mr Pudge – and I must admit I'd expected a little more. I felt choked by the smell of soft, dirty money.

'I celebrated by coming in her mouth,' he said. He snuffled in appreciation of his own sleazy revenge. One of the lads, that lad. Smoke a cigar. Too scared for the weed. Power always bowed to pleasure.

I'd met Blairy before. You couldn't help meeting him in those days. With his eager grin, his love of rote-learning, he was a quick study. He had well-learned pieties and a self-important grasp of simple ideas that he believed people could understand under his tutelage. Mr Blurr the History Master. So proud to have Bill Clinton for a colleague he might almost call a friend. To give away the prizes. My fellow Christian. My pal, the slut.

To be fair, they didn't like knowing I was there that time and I didn't get invited twice. They became a bit self-conscious when Barbi told them what I did for a living. 'But really he's an old rock and roller, eh, Den? We go back a long way. Down the Limbo, when everything was happening. Chilli Willi. Rockpile. Doing the wop-wop. Doctor Feelgood? Remember? The last kick of the real old heavy rock, man. Kaptin Klix, man. Remember?'

'When rock and roll *was* rock and roll,' said Bill in his Elvis Presley voice. 'Uh, huh, huh.' But you could tell he was stumped. Deep Fix? Fix? Made him nervous. He could see himself losing the bigot vote. He'd never heard of us. How could he have? We were Barbi's fantasy team. Our patron had turned a few excited memories into a guiding myth.

'Cool,' said Barbi, closing his eyes. 'The deepest fix . . .'

'Pricks?' said Clinton. I think he was casting around for familiar territory.

That's what he said.

I made an excuse and slunk.

A yellowpress jackal like me is never at ease in the company of the world's monumental lions.

That was when I went up to the Mill, desperate for comfort.

Tubby knew it was me. 'Did you get the 135?' he asked as he opened the door. 'You must have had a clear run along Fortess Road.' He had to be horribly telepathic or have CCTVs all over London. Retaliative strategies? He and Brian Eno had been pretty thick once. We'd been produced by Eno, in fact. Calvert's solo album *Lucky Leif and the Longships*. I played banjo on it. Wonderful job. But don't ask me how that Eno brain thinks. What angles those ideas are coming from. God knows what Tubby was thinking by that time. He never let me see much of what was on those screens of his.

Probably because of what was happening to him. He'd been awake too long. About seven or eight years. It was beginning to show. He looked pale and puffy. He gave me a hug. Even if he looked like shit his cats were as sleek, muscular and quick as ever. Tubby would have to be a lot further gone to start sacrificing his cats. And clearly someone was keeping things clean. There was still a lot of fancy food in the fridge and not all had antique sell-by dates. But there was, I'll admit, a distinct sense of being in the Führerbunker a day or two before the Russians started forking out the remains of the Goebbels children.

Almost the only light came from his murmuring, shifting screens. It made the insides of the Mill seem even more of a shadowy vault, vast and gormenghastly. Oddly quiet, as if he was listening for something outside.

He wanted me to cook a meal. He said he was starving. So I did some American lamb. God knows what they feed and inject into their sheep these days, but it's produced the best lamb in the world. We were lucky. It hadn't turned to mutton in the meantime.

We ate it in the kitchen. It was tough and tasty.

'You're avoiding me, aren't you, Den?' He helped himself to more potatoes.

God! Not another fucking guilt trip. 'No. Of course not.'

'Yes, you are. Everybody is. Except Paul Frame. He's too fucking pious by half. You're avoiding me because I'm barking barmy. I can't say I blame you, Dennis. I am barmy and I'm terrible company. But I know you're not against me. I know who *is* against me . . .'

His screens skipped and winked, casting edgy cold light over our faces.

'Come on now, Tub. Para-bloody-noia, man.' For some reason, sitting in the semi-darkness at the table, I made a peace sign.

'No.' He helped himself to Brussels sprouts. 'I mean I know. I know you're not lying. And I know what they're planning against the Mill. I know everything. Ha, ha, ha.' He raised a fork towards his face. 'Information, me. Our age's greatest asset. Corporations are already more powerful than some nation states. They can do anything they like. Pure multinational feudalism. And what have we got in place to counter that power? It's our only weapon. Our shield. Infor-bloody-mation,

Dennis. But what good will it do me against brute greed, all this information?'

'Overload.' I stirred the mint sauce. 'Information overload. Paranoia. You're not making sense, Tub. You, of all people. This isn't good. Listen to me, eh? Loopiness in extremis? Funny Farm Road? Take a break, Tub. Do some drumming. Get your kit out.'

It was a daft bit of inspiration, but, for that moment, it worked.

Tubby only had to strip off some dust covers, tune up his snares.

I still had the Rickenbacker and the Gibson with him for safe keeping. We started off slow. *Blind man, walkin' across America, I said, blind man, walkin' across America . . . I got a razor, man, I got a shiv that's a cinch . . .*

Soon we were feeling something. We were getting as close to spontaneous as we'd been in a long while.

Blind man, American man. Blind man walkin' through the land . . .
See them dancing through the land
Followin' the dealer man
They are laughing every one
They think they're having fun

Never felt more like slinging the booze.

Cause I never thought
That I'd ever lose
Your love
Babe.
Lord, have you seen my milk cow . . . ?
Going down to cowtown, to get my hambone boiled . . .

Jesus, I thought to myself, even as my fingers shaped the familiar chords. Is this what it's come to? *Dealer, dealer man, what have you got in your bag today, what have you got to turn me on again . . .* A fucking dirge. *Be-bop-a-lu-la, she's my baby . . .*

But then Tubby's drums kicked in like for ever and he was driving it so hard I began to feel my adrenalin coming back. What had been suppressing it? Coming back and sliding straight through my fingers to blend with that old blue and white Les Paul and make the sounds its maker dreamed of. Ta-da-dat-da-da . . . Ow-ow-owwwwwww . . .

Sixteen years old, with a death rattle in her throat . . .

Swinging the blues.
The cats thought it was cool.
For me, it felt like an evening off. A bit of real life again.

I was lost, lost on the merry – lost, lost on the merry – lost on the merry-go-round . . .

The last band, playing for the end of the world.

A few nights later, I was back at Barbican's gothic cast-iron cage of folly, sitting in my dentist's chair, rolling his joints, playing with his toys. Outside, the black river, yellow stains, the steady lights of the further bank. In the BBIC building there were still lights in the restaurant. He'd just had a party with the United Nations, he said.

'What, all of them?'

He was relaxing, stripping off his jacket, moving towards his fancy instruments, his elaborate bong. Behind him were the silhouettes of dimly lit office buildings, between them the river.

'Most. Rosie was in thick with Uganda when I left. Those African types can be so bloody aggressive and in your face. I mean, I don't own Africa. I wasn't responsible for the slave trade. I'm not in charge. She knows I have a hard time with that sort of thing. She helps me out wonderfully. Takes it all off my shoulders. What a warrior that woman is!'

He picked up the Black Falcon. Picked it up like a ceremonial sword, or some ancient sceptre. Revering it. I half-expected him to begin a spell right there on the spot. I wondered if he really was from Transylvania.

The black Epiphone was a 40/54 modification. Said to have been given to Leadbelly, it had definitely been swapped by Little Memphis Fats, on tour in England in the 1950s, for some Marshall amps and a couple of good speakers. It was rumoured to have been owned by John Lennon, but there are no pictures of him with it. Alexis Korner played it for a while. It was Korner who had sold it to Cochrane near the end of Eddie's tour. Alex Harvey, another old Star Club vet, got it next and loaned it to Kingsize Taylor. It didn't suit Kingsize, who can be seen playing it on the cover of *Hamburger Hell.* Hornsey sold it to Long John Baldry, who really pulled the most out of it, though you sometimes thought John was so thin the monster guitar would actually drag him off his feet. You can hear it on that weird Canadian record he did, *Hoochy Coochy Peter Pan.* After that Bill Wyman had it, charity-auctioned it, and it went into a private collection. How many businessmen secretly wanted to handle these symbols of sexual potency? A bit like saddle-sniffing, really.

I must admit the Epiphone pretty much played itself. It had all the craftsmanship of their best jazz guitars, with the double resonator giving it a bulky, unserious look, with modified Humpbacker Gibson pick-ups, done in the Gibson workshop at Kalamazoo and better than a 1958 T335.

Worth the money? Who knows? The guitar was unique, like the best Strads, and had been the work of loving craftsmen through all its modifications to the acoustic/electric wonder that it was. Heavy as lead. The history of American music was all there in the Bird. Roll your fingers on those thrumming hi-gauges, squeeze out the rumbling, grumbling bass moan, the wild trebles, squealing, squeaking, oinking and shrieking into one long, much-bent wild harmonic. Rockin' pneumonia and boogie-woogie flu. I played the Black Falcon. In fact I wouldn't let my cousin have it. It became an important consolation, that guitar. Barbi plonked away on rhythm. His Fender had cost him a little over fourteen thousand at auction. It had only been used by George Harrison on *Abbey Road*. The Falcon felt like you were playing a harp in heaven. Well, a lot of harps, really.

I still wasn't entirely sure of everything Barbi was buying. Authenticity as well as potency? Authority? What had their predecessors bought to prove their reality, their manly provenance? Guns? Big game? Mussolini used to pose with tractors, aeroplanes and other bits of fast nasty machinery with sharp corners. In jodhpurs. They wanted to be soldiers, in those days. To wear big boots.

It was creepy. Barb was oddly flattered by the attention he got from these politicians. He had a feeling they were only after his money, but he wanted to believe they admired his style.

'Bill said he liked the idea of forming a band but we had to keep Tony off the harmonium.' He seemed to be on some kind of desperate high. He hit me on the shoulder.

I had the feeling he was brothering with me again.

He started the drum machine. He handed me the black axe.

Barbi didn't quite get around to forming a rock-and-roll band with Billy the Cocksman but he came close. I was amazed. They really had fantasized about it with Blairy. That's what they were actually talking about when the world was in crisis. You could say it was reassuring, really. All a few months before the UK elections, when Tony was schmoozing with all the big guys, cheering up business.

It was amazing to me how these politicians and schtickmeisters, who had spent their lives on ambitious careers, wizards of manipulation and spin, who could squeeze approval from stones and shaft whole nations, who had more spare power than Portadown, longed to be mistaken for the rock performers their teenaged selves had dreamed of. What fuelled this compulsion to hang out with the real heroes of their time? Their own uncertain grasp on reality? Maybe they sensed that all they had was earthly power. They knew nobody wanted to *give* them their souls, that people had to be tricked into deals like that. But if you were Bruce Springsteen they would be queuing in droves to offer themselves up to you. You would have something they really wanted, rather than something you'd made them want. Voluntary souls. What a novelty. What a feast. Popular for your Self. Your actual Self.

Bill and Tony and Barbi and all the other populist politicians and business monsters knew in their bones that their eminence was unearned and largely spurious, created by spin and circumstances, by their own and other people's greed, by more hype than a roomful of artists formerly known as Ponce, by almost divine good luck.

They knew how to court popular power, but they didn't know what it was like to be popular for what you did, rather than for what you said. They had run under too many flags of convenience to have much serious belief in their own authenticity. So, in some cargo-cultist knee-jerk response, they found excuses to be photographed with the people whose interests they were serving, some ex-artist-turned-business-performer like Colonel Stevie Wonder or General Phil Collins or some other officer in the new corporate Salvation Army. Frequently flattered by admiring flunkeys, these great captains of industry and finance embarrassed themselves and their dear ones by appearing on stage with a musical instrument and some puffed up old Van Morrison or other in the pretence that they'd been coaxed into it to serve a charity. Big do's. Big do here. Big do there. Literature and the Arts. Computer-generated guests. Braggville. Rock-and-roll suicide.

These functions always had Salmon Rushdi turning up at some stage. First the security presence. Then the appearance. Then the applause. Rushdi was the first author ever to be fully consumer-rated. He was an adman prophet. There's an advantage to having a price on your head. You know your own worth.

In fact, it must be nice to get approval just because some idiot philistine politico takes against you. Bit like Solzhenitsyn, poor bastard. They were glad to see him slipping back to his security dacha. Writers are supposed to claim moral authority, not actually own it. Puts both their feet off the tarmac with the engine revving. Easy riders, these days, right? It's not fair on those readily inflated egos. My main problem with the Rushdi presence was the same as with the royals. You couldn't get in the fucking toilets when they were around. Salmon, of course, was just out for some petulant air. While presumably fundamentalist assassins slunk behind the draperies, ready to fling themselves at him from every corner. Trying to poison his Chardonnay. Meanwhile Iranian journalists and Russian journalists and Mexican journalists and Irish journalists and Nigerian journalists and Kurdish journalists and Kenyan journalists and Serbian journalists and Dutch journalists and German and French journalists were being knocked off by the dozen out here. Out here in the real world. Knocked off by the family-load.

Peace! Sunshine. Feelgood.

Maybe those scowling Republikans were right and Tony, Bill and Co were just decadent children of the alternative society, but it was more likely the boys were just boys. Just the boys. Bland boys. Grin boys. Quiff boys. Smart boys. Premier boys. Dreaming boys.

KERANG!!!!!

And it didn't get much better, either. Not for me.

After Bill went home, promising to bring his sax round next chance he had, Tony ran off to be Mr Nicely Persuasive and various privileged heads returned to their estates. Barbican thought Tony was a great guy. They spoke the same language, enjoyed the same things. The kind of socialist you could do business with. In fact, he'd always been a bit sympathetic to Labour. He was still sparking. As he moved in and out of those bars of light, he kept going back to his music console and the guitar beside it in its stand. The black Epiphone fascinated him. He was forever picking it up, getting a feel of it. He was so awkward with it, the guitar actually took on an alien cast, while Barbi moved his spastic body, stiff as a Mountie, in imitation of the life he'd longed for as a lad and could now possess. The guitar still had more obvious vital signs than Barb, though he did glow a bit when he was handling it, as if some of Cochrane's vitality had transferred itself to him via the instrument. So maybe it was worth the four hundred thousand quid.

He could do an F shape up and down the neck and just about keep time, but that was it. No twang. I did him a bit of twang. I got him a twang pedal. Just like Eddie. I showed him how to work the wah-wah.

Barbican had his own stage. Against the inside wall was a huge Wurlitzer electric organ, reclaimed from the Rotunda, Torquay, complete with triple consoles, two thousand shades of neon and enough bells and whistles to do the soundtrack of *Intolerance*. The whole bloody pop shop – the guitars, a drum kit, drum machine, synthesizer laid out in such a way as to attract Barbi's dreams back from the dead.

It was getting weirder and weirder and I probably didn't help keep myself in focus by drawing increasingly on Barbi's supply of custom drugs and superskunk, not to mention some of the best Mood Indigo acid I'd had since 1976. When Barbi had first sold it to me. The Mood also helped me enjoy the mellow company of the dancing classes. My subjects. I was still doing my night job.

People moan on about how the club scene is mindless, anti-intellectual. They don't understand how people can have faith in the power of dancing. There are entire nations and religions whose idealism is vested in very similar practices. Consumerism took over the pop dance world very early: it was almost the same thing – and now they all talk the same language. Icons and tags. Labels and designs. Yet even this language, because its users can't bear not to communicate, gradually takes shape, starts to do jobs – to question, challenge and explain. It's hard, though. It does your head in trying to understand it. You might think it's better to come back in about two hundred years.

Monday. Rise late. Dine early. To the Cage. Any news of Rosie? Any news of something? Nothing great. Play with Barbican. And so, drugged, to bed.

Tuesday: same.

Wednesday: ditto.

Then one night I turned up and here's Paul Frame, the same old Paul, handsome as ever in his jeans and denim shirt, his hair falling in a neat quiff, tickling the ivories, squeezing some oomphy noises out of the big Wurlitzer. Lights are rippling. He's giving it some stick. Neon heaven. Growling and whimpering, gasping and wailing. *Oh, I do like to be, down by the riverside . . . Workin' hard on the chain gang . . .* Then they're playing an old Deep Fix number – *Lost on the Merry-go-round.* Or rather, Paul is playing and Barbi's strum-posing.

I go over and pick up the Epiphone. I don't even question it much. I know what I have to do. And it's better than hurting.

I tuned up the Bird, because it was there and nobody else was playing it. They knew in their hearts it was mine. And I started joining in. My old numbers. Gilmore's old numbers. Calvert's old numbers. Charnock's old numbers. Pavli's old numbers. Until we were entirely ignoring Barbi and pumping the volume on the drum machine to make sure he didn't distract us. He seemed perfectly content – posing this way, strutting that, all contained in a kind of audio-condom.

Paul and I nod and play the old familiar tunes. We know our place. As mighty commercial empires rise and fall, as fortunes are made and lost on the stock market. As dreams are ruined and nightmares brought to life, as populations rush from disaster to disaster, we play on. We can pretend we're doing something else but we know we're part of Barbi's very own skiffle group.

Only Barbi talks of 'us' getting 'back' together again . . . All we need to form a band is Tubby, Calvert, Pavli and Charnock. No way, we say.

Pavli had always been a loner. At the height of his reputation as one of the three best bass players in the business he gave it up to do a degree course in the cello. Then he became manager of *The Economist*'s used-book store and got to specialize in economics, moved to Wales with his new business, married into a bookshop, got a nice kid, and now plays bouzouki in a restaurant in Aberystwyth. Happy as a clam. Why come out of that to be part of Barbi's wank? Calvert was dead. Charnock was a half-crazed best-seller, writing literary Westerns from his vast Texas estate. Gilmore was lost in New York.

Tubby wasn't worth asking. It would be an insult. Besides, the only reason I was doing any of this was so I could be near Rosie – who wasn't anywhere close. She was in all the papers – other people's pix – though I was never once at a function where she was supposed to be without her failing to turn up – and appear elsewhere apologizing for the fuck-up she seemed to be engineering for her own amusement. I didn't like it. I didn't like being hated. It was freaking me out. My judgement was all over the place. Rosie! Rosie!

I got all the good Di shots. Nothing ever on the light of my life. I was drifting all the less intentionally. I was beginning to doubt that I had my own identity. I just borrowed what I could from other people.

I was working at the Westminster Room, doing a *Tatler* job, enjoying a free drink with George, the old Greek who really owns it. He was another good source for me and I kept him supplied with the Nat Shermans he loved to smoke. They were hard to come by in England.

'You know what these boys want, Denny?' He was chewing on green peppers and spitting seeds into his hand. 'They want to have lived. They're still trying to find out what feeling is. They've traded everything human for their power, and still feel empty. In Greece old fellows start taking young wives and go hunting and boast of non-existent exploits in the war. In America, every banker is suddenly a Viet-vet. They want their words to be real. They'll go to almost any lengths. They want our authority for their words. They want our experience.'

'Ours?'

'Believe me, yes. Soon they'll have a way of siphoning it out of our minds and into their own. With a chip, Den. Our essence. Our identities. Authenticity on tap.'

'Well, they won't have much luck when they get to siphoning mine,' I said.

Raves and balls. Clubs and galas. Those glitzy charity gigs seemed to come along every week and all I had to do was cover the follies of the rich and famous. Thighs and sighs. I didn't do much news stuff at all. Norrie told me that I did the bums and boobs where I used to do the bombs and blunders. And there were plenty of bombs and blunders. Too many for me to deal with.

And pies. Remember Bill Gates, pied in Paris? That other rash of pie-terror during the mid-nineties? I thought for a while that Tubby was back in business and I began to cheer up. But he denied it when I spoke to him on the phone.

'I don't have that kind of fun any more.'

'So who is pie-ing these bastards?'

'The Belgians?' he suggested. 'They have a more permanent sense of guilt.'

'Then what's your equipment for, Tubby? What use is it? I know you're doing something with all that info. You can't help yourself.'

'I'm defending the Siege Perilous,' he said. 'Didn't I tell you?'

I wouldn't want to get into that again, but I found myself saying urgently, 'Tubby, you no longer have a life.'

'I have more than I need,' he said. And put the phone down.

And the bombs blow up our hope, and the bombs blow up our dreams . . .

Next morning, early for him and for me, Barbican was on the blower. He said he hoped to meet Rosie for lunch at Blue's. Would I like to come there?

I did my best to control myself. My heart began to beat rapidly. It was ridiculous. I tried to prepare for disappointment. But I was already anticipating what I would say to Rosie as I got dressed. More carefully than usual.

Barbi hardly ever met me in public. I was a bit surprised, but thought maybe Rosie had suggested the lunch. Blue's was Barbican's own restaurant, on top of the BBIC tower, across the river from The Cage.

Begg Tower rose above the Globe at Southwark. Bronze and golden stone. A marvel of Barbi's own special architectural tastes, it had been built on the site of Marriage's Old Wharf, the scene of several murders. Its view of the river had an unnaturally clear, sharp quality. As if it had been cleaned up and tinted.

In spite of my careful toilet you could tell they didn't like the look of me when I arrived at the reception desk. Then, of course, they were falling over themselves to fawn on me as soon as they realized whose guest I was. The advantages of power. It wouldn't take much to get used to it. And think it had something to do with people liking you.

Blue's hadn't always been on top of Begg Tower. I used to go regularly when it was Anville Street, Whitechapel and had been run by the famous fighting rabbi – Howard Blue – who had survived Bergen-Bergen to become amateur heavyweight champion of England. Blue's had been incorporated into the remodelled Tower. Tile by tile, booth by booth, steel fixtures and advertising boards and all, seamlessly, like matter transmission. You wouldn't have known it had moved. Barbi had builders who did that sort of work exclusively. Restoration, reclamation, removals. Rabbi Blue now owned a posh gym in Tudor Hamlets, getting a lot of the Hampstead Garden Suburb crowd. He complained that running a fish restaurant meant he had to get up almost every morning just to get down to Billingsgate before dawn. Some people loved that life, but he couldn't stand it. Tudor Hamlets could find their fish elsewhere.

Blue's was still fish. Only fish. Grilled, steamed or fried fish in matzoh flour. Chunky chips, boiled Cyprus potatoes. Salad. Portions of peas. A starter could be a salmon knish, but more likely gefilte fish. I'd have some good grub, at any rate, and some dubious company. This was where the City did its lunching.

The big blue tiled hall had belonged to a Jewish charity before Rabbi Blue turned it into his famous restaurant. The gold-leafed Hebrew homilies, the intricate scrollwork, the old-fashioned aquariums on the blank walls, the blue, opaque glass, were part of the place. In the old days, you felt like you were eating in some faintly holy spot, as if the food had been blessed. Here, in a perfect and sensitive reconstruction well above street level, with light flooding in as light wasn't ever meant to flood, it looked like a film set. A fairly noisy one at that. The governing classes aren't quiet amongst themselves.

Rosie wasn't at the table, which was clearly the best in the place, secluded but with a wonderful view of the river. I sat there by myself, holding a menu about twice the size of my torso. I didn't bother to read it. I was going to have the Dover sole. I never miss an opportunity to have a good one. There can't be that many of them left now.

Then I saw Barbican come sailing smoothly across the floor. He lifted his hand in a general greeting, an all-encompassing curve of the lips. I think he was buoyed up by the admiration and good will of his employees, because it did seem to me that he drifted like a balloon, just above the carpet and settled lightly in the chair across from me. He was sorry he was late. He was involved with the Millennium Dome committee. Had I heard about that? No? It was going to be fabulous. He called for a glass of water and took about eight pills. 'Rosie worries if I don't. Did you know there's another bomb scare on?' He was worried because there was some talk of blowing up Oxford Street and he'd recently taken discreet control of Virgin and her megastores. 'The sky's not really the limit,' he told me. 'Satellites and planes, telegraphs and trains. That's what it's all about. Transport and communications. Same as the nineteenth century, really. Only the commodities change.' He beckoned a waiter over and murmured something rapid at him. The waiter apologized and removed the glass of water.

'Apologies from Rosie,' he said as he raised his napkin. 'She'll try to get along in a bit. She says to start without her.' He had just come away, he said, from the Dome site. 'A real winner, Den. If the bastards don't bomb it to bits.' There had been another scare that morning, but no blast.

I took a grip on myself and decided to enjoy the lunch. 'So what's Rosie up to? I was looking forward to seeing her.'

'I especially was hoping she'd be here, too. But we have a crucial meeting with Clearwater and she can handle it a lot better than me.' Barbi sounded almost disappointed himself. 'Still, we can put it to her later.'

'Put what?'

He was used to that. He ignored me automatically as he glanced over the menu. I ordered my sole.

It wasn't until the main course arrived, after a bit of chat about some of his rivals, whom he'd judged with easy scorn.

'She's agreed to be our singer,' he said.

I laid down my fork.

'Rosie's terrible! She's tone deaf.'

I regretted that. I didn't want to put him off. This could be my one chance to see her.

'That's not crucial these days, Den. You know that better than I do.' Barbican wasn't worried. 'They have vocoders and stuff. She'll sing like a dream, if necessary via the wonders of modern electronics. You know that, me old strummer! Better than I do.'

'OK,' I said. 'Sounds OK.' I looked to see if Rosie had come into the restaurant. Nope. Just the feeding suits and skirts.

'More than OK, Dennis. This could be the biggest and best charity gig of them all. Not just Deep Fix back together – but the Beatles and the Who.'

'What? Supporting us?' He had to be fixing E.

'Could be,' he said.

Now that's what I called awesome power. It scared me shitless.

'Charity gig?' I was slowly coming to.

'Just a possibility,' he said. 'You know? The Deep Fix's final concert?'

'We had our final concert about ten years ago. Nobody turned up.'

That just amused him.

'Nobody was that interested in our *first* gig.' I was starting to feel chilly.

'They packed Wembley.' He was eager, persuasive. 'Filled Hammersmith Odeon regularly.'

'That's a sure sign you had one big hit and kept a very loyal fan base. Besides, we never packed Wembley. We were lucky to fill the first five rows.'

'Don't put yourself down, Dennis. You were one of the great guitarists. Only Paul Frame was better. It wasn't that long ago, my old mate, you couldn't open *NME* without seeing you leaping all over the centre spreads with that Gibson of yours.'

There was a reason I hadn't kept my old news cuttings.

'If we packed Wembley, Tower Bridge will be a doddle.' He leaned back, cheerfully sipping his wine, the monarch of all his mind surveyed. 'A bloody doddle, my son.'

He wouldn't tell me any more but my sense of trepidation made me very uncertain.

'And Rosie?' I asked.

'What do you mean?'

'She'll definitely sing for us?'

'Definitely,' he said.

So I decided to think about it. A few rehearsals would be all right and I could always jump ship once I'd got to see Rosie and straightened things out between us. But then, as I looked around me at the feeding plutocrats and started to think about it all, what was I really being asked to endorse? I felt sick.

'That fish seemed a bit off,' I said. 'Did it seem off to you?'

'Pulled out of the sea last night, Den. I insist on it. I frequently go down to Billingsgate myself to pick the fish.'

'Come off it,' I said, 'that's Rabbi Blue's story! You're pinching it!'

He laughed aloud. 'Fair enough.' He sighed.

What was all this bullshit? Was he just trying something on with me?

Was he in competition with me and I didn't know it? Did he think there was another man? Did he think it was me?

In which case, no contest, it had to be Paul Frame.

This wasn't doing my digestion any good.

'I was wondering what you thought about talking to Tubby,' said Barbican.

When he got up to go to the private bathroom, I checked to make sure his feet were actually touching the ground.

Before we left the restaurant he took me to the window and made me look down at the strangely blue stretch of river. You could see all the way to the brown swirling bottom muck in which shapes sought the little darkness they had left.

'CW technology,' he says. 'Gets rivers sparkling bright in seconds. Our chemistry bods came up with it. An economical solution to industrial pollution. A few drops of that stuff and you have near-drinkable quality in moments. Of course, the effects dissipate, but think what we'll be able to do with the oceans and lakes. The whales and dolphins will all be saved – and we'll be able to see them better, too!'

'Will we have to start feeding them?'

'Those same research departments are already working on ways of replenishing the biosphere. We're paying a fortune into the voluntary sector, of course. Don't worry, Den, all your furry, feathery, blubbery friends will be safe.'

'You always say that,' I said.

Over my head, sang Calvert, on that last album. *She asked me if I'd watched the movie, where the hero loses his soul. I told her I didn't find that groovy, I'm more into rock and roll . . .*

It was like that bit in *Body Snatchers*, where Donald Sutherland realizes there's only him left. I mean, I really didn't have any friends.

I needed Calvert or Pavli on this one. As it was, I decided to get to the Mill as soon as possible and find out what Tubby thought.

Over the next few days I phoned the Mill a lot. I left messages, but Tubby wouldn't get back to me. I began to worry about him and, after three days of this, decided I'd better check to make sure he was OK. I took a taxi there in a hurry. I remember running up the hill in the semi-darkness, just as the last bit of red skyline faded into a deep blue twilight. The Mill still looked like a Grot set exterior for *Captain Blood*, stark and black against that vivid gash of scarlet, the vanes turning very slowly, with what felt like meditative dignity, as if the Mill were the engine of the world.

I had trouble getting through the gates and up to the front door, leaning on the bell, looking up into the mouth of the camera as it swivelled to focus. 'Hi, Tubby. I just need to make sure you're OK.'

It got worse.

There was no reply.

I began to wonder about calling the police.

Then a disembodied voice, almost a whisper, came from behind the big church doors. It was Tubby. 'Fuck off, Den. If you wouldn't mind. I can't say any more. Just fuck off for now, OK. Phone me in a few days.'

I tried to talk to him, explain that he was behaving like a loony, what I needed to talk to him about, but he wouldn't respond. At least I knew he wasn't dead.

I went and sat on one of the battered benches in Tufnell Park. It wasn't a bad place to settle and take a breath. My world was getting less and less real. Everything was happening to someone else. The real Dennis Dover would never have fallen out with Rosie. The real Rosie wouldn't have had any trouble understanding what Dennis was trying to preserve when he took those pictures. So who were we? Simulacra? Virtual copies of ourselves? Had Barbican's agents bid top dollar for the originals at Sotheby's?

As I sat there wondering if I was plastic I saw a figure go by out of the corner of my eye. It was a familiar outline and, turning, I saw it was Flicky Jellinek. I had the impression she'd just come out of Tubby's and was walking rapidly down the path towards the Whittington Park entrance. Was she why Tubby hadn't wanted to see me? I started to get up.

Flicky Jellinek was now MP for Fletchley West, winning it for Labour in that sensational by-election. She had come up rapidly and was in the shadow cabinet and wouldn't last a month in Blairy's real world. She resigned after two months. But at the moment she was a star – spokesperson for Trade and Industry, all that – and a radical, a coherent feminist. She had become pugnaciously outspoken since getting into mainstream politics via Greenham, and I loved seeing her scathe the opposition – which often included her party colleagues – wherever she lifted those huge, brown eyes and transformed herself effortlessly from Bambi to Whitefang in a stunning instant.

I stepped lightly down the hill and fell in beside her on the path. 'What was all that about?'

I made her jump. Her head began to turn. I raised my hands and backed off. 'It's me, Flicky. Friend.' I was afraid she knew oriental martial arts that could snap my head off my body like a poppy off a stalk.

She slowed down when she realized who it was. 'Oh, bugger,' she said. 'Oh, fuck.'

'You're not hurting my feelings,' I said. 'I'm used to being unpopular. Why are you so specially displeased to see me?'

'Of all fucking people. Don't do anything with this, Dennis.'

'Do? I'm Tubby's friend, Flicky. I'm only worried about him. What's going on in there, Flick? Why did he tell me to go away?'

'He doesn't want you to pick up anything.' She was walking rapidly again now.

'What's wrong with him?'

'Bit of flu.'

'Well, I can look after him. I'll be glad to. Make myself useful. Get in the Lemsip. I'm at a loose end, anyway.'

'Believe me, Dennis. He insists on being left alone. He especially isn't having anything to do with old friends. He says he needs to think. He needs to sort some stuff out. He'll phone you soon, I'm sure. Don't think I haven't talked to him.'

'Well, it's not wholesome, Flick. It ain't healthy.'

She softened a bit as we got into the car park.

'What did you want to see him about?' She put her key in her Volvo.

'Nothing,' I said.

'Just dropping in?'

'That's right.'

She got the doors open and threw her bag in the back. She sighed. 'Can I give you a lift somewhere, Dennis?' She wasn't enthusiastic. 'Well?'

'That's very generous.' I went round and got in the passenger side. 'Which way are you going?'

'West End,' she said.

'That'll suit me fine.'

She grew friendlier as she drove. She said she had a margin. She'd take me home to Brookgate. By the time we were near King's Cross she was a lot more relaxed and asking after old friends. 'And what about that big Frenchman you're so pally with? The journalist. Got that prize.'

'Fromental's back in Africa as far as I know. Doing what he has to do.'

'Oh, right.' She paused as she began the complicated route to get her to Gray's Inn Road. 'Right.' She did a quick dog-leg, avoided a road island, two taxis and a junkie and somehow we were up near the old Camden Town Hall and I was almost home. 'So he's still in Africa, you think?'

'Are you trying to get in touch with him?'

'Oh, no,' she said. 'Here we are.' And she stopped her car firmly at the little alley just above Verulam Street, which would take me all the way home to Fogg Yard. I admired her economy. I kissed her cheek, wished her well, told her to call me if Tubby needed anything, and got out. The lights of the newsagent glossed the pavement. It had been raining here.

'Thanks, Flicky,' I said. 'Don't take any wooden envelopes.'

'You wouldn't hurt Tubby, would you, Dennis?' The window buzzed down and her face was anxious. A genuinely frightened Bambi.

'He's my friend,' I said. 'You know me. I can only do friendship one way. Why would I hurt him?'

'I know you wouldn't.'

'What is this, Flick? Has he gone completely barmy at last?'

'Well, put it this way – he's not locked up anywhere yet.' She gave me a funny look before she closed the window and spun the big car back into the traffic.

She'd known a little more than she let on, I think. But what difference did it make? I now didn't have Tubby, either.

I strolled home through the concrete-and-glass graveyard that was modern Brookgate, let myself into my flat, took about ten moggies I had left over from an old girl-friend, and went to sleep.

I'm not sure I want to tell you about the dreams.

Luckily a couple of demonstrations came up in the next few days and I didn't have to be a sensitive individual for a while. I just went and snapped the angry people. Almost like old times. I got some wonderful shots, which the magazines and papers are still using, but it didn't really change much for me. Everything was still happening to some other Rosie, some other Dennis. Everything was still profoundly wrong.

Unreal trips to Barbi's fantasy paradise. Playing the Black Bird, marking time, waiting for Rosie to turn up. If she was going to be our singer, she ought to be rehearsing. I hardly questioned what I was thinking. If I was thinking. *Playing in a band, you don't understand where the time goes . . .* Paul Frame came when he could. He'd grown a beard and looked like Jesus again, only more clean-cut. He couldn't help looking saintly. It was partly his natural neatness, partly his gaunt, suffering look. He was off to Calcutta for a photo opportunity, into Hong Kong for a crowd scene, over to Hiroshima for some pious head-lowering. Back to London, back to the Cage and the Wurlitzer, until one night he brought his old TS335 and then we really started playing. I hated the bastard. He condescended to me. Everybody enthused about meeting him. How down-to-earth and natural he was. What lovely hair, what lovely eyes. What a heart! Big as the world. What a fucking wanker! But we could bring out the best in each other's music. And we did. Sometimes savagely. Barbican hardly noticed. He was concentrating on his Fender's swing. Still no Rosie. Though she really intended to turn up, Barbican knew. It was just that she was so fucking busy. Hard work being Mrs Tycoon. He nodded to himself when he told me this. Bloody hard work. He was impressed. A dynamo, that woman. He was getting noticeably plumper, more relaxed.

The bombs blow up the churches and the dead give up their graves . . .

One morning, far too early, the bell rang at Fogg Yard. I opened up to find the doorway filled with Fromental. A pretty ratty, ravaged-looking Fromental. The Hulk on the run from the chain gang.

'Speak of the devil.' I'd been talking about him again to Norrie over a curry in Trinidad Street the night before. Not much of a coincidence, really. 'How's Africa?'

'Fuck Africa,' he said. He ducked into the hall.

I was very glad to see him. I told him I'd get some breakfast together, but he mumbled obscurely, took a couple of massive Frankenstein steps towards the spare bedroom, flung himself in and slammed the door behind him. A few moments later the flat was shaking to his familiar snores.

He hadn't been in Africa. He'd been on Morn with Pinky Fortnum.

'Morn?' We were in the Chinese chippy in Theobalds Road. He was stuffing down haddock faster than a pregnant penguin. He always ordered haddock in England because it amused him. Something to do with that Tin Tin strip he liked.

'You'd think an island would have good fish, man. Jesus Christ. Frozen fish fingers everywhere. What is that place?'

'Morn?'

'No, man, the Doctor Who refinery there. That we tried to get to. Nobody there now. Deserted, man. The whole complex. It still seems to be working, but not a human being in the place. What's it called?'

'What, Pilbeam? The house?'

'No, man. The peninsula. All that satellite tracking stuff. You know.'

'So did you get to interview Pilbeam?'

'No, man. The dude's a recluse. He didn't want to see us. He's like the fucking Phantom of the Opera, man. There's a guy who's seen too many Saturday serials. But we got all we needed.'

'For what?'

'For the exposé, man.'

He'd been obsessed with Pilbeam since we'd try to go there. When he discovered that Pilbeam had African interests, he decided to start tracking it all down. Pilbeam's African companies weren't especially bad and seemed to offer outstanding conditions to their staffs.

'So what's he doing? Running secret banana plantations in South America? Mines in Africa? Heart of Darkness stuff?'

'He's an exemplary employer.'

Fromental sounded almost resentful.

'Salaries adjusted automatically to inflation and real costs. Great health plans. Retirement funds. The lot. Plenty of options. Health insurance not tied to the company. Best-paid workers on two continents. A fucking old-fashioned philanthropist.'

'So no story.'

He brightened suddenly. Mithras ascending! 'Oh, no, Den, my old pard. Lots of story. Lots and lots of story. And pictures. More than you could ever hope for. This is a big one, man.'

'Big in what way?'

'Global, man. Fucking global. Governments will fall, man.'

I couldn't help myself. 'And you got Pinky taking the pictures?'

'No, man. She was part of the cover, that's all. My way to Pilbeam,

you know. She's lived there for a few years now. In his old house. He's
been abroad most of that time. Oh, man. Pictures, man? Believe me,
there are plenty of pictures.'

'What the fuck have you dug up? Porn? Paedo?'

'Nothing so ordinary, Dennis. You wouldn't believe it.'

As we walked back to the flat he told me some of the story, how he
and Pinky had got invited to Pilbeam's house, how the owner stayed long
enough to give them carte blanche, then left in a large Duesenberg. He
had directed them to his private cinema. A movie was already running.
A home movie, some of it spliced from high-quality CCTV, evidently
hidden cameras, secretly shot footage.

'What? Sleazy?'

'Some of it. Mostly ridiculous.'

'Anyone we know?'

'Oh, shit, man. It's an all-star cast.'

'Who, for instance?'

I made us some coffee and he rolled us some of his special Ghana
Gold. Of course, it's stale news now, but at that moment you can
imagine what those revelations sounded like. Heard for the first time. I
didn't really believe him. He had to have cracked. All they were really
doing was playing an elaborate businessmen's Dungeons and Dragons,
with the odd iffy or plain weird fantasy thrown in. Film One of the
famous Set of Seven. Edited on to V-tape, three hours each, on and on
and on. Prelates and presidents of multinationals. *Boy's Own* foolery,
mostly. More silly than sinister, much of it. But it was the goods on every
government minister who had ever accepted an invite to Morn and let
their hair down. Eat your heart out, Cliveden. Pilbeam must have been
recording it for years. His place had to have been designed to
accommodate all those cameras in all those positions in all those rooms.
Building up a vast file on the follies of the rich and famous. Games,
ceremonies, conversations, all far more damning than the sex stuff,
which was actually relatively discreet, sometimes touching, but certainly
revealing. A kind of devil's-video version of *People*. The same cast,
different plot and scenery. Pilbeam scarcely featured in any of it. It was
who Pilbeam had recorded, and what he had recorded, and when he had
recorded it, that was the white-hot lava bubbling and grumbling and
getting ready to blow out of that particular volcano.

'Enough material, man, to give the *Sun* headlines for the next hundred
years.'

'Why would Pilbeam let you have this stuff?'

'My guess is, man, that Pilbeam and Barbican Begg have fallen out.
And Pilbeam has blown the whistle on his old pals.'

It didn't sound right to me, but I didn't care much, either. 'Are you
sure you haven't been set up for something?' I asked him.

'Set up?'

'Doesn't it sound a bit easy? You prod and probe for years, getting nowhere, then suddenly something like this falls in your lap?'

'You read too much fiction, Den. This is the reward for all that patience. Coincidences happen in real life. This didn't come suddenly. Pilbeam knows I've been after him. He might have thrown me this in order to put me off some other scent.'

'Like what? You've just told me he runs a clean business. How bad can he be? Even if he's a drug baron, he seems a very pleasant one. I bet he wants you to use that material in a certain way. To help some plan of his own. Probably against a business rival. You've been set up. No other reason, pard.'

'Well, maybe his plan and mine work out the same?' Fromental was a bit frosty. He thought I was putting his scoop down.

'It's a great story,' I said. 'It'll run for your lifetime. But I'd just like to know why he suddenly gave you all this material.'

'He's been collecting it for ever, man. He hates these bastards as much as we do. He just wanted to be sure it got into the hands of a serious journalist. He's been biding his time.'

'And you're sure the footage of Barbican is the real thing?'

'Absolutely, man.' He waved one of his little unsmoked bidis about.

'So what will you do with it?'

He nodded. 'I know what you're saying, man. What do we become when we sell stuff like that?'

'Maybe something Pilbeam himself doesn't want to become.' I was sure he was being set up and I felt more involved than normal. I didn't want him to discover himself all alone and covered in shit in a week's time. I'd seen it happen before. 'Did you bring any of the tapes with you?'

'Impossible. I don't know where they are. He screened them from a security box.'

'Oh, shit,' I said. 'This is a waste of time, then.'

'I do have the eight-by-tens. Or some of them.' He went back to his room and came out in a few minutes with a fat, old-fashioned linen envelope.

I had a look at them. Follies of the famous. I couldn't help laughing.

'What the fuck are you going to do with these?'

He shrugged. 'We could show them to the subjects. See what they had to say?'

I started to laugh again. The phone rang. It was Barbi, inviting me up for another session at the Cage. I was taking a varda at a picture of him losing his hood during a strenuous session of the New Teutonic Knights or whatever they called themselves. They looked like Ku Klux Klan in those pointy hats and robes. The only difference was that their robes were designer items, in seasonal colours, while the Klan's had a distinctly modified-bedsheet style. A rich man's Klan? But there were black guys in it. And Chinese and Japanese guys. So it probably wasn't linked closely with the National Front or the White Defence League or whatever. More like some kind of businessmen's frolic. One of those excruciatingly boring bonding, relaxing, getting together, being fathers, being sons, being brothers, being guys, guys, guys, guys things. Wongo-fests. Testosterone turns. In funny costumes. Dancing round the tom-tom, the dick-dick and the harry-harry.

'Feel like lifting the axe tonight, Den?' said Barbican.

I was laughing when I agreed. He said it was nice to hear me so cheerful for a change.

And, of course, when I arrived, Rosie was just leaving. At least I saw her in the flesh this time.

She didn't speak to me as I held the door for her. 'Sounds great, Bee, darling,' I heard her say. 'I already know the words. So that's all right.' I wasn't there. She made it clear.

I had rushed from dope high to trembling, stomach-turned misery. 'Rosie?' She'd gone.

Barbican was grinning and shaking his head. 'What a powerhouse that woman is.'

I was a bit more than confused. So I threw what I thought was a rock into the pool. 'Sorry I'm a bit late,' I said. 'I was seeing a friend of mine. He's just come back from Morn. He was a guest of Hornsey Pilbeam's.'

'Oh, really,' Barbican picked up his Fender and switched on his electronic tuner. 'How is the old bugger? Still as reclusive as he was? I haven't seen him in years.'

I watched the rock sink without a ripple.

I was even more convinced that Fromental was being set up for something. All I had started to worry about was how it would look to Rosie. I'd already decided to distance myself from my friend's obsession. I hadn't sunk yet to selling someone else's pictures to the papers. I wasn't going down that road.

I was happy in the cul-de-sac I'd made right here.

Playing the Bird. Singing the blues.

I think it was that night that Barbican said he'd definitely got the gig booked. He'd had to pull a string or two, but we were all set. The only thing we had to do was be there on the night. As usual, he was the only one of us who seemed really happy. I had begun to envy him. Another week or two of this and I'd start wanting to be like him, play like him, sing like him, the jungle VIP.

He told me to come to the Cage at noon tomorrow and he'd show me what he was talking about. I agreed.

I was drifting. Freewheeling. Free-willing. Lost. Gone. Nothing.

When I got home at dawn that morning Fromental had already left for Paris on an early flight. He had some French newspapers and TV stations to talk to.

It's like that box in Kiss Me, Deadly, he wrote in his note to me. *Pandora's box. That will release the furies on the world. I'm no Mickey Spillane. I need to get some advice, Den.*

I knew what he meant.

A bit melodramatic. But it did seem that he had his thumb on the lid of a very big can of worms. A can that, at another time, I'd have been delighted to open with him. It was just what we needed to challenge the corporate ship. But at that moment I was praying that nothing Fromental did would rock the dinghy for me and Rosie.

Home. Too little sleep. A snort or two of some unusually nice Iraqi Silver and I was revving my engine, ready for lunch.

Barbican's Morgan was in the forecourt when my taxi dropped me off. The curve of the big mudguards reminded me of something I'd seen in the pictures Fromental had insisted I look at. The passenger door snapped open and Barbi's smooth, confident hand gestured me into the seat next to his. He was looking lively and alert. In a wide-eyed, red-rimmed, bloodshot sort of way. I don't think he'd had any sleep at all. He was also, I guessed, wearing some subtle make-up.

I wondered if Barbi would offer me some of whatever he was already on. It certainly made his eyes glitter and his nose run, as well as drying his lips and swelling his tongue. Good stuff. But it wasn't forthcoming. He was far too canny ever to be found with drug shit on him.

On the other hand, he didn't even have a bodyguard in the boot as he drove me through the grey southbank streets into what was left of the Borough and then did some speedy business in Tooley Street, David Street, Hallelujah Parade and the next thing I knew we were crossing the river via Tower Bridge and zooming down into some mysterious car park I'd never known was there.

A flunkey took the keys and disappeared with the motor. In the semi-darkness Barbican showed off his expertise, showed me he knew where he was. He flipped a switch, he found the elevator, he found the lights and the right buttons, and we went up with a swish of efficient machinery. You could smell the mechanical past. Floor by floor, the note of the machinery changed, until with a long, rather dignified shriek, it stopped at the top. We emerged in a room full of white-painted Gothic wood. As if the Baha'i people had decorated a church. Very sharp. Except there wasn't an angelic cleric waiting for us but an old-fashioned British Beefeater, in full bloomers and ruff. Who, I'll swear, pulled his forelock when he saw Barbican emerge. He wasn't sure whether to salute me, that honest Yeoman, but did it in the end.

Where the fuck was he from? Had he wandered in by accident from the Tower of London? I'd learn later it was some sort of heritage stunt, to keep tourists coming.

'MR ALFORD AND THE OFFICER SEND THEIR APOLOGIES, SIR!!!' he bellowed. A deaf sergeant-major? 'THEY'RE STUCK IN

TRAFFIC, SIR, AT THE ELEPHANT, SIR, AND SHOULD BE WITH US AT ANY MOMENT!!!'

'Well, let's just carry on up to the experimental control room, shall we?' Barbican forged ahead while the Beefeater, fingering his ceremonial pole, considered the protocol. 'They can join us there.'

I don't think he had any official authority. But he was so used to leadership and we were so used to being led that we just followed him up the narrow spiral staircase until we had reached the top of the north tower and at the top found ourselves in one of those four mini-towers clustered around the main turret. It was raining outside now, the wind whipping across the grey waters, smearing the concrete, stone and dirty brick on both banks. The cold little room glared with white light. It was full of electronic equipment, including a bank of screens showing the bridge itself from every possible angle. It would be hard to plant an orange pip without it being spotted.

You couldn't see that much of the actual river and its banks without going up close to the narrow windows and looking out, down into the Pool. A big barge was going by, heading for the Isle of Dogs. Its vivid canary tarpaulins stood out against the grey water, the mud-coloured hull. On it part of two words were picked out in glaring royal blue: – OLD – AGE. The bridge was a wonder of Victorian engineering and that strange Home Counties socialist picture of the future Morris and Co had given us, where we'd all live in medieval castles and make artistic chairs. Ever since then the British had been trying to recreate a mythical past in the name of a visionary future.

Barbican spread his large, plump hands across a console. 'This isn't the main control room, of course. This is the old monitoring station they've adapted. The real stuff's downstairs. But this will replace it by next year. Mr Alford can tell you more about it, really.'

'ALL COMPUTERIZED NOW, SIR!!!' bellowed the Beefeater suddenly. If he was a decade or two younger I'd say he had boombox fatigue. 'ALL DIGITAL, SIR.' He was proprietorial, though clearly he saw the electronics as something faintly alien, almost shameful.

Barbican gave him fifty quid and asked him to get us some sandwiches. To keep the change. The Yeoman of the Guard wasn't too sure about leaving his post, but was reassured by Barbican's natural assumption of command. He had no real idea, I suspect, who had authorized Barbican's presence, but knew that this was someone who hobnobbed with the royals and top soldiers, so he had to be OK. Almost as good as Prince Bigears.

Once he had gone, Barbican began to grin. He babbled something about mixing desks, equipment, accoustics. He laughed and showed a lot of well-tended teeth. It was as if Death had just pulled the Maiden at the local Wake. He was jubilant. Well in. His soft hands cruised the knobs and levers, the sliders and stops, and suddenly the TV screens overhead were on. We could see the traffic moving slowly over the bridge. He touched keys and twirled dials to show me everything the cameras could see and do. He picked out a squadron of Household Cavalry trotting along the Embankment. He zoomed in on a police van going up Tower Hill.

'But this is where the real business is,' he told me, coming back to the console. 'This is what will work the bridge itself.'

He turned a key on the deck.

He positioned a few sliders and frowned as he reached to flip a set of switches. 'All clunky old-fashioned electrical underneath the sophisticated electronics,' he said. 'It still has to be relayed. But you should see the incredible Victorian engineering here – it's magical, almost. Our companies helped install this stuff. I can raise the whole fucking bridge if I want to, just by doing this.' And he snapped some switches and moved a lever.

You could hear the result from up where we were. A kind of startled mechanical swearing. A huge screech. Some bumps. A lot of hooting and shouting.

And you could see it on the screen.

Just as the Beefeater came back with the sandwiches and started to have his seizure. I saved the sandwiches and began to lay him down. A phone rang somewhere. It sounded agitated.

A slick-looking goozer with too much Brylcreem and a terrible tailor, his face cold as a hatchet, came bursting in, followed by a uniform with a lot of gold on it. Mr Alford and the officer, I guessed.

'Oops,' said Barbican. 'Oh, fuck!'

He had only raised Tower Bridge a few feet and nobody had been killed, but several cars were rolling backwards off the road and someone had fallen in the river but was being fished out. A bus had almost gone over. Two women had minor injuries.

TOWER BRIDGE DISASTER, MANY INJURED. AMAZING RIVER RESCUE. SCHOOLBOY FEARED DROWNED. As the *Standard* put it that afternoon.

It was, of course, the lead news story. The BBC report said that the action was almost certainly the work of the IRA. Various government spokespeople and technical boffins argued variously for technical error, human error and hackers manipulating the system from a distance. So many balls spinning, so many narratives twisting, it made you dizzy. Well obscured within hours of the event. And no serious harm had come to anyone. The missing boy hadn't actually been on the bridge but was found doing his homework at a friend's. Nobody drowned. The women were patched up with sticking plaster. They were laughing about it. It would cost you a couple of quid to get a thrill like that at Alton Towers. They were certain it was a technical error. What would the IRA want with Tower Bridge?

So we all saw what happened and not one of us told anyone the truth. Not a whisper to the press. It didn't occur to most of us. Most of us never got second chances. Barbican had as many as he needed.

It was Barbi's people who had come up with the IRA story, but I could tell he was shaken. He'd almost killed those women. Mr Alford had been beside himself. He'd taken a lot of keeping quiet. A big Prozac shot up the jaksi and another one to his bank account. But mostly he blamed himself. They had all kind of procedures in place designed to stop exactly that situation. And they hadn't meant a thing in the end. Captain Sallis, the officer, could hardly speak to Barbican, he was so beside himself.

'Another few feet and it would have been extremely serious,' he murmured soberly and decently to me, his eyes on the ground. 'I mean, honestly.'

Serious enough for most motorists. As a result, the police put a road-block at the approach to the bridge. Kept London crawling for months.

That's what showed me how far from reality my cousin had gone. But it didn't mean as much as it should to me. Probably because I was about the same distance off-planet as he was. Maybe not the same address, but definitely hanging out with the Lost Boys in Never-Never Land.

'Anyway,' Barbi said briskly, putting a passing embarrassment behind him as he drove me back to the Cage. 'That's our venue. What a trip, eh?'

'Venue? You couldn't get the band in those little rooms, let alone an audience.'

'No, no. We do the gig *on* the bridge. In the middle of the bridge. But we need Tubby to drum for us.'

There was your problem, I thought. I knew Tubby too well. He'd never agree to work with Barbi, or any of the rest of us, for that matter.

So I wisely ignored that particular statement. Gibraltar would have to tumble before Tub was ever our stickman again. I felt a touch of my old sardonic levity. I couldn't help taking the piss.

'So the audience is, what? Paddling about in lifebuoys?'

'Boats, Den. A flotilla that stretches all the way across and all the way back to London Bridge. Floating seating, see? Moored either side. It'll work. I have guys sorting all that out now.'

Yeah, I know, pards.

I'm a cynic.

Barbi now has a simulacrum of Deep Fix ready to perform from a stage erected at the centre of Tower Bridge. It will be lit by searchlights on either bank and from the nearest bridges up and down river. Not the best acoustics. But it will sound like a dream. He guarantees it. We'll be like a modern Handel or someone. We won't be dwarfed, he reassures me. They'll able to see us on projection screens all around. 'Larger than life, Den!'

I didn't really care one way or the other about his grandiosity. *Turandot* in Peking, *Tosca* amongst the pyramids, *Parsifal* in the Black Forest. It was getting pretty familiar. But I wasn't sure about the practicality. In fact, it was obviously impossible. I wasn't going to have to refuse the gig because there wasn't going to be a gig. I was convinced he couldn't pull it off. They'd never give him permission. Especially after that near-disaster. I didn't much care, one way or the other. All I knew was that sooner or later I was going to be standing next to Rosie and she would have to speak to me. That was my only goal. The means to that goal weren't important.

And, of course, intrepid journo that I am, I didn't report a thing about the Tower Bridge incident. It didn't even occur to me. I let them cover it all up. I let them go on saying it was the IRA, or a system glitch. I didn't even see it as an abuse of private power.

That's how it happens to you. You don't know how it happens to you. Suddenly you're on their side.

CHAPTER TWENTY-SIX
The Set

I was too old to be as wonked off as I was. Barbican's herbs and pharmaceuticals were doing me in. Getting through to my marrow. Damaging my nerves. I couldn't imagine how he was holding up. Maybe personal trainers and personal drug therapists helped. All I had was my own judgement. Which was even more fucked than usual.

In the past I'd always relied on running out of money to control my drug intake. Now I was getting most of it free, lab-quality, and I'd reached a point of desperation. I couldn't believe I was being this stupid over Rosie's misunderstanding. My self-respect was down the drain and it had taken my self-control with it. But, when I could remember my own name and possibly which country I was in, it had me searching back a lot. Going over the past. Me and Rosie. Kids. Teenagers. Adults. So much of the time thinking and acting as one person. I'd die for her and I'd always assumed she felt the same about me. Apparently not. This was a serious shock. Surely she owed it to me to let me know if the kid was mine? Or maybe she didn't owe me anything? Somehow I couldn't believe I'd done anything that bad. Maybe that's what she hated, that I was incapable of seeing my own character, my own guilt?

I stopped hanging about near their Oxfordshire house after she'd had me arrested twice. Rosie had me arrested. It felt like your Guardian Angel had suddenly turned rabid and bitten you.

Naturally, my pictures got better and better. I was losing myself in my work. Bosoms and black ties. Expensive underpants. Knickers and stockings whose cost would feed a small country for a year. Cashmere. Mink. Silk. Linen. Only the best for the idle rich. Carmine shine, sweaty hair. The usual open mouths. Flash. Flash. Snap. Snap. Famous farts and top tarts. Exclusives. Nothing but. I didn't have to sell anyone anything. They were coming to me. Not doing me much good, either. Worse than rock and roll. Easiest money in the world. Easy money. Money. Running on drugs and ego. Easing down on skunk and E. Sailing up on whizz and charlie. At least I wasn't speedballing any more. That's what I said. That's how I could tell I was sane. I only took drugs I could control.

You know how unreal it got towards the end of the Tory years. The press at least gave the impression of a decadent court falling apart in all directions. Whole files full of scandals. Political scandals. Royal scandals. Scandals of the rich, famous and famous-for-being-scandalous. Rome in her collapse. Bread and circuses. The end of a world. And I was there to prove it.

There wasn't a cabinet minister I hadn't caught somewhere doing something rotten, if it was only kicking a neighbour's dog. There wasn't an irresponsible man or woman in responsible office I hadn't snapped enjoying a holiday at someone else's expense, or with someone else's spouse, or doing something perfectly innocent but that was *presumed* to be niffy. Because this was a very dead establishment. And having been too lazy to vote it out, we now had to chase it out. Not that the potential replacement looked very promising, even when shined up a bit with Thatcher-polish. All the lather and none of the soap. Say what you like about Fox the Younger or the Iron Duke or Benjamin Disraeli or even bloody old Abraham Lincoln or Woodrow Wilson, they had their own ideas and wrote them in their own language for their own public. Universal management-speak sounds efficient in the abstract. In reality it's about as useful as Scientology-speak or Baptist-speak. It doesn't work very well in politics, either. They offer us neat grids, to help us understand the chaos of the real world. So what happens when the grid doesn't fit the reality? Well, obviously, there's something wrong with the reality. Off we go, Yankee Joe. We borrow the language, we start thinking the thoughts.

And you know how hard and irritating it is for journos like me when it's my flashbulbs paying for their Christmas trees. People have always protected their power with piety and appeals to common decency, as if their public fictions were just ordinary. As if they weren't deeply involved in power politics. As if it wasn't the public's money buying the bricks in the walls these heroes throw up at the first swelling of their self-important heads. I pointed that out in court two or three times. The jury liked it, but they didn't like me much. So I was done anyway.

The papers always cracked the hike. You never paid your own fines in those days. There was a general understanding that it was in the public interest for people like me to claw down the rotten fabric and prepare for the new. We might have guessed the new was going to be the old fabric patched up, rather than the fresh-spun cloth we'd been promised, but there you go, that's us, the public, for you. Admiring the Emperor's new clothes again. All went by in a toney blur. Moments of optimism. Moments of fear. This year's twist of Essex fash. I could give them what they wanted. An instinct for crap. I could do it in my sleep. Yet all great Neptune's mighty waters weren't getting my hands very clean and I had a feeling that for every time someone slapped my back at the *Graphic*, Rosie lost a little more respect for me, was pushed a little further away.

No action without a reaction. I seemed determined to prove her right in everything she'd said about me. I was a creep. A bullshitter. I was getting slimier by the day.

Of course she'd been one of the main people to put me on the road to Slugsville. She'd set me up in contacts for years. I had more runners than the two-thirty at Aintree. I couldn't have got half the shots I got without Rosie's initial help. And Barbi was still slipping me the dope as, occasionally, was Tubby.

Twice since I'd gone up to the Mill and been turned away with the same words. He couldn't even be bothered to come to the door.

Evidently Tubby didn't trust me any longer. Who could blame him? He probably didn't like who I was hanging out with. Even though I'd tried to explain to him what I thought I was doing, he wasn't buying it. He was losing weight and didn't care. The few times I saw him he was always with Flicky Jellinek. He didn't seem to have other lady friends any more and there was something about Tubby being part of a couple that excluded me even further. Not that he was admitting anything. He described Flicky as 'an associate' once. I started to get suspicious and realized that now I was beginning to look on one of my oldest, soundest mates as potential foto-fodder. I gave that one up as soon as I sniffed it, but I didn't like myself any better for having the impulse in the first place. Hang around the Grand Consumer and you get increasingly predatory. Yet I did feel there was something worth nosing out at the Mill. Not necessarily anything against Tubby, but just discovering what his real twists were.

The Mill looked spiffier than it had done since 1800. With those white sails spinning on a wet and windy day you could imagine how it had been in its mighty prime, when it was the finest piece of cutting-edge technology around. A capacity that could produce flour faster and cheaper than at any time in history.

Those sails made a lot of noise, turning the squeaking reluctant machinery, swish, swish, swish. Screech, grumble, yelp. Sometimes the velocity of the sails made the whole place shake and groan, like a spaceship taking off. It had a slightly disturbing atmosphere. There was a bad story attached to it now. No skinhead would go near it. But there was something else mysterious about the place. Something going on. Did Barbican still threaten it? Or was it secretly under Barbican's control? Was Tubby now merely the custodian? Did Barbican own it without Tubby knowing? Did Tubby know but wasn't letting Barbi know? That's the sort of thought I tended to get at that time. You can say it was unlike me, but almost everything I was doing was unlike me. So what was like me? Not a lot. I was doing things I would have sneered at a year ago. I was full of self-disgust, but I was also full of disgust for pretty much the rest of the world, too.

Blind man, walkin' across America.

Music was always a comfort. I started staying at home when we weren't rehearsing. I'd sit and listen to Guthrie and Leadbelly and the others, as if a return to my musical roots would also provide a clue to where I'd gone wrong with Rosie.

Bring up your little fifth string, there, and put her in the right gear. That's nice. Okay, boys, let's go. Doc Watson. He was on one of Martin Stone's old albums. Martin told me that by way of an intro for his fiddle playing Doc'd tell you he's going to do 'Three nicks and a noo' or a 'Nick, nick, noo'. *I'd rather drink muddy water from an old Oklahoma bog, than go down to Texas and be treated like a dirty dog. There once was a Philadelphia Lawyer, in love with a Hollywood Maid. If you ain't got that do-re-mi, pard, you'd better go back to beautiful Texas, Oklahoma, Georgia, Tennessee* . . . Did you know both Woody Guthrie and Duke Ellington were professional sign painters? One of the things those two disagreed on was the race issue. Duke didn't think coloured folks were ready for freedom yet. *Many a lesson I have learned, in those Oklahoma hills where I was born.* Angry songs become half-remembered riffs. All that spilled blood. *Take The A-Train. Goodnight, Irene. Ludlow Miners' Strike.* All that history. Forget it. It messes up the pitch.

This was the beginning of a bizarre miracle.

Rosie arrived. At last. Everything I'd been waiting for. And I still couldn't approach her. I'm not sure I would have recognized her. She'd insisted on wearing the costume she planned to wear on the night. She still wouldn't talk to me. In her mask and all-engulfing gown of peacock feathers, fancy pheasant and ostrich feathers, all kinds of feathers, she could have been a Mexican goddess. It was her, all right. You couldn't mistake her profile, even in the shadow of that curved beak. She was wearing more make-up than Barbican. She talked to everyone else perfectly civilly, but somehow she managed to exclude me without them really understanding what was going on. Why should they understand? She wasn't their twin.

Or ex-twin.

Not that she bore a strong resemblance to a human being, at that time. She was initially just going to do one number with us, the *Hawk Mother* song, Calvert's fierce poem of maternal love, which he had originally thought of for Hawkwind's *Earth Ritual* but eventually did with us. He'd never recorded it in a studio, just on his creaking old TEAC. He'd used some Max Ernst picture for his inspiration.

So we started off a bit hesitantly. Calvert hadn't left any sort of real demo, just rehearsal tapes. We'd fleshed the song out and scored it from those recordings. You couldn't deny his talent, but his methods were bloody awful. You had to second-guess what he was doing on the tapes. I was afraid it was going to be a total disaster, but Rosie, disguised in her glaring painted leather mask, bristling with vivid quills, her flowing feathery gown of a million colours, her basalt eyes and dark, cruel lips, gave it attack and reality. I was very surprised at how good she was. She had to have been rehearsing the song for months. Maybe not. She just could be one of those talents which only really perform well in character. Playing a part, they're perfectly unselfconscious. Whatever part it was, she was playing wonderfully against Paul's spareness. They made a great contrast, her in her feathery splendour and him in his tight blue shirt and jeans, sneakers, Mr Clean-cut as always. He couldn't help himself. But then, neither could Rosie. She was coming on like a pro. Putting her whole body into the music. Prancing like a triumphant Fury. Dancing the way she normally only danced at home. I'd never have believed it. Only Siouxsie Sue at her best could match her.

Her voice, as thoroughly disguised as her face, brought the song in with amazing assurance. Barbi was beaming at her. Like I always knew you could do it. Had the disguise been his idea? I couldn't credit him with a good, simple, sensitive solution. It was a definite winner, though. But we were still lacking something. A certain substance was needed to complement Rosie, to make the song as good as it could be.

I said this afterwards, getting so close to Rosie I could feel her heat. But she brushed me off somehow. Barbi was impatient. 'Don't worry, Den. We need Tubby. He'll be here tomorrow. There was no point in his turning up today.'

What?

Either he'd had a Tubby made or Tubby had been rewired in Barbi's cloning studio. It wouldn't happen. This was another example of Barbican's decreasing grip on reality. He was really getting odd, losing his judgement in little things, hesitating. He was nothing like as confident as he had been all his life. Weird. But maybe I was just seeing a private side of the Grand Consumer. A softer side. The side Rosie saw.

'Well.' I paused as Rosie disappeared across the floor and out of the main doors. She managed to offer a friendly wave to everyone except me. 'We need a live drummer, that's for sure.'

Maybe Tubby was going to send us some ace up-and-comer he knew?

I tried to phone him that night, but I got his answering machine. It didn't say anything about open houses any more. It didn't say when he was likely to call me back. It was courteous, but clear. Tubby didn't want to be bothered.

I did a couple of jobs at the New Crystal Palace and snapped the rising Dome, the London Tit. More land was in the process of being cleared. Not that you could clear much of that mephitic aura away. This was the bit of swamp even Londoners hadn't wanted to build on. The NCP had become South London's biggest club. It even brought the international wankerati across the river. Impressive rep.

Fromental dropped in with his suitcase. He made a phone call, looked disappointed, then asked me if he could stay a couple of nights. He had already published a few of the Morn pictures in the French papers, mostly of French bureaucrats. The French forgave their ministers' mistresses but weren't too happy about them dressing up in baby clothes and getting spanked. Everything they feared about the Anglo-Saxon influence. The pix were receiving a lot of attention. Fromental claimed to have brought down the bastard who had set the Rwanda policy into motion. It had been his main object.

The guy had shot himself. You can always rely on a good conservative to take the conventional route. Just the Lodge costume had lost him his credibility. The robes and the hoods, the Maltese crosses, though traditional, looked too much like the KKK. The other French guy promised he wasn't a fascist, that the KTO was a Lodge with no religious or political affiliation. He didn't resign for that. It tipped his career over the edge, though.

Fromental was jubilant. The British and American KTO members hadn't started appearing in the papers, yet, but they had an idea the French pictures were part of a larger series in which they were almost bound to feature.

'You planning to blackmail these bastards into something? Confessions?'

'They don't even know it's me,' he said smugly. 'They only know it's payback time.' He was just sitting in his rocking chair and every so often giving the fire a poke. 'The stuff could be coming from anywhere.' Most European governments had representatives who had accepted Sir Hornsey Pilbeam's hospitality. Now that hospitality was looking a lot less generous. I wasn't the only one to make the Cliveden comparison. A few others went back to the Christine Keeler story. There must be quite a few sweating famous faces at the moment. As usual, the whole of the Belgian cabinet was involved. The rest of the KTO and guests were fairly evenly divided between church, government and business. The odd minor tyrant. Pinochet. Some Nigerian generals. Not too many members of the press, though some. Rupie Moloch himself, looking joyless as usual. Enough to make you laugh but not enough to ruin him.

'There was a lot more on the videos,' said Fromental. 'He must have had hidden cameras all over the fucking place. And the means of beaming it around the world. Pretty good, eh, man? Why should Satan have all the best songs? Pity you never went, Dennis, when you had the chance.'

But I was relieved. Who knows what temptations Pilbeam would have put my way if I'd accepted that invite to Morn all those years ago? I'd been saved by luck and lust rather than good judgement.

Fromental remained obsessed with Pilbeam himself. 'He's covered up all traces of his previous activities. Oh, there's a perfectly ordinary biography. Working-class, from Mossthorne in Yorkshire. Starts a little spare-parts business in the 1960s, mostly electricals. Gradually builds business. Harry Pilbeam. Becomes Harvey Pilbeam. Big contribution to Tory party funds. Then Harvey Pilbeam, OBE. Then Sir Hornsey Pilbeam. Sudden retirement to Morn. Expands business, mostly into Africa. Still basic automobile parts, particularly lights and electrics. Builds factories all over Africa. Local skills. Local everything. Everybody liked him as a business associate. Nobody really knew him as a friend. He could have been a saint or a demon, man, but I don't know. He's left me the goods on all his colleagues and less than nothing on his own life.'

'Maybe he's dead?'

Fromental moved his shoulders in an uncomfortable shrug. 'Maybe, man. Maybe he never existed.'

'You told me you'd found all those papers. Birth certificate. Deed poll stuff.'

'Well, he seems a bit of a split personality, man, that's all I can say. I don't know. From provincial businessman to eccentric recluse in one easy step. What happened to him? Was he possessed? It's almost a ghost story, you know, man?'

'There's too many fucking dead souls coming back to life these days,' I said.

I wondered if Barbican was getting nervous.

With that in mind, I arrived at the Cage early next time. I wanted to talk to Barbican about it, just to see what his reaction would be.

'Oh, if that's the best they've got,' he said. 'It all happened years ago. Nothing for us to worry about.' He thought I'd been down there with him. It was amazing how often I'd been around in his memories. It made me feel really important. Like a favourite slave. Or an ex-wife. Dead souls, eh?

I clocked the drum kit. It was familiar. But I didn't put it together until Tubby arrived and waved at me with his walking stick. Tubby? He was wearing a Crombie overcoat, dark green scarf and deerstalker. He wasn't that tubby any more. His clothes hung on him.

I was astonished, but I kept my face. 'You been getting to the gym a lot, Tub?'

'I've missed your cooking, Den.' His hair was dyed in an Elvis flop. He looked handsome but awful. A shadow. The loose clothes emphasized his appearance. He was almost clownish. I think he was wearing make-up, too. Pagliacci with a set of drums, including the Burundi tom-toms he had got on that trip with Ginger Baker. I started to say something, but he winked and walked away. 'Don't ask—'

He went over to the kit, stripping off his street clothes. Dropping his coat behind him, he picked up his sticks and started. His body and arms went through familiar movements – snaps, bounces, rolls, runs, raps, brushes – cymbal runs, bass drum harmonics. There weren't many better than Tubby, so even his casual practice rolls sounded better than most people's best. I can't say it felt bad to hear them.

It's raining, raining in my heart . . .

Rosie turned up in full costume as usual. She was with Paul Frame. Nobody seemed surprised to see Tubby. What could I do? I played the guitar.

We ran through *Hawk Mother* and it was getting very tasty, but a lot of my attention was still on Tubby. Why the fuck was he sitting here jamming with the man he regarded not only as his own greatest enemy but as the Antichrist incarnate?

There was no doubt, once he started, that his drums had been what we'd needed. It felt very good. Not one of us had to speak. We were there. All we did was *Hawk Mother* that night. Even Barbican's gimpy guitar couldn't spoil it. He seemed the most satisfied. Then he called the session to a sudden end and said he was sorry but he needed a word about something else with Rose and Paul. A Three Saints communing thing, I said, when I left with Tubby. He offered to give me a lift in the taxi he'd ordered. Brookgate was on his way, he said. He sat back in his seat. He wound down the window. It was raining slightly.

'What on earth are you doing, Tub? You swore you'd never deal with Barbican again. I mean, he put those skinheads on to you.'

He snuggled into his coat and wouldn't meet my eye. Had he got cancer? AIDS? 'Barbican talked me into it. We're all having to dance about a bit in the face of inevitable progress, aren't we, Den?'

'Me, I got tricked into this. Well, partly. But you didn't need to do it at all. Did you?'

'Well, partly.' His humour came back for a moment. His face was loose skin. He looked like a suicidal bloodhound. 'So I'm partly finessed into it, one way or another. I need some time, Den. The pressure's temporarily off if I do this. So I buy time with my body and talent, but not the Mill and not my soul. It's the best I can do. But we're still heading in the same direction. Does that make sense?'

'A bit. I'm not judging you, Tub. I'm just confused.'

'And so you should be, Den.' He grinned and patted at my knee.

'That was exhausting.' He fell back as the taxi turned up Tower Hill.

We didn't say much more until we got to Holborn and Gray's Inn Road. I climbed out, waving a fiver at him. He waved it away. 'See you tomorrow,' he said.

But I took a few days off. I couldn't stand any more of it.

Was it me, or was the world going through one of its quick changes? The conscious and the unconscious swapping places?

I went to bed. I told everyone I had flu. I watched the telly. When a story came on about ultra-rich billionaire Barbican Begg, 'whose eccentricities rival those of the great Howard Hughes', I started looking for the remote. He'd lit up a spliff at a big Savoy charity do. In aid of the NSPCC, I think. With a few minor crowned heads about, the Michaels of Kent and so on. Most of the guests wouldn't have known what a reefer smelled like. If Barbi had rolled his own, it had probably fallen apart after he'd taken a couple of drags. But I think it was his unrepentant surprise at their dismay that really worked them up. I didn't hear any more. I'd managed to find an old Alan Ladd movie.

I heard the odd snatch of the story as I surfed through my days off. Barbican surrounded by flunkeys giving a press conference outside some building. They seemed to be dragging in a lot of other, mostly unrelated, anecdotes. Did he approve of moves to legalize pot? Did his FamCo plantations in South America and Asia grow the stuff? A fulsome apology to all concerned was duly published. Along with a statement about it being a herbal cigarette, but someone had misunderstood and he'd gone along with the joke. A couple of million for the abused kiddies. Happy endings. Story over.

Then, quietly, some writs started settling and silencing. Barbican Begg was now too well established a character to disappear completely from public interest. By the time I was going out again, I saw the tabloid headlines. The Lord of the World wasn't exactly getting a bollocking. But he probably thought he was popular for the wrong reasons. He'd become a Toking Tycoon. A Coke-Sniffing King of the Market. A loose-living, easygoing open pocket, financing half the world's charities. A reefer-puffing high-roller. A billionaire playboy philanthropist. A lad's lad. A man of the people, with the tastes of the people. A drug-crazed rock-and-roll pervert. A Betty Forded clean-up kid, ready to preach the appropriate pieties. A lonely monk. A lucky bastard. It depended which tabloid you believed. Most were benign. He owned a couple of them. Between them, the media had him playing more characters than Peter Sellers. There were plenty of strands to follow. Plenty of interest in the rich and powerful. Were the Three Saints breaking up? Was Rosie having an affair? Was Barbican gay? I had a feeling that Barbi's counter-PR hadn't really started yet.

Still, from being more or less unknown to the general public, Barbican had quickly become a hero of his times, a key character of the *People* and *Hello* long-running soaps. Everything he said and did was of interest to the public. They were ready to love him. They didn't want us to pry too deeply. They didn't want shots of Lady Thatcher actually giving Willie Whitelaw the famous blow job and they didn't want to see Barbican slipping the needle into his own veins. If he took drugs, people preferred to see him as their victim, as wrestling with a problem. Putting on a brave front.

Generally, the public prefer to make up their own stories when it comes to speculating about those private public lives. They want you to supply them them some verification of what they'd do, if they could. So, unless the character is being kicked off the series, you go easy on the spike marks. Bring up some extra sex instead. Barbican Beats Coke Habit. My struggle with drugs. Barbi Fears Rose Will Leave Him.

Billionaire tycoon warns of drug use. Billionaire tycoon safely one of us again. And suitably heroic. The public wants enough innuendo, enough information to start their own private fantasies running. The public ascribed the motives and determined much of the plot. Readers described incidents and people as if they knew them personally. *National Enquirer* to the *Daily Star*. Supermarket to shining supermarket. That's when you know you've arrived.

The bedsheets weren't much better. Some reckoned his exploits upset the market, others said he gave it a boost. There was some iffy stuff hinted at in Southern Asia, but there was always iffy stuff hinted at there. In the financial pages they speculated on power, not personalities, and Barbi's image was translated into market confidence and market panic. But that image remained essentially a private Barbi, forever obsessed with his businesses, his authority, his ownership.

Via the red-tops, however, our public Barbi felt remorse, pain, horror, physical danger and bliss. The people were doing his living for him. He expressed and experienced more emotion than his real-life circuits could ever carry. Men speculated on who they'd fuck if they were him. Women speculated on how they would fuck him. If he had ever known real love before. He couldn't lose. He was the next President of the United States. He was the Prince of the Morning. He was, they insisted, a latter-day saint.

When I next turned up at the Cage, Barbi wasn't looking like much of a hero of our times. He and Paul Frame had evidently had some kind of fight. Rosie was as self-contained as always. But they were getting the treatment I was used to. What I wasn't used to was seeing the Three Saints at odds. I looked to Tubby for an answer but he was concentrating on his rimshots. Nothing said. Lots of atmosphere, though. As usual, I went straight to the Epiphone and started tuning it. What the fuck was all this about?

Tubby stopped his rimshots and that was that. Nobody else got anything going.

Paul Frame and Rosie suddenly started leaving. Barbican turned to me.

'Den. We need to talk. I'll phone you. I've got to go across the road.' He meant his company offices. 'Let yourselves out, yes?'

I stayed behind with Tubby and did a few bits of fancy rhythm stuff but the depression wouldn't lift.

'What the fuck's that all about?' I asked Tubby.

Tubby shrugged. He started putting on his coat. 'Something in the papers, I think. Who knows with that bastard? He's all over the place. Rosie's trying to stop him doing so much dope. He must be getting through an ounce a day.'

'We're helping him,' I said.

'Not that much. Not even you, Den. Up like a rocket and down like the stick, Barbi. It makes me nervous. He could do something drastic. He could set Jocky on me again.'

But Jocky was still enjoying the sun. He'd briefly been at the Cage, I heard. Barbican wouldn't talk about it. He said everything was sorted. Jocky had only come back for a day or so, then he'd had to go to Australia, and now he was in Fiji somewhere, checking out the BBIC summer-vacation facilities. They had a booming business in bad-boy camps. Half their clients arrived in handcuffs. It was, Jocky had told me, a good basic money-spinner, an extension of the booming US private prison business, but with fewer petty restrictions. They'd been sensible to get in early.

'Crime's an important part of our expansion,' Jocky had told me a couple of years before. If that swine had had only a flash of irony, a touch of self-mockery, I could have taken to him better.

This time I picked the territory. Barbi didn't like it. When he phoned next morning I told him I'd see him in Turpin's. He said he was under doctor's orders. He could only have a light salad and some table water. I didn't care what he ate. I was getting sick of being summoned.

Turpin's at lunchtime was better lit but had worse food. I ordered some worms but they weren't hot enough. There was some argy-bargy with the waiters and then Barbican said he didn't have much time. He wanted some advice.

It turned out that one of his guys on the *Independent* had spotted a possible pic they were planning to use if they could get their story right with the lawyers. 'It allegedly shows me in a KTO costume, taking part in some silly ceremony. Fun at the time. Nothing serious, but it's embarrassing. And the press is making too much of the KTO. It was just an informal way of getting to know people. Business schmoozing. Dressing up. Like a charade. Well, I've got someone working on that. One way or another I shouldn't have much more trouble. I'm really getting sick of the press, Den. We all are. What are we going to do about it?'

I couldn't help him. I'd only caught the headlines by mistake. I read comics and watched old movies, me. I said words that I never thought would come out of my mouth. I said he should be all right. If he hadn't done anything stupid, he didn't have anything to worry about.

'Oh, come on, Den. Everyone's done something stupid at some time. Haven't you? Get human. There's a limit, a line in the sand. We all know where we should draw it, really. What public good is served by this kind of invasion of privacy?'

Maybe it emphasized the discrepancies, I said. Between the kind of freedom he enjoyed and the kind of freedom available to the average citizen. Who'd said that Fourth Estate was democracy's strongest card?

He wasn't happy with that. 'Well, anything can be interpreted,' he said. 'Can't you sniff around the Wharf for a bit? Talk to a couple of people?'

'Sure,' I said. Anything for an old mate. A fellow musician.

I didn't get to the Wharf that day. Instead I went to Forbidden Planet and bought a fresh batch of comics.

Whatever was going wrong for him in the real world, Barbican was getting a lot more confident as our rehearsals continued. Rosie seemed to be feeding his ego in some weird way. He didn't defer to us quite like he had at first. He couldn't help himself. Taking over was all he understood. With us, too, he'd become the Boss. Now he was Bruce bloody Springsteen. Coming to the front. Strutting his stuff. Stomping his fuzz. Born in the USA.

I felt relieved. The aggression that had won him several empires was what I liked to see in him. It's what I had some idea about. The gentler Barbi was perfect for *People*, but lousy for *Last Merry-Go-Round*. He started to slam out those chords. Not very accurately, but they began to get a bit of power. We encouraged him, where we could. Where he got in the way, we just turned him down. It's an old band trick. Let the bastard do what he likes. Just fix it so no one else can hear him. Mix him out. Make sure he gets plenty of him in his cans or his monitors.

In spite of my advice, Barbi carried on his campaign. When the world returned to some sort of focus I read in the *Guardian* how BBIC had taken out a writ against Graphic Developments for alleged outstanding debts. GD, who were Fromental's UK processors, had had their stock seized in a kiddy-porn raid. It all fell apart, of course, in twenty-four hours. The police apologized and gave the stock back. But somehow the important negatives weren't there. GD didn't feel very good about that. They came out of it effectively silenced, because if they talked of missing negatives everyone would know what to think. I couldn't believe Jocky was on holiday. These were his trademarks. Barbi must have a lot of Jockys, though, making sure all the races came out with the right result. Bought them second-hand off Moloch.

To me it seemed a crude, poorly planned strategy, lacking Barbi's usual finesse. He normally only used Jocky for the less legal side of things. But it worked, I suppose. Everyone in England shut up for a while. Caused a bit of a stink, like John Major's silencing of the *New Statesman*. Also forgotten in a week. Speech is free. Publishing it costs a bomb.

I didn't give a damn whether a few old pix of Barbi in his socks and suspenders or got up to look like an extra in *Birth of a Nation* were published or not. I'd stopped getting serious about the world and while he may have been embarrassed, he was powerful enough to ride any problem, except possibly paedophilia or murder. By and large tycoons, owning as much media as they do, aren't as answerable as politicans. Only Captain Maxwell never made it to that safe place above the law, those heavenly Cayman Islands. The others learned from his experience. I wonder if Maxwell wanted to be the Frank Sinatra or Tony Bennett of the billionaire community. Was Maxwell up on deck singing into an air-mike the night he went over the side? *I did it my glub* . . . Maybe his generation fantasized about being crooners, rather than guitar heroes. Karaoke captains of industry? Air-guitar aces of the Stock Exchange in battle with the Bjorks of the Board Room. Rock that currency. Roll that stock.

Next rehearsal Barbi arrives engulfed in a kind of weird leather jumpsuit that he says he's going to wear for the big gig. It's like a spacesuit with neon trimmings. Tubby and I believe he's worrying about his weight and how to disguise it. We tell him it looks great.

That night we got a bit more ambitious. We did *Granny Junk* and *Sniff Her All Up* until Barbican got unhappy and reminded us that this *was* a rednose for drug rehab. He'd got Tower Records to sponsor the whole thing and they'd been a bit unsure about the band's name and old rep in the first place. United Artists were going to reissue our backlist albums to coincide with the gig and all profits would go to DrugFree, the private rehab chain. I wasn't entirely sure why our profits would go to a profitable private company but the public didn't complain and only NuLabor were initially piping on about debasing one of London's best-known heritage sites, before they realized that the idea was too popular to have principles about. At this stage the public was about to fall in love with NuLabor. The moodiest, most socially aware rock-and-roll bands were on their side. 'We don't have to give them much, pards,' says Barbi persuasively. 'But ease up a little on the drug references, OK?' Even these pieties didn't bring us down. We changed the words and kept the music.

After that we hit a bit of a low, though the people who dropped in on us didn't notice. Tubby and I were fascinated by how Barbican charmed people. It's something I've always clocked. People are forever telling you how 'charming' some tyrant or political rabble-rouser or nasty journalist is in person. It never surprises me. Hitler was charming in person. Some ladies thought his attentions were a bit creepy, but generally they loved him. Half of his early funding came from them. People don't get that power without some sort of charm, unless they're born with it. From our distance, we watched Barbi making friends and influencing people. After that little attack in the HoC we were suddenly visited by people granted special privileges to hear us rehearsing. Barbi asked us not to play anything too heavy. We had a whole bunch of NuLabor politicians, a couple of significant Tory backbenchers, some business people, but not press. Barbi knew when to bring in the press and how to handle them. For a while Tony Blair was a regular visitor at the Cage. He was probably more interested in the Begg billions than the Begg fantasy rock band, but he brought down a bunch of cabinet ministers in waiting. Gordon Brown kept saying 'gruel' or 'cruel' or 'cool', we weren't sure. His grin was fixed, enigmatic. Peter Mandelson was very keen and Tony was showing so well in the opinion polls he was glowing with glorious self-confidence. He was very encouraging. He already had hopes for us, a promise that one day we might also be him. He told Barbican how he'd had his own band at university, how he'd been a huge Deep Fix fan since he was a student. How, if we ever needed another member, he might give up leadership of the Labour Party. But maybe he should do what he knew best. This country certainly needed a 'deep fix' if it was to get back on the right road again.

Rock on, Tony, says the NME.

That faded away after a while.

And then we started doing *The Brothel in Rosenstrasse*, with Rosie singing the words rather than me or Calvert. And suddenly the song was working in a way it had never worked before. Rosie started to give it a sort of Marlene Dietrich treatment. She got husky. She started to slink. It was magic.

Frau Schmetterling says – that all her girls are ladies,
She won't hand out keys – to anyone who's shady . . .

Her lips brushed the mike. Something happened in the depths of the monitors. It got serious. It got sexy.

We were all into it, even Barbican, who was patting out the basic chords, that clean, complex sound we'd inherited from Pavli, lots of cross-rhythms, tekno-romantik. And then suddenly, out of nowhere, like that Saturday under the motorway years ago, when I'd met Julie, it took me over. My body filled up with something I hadn't felt in years. Not really. Not like this. Oh, no!

It was ecstasy.

It was lust.

And it was lust for Rosie.

I looked at her dancing in front of me and I stopped breathing.

I couldn't stand it for long. I almost felt sick. This was really too much. It's like God was delivering St Anthony's and Job's burdens at the same time. I didn't want to feel any more than I felt already. I was already feeling too much.

It's all in good taste, you musn't seem a waster or a scoundrel . . .

Barbican was getting excited, I could tell, while Paul Frame, who was doing the bass part, and Tubby were picking up a fresh vibe. We began to work together in a new way. Even better than the best of times. And all around Rosie. All around this incredible performance as she strutted and slunk about on the little stage. Around her voice and my guitar, because there was no doubt that that was the dialogue that was running and it was what you had to follow.

The Brothel in Rosenstrasse. All our girls are clean and game.
The Brothel in Rosenstrasse. You don't have to give your right name.

It was like my central nervous system was wired up to my guitar and my guitar was wired up to my id. Closed-circuit sensitivity. I was shaking with the power. I was the power. I was ALIVE!

Oi-wowo-oi-oi . . .

Fingers, lips and tongue. A million senses in unison. A total experience. The old druggy eldorado.

Don't speak of despair or anything that's seedy,
Please don't admit you're cynical and greedy . . .

You could tell from Barbican's expression – his closed eyes, the way he was shaking his head, the way his nostrils were flaring – that he was getting everything he wanted. The old buzz. The old smell. The old sweat. The old underpants. I could almost see the stain in his crotch.

Your manner's refined, your role's clearly defined . . .

Rosie, of course, remained totally enigmatic. She was freaking Paul a bit as she strode and gestured and smiled with those black, harsh lips.

At first I couldn't believe she was looking at me like that. Her eyes staring directly into mine. Making more contact than she'd made in months. I made an almost tentative response. And she gave me my answer. As if all the emotion between us, all the love and all the attraction that we had refused to acknowledge, was coming out in that one strange number. Because there was a kind of hatred in it, too. It was carrying everything. I was completely absorbed. Only Tubby seemed to have some real idea of what was going on. The others just thought we'd hit a good moment.

If an audience had seen us then, they'd have said that Rosie and I had something going. This was that particular chemistry you only occasionally got on the rock-and-roll stage.

The Brothel in Rosenstrasse. All our girls are keen to please.
The Brothel in Rosenstrasse. At reasonable fees.

What the fuck was all this? Oh, oh, oh! Ho, ho, ho!

I was even more in its grip than I had been when I was doing that gig with Martin, Nick Lowe and the others. Because this object of my affections was singing back. Singing as well as anyone could. And she was dancing.

At the beginning we'd felt a lack, even with Tubby's wicked drumming. Not enough cross-rhythms. Paul couldn't do it. We really needed Charnock or Pavli on bass. Then, degree by degree, Rosie began to supply the missing rhythms with her increasingly assured dancing. This was how it always should have been. How we all wanted it.

I looked into her hard, hawkmother eyes and I saw a terrifying promise that had no memory of our old relationship. She looked at me as if I were prey. There were questions in every bend of every note I sent her, but there were no answers, just statements.

Please don't speak of despair or anything that's seedy,
Please don't admit you're cynical and greedy.

I'd looked over to Tubby, who was keeping us all together, refusing to take his attention off the job in hand. As usual, he refused to meet my eye. He lifted his arms and brought the sticks down suddenly, finally.

And then it was over. Rosie stopped. Done. Good rehearsal. Thanks, everyone. Back to being Dennis's personal icebox. I started to approach her but then suddenly the three of them, Paul, Barbican, Rosie, were back in a private Three Saints Big Hug situation and Tubby was winking at me as he left.

I hesitated, meaning to follow him.

'Not now, mate,' he said.

So I stood there like a fool for a few minutes and then I went home. I could hardly walk. I was shaking all over.

I didn't go back to the Cage for a while. I wasn't going until I had some of this sorted out in my head. I said. I got some work from *Poke*, that gents' lifestyle 'zine.

I had a whirlwind three nights in the Adriatic. Four famous film stars, three dodgy Members of Parliament, two company directors (together), two cabinet ministers (separate) and a Welsh councillor who had recently declared bankruptcy and put up his terraced house as his only asset but who seemed to be the maestro of a nice little Turkish hacienda with an unpolluted view of the sea. Owens Pasha got me a lot of mileage. Then some Turkish heavy told me he had a message for me and I didn't bother to ask what it was. I went back to Paris and tried to find old friends, old flames, without much luck.

It was nearly a week before I could risk another rehearsal. Barbi and Paul were glad to see me.

Barbi had put on weight. He seemed to be making an attempt to hide it with a little discreet make-up. 'We needed you, man. We got our bass player promised, but it still isn't sparking. You're the only one can work the Epiphone.'

I took it as flattery.

'Just in the nick of time,' said Tubby from his chair. 'We've only five days to go before our first gig.'

'Gig? What, Tower Bridge?' I was settling the strap of the Bird while the Three Saints went back to huddling around some coffee, like US footballers deciding a game plan. *Dream, dream, dream* . . . Fingers settling in the old riffs, the old snatches of melody. The stuff you wanted so desperately to play when you were twelve. Playing through your past, your career. *Isn't it delicious?* Tubby wouldn't look at me.

'*What gig, Tub?*'

Tubby was grinning like Jaws. 'Pre-publicity. An HBO tape. Stuff like that. Anyway, we're doing it down The Whisky Twist.' This dead man laughing at me.

'The what?'

'The old Limbo.'

Oh, fuck. Even if the crowd all fucked off they'd leave enough BO behind to applaud us. 'Does Barbi own that, too?'

'I'd guess he would. Wouldn't you?' Tubby leaned down to sort out his sweat rags – torn-up St Michael's knickers – and spare sticks. 'That was a great session last time. Do some of that again. I'm really enjoying myself.' At this rate he'd return to life by the century after next.

It probably wasn't exactly enjoyment I felt. But already I could smell her, through all the other scents. I could smell her and I could almost touch her. My fingers brushed an imaginary thigh. It didn't turn me into a predatory monster. In fact, it tended to freeze me. I had no desire to control anyone or anything. I didn't want to own her, or fuck her, or anything. I just wanted to be with her. But the one time when she looked up from the huddle and her eye met mine, she was frostier than ever. It was as if all our pent-up feelings – the best and the worst of them – were going into the music, and there was nothing left for any emotion outside of that. I felt as if I had a permanent fever, unable to tell anyone what was wrong, yet constantly finding it hard to focus. Nauseated only when I wasn't playing in the band. It made me feel exhausted. Like making love on crack.

As far as the outside world was concerned, the rest of us were still the Three Saints' backing band. Has-beens brought back to life by the holy power of St Barbican, St Rosie and St Paul. It was obvious who was supplying us with our energy. Somehow the fact that Barbican had never been in the original band wasn't touched on by the publicity. The memory of the media could be relied on. It's as good as the average two-year-old's. So they can't be blamed for a few muddled facts, for relying on the press handouts, for having only the vaguest memories of what happened last year.

Again, the Bird was playing me.

We went through another blues run and did *Trouble in Mind* for a few bars.

Barbi and Co were still talking. I stopped and shouted across the room. 'What's all this about a gig, Barb?'

'Oh,' he said. He gave me a professional smile. 'It's just a pre-publicity thing. Nothing serious. Just to show them we aren't wankers. That we're proper musicians.'

'Eh?'

'It'll give our Tower gig extra authenticity, They'll know we're a real rock-and-roll band.' This was from Tubby. He glanced away before I could catch his eye.

'How many gigs, Barb?' This was outrageous. This was supposed to be a bit of fun, an amateur night out for charity, not Barbi's way of getting popular with a new public.

'A few selected London venues.'

'Well, you know me. I'll do them if there's nothing else planned.'

'You're so fucking dedicated!'

But Barbi understood his game. He'd already put some publicity out. Nothing untrue. It gave us a slightly more heroic past than I remembered. And if I didn't turn up, there would be a whole lot of stuff about it. I'd look like a creep. Or a bastard. Or a scrooge. Or a moody git. Feuds would be concocted and fiction would rule my life again. So the sooner we scotched the story in the tabloids, the better.

Easy rider, see what you done done . . .

Anyway, the whole emphasis is changing. I don't think Barbican has a notion of what's happening, but Paul has an idea and Tubby's certain. You can tell from their playing. And we all know we're getting better than we ever dreamed of being. It's bizarre. Rosie's suddenly our star, giving as good as she gets, and we're playing for her. We're not Barbican's backing band any more. We're Rosie's. And proud of it. Barbi only knows it all sounds wonderful and he's still happily convinced most of the attention is on him. And then we get our bass player.

Lemmy Kilmister turns up on my doorstep at four in the morning and he's got his Rickenbacker with him. He's come back to London to get his cowboy boots repaired and he's going to do a gig with us, he understands. The old rocker's held together with black leather. He has bolts through bits of him. He's all studs and animal skins. His face comes out of a gene-pool that was started before the dawn of time. He's full of jokes and happy contempt for almost everything. Especially if it's English. He dumps his bass and bag and is gone almost as soon as he's arrived. Scoring something somewhere. He didn't come home in the morning. I left the key where I'd told him, behind the pipe.

I saw him next at the Cage, plunking out a few new rhythms for Rosie. We'd all worked together quite a bit on various albums and he'd recorded a couple of singles with us, before either Charnock or Pavli joined. He was just what we needed. His own band was known for its basic, heavy, head-banging qualities, but Lemmy could do really subtle work when he wanted to. He formed Motorhead about the same time we formed Deep Fix, before we had a regular bass player, and he'd been on several of our early singles. I was beginning to think I'd wandered into *The Magnificent Seven: The Rock Show.* Except there were only six of us. All we needed was Yul Brynner on lead and Paul could concentrate on keyboards. Or maybe that was *The King and I.*

Anyway, Lemmy was just what we needed. He was due to go back into the studio with his own stuff just after the Tower Bridge gig, so this suited him. He was laughing after that first evening, when we went home together. 'So that's what it's like to rub shoulders with the Great White Shark. Poor little wanker. Still, it's all right to be playing again with you lot. I'm enjoying it.' He unfolded a newspaper, pulled down the seat in front of him, spread the newspaper over the seat and put his manky old white cowboy boots up. This was one of the few people the punk movement had any time for. He was one of the smartest, most eloquent people in rock and roll. And he was a gent. I remember a time when some lordy got infatuated with us and offered to put us all up at his manor house, somewhere in Yorkshire, after we'd done a Leeds gig. Apparently the lordy's housekeeper and nearest and dearest had been very chary of the country's most notorious drug band turning up. They went out for the evening. The lordy and the band came in after the gig, when only the housekeeper was up. Lemmy, of course, was all courtesy and appropriate humour, apologies for keeping her away from her well-deserved rest. We went to bed. And next morning when the household got up, he'd lit the fire, got the kettle on and was preparing the cat's breakfast. His stage persona was just a version of himself, no closer to the norm than Rosie's strange hawk-woman costume. It's what we sell of ourselves. Our fantasies. If we sell more than that, things start to get dodgy.

Barbican wasn't using make-up as a stage disguise, but he was trying to hide the bags under his eyes, the lines in his face, and he had definitely dyed his hair. Burning the candle at both ends. Too much business by day and rock and roll at night. A bit twitchy sometimes. He was beginning to look like a cartoon version of himself. I'd never seen him so blond. Did he check himself out every morning, wondering how he was going to appear on stage? The rest of us didn't give a crap about that and never had. We came from an era when signs of personal vanity could lose you too much street cred. Barbi knew that appearance was everything and was worth millions in the bank.

When Lemmy made a crack about us all needing wheelchair access to the stage if we were going to get on it, Barbican grew very serious. He said the age thing was a load of rubbish. Nobody got greylined, he said, at BBIC. Experience was what counted. Who could guess Rosie's age, for instance? She was ageless. As beautiful as ever. And we were, even the oldest of us, a good ten or fifteen years younger than the Stones, and look at them.

We knew we were old farts. But we also knew we were clever old farts. We didn't give a shit if our laughter lines were showing. Even Tubby had lost any interest in himself, apart from his hair. Paul never wore anything different, ever, than his jeans and denim shirt, and he was still very handsome. Chiselled, gaunt, self-contained and getting more like Max von Sydow with every passing day. At this rate we'd be playing chess on the beach together. I never had any problem wondering what Rosie saw in him.

The strange thing was, as the rest of us got it together, Barbican seemed to be losing it. Not the music. He was growing fairly competent, as if all the concentration and energy he'd devoted to his career was now going into his playing. He was putting on a lot of weight and seemed increasingly blocked, less and less interested in the world around him. And the newspapers were beginning to spot something too. The financial heavies started running stories referring to the 'fault lines' in the BBIC empire, the grumblings of high-level board members. I asked him if everything was all right. He insisted it was. The papers were just out to get him, he said, like they were out to get everyone in this country who had managed to make something of themselves. At one point he started to sound like Baroness Stoneybroke extolling the virtues of the ugly sisters over Cinderella, that shrill, self-righteous rising note which everyone seemed to get from her. It made people sound like Cairo pornographers explaining themselves to the police. It was aggressive, but it didn't have a lot of authority. Like Mrs Thatcher talking about our nation's historical relationship with China that she hoped to restore. I never could get that one. Must have alarmed them silly. No wonder they started clamping down on Bibles and opium. Odd how the natural racism of these people is translated into their public speeches. Clinton's African pronouncements are gems of their kind. White liberal insults, one after the other. Those American blacks must be so used to being condescended to, they think any whitey who grins at them is on their side. They loved him. They thought that guys who do drugs and fuck a lot of women are natural niggers. So did the Republicans. That's why they got so close to tarring and feathering him.

Blind man, walking across America . . .
Don't see no pain.

We seemed to slip naturally into the gig. We got down there and apart from a few bits of neon and a couple of strobes, the Limbo hadn't really changed very much. It still smelled of damp, urine, cigarettes and alcohol. That would be swamped, after a while, by the smell of the customers. I didn't feel nostalgic. I just felt a bit depressed. The famous guests started turning up, being cool, being their old selves. Everyone was being their old selves. Handshakes. Assurances of never-ending roots. David Bowie. Dave Edmunds. Patti Smith. Sugsy. Elvis Costello. People you respected. Their fame alone was enough to set the press guys buzzing and snapping. I knew what they were getting. It was irresistible.

But then it was real and we were doing it. Starting a bit cold. No nerves. Even Barbican behaved like a pro on that crowded little stage, keeping back near the dressing room door and letting Rosie to the front, me and Lemmy behind her, Tubby in the middle, Paul to his left on keyboards. And we never looked back. We gave them the best gig they'd ever heard in that tiny space. We blasted them to bits. We left them limp and grinning. We hit them with some good, solid rock and roll. And then we gave them *Brothel in Rosenstrasse*.

Combined with Barbican's publicity machine, our performance convinced almost everyone. Paul's guitar was its old, edgy self. His keyboards were sharp, dynamic. Rosie had never been better. Everyone else was better than perfect and that old Epiphone was still playing me, still playing me for Rosie. A sensation I was getting used to.

At the end of it all the faces came up and gave us their blessing. Nobody was embarrassed, but you could tell they were wondering if we'd been this good when we were going out regularly. Good as we were – and it had been Paul's and Tubby's twin talents that drove us then – we'd never been as good as this. And, of course, Barbican got a fair share of the credit.

Even the *NME* was amiable. By that time, anyway, they were supporting the Blairies and looking around for a cool millionaire or two, so they could show they weren't biased. Barbican fell into their laps. We were just what they were looking for.

DEEP FIX COME BACK ROCKING!

They put us on the front cover. It was as if Richard Branson had joined Yes. We'd arrived almost before we started. Everyone had heard of us, of course. They always had. They'd always known we were good.

We could have been any old bunch of has-beens. I think they were looking for signs of oldsters who hadn't completely sold out the seventies. Naturally, in our last two years as a band they had splashed their contempt for us all over the place. My guitar had been 'ragged' and Paul's 'mechanical'. Tubby wasn't a patch on Moon. Pavli was too pretentious. Charnock was too basic.

Now, though, we were a receipt against melancholy. We were the real thing. What the Beatles and the Who and especially Oasis had failed to be. Kept our roots. Kept our faith.

That's how big the lie was getting. And I pretended it made me laugh. Now we had all the lifestyle mags doing pieces on us. *Poking* one minute. *Poked* the next. *Poke* loved me. I was one of its own. People who were prepared to be sceptical of Barbi remarked on his excellent guitar-playing. Even famous guitar-players said they were surprised at his skill. Nobody remembered the real story. We had a better one than that.

They all talked about Rosie. They talked about Barbi. They talked about Paul. This was the Three Saints revealing their roots in popular culture. The Princess of Wales had to start coming up with some good charity stunts just to keep her place in the headline league.

We really had never been this good. Tubby was as surprised as I was. I asked him one night: had we made a deal with the devil?

'Oh, definitely,' he said.

Paul's keyboards and guitar had their old, nasty oomf. He stood there with all his authority back. Tubby lost another pound every time he did a set. Lemmy was giving it this meaty, complex bass. The Epiphone was playing me better than ever. Barbican hardly had to be turned down at all. And Rosie had transformed herself into a rock-and-roll genius. Another Annie Lennox. In that costume she insisted on wearing at all times, she was an astonishing image of glittering plumage and vivid leather. When she did *The Greenfly and the Rose* and *Lord of the Hornets* she brought things out of those songs that nobody had seen before. But even that was nothing once we hit *Brothel in Rosenstrasse*. Lemmy's long, seemingly simple bass intro, then the drums, then guitar – yow! – we were even better than our best. The number went over so well at those preliminary gigs that they wanted to bring the new version out as another fund-raiser.

So we did it as a single. The original had had *Another Quiet Day In Auschwitz* on the B-side. This time it was *The Greenfly and the Rose*, sung by the Rose herself. And played by her happy greenflies. It came out a week before the Tower Bridge gig. But I insisted that the money went to Womankind Worldwide and the Southern Poverty Law Center, not the drug-rehab clinic. Nobody objected. I hoped to see something encouraging in Rosie's eyes, but the stare was as bleak as ever. I might have been her prey. She didn't even remember that stuff any more.

I got nervous and suspicious when the single went straight to number one. Worth remarking. I wasn't used to that kind of success and it felt too easy. We did a *Top of the Pops* and a couple more MTV spots. It was the combination of everything the public loved, including a hint or two of sex. *Brothel* got banned on US radio stations. Church groups objected. Papers ran 'for or against' features. The irony was explained in *The Times* and dismissed by the *Telegraph*. A fucking pop song got more analysed than *War and Peace*. That release generated its own story, while the main story continued on. Where was the famous Brothel? What was it? Who had used it? Based on real experience, we said. A signal for them to make up their own versions. Their versions were never as complicated as the real ones. If you read the story now you'd learn how I'd been found in obscurity, reduced to the lowly status of photo-journo, until Barbican gave me a new guitar and put me on my feet again, playing in a band where I belonged. Redeemed by the household gods of Commerce. Tubby had been a recluse-financier – a kind of minor Barbican – while Calvert and Charnock, Pavli and Gilmore, White and Kumo, Lloyd Langton and Simon House – all on the old records – had vanished.

The twist now went that back in the old days, when Barbican was carefree rock'n'roller Jack Begg, Lord Barbican, his powerful uncle, had decided that Jack would inherit the Barbican fortune and its weight of responsibility. Jack had hated the idea. All he'd wanted to do was be the next Elvis – as he was already tipped to be. Alas, Lord Barbican exerted mighty pressures on Jack and his mother until they had no choice but to give in. Then, broken-hearted at Jack's making himself hostage to the City, Rosie decided to go to help the less fortunate in Africa. The Deep Fix had lost its stars and would never be the same band again. A few years later Paul, too, threw in his career to go to help the unfortunate black man. It was suggested that I had overcome a drug problem by starting afresh as a photog. Lemmy had been lured back from success in Las Vegas. Tubby's conscience had been spurred by Barbican. Now he realized it was time to give something back to the public.

It all went together fairly well.

Fate, circumstances and Barbican's determination to help drug abusers help themselves had brought us back together, making music that was better than ever. Which was the only bit of truth in the whole concoction.

And I couldn't start rocking the boat at that stage, could I? And Tubby didn't want to. For whatever reason, he sunnily agreed to whatever crap the press told him was true about him. Years of drug-rehab in a lonely, desolate house patrolled by leopards and panthers. Brought back to sanity and the light by the Three Saints.

Red-tops, rednoses, red hands.

Blind man, walkin' across America.

I suppose it's easy enough to reinvent yourself in a more popular fashion. Everyone does it these days. They lose their old personality and they come back as a Holocaust survivor, a Vietnam vet, a hippy outlaw, a cardinal. A sympathetic victim. A hero. A survivor. The business of the world is show business. Why do people grope so greedily for public approval? Why do they need it? Howard Hughes never needed it. As far as I know Zaharoff the Armaments King never hired a PR. But this new generation of world-eaters seems desperate to get elected, when they already own the party.

The older and more famous they become, the more lies they start telling about themselves. Most of these people are nerds in the first place, more interested in power, manipulation and fame than in living much of a life. It's all they've ever known. Real life at a distance. The mud sticking to the Feragamo size nines. Once they have the power, they start casting around for the best life they can buy. *Consumer World's Pick of the Lifestyles, from Modest to Totally OTT Psychedelic Rockstar . . .*

Rather than an obsessive fascination with money and power, you actually always had this real rock-and-roll person lurking away in the backbrain, wanting to do nothing but make music. Instead fate carried you into a life of rapacity and insane greed, of rationalized genocide and market-driven wars. Think of the widows and orphans who would have been so happy if Barbican had only listened to the beat of Tubby's drum.

Anyway, someone like Robbie Wilson and a member of Blur said Calvert had always been their model, while Poppy Space said ever since she was a little girl she'd been inspired by Rosie's saintly lifestyle. All this was spun into an endorsement of the current bunch of pop stars for Deep Fix. Calvert and the rest of us got a little bit of space as background characters, but basically the stories were about those authentic Rockers, The Three Saints.

You can always start a story, but you try stopping one. By the time you realize what's up, they've become official. Anything you say that's different, your own reality, becomes a matter of footnotes and of contradiction, your inclination to mythologize.

If you try to tell the true story, you're dismissed as crazy. Interviewers get impatient with you and swear they'll never have you on their programme again. Why are you making trouble for us all? What axe are you grinding? So you keep your mouth shut. That's right, boss, the sixties was all about *A Whiter Shade of Pale* and flowers and free sex and peace and love, right? And it all ended in tears, right? And the seventies was all Malcolm McLaren, Sex Pistols and outrageous punk stuff, right? And that burned itself out, right? And the eighties was the rise of disco, right? And people got miserable, right? And the nineties was trashy repro and sampling, right? Heading for the year nothing. The year of the missing memory. No music. Just one big drum. One beat. One dance. One happy song. Right?

Oh, and I got off with Poppy Space, that night, after the Limbo gig. I didn't have my old charisma back, but I was close enough to the real money to seem sexy again. The irony was that Poppy was like a quintessential airline hostess. But I wasn't getting the same buzz. She didn't want me for the old reasons, and I didn't really want her at all. As we found out.

I saw Fromental at the gig. He came down late and only heard our last three numbers and a couple of encores. He was impressed. 'You have a secret talent,' he said as he got a lift in the limo Barbi had laid on for me and Lemmy. 'But you, man, and Rosie – that's the real thing. Or seems like it. I thought you said you weren't very good friends at the moment?'

Poppy was sitting on my lap at the time. She was a stickler for the conventions.

My place was getting so filled up, I had to go to a hotel with Betty Pepper the next evening. Jenny Sage had a place of her own. They all talked the same. They were all lovely girls. But it was the same problem.

I only felt alive and sexy when I was playing those numbers. This was a rotten irony, given that Rosie believed me to be Number One to Hitler's Number Two in the world-class bastard stakes. I'd have had better luck with Princess Di.

Who was coming to the gig. Along with a couple of other minor royals, perhaps HRH Princess Margaret, Patroness of DrugFree, who hadn't cancelled. She'd been heard to complain that she herself never got any free drugs out of them. Maybe she was hoping for something on the off chance. The safety engineers had checked everything. The moored boats, on which the audience area would be set, were designed to move with the tide, to settle slowly down or up as the river rose and fell. It was a complicated operation, but they seemed to have it in hand. The audience would feel only a gentle, floaty-boaty sort of sensation, as some tosser in a striped jersey told us.

Barbi took me out to the site. There was no sign of Mr Alford or any other embarrassing witness to that earlier over-enthusiastic episode. A bloke in a yellow helmet explained things to us. Our stage would be set up directly in the middle of the bridge, with lights focused from both banks and from above. There would be a vast screen behind us, with back projection.

I got bored. We'd gone through all that stuff with the designers. How the stage would be fixed on the bridge. For safety it would be set well back from the parapet and raised so that the audience got a decent view. No chance of anyone falling in. Plenty of room for prancing about, lads, and doing your stuff. Rock and roll, eh? I used to love you when I was at school.

They told us how we'd be lit, what Dave McKean's images were going to look like on the back projection, how we'd be miked and monitored, where we'd have to stand, where we could and couldn't be seen. The screen behind us would curve, like the sail of a clipper. Sometimes it would show us larger than life. But there would be other TV screens everywhere relaying the gig. It was going to be televised worldwide. Cameras here, cameras there and there. Guys with cameras based here and here, just don't kick anyone in the head, ha, ha.

Barbican cheered his troops on. He told them that they expected to raise more money for drug rehab than any previous event. Had he got these guys to work for nothing, too?

I was still a bit unhappy about it all. To me 'drug rehab' was the other end of the drug business, a way of making even more money out of the addict. Or the kid caught with a couple of reefers who was deemed to have and be a 'problem'. Lot of business there. Especially in the States. The prison business. The legal business. The enforcement business. The shackle business. The Drug Enforcement Agency business. The Betty Ford business and all the other businesses that had mushroomed with the coming of Reagan's War on Drugs. He knew how to create a mushroom bureaucracy, that guy. Spend the most of our tax dollars. Bigotry had become an essential part of the world's economic engine. When Tubby told me to lighten up, I knew I was on my own.

After we'd made our second visit to Tower Bridge, Barbi stopped at his Morgan and apologized for not being able to give me a lift. I said I didn't mind. I felt like walking home. It wasn't that far.

He reached into the car and came out with half a bar, wrapped in a Harrods plastic bag. I could smell it. I checked to see if he was setting me up. But he'd been careful. Nobody saw us.

'What's this for?' I said.

'Our ship came in,' he said.

'You're not still dealing, you stupid bastard?'

'No. But Jocky was doing this on the side. Flying under my fucking colours, the little brute. In my yacht. Which, luckily, isn't registered here.'

'So you confiscated his stock.'

'And turned him in to the Indonesian authorities. Got the yacht back untouched.'

'Bloody hell!'

'I don't like what you said he did, Den. We're mates. Always were. You're family. Fucking Jocky's just an employee.'

'When's he coming out?'

'Whenever I say. He hasn't been sentenced yet.'

'So what's he likely to get?'

'Whatever I tell them. We have a lot of friends and partners in the Indonesian establishment.' He winked at me, pushed the block towards me and eased his somewhat corpulent self into the shrinking seat of the Morgan.

Fucking what?

I had half a mind to drop the hash where I stood and walk away from it. That's how paranoid I was getting. Instead, since my place was pretty full, Poppy never having left and Lemmy having nowhere else to stay, I went over to Maddy's and dropped it off with her to be on the safe side. She was yummily grateful. I'd come just in time, she said. That disgusting Zeta had promised absolutely he'd have some skunk for her by last Tuesday. Stay and smoke it with me for luck, darling. I said I'd try to get back later, if that was all right.

'More than all right, darling.' I was turning her on again, I could tell. 'I never realized you were such a great musician.'

'It's Rosie's dancing and a very good guitar,' I told her. But I was enjoying the flattery, even though I hadn't even seen her at the gig. She was just the artificial shot in the prenumbed arm I needed.

She was drinking strong bourbon and I didn't have time to catch up. And even she couldn't get through a half-bar in a day, which was how long I might be.

As it was, Fromental was up and wanting to talk. In a day or two he was planning to make another trip to Morn. He was selling a lot of papers on the Continent, but the UK and US weren't getting too much fallout. 'I need those movies,' he told me.

In the end I took him with me to Maddy's to collect her and the hash. But she wasn't in any condition to go out. Fromental asked me who she was. Her new million-dollar Mexican face was obviously working. I never could see much difference, except she sometimes seemed trapped behind a lifelike mask. I had managed to get my flat a little less full. I could sleep at home. I made a vague introduction and let nature take its course. I left them half the half.

Lemmy was either asleep or off somewhere, so I made it to my room, undressed and just fell out. I wasn't giving myself enough time on my own. I needed a huge amount of breathing space if I wanted to think at all.

Before I had a chance to formulate any coherent idea of what was going on, I was back in the swim again. I wasn't a superstar, but I was a star. Thanks to the power of the pound. The domination of the dollar. Even in that reflected saintly glory I was suddenly more famous than Michael Jackson. I got soft-focus photos in the glossies. Nobody doing unto me what I'd done unto others. We were enjoying a lot of free lunches and it made me uneasy. But fame makes you famous and people love your fame, so there you go. Suddenly I had more girlfriends than I could count. Just the kind I lusted after. But they liked me for the wrong reasons and my lust went away. For the first time in my life I was having trouble with Mr Wongo. They were loving me for my millions, not my lowly origins, not my imagination, not my talent. Not my stink.

It's all right, all you creditors. Don't start writing out the invoices or phoning up the writ-servers. I never had any millions. At least, not long enough to count them. I'm not twisting you. I didn't have to go down to Skerring because I'd stashed a secret fortune there . . .

Lemmy had left a *Times* in the kitchen, so I started reading it as I made myself a decent cup of tea. Stuff about our last gig. The usual tone. Some teenager talking about us as if we were the lost Beatles. BBIC being 'overvalued'. A reference to the board's increasing dissatisfaction with its 'showbusiness chairman'. Dissatisfied they may be, I thought, but no way will Barbican let one of them gain ascendancy, unless it's at his discretion. Still, it seemed he was playing a dangerous game. What would happen if he and those few others suddenly got economic cold feet? Had Barbi been so distracted by sex and drugs and rock and roll that he'd left his business interests vulnerable to attack? I found that hard to believe. Yet that appeared to be the underlying message of the story I read. Rosie would never allow it to happen. She wouldn't let him get so out of control. Would she?

Anyway, the big day, Sunday 23 June, had been hyped so much in the media that I was starting to hate us. That morning, early, me, Paul, Tubby and Lemmy did a sound check. We worked out a few bits and pieces with the roadies. It was a nice, sunny day. Crowds were already getting positioned along the banks all the way back to London Bridge. The stage actually did have wheelchair access: two sloping sides that we could, if we wished, run up and down, but they were mainly there for the convenience of the cameramen. The river on both sides, from Blackfriars to the Isle of Dogs, was tranquil. There were even anglers on the south bank below us. The tide was low and revealed the gravel and mud of the bottom. A few beached barges and a couple of light boats. Two kids mudlarking in the shallows beyond the police cordon. A bunch of gulls. The sun catching the granite and making it glint and sparkle. The high concrete bunkers lining the banks, where I'd known only slimed oak and dirty brick, gave the impression of defences, as if the city was expecting attack from the river. I looked down towards the Isle of Dogs, half hoping to see Viking longboats beating up towards us. But it was only a couple of toxic-waste barges heading down towards the estuary.

I went home. Fromental had left. He was still questing after his own rather seedy holy grail. Lemmy had gone into Soho. I was glad to have the place to myself, to sit in my underpants looking out at the graveyard and the weirdly warping church beyond. I'd no idea what materials they'd used in its cladding.

I'd be glad when the gig was over and we could all go back to normal, whatever that was. I'd had more than enough. There was no way Rosie was ever going to speak to me again and here I was behaving like a middle-aged wanker just on the off chance. And now, with the sexual buzz, I just wanted to run away and hide. Or sleep it off. Or think about it.

As soon as I could I'd return to the mindless life of a happy snapper. I'd go to parties every night and be picked up by Lacey Moloch wanting a bit of cockney oompah.

Meanwhile, one more run on the emotional roller coaster, one more night of erotic torment and I could give Barbi his guitar back and return to snapping wankers rather than being one. I'd decided I was going to try staying at Les Hivers again. I couldn't bear to be in the same country as Rosie. Especially not now. Lusting after her the way I did was almost like lusting after your own sister. I had to sort this out.

I left it until the last minute before picking up the Epiphone and going out into the street to look for a taxi to take me to Tower Bridge. Cabs weren't so easy to find on a Sunday since Fleet Street had moved to Wapping.

Barbican wasn't there when I eventually turned up. The gig was being opened by a couple of teeny acts, presumably to reassure the Princess of Wales who was already there. The TV cameras were concentrating on her. You could see her on our TV monitors. Grace personified. You could tell. I always knew when she, Princess Margaret and Salmon Rushdi turned up. About eight rows of seats were filled with security guys. They knew one another. They chatted out of the corners of their mouths while they looked around them, trying not to move their heads. They murmured laconically into mobiles and walkie-talkies. Diana was all easy smiles and quick shy hand grabs. Margaret sat as if freeze-dried, enduring something, and Rushdi seemed to be talking to himself. Prince Andrew and the Duchess of Essex (*La Belle Dame Sans Frontières*), a few more minor saints and the usual charity comedians and actors. Richard Attenborough, Glenda Jackson, Kenneth Branagh, Emma Thompson, Anthony Hopkins, John Cleese, Melvyn Bragg, Janet Street-Porter and a bunch of other media lords and ladies. No wonder the police were about a mile deep in all directions. Barbican had got a better audience than a Royal Command Performance. Not, of course, Deep Fix's normal or natural audience, as they might soon discover. Still, you couldn't say Barbi didn't get what he wanted.

There were now thousands out there. A lot of ordinary people were lining the embankments, office buildings and so on, but the entire river in front of us was this linked platform, floating on dozens of barges, on which chairs had been fixed for the great and the good, for the high-payers. The seats were filling up fast. I'd never known an audience like it. The Space Gals were already on, doing their Abba impersonations.

When I got up to the little tower they'd given us for a dressing room the Pepper Boys had just come off and were in and out of the toilet, giggling and snorting huge lines of something. I think they were getting a thrill out of doing something naughty in a public building. In their identical navy blue singlets and shaved hair, they looked like Sea Scouts having a secret smoke behind the wheelhouse. We tried a conversation, but it failed. Their references were all to Shirley Bassey and Dusty Springfield. They definitely saw us as old farts. Gordon van Gelder was going on next. Then it would be us.

Lots of time. I went over and unpacked the Epiphone just as Rosie arrived in full kit as usual. She was clearly nervous. She paced about and kept looking for things in the bag she carried. I wanted to comfort her, the way I used to. I could always calm her down when she got anxious. Then Paul turned up, tight-lipped and a bit pale, and put his arm round her. But she didn't want it. She started pacing again.

Paul was polite enough but wouldn't really look at anyone. Tubby arrived next, then Lemmy. We were all fascinated by what we could see through the windows and on the TV screens – the weird seating, the size of the audience, the way lights and sound equipment had been positioned. We could see the stage that from here looked a lot closer to the water. But there was no danger of falling off, because of the parapet.

I asked a Pepper Boy what the stage was like.

'Amazing, man. Great acoustics. You'll sound wonderful.' He was just starting to ask me if I'd known Alma Cogan personally when Paul's mobile went off and he answered it.

'Barbican's been a bit delayed, but he's on his way.'

I was surprised. I'd expected Barbi to be the first there. He was the one who wanted this, after all.

We were all tuned up, ready to go and do it. It wouldn't be any major disaster if Barbi, who was essentially a passenger, didn't make it. But I think that's what most of the posh audience was waiting for. Him and Rosie, anyway.

Barbican arrived when Gordon was on his last number, *Brussels*, which had won the Eurovision that previous year. I wasn't nervous, but Rosie still seemed agitated. Barbican was sweating. He was wearing an overcoat and carrying a case. He kept glancing towards Rosie. She seemed to be giving him the treatment I usually got. You wouldn't think one woman could generate so much ice.

Hard-hearted Hannah, the vamp of Savannah, the meanest girl in town . . .

Barbican did himself up a pair of footballers' lines, snorted them noisily without offering any to anyone else, rubbed his nose and took his case into the toilet with him.

He came out in his leathers, looking steadier though still bloated and reminding me of the Michelin Man pretending to be Meat Loaf. He looked even fatter than the last time I saw him.

Gordon was still finishing off downstairs. You could see the audience applauding him on the dressing room monitors. Then Hugh Grant came on and told everyone to stay calm: Deep Fix were on their way. I think that was the year our Jolly Englishman was caught in his famous, even more farcical scandal in LA so he was very popular with the audience. We saw Princess Di on the monitors, giving it some shy, wry handclaps. What a politician that woman was! I wasn't sure whether the applause was for him or for us.

Barbican was moving awkwardly in that weird leather spacesuit. He brought his elbows sharply to his sides and the neon began to buzz and run all over him. It made one of Queen's ideas seem almost tasteful. I wasn't sure it was working, as he hoped, to draw attention away from his portliness. The suit might have looked all right on Elvis Presley circa 1955, but Barbican was more an Elvis circa 1975. He didn't seem to realize that the costume made him look like a Telly Tubby rather than a Talking Head. And who was going to tell him? Rosie was the only one who could have done it, and she seemed to think he looked pretty spiffy, too. At least she shared a look with him, which was more than she'd done with any of the rest of us.

Barbican laid out the remains of a paper on the back of his Fender case and chopped the stuff up crudely. I did a bit, but I wasn't even sure what it was after I snorted it. I went easy. You never knew what people were selling him. I wondered what else they'd found on Jocky's boat and why they hadn't confiscated it when they arrested Jocky.

We went down in two lots, via the elevator. We had security people lining the way right up to the stage. Security guys surrounding the stage. Helicopters and whatnot everywhere. River police boats cruising. Beams of light swinging about. A lot of scarlet-and-gold uniforms. You could tell how important we were and how much money we were worth. Barbi's PR people had done their job well.

There was a lot of general crowd noise, machinery going all over the place, but we couldn't see much. We made our way up the ramp, over the cables, and onto the stage as the lights found us. Cameramen crouching and scuttling. We squinted and waved. There was a huge response. We couldn't see a thing out there as we took up our positions by our mikes.

Once I was on stage, I was working. Everything was concentrated on the gig, on what the other members of the band were doing. The audience can give you energy, but you're not at that stage playing for them, unless you start the set with some popular number they all like. But we were doing what we'd always done, slowly feeling our way into it. Doing the folky, moralistic *Dealer Man* and then getting everything going, nice and energetic, with a steadily more confident version of *Sixteen-Year Doom*. The Epiphone loved a crowd. She seemed to respond even better than usual.

To everyone's relief, it was going well. Even Barbi's weird, flashing costume wasn't particularly intrusive. Sometimes you couldn't tell him apart from McKean's equally weird back projection. Collages of the urban world. Sepia glimpses of the future. Barbican stood at the back and to the side of the keyboards and it was Rosie, stage centre front, who was getting all the attention as she pranced and pounced to the basic blues we were ripping out for her.

Sixteen years old, with a death rattle in her throat. She's hoping to get bad habits . . .

We couldn't see much out there now, though the roar could have been the sound of the world ending, the river on fire. The applause seemed to be coming from the whole of London. It was pretty generous of the people in the front seats to be clapping at all. Most of them at some time had been victims of my trusty lens.

All easy chords for Barbican, those numbers, so he could be seen to be playing. He didn't want anyone, he said, to think he was faking it.

Then we did *Dodgem Dude*, which had a special spot for Barbi to demonstrate the little riff we'd taught him. He got a lot of applause doing it.

Having established our leader's musical credentials, we took off into the spacey, pompy *Star Cruiser*, followed by *Lou* and a couple of guitar numbers that left Barbi chording quietly away in the background, while me, Tubby and Lemmy had the time of our lives. Only Paul was playing a bit mechanically, as if his whole heart wasn't quite in it. Even then we were really delivering. Nothing too druggy, but enough of an edge to give the posh seats a bit of a frisson. Charnock's *You're A Hero* and *Playing in the Band*, Gilmore's Sam Shepard song *Marlene* and then *The Greenfly and the Rose*, with Rosie coming into her own and the crowd along the embankments going wild.

All good things must end, the straightest rose will bend . . .

Suddenly it was personal. I'd never really listened to the words before. I'd only done the choruses and the middle eight.

The baccarat, the flame-red superstar . . .

Her feathers swirled and blossomed as she gave purring emphasis to the lyrics.

. . . their tiny jaws, munch on planet cores . . . Their complex eyes examine the skies . . .

She was making the song angry and sexy at the same time, but this time her magic wasn't working on me. She was playing to Barbi, who had a simple shape to play and didn't have to concentrate on his guitar. He grinned like a spaniel.

They eat the jungle leaves, consume the wheat in sheaves . . .

Strobes stroking the old stones of the twin towers. Pastel light playing over the audience. Coloured spots picking us out. We were playing the best we'd ever played in public. We were very pleased with ourselves. At last Paul Frame was relaxing and adding some ideas.

The greenfly and the rose. The greenfly and the rose.

Paul's guitar got lyrical. He was building colour and depth with every note and the Epiphone was picking up on his harmonics. I hoped someone was recording this. I was finding things I could do that I wouldn't have believed a few hours ago . . .

They lick the plate of space . . .

At night the aphid's dream, a micro-locust dream . . .

And Barbi's electric suit is going off as if it's just won *Wheel of Fortune*.

On the crest of the applause for that one we go into Rosie's version of *Lord of the Hornets*, *Mary Rivers*, *Clone Her* and *Rolling in the Ruins*.

It's her show.

Isn't it delicious, there's a red sun in the sky. Every time we see it rise another city dies.

Rosie dances in and out of the light, a wild, arrogant hawk, her husky voice following the harmonics to weird chilling effect. This is as good as it gets. One fucking gig in my career, at any rate, to be reasonably proud of.

But then we start going into *Brothel*. We're getting near the end of the set. I don't want it to stop. That long bass intro starts every vein in my body throbbing and I'm suddenly zonked with an emotion too powerful to hold. I step back, dizzy. I gasp. This is too much. This is magic. Lemmy keeps the bass running and Rosie dances. She dances with such incredible sensuality that she entrances the whole band. She entrances everybody, including the security guys. We can't stop watching her. All we care about is playing to her. Playing to her rhythms. Playing to her dark, sardonic muse. We're all in love with Rosie. There's nothing she can't do with us. Nothing she can't make us play.

Behind us the bizarre back projection throws busy, multicoloured shadows over us, making our faces writhe and seethe. Old Gilray prints of Londoners. Prints of rioting mobs, pix of Rwanda and Bosnia, the old sixties mix. New to most of our audience. Bombs, mines, mayhem. Rock and Roll. The audience is cheering. Even the front seats are rocking.

Tubby's a demon of blurred action. Paul is Ahab riding the long boat, doomed, mad and proud, his Gibson held like a sea-lance. Barbican looks like a barmy robot, running up and down the ramp, making that Gibson clack and squeal, showing off in the way his mother had always hated. Lemmy stands there, legs spread, head up, eyes shut, fingers plucking a throaty, sensuous boom. And my Epiphone is slinky, sardonic, relentless. I've never heard sounds like it.

What an instrument.

Musicians I've known have talked about it, but I never thought I'd experience it myself, that sense of you being the guitar and the guitar being you. No difference. Every subtle emotion you felt, you could express. And it was aching with love. It was yearning for Rosie. For everything we'd had and everything we might have had.

Raw as I was, I could still respond to Tubby's insistent drum. He was keeping us all together, just as he always had.

They wanted an encore, but we were saving that up. So we went straight into *Hawk Mother*.

Rosie's costume glittered and rustled. Her mask glared into the audience as she began to spit the introduction.

Mother of hawks. Eater of Sons.

And Tubby's sharp, nasty, accusatory drums set a sinister tone as Paul's guitar cut in with furious aggression.

Mother of Death. Killer of Fathers.

This was too fucking good for the front rows. I wanted to be at Wembley or the Rainbow or anywhere that had a proper audience. But the big screens were spreading it across the nation. Nobody who saw that gig will ever forget they were there. Not necessarily because of our music. That was the fucking irony of it all. One gig you felt you could recommend to your friends and it falls into the shadow of a mystery. The video was withdrawn. All kinds of daft legalities. There are a couple of iffy bootlegs, too.

Rosie was on fire, her costume was moving so rapidly, so wildly in the strobing light. Barbi was a sort of grotesque amanuensis, running about behind her, rushing up one side of the stage and down the other, the roadies having to work like buggery just to keep his leads from tangling. It was like Devo meets The Acid Queen.

Even I can enjoy a lot of that set and usually my own records or videos depress me. They don't show the video that often because of all the ridiculous legal shit, but you can occasionally catch a bootleg on a Swedish satellite station at five in the morning and you see the same clips whenever they revive the story. They weren't ready for the big news story and most TV crews missed it.

Everyone watching it on those giant V screens or who saw the tape knows better than I did what actually started happening then.

Hawk Mother's now all dance and instrumental. Every one of us is joining in as we play. Barbican has gone frantic. He rushes up and down. He runs in front of the bewitched security guys. He jumps on the parapet. You'd think he was Ted Nugent or somebody. Or Marco on whizz.

The crowd's voice dies away and there's nothing but the music now. Even Barbican's frequent discords, as he tries to keep his fingers in the right places and do all the rockstar poses, are so muted as to be no problem.

The audience is raving and stamping. Baying. Again I get the idea they're salivating. Maybe they want to complete the evening by eating us.

I was leaning back, eyes half shut, enjoying the sex, enjoying Rosie, enjoying the sounds that were pouring out of me. Enjoying a moment that would never come again. I heard a noise and looked up, wondering if they were starting the fireworks early. But nothing much had changed in the sky. I couldn't see very well against the glare of the lights, but I guessed something was happening on the platform. I looked around to see if anyone knew what was going on. Nothing. We were still playing. I started doing those long, bendy notes for the last part of the song. But I can see the roadies are beginning to look worried and the security guys are talking into one another's heads. Maybe they're worried about snipers taking Barbi out as he struts like a prince up and down the parapet. I glance over to Tubby and grin.

Another noise and I realize the audience isn't cheering. It's a shout of horror. Barbican isn't on the parapet any more. I look for him in his usual stage position, but he's gone.

Suddenly Tubby and Lemmy have left the stage and are running to the edge, trying to look over.

I couldn't believe it. You can see it clearly on that one famous video clip. Barbican's the star of the moment. His neon space suit is pulsing and blazing as he bangs out his chords.

Then there's that snapping noise, like something breaking, not really a shot. And Barbican's plunging headfirst towards the water, right in front of the People's Princess and HRH and Salmon Rushdi and all the other luminaries. Barbi's swallowed by black water. A few spurts of multicoloured neon. Some of the audience rushes forward to the edge. They start the whole platform bouncing in a peculiar rhythm that won't stop.

Barbican sinks like a stone. The neon flickers and flares beneath the surface, moving swiftly away on the outgoing tide. Is he swimming? Is he dead? Maybe that was a shot, after all? A couple of security guys strip off and jump in after him. Meanwhile the audience on the gigantic raft are beginning to panic. One of the links breaks and a gap appears. Water splashes in. Another break. More water. A thin layer of water begins to cover the platform. This is going to be the worst disaster the Thames has known since the *Marchioness* hit the *Bow Bell* if those people don't get off in a hurry.

Hugh Grant's on the microphone, asking everyone to keep calm. There's a moment of quiet, then another snapping sound and then they're all lunging towards the sides. Some goozer heroically saves the Princess of Wales. Princess Margaret refuses all help and has to be rescued forcibly by Prince Edward and Bob Geldof. It's a total shambles.

It goes on for about half an hour's worth of tape. It's a wonder nobody's killed. A few minor injuries.

And, of course, Barbican has vanished. The river police start looking for him. Frogmen go down. Nobody can find him.

'A bit of an anticlimax, really,' says Rosie, coming up beside me for a moment. 'Still, it was a good gig up to then. You were great.'

I look around. Was she really talking to me? I see her going back towards the North Tower with Paul Frame. Tubby has put down his sticks and is walking up to me. Lemmy joins him.

'Jesus,' says Tubby. 'I hope he's not dead.'

But he was. Three days later they found a corpse down at the estuary. The eels had had a good nibble and it was a bit hard to recognise the face. But that weird stage suit was enough to identify the body and Rosie confirmed that it was that of her late husband. So they had a wonderful service for him at St Jude's, Lancaster Gate, then burned and urned him at Kensal Green, in that huge mausoleum containing the first Lord Barbican. The *Sun* reported that they had hard evidence Barbican had been shot by Arab snipers. They also claimed that Rosie was pregnant. There would be a Barbican the Third.

The stories would get better than that. Barbi's flashing stage suit was really a signal to the flying-saucer people to carry him away. And so on. Conspiracy theories of all kinds. But nobody in the grown-up world really believed them. What they did believe was that Barbican Begg had overreached himself and had fallen to his death, leaving behind him the largest financial empire the world had known. They wondered what his widow and sole heir would do with that extraordinary empire now. Rosie made lots of statements about how she would run BBIC exactly as her husband would have wished. Most people didn't want her to run the company at all. They wanted to see her back on stage, doing *The Greenfly and the Rose*, *The Brothel in Rosenstrasse* and *Hawk Mother*. They understood, of course, when she said that the whole memory was very painful to her and she would never again be able to appear on the public stage.

Which scotched any fantasies I might have had.

I wasn't. I am. I won't be.

Lemmy made his record and eventually went back to LA. Tubby retired to the Mill, now refusing all visitors, and Paul Frame returned to Kinshasa and became some sort of unofficial ambassador. He turned up wherever they couldn't get Nelson Mandela. He alerted us to famines and floods and the poor starving survivors so few of us had the will to help. The Labour Party became NuLabor and won a vast majority by assuring everyone that not only would things stay the same, they would stay the same but better. Rosie schmoozed with Moloch and Rosie schmoozed with Blairy and Rosie did just as she promised and continued her husband's business policies by gobbling up yet another chunk of the world. There were no more rumours about BBIC being in trouble. In fact BBIC, the last anyone checked, was more powerful than almost any single country in the world. Its only main competitor was the United States. There was talk of a merger. Many spoke admiringly of Rosie, the way they had of Maggie. Just what the country needed. A new Iron Lady. Some Americans had suggested she run for President. She said she'd rather not give up her power.

About a month after Barbican's funeral, they held a memorial service for him. I was the only one of the band who could attend, apart from Rosie. They held the service at St Alban's, Brookgate, which was a bit like saying a prayer for Adolf Hitler in Coventry Cathedral. But nobody mentioned anything except me. When the service was over and all the great and good stood about discussing my cousin's spectacular (and rather flashy) end, I managed to slip up beside Rosie. She couldn't pretend I wasn't there and people were already treating us as a pair – the two band members who had been there when Barbican fell.

At last I was able to murmur a few words to her. 'Rosie, whatever you decide afterwards, give me a chance to talk to you.'

'Absolutely,' she said brightly, and handed me a card. 'Give me a ring next week.'

I rang her. That was when she told me to get in touch with Captain Quelch, the skipper who'd taken Barbican from France. I was on the trail at last. A trail that led to Little Cayman and a couple in a hammock. And from there to Skerring.

Believe me, pards, we're living in an age of myths and miracles.

CHAPTER TWENTY-SEVEN
The Plot

I went back to London once after I settled in Skerring. I had to sort out the details of handing Fogg Yard over to Fromental. The town was full of the news of the Harrods/Marks and Spencer merger. Certain M&S branches were being converted to Harrods Food Halls. Now everyone could have a posh store in their high street, with plenty of parking for their mini-Rolls.

I bet they had to work for it, though. Two jobs per parent and something extra on the side to pay for a baby-shaker. What happened to the problem of leisure they used to write about in the early seventies – how by the year 2000 we were all going to be doing more hobbies, having more holidays, going to more places, doing more sports, more voluntary work?

They solved the problem of leisure. Now everybody goes to the shopping mall. It's the only time the family ever gets to be together.

Brookgate didn't look any better for the new Iceland and Kwik Save. The fake market stalls were gone. Shops closed or on their last legs. Desolate. Fucked. Nothing. Everything was peeling, twisting, fading, falling down. Fogg Yard looked weird, a tiny bit of authenticity in all that rotting fakery. The view hadn't improved. Even the railings around the family grave were rusting. Barbi's cosmetics were collapsing faster than Dirk Bogarde's mascara. The legoed bits of the church were warping and melting like a jelly left out in the sun. I was glad to get the train home.

That's how bad it was, pards. Skerring was now home. And I was relishing it. The greyness, the miseries, the audience at the pub who loved the blues as if they were hearing them for the first time. I started playing at the Golden Bowl roadhouse, where Skerring Lane joined the A23 to Lower Bleading. The crowd didn't change much but the landlord seemed pleased. Then I did Saturday nights at The Garnett Arms, down on the front near the pier, with a band called The Tejano Cajuns. The sons and daughters of the hippies who'd settled here in the seventies and eighties. Great Stiff fans. I only guested with them when they did Skerring. They could get gigs easily and went as far as Portsmouth and Croydon. I didn't play anything to draw attention to myself. Nothing to remind anyone of those final gigs with Rosie. I couldn't imagine I'd ever play that well again. I daren't bring out the Black Bird I still had. No one had asked for it back. I used my old Yamaha. I was quite happy doing lead in the background while Johnny Bledsoe, a milkman from Tarring, sang in a voice that made me nostalgic for my dad's old skiffle records. I worked for meals and beer. One gig a week and they let me eat lunch there every day. There was quite a lot of barter going in Skerring and that, of course, suited me, since I didn't want the tax people to know where I was. During the daytimes I'd go into Worthing or one of the other towns that still had some tourism, mostly coachloads of retired people, and pick up whatever cash I could. A quick polaroid on the promenade. Two snaps for a fiver. 'Thank you, young lady. There's a smile to gladden the eye.' To the sets of NHS choppers displayed for the day. To the old dears, the old codgers, looking for the quiet familiar security of a stroll along the front. A little bit of reassuring memory. A taste of the comforts they remembered. In a lot of cases I knew I was taking maybe the last photo of their lives, wondering how many of these memories would wind up in a recycling bag as weary survivors tried to value some relative's ordinary relics.

No photographic jobs for me in Skerring. I didn't have the heart to try to work with those abandoned pensioners clutching at one another on the crumbling tarmac of the eroded promenade as the sea-spray and the rain threatened to engulf them.

Sweet Honey Lane had been Skerring's most famous thoroughfare from when it had been the village street, but now it was just second-hand shops, funeral parlours, florists and bent solicitors. Skerring's only viable services were all for the dying and the dead. There were a few depressed kids, but they usually killed themselves or ran away to Brighton and Eastbourne.

Ron Blewitt, the only other professional photographer in Skerring, specialized in portraits of the recently deceased – like modern death masks, he said. It was an art. They were all the rage in Skerring, which had whole grim folk epics of her own. They'd never be universal or even collected because they were so boring and repetitive. Christmas and the other holidays went by largely unnoticed, since they had become expensive luxuries for the poorer consumer. But there was one big event that didn't have a single commercial greeting card for it anywhere in the world. Skerring's very own 'Billy Day'. On Midsummer's Night, every year, the Skerrings celebrated Billy Day. Alternately they burned in effigy the Pope, who was always represented in blackface, and another effigy called King William the Fifth, whom they dressed in women's clothes. I was pretty sure the ceremony had been going on from before anyone in Skerring had ever heard of the Pope or the entirely mythical transvestite

King William, but both were burned affectionately with equal relish, reminding me of Tubby's old Jack and how Tub had let the whole tradition fade away as he gave more and more of his attention to resisting Barbican's rapacity. To destroy the fabric of our common ancestry The Grand Consumer hadn't even had to wipe us out. We were doing the job for him.

The Skerrings weren't a particularly grim lot, but they were very inbred. They had been here since they landed with the first Saxons, content to pull up their boats on the shingle, build a village and never venture inland without a very good reason. During the seaside holiday boom, which began in Victorian times, they had catered gladly to visitors and any remaining adventurous Skerring spirit had run off long since with a holidaymaker. All that was left was the fundamental bloodstock, about as conservative as it was possible to get without turning to stone.

Billy Day usually ended with the rain putting the effigy out and someone pouring petrol on it and setting fire to something else as well. Which usually burned a couple of bystanders. It was the big day of excitement for Skerring-on-Sea. Since the cottage hospital had closed, an ambulance had to come from Worthing to take the victims to Worthing General, so it felt like recognition from the outside world. Some proof that we really existed. I'd usually be asked to buy that week's *Argus*, if I was going into Worthing, so they could see if they got a mention, but they were used to disappointment. The *Argus* rarely mentioned Skerring at all. It was West Sussex's shameful secret. Skerring gave the *Argus* no advertising and sold no copies in the town's remaining newsagent, which only stocked special orders since it was off the usual delivery routes and had no sale-or-return arrangements with suppliers. TV was a dodgy affair. Our configuration between the Downs and the sea also gave the beach its distinctive smell. Nobody had yet put up a dish. We got BBC local radio, of course, if the cloud cover was low enough, and sometimes a Skerring resident would call in to a chat show. There was always the same response. 'You're from where, dear? Oh, really! I didn't know Skerring was still open. Ha, ha, ha. No offence, dear. So what's happening in the town that time forgot?' In tones of undisguised contempt usually reserved for their comments on baby-batterers and boy-buggerers.

It was scarcely our fault that the miniature Sargasso lying off our shores attracted almost anything that would rot and was permanently covered by clouds of noisy carrion birds. There had been attempts to cost a clean-up, but everyone knew how expensive it was and how it only worked for a few months before the bobbing carpet of filth returned with its squawking gulls and crows. That's really why the town was so poor and why it was so rarely visited.

That suited most of us. You quickly got used to the smell. Some

people liked it. Ron Blewitt said it was the stuff of life. Amniotic
developing fluid. A rich mix of everything in the world come back to the
sea to start all over again. Ron was the only native Skerring of a mystical
disposition. He probably got it from his mother, who came from
Ferring.

While Skerrings discouraged interest in their town, they also felt
slighted at being ignored. Nearby towns considered themselves a cut
above Skerring anyway. But most of us were glad of the invisibility. The
boarded-up shops were a bit prominent where you came off the A23 and
went towards Chichester, but the residents had regrouped around the
old square with its clockless tower, and the seafront near what remained
of the pier. As the original Skerrings died out and their children and
grandchildren fled, these areas were increasingly occupied by old
hippies, cranky retired natives, French students (high turnover), a few
settled travellers and about fifty assorted mystical and evangelical cults
of an average of eight members (counting children) each.

On Sundays I did a kids' show in an old Pierrot costume at the end of
the very short pier – playing the banjo and singing all those old songs my
grandad and Norrie had taught me. I was a major hit. Because of the
awful reception, electronic entertainment hadn't become incorporated
into Skerring culture, so even videos were only popular with a few V
buffs. Most people couldn't afford anything new. The old Skerring
Grand cinema didn't even make it into the era of sound. My mother's
psychic friend Ethel Masters played the piano there until 1958 when the
roof collapsed under an unusual weight of snow.

I was just where I felt like being. About as isolated, anonymous and
secure as it was possible to get in modern times. Everybody called me
Denny Cornwall, the name of my mother's seventh husband – she was
always Mrs Cornwall in Skerring – and that suited me perfectly because,
not long after I'd given Jean-Luc his rent book, letters started arriving
from the Inland Revenue about my lapses of payments. I owed enough
to cover at least half a cruise missile or fund a South American dictator.
I had better cough up, plus billions of sheets of interest, or the men
would be round to break my fingers and feet, just as a warning, or words
to that effect etc. etc.

They'd take proceedings? Bankrupt the man with a couple of cameras
and an astonishing guitar he hadn't given back yet and didn't dare play
in public? They had to catch me first and the mortgage was now being
paid directly by Fromental. Everything was in his name. After he'd
forwarded a couple of the Inland Revenue letters, I told him to send
them back 'Addressee unknown'. Which he did, and life returned to its
own slow, normal rhythms again.

Of course, I wasn't living with my mother. That had lasted a couple
of weeks. She couldn't help herself and neither could I. The morning she
followed me into the toilet in order to keep telling me the same story she

had told a million times about her friendship with Myrna Loy and how Myrna had said she was a saint to put up with what she put up with, I lost it. I yelled at her. And then felt like a wonker for making her cry.

So we sorted it out. She calmed down. She didn't want me to leave. It was all her fault. She knew. It was because she felt so miserable, knowing that I didn't really love her and so on and so on. The music goes round and round. Some of the time you dance to it. Some of the time you get sick of dancing.

I moved round the corner to the Beach Hotel, which was glad of any trade, and paid by the month. That way I also got my linen changed and had a kitchenette with a microwave, which was all I needed. I had a suite on the second floor overlooking Skerring's stark, faintly threatening ocean. Her crowded, cawing horizon. Two bathrooms, one used as a darkroom. Some of the rooms were let to DHSS people, but the only other more-or-less permanent guests were myself and Gordon Reynsham, a Skerring native who had toured for England and returned to his roots. For a while he had travelled to Goring, where he was cricket pro for the Lloyds Bank team, but interest in cricket fell off with Sunday opening and he now did a mail-order business in bootlegged tapes of famous matches. He let me use one of his postboxes at the newsagent's, in the name of Cornwall, and collected my mail when he picked up his orders for *Stolen wickets and Forbidden boundaries*. He had the whole basement and was technically the caretaker.

The Beach was a crumbling deco building put up in the days before the Great Depression when everyone was trying to attract the bright young things to their resorts, and after they believed themselves clear of the so-called Skerring Sargasso, the festering weed. There was never a year when they could fill the place or sell it, until the 1950s when slum landlord Peter Rachman came down to Skerring with Mandy Rice-Davies and bought the whole thing for a pittance, so they could have somewhere nice to stay at weekends.

They stuck it for about a month, then Rachman sold the hotel on to some posh beatnik in Soho who paid a fiver for it and who now lived in Las Cascadas and didn't really give a damn what happened to The Beach as long as it didn't cost him anything and squatters or rats didn't become a problem.

My mail wasn't much. Usually Jean-Luc sending me my share of some second-rights sale. I had no means of getting the dosh the papers paid for reusing my old stuff so I let my agent send it to the Revenue, hoping a few bones would convince them that was all I was worth. But those bastards always knew what they would do if they had my kind of money, so they were probably convinced I was already waiting for my turn in the hammock on Little Cayman.

Like almost everyone else in Skerring I'd lost interest in the outside world and made no effort to keep in touch with what was happening.

Gordon even had a computer, but he used it only for his business and for looking up cricketing information for what I think he called *ballsearch@hotpoint.com*. Jean-Luc always put anything he forwarded into another envelope addressed to Dennis Cornwall, so even Gordon didn't know my real name. It made me feel very comfortable and safe and I knew Skerring was where I loved to be. The skunk that my step-brother was growing in his loft might have helped with that sense of contentment, spending as much time as I did just lying on the beach and inhaling the bizarre mixture of odours the wind blew remorselessly inland.

A lot of weed went by and I caught up on some books I'd always looked forward to reading. I did a bit of painting. And, of course, I wrote my memoirs. But that was all in the first few months. After a year or so I'd lost interest in everything except old comics. I followed the adventures of Dan Dare who had been Pilot of the Future years before I was born. There was a certainty about those old *Eagles* and *Lions*, an unexamined agreement, like you heard on a lot of those old BBC tapes Norrie got for my grandad. Was that a coherent culture? No questions asked?

I came off the beach one evening (*Dan Dare and the Purple Planetoid*) to find Gordon waiting for me at the old reception desk, where he sometimes set up his terminal. You'd think the place was a proper hotel sometimes. He gave me the usual junk mail and then showed me a couple of buff envelopes addressed simply to Mr Dennis Dover, c/o Mrs Dover, Skerring-on-Sea, West Sussex, WC4 6N2. 'You were the only Dennis Mrs Whitbread knew, but she'll send them back if it's a mistake.'

I told him it was OK and murmured something about one of my cousins thinking I had his family name, told him I'd send them back and burned the buggers.

But there were two more the following week. This time I took them to my room and steamed one open to see what it was about.

They were claiming I owed them £250,000 down, which they'd be glad if I paid by return, etc. The usual crap. So I sent those back to Fogg Yard and Jean-Luc sent them on to an address he had in Majorca and they sent them back. But I was a bit uneasy. There were never many fresh faces in Skerring at any time and whenever I spotted a stranger I suspected it was a Revenue Officer, Special Enforcement Squad, hot on my trail. Logically it would take them a year at least to find me. I was content in a depressed sort of way. I wanted time to stand still. I was prepared to pay the price of retreat into the past. Pretty much by accident I'd found the perfect hiding place, made all the more perfect when the train no longer had Skerring on its regular run but only on Wednesdays and Saturdays to comply with some agreement with the government. Then the bus stopped and it was hardly worth my while going into Worthing, so I became even more cut off than I had been.

There seemed an unending supply of 1950s comics from the Old Skerring Bookshop, whose owner Percy Clacton never left the pub next door. You just took what you wanted from the shop, went into the pub and gave him the money. 'Thanks, laddy,' he'd say. 'Happy reading.'

The only really unpleasant rumour I'd heard was that the Inland Revenue was thinking of building extension offices to its Worthing HQ. And the cheapest land for nearby sites was in Skerring. There was talk that they were moving the Execution Department, already partly operating outside London as a semi-independent arm of the Enforcement Division. These departments were only slightly less sinister than they sounded. The titles were invented by the same kind of guys who thought up *Cheka* or *Gestapo* with the intention of deliberately scaring the shit out of people. They employed all the techniques you'd condemn when crooks used them. They were the heavy squad who travelled in black cars with mirrored windows. They spoke softly and they were very self-righteous. They didn't like people making jokes or telling lies.

They found me, of course, on a Friday night after I'd been gigging with The Tejano Cajuns at the pub. I was sitting with my back against one of the cast-iron pier supports looking out to sea at the faintly glowing horizon and eating thirty pence worth of horribly floppy Skerring-style chips from the *Union Jack* ('Say No To Europe') *piscatorium*. My stepbrother had heard a rumour they were fried in human fat. Non-foreign, of course.

The Three Revenue Officers were like something out of one of Fromental's Tin Tin comics – two men and a woman all wearing the same shade of grey. Identical suits, two trousers, one skirt. Oxblood brogues. The woman had thick lips, like uncooked liver, bottle glasses, an intense manner, dull page-boy hair. One of the men could have been her brother, while the other was plumper, pastier, the sort of character who Dan Dare's chums would have spotted immediately as a victim of self-abuse and other types of beastliness. Framed against the moonlight, they came crunching over the shingle towards me.

It looked like a fair cop. Had someone turned me in?

They all leaned down to peer into the shadows at me.

'Mr Cornwall?'

'And 'ood wanter know?' I said.

'We represent a firm of solicitors. Is your cousin Mr Dennis Dover?'

'I've got some distant Dovers in the family,' I agreed.

'Sorry to bother you, Mr Cornwall.' The woman's lips made some sort of writhing motion. A smile? 'I hope you can help us.'

'Fire away, marm,' says I, still in the local accent, round a mouthful of chips.

'We were wondering if you could get a message to your cousin Dennis Dover,' said the thin-lipped man.

'The photographer and guitarist,' said the fat-lipped man.

'If I see his Uncle Norm I might.'

'Does his uncle live here?'

'Distant,' I said.

'Do what?'

'Distant. They're from up London. They'll be in Brookgate.'

'Not any more,' said the thin-lipped one. 'He did a bunk.' And then he tried to pretend he hadn't said anything while the other two glared at him.

'Just in case.' She handed her card into the semi-darkness while I finished the last bits of salty chip. 'Do you expect him back any time soon?'

'Back?' I said. 'He'd never come here. He swore he'd die in agony afore he set foot on yon station platform. Yon's a Londoner, he is.'

'Well, if you hear from him, perhaps you'd let us know.'

I accepted her card.

'Could be something to his advantage,' said the thin-lipped one, as if to an idiot.

'What for?' A local expression.

'Just ask him to get in touch. We'd be ever so grateful. His mother said he was working on a space shuttle and wouldn't be home for a while. Then, we gather, he'll be rehearsing with Paul McCartney in a new band. But we'd like a word with him before that.'

'Oil rig,' said the woman. 'Not space shuttle.'

'That sounds more likely,' I said.

I'd realized they were out of their element, believing themselves victims of a wild-goose chase. They'd spent the best part of a day with my mother who would rather climb a tree to tell a lie than stand on the ground to tell the truth. They were shell-shocked. They thought they'd been pumping her. Now they hardly knew who they were. They carried massive square cases and were shivering in the faint, noxious mist from the sea. They'd missed their connection, they said, and they couldn't get a taxi. A car was coming from Worthing to collect them. By the pier. Meanwhile they were following any leads they could. They were sorry for disturbing my meal.

When I saw my mother the next day she said not to worry, she'd put them on a false scent. She'd sent them on a trail from Aberdeen to the Shetlands to Norway, she said, but my guess was they were back in Worthing, regrouping.

Not much later I was at The Garnett Arms playing 'our favourite old time R&B hits', as the blackboard said, when I looked out into the audience and there she was, with a woman who could have been her sister, looking a little more County than Country. Bobby MacMillan. She came to stand round to the side and winked at me.

I was feeling very paranoid. Was she now working for the Revenue? Was that how she survived? Under some sort of protection programme?

She was wearing pearls and a dark sweater. Riding breeches. Had she turned Barbican in? Or been involved in his murder-masquerade? Or had she known so much she'd scared him into pretending to kill himself? None of it seemed likely, even to my pleasantly deadened brain.

Anyway, there was no escaping Bobby and the pard she introduced as Cousin Jax. They'd been out for a drive from Lansing Boise (which the locals called Lancing Boils) and thought it would be a laugh to go into Skerring, since nobody ever did and there was talk of drugs and dancing and stuff going on there.

So we go back to The Beach and Cousin Jax gratefully picks up a quarter-ounce of skunk from me and tells Bobby she'll drive round in the morning to get her for their hairdressing appointment in Brighton.

Bobby loved my place at The Beach. It was probably the sleaziest gaff she'd ever slept in. Even the loud Vs from the deafer pensioners seemed to excite her. 'Oh, God, Den! I've been so fucking bored!'

She was stepping out of her jodhpurs.

I'd forgotten she'd been born, raised and married near Skerring.

'Home turf,' she said. 'Skerring used to be our nearest town by bus, so me and Jax used to come here as kids. It hasn't changed much.'

I told her about my pursuit of Barbican to the Caymans where I'd found him alive and hearty. She believed me. No problem. She'd wondered more than once, she said. That was a reason for staying away from the public eye. In the course of the night and early morning, between energetic sessions, she filled me in on her own vanishing act.

'He got so weird that I was actually scared of him. He could seem very barmy sometimes. You know. You wouldn't be shocked if you discovered he'd killed someone. Or, at least, Jocky had. At one point I changed my name and moved to Chichester, then back to Lansing Boise. But Jocky found me, anyway, and there was a bit of bargaining. I felt like some gangster's moll on the run, sweetie. Filled my knickers more than once. I'll swear that bitch Rosie Beck had a hand in it. In the end they got my share of the Leases.'

'*Your* share?'

'I'd gone to a lot of trouble and expense to track down Billy Fairling, establish his ancestry and his rights to the Leases. It was working well, too. But bloody Barbican wanted to be the big IT. Wasn't satisfied with what I offered him. And all he had to do was bankroll it. He wanted to control it all, do it all and have it all. By the time I'd been married to him for a few months I knew his methods and I knew how ruthless he could be. I also knew I couldn't satisfy his needs. His appetites. That stuff. And you know me, Dennis, I'm no prude. Anyway, by that time I'd started my affair with Paul Frame.'

'What?'

'Rivalry at first. I thought he was Rosie's squeeze. Turned out they hadn't had anything going for years and years. Not since she'd had his baby. When she was a teenager.'

So who had the truth of it? I scarcely cared any more. 'Kim? Was that the kid's name?'

'Could be, darling. Little girl. Came to the Mill once. Thanksgiving? Anyway, Barbs got sussy and I got even more scared. Paul wouldn't come with me. Wouldn't stand up to Barbi. Duty called and so forth. Needs of the fucking Hottentots more important than mine!

'So when it started getting nasty I buried myself away where the photogs couldn't reach me. I mean a long way away, until Jocky found me again. But by that time I wasn't really fighting any more and he knew it. We did a trade. No scandal but the divorce went through on Barbican's terms. I couldn't afford to hang on to the Leases. Forty-two fucking million was all I pulled out of it! A lot of which was swallowed when Lloyd's and Barings collapsed. And that conniving bastard Rosie Beck getting her hands on the lot. She was always the same – sweetness and light, until you crossed her. Then you'd better watch out.' I said it was a side of Rosie I'd only recently seen. Barbican had thought her really good for him. She'd changed him.

'Changed him, all right. Filled him full of crack and God knows what and turned his brain to jelly. Went along with all that nasty stuff he liked. Then got him to do whatever she wanted. Make an absolute arse of himself. Almost lose his entire fortune. Drove him to lunacy so that he really thought it was a good idea to fake his own death in public after doing a rock-and-roll gig that was watched by millions. I mean, he didn't think up stuff like that on his own, Dennis.'

'Well,' I said. 'He did a bit. He was a sort of rock-and-roll wannabe. You know, he wanted our rough spontaneity or something.'

'It was Rosie's fantasy.'

'I don't think so. I worked with the wanker. He paid over a quarter of a million for a guitar he couldn't play. They do, apparently, those blokes.'

She agreed with that. She'd pulled more of those stockies, in their striped shirts and fancy braces, than most. All they ever dreamed of was strutting across the stage like Mick Jagger with nubile lovelies tugging at their bell-bottoms.

But, she insisted, Rosie had played on Barbi's weaknesses. Got him so he didn't know his anus from his elbow and actually managed to inherit everything without even having to murder him. Lady Macbeth of the Monument, that woman. But, although she'd suspected the truth, Bobby was really disappointed to know I'd photographed Barbican alive and well in his hammock. She'd really hoped Rosie had killed him.

I wondered why I'd never had a hint before of this side of Rosie. All the years, from babyhood upwards, inseparable, nothing protected, feeling as if we were the same person. Warm, intimate, frank, loving. But then, bingo, she turned against me. I couldn't imagine doing that to her.

'So you and Rosie didn't get on at St Paul's?' I wondered.

'We weren't in the same year. But she was very stuck-up even then. Talking eighteen bloody languages and trying to persuade everyone to go to Africa and be a bloody leper-kissing nun. The teachers thought she was marvellous, of course. The Victorian heroine returned. Just what the school needed. Snotty arse-licking cock-sucking cunt-sniffer, I say. Sorry.' She'd been trying to turn me on. It usually suited her peer-group pulls. 'I forgot you're a working-class prude. Ooo!'

Later she told me she'd learned her lesson. Keep a low profile and enjoy familiar pleasures. I was an unexpected and very welcome treat, she said. She'd be OK, barring a big crash. The remaining few million were well sheltered and she was living on the interest. Which was enough to keep a couple of horses and do all the repairs to Lansing Boise. Daddy had died shortly after that Coca-Cola bubble burst, taking his last few thousand with it. 'Bit of a trauma, Daddy going. Luckily I still have Boise. Come and stay for a few days. Be my new daddy.' She hissed happily at me like a body-snatcher, a friendly cobra. Her lovely lips brushed my ears. 'I mean, you don't have a day job, do you?'

'So how's Rosie spending all that dosh?'

'Making more dosh, darling. Until billions become casually tossed about. That feels very good, darling. That feels like real fucking power. She runs the fucking world. And she's worshipped by these mummy's boys, just the way Thatcher was, except she's fucking Thatcher, Soros and bloody Diana combined. That isn't girl power, Dennis. That's *power* power. She controls continents, not countries. She could have us killed and get away with it.'

I didn't argue with that. But it didn't make my judgement any better. I began to consider the possibility of becoming Bobby's fancy boy. What the fuck did I know? What the fuck did I want? Nothing.

But some instinct saved me for the moment. I told her I had professional commitments, but I'd be glad to come over for an evening or two.

'Well,' she said, with that sly, slanted smile that I think she modelled on Lauren Bacall. 'Working for a living, eh? You must be the last person in the world. What the fuck is there to do in Skerring?'

'General entertainment,' I said. 'I'm the town clown.'

'And you play in that band. What do you get? A tenner and free beer?'

'And supper.'

'Come and be my plaything for a bit.'

'It's tempting.' With the Revenue breathing down my neck, it might be worth considering a slight change of location.

'OK,' she said. 'Let's do it.'

'Why were you so scared of Barbi?' I asked. 'I mean, do you really think he was convinced he was ruined? That he killed Jocky, then got Jocky's corpse up to look like him?'

'If he was driven barmy enough with drugs and strong sex,' she said. 'They were always his weakness.'

'What kind of sex?'

'Oh, extreme stuff,' she said. 'It finished me, Dennis. If you don't know, you won't want to know.'

'Jesus.' I didn't want to know. 'What about Paul Frame?'

'Paul's sweet, I think, But no doubt he was useful to Rosie. Maybe she started schtooping him again. Maybe that was his job. Relief from Barbi's demands. Probably. Though maybe that's her thing, dear. I mean, we all have our little weaknesses, don't we?'

I didn't want to remember my little weaknesses, either. Nor did my churning stomach. 'So what hold did he have over you? Not just threats, surely. Pictures?'

'Too much in the end,' she said. She filled me in on some more details, before her divorce, before Rosie's decision to marry Barbican.

She'd become seriously worried after that first visit from Jocky. She recognized the codes. Sending Jocky was always Barbi's way of telling you this was a blitzkrieg, that he was ready to fight on any terms and for ever.

She'd angrily gone out to Rowe Island, a former colony in the middle of the Indian Ocean, which belonged to BBIC. It had been Bobby who'd appointed the manager there, so she felt she could trust him. Rowe Island was all phosphates and rival Chinese and Muslim workers. The manager proved to be OK and she'd lived there quite happily, negotiating by untraceable e-mail. Then there was some local religious trouble.

That was how Jocky tracked her down. Came out in one of those little skyships, unscheduled, that they ran for a while. The manager was fired and Jocky put himself in charge. Bobby left for Bangkok, was briefly mixed up with an errant banker who suddenly disappeared and scared her. Anyway, she said, she couldn't get on with the weather. Took the steamer. By this time she was frightened enough to be grateful for whatever she could get out of her losses and disappear down to Lansing Boise, to enjoy full security and the occasional bonk with some married hooray henry. The setbacks had come rapidly.

'And then, of course, Jocky had vanished. Barbican seemed to be dead. I wasn't nervous any more. But I was fairly broke. I got used to it. Now I don't mind. Especially since I've met up with my favourite oompah-man.'

I started looking around for escape.

But somehow, when the Morgan appeared outside the doors of The Beach, I was there with my little overnight bag. I'd agreed at least to see the place.

'Boise needs a new master,' she said gravely.

Jax, driving, burst into girlish laughter.

It became a bit of a habit after that. There were consolations, but the worst was that I got to see too much V. Nothing wrong with reception this far inland and a discreet dish gave Bobby the world. She was also addicted to *People* and *Hello* and the rest. So, against my will, I caught up with the doings of Rosie and Paul. Rosie was very big in the City. In fact she was very big everywhere. Presidents and bankers consulted her. She was admired as much for her firm, ruthless dealings as she was for her success and her beauty. Even touching fifty Rosie looked wonderful. Queen of Olympus. Paul Frame was still being saintly, trying to get a reconciliation here, a peace plan there, an agreement, an accord. You couldn't fault him for trying, but the peace never seemed to last after he left. He was always there, though, for the front-page reconciliation, the TV spots. Whenever the PM needed an effective-looking authentic hero for a photo-op, Paul was available. It was a bit hard to work out how Paul still tried to stop the fighting factions but never addressed the fact that we, the civilized nations, were supplying them with the guns. I was very glad I'd given up all that political shit. It just hurt my head and made me feel frustrated. Good old Paul, I said. Good for him. He's trying, anyway. The effect usually lasted long enough for the PM to get a bit of mileage, claim a bit of credit, increasing his profound self-satisfaction. You've done everything you can for them and these people still go on behaving badly.

Paternalism was definitely back in style. Hand in hand with the new imperialism. *Hand in hand with horror, side by side with death.* Never forget how popular Mussolini and Hitler were with Americans before WW2. They used to praise Roosevelt by calling him the American Mussolini.

All you could do these days was keep your head down and hope for the best.

Bobby's restored early Victorian manse didn't welcome me. The staff treated me as if I was just one of a succession of stable boys who would have been best fucked in the outbuildings where they belonged. But Bobby did tell me a bit more about what Barbi had been up to in those last months. Now she knew he was alive, the rest made more sense to her.

'He was getting a bit flashy even when we were first married. Nothing spectacular. But he used to reminisce a lot. You know, go on for half an hour in board meetings about a totally irrelevant event that happened to him as a boy. What good I was to him as a wife, I can't imagine. He bored me stiff and I bored him limp. Maybe he just didn't want the scandal of having mistresses or whores. Maybe he'd just wanted to get his hands on my Leases.'

'Why did Jocky stay out there around the Islands?'

'Exile, I think. I know Barbi discovered that Jocky had done something very shady. This was after we divorced. For some reason Jocky got him angry and that's how he punished Jocky. Jocky hated Indonesia. He had to stay out there. Barbican was funding a lot of the East Timor operations, which would normally have been Jocky's cup of tea. Occasionally he was allowed to go to Australia. But he took advantage of Barbican, as I understand it. He made the most of his situation by doing some large-scale drug smuggling on the side, using the immunity given to Barbican's well-known yacht, *The Teddy Bear*, by friendly, sweetened officials. South America or South-East Asia, he was never bothered by customs.'

As those economies crashed, Barbican needed someone with a steady hand on the tiller, but Jocky had become distracted with his own business dealings. So in the end Barbican had turned the guy in. But not before he'd confiscated the cargo for himself.

Meanwhile all the fake scenery, including Jocky's, fell down. Ancient banking houses collapsed in shame bringing ruin to millions.

'So what happened, then? How did he get free?'

'You must be the only person in the world who hasn't got their own theory about this story,' she said. 'You really were vegetating, weren't you? Anyway, it's all blindingly obvious now.'

The corpse Barbican had used as a substitute was, of course, Jocky's.

'Jocky died while helping the Jakarta police with their enquiries. Heart attack, apparently. His body was secretly sent back on ice to England as a special favour to Barbican.'

'Before the Tower Bridge gig?'

'At least two weeks earlier.'

'So the body they identified as Barbican's was actually Jocky's. It just needed preparing. Rosie must have been in on it.'

'It was probably Rosie's bloody idea. If you took those pictures of yours to the police, plus the rest, they'll dig up the grave and find Jocky.'

'The bastard,' I said. 'He was cremated.' But I felt a flicker of triumph. Further proof that I'd been right. 'The bastard! What was it he wanted? One last moment of public adoration before he disappeared from the world? Sounds the sort of crap he'd think of on his own.'

'Once an available corpse came up,' she said. 'He wouldn't deliberately murder anyone. He'd rather not know about stuff like that.'

'Oh, it's too fucking grotesque!'

'Is it?'

I was certain.

'Any more than what's going on in the rest of the world?' Bobby laid out a couple of sparse lines for us.

'Probably not. That's too fucking grotesque as well.'

'I see what you mean,' she said.

'So Jocky's corpse was just what Barbi needed to put his barmy plan into action. Because Barbi was scared. Of what? Exposure? What? What couldn't he control? Bloody hell, Bobby. It's not normal to fuck about with people's corpses. You have to be well up your own bottom.'

'Well, he wasn't normal, was he? For years he talked about faking his death. It was his pipe dream. To put everything behind him, live the simple life on some tropical island. You know. He also wanted to be a rock star. He was obsessed with what he called his Worst-Case Scenario. He said he'd rather die doing what he'd always dreamed of doing. I wouldn't go along with any of it. Rosie didn't have any trouble. She seems to have encouraged him.'

'He changed that much?'

'Not really. He just got more exaggerated, more fantastic. Maybe owning that amount of the world does that to you. But I had a feeling she was pushing him towards the edge. I think she egged him on to do that silly rock-and-roll nonsense – those childish obsessions with reorganizing the world – all those drugs. He just did a moderate bit of coke and hash when I was married to him. He got obsessed with vitality, with risk-taking, keeping ahead, getting good publicity, making the spin go – getting people to believe his lies so that they act to make the lie seem true. It's the art of politics these days. Rediscovering his true self, he said. It had to be Rosie filling him up with all that hippy crap.'

'Well, she seems to be as hard as he is now.'

'Oh, she was always that. She has an absolutely vicious reputation in the City. Far worse than Barbican's. The female of the species and all that. She's doing stuff, I hear, that a lot of people really don't like.'

'That bad! Are they trying to stop her?'

'They don't dare. BBIC's too big a boat to start rocking. It would be like knocking the Earth off her axis. It could make huge, unpredictable tidal waves at a time when people set more store by predictability than common sense. She's made the corporation four or five times bigger now than it was when Barbican was running it. I mean, they all call her Lady Barbican and she has no right to a title like that. Lady Rose is what they should say, but she won't let them. It's Lady B or nothing. I've seen politicians and merchant bankers go purple when they mention her name. But for most of them she can do no wrong, it seems. She was always a goody-two-shoes, even at school, but she didn't like to lose. She's got away with stuff even Maggie or Tony couldn't swing.'

'Like what?'

'All kinds of shifts of capital, moving centres of power, whole countries getting vast brown envelopes in exchange for God knows what. Moving the World Bank HQ to London. Laundering stuff, I'm sure. Using all the contacts she got when she was doing her charity work. Drugs are bound to be involved. Anything that can be done under the counter and behind the scenes, that pious cow will do. Democracy's a laugh these days, Dennis.'

'Is she still in with that NuLabor lot?'

'Thick as thieves. They learned from Barbican and from her. And Paul Frame's still picking up the Englishman's burden and doing something for the lesser breeds without the law. Who is anyone who doesn't accept their economic view of things. Waste of a damned good bonk.'

To hear Bobby accusing capitalism of aggressive imperialism was such a new experience I almost forget what else she was talking about.

'They make Attila the Hun seem like Saint Francis of fucking Assisi, darling. Honest, Dennis, I'm sick of them all. That's why I stay down here. Though how long it will be before they ruin it, I don't know. They want to stop fox-hunting. Anything to distract people from the real issues. They don't care how many millions of people they displace, but we mustn't chase the poor ickle foxie-woxies, must we?'

Well, I wasn't exactly pro-hunt, but I'd long since learned to keep my opinions to myself in Skerring where people had the political views of the average seventeenth-century kulak.

This was all a bit depressing. I'd half-hoped Rosie would somehow redeem Barbican's horrible career. Instead it was pretty obvious that absolute power had done its absolute dirty work on her. She'd turned into the Daughter of Fu Manchu. Making no friends and needing none. As all the ex-commies crumbled and scrambled for handouts or turned on one another in a fury of disappointment, she steadily moved in on their utilities and services – internet providers, telephones, power, transport – until Russia, parts of the Balkans and most of Eastern Europe were branches of BBIC, with only the odd local dictator holding out against the development of essential markets.

Which was where NATO came in, when the job was too big for Jocky.

Bobby was cheerfully cynical. 'Modern capitalism isn't about supply and demand – it's about *demand creation*. Just like the drug trade. It's no coincidence they obey almost identical rules. And have so many identical beneficiaries in the financial world.

'Which reminds me,' she said. 'I've got a couple of ships coming home next week. If you're interested in a few blocks of Moroccan, let me know.'

'You're smuggling now?'

'Don't be daft, Dennis. I just put up the capital. I've got to build back somehow.'

To be honest, Bobby didn't do what she used to do for me and she probably felt much the same. But she was pretty insistent about me staying at Boise and it wasn't easy in Skerring to find an excuse.

I was sneaking back into The Beach a few Fridays later, hoping Bobby hadn't decided to come to pick me up for the usual weekend, when I noticed that the old lounge and bar were filled with weather-beaten-looking characters in headscarves and cloth caps, as if they'd just wandered off the set of the *Return of Doctor Zhivago* miniseries.

Glasses flashing like semaphores, Gordon flew up from the basement to say that it was bound to come. The council was forcing bloody gypsies on us now. I couldn't understand their language, though they appeared to be Muslim, and it looked like the most they owned were the clothes they stood up in. I'd thought gypsies were all Catholics. Old buffers, grannies, mums, kids, a few scowling men. I hoped they didn't have any fucking ethnic instruments on them, I said. I was looking forward to a couple of hours' peace and quiet before the gig. They turned out to be orderly enough, watching the snowy pictures on the old V. I guessed they were Albanian gypsies. I wasn't sure what Gordon was worried about unless he was afraid they were going to steal his chickens and abduct his babies. He said it wasn't his job to look after them. 'And, oh,' he said, 'I forgot. There was a chap looking for you. A bit iffy, if you ask me.'

'Bugger.'

I decided to go down to The Garnett Arms. No customers. Only Tommy Pane, the landlord, behind the bar.

'How do, Denny.' A conspiritorial wink. I'd told him to let me know about strangers who might come looking for me.

'Bloke asking after you, Den. By name. Dennis Cornwall, he said. Gave a good description. I told him to try in Worthing. Bloke like he described plays over there at the Mississippi Grill.'

'Thanks, Tommy.'

'I'm not sure he believed me. Told me his name but it didn't stick. Sinister-looking cove. Mafia chap. You into the Mob, Den?' He laughed. The idea of Skerring attracting Mafia notice was ludicrous. 'Wouldn't like to be on his bad side, though. Bloody monster.'

'Foreign?'

'Either that or from up north.'

'Fromental? Is that the name he gave?'

'That's it. Very likely.'

Jean-Luc came in during our second half, around ten o'clock. He looked like he'd been in every pub on the West Sussex coast. He sat quietly at the back, raising his massive eyebrows at me, his hand engulfing a shant of mild. I winked at him. What else could I do? I hoped he hadn't brought bad news.

When the set was over and I'd had a word or two with the audience, I went to where he was sitting under a nicotine-stained poster of the Players' Tar. He was chain-smoking his bidis as usual. I couldn't help myself. I hugged at him, slapped at him. I didn't care what his news was, I was just very glad to see him. 'Have you come to pay the rent? Anything wrong with Fogg Yard? Roof need repairing? You could have phoned, you know.'

'Not really, man. The entire site's being rebuilt again. You know.'

'That crap Barbi put up wasn't going to last a year. So it's more concrete-and-marble office blocks, eh? And that's the final end of Brookgate.'

'Seems like it.' He was looking around at the brown paint and panelling, the gloomy old ads. 'So do you prefer it here?'

'By and large. At least it's pretty much the same as it always has been. What the fuck are you down here for, man?'

'I just felt like a visit, you know. With everything that's going on between NATO and the Balkans, I wanted to get away and see you.'

'Nowhere better than Skerring for getting away. Nobody knows what's going on down here. I did see something about Yugoslavia. A sort of civil war, is it?'

'I don't believe it,' he said. And insisted on briefing me. I knew that for some time the Yugo authorities had been up before the UN beak for torturing Kosovar Albanians and I'd seen that there was some sort of resistance movement forming in Kosovo, but that was about all.

Anyway, Jean-Luc filled me in on the Serbian faction he called The Black Hand – his theory was that Milosevic was really the chief of a modern version of the secret society that had effectively begun the century's troubles.

'Bastards, man. Fucking bastards. They like what they do. So all the bastards on the other side become freedom fighters – Kosovo Liberation Army, you know.

'There's more propaganda coming out of this than in the whole of World War Two, man. Very hard to get straight answers. Anyhow, the Americans decided to support the Kosovars. To show they were pro-Muslim. They got petulant when their tactics didn't work in Belgrade and decided to display their power, get rid of some decaying warheads and make sure the local bandits had some idea of what they were defying. The UK had taken the American line, as well as the hook and sinker, and all the other countries who depended on the US for much of their own trade had fallen into step, some a bit reluctantly.' And another Crusade was on. Jean-Luc said the sententious self-righteousness emanating from Washington and London was so dense you could feel it on your skin. Unlike Rwanda, this genocide was widely and constantly reported, not as the actions of Christian Serbs against Muslims, but as an attack on the 'ethnic Albanians'. It was almost as difficult to get public support for Muslim peasants as it was for Christian Africans. And they did their best to keep down the reputation of the KLA, as well as trying not to mention how the KLA were running the biggest heroin racket in Eastern Europe and were perfectly capable of murdering their own people in order to maintain American sympathy.

'It's a mess, man. They're using the old techniques. The Americans never lost the trick. You demonize your opponent and find a "victim" you can liberate. Hitler liberated the Sudeten Germans from the Czech yoke, remember? This is the most controlled war I've ever covered. So much spin from so many friendly soldiers and concerned politicians it feels like a fairground ride gone out of control. They really want us to think their way, man. Now why should it be so important? Do they expect this to escalate? Do they want to extend it? Why are they so busily trying to control all the media?'

I'd already lost interest. 'I'm not that paranoid,' I said. 'I believe that most things are accidents and that most elaborate plans generally cock up. Maybe they think they're doing right. Clumsily, but sincerely.'

'Of course they think they're doing right, man. It goes with the package. Puritan cultures, Puritan language, Puritan logic, Puritan self-righteousness. That's what powered the Norman conquests. It's what helped rape Africa and conquer China. Guns and Bibles, man . . .'

This was making me very tired. I went up to the bar and got us a couple more shants of mild. Trying to change the subject didn't do me much good, either.

'Have you seen anything of Tubby?' I asked. 'Or my friend Norrie Stripling?'

'Norrie? Oh, man, that was it!' He snapped his fingers. 'Your grandfather left a message on your phone. He didn't know where you were. Norrie's dead. Heart attack in Drury Lane. Dead on arrival at St Pancras. Sorry, Den. I thought you'd have read about it in the papers. They ran a lot of obituaries. And on the V and the radio and everything. He was a popular guy. Last of his breed, they said.'

'That's right,' I said. 'He was.'

Jean-Luc was drawing concerned brows together. 'So you don't know about Flo Fortnum, either?'

'Go on.'

His sigh threatened to put out every light in the house. 'Well, you know, man. She hanged herself. After all that Millennium Dome scandal. Off one of the central spars. She felt it was all her fault. She'd been in charge of fund-raising after those NuLabs were fined and fired, you know.'

'How much did she raise?'

'Nothing. In fact, some backers withdrew.'

I felt seriously sorry for Flo. She might, after all, be my ex-wife.

'I didn't even hear about the funeral.'

'There wasn't one. She recovered. Always the opposite of the effect she desires. However, man, listen – the rope seriously damaged her vocal chords, so—' he broke into a grin at the same time as I did '—she won't be able to lobby for any more good causes. I think she just married a minor Forte. They're planning to open an upmarket Italian restaurant called Little Venice.'

'What, by the canal?'

'No, man. That's just the name. Leases are astronomical in the actual Little Venice. All bought up in that big deal BBIC did with the Church of England. You can't get them. Flo and Florent have bought a nice place just down the bottom of Whittington Park. Near Tubby's Mill?'

'They'll never make a go of it there. Even pie shops fail.'

'It's one of the few areas that hasn't been gentrified. But they're already calling it Tufnell Village.'

That made London even less attractive. I asked after Maddy.

'She's in South Africa helping build a new theme park: Six Flags Savage Safari. Like a virtual Disney version of *Heart of Darkness*, you know. They've got John Milius doing the scenarios.'

He lit a fresh bidi. 'It's going to bring millions of jobs to the Cape Town area. Billions of dollars. Much-needed tourism. You know, man. The usual remedies. National parks and game reserves find a franchise from Disney helps them keep costs down and attracts more visitors. Good security. No chance of *interahamwe* getting in and carving up the punters.'

Maddy and her partners had successfully completed an *Egypt Experience* near the site of Memphis. The daily chariot races – Egyptians v. Nubians and so on – were hugely popular. They'd been the most successful feature in the *Rome Relived* theme park Maddy's company had co-built with Disney and the Vatican business office. 'And they're doing a *World of Bacchus* park on Lesbos,' said Jean-Luc, 'which I wouldn't say was entirely appropriate. And they're negotiating with the new Iraqi blokes for a *Haroun-al-Raschid World* outside Baghdad.'

'I think I'll stick in Skerring World,' I said. 'It seems to be the only way of avoiding the *Pax Pizzahut*.'

'There are other places still just as real,' said Jean-Luc. He checked his watch. 'Lots of them. But you've turned your back on them.'

'The only gun I've seen in Skerring is a BB gun that our copper took off one of the kids. The only mangled corpse I've seen was a seagull that got trapped in a fan. That's the reality I want, Jean-Luc. Ordinary, old-fashioned English, grey, boring, bloodless, unviolent, gunless and by and large poor enough to be free from the interest of corporate investment. I'm happy I'm living in the next best thing to an Ealing Comedy. An Ealing Tragedy.'

The vast Frenchman rose and swept up the glasses. 'Well, man, you're fucking lucky, aren't you?'

'Am I? Time travel comes with a price, man. And you have to pay it, no matter which way.'

'You're depressed out of your skull, admit it, man.' He began to move towards the bar.

'True,' I said. 'But quiet desperation's the best I can expect. I'm not greedy.'

'That's the point.' He lumbered off and came back with two pints of M&E. 'It's what I wanted to see you about.'

'I thought you were just down here for a day or two off.'

'That's right,' he said. 'Before I go to Kosovo.'

'You're still involving yourself with all that shit, are you?'

'It's my living, man. I go where the papers want me to go. Besides, I'm the only guy with a secret way in. That's why I need you with me.'

'Hold hard. What?'

'I can get us in, but I need you to take the photos. I have a new Sharp pocketbook V camera for you. Stills and movies. Studio quality.'

'What the fuck is that?'

'Jesus, man. Who are you, Rip van Winkle? Everyone's using these – carry it in your pocket. Nobody guesses what it is.'

'In your pocket?'

He reached into his jacket, pulled one out, flipped it open and put it in the palm of my hand. I watched him watching me from the tiny screen.

'You don't need me to use one of these.' I was fascinated. Everything automatic that previously had to be considered, everything else digitalized, on screen.

'Not true, Den. It's like a good musical instrument. Anyone can strum a tune on it, but it takes real talent to get the most out of it. Just like you were doing with that Black Bird.'

'Flattery's another thing that won't work.' I handed the Sharp back to him.

'We have to bring back pictures, Dennis. The job depends on it.'

'Then take some.'

'You know what they're expecting, man. Your eyes. Quality stuff, not the kind of rubbish any peasant can shoot. This'll put your foot back in the door.'

I must admit I hadn't felt so important for years. 'Now I'm enjoying the flattery,' I said. 'Don't stop. But I ain't going to fucking Siberia . . .'

'Kosovo.'

'Serbia,' I said. 'The whole fucking place is gun-happy. Let them get on with it. Sooner or later they'll sort themselves out.'

'I didn't say I approved of the war, Dennis. I just want to know the truth about it. I'm always suspicious of wars that are supposed to free some minority or other. Remember the American Civil War? The Indian Wars? The Inner-City Wars? They've hardly changed their tactics since they started. But because of the amount of spin they're putting on it, I get suspicious. Don't you want to know what's really going on?'

'What's really going on, man, is that I do two nights a week here, one night a week at the Golden Bowl. That and the bits of second-rights money I get keeps me in beer, dope and comics. I get my grub free, mostly. No transport costs. Low rent. Regular millionairess girlfriend who bonks me blind. Why should I want to go to some Ruritanian state and get involved with a bunch of Balkan brigands?'

'Because you're a Rassendyll!' His grin was magnificent. A conscious Porthos. 'The money will be very big. First authentic pictures out of there.'

'What's more, I'm probably still on a black list – a lot of black lists. People will lose interest when they know it's me.'

'Don't be ridiculous, man. They forgot all about you three days later. Your problem is that you think you're better known than you are. You could go anywhere in London and nobody would have heard of you, would even know how you stayed alive. You can sink into a dirty-old-man existence down here, or you can get back in the field and do what you were meant to do.'

'Chew grass,' I said. 'I'm in a field already. I have all the money I need, pard.'

'Not enough.'

'Enough.'

'Not enough to keep you out of jail. The tax laws are a lot tougher now, man. They're going for the American blitzkrieg style just at the point the Americans have realized it doesn't work. That's your country these days, man. Buying second-hand systems. Faulty ones at that. Don't your guys have any ideas of their own?'

'Why should they? They're rewarded for their ability to cling to their orthodoxy, no matter what. The maintenance of orthodoxy obsesses the government which sees its own power dependent on that. Have you listened to cynical schoolkids lately? They know fascism when they smell it. They suss programmatic politics.'

'A shame they couldn't have been this single-minded when they were socialists.'

'They were. That's what threw us into Thatcher's arms.'

Alarm bells were ringing like Christmas Day. I didn't want any politics. I was tired of my own idiotic ideals, my own puritanism, my own naïveties. My own foolish misunderstanding of everything and everyone, especially Rosie.

I didn't want any more trouble. I told him all this again.

'Man, you're wasting your life down here. Wasting your talent.'

'Well,' I said, 'it's familiar and familiarity's all I want these days. Backwaters. I've seen too many twists. Too many changes, Jean-Luc. We thought we could stop another Holocaust by making laws. The universal declaration of human rights is worth fuck all. To get anywhere there has to be a greater common will towards peace and civil order. And that's why we'll never get it. Why only the very rich will be able to afford peace of any kind. It's free-market demographics, pard. The Grand Consumer berserk.'

'Fuck, man. This place isn't a backwater. It's a septic tank.'

I let him buy me another pint of mild. I looked around the pub. It hadn't had any major redecoration since VE Day. It stank of fags and beer. Everything had a heavy patina of nicotine. Its floorboards creaked and its bar was grubby. Even the dart board had been punctured too much. Half the time you used it, the darts fell out. Low aspirations. Low expectations. Nothing wrong with that. The twentieth century's high aspirations, its big expectations of itself, had got us into the mess we were now in. How many big-headed bastards had swaggered across our screens since 1917, knowing exactly what to do to end all our miseries? Most of them weren't like Milosevic. They had bigger dreams than a Greater Serbia.

I wasn't going for any of it. I shook my head.

He was staying over in Brighton, he said. He'd rented a little Honda. He had to know about this job in two days, latest. Or he lost his chance. He had to be at a certain place at a certain time.

I took his card. 'OK,' I said.

He could tell I was only humouring him. 'Don't live the rest of your life in blinkers. This could be your last chance, Dennis, man.'

I told him I didn't know I needed one.

Next day at lunchtime in my wobbling old hotel bed, bonking while staring through the big bay window looking out on a beach that might still have been waiting for Hitler to land, with its rusted machines, tank traps and abandoned artillery bunkers, I wondered if this really was the future. Bobby always got randy on a Saturday around noon and she knew I was usually still in bed. I'd made the mistake of telling her the Revenue was after me. She had an instant solution.

'Marry me.' She lit a cigarette. 'Vanish. Change your name by deed poll to MacMillan. Then nobody will have a clue, darling! And we'll live happily ever after. At Lansing Boise.'

I could get some sort of gloomy satisfaction from Skerring's grey hopelessness, but the idea of ending my days as a squire of some local manor didn't do anything but embarrass and frighten me.

'OK,' I said, 'I'll think about it.'

'Don't say no, Den. We're perfect for each other.' She sat up in the sheets and put out her gasper.

'It's worth considering.'

After she'd left, I lay in the sweaty bed going over my few dreary options. When I'd showered and dressed, it was almost closing time. I thought I might get down to the pub for a swift one. As a matter of habit I took the old service back stairs down and was leaving by the side entrance when three figures stepped out of the shadows, their glasses baleful, their suits threatening. It was the Enforcement Trio.

'Mr Dover?' they said.

'Fuck,' I said.

'You are Mr Dennis Dover?'

They sounded like cops. I suppose they were cops.

'Whad noo?' I said, remembering I was a local. 'Nerdy turdy, eh?'

'We'd like a word.'

'Fuck you,' I said and walked through the door to the outside. Even the drizzle didn't comfort me. They were following me. I broke into a run. They had their huge square file cases. It was obvious that they couldn't catch a blind sloth carrying those heavy weights.

I put a couple of streets between me and them and stopped. What the fuck was I doing? Where the fuck could I find a better hiding place than this? I turned up the collar of my coat. I went back to the front and crunched down to the pier to hear the listless, unhappy waves. Why the fuck had I run for it? Why had I let them bluff me?

There were footsteps behind me. I knew I couldn't be seen from the shadows, but I turned cautiously. It was my half-brother, wearing two cardigans and a pair of baggy cords.

'What do you want, Bernie?'

'Blimey, Den. Nearly gave me a heart attack. Mum sent me to find you.'

'Mum?'

'She heard what happened. She said you'd be best off coming to live with her and the Colonel. They're getting a caravan somewhere on the Downs. They could buy one that was a bit bigger. The Colonel's thinking it over.'

'She's not back with that old horror?'

'Whatever you think of him, he's had a distinguished military career. If it hadn't been for Lloyd's going he'd be back living in Mayfair and so would Mum.'

'They'll find me at mum's as easily as they found me at the hotel.'

'Mum knows that. That's why she's got it all worked out. You leave your clothes on the beach tonight – you know, like they've driven you to suicide – then you go round to Mum's who'll sort you out with some of Marlene's clothes.'

'Hang on. What?'

The idea was that I would probably fit into my simple half-sister Marlene's clothes and pose as her until the danger had passed. Marlene had left it all behind when she went to Jamaica with that Rasta. I wasn't sure we were the same size.

'It wouldn't work,' I said. 'And if they caught me looking like that it would be about as ignominious as the death of Mussolini.'

'What, the old bayonet up the jacksi?' he said, and winked.

That was Edward the Second, I told him. Or Geronimo.

I said to go back to Mum's and let her know I was going up to London for a day or two, to throw them off the scent.

'Good idea,' he said. He sucked at his teeth. 'I'll decorate your room for you. Make it more feminine.'

Next morning I took my stuff round to Mum's, got Gordon to give me a lift into Worthing and caught the train for Brighton. Jean-Luc was staying at The Grand, where the IRA had tried to blow up Thatcher and Co. He was happy to cut his stay short.

'We can only hope,' he said, 'that they don't come looking for you in Fogg Yard before we get a chance to leave.'

'Maybe I could stay at Tubby's?' I suggested. I was keeping this option open. I didn't want to go to Fogg Yard. Tubby's really wasn't an option.

Since that gig, the drummer had grown so reclusive he had no interest in his old pards. Maybe he couldn't be friends with Rosie and with me.

'Tubby's got a lot on at the moment.' Fromental gave a kind of snuffling snigger.

'Don't tell me he's back playing.'

'Not exactly, man. He's engaged.'

'As what?'

'To Flicky Jellinek.'

It felt very strange. 'It was on the cards,' was all I could say. I felt excluded. I felt abandoned.

'They're good together.' Fromental told me.

Was Bobby MacMillan really my only likely future?

Even when we were on the plane for Budapest I didn't feel that I'd left any of my troubles behind. It seemed to me, as we flew towards a conflict beginning to terrify me, that all I could do was drift with the twist. Go with the flow. Let the winds of limbo blow me wherever they fucking felt like. I didn't give a damn.

Budapest to Sofia. Smooth flight. Bumpy landing. I'd asked Jean-Luc what had happened to his Pilbeam story and a big frown had crossed his face. He'd started to say something, stopped and gone to sleep. What had he found out?

Sofia airport isn't as bleak as others, but it's not the best place to be stuck waiting for some kind of commercial transport plane making a flight to Sarajevo. Jean-Luc told me reluctantly how he'd been wrong about Pilbeam. He was a good guy. I asked him how he knew that. He had a few drinks and smoked a lot of bidis. He was thinking over stuff. I knew he wanted to tell me. I knew he felt he should tell me.

'Come on,' I said. I sipped something cold and coffee-like. 'Who's told you to shut up? MI5? CIA?'

This made him start to laugh. First a snort. Then a series of snorts, then the full quake.

'Tell me who Pilbeam is,' I said, 'and what it has to do with Tubby.' Only a hunch, but it made him relax and think some more. We took turns checking at the office. The plane we needed wouldn't appear on the ordinary passenger boards. You had to ask in a special room.

'Oh, man,' he said. 'They didn't know I was going to see you. I didn't know, really, until this job came up. So nobody really told me not to tell you. But they sort of wanted to keep you out of it.'

'Keep me out of what? Who? The band?'

'Sure man!' Another snort of laughter. 'Oh, shit, it can't be important now. But, you see, Tubby *was* Pilbeam, man. At least, in all the important senses.'

I didn't have an inkling what he meant.

'Was him? What do you mean? That was his real name?'

He told me how the real Pilbeam was an amiable chap who had relocated to Skipton years ago, tax free, and bought the castle. Loves it. Keeps it up properly. No restorations. He's very popular in Skipton and the Dales. Known as Martin Hawthornthwaite. Breeds horses up near Dent. Changed his name by deed poll. Matter of public record if you looked. Jean-Luc had looked. All kosher.

'I talked to him, man. I had tea with him at his castle. Nice guy. Asked me not to use the interview, though, to keep his secret. He and Tubby have a lot of similar ideas. He's very happy with the way everything's gone, at least so far.'

'Happy with what?'

This got a further thoughtful frown from Fromental while he enjoyed some inner debate. 'With the idea. He and Tubby support the French policy, you know, of encouraging small, independent businesses. Maintaining strong, responsive public services. It seems to be working for us, these days. Though I can hardly believe it.'

'Wouldn't know,' I said. 'Can't understand politics. You still haven't really explained what Tubby had to do with Pilbeam, man.'

'Tubby bought Pilbeam's name and his island, basically. He put up the communications complex. It was the most sophisticated in the world. Still is.'

'The whole of the Isle of Morn is Tubby's?'

'Effectively. But all he was interested in was the communications side. He was relieved when Pinky Fortnum agreed to go out there and keep an eye on things.'

Some kind of wailing had broken out in the gents' bathroom. We went to take a look, but whatever it was had stopped by the time we got in there. We heard two whispering voices from one of the cubicles and then a dirty cardigan was thrown over the partition. I stood side by side with Fromental at the urinal.

'So,' I said. 'What the fuck would Tubby want with another communications complex? Anyway, I thought that was where Pilbeam was throwing his wild parties. That house of his. Where you got the photos.'

'All Tubby. Mostly at remote. He set the house up exactly for that purpose, so he could get the goods on the powerful. He didn't plan to blackmail them, of course. He was just trying to counter people he thought were out of control.'

We zipped and skipped. Leaving the Gents, we found the airport even more deserted. I began to wonder if there really was a plane. Or if it really was an airport.

'This is nuts.' I wanted to go back to Skerring and marry Bobby. 'Tubby did all that without a word to me? One of his best friends?'

'For that reason, I guess. Didn't want you mixed up in it.'

'Didn't trust me to be in on it.'

'You can never trust a journo, Den. You know that. You don't expect people to trust you. Or me.'

'Tubby should have trusted me.' I felt even more childishly upset. As if every certainty of my life, even the smallest, was being devastatingly challenged. I sounded like a fool to my own ears. 'He's always been my mate.'

'And always liked to control. You know that. Maybe he didn't need you in on his secret? Maybe he didn't want any friend compromised?'

A guy in a red shirt with blue flashes on it started waving urgently at us from the office. Then he yelled and pointed towards the door we were supposed to go through. We'd done all the million passport checks. We picked up our stuff and ran out onto rainy tarmac.

A surprisingly modern plane. A Fokker. And the passenger accommodation was more comfortable than a regular airline's. The pilot shook hands with us. He was a big, wide-faced, blue-eyed Slav with his cap on the back of his head, who kicked the plane into the air as if he was urging on a horse. It was like being flown by a Cossack. He didn't know much English. The cabin was noisy and it was hard for us to go on talking. I shouted into Fromental's ear. 'Has this to do with Tubby's pie-throwing campaign?'

'A development, I think. You know how long he's considered Barbican the devil incarnate. As soon as Barbican tried to get hold of the Mill, Tubby seems to have stopped being Mr Nice. There's a lot of evidence that as well as using me to distribute those pictures and start putting the wind up the politicians and business people, he fed Barbi a lot of misinformation, especially around the time Barbican married Rosie. But it all goes back twenty years or more. He's been gathering information, sending out information, distorting information . . .'

'Distorting?'

'I think the reason Barbican started losing his judgement was because Tubby had hacked into his whole communications system, man. Tubby could doctor any information coming in to BBIC. He could send misinformation. On which the company would then act. This, of course, meant that they made a lot of wrong decisions. Seemed to get flakey. Tubby could give the impression that the BBIC empire was disintegrating. And who was now controlling what. And whom. Even when Barbican discovered the truth, he could not be sure of it any longer. While he was drumming as part of Barbi's backing band, Tubby had been bashing away at Barbi's judgement.'

'And Rose?'

Fromental shrugged. 'I think she was hungry for power. Willing to get it at any price.'

The same thing Bobby had told me.

'You're not suggesting she planned to kill Barbican?'

Fromental smiled. 'Oh, no, man. I'm sure she didn't push him. But I bet she encouraged him to jump . . .'

Then the plane began screaming and the pilot pulled heavily on his controls, shouting something Slavic, laughing wildly and shaking his head. We bumped out of that one. It seemed the peaks of mountains were a few feet below us.

Tubby also being Pilbeam explained quite a bit. Why he wouldn't come to the door when I visited him. He'd probably been on Morn. And his voice had been a tape or a remote. The way he scared the skinheads. I hadn't even guessed. But that was why Flicky had begged me not to say anything. She thought I'd seen more than I had. She definitely overestimated Dennis the Dumbo. Of course she'd been Tubby's go-between.

It was ludicrous. It was sickening. Imagine someone of my age realizing suddenly that he's been betrayed. The victim of a fairly complicated conspiracy made up by his dearest, most cherished friends.

I was ready to get back to the dull ache that was Skerring rather than stay on this roller coaster of emotions. Clearly Rosie had been in on it with them, too, Why would they want to spend so much time deceiving me? I'd never betrayed them. I was, if anything, childishly loyal. Was taking those pictures of Kim that bad a crime? Or had Rosie created the whole thing? Not to harm Barbican, but to ruin me? This was paranoia of a kind that wasn't natural to me and I suppose it was all the harder to take. About an hour before we landed I started pulling hard on the Starka vodka the pilot sold us. He ran a sort of rough-and-ready duty-free service.

I got moody. Self-pity on that scale is incommunicable. Jean-Luc clearly regretted telling me anything. He kept apologizing, trying to reassure me that everyone must have meant well. Explaining events in the best possible light. He'd never been over-quick on the uptake where human relationships were concerned. On the other hand, was I?

Sofia to Sarajevo. A mess. But we eventually met up with Micky Kay, the people smuggler, our guide, whose English was mostly memorized from the less complex Arnold Schwarzenegger movies. Our way in, Jean-Luc had been assured, to Kosovo. I didn't give a crap. I felt that I'd be better off dead. Unexpectedly, I started to grieve for Norrie.

We travelled through that night. Nothing fancy. Micky had slipped us some documents in Russian. He assured us that they showed we were friendly, pro-Serb correspondents. Even I, in my joggled state, could guess what that would mean to the average Serb Black Hander, most of whom couldn't talk decent Serbian, let alone anything else. Milosevic had banned journalists from the region. Which gave us all some idea of what was going on under cover of the NATO bombing, just as the Final Solution had had to wait until the Second World War was in full swing.

We were now in constant danger, either from NATO bombs, Serb gestapo or KLA grenades. Why were these risks worth it? Jean-Luc was nuts. I wondered how much to believe of anything he told me.

Then we were out of the truck and slipping through cut wire, under wooden fences and through ditches, all in the darkness with the occasional help of a low-powered torch. Soaking rain. Into another truck. Blankets. Shake of hands, exchange of cigarettes, reassurances in broken French. On our way in, don't worry. And I'm thinking to myself, all I want to do is get back to Skerring.

Then I remember that I can't go back to Skerring. Not to what Skerring once meant to me. I'm sinking so fast into depression I'm becoming a risk to the others. So I pull myself together with a bit more help from a couple of joints and a bit of opium. I'm now convinced we're being set up by these bastards. Playing straight into Milosevic's hands. At this rate we're going to wind up looking dazed and bruised on *Belgrade Tonight*. I hardly have anything to say to anyone. I don't trust Jean-Luc any more, let alone the Yugoslavs.

The idea is to get into Priština, keep our heads down and see what we can. Then we slip out into rural areas. If challenged we speak French and wave Russian papers. It didn't seem much of a cover to me. I wondered who'd set it up.

Fromental was doing everything he could to make me feel better, talking and talking and talking, the way only tired people can. He told me how 'Pilbeam' had completely reproduced all Barbi's communications systems. He could create a virtual world of dodgy but authoritative info. Every kind of misinformation, including the weather. Controlling the smallest detail. And, of course, Rosie was doing her bit at the other end!

Naturally.

'That's why she married him, man. That's why she put up with all his bullshit, all his fantasies, everything, eh? To get control of the BBIC empire. Lady Macbeth and Salome and Nana and Camille and Medea and the Thatcher, all rolled into one, that woman! And now she rules the world, man. For all we know this war is on her behalf. She's certainly powerful enough to engineer it.'

Jesus, I thought. I tried to find something in myself that echoed what Rosie must have been thinking and feeling. It had never occurred to me that we weren't the same. Yet I kept receiving proof that she was about as different from me as you can get. When had she changed? Did she present her 'good' face to me and her 'bad' face to Barbican? Was she that nuts? That conniving? It meant my instincts since boyhood had been shit. Fuck. She must have laughed herself silly at me sometimes. Sod her. I didn't give a bugger's.

However, by the time we're being rowed down a dark, narrow river between high, orderly banks, in a freezing cold night, without a clue where we are, I'm seriously wondering if this is better than giving myself up to the Revenue.

I'm too old for any of it, I'm thinking, as we get out of the boat and begin to follow, at the guide's urgent insistence, in the leader's footprints. It's like a kid's game. What the fuck is it all about?

I wondered what it would take to make me get as ruthless and calculating and downright vicious as Rosie. When had it happened? Nigeria? Or before then? A hardening of the soul in the face of too much human pain. When did she go from selfless angel to selfish demon? Or had she always been closer than I realized to hating the people she tried to help? An echo of *Caligula*?

In spite of all the crap Fromental's on a high. We're the only journos to bust through the security barrier and get into Kosovo. I've started to realize he's barmy. Competing with himself for a scoop. What was the risk of a little personal safety, when you could report what was actually going on and find out if it was more than the old Balkan blood-feuding jacking itself into the late-twentieth century with the methods and weapons we'd created over the past few years? Blood for blood. Blood for blood. Fromental thought they'd never gone away. 'Pig-ignorant peasants, man, come up with pig-ignorant ideas. The sooner we concrete everything over and eat food produced by alert, well-educated urban technicians, the better. This isn't a world that has any use for peasants and that's why they're so resentful. Meanwhile, if there are no Jews around, they'll find a few gypsies to take it out on.'

Jesus, I thought. It's too late to save any of these fuckers just by trying to tell the truth in a newspaper. He was as much stuck in his past as his peasant relatives.

Blood is blood. Blood will out. Blood will tell. But we're not sure how that relates to the AIDS epidemics that flood like rivers through those communities of blood.

A tip for viewers at home, though. If you think you heard something on the noon news that either changes or disappears by the evening news, there is nothing wrong with your judgement. If you heard it, remember it. It's probably true. You can believe your ears.

There weren't enough clear-cut issues for this to be a just war or any other kind but one to swell the coffers or the egos of the wonkers who declared it.

I wasn't learning anything new. I wanted to go back a year or two and stay there. I didn't want any more life. Or death, for that matter. I wanted nothing. I wanted Skerring.

Jean-Luc is whispering to me how they're taking us to a mass grave, how the road's been mined and the guy with the AK-47 ahead of us has memorized the route. But we must be careful to do exactly as we're told. Then the world starts roaring around me and I lose control of everything. I'm adrift on a burning wind that sears my clothes, tears stuff from my body and starts gnawing on my right foot. I try to reach for my cameras, thinking to protect the lenses. I feel a weight on my upper body.

I struggle underneath it but can't get out. Can't breathe. Start losing it. The cameras will be ruined. Must get it together to roll over on them.

I knew I'd stepped on a mine. I felt that slight yielding just before it happened. I was almost relieved. Joining the dead. If not happy, at least I'm no longer unhappy. I feel almost glad.

At least until the pain begins to come back. I can't understand why it doesn't kill me. Everything has to be broken.

And then I pass out.

Blind man walking down the line. Blind man singing for his time. Blind man walking across the land. Blind man's soul got the blues in his hands. Blind man. Blind man. Blind man's blues.

Blind man hopping across Eastern Europe. For a while, as I understand it, I became collateral. Eventually someone bought me, took me out of a field hospital in Macedonia and got me as far as Athens. I didn't really know much of this. Fromental was gone. Probably killed by the same mine. From time to time my feet started hurting or I felt an itch under the bandages over my eyes, but mostly I was out of it. I probably had more morphine jabs in those few weeks than William Burroughs had hot dinners. It made me hallucinate, of course. And when I was awake I heard people talking about how my brain had been fried. That helped. It would take more than a few shots of junk to fry my fucking brain. I told them while they were at it to fry me some bloodworms. Everything looked like bloodworms. Living, writhing, slipping about under the bed. Except I was blind. I couldn't find them. It was a weird feeling, seeing things while you were blind.

My fingers and toes were the bloodworms, slithering across the sawdust of Varney's. Or were they my guts? Or the pig's? But the pig was trotting across Tower Bridge with a Union Jack sticking out of his arse. And I slipped back to that pig race I went to in Missouri somewhere, when I was doing the pix for a Mark Twain feature. Those pigs were addicted to cookies. It was what made them run. But they ran as fast as a pig can run. Anything for an Oreo. The people who put on the races didn't want to get into trouble so the pigs were segregated. White pigs weren't allowed to compete against black pigs. Black pigs, legend had it, made the best worms. I could feel the warm, bloody oats in my mouth. But there was something else in there as well. Something that tasted bitter as steel.

It was now obvious how these fake friends, these cynical relatives, had been out to get me for years. All of them lying to me. Excluding me. Not letting me know what the fuck was going on. Tricking me over and over and over again. Tubby, Rosie, Paul Frame, even Fromental and Flicky Jellinek, had thought me such a wonker I couldn't be trusted with what the rest of them knew. Great. My self-esteem wasn't the pristine thing of beauty it had once been. I probably was a wonker.

I'd definitely been the biggest prat in history, if what I suspected was true. There was a strong possibility that every lead on a story any of them had ever given me was a nail in some competitor's coffin. I was the unwitting hatchet man. Just another rung on Rosie's ladder as she climbed up the sky to eat the universe. If I'd been so wrong about her and so wrong about me and so wrong about almost everyone I knew, what the fuck was I worth?

I demanded the right to die, to decide when to terminate myself. With deliberate mockery my guards jabbered nonsense at me.

Around that time I was transferred to Geneva. You could tell it was a step up by the smell and feel of the sheets, the efficiency of the staff, the crisp voices, the rattle of steel. And I could understand their French. The food smelled better, too. But this was all to lull me into false security, I decided.

I began to object. They were planning surgery. I knew this invasion could do me no good. I told them to keep out of my body. They had no authorization. No papers.

I went back to Kosovo, but this time I was wrapped in a huge, warm duvet. Floating a few feet above the tops of fir trees, looking down on black walls, strings of pale smoke. I remember Fromental remarking that most of the cruise missiles involved were close to the end of their use-by dates and they had to be dumped somewhere before 1 January 2000. One of those win-win situations, I'd said. It was as if he was next to me, rather than circling the moon. I had a feeling he had caught the worst bit of blast. Now, he said, they can send all their out-of-date and inappropriate pharmaceuticals and medical supplies there and write them off against their taxes. Burroughs-Wellcome or Glaxo-FamCom had sent nothing but an unpopular brand of pile ointment. And the Americans had added sententiously that it was Serbia's business to clean up the mess. Now that's nerve.

The radio's on.

'What? The war's over already?'

'Been over quite a while, me old son.' The English orderly said he'd get a television in now I'd made such good progress. Fromental, an embarrassed ghost, an invisible rabbit, vanished. 'We won. Naturally.'

The nurse's motive for being friendly was also beyond me. I decided to pretend to trust him, until I found out a little more. Did he hope to inherit something from me?

I was in a desperate situation. Trapped in a hospital, deep in the heart of Switzerland, and blind in both eyes. Bang went the chances of getting my old job back. On the other hand, a career as a blues singer might take on a bit of extra authenticity.

I then started to wonder if this wasn't some payback from Rosie. I'd been set up so frequently in the past, it would have been a matter of easy habit to set me up now. Rosie didn't want me drifting around because I was the only one who had really known her, could tell people how the changes I'd glimpsed in her after she'd married Barbican had been almost sinister.

Wasn't that barmy? Bobby MacMillan had said Rosie was always like it. Only muggins hadn't noticed. I'd idealized her, I suppose, the way some girls idealize their brothers.

At first they told me I might not have to be blind for ever, that there were new techniques that could almost certainly save my sight.

I got a bit euphoric, I think, after that. I'd believe anything. Maybe they changed my drugs. Whatever, I felt better than I'd felt in ten years. It was as if all my innocence was coming back. It was like living in one of those nice, reassuring environments, safe and clean and rational, that you get in Wells and Clarke, where everyone's civil and the great struggle for liberty and egalitarianism has been won. Always a bit dodgy in reality, but here it had the authority of those books Rose and I had read as kids. The rational future. It even seemed that the V was contributing to my fantasy news of the US implementing an astonishingly democratic, progressive and humane national health service and doubling spending on education, setting up an independent public broadcasting system funded by public licence and free of all government and business controls, bringing in the funds to challenge the BBC and CNN, establishing a low ceiling for campaign spending and strict limits on contributions.

I forget who they said the new President was. He didn't sound familiar but he spoke in complete sentences and his Congress was made up of new faces, too. It was probably a movie I was confusing with reality. Difficult to tell sometimes in my situation. Still, I got euphoric, even though it was probably only some pious SF series I was watching – or even inventing in my own head. It was a great series, anyway. The North and West started making massive, serious investments in the South and East and some countries were already beginning to emerge from their misery. The cynical certainties of the despairing began to disappear, leaving fundamental extremists with no constituency. It was like those montage scenes in *Things To Come*, where straight-backed volunteers start to rebuild the world – or those old propaganda films from the New Deal, featuring fresh-faced farmers marvelling at the coming of electricity. Not very different to the United Planet of the Dan Dare comics I'd been reading down in Skerring. Maybe that's where I got it all from, that vision of a mutually respecting civil and civilized world, judging itself by its best ideas and actions.

Not much different from the world we all want. That common dream. That place of peace and good health we were promised as the prize of our progress.

They got me a Walkman and some miscellaneous CDs, most of them surprisingly close to my tastes. I'd always liked the Colombo Brothers, Bal Taborin accordion from the thirties and forties. But halfway through the first track I thought of my ruined Les Hivers and fumbled the CD off. Through trial and error I found out that the Walkman was also a recorder. It didn't take me long to work out the right buttons. That Calvert album I'd loved now depressed the shit out of me. There was even a CD of our last gig on the bridge. I stopped listening to everything but an old Zoot Money album. What exactly were they trying to do to me?

The eye operations got increasingly painful. My whole body felt as if it had been blown apart. I couldn't stand it. I suppose they put me back on the junk.

At some point it occurred to me that the hospital staff might be lying, that all this utopian illusion was induced by them to control me, perhaps kill me. I had no one I could confide in, but I began to feel that, if there was no escape from my enemies, I might as well die. It was the last thing I could control. I began to retreat, down into my own miserable, self-loathing, self-deluding, self-pitying heart.

I think I became conscious of them deciding to send me home to London because that's what they were testing me for, to find out if they could take me to the next stage at the New Royal.

I didn't give a damn. I was glad to be going back to my own turf. Even blind I could probably find my way to some sanctuary. Get away from them. Get back to Skerring and my mother and Bobby and let Bobby pay off the enforcers. I heard them say they were going to have to fly someone or other in.

I didn't even wonder who was paying for all this expensive private care. Still dumb, eh?

I'd gone through life in a dream, imposing my own ludicrous fancies on people and places, not once looking into my own motives and actions, though pretending to. Now reality had brought me up short. Never really sympathetic to other people. Deceiving myself that I was somehow above the herd, its moral superior.

What was the difference between my arrogance and the arrogance I despised? I was a populist, I said. I spoke for the community, for the mob. But where was the mob? Had it been destroyed at last? Or was there a new mob now? An e-mob?

On the V. That serial still running. Through various civil actions, we were marching against the fortresses of privilege. We were taking back our public rights, our real democracy.

Or maybe not.

What a trick those utopian nations had been, from eighteenth-century Americans and Frenchmen with their idealized democracies of good-hearted gentlemen, through Communism and Fascism, those triumphs of the proletariat. And now more and more specious talk of Third Ways, of modifying the effects of unregulated corporatism without stopping its voracious progress, insisting on its uses as an engine of profit, of material change, of social improvement. Everything had proven a betrayal. It had been a century of betrayals. We'd betrayed every promise we had made to ourselves. All we had learned at the end of it was how to hide or forget our shame. All we had earned was guilt.

A confused transition. Reassuring voices. Different textures. Movement. I was on a plane or helicopter. More road travel. I tried to make my senses sharper. Were we in London? Or was this another deception?

Hard to say how much time passed. Tones change. The language gets easier to understand. This was definitely England.

Flashes in my head. Images of friends, favourite places, like watching an old montage.

Then I was on the road again. I felt myself slipping in and out of a stupor as I went from bed to trolley, to ambulance and back again. More reassuring murmurs. I felt like a calmed lamb in a slaughter-house. Enough to make anyone anxious.

Smells of roses, fresh-cut grass, summer rain. The country. Hardly any traffic. A river somewhere. Or a fountain, maybe. I sit outside. Someone holds my hand. We don't speak. I begin to cry. Then I'm on my own again and I hear them whispering out there. Too much nerve damage. No way we can save anything. There are a few other tests we can try.

Back-projected in my skull, I was being shown a series of Mickey Mouse cartoons. The silent black-and-white ones when Mickey was still an anarchist with a huge, wicked grin. Everyone was running about hitting everyone else. But they seemed to be enjoying themselves. My mind slopped in my skull, half-full of mystery. Paradox was a balance. Paradox was the truth. This time my laughing fit lasted so long they thought they'd try to find another new treatment.

It wasn't just my eyes, of course. They were rebuilding me. I was going to come out of hospital as the Bionic Man. Or maybe the person who came out wouldn't be me. Maybe they hadn't got to my brain yet. I was being regrown in a lab.

I'd made it as clear as I could in my clearest moments that I didn't want any visitors, yet as soon as I got to the New Royal Eye it seemed there were a whole lot of aliens in the room. Filling up the entire space. They had wired my mouth shut, presumably to keep me from telling what I knew. I could tell them a lot. A lot about blood. A lot about greed. And power. And corruption. But they didn't want Dennis Dover, intrepid photog and journo. They wanted Dennis Dover, Class One Dope, whose stories were only as good as the friends who fed them to him. Just a piece in the game they were playing to bring down the King and put the Queen in his place. I don't know why I thought my experience unique. It's a common enough story. Watch your former comrades take a bung. Feel a friend shaft you for a fiver. See the only woman you ever really loved turn from Mary Poppins to Medea in one easy move. In my rational periods, which were few, I tried to trace the moment of Rosie's change. But it just didn't come. Nothing resonated quite right. So was Bobby closer to the truth and Rosie had simply never revealed that side of herself from the age of nought to the age of forty-five? Why? Because she wanted to please me, be the same as me? If I could, I would have shaken my head. No sense there. Barmy as I was, I should be able to look back and say 'Yes, that time we were mudlarking' or 'That time down the Limbo', or 'That time in Zaïre'. But I couldn't.

It crossed my over-medicated mind that Rosie's evil double had killed her and taken her place. That would explain why she didn't want to go on seeing me, because I'd guess the truth. So she invented an excuse. Same reason she wore a mask to gigs. And that would be why I got such a strong sexual buzz off her, and it would explain her improved singing voice. By God, her speaking voice had been close enough to fool me. But there again, it had happened suddenly, so the Rosie I met at the live bird market wasn't the same as the Rosie I met a bit later in John Adams. Paranoid as I could get, even that didn't quite fit.

What did fit was how she'd played Barbican. If she could fool me, she could easily fool him, especially if she was pandering to his sexual fantasies as Bobby had said. And she'd worked on his judgement, I could see that. And weakened him further by encouraging him to take more and more drugs. While Tubby was feeding him fear of exposure *and* financial ruin. So that Barbi compounded mistake with mistake. Great if you could pull it off. But why do it just to take over an empire and run it exactly as Barbi had run it on false sentiment and real rapacity? Fromental said she had more power in the US than any political party and far more power than the President. Her companies must have owned two-thirds of Washington after she'd taken over Monsanto and United Fruit again. They'd been lost in one of Barbican's loonier responses to Tubby's virtual info. She could do anything she liked with the world and she chose to leave it alone, make a profit, be the biggest bug with the biggest ball of dirt on the planet. Maybe Barbican had infected her with something? GM gobblebugs? Or were they really building a secret rocket ship to take them to a new planet they'd bought?

AIDS would change your attitude. Maybe that was it, though. The reason for her betrayal of us. HIV, anyway? Was that how Kim came by it? Or maybe some sort of terminal illness?

This was getting stupid. An entire circus of clowns, still in black and white, performed before me. I hated circuses. How much more fantastic could it get?

Watching the clowns I had another idea. Clones! Tubby had cloned us all. The reason I was here was because they were in the process of making a series of me. Maybe I was already one of a series? For when they needed a really dumb pet journo to do their dirty work. I began to get paranoid again. How did I know I'd really even stepped on a landmine in Kosovo? That could be a virtual memory. In fact everything, including this, could be a virtual memory. A detailed construct. All of me. And they'd blinded me so I couldn't escape. There was still no one I could confide any of this to, of course. Every so often there were 'visitors' whom I knew to be staff members dressed up. Like clowns, I said. One as 'Tubby', another as 'Fromental', a 'Paul Frame', a 'Flicky Jellinek', a 'Pinky Fortnum', even a 'Rosie'. I told them I might be stupid but I wasn't that stupid and to fuck off.

Fromental was definitely dead. It was half the rest of them who weren't really dead or were really someone else or whatever. Next, one of the doctors would turn up near the bed saying he was 'Barbican'. Barbican I could be sure of. He really was back from the dead. As, of course, was I. *Because I am dead and a friend of the dead.*

On the other hand, I thought, as I listened to the V, I could be in the world of the dead already. Apart from sharp pains in my feet and sometimes my eyes, there was no real evidence of life. And every sign I'd died. Even the news on the V gave that impression.

I could be constructing my own world from the fragments of memory and desire that remained after the shrapnel went into my head.

As I lay there I'd hear about a society in which, almost every week, some fresh advance would be made in legislation, some fresh will would come from the politicians to tackle the problems of prisons or regulate the activities of monopolies and mega-corporations. It was like the great age of progressive Victorian politics.

It was just a lot of sci-fi, of course. Some kind of therapy they were giving me. Rosie wouldn't allow it to happen. She was too powerful for any government or any nation's public to fight. So if I wasn't being brainwashed or fantasizing, this had to be mock legislation, without any financial backing or real effect. Feel-good legislation. Whatever it was, unless I'd lost all judgement, it had improved the political rhetoric. The pieties and faux frankness of NuLaborism had given way to a much more convincing tone. Either that or whatever shreds of brain I had left had finally worn to nothing.

I dreamed I'd found the Epiphone, the Black Bird, but it wasn't the original. It was a beautiful fake. When I played it, instead of singing back to me it merely translated what I was playing into familiar V jingles. Diamonds or carrots. You'll find them all at Harrods. Come and park at Marks and Sparks. Something to do with the M&S/Harrods merger.

Later I began to realize that all this happy shit, all this social progress, was just propaganda. That BBIC had actually taken over the BBC and all other V companies. Outside the laboratory where I was a guinea pig, the world was a wasteland, its last substance sucked from it by corporate greed. Now reality was what they told me it was. I'd seen the whole episode on an original 1960s *Twilight Zone.*

Anyway, that's how banal your imagination gets on too much morphine and whatnot. It also makes it hard for you to separate any real conspiracy from the imaginary. In my more rational patches I continued to do my best.

Some smooth posho came in to have a chat. She was rabbiting a lot of tosh about nano-technics and I agreed amiably with everything she said. Yes, boss. That's right, boss. Anything you say, boss. Just as long as you go away, boss. She talked about seeing everything in black and white and I said 'It's the problem with the world today, boss. Polarization, right?'

Now I'm having to swallow philosophy. Yes, boss. Too right, boss. Anyway, she murmured sentimentally and put her hand on my arm. She called me a pioneer. I became alert at that point. Far too late as usual. Do you mean guinea pig? I asked. Of course not, she said.

I got a bit jumpy. I started listening for traffic sounds, asking nurses odd questions that would help me place myself, ready for the getaway. I might as well have saved the effort because within a couple of days I'd been premedicated into Narnia, back with the delusions and hallucinations again. In my delirium they became more sinister. Shadowy figures of Rosie, Tubby, Fromental, Paul appeared around me frequently. I felt like Macbeth trying to get a bite in between ghosts. I told them to fuck off and stop trying. If nothing else I was wise to them now. Then I attempted to convince a nurse that I had a secret horde of krugerrands at my apartment if he'd get me home. He said he couldn't help. Krugerrands weren't legal tender any more. He was lying, of course. But then, so was I.

'Besides which,' he said, 'your operation's coming up. You'll be able to get yourself there in a few days. A couple of weeks.'

Sure, I said. Fuck you. They still thought I was as dumb as ever. I'd heard them say too much of the optic nerves were damaged. The tests had proven that.

I fell into sleep and something bad started happening to my head. Slivers of pain, wires of agony lying against my eyes, slipped into my ears, needles in my brain. Sinuses. Nerve sheathing. This was it. My panic was almost totally repressed. I didn't care, but I knew this was my last moment to say goodbye to what was left of me before I became a cloned 'me'. Maybe the clones would be happier, I thought.

The sensation turned to gold-and-silver shards, as if every piece of shrapnel that had gone into my skull was being vibrated. Zig-zags. Zips of refined agony. Balls of pulsing scarlet horror. Lines of crimson crisscrossing in exquisitely complex patterns of pain. I had to admire my torturers. Red advanced. Green retreated. No old-fashioned bludgeons here. I watched something move in the fog. One of those big old double-decker trams my dad used to drive. But this wasn't new. This was a film. I recognized the actors. I'd seen them a million times on those old rerun channels. This was long before my day. I knew the film though. Or was it my father's past I was watching? Or maybe my mother's? That was it! They were installing the memories.

I started looking at other old movies, all black and white. Ealing comedies. London Films. Dramas with James Mason and Margaret Lockwood. I recognized them from their backgrounds, the parks, the woods and lakes surrounding the studio. I didn't actually see the stars, but I heard their voices from time to time.

The Wicked Lady. Rosie Begg was in Margaret Lockwood's part and Fromental or sometimes me was James Mason. Best pair of laughing rogues who ever earned a living from the High Toby. Your watch, sir, if you please. Dear lady, keep your trinkets with my compliments. Brought low by misunderstandings, by the greed of others. Just like me and Rosie. Except it was now obvious she had been deliberately supplying half the misunderstandings. And the greed.

She had never given me a chance to explain myself because she had no need or desire for the truth. She just wanted me in a useful position. I loved that movie, though. 'Will he live?' How many love-lost women have asked that question? 'Will he see?' I could hear Margaret now.

'Not in quite the detail you and I see. More like a cat. Mostly monochrome and two-dimensional, but perfectly useful. We're hoping to get colour later.'

Were Margaret and Sam Kydd talking about V sets they were buying? DVDs? Something advanced and digital? Or early PCs? This wasn't in the original. And James Mason would have uttered a gentlemanly snort at the notion he might know anything of nano-technology. Haven't played a scientist or a surgeon in years, dear boy, unless you count Polidori. Did you say nano-optics?

I phased out on him. I went into another deep, deliberate sleep.

Margaret Lockwood turned naturally into Rosie and we were side by side again, King and Queen of the Road, ready to rob any tram that chanced to cross the heath at night. And when our daring pursuits were done, we'd ride home to Brookgate and our old refuge, The Hare and Hounds.

Comrades in the same cause. As we'd always been until Rosie married Barbican. That had to be the point of change, after Ken Saro Wiwa and Ibram-al-Rikh' were killed. The serial betrayal of Africa. She had decided that there was nothing she could do to beat them. So she might as well join them. Just like Caligula. And then she'd perhaps turned her self-blame against me. Were her responses to my pictures aggressive because they reminded her of what she'd given up?

There I was, back on the familiar merry-go-round, thinking about Rosie.

A large hand fell on mine. I shuddered. For a moment it was as if Fromental had come back from the grave.

'Jesus, man, they did a great job on you.' Fromental's voice all right. 'A technological miracle.' Convincing, too. It was a relief to go along with the pretence.

'You watch it, you bastard, or I'll jump out of this bed and give you a good kicking.'

That laugh, coming up like lava from the earth's core, couldn't be reproduced.

'How, man? Will you stand on one leg and kick me with your stump or stand on the stump and try to kick me with your foot?'

It could only be Fromental. Nobody else was that unsubtle.

'One foot?'

'Oh, shit, man. Maybe you're still not ready for the news. Oh, fuck. I'm sorry. You've been out of it a long time, man. Coma. Then raving crazy.'

'I've only got one foot?'

'Well, you know, man. What can I say? You stepped on a land-mine . . .'

'And what about my eyes?'

'Blind, man.'

'Yeah. How blind?' While he was blundering along I might as well make the most of it.

'Well, man, you'd better ask some of these doctors, you know. They've done all this great new surgery on you, man. You were really hit, you know. But nothing immediately vital. Saved my fucking life. You took most of the blast. Which wasn't a grade one, apparently. KLA got us back to Macedonia. A lot of shrapnel. Most of mine in the fucking backside. But we made it through. You went to Switzerland. I went to Hackney.'

'Hackney?'

'Best facilities in the world nowadays, man. You've really been out of touch. I thought you were supposed to have a V and a radio in here.'

'Come on! Hackney!'

'They took good care of me. And today they told me I could come over to visit.'

'Well,' I said, 'it's nice to see you. I'm glad you're not dead.'

'I'm sorry about your foot, man. And, you know, the other stuff.'

'Don't worry. It's a lot better than I thought. You're still alive. I've lost a plate but I've gained a mate.'

'It's karma,' said Margaret Lockwood from the other side of the bed, 'for all those tricky Diana shots you sold. I always heard wanking turned you blind.'

'Just a bit short-sighted,' I said. I was on overload. Footless. Blind. Rosie at my bedside? If I hadn't been tranked, my heart would have bust out of my reconstructed ribs. I didn't care what had happened in the past. Every pain vanished. She was there. I'd have given up any limb and organ to die reconciled with Rosie.

I turned on the hard pillow and something flickered, then shifted into focus. Black and white. Two-dimensional. Like an old movie. Is this what they'd been talking about? Could I see or was it a subtler form of brainwashing?

And there she was. I could see Rosie. The old, familiar, smiling Rosie. But it was Rosie in one of those Margaret Lockwood movies. She was holding out her hand to me and making me very confused. Sharp contrast. And turning me on again. And me wondering why my leg felt lighter and as my wongo went wacko and thinking she couldn't possibly want me now and how could she care that much about me if she was prepared to put me through so much shit and then I felt guilty about taking those photos of Kim and I burst into tears.

I lost focus. Her image began to melt. A million years of pain ceased to be.

'You've caught me a bit off balance.'

How could I forget so much misery so quickly? And how could I forgive her for what she was doing? I tried to turn away. I reached up to wipe my eyes and hit a bar of plastic.

'They look just like ordinary shades, man, don't worry.'

'What do?'

'The circuits they use to connect the images to your eyes, man. Mostly electronic surgery. Projected images. Tiny transistors, man. You never saw anything like it.'

Things were back in focus as I blinked off the tears. I saw Fromental looming down at me. He was Boris Karloff wondering why the little girl wasn't moving any more.

'How do I look?'

'Pure James Whale,' I said. 'This is cool.'

'He's still, you know, feverish.' Fromental looked across the bed at someone.

'I'm sorry,' I said. 'I hadn't believed you existed.'

'You're right,' he said. 'I'm really a giant invisible white rabbit.' He bent to put a kiss on my unfeeling forehead. Then he left.

Another figure came up. Someone out of that great *Pickwick Papers* with the whole Ealing repertory cast. Sam Kydd. James Hayter. Nigel Patrick. Donald Wolfit. Hermione Baddeley, Hermione Gingold, Kathleen Harrison. Mr Pickwick was Tubby Ollis. Dorian Theakston. Hornsey Pilbeam. Something of a habit, changing names. A recluse? An actor on life's stage?

'Wotcher, Tub,' I said. It was funny what a bit of eyesight could do for your paranoia. Black-and-white and two-dimensional, at least I had perspective. I was my old gullible self again. Almost. There were probably other bits missing they hadn't told me about yet. For that matter, I had a feeling the batteries weren't cheap. I was going to have to earn a living. Still, all they needed to do was build in a camera and Bob's your uncle. One blink and you're snapped. Digital brainfun.

'You've come a fair old way since I last saw you.' Tubby looked as if he was crying. 'I thought I'd lost the best cook in London.'

'I can still make the plummiest duff on the Spanish Main. And stuff a boy in a barrel of apples. All I need is a crutch and a parrot.'

'We won't overdo the sea-cook jokes. Or the Robert Newton impressions. Even if they are therapeutic for you.' Tubby had recovered himself. And got back to normal weight. Had he and Rosie really conspired to kill Barbican, or at least to drive him to his fake suicide? They both looked a lot more relaxed than I last remembered. Why shouldn't they? Between them, they owned the whole sodding world. Shiny and sleek in their colour versions, I bet. 'I'm sorry we didn't tell you anything, Den. We already had a deal that we'd carry the whole burden of this because secrecy was crucial. There was nothing for you to do, not then. We'd have asked you and told you why, if you could have done anything.'

'So everyone else had a job but me.'

Tubby couldn't answer. He knew I wasn't angry. I was just asking.

'Fair enough,' I said.

'There was another reason,' said Rosie. 'More to do with you and me.'

'You can tell him all that when I'm gone,' said Tubby. He put his head close to mine, looking into the little cameras that were now my eyes. 'But I'll tell you this, mate. Nothing Rosie did over the last few years was easy. Nothing was done to hurt you or to make things better for her. We had a plan. We put it through. And, by and large, it seems to have worked.'

'So now you're the two biggest maggots in the Stilton. Great.'

'I'll let you sort that one out for yourself,' he said. 'I'll see you at the party, if I don't see you before.' A wave. He was gone. Just Rosie now.

Just Rosie and me. I risked a head turn. There she was. Fifty-something and beautiful as she'd ever been. Still stirring my battered, reconstituted loins. Whereas I had been technically modified and probably looked like RoboCop's ugly sidekick, Scrapheap.

'Welcome to the future,' I said.

'We could do some more of that sometime,' she said. 'When we felt like it. Make some music.'

'You've improved,' I said.

'I got lessons from Paul.'

'How's Paul?'

'Out there being saintly. He can't help it. As always, he blames himself for his wife's death. It makes him feel better. He does a good job.'

'What? Easing the worst effects of corporate rapacity?'

'Still teasing out the subtleties, are we, Den? The world's changed a bit since you last stepped on a landmine.' She came and sat on the bed. I was filled with a mixture of lust and self-pity.

'I'd better apologize,' she said. She was everything she'd ever been before she married Barbi. She was close, intimate, easy. It was all she needed to say. I believed her. I didn't want to do anything else.

'What the fuck are you up to, Rosie? How could you have fooled me for all those years? Made it seem my fault? Make me waste all that wonking time.'

'It wasn't that long,' she said. 'I was genuinely pissed off with you for taking those pictures. Of course I worked it all out, once I really knew what Jocky was like. In the end I was glad you took them. You weren't in any terrible pain, Den. Not like the world was in.'

'Fair enough.'

'I had to use that passing anger with you to make a clean split. Something that couldn't be mended. At least until later.'

'Clean split?'

'I had to have you out of it, Den. You were getting too close. You were starting to read my mind.'

'You've never objected before. You can read mine.'

'I couldn't have anyone involved who wasn't crucial to the plan. That meant everyone but Tubby.'

'And Paul. And Flicky. And Fromental.'

'Paul and Flicky hardly knew anything. They were just ready to go along with what we were doing. Fromental wasn't involved. He just started finding out too much. And you were getting too close too fast, with that Pilbeam stuff. We were manipulating everything, Den. I'm afraid we manipulated you. Cruelly, I'll admit, sometimes. The others couldn't read my mind, Den. You'd have guessed everything in a minute. It's what we were all afraid of.'

'What? You couldn't trust me?'

'I didn't want to. It's a burden. Den, believe me. I wanted you as clean as possible at the other end. Someone I could come home to. Someone I could marry, maybe.'

The picture started warping again. *It Always Rains On Sunday*. These buggers needed a set of interior wipers. I could hardly see her. She seemed to be upset.

'I wouldn't have betrayed you, Rosie. Never.'

'Never deliberately,' she said. 'I love you, Den. Nobody knows you better, eh? Or me better? Neither of us is a natural for keeping secrets. I'm better at it than you, yeah?'

'Marginally,' I said. 'I think we're about even where porkies are concerned. Bobby MacMillan tells me you were a bitch at St Paul's.'

'Ask her why sometime.' Rosie grinned. Then she laughed.

'So you sent me off on all those stupid stories. I still don't like it, Rosie.

I mean you were really dissing me. Besides, you're still married. Remember?'

'No,' she said. 'I'm a widow.'

'No,' I said. 'You're not. I've got the pictures to prove it.'

'It was after you took those pictures.'

'When?' Suspicion came snaking back.

'About two minutes after you'd snapped your last roll.'

'How did he die?'

'A big bag of sand fell on him. Straight out of the sky and whacked him on the head. Killed him instantly. Duchess of Essex hardly scratched when the hammock broke. She was in shock. She described a flying saucer. She said they were attacked by aliens. She says she remembers how one of the aliens looked.'

'Oh, no!'

'Yeah. Bright green, apparently, huge mouth, a frog. Kermit? The authorities seemed to think the sandbag was a counterweight on the hammock and their violent activities brought it down on them. The inquest went on for ever. Stories in the press. She came back to London. Then it was over. When the Caymans got nuked.'

Back to the Twilight Zone. I'd been right, after all. This was a construct. Outside was nothing. A nuclear wasteland.

'Low fallout, no great harm done. Bit of a mistake by the US. But it cheered up the gay community. Turned the tide for us, too.'

'You really have been playing some games, haven't you?'

She grinned. 'Not just me,' she said. 'Still, all's well that ends well, Den. We're nicely past the messy stage now.'

'So the Duchess survived?'

'She left long before the take-out. Of course, your pictures finally got published. Some people think she socked him when he got too amorous. She's very popular on the V. Suspected killers always go down well with the public. She does a cookery show. Everything.'

'So you really do own the world?'

'Well.' She seemed embarrassed. 'I owned it for a while. I don't own as much as I did.'

'You've lost control?'

'Just say I've given some of the control back. Den, I wasn't getting anywhere lobbying for the voluntary sector. Yet more and more was being put on our shoulders as big business refused to accept, or minimized, its responsibilities.'

'Don't tell me!' I couldn't believe it. 'You were working from the inside all along? You meant to force them to take responsibility for the world they'd created?'

'If you like. The service sector is now the best coordinated it's ever been, employing more and more professionals, and it has the experience of working in Africa, say, or South America. All it needs is appropriate regular funding to move from shoring up failing structures to building a solid new infrastructure. Schools, hospitals, roads. We're able to guarantee those funds. And make sure they get used appropriately.'

'Lady-bloody-Bountiful. You're not exactly giving power to the people, are you? You're just trying to make things a little better. Sanitary housing for the workers. Gawd bless you, your ladyship.'

'If we were doing just that, maybe. That's why we also back independent political candidates in all the democracies. They make the laws that in turn determine how we use our funds. They've also pushed international law to new reforms so that we're developing a universal income tax which will have to be paid wherever you live in the world. Somehow it works out for everyone.'

'It's still consumerism driving everything, isn't it?'

'Not since we made so many of our companies responsive rather than aggressive in their trading techniques. We take reasonable profits from quality goods and services. But when the economy isn't driven by consumerism there's less discrepancy in salaries, for instance, and a greater number of people sharing similar experience and ambitions. Money has the effect of dividing people, Den. Monetarism is a philosophy of division. We don't need to run those simple engines any more. We have a dozen different systems going in different places, some a bit experimental, but all appropriate. We never lacked ideas. Now those ideas are being backed. The fact is that BBIC alone had the power to change the rhetoric, the debate and the political will. To demonstrate that it was possible to keep a decent economy and a decent quality of life, that the more we shared the better things became. Haven't you been getting the news?'

'I thought it was all bullshit. I'm full of drugs, Rosie. How long is it? Since I stepped on the mine?'

'Quite a while. They didn't think you were still alive. What with your stay in Skerring you've missed a lot of the saliencies, haven't you?'

'Were you really trying to drive Barbi mad?'

'Well, wreck his judgement, that's all, so he'd be glad to hand over control to me. That's why I encouraged the sex and drugs and rock and roll. The things he'd always dreamed about. He started to value them more than he valued power. Music. Food. Love. I gave him excess of it. Oh, and drugs. Meanwhile Tubby was playing havoc with Barbican's communications while I knew what was really happening. That way I was gaining more and more power. But Barbi got seriously worried when he heard what had happened to Jocky. And then Jean-Luc's pictures, which Tubby had been taking for years, planning on this moment, plus his certainty that he was going to be plunged into ruin and shame, made him fake his own public death and take the waiting helicopter from the BBIC pad to a Lear jet at Stansted, all cleared for take-off. And away he went, to France, then Tahiti, ultimately to become a remittance man in the West Indies. And Jocky, already bashed, identified as Barbican, nicely cremated at Kensal Green.'

But Rosie had had more plans for Barbican, including public humiliation, and that was why she'd put me on his scent. Unfortunately the death of Princess Diana, some wild cards played by an American president who seemed to like to let off rockets whenever he was feeling depressed, the consequences of those actions, a new government rhetoric, had set back their plans. The escalation which took out the Cayman Islands brought a lot of people to their senses.

'That's when they seemed to realize it. Just because they felt self-righteous they might not be right.'

'So all that stuff I heard on the V is real. All those improvements. Everything we ever dreamed about . . .'

'*Things to Come*, Den. *Roads To Freedom*.'

I started laughing. 'I said it couldn't be done.'

'It's working so far. There are always unexpected consequences to every action, particularly when you're trying out new ideas, but we seem to have a handle on it.'

'So what you're telling me is that you and Tubby, with some woman's wiles and some fancy communications equipment, achieved world revolution?'

She gave it her consideration. 'More or less. The same vested interests exist, but there's a more knowing public to deal with for a start. Communications are the lifeblood of democracy, Den. Otherwise there's no democracy. So, do you want to get married?'

'Jesus, Rosie!'

'I'd been meaning to ask you before I decided to marry Barbican. I had it all planned. Then it just got too much, so I had to go on to the next plan. Put you on the back burner, so to speak. That's the reason I really wanted you distant from everything I was doing. I wanted you really clean. I wanted you out of it so I could come home to someone I loved, someone who hadn't been part of all that shit.'

'Me? Clean?'

'You can't help yourself, Den. You're like a cat. You just never can let yourself get that dirty. Can't you see the problems you would have faced if I'd have included you?'

'You're not dirty, Rosie.'

'Not now,' she said. 'Not here. Not with you. See? I *was* saving you up. Den, I want to marry you.'

So I said yes.

When she'd left I got this Walkman and started recording the rest of the story. I'm still not sure how it'll work out. For one thing, I haven't yet told her about my part in Barbi snapping up the Huguenot Leases. Maybe she won't feel so badly towards me now that Brookgate's a lot better. It'll never really be home, but it doesn't look at all bad, these days. Not in black and white. It's got a decent market back. Proper business. And the rest of London has a tangled, organic feel again, as if the roots have restored themselves. I'll swear some buildings are beginning to regenerate. Levels of aggression have dropped. There's a different buzz, vital and optimistic.

They finally got rid of the Obscene Publications Act and put through a decent Freedom of Information Act. Drugs decriminalized and regulated. If the monarchy abolishes itself, as it's suggesting, Charles Windsor will become an expert on reproduction architecture. Buckingham Palace will become an art gallery and theatre. There's some talk of doing Old Time Music Hall, which will please my grandad, who reached his 100th birthday last week, who reckons his new sheltered housing in Brookgate is better than his previous place. But there's another proposal, that the palace become the HQ of the WMF, now massively funded from the UK and therefore relocated in Europe.

All Rosie's doing, of course. It's going to feel funny being married to the most powerful person on the planet. But I can probably get used to it. Better than living in Skerring. Better than marrying Bobby MacMillan. Which, in fact, Paul intends to do, never having lost his lust for Bobby. A perfect partnership of opposites.

Of course, this could be my elaborate hallucination. For all I know I'm still really hurtling in various directions through the night air of Kosovo and haven't come down yet. Or I'm in some crappy hospital waiting until a passing nurse remembers to straightline me. But if it's an illusion, it's good enough for me. I'm looking forward to getting married. I'm tired of being single.

We're going to do it at St Alban's, Brookgate on Thanksgiving Day, so we can make Tubby's party double for the reception. It'll be a triple wedding, in a way, all on the same day. Fromental and Pinky Fortnum at Kings Hall, Tubby and Flicky Jellinek at St Jude's, Gray's Inn, where Tubby's parents were married.

We'll walk up to the Mill, in her enduring magnificence. She's worn enough now, and experienced enough, to look all of a piece, with those great sails held by thick hawsers against the winds. We turn and stare south across London. Then we go in. Our surviving friends will be there, and some of our enemies. Jillian Burnes will come, in her stately glory, but Felix Martin will still be in traction. Freddie Earlle says he got hurt in a golfing accident. Fell into the thirteenth hole. Maddy La Font will be there, handing around brochures of her newest worlds and parks. I shall miss Norrie Stripling but there's a strong chance, if we have enough of Tubby's kif, that we'll see his ghost and maybe resurrect a few other absent pards. My mother's coming up and most of my relatives. We even invited the Three Enforcers, since Rosie paid them off with the petty cash and they're all apologetic smiles now, instantly trying to reinvent themselves as old friends. But nobody's asked me if I feel uncomfortable earning less than my wife. Grandpa says he'll just come to the wedding. He doesn't feel like parties now Norrie's gone. He's hoping for great-grandchildren. He'll probably get some, but they'll be most Rwandan. We know Jimmy Lakeforth will honour us, and V.J. and Ray. Sonny Shapiro and his lady. Mr and Mrs Stoker. Lemmy. Pete Pavli. All the surviving band members. We'll do our best to invoke Calvert. We finally found Steve Gilmore. Charnock's promised to rent a boat and come from Galveston. He won't fly since he wrote that book. Paul Frame, bearing his sainthood like a cross, with Bobby MacMillan. We'll miss Barbi, I think. So we'll drink a toast to him. After all, though he couldn't be officially dead twice, I am technically guilty of his manslaughter and certainly the main beneficiary of his death. And not one suspicious sniff. I have a lot to thank the Duchess of Essex for. We've each contributed to the other's career.

At some point Rosie and I will leave the main party and climb the spiral stair until we reach the gantry to the gallery, which encircles the Mill's mellow brick. We'll push open the big grain doors and step into the autumn air, breathing the rich scent of the centuries, looking out over a city that glitters and vibrates with a new optimism, a positive energy, a will to become, once again, the best and most progressive, the richest and the greatest city the world has ever known. The hub of all our histories. Forever glorious. Forever golden. Forever just.

And we'll embrace, of course. And we'll kiss. And all the bells of London will start ringing their familiar chimes. Happily ever after. St Clement's and Old Bailey. St Paul's and Westminster. St Mary-le-bone's and Kensington and Bow. A great celebration of our enduring blood, of our will to justice and equity. Of the power of love.

Myths and miracles, pards. What would we do without them?